"THERE HE IS!"

Marguerite followed the direction of her mother's pointing finger. She could feel her breath gathering in her chest as if her lungs would burst, for she was gripped by tension at this pivotal moment in her life.

It could have been argued that she had been conditioned since birth for this sighting, that she had been primed by her mother's romantic tales and her teacher's exotic myths to be more vulnerable than she might otherwise have been at a highly emotional period in her life, but she held to the belief then, and ever afterwards, that she could have been shown a thousand handsome faces and not one of them would have made her fall as completely in love as she did that day with Augustin Roussier. . . .

BOOKS BY ROSALIND LAKER

The Smuggler's Bride
Ride the Blue Riband
Warwyck's Woman
Claudine's Daughter
Warwyck's Choice
Banners of Silk
Gilded Splendour
Jewelled Path
What the Heart Keeps
This Shining Land
Tree of Gold
The Silver Touch
To Dance with Kings

To Dance with Kings

ROSALIND LAKER

BANTAM BOOKS

NEW YORK · TORONTO · LONDON · SYDNEY · AUCKLAND

This edition contains the complete text
of the original hardcover edition.
NOT ONE WORD HAS BEEN OMITTED.

TO DANCE WITH KINGS

A Bantam Book/published by arrangement with
Doubleday

PRINTING HISTORY

Doubleday edition published February 1989
Bantam edition/January 1990

ISBN 0-553-28284-0

Published simultaneously in the United States and Canada

Bantam Books are published by Bantam Books, a division of
Bantam Doubleday Dell Publishing Group, Inc. Its trade-
mark, consisting of the words "Bantam Books" and the por-
trayal of a rooster, is Registered in U.S. Patent and Trade-
mark Office and in other countries. Marca Registrada.
Bantam Books, 666 Fifth Avenue, New York, New York 10103.

To My Granddaughter, Jenny

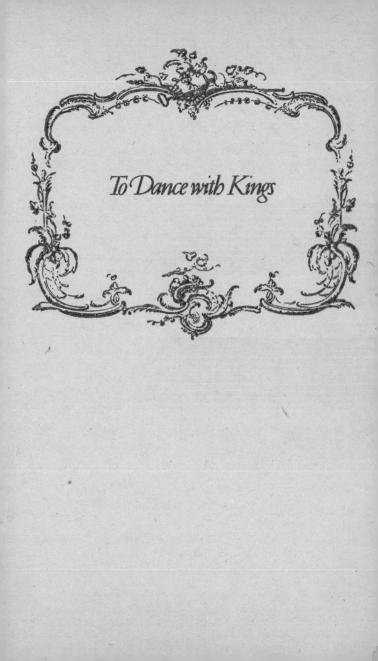

To Dance with Kings

One

With the crimson, emerald and purple plumes of their hats
streaming out behind them, four young men rode at speed
into the village of Versailles one May morning in 1664,
scattering squawking geese in their path.

"We should have been here hours ago," Augustin
Roussier yelled to his companions, making his horse rear as
they halted to view the busy scene. "All the best lodgings
will have been taken by the look of it!"

The rutted streets were crammed with elegant traffic
more at home in Paris, from which most of them had
come, than in these countrified surroundings. The sun
glinted on gilded coachwork and harness, the warm air
hazy with dust thrown up by wheels and hooves. Six hundred of the nobility had been invited to the first grand fête
ever to be held at the nearby hunting lodge, which was a
small place with only accommodation enough for a few of
the King's special guests to stay.

"Is it any use trying the inns to see if there's a room left?"
asked one of his companions as they moved their tired

horses forward at a more restful pace. "There are three hostelries, I believe."

"I'd say we've lost that chance, Léon. See! Even those miserable hovels have been taken." Augustin flicked his gloved hand towards some old stone houses they were passing. Well-dressed arrivals were stepping fastidiously inside, never having set foot in such humble places before, their servants carrying in their boxes and baggage after them. "Those we left behind us on the road will be lucky to get a stable at this rate."

He was the natural leader of their high-spirited group. They had become friends during their initial year's service with the First Company of the King's Musketeers, a duty expected of every young courtier who wished for promotion at Court. Not yet twenty, born of Huguenot stock and of a father with powerful financial interests, Augustin was tall with a straight bearing and a good physique, his looks dashing and debonair.

Like most youths of his age, he scorned the fashionable full-bottomed periwig and wore his own hair, which was thick, curly and long enough to rest on his broad shoulders in the modish style. Its luxuriant growth, black shot with blueish lights, framed features hardening into the square jaw and prominent nose of his forebears. Beneath thick brows the narrow eyes were a curiously brilliant green and there was a lusty eagerness in the lines of the wide mouth. As always when he was with these particular friends, Léon Postel, François Esconde and Jacques de Fresnay, any excuse for a prank or horseplay was seized on with relish. They had enlivened the ride from Paris with a number of diversions, such as racing each other dangerously, swerving in front of coach horses and flirting with pretty women riding together in the lumbering equipages.

"At least let us stop for a swig of wine first." François eased a gloved finger around the inside of his lace-trimmed neckband, his freckled face gleaming with beads of sweat.

"Agreed!" Jacques, hawk-faced and fair-haired, made exaggerated gasping sounds. "I'm parched from the dust of the ride. There's a wineshop ahead."

"We can't afford to stop yet." Augustin twisted in his saddle to signal his own servant forward from the retinue of valets who had now caught up in the rear, bringing with them the extra horses with saddle hampers and chests of clothes. "Get a few bottles of the best wine this place can provide," he instructed, "and follow me."

The wine, coarse and rough though it was, proved welcome when the search for accommodation brought no result. While the servants did the knocking on doors, Augustin and his companions tossed it back from their silver travelling cups. Its potency took full effect as the rising heat of noon combined with their deep thirst, Léon's swarthy complexion almost reaching the same hue as the wine itself. All four of them became more boisterous and everything seemed excruciatingly funny to them. There was plenty to amuse as women accidentally set satin-shod feet into cow dung, sometimes causing a loss of balance amid squeals of temper and dismay, and fellow gallants, who were no more used to inconveniences than they were themselves, sprang off their horses to kick and cuff their unfortunate servants for failing to get a room for them in the last of the tolerable property.

The local priest had opened his house for some of the women out of sympathy for their plight, but he ran like a schoolboy, his black robes flapping, to lock the doors of the twelfth-century church before anyone thought to bed down there. He knew as well as anybody that there would inevitably be drunkenness and every other kind of indulgence before the royal fête was at an end. Augustin, laughing, wheeled his black horse about with a sheen of flanks to the church steps and leaned from the saddle to offer him a cup of wine. It was refused with uplifted white palms before the priest went scurrying back to his house.

Gradually the search spread from the centre of the village to the outskirts. Versailles, situated as it was on the main road between Normandy and Paris, was better able to house travellers than the neighbouring hamlets, but already some people had set off for Clagny and Saint-Cyr and Trianon in the hope of snatching up the best accommodation there, not knowing that they could not expect even a moderation of comfort in those poverty-stricken hamlets.

Augustin's servant, dodging in front of one of these departing coaches as he returned from a row of mean-looking stone cottages, gave his information breathlessly. "All rooms have been claimed, except in the end one where the housewife is in labour and nobody is being accommodated."

Augustin raised an eyebrow incredulously. "Do you mean that space has been found at last and admittance refused?"

"The woman is almost at birthing point—"

"Out of my way!" Augustin swung himself down from the saddle and turned to the other three with a sweep of his arm. "Come along, my friends! If this were a royal birth, it would be our noble right to witness the delivery! A peasant woman has no cause to keep us out!"

He made for the cottage. Whooping and shouting as if going into battle, the trio dismounted and rushed after him. The door was on the latch and he flung it wide as he entered, those in his wake following close behind, the heels of their riding boots ringing on the flagstones. They found themselves in the single whitewashed room that served all purposes. Sparsely furnished with a rough-hewn table, a dresser and benches, it was stiflingly hot, the windows tightly shut. A midwife swung around from a bed in the far corner, her sleeves rolled up above her elbow, her apron soiled and her sweaty red face a mask of outrage at this intrusion. Deftly she flicked a corner of the sheet over the bare updrawn legs of the groaning woman she was tending before taking up a belligerent stance with feet apart and arms akimbo.

"Messieurs! You must leave this instant! Madame Dremont is unable to wait on anyone and there is no place for you here."

A scream of torment compelled her back to her charge. The woman in labour, regaining her breath, raised her head weakly from the pillow. "Who has come?"

The midwife reached out to pull the ragged bed-curtain across and block the view, but her action came too late. Jeanne Dremont's pain-filled eyes became drenched with horror as she saw the four youths advancing towards her. She began to shriek hysterically, releasing the labour rope strung across the bed to clutch frantically at the midwife's hand.

"Make them go away! Have I not endured enough this day?"

Augustin thrust the curtain far back on its rings and looked down at her. She was about thirty-five but looked much older, her gaunt bones having taken over from the bloom of youth. Her faded hair, with some traces of red, was darkened by sweat and her lips were drawn back grotesquely in her mental and physical agony. Compassion for her moved him.

"Don't be alarmed, madame," he assured her kindly, the wine making his tone jocular. "We don't want your bed. Some clean blankets and fresh lice-free straw will suffice for us."

She drew breath and tried to answer him, seeing he meant her no harm, but a new wave of pain defeated her, cutting her through. It was hard not to believe she was caught up in a terrible, whirling nightmare. Young male grins and laughing eyes were at the side of her bed, cheering her on as though she were a racehorse nearing the winning post. She did not know that the Queens of France had to suffer the same public witness. The midwife, no time left for argument, had elbowed her way free to be ready for the moment of birth and was coaxing her towards it amid the uproar. All decency had flown. Even a doctor delivered under a modesty blanket, but whatever had been covering her seemed to have fallen away. She heard her own ear-splitting scream as she thrust against the final ripping apart of her body, her back arching like a bow. With a rush the baby came. As its wail went up there was a burst of applause from the noblemen. The one she heard addressed as Augustin gave her the news before the midwife had a chance.

"It's a girl! You have a fine daughter, madame!"

In exhaustion, she let herself sink deep into the mattress of goose feathers, eyes closed and a smile on her lips. She no longer cared about anything else. The baby's lusty wailing was music to her. After several stillbirths and more miscarriages, she had a living child. "Give her to me," she implored in an exultant whisper.

The midwife had cut the cord and wrapped the infant in a piece of linen. When she would have handed her over to the mother, Augustin snatched the human bundle away and swept the newborn infant high into the air, regarding her fondly.

"You're like a crumpled little flower, mademoiselle," he joked, making swooping circles with her. His friends came to gather around, laughing as they shoved and pushed each other. In the bed Jeanne reached out her arms, gripped by panic at this new turn of drunken horseplay. She was terrified they might start throwing the infant to each other like a ball.

"Let me have her, sir! I beg you!"

He took no notice, continuing to address the baby whose pouched lids blinked at him over an unfocused gaze, her lungs continuing to give forth a newborn cry. "A bloom from the meadows and dung-heaps of Versailles, that's what you are, *ma petite*. Marguerite is a name that would suit you. Yes, I name you Marguerite." His friends cheered noisily. Jeanne would have struggled from the bed if the midwife had not restrained her. "In seventeen years," he continued laughingly, "Jacques and François and Léon and I will be back to court you. Pay no attention to them. I'll be the one for you. In the meantime here's a token of my good faith." He had a louis d'or in his pocket and as he gave the infant into her mother's arms he pressed it into her tiny fingers. "See how she clutches it, madame! She'll be an expensive wife for a man to keep when the time comes."

Jeanne, whose tears had been streaming down her face in her fright, turned her shoulder to him as she settled the infant protectively against her. He bowed to them both and pulled the curtain across to leave them on their own with the midwife.

When Théo Dremont hurried home from work there was little hope in him that his wife's labour, which had started in the early hours before sunrise, would have proved any more productive than on previous occasions. After each one Jeanne had become more difficult and at times quite strange in the head. He had had to take a stick to beat the sense back into her too often for his liking, but his reputation in the village had to be considered and no one respected a man not seen to master domestic upheavals in his own house. After a few months of constant weeping, Jeanne had adjusted once again. If after every disappointment she was a little less stable than before, only he knew it.

His mouth fell agape as he stopped in the doorway of his house and saw its disarray. There was no sign of the neighbour who should have had a cooked dinner ready for him. Instead two dandy menservants in doublets and petticoat breeches with ribbons at the knees, aprons about their waists, were removing from the table the remains of what appeared to have been a grand meal judging by the number of chicken bones and emptied wine bottles.

All the windows stood open and under them were four mounds of clean straw that had been shaped into beds, with a satin-lined cloak on each in lieu of blankets. A row of riding boots, newly polished, stood beside some travelling chests stacked against the wall. From the scaffolding around a barn he was building for a farmer, he had seen throughout the day the nobility descending like a great flock of peacocks on the village and he realised full well that his cottage had been taken over. Yet the question still burst from him.

"What's going on here?"

The two menservants looked condescendingly at him. They had seen their masters rigged out in best clothes and off to the royal lodge before they and their fellows had cooked and enjoyed a good meal themselves out of supplies brought with them. Although of peasant stock, they adopted the rank of their masters in the hierarchy of the servant world and thought themselves well above this thick-shouldered, coarse-featured artisan in his dirty bricklaying clothes. The taller of the two pointed to a leather purse on the windowsill.

"That's your payment and there'll be more when our masters are ready to leave."

Théo snatched up the purse and tipped the contents into his calloused palm. His eyes gleamed. The longer the King's fête lasted the better as far as he was concerned. As he pocketed the purse he remembered what had brought him home with more haste than usual. He looked towards the bed. The curtains were drawn and there was silence. With a depressed sigh he turned to hang up his hat, only to find every peg taken up with riding coats and headgear. He put his own hat on the floor. Crossing to the bed he drew back the curtains, expecting to find Jeanne lying stark-eyed and immobile with disappointment. Instead she lay sleeping, a babe in her arms. His sharp intake of breath roused her. She opened her eyes on a smile. There was an eerily bright look to her face that he had never seen before. Somehow it unnerved him.

"We have a daughter, Théo. Her name is Marguerite. That's pretty, don't you think?"

He forgot that moment of unease. It occurred to him that having proved herself a woman at last she could at least have presented him with a son to be named after himself, but better a daughter than nothing at all. Let the name be whatever she fancied. Leaning a hand on the bed, he bent across to touch the cheek of the slumbering infant with a forefinger.

"Marguerite, eh? Has she strong lungs?"

"You'll hear that for yourself soon enough."

"Did all go well at the birth?"

Jeanne lowered her lids. If she told him of the noblemen's behaviour he would be enraged, but he would vent his anger on her. She had not been his wife all these years without knowing how his moods took him. The midwife, a kindly and understanding woman, had willingly promised to keep silent on the subject.

He had not kissed her or his daughter and neither did she expect him to. With men like Théo outward demonstrations of affection belonged to courtship and ended once the early days of marriage were over. Her lot was that of most women in the village and yet she knew herself to be different from them. Something in her nature, which she could not always control, strove for an outlet beyond her comprehension and frequently confused her. Even now it was soaring through her, silent and alarming and powerful, as if through her newborn daughter it might come to fulfilment. She put her lips to the soft down on the infant's head.

"I forgot all the bad moments as soon as I held this little one in my arms," she answered evasively.

"Good." He went as far as patting her shoulder surreptitiously, uncomfortably aware of the presence of two strangers in the room, albeit they were clattering about their own business. At heart he was a shy, well-meaning man, best suited to a quiet life, and it was temper at his own inadequacy in the face of anything he could not deal with or understand that brought about his harsh treatment of her at times. In his own way he was as fond of her as she was of him. "Am I to get any dinner?" he inquired on a practical note.

"Those servants brought me food and I asked that some be left in the pot for you."

He flicked the bed-curtain back in position and she sighed with relief. For a little while longer this bed was a sanctuary for her and her child. Never again would they be alone and undisturbed as they were now. She wanted so much for this infant's future. Not a marriage like her own that was drudgery and beatings and the constant threat of starvation when there was no work or the time when Théo was laid up for weeks with a broken leg. He still limped, for in spite of the carpenter's splints it had not set properly, and she was always worried when he was up on scaffolding in case he lost his balance.

Turning her head on the pillow, she looked towards a crevice between the stones of the wall. She had hidden the gold louis there. It had been given to Marguerite and should be used when she had need of it, however distant that time might be. It had not been a lie to Théo when she said she had forgotten much of what had happened at the birth. Somehow the nightmare had faded as if it had been part of the labour pains. All that remained vivid in her mind was the image of the young man in his lace and leather and fine cloth coat, the man whom she now knew to be Augustin Roussier, paying compliments to her daughter. She had seen kindness in his eyes. Who was to say he had not meant what he said about returning in seventeen years' time? It would be a thought to strengthen her hopes for her child whenever existence was particularly bleak and their stomachs ached with hunger.

It had been Augustin's suggestion that he and his companions should walk to the fête and they willingly agreed. They were a good foursome and rarely fell out over anything these days, but when they did their quarrels were fierce, for all four had strong temperaments. Yet the bond formed during their service as musketeers bound them in honour as well as in friendship. Early in their acquaintanceship, after swords had been drawn in a violent dispute over a woman, they had made a solemn oath never again to poach on one another's territory once a verbal claim had been made. As they were all gentlemen born it was a pact that could never be broken, no matter how testing the situation or how luscious the woman concerned, and subsequently it had kept their friendship intact.

They strolled with the fashionable strut that gave a swing to their short silk cloaks and an additional arrogance to their posture. Maybe this walk had evolved generally through the wearing of bucket-topped boots, but even in buckled shoes, as they were now, men of fashion and authority walked in this manner as if they owned the world and everyone in it. It reflected the whole structure of their society, for France was the most powerful and prosperous state in Europe, unified and centralised in the King himself.

If anything the spirits of the four friends were even higher than earlier in the day, and they laughed together and chaffed one another good-humouredly, feeling refreshed and full of energy. They had bathed from buckets of water in the ramshackle outhouse before returning naked and dripping to dry off in the cottage. There they donned clean linen and hose and the rest of their finery, which consisted of knee-length silk coats over full-cut breeches, and on their heads wide-brimmed hats with huge nodding plumes. A patch or two on chin and cheekbone to give drama to their looks and finally each took a differently coloured spangled mask, fashioned like a face in vivid satin and mounted on ivory handles, to make them part of the magical theme of the fête, which was entitled *Les Plaisirs de l'Île Enchantée.* It was being held in honour of Louise de La Vallière, mistress of the King, even though his wife and mother were to grace the proceedings with their presence.

As the gates of the hunting lodge came into view, Augustin's mind flicked back to the only time he had visited here before. That had been three years ago in the early summer of 1661, the weather as balmy then as now and the occasion the first party held here by the King for a group of close friends, whose ages ranged from eighteen to the King's own age of twenty-three. Augustin, newly arrived at Court and to whom the King had spoken only once, was puzzled as to why he, then only sixteen, should have been included. The most likely explanation was that a few weeks before, his father had done the King a great service in a matter of finance and, as a form of appreciation, the son had been invited to the party instead of the father, whose austere manner and middle-age would have been thoroughly out of place.

The lodge, which could be reached in just over an hour at normal speed from Paris, was the King's own private property and stood on a slight rise overlooking the village and the countryside beyond. Built of warm russet brick and creamy stone, roofed with blue-grey slate, it was a small unpretentious mansion that had been designed originally as a male preserve for the late King, Louis XIII, from which he and his fellow huntsmen rode out to enjoy the chase in the surrounding forests and fenlands where stag and other wild game abounded. In his last days, not knowing death was near, he had expressed a wish to retire there as soon as his son was of age and devote himself to his spiritual salvation. Instead, when he drew his last breath, his son, the new King of France, was still only five years old.

Except for sharing the same consuming passion for hunting, which had been ignited in him in the forests around Versailles when he was twelve, Louis XIV had grown to be quite a different man from his father, being dedicated as much to pleasure as to his royal responsibilities. Through the lodge's happy associations with his early youth, only joy and relaxation known within its walls and environs, he had begun to see that it could be a delightful centre in which to entertain those he liked best. Being away from Court, what better to ensure that married partners were never invited together to these small, informal gatherings. It would enable him to leave his wife of a year in Paris and add to his own and everybody else's sense of freedom while at his beloved lodge of Versailles.

Augustin had learned a lot about life at that party. An exciting and throbbing sensuality had prevailed throughout the whole three days and nights, generated by lavish hospitality, the excitement of good hunting and the exuberance of sophisticated youth. Liaisons were many, but discreet, so that nothing marred the harmony that prevailed under the lodge's roof or in the grounds where the festivities were held, there being no salon large enough within to hold feasting or dancing on any scale.

Although since his first visit Augustin had never again been invited to one of these exclusive parties, a royal obligation having been fulfilled, he continued to take an interest in the lodge and looked forward to seeing what changes had been made there in the interim. As he and the trio with him approached their venue, the sound of music drifted out from the grounds to meet the stream of arriving guests. The precincts of the lodge had a welcoming aspect. Semicircular ramps enclosed an opening forecourt as if to embrace whoever entered the gates, which were set between two small pavilions that echoed the warm russet brick and creamy stone of the lodge itself. East-facing, it further emphasised a hospitable aspect by enclosing three sides of a black and white marble quadrangle, the Cour de Marbre.

Augustin was struck at once by the sumptuous new embellishments of the mansion. One and a half million livres, a sizable fortune, had been spent on interior redecoration and on extending the gardens on a vast scale. The iron-work balcony, which ran above the central entrance and under the windows of the first of the upper floors, had been marvellously gilded, as had other ornamentation that lent itself to this new splendour, all of which shone brilliantly as if the King had chosen to emphasise that his royal device was the face of Apollo, the sun god, whose very rays had been captured to shine out from this country abode.

Dancing in the gardens was already in full swing. There were as many areas in which to dance as there were to feast or gamble or just rest and listen to the music, for rooms had been created within the gardens, sometimes at a sunken level and also by the clever use of box hedges and trees, arbours and blossoming archways and delicate trelliswork, each area spectacularly furnished and hung with silken drapes and tapestries. A long rectangular lawn, known as the Tapis Vert, led down to the gleaming lake, the Bassin des Cygnes.

As dusk fell many thousands of candles, and almost as many flambeaux, glowed to give flickering wells of light and pools of shadow in which people milled about, the sparkle of jewels almost matched by the gleam of satin and silk and brocade, while fountains captured the brilliance in their spray. Those taking part in the enactment of the legend of the enchanted isle, which had inspired the fête, wore exotic headgear and fantastic costumes, giving an added magic to the scene. Almost everyone had a glittering mask on a handle which, like those Augustin and his

friends held, were used only for effect and not to disguise.
After greeting acquaintances and mingling with those
they knew well, the four companions gradually split up to
take partners into the dancing.

Out of gallantry, Augustin first asked the King's mistress.
As a lanky youth he had bowed to Louise de La Vallière at
that first party he had attended at Versailles. She did not
remember him from then and there were too many at
Court for her to know him by sight or name, but she smiled
and chatted as if she did while they turned and twirled in a
gavotte, her skirt of green and silver swirling like the
waves of the sea. She wore her golden-brown hair in the
fashionable style adopted by most women present, that of
a smooth-topped head with a middle parting and bunches
of curls bouncing out over the ears to reach to the shoulders. Her single lovelock, arranged to fall below her right
breast, sprang in and out of her cleavage in a dance of its
own.

"Isn't it a splendid evening?" she said to him. "To crown
it all we shall soon have a moon as bright as a silver ball."

He responded to her small talk, wondering if she knew
that in spite of her being the royal favourite, the King, an
insatiable womaniser, was no more faithful to her, according to Court gossip, than he was to Queen Marie Thérèse.
At that earlier party the King had been newly in love with
this modest young woman whose arched eyebrows over
large azure eyes gave her a look of pleased expectancy at
whatever was to come and whose inviting mouth had a
provocative dip in the full lower lip. Then it had been
difficult to decide whether Louise or the lodge held precedence in the King's heart, for it was obvious then, as it was
now, that he was enraptured with the small mansion that
he had already set in gilt as if it were a precious gem.

The King, wearing a gold helmet with flame-coloured
plumes, had come directly into Augustin's line of vision; a
dignified, impressive young man with a natural majesty
that made him a dramatic figure even when in more sombre clothes and not arrayed as he was this evening as
Roger, the hero of the legend, in cloth of gold, a jewelled
sun blazing from his silver breastplate.

He revelled in lavish entertainment. The hedonistic side
of his complex character needed a constant outlet in lively
company, amorous women and ostentatious pomp and

ceremony. In contrast, when in council with his ministers or when dealing with affairs of state, he was stern, severe and cold. He did not spare himself in long hours of work. On the battlefield he was a formidable warrior.

His features revealed the strength in him. He had the Bourbon nose that was long and thin, flaring out into sensual nostrils, his upper lip adorned with a thin, black moustache. His glittering eyes, heavy lidded, missed nothing, or so it seemed to the nobles who found their plans thwarted or their cunningly devised schemes set awry. Once they had expected him to be malleable as a ruler and easy to control, but he had soon shown them that he was otherwise and did not trust them.

Their lack of respect and open quarrelling during the uprising of the nobles, known as the Fronde, in his early childhood were still a thorn in Louis's side. He was resolved that never again should there be an aristocratic threat to the Throne of France. Paris would ever be associated in his mind with that painful upheaval and he liked the Louvre least of all the palaces in which he held court. But cities had no charm for him in any case. He was an outdoorsman, happiest in the open air and especially here at his lodge where he could ride and shoot and hunt to his heart's content. He was already beginning to see that in this place he could create a new seat of power away from all the old intrigues and past bitternesses such as clung not only to the Louvre but also to the palaces of Saint-Germain, Fontainebleau, Vincennes and Chambord among others.

He noticed that Louise had finished her dance with Gérard Roussier's only son and was being brought towards him. Smiling, he gave Augustin a regal nod and held out his hand to take his mistress's fingers into his. "I've been looking for you, Louise. We haven't danced for an hour. It's my turn now."

Pearly tears of love welled up in her eyes. She could weep as easily from joy as from sorrow, tears spilling from her at the most disconcerting moments. It was a trait he had found endearing in the first flush of passion. It touched him now, inflamed as he was by the warmly erotic atmosphere of the fête, and he forgot the recent times when he had come close to being irritated. He led her with a loving clasp of fingers into a *danse à deux*, the Slow Courante with its graceful turned-out position of the toes at which he excelled. A superb dancer, acknowledged without flattery to be the best in all France, he was ably partnered by the lovely Louise and everybody else drew back to watch. If his gaze flickered from one pretty woman to another in the clustered spectators, it was not obvious and Louise did not notice.

After the spectacle of the evening was over, a mediaeval tournament fought in the glow of crystal candle-lamps, all six hundred guests sat down with the King to a banquet at long tables. Masked and costumed servants, looking like creatures from the fantasy island, held aloft greenery-adorned silver candelabra behind every chair. Augustin found himself seated next to a witty young woman who made him laugh. Before they had finished the first course they were on familiar terms. In the middle of the third she drove her little red heel wickedly into his foot, ready then and there to lead him to her bed in the hunting lodge. The lengthy duration of the banquet only added to a mutual and delicious anticipation that reached a satisfactory conclusion later in the night. She clawed his back like a cat and shrieked her ecstasy on a high-pitched note that must have echoed through several walls.

Down in the village, Jeanne heard the first crackle of fireworks in the distance and through the chinks in her bed-curtain she was bathed in a rose and silver glow. Careful not to disturb her sleeping infant, she sat up to draw the curtain back until she could see the windows and watch the interior of her home change colour as if some wizardry was afoot.

She was alone in the cottage. A neighbour had come to settle her and her infant for the night and see to their needs after the servants had bedded down in the outhouse loft. Théo was with them, not having dared to assert his right to sleep under his own roof when four nobles had staked a claim to it. When the rainbow hues of the fireworks finally subsided she lay back again on her pillows and tried to sleep. It was difficult, there being so much joyful excitement in her over the events of the day.

Eventually oblivion did come, only to be broken when the two nobles, Jacques and François, returned to the cottage, their laughter and talk and the thumping of their

footsteps awakening Marguerite, who was only quietened
when put to the breast. Through a ragged gap in the curtain Jeanne saw to her surprise that Léon was already back
and lying on his straw bed fast asleep. She liked him for
having taken care not to disturb her, but it was Augustin
who had given her a sense of destiny.

He did not return that night. She did not see him until
morning when he reappeared to bathe, be barbered by his
servant and don fresh finery before departing once more
with his friends until the next night was over. It proved to
be the pattern of their days. They ate no food at the cottage, feasts being laid on between nonstop entertainments
from breakfast to midnight suppers. They frequently forgot her presence, as the servants did on occasions, and
there was much open talk that would have embarrassed a
more innocent woman. Jeanne listened keenly, wanting to
know as much as she could about the customs, pleasures
and escapades of her so-called betters. She did notice that
Augustin had become quieter and more reticent than the
rest. None of his companions appeared to be aware of any
change in him, but she, watching him as she did, saw how
often he was lost in his own thoughts, paying no attention
to the bawdy talk around him.

For Augustin the fête had become a search. He had said
nothing to his three friends, not wanting them to gibe him
for his foolishness when there were any number of beautiful women for the taking, but he had had a glimpse of a
female face he could not forget. Young, sparkling, with
huge long-lashed dark eyes and the innocent aura that
proclaimed a virgin.

It had happened on the second night during Molière's
play, an extravagant production in which the King continued to play the role of Roger, whose love for the heroine
echoed his own passion for Louise de La Vallière. The
theatre had been specially constructed in one of the silk-
hung groves where those too late to get a seat could take
advantage of the cushions and Persian rugs spread out on
the grassy slopes higher up. Augustin, seated with merry
company on a rug at the side of the grove, could look down
into many faces in the audience. While applauding a scene,
he happened to glance along one of the rows and sighted
her. Illumined by the glow from the stage, enthralled by
the King's performance, the girl was leaning forward and

laughing in her delight, her bejewelled hands clapping enthusiastically. Then she sat back as the play proceeded, never taking her gaze from the unfolding drama and not knowing that he could not keep his eyes from her.

He judged her to be sixteen or seventeen, just a little younger than himself. Her profile was exquisite, her hair a light chestnut and full of curls. He had already made up his mind to find a way to speak to her at the play's end.

Yet when the actors had taken their final bow and hundreds of people began to move away from their seats the crush made it impossible for him to get through to her. He did get near enough to see that she was just as enchanting at close quarters and caught her clear voice as she addressed the middle-aged man who flanked her protectively.

"I'm so glad you let me come, Papa! Wasn't it splendid!"

Then a few moments later, quite without warning, she turned her head abruptly and looked back at Augustin, seemingly as surprised by her action as he. He could only conclude that away from the spell of the play she had been seized by the sixth sense that can tell someone when he or she is being closely watched. Whatever the reason, their eyes met and held, hers growing wider, his more intense. A blush soared into her cheeks and she looked hastily away again. To his exasperation more people made a solid block in front of him, putting a greater distance between them. Yet she glanced back once more, giving him a mischievous little smile, and then in the surge of the dispersing audience he lost sight of her completely.

Since then he had searched for her everywhere. With such swarms of guests and a variety of entertainments going on everywhere it was like looking for the proverbial needle in a haystack and he had no success. He had no means of knowing who she was or where she had come from, never having seen her father before, but she had touched a previously unplucked chord in him, leaving him restless and desperate to see her again.

The third and last evening of the fête arrived. Having looked in vain among the dancers and wandered through many of the open-air bowers and rooms he came to the bank of the Bassin des Cygnes where everyone was gathering for the final enactment of the enchanted legend. There was applause as the realistically constructed palace of the

Enchantress, its silver turrets gleaming, began to float
swanlike across the water until it reached the middle of
the lake. With a fanfare of trumpets the golden figure of
the King sprang up onto a gilded platform to confront the
Enchantress in her den. As he flung up his arms, drums
rolled. To a crescendo of Lully's specially composed music
the magic palace became engulfed in flames while overhead the first wave of exploding fireworks flooded the sky
with an ocean of multicoloured stars.

Augustin took advantage of the fireworks' brilliance to
climb onto the plinth of a statue and scan the faces of the
spectators. His sudden exultation at sighting his quarry
gave way to dismay when he saw she was departing. Now
that the climax of the fête was over her father was getting
her away as quickly as possible, helping her into one of the
little open carriages used for viewing the park.

Augustin leapt down from the plinth. By the time he was
through the crowd the carriage was bowling away down
the Tapis Vert. He sprang into a run in its wake. People he
met stared after him, laughing and calling out. He knew
there was no chance of catching up with the carriage, but
he hoped to be in time to discover the girl's identity before
she left by the main gates.

He was too late. When he arrived breathless in the courtyard the abandoned open carriage was being taken away
and a travelling coach was disappearing beyond the palisades. He questioned several grooms and outdoor servants
as to whose coach it was, but none was able to tell him,
which meant that the girl's father came rarely if ever to
Court. She probably lived far away. He would have liked to
know her name. Her lovely face was imprinted on his
memory. He could only hope that one day he would meet
her again.

With the end of the fête the King's hospitality took on
the style usual to such gatherings, with hunting parties in
the morning and the rest of the day taken up by extensive
gaming sessions, dancing and music and acting, either by
courtiers and their ladies or a professional band of players.
In this case Molière's company had stayed on.

Jeanne had become used to the four young men and
their servants occupying her home. Augustin, whom she
observed still had reflective moments, and his friends al-

ways returned to the cottage after the morning's chase to
change out of their riding clothes and bathe before putting
on finer garments again. So much bathing astonished her.
She had always understood that the rich were no cleaner
in their habits than peasant folk, in spite of having access to
hot water whenever they wished, but the reverse had
been proved. Her cauldrons had never boiled so much
water in all the time she had had them, or even when her
mother-in-law lived here before her. The servants were
kept hurrying with buckets whenever the young nobles
chose to strip off and bathe away the sweat of exertion.

By this time she was up and about her domestic chores
again and engaged once more in the fan-making she did
for a shop in Paris, the owner supplying her with the materials. It was poorly paid for the amount of skill and time she
put into the work but it was a much-needed supplement to
Théo's meagre income. Usually the spread of a fan, known
as the leaf, would be in silk or satin or vellum if it was to be
painted. Jeanne was not an embroiderer and often fan-
leaves came already embroidered by other outworkers.
Then these in turn would be stuck onto sticks of bone or
ivory or aromatic wood and pleated before the final clip-
ping together and the last additional touch of a tassel or
ribbon streamers to the ring.

While dealing with the orders delayed by her confine-
ment, she concentrated on making a fan of her own choice
from a leaf of silk surplus to supplies she had saved from a
long time back. She had to use every minute available
between attending to her baby and carrying out necessary
domestic chores, for she wanted the fan completed before
Augustin departed. At least she was spared the cooking, for
the servants shared their own meals with her and Théo.
They were far more agreeable to her than they were to her
husband, who made no secret of disliking their presence,
although he bowed almost to the floor if one of the nobles
should cross his path.

When on her own with the servants, she took advantage
of their geniality to find out more about life at Court. It
came as no surprise to be told that marriages in aristocratic
circles were made entirely for wealth, rank and property
and she thought it no wonder that couples went their own
way once the knot was tied. Who could blame them? Yet
she could not stop her eyebrows lifting at the tale of the

nobleman who had walked by chance into a rose bower at the Fontainebleau palace and found his wife rutting with her lover. His only concern was that someone else might have discovered them instead of himself! It appeared that to invite scandal was in poor taste, which was why the ladies at Court went to great length to conceal adulterous pregnancies. The Court had evolved its own rules of conduct and etiquette over the years and it only brought disgrace and even banishment to flout them.

"What of the King?" Jeanne asked, adding a dab of blue to the scene on the fan's silk that she had pinned out on the table. "Suppose the Queen took a lover?"

It was Augustin's valet who answered her. "Strictly speaking it is treason in any country to cuckold a king. As it happens, in spite of it being a political marriage, Queen Marie Thérèse is in love with King Louis and there's no question of her straying."

"Yet he—"

"Ah, that's a different matter. Even the Church accepts that the King is entitled to a titular mistress and she is treated like another Queen at Court."

Jeanne chose not to comment. It was a man's world and nobody knew better than she that women were put on earth to submit to men's dubious standards. "What happens to the mistresses of rich men when they are no longer desired?"

Under her lashes she watched the servants glance at one another in amusement as if they had a fund of jokes on that subject. Again it was Augustin's servant who replied.

"Usually the ladies receive jewels and single women of humbler origin are given a dowry large enough for them to secure bourgeois husbands."

That was what she wanted to know. She hugged the information to herself with satisfaction and asked no more questions. When the painting on the silk was finished she enlisted the help of the priest, who had called to see her and the baby, in the spelling of *Marguerite*, for she herself could neither read nor write. Under his direction she copied his fine lettering with her particular skill. When she had done, she asked him a question that had been troubling her.

"There are four nobles staying here, Father, and I've heard the one named Monsieur Augustin Roussier referred to once or twice as the Huguenot by the servants. What does it mean?"

The priest's face took on an immensely grave expression. "Huguenots, my child," he informed her heavily, "are Protestants. The term is of unknown origin, but it is applied by Roman Catholics of France to our lost brothers and sisters who follow the so-called reformed faith. Have you never heard of the massacre of Saint Bartholomew's Eve?"

"No, Father."

"It was a terrible time, but deemed necessary to put down the Huguenot nobles, who had their own private armies then. France had been torn apart by religious violence for far too long. Over thirty thousand men, women and children were put to torture and the sword." He saw the flicker of horror in the woman's eyes and put a reassuring hand on her shoulder. "It happened a long time ago, my child. It is due to the magnanimity of the King's grandfather, Henri IV, who passed the Edict of Nantes to protect them, that they have religious liberty and equal civil rights with Frenchmen of the true Church today."

But here and there pockets of resentment against the Huguenots continued to simmer, he reflected. It was his hope that forces would not be released against these Protestants again, but this was not a matter with which to trouble the head of a simple peasant woman. He closed the subject by getting up to leave.

Jeanne showed him to the door and bobbed respectfully as he departed. Returning to the table, she sat down deep in thought. It had been a shock to hear that Augustin was not of the Roman Catholic faith into which her infant daughter had already been baptised. Then sensibly she reminded herself that it was not as though there would ever be a marriage between them. It was only in legends that the prince married the beggar maid. Instead, from what she had learned from the servants, her aim was to see Marguerite as Augustin's mistress until such time as he gave her a handsome dowry, when she would be free to marry well among the bourgeoisie—and for love if she so wished.

Taking up her paintbrush, Jeanne finished her design and waited until the paint was dry. That did not take long.

Then she set to work to put the fan together with ivory sticks.

The festivities closed as they had started at an afternoon hour. Soon afterwards the streets of the village were jammed with departing traffic. Augustin was the only one of the four nobles who had the courtesy to say farewell to Jeanne. He happened to be the last to leave the cottage, for the others had wanted to be among the first on the road to reach Fontainebleau, where the Court was to reassemble, while he was going to visit his home near Le Havre, a flourishing commercial port on the Normandy coast.

"I wish you and your daughter continued good health, madame," he said to Jeanne. "My compliments to you both."

He would have turned to leave but she stayed him. "Monsieur Roussier! One moment please." She handed him the fan. "It is a keepsake to remind you of this royal fête at Versailles."

He smiled as he took it from her. "Is it for me to hand to the lady of my choice?"

"Perhaps, monsieur. If you should ever wish it." She watched him open the white silk fan, not as a woman would have done with a graceful flick of the wrist, but in a masculine way by taking the main sticks and spreading them wide. He reacted with surprise.

"You are an artist! This scene is very fine." It showed the royal lodge, not as it was now with recent embellishments but with its original appearance, as he had seen it on his first visit three years before. Bathed in a sunny light, backed by the gentle blue of an early summer sky, it was entwined as in a frame by garlands of tuberoses, jasmine and the lilies of France spread out on either side. Then he noticed more. Wrought into the central garland of marguerites, as if in silken ribbons, was the name of her daughter. It stabbed his memory. His wild promise made in a drunken moment returned to him. He drew in his breath in sharp reaction to the woman's presumption. Any one of his friends would have cuffed her to the floor and hurled the fan away, but he was levelheaded enough to accept he was not without blame. He folded the fan without further comment and slipped it into his pocket. Unbuckling the purse on the belt of his riding jacket, he put it on the table. "This is all I have to give you in return, madame."

"I thank you, sir."

He went from the cottage with his mind relieved, feeling that he had paid her off and there was nothing left with which to reproach himself. She picked up the purse and held it to her as she crossed to the window to watch him mount and ride away. On her face was the radiant, rather curious expression that had made her husband uneasy when he had first spoken to her after their daughter's birth. He had not recognised it as the reflection of an obsession already rising in her.

As soon as Augustin was out of sight Jeanne turned back into the room, looking down at the purse in her hands. It was weighty and there was no telling how much money it contained, enough in any case to store away until Marguerite had come to womanhood and was in need of some fine clothes. Not for a moment did it occur to her that Augustin had been settling his conscience. She saw the purse as yet another token to strengthen the promise made. Everybody knew that no true nobleman ever broke his word.

Augustin forgot the whole disturbing incident before he was out of the village. When it grew dark he put up for the night at a hostelry. His valet, who had accompanied him, brushed and folded his riding clothes when they had been discarded and Augustin was already asleep. Finding a fan sticking out of one of the pockets, he recognised it immediately and supposed his master had purchased it to help that peasant woman in her poverty-stricken circumstances. It was a fine fan, and had the name of Marguerite not been incorporated it would have made a pretty gift for any woman.

He put it into one of the studded leather pockets in the travelling chest. There it remained, never asked for or remembered by either master or servant and it was to make many journeys before it came to light again.

Two

Jeanne did not relinquish her dream. On the contrary, it strengthened within her until at times she had to laugh aloud at the sheer wonder of it. Théo beat her cruelly several times, made angry by her inexplicable chuckling to herself and the shifting gleam in her eyes as he had been by her postnatal tears in the past. He called in the priest, fearful that the devil had taken control of her wits. Fortunately for Jeanne, the kindly priest had always shown sympathy for the hard lot of the peasant women in his parish.

"Put your fears away, my son," he advised Théo, "and count your blessings. What woman wouldn't have an excess of happiness over a strong and healthy child after so many barren years of disappointment?"

It was true that Marguerite was thriving. Her dark birth hair had given way to curls of reddish-gold, the tint that had been Jeanne's own before premature greyness had dulled its sheen, and her eyes, large and round, deepened to a sapphire-blue.

"You're going to be beautiful," Jeanne cooed to the infant whenever Théo was out of earshot. "One day I shall pay for you to be taught to read and write. Oh, yes, I have the money for that. You'll see."

Jeanne's complete happiness was marred by one irrational fear that she could not dismiss. It was that she herself might die before she saw her daughter reach womanhood, and then all those marvellous hopes would come to nothing and Marguerite's life would be no different from her own. Since further pregnancies presented the greatest hazard to her life, she consulted a local wise woman and afterwards had no more worries on that score. If Théo continued to hope for a son he did not mention it and she never brought up the subject. Yet the black shadow of a possible early demise continued to lie over her, returning to haunt her in unguarded moments. It made her decide that as soon as Marguerite was old enough she would start instilling in her an aim to rise out of drudgery at all costs while, at the same time, preparing her for what had been decreed at the time of her birth. Then at least the girl could stand alone if deprived of a mother's care too soon.

The royal lodge became a focal point of interest for Jeanne. It was her only tangible link with Augustin and therefore must be observed as closely as possible, anything of importance happening there being more than likely to have some influence on her daughter's future. Being a local woman, she had known the building all her life, which was why she had been able to paint it on the gift fan with such ease, drawing on its image in her mind with none of the finer details overlooked.

As a child she had seen the old King many times, and Louis XIV in the saddle was a long-familiar sight. She could remember him riding to hounds as a boy in the company of Cardinal Mazarin, who had trained him in the duties of Kingship. There had also been countless occasions throughout the years when she had watched in envious hunger as stag and boar, swinging suspended from poles slung across the shoulders of hunt attendants, had gone past to feed the already well-fed at the lodge. Feathered game was bagged on other days, sometimes so many that the bearers seemed cloaked in them. Only the nobility had the right to hunt. The penalty for anyone else trapping something for the pot was death, which was how her father had met his end when starvation was staring him and his family in the face. It was no wonder the royal sport remained virtually unimpaired by poachers.

With some local people employed in menial tasks at the lodge and in digging and weeding the gardens, it was not hard for Jeanne to keep abreast of events there. The village grapevine positively hummed with news at certain times, such as when the royal architects appeared shortly after the grand fête to examine the soil, make sketches and notes and investigate possible new supplies of water, which in itself had always caused problems at the lodge. Before long it became apparent that some major rebuilding was to take place.

The King visited frequently for consultations on the spot with the chief architect, Monsieur Le Vau, whose work he was known to admire. Everybody in the village, as well as those in higher circles, expected the lodge to be pulled down and replaced with a new building entirely. Old people in the village remembered it had happened before when the old King had found the first lodge he had built in 1623 too small even for his simple requirements and had had it replaced with the present charming little *maison de chasse* some years before the present King was born. But it soon became known that Louis had no intention of pulling it down. On the contrary, it was to be enveloped by an extension on three sides, juxtaposing the new residence with the old.

"If fate or fire should raze my father's lodge to the ground," he was heard to say on one occasion, "I would build it up again exactly as it was."

Théo, who knew about building, scratched his head that the King should be so infatuated with the lodge as to authorise its enlargement on a site where the ground had always been bad and inclined to shift. His sympathy was with the architects, who had countless difficulties to overcome.

Le Vau lost no time in making moves to carry out the royal wishes. By the time Marguerite could take a few steps alone, a great pump and water tower had been erected to solve the supply problem and the ground had been marked out and dug up in sections until at last Le Vau's satisfied nod had sent the word that everything was ready to build what was already being referred to as the King's Château, his country seat.

Yet in spite of the constant flurries of activity as architects and engineers came and went, little more happened until after the King had given another grand fête on a scale even more spectacular than before. Jeanne hoped that Augustin might reappear, but although the village was just as crammed as in 1664, it seemed as if many people were choosing to make the journey daily from Paris rather than face bedbugs in dubious country quarters. Three-year-old Marguerite was never to forget the excitement of being taken at night to a vantage point to watch the fireworks and then, as a finale, to see flaring up in golden stars just above the treetops the double reversed L for Louis the Sun King.

"Look!" she cried, pointing her little finger. "The King is writing in the sky!"

Around her everyone laughed and her mother hugged and kissed her, telling her she was a clever girl.

Not long afterwards, life in the village of Versailles changed completely as every able-bodied man not otherwise gainfully employed was given the chance of working on the new extension. Théo was one of the first to sign on, able to see there would be work in abundance for a skilled artisan such as he. In the vast open space in front of the gates of the lodge, already spoken of as the Place d'Armes, workshops sprang up for every branch of the building trade as thousands of workmen poured into Versailles from all parts of the country. Cranes and winches were brought in and scaffolding erected to encase the russet and cream lodge. Hundreds of huts had been put up with speed to house the tremendous work force and there were food kitchens to feed them, women from the district being taken on for the task of cooking and baking.

The majority of the masters of the trades chose to live away from the men in their charge by staying in local homes, which that way brought extra money into the villagers' pockets. In spite of the heavy taxes, which never seemed to ease, times looked better, at least for those engaged in any work related to the building at Versailles and also in Paris, where the Louvre was undergoing similar reconstruction and alteration. Some said that whenever the King was not at war he was possessed of a building fever, for even Paris itself was being remoulded under his direction to become a fitting capital for a great nation, and the new avenue to be cut through the heart of the city at Le Nôtre's design was to be known as the Champs-Élysées.

It suited Jeanne to have Théo at work on the site. While confined to her fan-work, her domestic chores and, above all, the rearing of her daughter, she still received firsthand reports on developments. It had soon become apparent to everyone, as the digging for new foundations began, that this was not to be a modest expansion but a project on a grand scale. Local people began to make Sundays after Mass the time to stroll to the Château and assess the progress since the previous Sabbath. Jeanne was always among them, her child on her hip. Usually they went on their own, for Théo said he saw enough of the site during the week and he liked to repair to the wineshop for a while and chat with friends over a glass.

As soon as Marguerite had been able to toddle around by herself, Jeanne taught her to pick up anything that fell accidentally from the long table at which she herself sat at fan-making. Marguerite's only toys were chipped or broken fan-sticks and a rag doll that she dragged about everywhere.

She was not very old before she learned to stir together the ingredients of the gum made to her mother's own closely guarded formula. It had been handed down to Jeanne from her grandmother, who had also been a fanmaker, and when skilfully applied it would neither mark nor harm the most delicate of fabrics when the sticks were fastened to the leaf. The foul odour that was emitted from the gum pot at its initial heating to blend the ingredients bore no relation to the dainty workmanship of fan-making itself. Sometimes a box of prettily pierced carved or lacquered sticks would arrive and these had to be threaded together by ribbons or cords into what were known as bisqué fans. Marguerite had nimble fingers and she was no more than six when she became adept at threading these up.

It was to celebrate her sixth natal day that a treat was arranged for her. It fell on a weekday, but as Jeanne had just despatched a batch of finished fans and the new materials had yet to arrive, she had a little time on her hands. It was Théo's suggestion that Marguerite should be taken to see the new arrivals at the menagerie in the Château's park where he was working on a new run. The King was elsewhere, but even if he had been at the Château there was no barrier to ordinary citizens enjoying the beautiful gardens as long as they did not get in the way of the building work or any new innovations being introduced to the park by the garden designer, Le Nôtre.

It was always a pleasure for Jeanne to visit there. Attracting her more than the statuary or the fountains that only played when the King was in residence, or the costly orange trees in their tubs, were the parterres, the laid-out flower beds that were as neat as embroidery in intricate designs, each bloom in harmony with its neighbour. It was said that Le Nôtre knew when a pansy was planted a fraction out of place and could spot an errant leaf in a clipped hedge as if it were a branch that had extended. Marguerite was fascinated by the evergreen trees clipped to the shape of tall cones, which flanked the paths of the parterres like soldiers at attention, and on this day she sprang into a game of hide-and-seek with her mother.

Eventually they took a path through planted woodland and came out not far from the shining water of the Bassin des Cygnes where the menagerie stood with its central dome for all the world like a little palace in itself. Théo, who had been watching out for them, had just taken his noon break with the other workers and he used the time to show them around, eating his chunk of bread and cheese at the same time.

Jeanne was overawed by the splendour of the setting in which an elephant, a dozen camels, several ostriches and some odd-looking sheep lived in their own quarters with extensive runs laid out as from the hub of a wheel. She followed at a slower pace behind her husband, who had lifted their daughter up in his arms in case she should be nervous of the strange animals on the other side of the gilt-tipped bars. It was quite the reverse. Marguerite was excited and eager.

She shrieked delightedly at the elephant and in the Cour des Oiseaux she stood on tiptoe, fascinated by the sight of so many exotic birds, the flamingos, toucans and birds of paradise, the parrots, hummingbirds and cockatoos. She made up her mind that if ever she should become as much of an artist as her mother, she would always try to include a lovely bird in her fan-design, either on the wing or perched lightly on a blossoming branch.

Being a child herself, she liked best to work on fans for children. She would sit beside her mother at the cottage table, her feet dangling, as she concentrated hard on the task in hand. She never felt envy towards the little girls better off than herself who would be given the fans. Without her knowing how or when, there had been subtly instilled into her by her mother a kind of anticipation that she could not as yet express, but which carried her through the disappointments and sicknesses of childhood as if they were minor inconveniences that had no true bearing on her life. It was as if she always stood on the brink of something wonderful and unknown. Instinct told her that with time her mother would reveal the secret to her, but in the meantime it remained a silent bond between them, enriching their relationship.

In spite of her obedience at work she was not an easy child to raise. There was a streak of wilfulness in her that fed on a strength of will inherited from both parents. At times she was infuriated by her mother's fussing with her long tawny hair, its constant bathing and brushing, and by the insistence on frequent bathing when nobody she knew gave any thought to such finicky refinements.

"You would bathe daily if you were a lady living at the Château," was the only reply her mother ever gave her. "So once a week in winter and twice or more in summer is not too often for a little girl under this roof."

She began to note how often her mother mentioned the Château. It was as if that mass of rising stone had thrown some kind of spell over her parent. None of her friends went as often to view the building with their mothers and fathers as she did with Jeanne. Yet the Sunday walks to the Château were never monotonous for her as they might have been for another child, because Jeanne always had some new tale to tell about it, based either on past hearsay or present gossip, or even Théo's latest reports. In spite of her complete lack of education, Jeanne had a flair with simple words, able to conjure up a picture for her naturally imaginative daughter, just as she was able to paint artistically with the primitive skill in her fingers, talents that would have been fostered to a higher level if she had been born into more affluent circumstances.

"The King has won a great battle. His soldiers marched across Flanders and all the flags waved," she said once, marching two fingers down her daughter's arm to the hand. "He would have conquered Holland easily if the Dutch hadn't let in the sea and flooded their own land. The King could not get across because all the fishes danced with rage at finding themselves in shallower water."

Marguerite liked to hear about the golden-haired young Dauphin, who was just three years and a few months older than herself. He was also an only child, none of his newly born brothers or sisters managing to survive the hazards that beset infancy, and he had his own suite of rooms at the Château for his visits as well as a white pony to ride. She was less interested in hearing that the King had a new lady to amuse him. He had taken Athénaïs de Montespan on campaign and when his former playmate, Louise de La Vallière, followed after them, he had sent her away in tears that fell from her eyes like dew and covered the grass all around.

Jeanne, entertaining her daughter with these tales, sometimes tried to estimate the cost of all that was going into the building of this great Château, but it was as impossible for her to imagine the amount as it would have been for her to guess the distance between the sun and the moon. One who knew the cost exactly was Jean Baptiste Colbert, the minister in charge of providing, through exorbitant taxes, the necessary monies. He had given up all arguments against extravagance and become resigned when he discovered that a curb he had tried to put on the King's spending had been baulked by advice given by a certain financier, Gérard Roussier. Considering it demeaning to his own position, he resolved it should not occur again. Although he would have preferred the monies to have been spent on the Louvre palace, he indulged every royal whim.

From the start the King had wanted the furnishings to be French wherever possible and to Versailles came red, grey, pink, black and white marble from the south of the country, furniture of solid silver executed by superb craftsmen, embroidered velvets, Gobelin tapestries depicting scenes of Louis's activities in peace and war as well as others of comparable beauty, and glittering chandeliers of French crystal. The artist Le Brun was supervising the interior decoration and he charged the best of artists and sculptors to create a setting as glorious as a casket of jewels. Above all, gold, the solar metal, was to predominate throughout.

The glowing face of Apollo, as well as the double reversed *L* for *Louis the Sun King,* appeared in gold leaf in the midst of encrusted decoration on doors and shutters and in ironwork. Ceilings rioted with gods and goddesses while masterpieces in gilded frames adorned walls hung with glorious Lyonnaise silks.

Only in the matter of mirrors had there been a problem. Venice had a monopoly in this trade, its quality unsurpassed and its secrets closely guarded. In order to pacify the King, who saw no reason why French glassworks could not achieve the same standard, Colbert had arranged the dangerous enterprise of smuggling eighteen Venetian glass-workers into France. This was done with the aid of the French ambassador to Venice, who would have had his throat cut and his body hurled into the sea if his deed had been discovered. But whether these glass-workers knew less of the secret process than they had boasted, or else had sworn between themselves not to reveal too much, there was no marked improvement in French products. Worse, French people continued to buy Venetian mirrors until the King passed a law prohibiting their import. It added to his chagrin when a mirror-smuggling trade developed as a result.

Colbert, who always shuddered inwardly at each new expense, grew grim-faced when yet another set of plans for a future extension of the Château was put into his hands for perusal. His dismay was boundless when to top everything he learned that Le Nôtre was to lay out a new town of architect-designed buildings to replace the old village of Versailles and make a fitting environ for the great Château. A wide central avenue of trees, to be known as the Avenue de Paris, would enable it to be seen from a great distance away, and on either side the new town was to rise. Two more gracious avenues were to approach at an angle, making the Château and its park the axis of a wide area of elegance and beauty.

The vast Place d'Armes, familiar as an open-air workshop for the multitude of workmen engaged in royal construction work, was to be flanked by two great stables to replace the present ones and house the thousands of horses and equipages required by the King and those invited by him. Just as it was once said that all roads led to Rome, it now appeared that in France at least, by direction of the King, all roads should lead to the Château of Versailles.

When the demolition of the village started, the Dremont family had no cause for alarm. Being on the outskirts meant that for a while at least there was no danger of the authorities turning them out of their home. As for the new owners and tenants of the property being erected, it was obvious that a far more prosperous category of people, such as bankers and merchants as well as those connected in some way with the Château, would be moving in and the character of the place quite changed.

Shortly before Easter of 1671 an honour was bestowed on thirteen poor families in Versailles. A little girl from each household was to attend the Chapel of the Château on Holy Thursday and Marguerite was selected to be one of them. Jeanne, ready to refuel her hopes for her daughter from any source, convinced herself that Augustin had recommended Marguerite as a candidate. It was an erroneous supposition, the priest having been responsible, but as the details of selection were never made public, Jeanne's cherished dream took a new surge forward.

She was almost delirious with happiness as she washed and pressed her daughter's best garment for the occasion. A new dress would not have been appropriate in the circumstances, particularly as she, with her secret hoard, was the only parent who could have afforded it.

"Why should the Queen wash my feet?" Marguerite had asked immediately.

"She is following the example of our Lord," Jeanne explained blissfully, "when He washed the feet of His disciples."

Afterwards, when the event was over, a few moments shone out for Marguerite above all the rest. There was the Chapel's richly decorated brilliance in the sunlight that poured through the windows, its warmth a contrast to the chill of the marble floor, she and the other girls being barefoot. Then there was the luxurious softness of the velvet-covered stools on which they sat in a row and the hammering of her heart against her ribs when the Spanish-born Queen knelt before each of them and her own turn came nearer. At close quarters the Queen looked quite young in spite of the sombre gown she wore, whereas the King was resplendent in purple and silver. Her hands were white and soft, the almond-shaped nails buffed to a polish and, in spite of bad teeth, her smile coaxed a response from even the shyest child.

There was no room in the Chapel for the parents of the candidates, for members of the Court occupied every inch of space. Jeanne, waiting to reclaim her daughter, scanned every face leaving the Chapel in the hope of seeing Augustin, but she had not sighted him anywhere. It did not shake her conviction that he had acted on Marguerite's behalf and she was encouraged to take the first steps towards her daughter's education. She had expected Théo to be the stumbling block, but he proved easier to persuade than she had expected. Her argument was that out of their improved earnings she could manage the fees, which would be small for the girl's instruction in any case, and that in the new township there would always be shopkeepers and other tradesmen to whom a wife able to keep their books would be a sought-after asset. Théo loved his little daughter in his own undemonstrative way and, providing any domestic economies for the fees did not affect his drinking money, he saw no reason why she shouldn't acquire some learning.

"Very well, wife," he consented with a nod of his head. "Do as you wish."

To his astonishment, Jeanne sprang up from the bench to throw her arms about his neck in a show of affection unknown for years. It stirred him and briefly what each felt for the other rushed to the surface just as if for a short spell they were young lovers again. Their relationship remained enriched by it, although out of their natural reserve neither ever referred to it afterwards.

Jeanne went to see the priest. He had retired, distressed that in his old age his little church should be demolished in Le Nôtre's grand design for the township. He had had pupils in his time, but he felt himself at seventy to be past taking on another. Yet he did not discourage Jeanne and recommended a certain Mademoiselle Printemps.

"She is a relative of the Desgranges family who recently

moved from Paris into one of the newly completed houses here."

Jeanne shrank back. "I couldn't approach anyone who lives there, Father, I'd be kicked from the door."

He thought this highly likely if she met anyone except Marie Printemps herself, who was a penniless relative compelled by circumstances to be dependent on her cousins, Monsieur Desgranges and his wife, an unenviable state since they were not charitable at heart. It would do her all the good in the world to have an interest of her own and a little financial reimbursement. "Would you like me to ask her on your behalf?"

The offer was gratefully accepted. The priest, knowing that the Desgranges would not allow a peasant child to cross their threshold, offered a room in his house for the lessons, for it was equally out of the question for Marie to go to the Dremont cottage.

Marguerite liked Marie from the start and the feeling was mutual. In spite of her charming surname, Marie was plain, bone-thin and past her springtime. Yet she had a gentle way that was appealing and she proved to be kindness itself in her teaching. Although the lessons took place only once a week, Marguerite's main task being to help her mother in fan-making, she learned well and quickly. Grammatical errors were soon erased from her speech. When the priest's servant brought refreshments, Marie showed her how to eat neatly without fuss and not to bolt her food.

"Let's go to the park for lessons today," Marie always said when the weather was dry. She believed it was good for Marguerite, confined to fan-making indoors for much of her time, to get fresh air and exercise whenever possible, while she herself enjoyed the sense of freedom it gave her to be among the spaciously set trees and flowers.

She never met her pupil's parents, reports on Marguerite's excellent progress being conveyed by the priest who also dealt with the fees to spare either side any embarrassment. Together Marie and her pupil came to know every inch of the park and they chose a different stone seat to sit on every time. Pleased with the child's intelligence and finding there an imagination already ignited by the mother, Marie regaled Marguerite with tales from Greek mythology, bringing every one of the many statues to life for her. The beautiful marble and gilded Latona fountain, placed at the foot of the wide steps leading down from the Water Parterres of the Château, took on a new meaning when Marie explained that Latona was the mother of Apollo whose own gilded fountain lay in a direct line away at the far end of the Tapis Vert, both tangible links with another Sun King who radiated from within the Château itself.

Louis entertained lavishly there between spates of building, and sometimes when the construction was in progress he found himself unable to stay away for long. In spite of the din of hammering and sawing, the film of plaster dust and often a quagmire of mud to ride through amid a maze of stacked bricks and timber and unplaced statuary, invitations to the Château had become the most sought after. It had nothing to do with the area, which many courtiers hated. It seemed incredible to them that out of all France with its fine scenery, its rich hills and valleys and forested mountains, the King could have chosen the dull and unhealthy land around Versailles with its low-lying mists and damp marshes for an additional country residence.

It was certainly true there was a high death rate among the workmen as a result of strange fevers believed to have been caused by the inhalation of peculiar odours that emitted from sections of newly dug earth. Some members of the Court protested they always felt unwell at Versailles, but neither they nor anyone else ever declined an invitation through choice. They might grumble about the inadequacy of the accommodation, overcrowding being the chief complaint, and always a large number having to stay in the growing township and elsewhere, but it had become the epitome of social success to be seen at the Château. People not invited on any specific occasion frequently feigned illness or put up some other pretence to escape the humiliation of being overlooked.

Louis, who thrived on the air of Versailles and the soft winds which blew down from the gentle heights of Satory, observed it all and under the hooded lids there was a glint blended of triumph and satisfaction. It was through the nobility's penchant for always wanting to be à la mode that he was manipulating them like puppets and making them dance more and more to his tune. Because of this, his

Château would have endeared itself still more to him for the extra power it had delivered into his hands even if he had not been enraptured with it already. He sometimes acknowledged to himself that he loved it more than any woman and this when Athénaïs de Montespan had a tight hold on his heart if not on his head.

"My body may be weak for the gratification of carnal desires," he said once to his mother not long before she died, in answer to yet another maternal admonition about his licentious ways, "but my brain is France and strong as iron, always under my command and immune to coercion of any kind."

It was the truth, for the whole makeup of his character made it impossible for him to be subservient to anyone, even when in love. With each passing year he seemed to expand into still greater majesty. Always awe-inspiring, he was able to terrify by the merest lift of an eyebrow or the sudden impatient tattoo of his fingertips. It gave him immense satisfaction to see the Court hang on his every word and scuttle to his will. In spite of the vast number in attendance, he knew far more about the majority of them individually than most of them realised. He took an intense dislike to those who made no secret of preferring Paris to his beloved Versailles, and he marked in his own mind against the ones who spent excessive lengths of time away from Court. In contrast, he respected the courtiers who, at a courteous level, were unafraid to disagree with him or to bring a controversial matter to his attention, and he always listened and considered, for at all times he tried to be fair and to judge wisely.

Among the younger courtiers, he looked for loyalty and a dedicated sense of duty. Augustin Roussier was one who had been noticed for bringing forward cases of injustice to Huguenots and no less for his valour on the battlefield. Louis, his memory jogged, was pleased to recall that this was the son of Gérard Roussier whose financial power he could still use against Jean Baptiste Colbert, his chief minister and adviser, if ever the need should arise.

As one year and then another went by Louis continued to observe Augustin. When the time was right he would show some mark of favour, but in the meantime he had other things to think about and there were plenty of developments at Versailles to keep a continual correspondence flowing between him and his architects whenever he was elsewhere. He had bought the hamlet of Trianon and demolished it to extend his park to the north, and Clagny to the south had suffered a similar fate. A little porcelain palace was being erected at Trianon and Le Nôtre had also enlarged the Bassin des Cygnes into a Grand Canal.

Between visits to the Château there was always a constant flow of movement from palace to palace, for the King never stayed long under one roof. Interspersed with these sojourns were the sorties into whatever war was being fought, for Louis was set on expanding the eastern border of France.

Warfare, with its military service, provided a different kind of excitement for the young men of the Court. When Augustin sustained a severe shoulder wound during the current Dutch campaign, he was forced to lie up in a sickbed in a foreign convent until fit to travel again by coach, although not in the saddle. He had hoped to meet the Court at Chambord, only to find it had already departed in the wake of the King, home again from his triumphal entry into Utrecht after its surrender to his troops, for Fontainebleau and boar-hunting. After a day's rest Augustin set off again through the autumnal countryside. There was no question of his joining the chase for, although his shoulder was healing well, it had to be dressed daily and any unnecessary exertion avoided.

It was a pleasure to meet Jacques again when he arrived at Fontainebleau and they greeted each other heartily. The bond of their friendship had been strengthened immeasurably since François had been killed in battle and since Léon's more recent death from gangrenous wounds.

"How will you pass the time of day while the rest of us are hunting?" Jacques asked him.

"I'm not here to stay this time. As you know, it is expected of any one of us recovering from campaign wounds to make an appearance at Court, however briefly, as soon as possible. My duty done, I shall go home to Le Havre. A visit is long overdue and I can complete my recuperation there."

"When shall you be leaving?" Jacques spoke as if he might have some special reason beyond a normal enquiry for wanting to know, but as Augustin answered him the moment passed without explanation.

"I'll be off tomorrow afternoon after I've made my bow to the King at the appointed hour. It will give me a chance to take a leisurely ride beforehand to see how it feels to be back in the saddle."

Like the King, he rode whenever possible. Often he joined the escorting riders when Louis untiringly covered in the saddle many leagues between palaces or cities. If Louis did travel by coach he invariably invited two or three women to travel with him, selecting them for their charm, beauty or wit. His mistress was always his first choice unless there was some good reason, such as a pregnancy, as to why she could not travel. For Augustin in his drive home to the coast of Normandy there would be only his own company. He had been in and out of love many times, but as yet he had not met a woman he cared about enough to take home to present to his father as his future wife.

That evening he and Jacques made their way to the stateroom where dancing was in progress. Side by side they entered the wide-open doors and stood to survey the scene, a striking pair themselves, the dark-haired handsomeness of one contrasting with the fairness of the other. Many a time this effect had aided them in individual conquests, but always they kept to that long-distant pact of never making a play for the other's woman.

The stateroom presented a colourful sight. The heavily carved ceiling and walls inset with paintings held, as if in a large rectangular box, the stately dancers. At the far end was a canopied chair for the King and in a gallery the musicians played, their music sometimes lost in the buzz of conversation from those seated around the floor. Princes of the Blood Royal, glittering with jewels, sat in the brocade chairs in a single row, while the princesses were accommodated in the same style on the opposite side. Nobody else sat in the presence of the King and when not engaged in the dancing, people milled about in the background. Jacques indicated a severe-looking woman of middle-age, a-sparkle with diamonds, who stood on the far side of the room.

"There's the Duchesse de Valmy. I must pay my respects."

"By all means." Augustin knew that Jacques's family and the Valmys were friends over many years. "We'll meet again later."

As Jacques left him, Augustin moved on through the throng of spectators, stopping to talk here and there with those he knew. In a lull of conversation, momentarily on his own, he looked towards the dancers. The musicians had just struck up a new measure and the King was partnering the Queen for the second or third time that evening, both of them grandly dressed in scarlet and black, the appearance of each complementing the other. She was transparently happy at his show of attention, for she continued to adore him. Light on her feet, she was proud that her dancing still met his high standards and occasionally earned his praise. To be complimented by the King on one's dancing was the aim of every woman at Court. Augustin, his gaze already drifting from the royal couple, fastened on a young woman who was as graceful as a gazelle and might well deserve the sought-after royal praise.

She was vaguely familiar to him. He was certain he had seen her somewhere before. Then it came to him. It was the girl he had first seen at the King's fête at Versailles. She had matured to an astonishing beauty, swan-necked and narrow-waisted, her breasts rising out of her bodice like small peaches. The new mode of drawing the hair back into a knot with falling side-curls, echoing the fastening back of pretty overskirts to more fullness at the rear, suited her patrician features, her complexion pale against the light chestnut of her locks and the swing of her diamond eardrops. A beguiling smile at her partner curled the rosy mouth and she looked luminous and chaste with an intriguing hint of unplumbed depths in the twinkling dark eyes that he remembered well.

He was filled with excitement. She charmed him no less now than she had at the fête. He hardened his stare to compel her to glance in his direction as she had done before. The moment came when she swirled away from her partner before linking fingers again. Her eyes met his and the look between them locked for a second or two, triumph in his and a widening flicker of surprise in hers. The dance carried her on and away from where he was standing. There had been no recognition in her glance and neither had he expected it. After all, it was he who had tried to find her and she had been completely unaware of his search. He waited eagerly for the moment when the music would tell him at which end of the floor he should be in order to meet her as she left it. He knew her partner only slightly, but enough to secure a long overdue introduction. Nothing should keep him from her now.

The last notes of the dance came and she dipped into a curtsey to her partner, her skirt a ripple of coral satin. She was slightly nearer the north end of the room. As Augustin set off purposefully to reach the gap through which she would come, he saw Jacques go from the Duchesse's side to take the young woman's hand from her partner. From the way they greeted each other it was obvious they were on close terms and knew each other well. But there was more. Augustin recognised on his friend's face that rapt expression that meant it was not just friendship he felt for her, his gaze doting as he led her to the Duchesse, who was beaming on them both.

"Who is that young woman?" Augustin asked an acquaintance who stood nearby. "Do you know her?"

"That's Mademoiselle Susanne Le Viger."

Augustin knew the name immediately. Jacques had mentioned the family many times over the years and was as well acquainted with the Le Vigers as he was with the Valmys. "How long has she been at Court?"

"Not long. No doubt she would have been here before and married long since if she had not nursed her sick father for a number of years. Since then she has been over twelve months in mourning for him. She is under the protective wing of her aunt, the Duchesse de Valmy, who presented her when the Court was at Chambord."

With fierce regret Augustin conceded that he could make no move towards Susanne Le Viger until it was established whether a serious courtship by Jacques was in progress. Whore or lady, it made no difference. The old pact still held, no matter what his personal feelings might be. He could make no prior claim on a chance sighting, particularly as Susanne would not remember him.

He watched them dance together. The fact that she might be already out of his reach again violently increased his attraction to her. Once he thought she glanced in the direction of where he had been standing, but it was probably wishful thinking, for she was animated and light-

hearted in her attitude towards Jacques, who was not able
to take his eyes from her.

Becoming increasingly impatient with the situation, Augustin left the dancing and made his way to the gaming
tables where he spent a couple of hours before retiring. He
was barely asleep when he was roughly awakened again by
Jacques dropping his weight down at the end of the bed.
The candles had been relit and Augustin blinked as he
heaved himself up against the pillows. Jacques sat grinning
widely, his back against the end bedpost, his long legs
stretched to the floor.

"Offer me your felicitations at once, my friend! I'm going to be married."

Augustin experienced a shaft of disappointment. Worse,
he felt rage. "The lady is undoubtedly Susanne Le Viger."

Jacques raised his eyebrows. "You saw us together, did
you? That's odd, because when I intended to present you
there was no sign of you anywhere."

"I didn't stay long. Somebody told me who she was and
you were oblivious to everything in her company."

Jacques laughed out of the exuberance of his mood. "I've
known her since my boyhood, as you may have guessed.
Not that I took any notice of her then, because she is three
years younger than I. Do you know, her father brought her
to that first fête at Versailles and I avoided them as much as
possible, seeking less respectable company as you can well
imagine. Then I saw her again after a long period when I
went home for my sister's wedding. To me Susanne had
blossomed out of all recognition. We began to correspond
and after she lost her father she seemed to turn to me
before anyone else."

Augustin drew a finger and thumb across his forehead as
if to stir his memory, seeking to quell the burning jealousy
that possessed him. "I recall your saying something about
that at the time, but you made no great issue of it."

"That was because I hadn't realised what was happening
between Susanne and me. Everything came to the surface
when you were away on that recent campaign and she and
I met again at Chambord. As soon as we were together
once more we knew we were in love. She's a marvellous
girl. I'm the luckiest fellow."

"Why didn't you tell me about this when we met today?"

"I hadn't spoken to the Duchesse then and the betrothal

was not yet official. I have just come from her salon." He shook his head in wonderment at his good fortune. "You're the first to know."

So that was that. Augustin forced down his own disappointment in genuine goodwill at his comrade's happiness and leaned forward to clasp his hand. "You have my felicitations! You have won a beautiful bride."

"I thank you. I want you to meet Susanne as soon as possible. Now good night to you."

"Good night." Augustin drew the covers up over his shoulder again. Jacques obligingly snuffed the candles and, whistling exultantly under his breath, left the room, closing the door behind him.

Augustin lay awake. The Court was full of lovely women and it was folly on his part that Susanne should again appear to outshine them all. All he knew was that there was a magnetism about her that he feared would always draw him. He shifted his position restlessly, unable as yet to lie on his left side, and punched his pillows viciously into a more comfortable shape. When he slept it was to dream lustfully of her until he awoke with a start, bathed in sweat, his desire for her even stronger than before.

When morning came he rose leisurely, took his bath and, still in a robe, breakfasted in his room on savoury soup served in a silver bowl with new-baked bread hot from the palace ovens. Afterwards his valet rebandaged his shoulder. Augustin liked peace at the beginning of a day whenever possible and was thankful his lot was not that of the King's, whose dressing at his *lever* in the morning and undressing at his *coucher* at night always took place in the presence of gentlemen of the bedchamber and other courtiers. Even when the King sat on his *chaise percée* he was not left alone for the few minutes of privacy that even the most humble of his subjects considered a natural right at these necessary times. It was a fact that the King, by long tradition, lived every minute of his life in public and was virtually never on his own, for with his insatiable sexual appetite some part of every night was spent in the arms of Madame de Montespan or one of his many other mistresses.

At half-past ten Augustin ordered his horse to be saddled for him. When he emerged from the palace he found a bevy of women of the Court in flower hues, plumes and ribbons on their hats, forming a riding party of their own, their menfolk being at the hunt. Some were already mounted in the forecourt, others still gossiping together on the steps, and he greeted those he knew as he descended to where his horse awaited him. He mounted and was about to ride off by himself when one of the women riders detached herself from those waiting for the rest of the party and rode towards him.

"Monsieur Roussier! Forgive me for delaying you, but we missed meeting each other yesterday evening."

He steeled himself to turn his head and look towards Susanne Le Viger. As he had feared, he received the same fierce shock to the heart at the sight of her lovely face, framed by the sweeping brim of her plumed, poppy-red hat, her smile dazzling. There was a morning freshness to her that was as captivating as the softer look given her by candle-glow. Involuntarily he recalled his dream of her with such implicit vividness that he assumed a hard expression as if somehow she might read what lay behind his eyes. Almost rigidly he doffed his hat and held it briefly to his chest. "You do me honour, Mademoiselle Le Viger. How did you know me by name?"

"From Jacques's description. In any case, he told me you would be riding alone today. I trust your shoulder is not too painful. I understand that you'll be unable to hunt for several weeks."

"Not as long as that, I hope. At the present time it's impossible to tell."

She flung out a gloved hand in invitation. "Why not ride with us today? I know I speak for all the ladies here when I say we would be glad of a gentleman's company."

He was not at all sure that she was not making fun of him. There was a brilliance in her eyes he could not define, and the other women were giggling and whispering among themselves as they brought their horses up around him. He knew from experience the state of mind of many of them. Bored, always ready for a new diversion, they would enjoy having a lone man in their midst to tease and entice. If Susanne supposed him to be too serious to take a joke well, it would be entertaining to show her otherwise.

Doffing his hat again, he bowed from the saddle to those gathered around him. "I'll escort you with pleasure, ladies." His glance returned to Susanne. "Pray lead the way, mademoiselle. We shall follow."

"Let's be gone then!"

If she had expected him to ride beside her she gave no sign of it and set the pace and direction. Great forests surrounded Fontainebleau and the procession of riders wound its way along a bridle path through the trees, he riding with the last of them. There was plenty of flirtatious chatter from his new companions, few of whom were intent on enjoyment of the open air. He soon tired of it. When he saw Susanne whip her horse into a gallop and break away through a natural clearing in the forest, he flicked his horse as well and went after her with some others eager for real exercise. Clods of soft earth and dry leaves flew up in their wake, while the rest of the party was soon left far out of sight.

None of them slackened pace until Susanne rode her horse through a stream, sending up glittering spray, and brought it to a halt in the shelter of a leafy grove. Everywhere the trees were turning to flame, the colour harsh against the sharp blue of the morning sky. Augustin found himself with just five women and as they dismounted and dropped down onto the grass, laughing and exhilarated, he followed suit. He chose to sit facing Susanne and next to a married woman, Madame Vermorel, as if it was her close proximity he preferred.

"We should have arranged to have a picnic waiting for us here," Susanne said with a sigh of pleasure, watching a flight of birds. She had lost her hat during the gallop and her hair was gloriously dishevelled. "This is a delightful spot."

"Let's do that tomorrow," Madame Vermorel suggested, putting her hands together girlishly. "I adore to eat alfresco."

Susanne looked casually towards Augustin, running a piece of feathery grass she had picked through her fingers. "Would that suit you, Monsieur Roussier?"

It would have been all too easy to delay his departure and accept, but he was on dangerous ground. Every nerve in him was keyed to the scented warmth of exertion that emanated from her, the rise and fall of her buttoned jacket over the swell of her breasts and the way her skirt had drawn taut to reveal the line of her thigh before she adjusted it where she sat on the grass. He shook his head without any sign of regret that he would be absent.

"I'm leaving Fontainebleau this afternoon. This happens to be a good time for me to go home for a few weeks."

"Won't that displease the King?" one of the other women asked.

"Not in my case. He knows I was wounded and would prefer me to be out of his sight."

They all understood. The King abhorred sickness of any kind. He was also intolerant of any physical weakness. Susanne knew her aunt dreaded to be invited to travel in the royal coach for a journey of any length, for the King had a strong bladder himself and expected everyone else to have the same. Nobody ever dared risk his disgust by asking for a necessary halt and suffered agonies in consequence.

"Where is your home?" she asked with interest.

"Near Le Havre. By chance I was born at my grandparents' residence in Luneray."

She looked surprised. "Isn't that a Huguenot stronghold?"

"Yes, it is." He noticed how she glanced away at his reply, lashes lowered, and guessed that her upbringing had included the all too common prejudice against the Huguenots. Much of that feeling inherent in her came from the general resentment throughout France, human nature being what it was, that the Huguenots had banded still closer together after their decimation through past massacres and flight to safety overseas. They had thrived through their own industrious efforts as craftsmen, tradesmen and shopkeepers; many were engaged in banking, shipping and other great commercial enterprises; few, even of noble blood, leading idle lives. For once her familiar attitude did not displease him, for it set a sturdy barrier between them that was of help in keeping him an emotional distance from her. The less they had in common the better.

Madame Vermorel touched the back of his hand lightly with her fingers. "Your parents will be overjoyed to see you, I'm sure."

He gave her a lingering smile. "How kind of you. I'm sad to say my mother died a few years ago. Fortunately my father retains good health."

Susanne came back into the conversation. "Have you brothers and sisters?"

He looked across at her almost as if he had forgotten she was there. "No brothers. I have one sister who is married to a Scottish merchant and lives far away in Edinburgh."

"Ah." She inclined her head sympathetically, understanding that he might as well not have a sister for all the meetings they would have these days. Then, her attention attracted to a point beyond where he sat, she sprang lightly to her feet. "Here come the rest of the party."

He helped all five women to remount. Susanne's fragrance swept over him, intoxicating his senses. Turning away, he swung himself into his own saddle, ignoring her words of thanks. The six of them waited until the procession of riders drew near and then rode forward to join up once more. As before, Augustin fell back to the rear, Madame Vermorel doing likewise. Although he tried to listen and respond to her chatter, his eyes kept returning as if magnetised to Susanne riding well ahead. Somebody had rescued her hat en route and the nodding red plumes tantalised him like beckoning fingers.

When they returned to the palace, he bade her au revoir in exactly the same courteous tones that he used towards everyone else. The last he saw of her was when she went up the horseshoe steps to the great entrance, engaged in close conversation with two of the party. If she did give him a backwards glance, puzzled and disappointed, he was not aware of it as he gave the groom instructions to have his coach waiting for him in exactly an hour's time.

Before the huntsmen returned from the chase, Augustin was on his way. He had ridden too long and too hard that morning and set up such pain in his shoulder that he was glad of the support of the firm upholstery. It would be a relief to get home.

The Roussier ancestral home, known as the Manoir, was an ancient stone building that had once stood alone, part fortress and part residence, its vantage point enabling a watch to be kept for raiders or invaders. With time the port of Le Havre had grown in importance for trade and the dwellings of the townsfolk had spread through the centuries to reach the gates of the walls that now enclosed the Manoir, its parterres and trees and fountains conspiring with ivy and wisteria to mellow and soften the gaunt lines of its structure.

Once the Roussier banking had been conducted from

the Manoir, but Augustin's grandfather had built a large pavilion, constructed around an inner court, for the chambers of finance. It stood some distance from the Manoir, although still within its grounds, and had its own access from the road, busy with traffic to and from the harbour. It was to these chambers that merchants of every trade came; ship-owners and sea captains; nobles who were in dire straits, perhaps through gaming, and many more who were prudent and wanted a safe haven for their money that would bring them accumulated profits. On the level that appealed most to Augustin, expeditions and voyages of discovery were financed and those that were successful added to the fortunes of Gérard Roussier and, indirectly, his son.

As Augustin had expected, upon his arrival he found his father in the great central chamber that was enriched by leather-bound volumes covering the walls from floor to ceiling. Gérard Roussier, a high-born man of immense dignity and intellect, was a daunting figure to those who came in request of a loan and few of them would have recognised him disarmed by pleasure at the unexpected sight of his son. As always, he was impeccably dressed, his grey periwig freshly brushed and curled, the lace fall of his neckcloth and cuffs crisp and pristine.

"What brings you home this time, Augustin?" he asked when greetings were over. "Are you in need of funds or is that sword-hand of yours itching to take a pen to ledgers?" It was a dry joke, referring to the fact that whenever Augustin was home he absorbed himself in the business and, between seeing old friends in the district and being entertained by them, he worked as hard as any clerk until the day he left. As to the reference to funds, that was as close as Gérard could come to outright humour, for investments made on Augustin's behalf gave him an income comparable to that of most men at Court and even covered the occasional heavy loss at gaming.

Augustin smiled. "I think you know well enough, sir, it's not debt that ever brings me back to Le Havre."

"I welcome you home. Your arrival could not have been more opportune. I heard only yesterday that your sister has given birth to a son. There is to be a celebratory banquet here at the Manoir this evening."

Augustin was relieved to hear that his sister was safely

delivered. He missed her whenever he came home, for their ages were not far apart and they had been close until her marriage had taken her far away to Scotland. Jeanette had understood more than anyone else what it had meant for him to be sent away to Court at the age of sixteen instead of going into the business, which was what he had always wanted. He had been taught the ins and outs of finance almost from the time he could walk and then, without warning, Gérard had made the devastating decision about his future that had barred him from it.

"Why?" he had protested vehemently. "My rightful place is here—at the Roussier banking pavilion!"

Gérard had given him a brief answer. "When you have served your year with the musketeers and another year at Court, I'll give you an explanation. Enjoy those two years. Sow your wild oats. Never waste a minute of life in regrets."

It was no wonder those two years were lived to the full, especially as at the back of Augustin's mind was the hope that with time he would be allowed to return, for who else would follow in Gérard's footsteps? There was not the least likelihood of his father ever marrying again to beget more sons, for these days banking was Gérard's sole interest in life.

As Augustin dressed for the banquet that would be celebrating the birth of a baby many leagues away, he recalled clearly his high sense of anticipation when his two years were up and he had come home again to keep that appointment for an explanation from his father. They had sat together by a roaring log fire, a decanter of wine on the table between them.

"Are you still enjoying life at Court?" was Gérard's opening after the wine had been poured into crystal goblets.

Augustin had smiled reflectively. There was nothing like a life of pleasure to ease an early disappointment and provide enriching experiences. He was more than willing to spend another year or two in the King's service before taking up the different excitements of the financial world, but he wanted to be sure that his place was waiting for him when the time came.

"It is all extremely pleasant," he replied. "I know the Court ways now, its protocol and its elaborate etiquette. I can call myself a courtier of the first order."

"Do you see a challenge in advancement there?"

Augustin's eyes narrowed warily. "Only by my own merits as I would expect to prove myself here. I would never join that vast flock of grovelling courtiers who run after the King every minute of the day, pressing for higher positions, currying favour, trying to catch his ear with flattery and virtually pleading for an audience in which to put forward their case or that of some member of their family. They swarm about him like bluebottles, cringing and obsequious to a sickening degree. The King is a patient man. In his place I would have thrown them out of my sight."

"He is also a clever man. Don't you see his political masterstroke? He has them all in the palm of his hand. He is an absolute monarch. All the power is his now. If you win his recognition by your own worth, you will achieve the ultimate for our Huguenot cause."

Augustin shot forward in his chair and thumped a fist hard on the table between them in comprehension. "So *that's* why you installed me at Court!"

Gérard faced him keenly. "I wanted to take you into banking with me from the time you were born. Any man in my position would, and more so when you began to show a quick brain and a natural aptitude for figures. Even the necessary spirit of daring and adventure was in you as in me and my father before me. It was hard for me to make the decision that I did. On the one hand there was a certain wildness in you, which I can tell still thrives, because as yet you are young and you would never have settled down among documents until your system was cleared of it." He took a sip of wine and set the glass down again. "Mercifully, your generation lives less under the shadow of Saint Bartholomew's massacre than those of us who are older, but never suppose its threat has been totally removed. History has a way of repeating itself."

"The King would never—"

Gérard interrupted, holding up his hand. "For all his licentious ways, the King is an intensely pious man at heart."

"That's true. He prays every morning before leaving his bedchamber, attends Mass daily at ten o'clock and is sincerely devout. Are you saying he might turn against us out of religious fervour?"

"I say only that it would be folly to be overconfident or to feel secure. That's why I sacrificed my own wishes in order to place you at Court. I had, and always will have, faith in your integrity. All the time a Huguenot is seen to be favoured with social invitations to Versailles and eventually advances to stand near the King, there are few who would dare to make a concerted attack on the Huguenot cause. You have it in your hands to gain the authority to serve the Throne and France by the best means possible, for thousands of innocent lives depend on your steadfastness and that of others like you."

Augustin looked down as he twisted the stem of the glass on the table in front of him, the jut of his chin showing that he had accepted the responsibility placed on his shoulders. "Why haven't you said all this before? On the eve of my leaving home, perhaps?"

"It would not have been fair to burden a mere lad with such a heavy duty long before time. That was why I chose to wait."

That was all a long time ago. Now Augustin gave a touch to the lace on his linen cuff and went downstairs to be with his father when the guests arrived. Sixty people sat down at the long banqueting table, some of them cousins or otherwise distantly related, the rest friends of the family. As the party progressed, Augustin took note of his father's exceptionally elated mood. He wondered if Gérard saw in the birth of his grandson his successor in the business, perhaps even as a reward for having sacrificed his most heartfelt aim for his son to a greater cause.

The next morning Augustin was up early and soon engaged at the pavilion in reading various contracts and documents that his father knew would be of particular interest to him. A few days went by before he was able to test whether his theory about the new grandson was right. A chair was always put for him in his father's chamber and he sat in whenever clients came to discuss their business. A merchant had just departed and it had been the last appointment of the afternoon. As Gérard locked away a few papers in his desk, Augustin went across to look out of the window at the plane trees.

"Although I'm committed to the task entrusted to me," he said contemplatively, "the tug on my roots becomes stronger every time I come home."

"I am confident that eventually you will overcome it."
Gérard slammed the drawer shut and turned the key. "You
know full well that all is severed for you here."

Augustin turned and stood against the daylight, his tall,
broad-shouldered frame in silhouette. "What if the danger
we fear from the King no longer exists? If time should
prove that any threat is a thing of the past, I would expect
you to open these doors to me in my own right."

Gérard had risen from his chair and he jingled the keys
in his hand. "You still trust Louis, don't you?"

"I do."

"Pray God you are right. If you have proof when my last
day at this desk comes, these keys shall be yours." His tone
was such that Augustin felt he had no hope in that direction.

Holding to his own opinion about the King, Augustin
should have been encouraged by the knowledge that he
was still his father's first choice as his successor if circumstances permitted, but his peace of mind was already disturbed by haunting thoughts of Susanne. In addition, he
found some papers in a file that listed recent incidents
instigating trouble against Huguenots in certain parts of
the country where the Edict of Nantes had always been
poorly enforced. Although he took copies for investigation,
he became increasingly restless, less absorbed in work than
usual and savagely impatient for his recuperation to be at
an end. With two or three of the family dogs loping along
with him, he went for long walks by the sea whatever the
weather, and drank more than was usual. His shoulder
finally healed, but had given a stiffness to the upper part of
his left arm that would always be there, not a serious handicap in civilian life, but making an end to his military service. He was getting ready to return to Court when a letter
was delivered to him in Jacques's hand.

He broke the seal and it told him what he had half-
expected. Jacques and Susanne had named their marriage
day. In spite of being prepared, jealous rage ran through
his veins and he realised that he had been hoping against
all odds for everything to have fallen through between
them. He might have crumpled the letter and thrown it
into the fire if it had not contained further information
written out of sheer goodwill. Jacques wrote that the King
had included Augustin in an invitation to Versailles. His

advice was that Augustin should make for the Château immediately whatever his condition, for the exodus of the privileged from Fontainebleau had already begun.

He broke the good news to his father. "This invitation is not just for some grand occasion as in the past when I've been included with hundreds of others. It appears I've made my mark at last in my own way."

"Well done!" Gérard was immensely pleased.

"It also means that I must depart at once."

"May God go with you, my son."

Since his coach had brought him to the coast, Augustin had no choice but to make the return journey in it, although he felt well able to ride any distance. It was when he reached Versailles where recent rain had created thick mud around some new roadworks that the coachman brought the horses to their slowest pace. To Augustin's surprise a peasant woman, who had been standing back to avoid getting splashed as the wheels went through puddles, suddenly gaped at him in recognition. Not having the least idea who she was, he stared as she plunged her clogged feet into the liquid mud, soiling her skirt-hems, and rushed to grab the edge of the window as she gazed up at him.

"Good day to you, Monsieur Roussier! I'm Jeanne Dremont. You favoured my home by staying in it at the time of the first grand fête."

He remembered her then. Hadn't he and Jacques and the late lamented Léon and François watched her give birth? It had meant nothing to any of them, but this creature seemed to think she had been honoured in some way. The coach was gaining a little speed, but she kept pace with it alongside, an almost demented expression of excitement on her thin, upturned face that made him wonder if she was entirely sane.

"How is your daughter, madame?" He had been reared in an environment where courtesy and kindness were paramount. Not all the sophistication of Court life had been able to take that from him and, in any case, none was more polite than the King himself, who would doff his hat to a kitchenmaid if he met her out of doors.

"Well indeed, sir!" She seemed beside herself with joy at his enquiry. "I know you will recall that you named her Marguerite."

"So I did." He smiled on the memory. How drunk he must have been! "Is she blossoming like her namesake?"

"Oh, yes. She is a beauty already and has learned to read and write." Her pride in her child was enormous and seemed to swell out of her. "She is being taught pretty speech and manners, too. You will not be disappointed in her when the time comes!"

The coach took a lurch forward onto harder ground and she was left behind, staggering a little to keep out of the way of the wheels. It saved her from seeing Augustin's expression of bewilderment and distaste. She hugged herself in her exuberance. He was more handsome than ever with the boyishness gone from his strong features, the green eyes more worldly, the mouth quite splendid. Marguerite could not help but love and be loved by such a man. Throwing back her head, she laughed aloud as if some part of her mind had taken off on wings of its own happiness. Passersby, their notice drawn by her strange mirth, saw her set off homewards at a run, mud dropping from her clogs.

In the coach Augustin had not recovered from this extraordinary encounter. That woman, a respectable artisan's wife, had spoken to him as if she were a procuress with girls for sale, her own daughter being raised apparently for his future pleasure. But why? What claim did she imagine she had on him? Then dimly he recalled some foolish promise he had made. And hadn't there been the gift of a fan with her daughter's name on it? Who could say what untold damage he had done to the placid existence of a peasant woman through the sheer thoughtlessness of youth?

At the Château the coach drew up at the place allotted to those of his position at Court. Those of higher rank could go further ahead. An etiquette of its own was evolving at the Château, almost as if an invisible web being spun to bring every noble still tighter under the King's control.

Augustin found he had been given one small attic room for his sojourn and he was thankful to be under the Château's roof, recalling again the inconveniences of staying in that woman's cottage. Strange that she should have made such an impact on him with her wild promise.

"Have you ever seen a fan among my possessions?" he asked his valet. This man had been in his service for the past two years, the previous one having been dismissed for idleness.

"Yes, sir." The valet prided himself on being able to put his hand on anything his master required, from a certain design of face-patch to a third-best pair of bucket-topped boots. The travelling chest was already open and he dived his hand down into one of the leather pockets to produce the fan, which he had wrapped in a piece of fine linen upon first discovering it, supposing it to be a sentimental keepsake.

Augustin took it from him and opened it. He was struck anew by how exquisitely the scene on the leaf had been painted and he smiled reflectively at the comparatively simple *maison de chasse* that the Château had once been. The main parts of Louis XIII's retreat were still as they were, enclosing the Cour de Marbre on three sides, although eight rose-pink marble columns and more gilded ironwork now added to the beauty of the East Front, while statuary and gilded ornaments graced the edge of the roof. Yet the old section was now truly enveloped on three sides by a majestic building in Roman style. Sand-coloured, its walls were enriched with statues and columns, its flat roof with the ornamented balustrade a complete contrast to the rising grey-blue slates of the preserved East Front. On the new West Front, which looked across the parterres and fountains to the distant Grand Canal, a recessed terrace with arches linked two symmetrically placed apartments, the King's to the north and the Queen's to the south.

Already these extensions were not enough, evidence found in the overcrowded quarters that had been assigned to Augustin, and he had heard from those he had met since his arrival that once again new plans were being drawn up. It was as if the Château had taken on a will of its own and nothing could stop its constant expansion or the beautifying of the gardens.

Augustin closed the fan again. He would keep it. It was an interesting souvenir of the past and would increase in novelty value as the Château continued to grow. The name incorporated in the ribbons seemed to stay with him as he handed the fan back to his valet.

"Make sure this is never mislaid."

As he dressed for the evening, his thoughts turned bitterly to Susanne and his lost chance. At least she and

Jacques were not at Versailles and by the time he met them again he might well have met someone else to stem those feelings for her. Wryly he thought of Marguerite. Hadn't he said he would return when she was seventeen? By his reckoning there were still eight years left to wait. He did not intend to wait as many minutes for some balm to his jealousy. With a flick of his cuffs he left his room to find his way through the sumptuous labyrinth to the State Apartment where everyone would be assembling.

Oddly the name of Marguerite stayed in his mind. It was like the sight he had once had of meadowland white with those namesake flowers as far as the eye could see, almost as though snow had fallen onto green stalks in summer and been dusted with golden pollen. Without being aware of it, he had begun to associate with beauty a misty figure waiting in the future whom he never expected to meet.

Three

Marguerite sometimes thought of the year when she was thirteen as being one of trouble. Marie Printemps started it all by falling violently in love and conducting a concealed affair with a portly, flashing-eyed Venetian being housed as a guest of the Desgranges. He had business at the Château on the matter of mirrors. Earlier, to the King's huge delight, French glassmakers had discovered how to make plate glass which, when backed with foil, became the first flawless mirrors ever to be made, free of air bubbles and giving a perfect reflection. He had ordered vast amounts of these mirrors, installing them everywhere, and they were to be the main feature of a new gallery being planned to link his apartment with that of the Queen's in place of the terrace on the West Front.

Almost overnight Venice was no longer hostile and the Venetian had come with an ingratiating offer of the full cooperation of the Murano glassworks in exchange for the secret of plate-glass making. Nobody knew what was said to the Venetian at the Château, but after being kept waiting for weeks to gain an audience in the right quarter, he ended up with a five-minute hearing and departed afterwards in a great huff. Marie, whom he had used for his convenience during his stay, was left distraught and pregnant. There were no more lessons. The Desgranges banished her to a convent where, after the baby was born, she took vows and was never to emerge again.

"Well, you had had enough learning anyway," Théo said phlegmatically to Marguerite, who was shattered by Marie's fate and angry enough with the Venetian to have killed him on her teacher's behalf given the opportunity. The fiery spirit in her, long suppressed by discipline in the home and her intense interest in her lessons, broke loose on a scale not seen since the early tantrums of childhood. She became tempestuous and difficult even in Théo's presence and he cuffed her for insolence on several occasions, threatening his belt if she continued to defy. Eventually he did use it a couple of times across her back, but it made no difference. She remained dry-eyed and rebellious over any punishment, took no interest in the stack of books Marie had kindly left her, and made careless mistakes in her fanmaking.

Jeanne despaired that the disruption of lessons and accompanying upset should have occurred just as her daughter was at the most vulnerable time of her life. In her opinion Marguerite looked almost ready to break loose and run. Equally threatening, boys had begun to hang around to see her, almost as if some invisible current had alerted them to the change in her, childhood left behind and young womanhood full upon her. As yet, the Venetian's betrayal of Marie Printemps still uppermost in her mind, she tossed her head contemptuously at them, but Jeanne could see the girl was not unaware and it was only a matter of time before one or the other of those equally gawky lads engaged her interest. Young girls were apt to become infatuated very easily. It became Jeanne's desperate hope that Augustin Roussier would reappear before the moment was lost. Marguerite was ripening fast, ready for her first sight of her future love even if it was too early for him.

Augustin's desire for Susanne, far from diminishing, had increased the more he had come to know her. Long after the Fresnay wedding night was over it continued to haunt him. Never before had he been repelled by the bawdy humour and riotous horseplay that accompanied the bedding of newlyweds. It had been all he could do not to break away from the shouting, drunken throng of men that had pushed, half-carried Jacques in nightshirt and robe to the waiting bride. Yet he had had to behave exactly as when he and Jacques had been at the bedding of other friends. To this day the scent of certain herbs, which had decorated the nuptial bed to ensure marital bliss and fertility, brought back the sight of Susanne, sitting up, pale and beautiful, against the pillows as they had propelled Jacques forward into the room. Her giggling attendants had encouraged the lewdness and he had seen the lovely rose colour come and go in her cheeks.

Due to his intervention, the groom's nightshirt had not been ripped from his back and the noisy crowd was kept at bay to allow Jacques to enter the sheets without harassment. As the groom's swordsman, it was he who closed the curtains on that side of the bed. He never knew what made him hold them apart for a fraction longer than those released on the opposite side, but he did and Jacques, shaking with laughter at some jest, failed to see the look that he and Susanne exchanged. In her eyes he saw abject despair and a yearning for him that reflected his long-held feelings for her.

The marriage had taken place at the Duchesse de Valmy's château and he did not see Susanne again for over a month. Then it was at Vincennes. She entered the salon where gaming was taking place wearing a velvet gown the colour of ripe apricots. He had looked up from his cards and it was as if invisible sparks crackled between them. For an instant her whole face blossomed and then the guarded look, which he was to come to know so well since it matched his own, settled on her features like a mask. Until that moment luck at the tables had been against him. It changed even as Jacques, exuberant and happy, brought her across the room to greet him and watch him play. He was reminded of the old adage that to be lucky at cards meant the reverse in love.

Since then they had conducted a curiously silent love affair, wished for by neither of them, never exchanging a word that could be questioned, avoiding each other whenever possible and, above all else, making sure they were never left alone together. In an environment where almost everyone from the King down never gave faithfulness in marriage a thought, he and Susanne, no better than the rest at heart, had created a little vacuum. There was no questioning her deep affection for Jacques. It showed in their ability to laugh together at their own secrets, her obvious pleasure in his company and the occasional surreptitious holding of hands in a cynical society that mocked sentimentality. All this only dimmed when Augustin himself drew near and a stronger, forbidden attraction cast a shadow over her, making her eyes shriek out an appeal for him to keep his distance from her.

There were times when he believed he had overcome his feelings for her. It was usually when he was absorbed in the charms of a new mistress or when the arrival of a pretty young virgin at Court made him think of marriage and his need of an heir. It also helped when Susanne retired to the château on her husband's estate near Orléans to give birth to twins, Jean-Paul and Catherine. Then he was away, travelling as the King's envoy in Italy. When he returned he saw her briefly before she visited Jacques at the war front as high-born wives often did and there was a healing absence again.

Yet the unobtainable continued to hold him in thrall, a mere glimpse of her bringing a resurgence of desire. Although to others, Susanne's interest and devotion seemed channelled solely towards her husband and children, Augustin knew through that special communication that exists between couples attracted to each other that it seemed inevitable that eventually there would be a flash-point. If the situation had been reversed, he did not doubt that Jacques would have felt the same.

When the Fresnays had been married for three years, Augustin found himself with them at a masque at Versailles, the Court having moved there for the summer. Everyone was extravagantly dressed and flaunting a variety of dazzling masks, the moonlit night hot and still and the dark shadows full of amorous encounters.

It had happened that the Venetian Republic, past differences forgotten, had presented the King with two ornate state gondolas for his Grand Canal. In boarding with a number of other people, Augustin and Susanne were separated from Jacques, who had become caught up with those on the companion vessel with the King and Madame de Montespan. The two graceful gondolas sailed slowly down the immensely long canal, fireworks splintering the sky and turning the water to liquid rainbows. Musicians played on one of the gilded sailing ships with silken sails and rigging that made up the little flotilla always at hand for these cruises, merry company on every one of them. Susanne and Augustin were aware only of each other, the exotic setting, the perfume and the flowing wine all heightening the communication of their senses.

She sat beside him on a seat draped with crimson and gold brocade that trailed its fringes over the side into the gently lapping waves. There was such passion in him that he could take no part in the conversation in which she joined, a brave attempt to keep the rising situation on an even keel, while he knew that everything remained as it was at that moment of revelation on her wedding night. He watched her in profile to him. She held up her spangled mask by its handle from time to time and he knew it was more to shield herself from his searing gaze than in the spirit of the masque. The soft lights played over her neck and the mounds of her breasts which rose above the pearl-encrusted square neckline; the diamonds in her hair surrounded her head with an aura.

When they stepped ashore after more than an hour on the water, the King's gondola was still far behind having sailed the full length of the cruciform canal, as well as to the north and south. Susanne made a broken little cry of protest as he swept her into the darkness of a path between the trees, his arm about her waist, but she had lost the will to resist and he brought her to the Enceladus Grove, which was deserted except for the marble giant straining for the heights of Olympus.

He took the mask from her hand and flung it aside with his own. Then he crushed her in his arms and lowered his head to devour her mouth, she responding with equal fervour, the long restraint of their ardour unleashed. She gasped, shivering deliciously when he ended his long and rapturous kissing to scoop down her bodice and possess her breasts, first with his ardent hands and then with his passionate lips until she could scarcely bear the pleasure of it.

He supported her as she swayed, his caresses everywhere, both of them becoming wild with desire.

He bore her down onto the soft leafy mould beneath the surrounding trees, the flowering shrubs a shield, and she was as frenzied as he, pulling at his shirt and breeches, utterly abandoned and beyond herself. He, all sense thrown at having her half-naked form in his arms at last, thrust and rammed into the luscious softness of her with all the power of his long, hard body. Their passion exploded simultaneously, sweeping through her again and again, unlike anything she had ever known before, and she threshed about under him, wanting these moments to last forever.

When eventually they lay still and breathless she ran her hands over his back and shoulders under his loosened shirt while he murmured his love for her between soft kisses. A sense of the passing of time reached her first and with it came a sudden terror of discovery.

"Someone might come into the grove at any minute!"

He brought her to her feet and she bit her lip at the disarray of her clothes and the delicious, never to be forgotten madness that had come upon them both. When she felt her appearance had been put to rights he, ready before her, would have taken her again into his arms, but she evaded him and sat down on the brocaded cushions of a stone seat, needing to adjust her thoughts.

"When can you meet me again like this?" He took the place at her side, sitting turned towards her.

"Never," she breathed, regret tearing at her for what must be denied. "This was something that should not have happened and must never occur again. There's too much at stake."

"Do you expect that we should go our separate ways again after this?" he demanded incredulously. "I could meet you in Paris. Or we could—"

"No." She was firm, not knowing from whence she drew her strength.

Suddenly enraged, he grasped her by the shoulders and shook her. "Why in hell's name did you ever marry someone else? You should have been mine!"

She retaliated swiftly, jerking herself from his grasp. "If you had continued to show the interest in me on the morning of that ride at Fontainebleau as you had the previous evening, I would have told Jacques I needed more time before coming to a decision. He had gained my aunt's permission to wed me, but I'm sure he would have respected my hesitation."

"I was powerless to make any move towards you that day."

She tossed her head bitterly. "Oh, yes. That musketeer pact with Jacques made when you were both only youths. He told me about it a long time afterwards when it was all too late."

"I wanted you the instant I set eyes on you."

She released a deep sigh, calmer and more composed. "It was mutual. I had been watching for Jacques and saw you as soon as you entered the salon with him. I remember feeling choked with excitement. I waited for the right time to return your glance, anxious not to display the eagerness in me."

"I had no idea."

Sadness lay across her eyes. "Until that time I had never known a disappointment as acute as when Jacques would have presented you to me and you had already left. I even arranged the riding party next day because he had told me you would be setting out alone. I believe now that if I had confessed to having fallen in love with you he would have released you from your vow."

"If only I'd known."

"It was hopeless in any case." She traced his lips with loving fingertips. "My aunt would never have allowed me to marry a Huguenot. While we rested on that ride and I learned of the insurmountable barrier it was such a shock that I seemed to feel my heart stop. Did you notice anything?"

"I remember that you turned your face from me."

"I was desperately afraid of having given myself away." Her hand with a glitter of rings drifted back to her silken lap. Somewhere beyond the trees the musicians were playing a piece composed by Lully especially for the nights of sailing on the canal, delicate and romantic in the still air. She spoke again on a pensive sigh. "Is it not odd that we should both care about Jacques for the same reason. He is a good companion to each of us. To you he is a comrade-in-arms as well as a friend and you have fought harsh campaigns together. I know from all he has told me that once you almost lost your own life in saving his."

"He and I fought well together."

She noticed her spangled mask lying near her feet where it had been thrown and she stooped to pick it up. Resting it across her palm, she twisted it restlessly, making small green moons dance over the marble floor of the grove. "I've never known anyone as kind as Jacques," she continued, her voice steady. "He sustained and comforted me at a time when I needed him most. I could never hurt him. Neither would you if you stop to think about it, no matter what you feel for me."

"I can't promise that."

He saw how she bit into her lower lip as if she were equally afraid, but she made a brave attempt to hide her doubts.

"We must go on exactly as before. Not by a look or a sign must we acknowledge how our feelings ran away with us. Jacques must never suspect. I'd go to any lengths to prevent destroying his peace of mind." She rose to her feet to leave the grove. He would have accompanied her, but she stayed him. "Allow me to go alone. The King's gondola should be coming back now. I'd like to meet Jacques on my own."

He let her leave, but not before he had kissed her again, the two of them locked together by the giant Enceladus while a sudden burst of fireworks bathed them in a silvery light.

She went to her children in Orléans shortly afterwards. Normally the existence of offspring did not disrupt the social life of a woman at Court once she had recovered from the dangerous ordeal of giving birth. Children were left in charge of nurses and tutors under responsible supervision, usually at a country estate. Susanne had chosen from the start to have her children with her whenever possible, and they alternated between Paris and Orléans according to whether it was summer or winter, the hot weather in cities bringing forth strange fevers and contagions.

When next she returned to Paris with young Jean-Paul and Catherine, she seemed to have a new control over herself and, as she had insisted in the grove, she made everything as normal as before. Since Augustin had always been a guest at the Fresnays' Paris home whenever they entertained, Susanne saw to it that he was there as often as before and it was only rarely that he caught a glance from her at an unguarded moment or glimpsed her face in a mirror's reflection that told him, without her wishing it, that nothing had changed. As soon as Jacques was off to the Dutch war again, she went back into the country as if to put temptation well out of her way. She had set a pattern to her life and did not intend to be swayed from it.

In December of 1678, the year in which the Dutch war had ended, Jeanne was gathering kindling in the woods when the hunt went by in full cry. It seemed like the answer to her prayers when she saw Augustin galloping just behind the King. Proof that he had risen in royal favour was in the light blue coat with the silver and gold braid that he wore. She knew that permission to wear these coats was given as a favour by the King and apart from entitling the wearer to follow the royal hunt other privileges would be his.

That evening after Théo had gone to the wineshop and Marguerite sat moodily at the table, one of the books Marie Printemps had left her pushed impatiently away, Jeanne decided that the moment had come to disclose the secret she had kept for so long. Putting aside her mending, she moved from her chair by the hearth to the bench opposite her daughter and folded her work-worn hands before her on the table. She was not without trepidation because, whereas once she had looked forward to confiding her secret to Marguerite, there was no predicting how the girl would react in her present state of mind. Yet the time was now. As always at moments of tension, Jeanne felt her nerves knot themselves and her voice came out curiously high-pitched.

"There is something I have to tell you, Marguerite. It has been unspoken between us for a long time. In fact, although you have been unaware of it, it goes back to the day you were born."

As she recounted everything, the joy in what she was telling overcame her nervousness and unconsciously she used the descriptive element that had made her tales of the Château and those who stayed in it so enchanting to Marguerite in the past. She conveyed a kind of magic in her words and as if weaving a spell she drew her listener into the romanticism she had created out of what had originated as an alarming, drunken prank. Her expression was elated and her eyes shone with the unusual gleam that would have sent Théo into a fury. It had never frightened Marguerite and neither did it now since her father was absent and she could use a tone, soothing and emollient, to which her mother always responded. In any case, she was captivated by what she had been told. A surge of rebelliousness at this settling of her future long before she could make her wishes known had succumbed almost at once to the romantic image of the handsome youth naming and claiming her from the moment of her birth. She could not stand out against it.

"What is his name?" she asked almost in a whisper.

"Augustin Roussier. He is your destiny, my child."

"It's a fine name. Does it suit him?"

"Tomorrow you should be able to see for yourself." Jeanne reached out and lovingly stroked an unruly tendril back from her daughter's intense young face. "He is more handsome than any of those marble gods in the Château's park."

Jeanne took care that they did not arrive too early at the gathering of the hunt. She timed their arrival for when a large number of spectators would be there, local townsfolk as well as members of the Court, for she wanted to keep Marguerite secure in a crowd where she could see but not be seen. After all, no craftsman wanted to reveal his creation until it was perfect, and the girl was at a leggy, young filly stage. Three years should do much for her face, which was not yet fulfilling its earlier promise, as well as for her budding figure.

Marguerite had never before had a chance to view at close quarters *la chasse royale*. Jeanne thought the horses of the nobility too high-spirited for safety, having once seen a bystander maimed for life by the kicking hooves of a restless mount. Now the vibrant scene with its moving colours and cheerful din set against the lush outskirts of the forest came fresh to the girl, who sensed that something of her own excited anticipation was at one with the atmosphere prevailing in the grassy dell.

A repast, which had been set out on long tables under a blue and gold canopy, was over, although enough food was left in the porcelain dishes to have fed many more than those who had already eaten. The gold and silver braid on the coats of the hunters glistened as they mounted or stood talking to one another, flicking their riding whips against polished boots, some women ready to ride with them. The hounds, straining at the leash, added their baying to the noisy chatter and laughter and the snorting and stamping of the horses.

Suddenly Jeanne, who had been craning her neck, gripped her daughter's arm. "There he is! That's Augustin Roussier!"

Marguerite followed the direction of her mother's pointing finger. He was in the saddle of a dappled grey horse, a straight-backed man whose blue coat set smoothly across broad shoulders, his face in profile to her, his serious gaze turned in the direction of spectators from the Court as if he was looking for one face in particular among all the others. Marguerite could feel her breath gathering in her chest as if her lungs would burst, for she was gripped by tension at this pivotal moment in her life. Then he, failing to see whoever it was for whom he had searched, swung his attention away and she saw the emerald glitter of his eyes as his glance passed unseeingly over the cluster of townsfolk in whose midst she stood. At that second her breath gushed out in a long sigh and her heart exploded into love for him. It could have been argued that she had been conditioned since birth for this sighting, that she had been primed by her mother's romantic tales and her teacher's exotic myths to be more vulnerable than she might otherwise have been at a highly emotional period in her life, but she held to the belief then, and ever afterwards, that she could have been shown a thousand handsome faces there in the dell and not one of them would have made her fall as completely in love as she did that day with Augustin Roussier.

He, waiting for the King to lead the departure of *la chasse royale,* had been looking for Susanne. The previous evening there had been one of those encounters that stirred up all his feelings for her again. He had watched her take part in what was virtually a ballet performed by the most graceful young women at Court, a display in the Apollo Salon of formal steps and graceful poses that formed part of the *Appartements,* the title given to the three evenings a week when the King and Queen mixed

informally with the Court during allotted hours of entertainment. Concerts, plays, billiards, gaming and dancing
took place in the magnificent rooms of the State Apartment. It was a charming sight as the dancers of the ballet
moved with perfect timing, their full skirts swishing out in
a gleam of silk and satin. Some evenings the dresses were
all in a variation of the same colour.

Augustin had glanced towards the King to see if this
particular ballet, being performed for the first time, was
pleasing his critical eye. But Louis's attention was not
wholly on the dancers. Augustin was near enough to the
canopied chair to see that Louis's dark glance kept leaping
to a window alcove where Jacques was engaged in close
conversation with Madame Françoise de Maintenon, a
good-looking woman with a superior nose and rather fine
eyes, who was witty, brilliant and deeply religious. Although she had not yet surrendered to the King, she had
won his favour, rivalling Athénaïs de Montespan and both
of them competing with the charms of innumerable other
mistresses taking his short-term attention in between. It
was wagered by many that she was destined to be the next
titular mistress since Athénaïs de Montespan appeared to
be falling from favour.

As plenty of smiles were passing between his friend and
Françoise de Maintenon, Augustin set off casually to interrupt the tête-à-tête and allay the King's jealousy. In a
Court where flirtation was a normal part of life and a
strong sensual atmosphere prevailed, it was natural sometimes for reactions to get out of hand. It happened even
when there was no cause for suspicion as now, for Jacques,
although a master of the compliment and the twinkling
glance, was known to be extraordinarily faithful to the
woman he loved. But the King was in a strange mood these
days. Augustin, being close to him, happened to know that
he was being pressured relentlessly by the priests to mend
his lustful ways and was well aware that Françoise de Maintenon was adding her persuasion. It seemed that Louis was
seeking to escape from all admonishments in excesses of
carnal pleasure, taking any comely woman he came across
in a deserted corridor or salon, and even slaking his impatient lust on the waiting maids of his mistress for the night
if she delayed in coming immediately to bed.

Jacques greeted Augustin as he approached. "Come and

join us, my friend. We are having a most interesting discussion on the language of flowers. Madame de Maintenon is quite an authority."

"Do you have a favourite flower, Monsieur Roussier?" she asked.

"The little marguerite of the wayside," he replied, tongue in cheek, the joke his own since Jacques would not remember why he should have made that choice. Even he himself was surprised that it should have come to mind.

His mission was accomplished; the danger of arousing the King's ire had been averted. Louis sat back in his chair and began to tap his foot to the rhythm of the dance. Before long Françoise de Maintenon returned to him while Jacques and Augustin waited for Susanne. When she came she declared herself to be in need of air after dancing in the warm room. A servant was sent for their cloaks, Susanne tucking her curls into her fur-lined hood, and the three of them would have strolled out of the Château through the West Front if Jacques had not been called back by someone who wanted to speak to him.

"Go on without me," he urged when they would have waited. "I'll catch up with you."

For Augustin and Susanne it was the first time they had been on their own since the evening they had made love in a grove. They both guessed that the memory of it was in the other's thoughts as they walked across the spacious terrace and down the steps to pass along the path between the vast frozen ponds, the Water Parterres.

They chatted as they went, keeping the talk to events at Court and people they knew. The next wide flight brought them down to the Latona fountain. It was playing its own music in a lyrical rise and fall, the jets shooting high into the star-lit frosty sky in a constant weaving of spray that created golden veils in the glow of flambeaux on all sides. She thought almost with despair as they halted by it that there was nowhere in the gardens of Versailles that was not intensely romantic either by day or night.

"Susanne," Augustin said softly. Even her name became an endearment when uttered in that way in these surroundings. When he took her hand into his she turned to him. She found herself unable to make any protest as he put an arm around her. Then she was crushed to him, their mouths recapturing the well-remembered ardour. For a few timeless minutes snatched from the barrenness of her existence without him, she surrendered to the joy of responding to his kissing.

No sooner had they drawn apart, their gaze locked, when they were hailed by Jacques who had appeared at the head of the steps and was coming down towards them. Susanne went to meet him and linked her arm through his as if to anchor herself once again.

"What a brilliant evening," he commented, looking up at the stars. "I think we have time to walk as far as the Tapis Vert before we need to escort Susanne in to supper."

She had been invited to sit at the King's table in the large anteroom where this meal took place every evening at ten o'clock. In principle and by long tradition going back over the centuries, the King's subjects were entitled to be in his presence at any time and to petition him on any just cause. People often journeyed for many leagues, sometimes making it a family outing in half a dozen wagons, to enter one or other of the palaces and see the King in his own surroundings. As a result there were always some of Louis's more lowly subjects gathered respectfully in the anteroom every evening at ten o'clock to watch him eat his supper with the royal family, the rest of the space crammed with the nobility. Nearly always some specially invited ladies would be at the table, all of them seated on tabourets, for Louis occupied the only chair, a fine one in rich red brocade.

His life followed a strict routine and he always dined at one o'clock in the afternoon with the Queen on her own, watched again by nobles and Princes of the Blood. His appetite was gargantuan, but he put on no weight and had no need of the fashionable purges that the Queen found beneficial.

Supper was considered a light meal as there were usually only three courses with five or six dishes to each. Neither was it a long meal, which was as well for Louis, because he never had any peace at it. As soon as there was a pause in conversation there was always some courtier bobbing forward to the royal chair, eager to catch the King's ear with a request. He was extraordinarily patient, considering everything asked of him while he put food to his mouth, not always with a fork, for he preferred his fingers and would wipe his hands fastidiously on a clean fresh napkin between every course. All the time there was violin music from the gallery, pieces specially composed to accompany the royal supper, which helped pass the time for everybody else. It was not unusual to see yawns being stifled.

When supper was over, Susanne rose from her tabouret as the King stood up and she curtsied with all the other women, their skirts spreading out around them like multicoloured petals. Louis bowed and smiled at them before going from the room. Augustin, standing back by the wall, saw Jacques go to Susanne and encircle her waist as he led her away. It was one of those times when he thought how much easier life would have been if he had never met her.

Yet in the morning, at the meet, he had scanned the crowds gathered there in the hope of a glimpse of her. He was unaware of a last backward glance thrown in his direction by a redheaded young girl as her mother, a coiffed peasant woman, hastened her away.

Marguerite felt a new phase of her life began in the grove of *la chasse royale*. In an adult manner she resumed her studies on her own, making full use of Marie Printemps's books. Her fan-making attained a higher standard than before and her talent as an artist flourished as a result. It was as if a door had been suddenly opened, showing her at last the path she was to take, and she was no longer confused about life and what it held for her. She had listened without comment when her mother had broken it to her that there would be no marriage with Augustin Roussier and the opportunities for that would come later. It came as no surprise. Her ears were sharp and enough gossip circulated about those at the Château for her to have a realistic attitude on that score. Gentle Marie Printemps and her fate constituted a clear warning. Only a doormat was cast aside. Marguerite resolved it should be different for her whatever her mother might have planned on her behalf.

To Jeanne's dismay Marguerite grew still taller in the ensuing three years and her looks, which had made her such a pretty child, had become too unusual to be remotely beautiful. There was no symmetry to give the loveliness that had been hoped for, her nose long, her chin too determined and her wide-lipped mouth as red as if she had

access to the paint used by the whores of Versailles. As for
her hair, that was the biggest disappointment. Far from
easing into the deep waves that Jeanne had always pictured in her imagination, it had all along tightened its curls
waywardly, making it difficult to control, and deepened
gradually to an impossible colour, a dark crimson shot
through with coppery tones. It broke combs and would
only submit to a brush, bouncing up even then into myriad
tendrils that refused to be tamed. In all Jeanne's life she
had never met anyone else afflicted with such a hue or
with hair of such rebelliousness although, in searching her
memory, she recalled that her grandmother had talked of
a forebear with hair like a witch's.

Far from looking forward to the girl's seventeenth natal
day, Jeanne began to dread it. She had promised Augustin
Roussier he would find a beauty when he came and he
would be disappointed. Nothing would be as she had
hoped. It was no consolation to her that the opposite sex
was attracted to the girl, because she had had the same
attention when she was young and knew the predatory
purpose behind it, men being made the way they were.
What worried her most was a certain uppishness about
Marguerite, which matched her defiant hair, and an air of
self-sufficiency that did not seem to fit in with what Jeanne
still hoped for her. In her present state of anxiety, Jeanne
forgot that from the start she had wanted her daughter to
be able to stand alone if anything should happen to her.

Shortly before Marguerite's natal day, a heavy blow fell
on the Dremont family. Théo was given six weeks' notice
in which to quit the cottage. It had finally been encom-
passed for demolition in Le Nôtre's layout for the extended
township. Jeanne, who had long since come to the conclusion that they were too far out ever to be affected, almost
collapsed when he broke the news.

"No!" she shrieked in protest. "I won't go! I came to this
cottage as a bride and Marguerite was born here. Why
can't the King be satisfied with what's been done already?"

"This day had to come," Théo answered, no more
pleased by it than she was, but knowing it was pointless to
rail against it. "As for the King, be thankful that he has kept
on building. I'd have been out of work these many months
if he had not continued to add to that great Château of
his."

Jeanne would not be appeased. She began to speak harshly of the King in a way that would have been foolish had she not kept her outrage to within the cottage walls. Old resentments built up in her out of past memories of hunger while he had hunted for pleasure, and also of her father's death at his father's command. Other housing was available, but she had set herself completely and illogically against leaving her home and the little garden she had nurtured, the produce of which had kept them from starvation many times. Marguerite believed privately that most prominent of all her mother's distresses was the fear that Augustin would come in search of her daughter at the cottage and find it gone with none to tell him where she was to be found.

Under the weight of this tension, which brought sleepless nights, Jeanne was a mass of nerves by the day Marguerite was seventeen. The importance of the date increased her agitation to a point where the shaking of her hands made any fan-painting impossible and she resorted to sorting fan-sticks at the table. She jerked up from the bench whenever an equipage passed the windows or when a rider trotted up. Marguerite, upon rising from bed that morning, had put on a new blue skirt and bodice that had been made for this occasion, but now she felt compelled to quell her mother's immediate anticipation, even though what she had to say would not be welcome.

"Monsieur Roussier won't come today. You must give him time."

Jeanne's question came sharply: "How do you know?"

"I have a confession to make. I didn't just go for a walk yesterday evening. I went to see the King at supper."

"What! I've forbidden you ever to go into the Château alone."

"I wasn't alone. Noémi Gadeau was with me."

"Worse! She's a little minx and not to be trusted." Jeanne was extremely angry.

"Noémi behaved herself. I threatened to box her ears if she didn't." Unbeknownst to Jeanne, it was not the first time the two girls had been to watch the King sit down for his supper in the public eye. The gates of the Château were never closed and the only provisions for entry were a tidy appearance, however humble the garments, that men should hire a sword from the porter for the accent of formal dress and women remove their aprons. The same rules applied to those entering the park, only pedlars and beggars being excluded there as in the Château. Marguerite and her friend in their homespun skirts and bodices, their caps crisp and white, had been passed through with everyone else. "At least I have obeyed you in never going to the State Apartment as lots of my friends have done."

"I should think not! Silly-headed girls at risk amid lecherous company!" Jeanne leaned forward to drum her closed fists on the table in demand for a satisfactory reply. "Why did you go to the King's supper?"

"I was looking for Augustin Roussier. If he had been there I could have expected him today, but I didn't want to spend endless hours in useless suspense." She spoke firmly, but there was a wealth of feeling in her words. "I don't think I could have endured it."

Jeanne, taken aback, still did not relent. "There are hundreds of people in the Château whenever the King is there. It was no guarantee of Monsieur Roussier's absence from Court just because you didn't see him."

Marguerite straightened her shoulders for what she was about to say next, knowing she must expect the full force of her mother's wrath. "From what I have noted, he is always in that anteroom at suppertime."

Jeanne went white to the lips. "How many times have you been there without my knowledge?"

"I haven't kept count. At least two score, I suppose." Marguerite's expression became suddenly desperate. "I waited over a year before I gave in to the temptation to try to see him again. I had to go there. I couldn't stay away."

"Have you ever tried to engage his attention?"

Marguerite was astonished that she should ask. "Never. I knew I had to wait until I was seventeen." Then, taking a tight grip on herself, she expressed her gravest fear. "We have to consider that when he does return to the Château next time he may have forgotten it is the year of his promise."

If anything, Jeanne turned even whiter and she crossed herself hastily. "Don't say that! You mustn't think it either. It's bad luck to doubt your destiny."

Marguerite shivered uncertainly as if a shadow had passed over her. Instinctively she reached her hands out to her mother, who gripped them. Although each drew comfort from the other, apprehension remained with them like something tangible. As they resumed work, Marguerite found it difficult to concentrate, for in spite of what had been said her mother continued to jerk upwards to glance through the window at every passing sound, making a new disappointment for herself every time. It was alarming to see how the little clash between them had increased Jeanne's agitation. Her hands were shaking almost as much as her head. It was as though some kind of nervous palsy was affecting her and she kept dropping the fan-sticks until Marguerite suggested she put them away and make some bread instead. It was a domestic chore she had always liked and she became a little calmer as she kneaded the dough.

It was early afternoon and the cottage was filled with the good smell of newly baked bread when there came the sound of some commotion approaching along the lane. A horse was being driven fast and wheels were rattling in their speed. Jeanne, who was still too restless to resume fan-making, had begun to scrape carrots for the evening meal. A wild look of excitement dawned on her face as the wheels drew up outside. Her hand, reaching for a fresh carrot from the little pile, became motionless in mid-air.

"It must be he!"

Marguerite sprang to her feet and swung around to face the door. It burst open and one of Théo's workmates threw himself into the room, his expression greatly troubled.

"Come at once, Madame Dremont!" he urged breathlessly. "And you, Marguerite! There's been an accident! Théo fell to the terrace from the scaffolding of the new gallery on the West Front. I have my cart outside."

Without a word Jeanne flew for the door. As she went she dropped the carrot knife into her pocket and reached automatically to snatch her shawl from its peg and throw it about her shoulders. Marguerite followed and clambered up into the cart after her. Neighbours, alerted to trouble by some sixth sense, came hurrying out of their cottages to watch them driven swiftly by, the carter's whip cracking over the horse's head.

"How badly is my husband hurt?" Jeanne croaked.

Monsieur Dumay did not turn his head. "All I can say is that he was alive when I left to fetch you, madame. It's not good. His foot became entangled in a rope and he tumbled from one height to another."

Jeanne moaned and clung tighter to her daughter whose arms were about her. When they reached the Château, Monsieur Dumay drove through the main gate, the wheels dancing over the large square cobbles of the enormous Cour Royale. Finally he reached the vast terrace of the West Front. Marguerite sprang down from the cart and her mother came after her. Work had stopped on the site and a crowd of workmen were gathered at the foot of the scaffolding. They parted to let the two women come running through. One of the masters of work blocked their way briefly to prepare them.

"I'm sorry, madame and mam'selle. There was nothing to be done for him."

Théo lay on his back with a coat covering his face. Jeanne flung herself down on her knees beside him and pulled the covering aside. There was surprisingly little blood, only a trickle from one nostril and a corner of his mouth, but by the awkward splay of his limbs it looked as if he had broken bones in crashing against some lower scaffolding before reaching the ground. She gathered his head against her and sobbed bitterly, wiping the blood away from his face with a corner of her apron, racked by grief.

"Oh, my poor Théo," she moaned, stroking his hair, his rough chin and trying to tidy his neckcloth. It took quite a time before Marguerite, her own tears making rivulets down her face, eventually managed to persuade her mother to allow Théo to be lifted up by four of his workmates and carried to the cart. Jeanne swayed as she rose unsteadily to her feet and the master of work as well as Marguerite gave her support as they began to follow the bearers ahead.

They had almost reached the waiting cart when there was a burst of hearty laughter a little distance away. Jeanne shuddered violently at this sound of mirth that degraded her husband's last passing from this place where he had toiled countless hours. Turning her head to see from whom the laughter came, it was a second or two before her tears cleared enough for her to discern the group of noblemen mounting the terrace steps in the company of the King. With a muttered exclamation, she wrenched herself away from those supporting her and stood looking towards the new arrivals on the scene.

Louis, who liked nothing better than to show off the beauty of his park and in particular the marvellous fountains, was returning from a short tour on foot with the English ambassador and some other distinguished guests, a number of courtiers in attendance. Usually the tour was by carriage, which enabled much to be seen, but the Englishman had wanted to walk and thus they had only managed to get as far as the Apollo fountain and back again. When the accident had happened they had all been too far away to have any knowledge of it and the fifteen hundred jets of sun-sparkling fountains playing throughout the park had literally drowned the distant shouting that had rung out. As Louis turned to guide his guests onto the North Parterre, one of them made an entertaining remark and he, always quick to enjoy a joke, threw back his head as he joined in the laughter.

In Jeanne something snapped. With a demented screech she hurled herself in the King's direction; her shawl flapping about her shoulders like the wings of a crow. Marguerite cried out in panic-stricken alarm: "Mother! Come back!"

She would havè dashed after her, but was swung off her feet as the master of work grabbed her by the arm and held her for her own good. He was able to see that something as terrible as the earlier tragedy was about to take place and it was too late for anyone to stop it. Already the King had halted and was staring in bemused disbelief as Jeanne came screaming abuse at him. Her shrill voice reached in all directions.

"You devil! You cold-hearted murderer! You don't care what has happened because you have no heart." She reached the place where he stood, but his aura was such in his rich sapphire-blue coat and hat and gleaming black periwig that she remained a few feet from him without knowing why, for she had no fear in her now totally unbalanced mind, her face contorted with loathing. "It's not enough that you must take my home from me and the little patch of land that has been our salvation when you would have had us starve, but now my husband has been killed to satisfy your lust for glory. You are a monster! An evil lecher as everyone knows! I spit on you!"

Her head shot forward and her spittle landed on the polished toe of Louis's right shoe. His upsurge of rage clamped his features rigidly and as his chest expanded with it, his most quiet and terrifying manner settled on him like a cloak, frightening the guards who had come at a run to draw the demented woman back. Louis raised a pointing finger at her, giving a deadly order in an impassive voice.

"Hand that woman to the Château police. She is to be flogged and thrown into prison. She shall never see the light of day again."

As she was seized he turned towards his guests, who stood aghast, and nonchalantly made some remark about the floral patterns they were about to see. It was as if nothing untoward had taken place. Yet inwardly he was seething. That such an incident should have happened in the presence of his distinguished guests was insupportable, even though his dignity had remained unimpaired. He was proud of his people's affection, the way they flocked to see him and the warmth of their cheers when he visited cities or rode home from yet another victory in the field for France, he the most godlike and awesome of men. No king ever had a setting more suited to him than he, monarch of the most powerful country of Europe, and it had given him intense satisfaction to see how impressed the representative of France's one-time enemy had been with the size and beauty of Versailles.

Then, ruining the day, that creature had burst upon him. Not since the loathed uprising of the Fronde in his boyhood when rebellious nobles and their peasant followers had stamped his hatred on Paris forever had he been subjected to such insults. He felt nauseous from the sensations of the past that she had revived. She had come like a ghastly spectre from those childhood days, dragging icy nightmares with her of when he and his mother had gone in danger of their lives. At least she would never emerge from the dungeons to rise up at him ever again.

As he led the way, discoursing on the flowers that he loved to see all around him, he failed to notice that one of his courtiers had dropped behind and broken away from the rest of the party. It was Augustin who crossed to the scaffolding where the workmen were returning to their construction tasks in silence, dismayed by the severity of the sentence passed on the distraught widow of their late workmate.

"What happened here?" he asked the fellow who was nearest. "What made that woman come screeching to the King in that manner?"

When told he hurried after her, compassion mixed with a certain sense of responsibility since he had recognised her, strange though their acquaintanceship happened to be. Already she was out of sight, having been rushed away, kicking and screaming, by her captors. Turning the corner of the building, he overtook the trundling cart in which the covered body lay and was in time to see Jeanne disappear in custody through a door before it was slammed shut against a girl who had tried to enter as well.

Slowing his pace, he watched her hammer with her fists on the door in desperation. He could only suppose that this was Marguerite. She had lost her cap in her struggle to get to her mother and her vivid hair hung loose and dishevelled down her back to below her waist. As her efforts failed, he saw her drop her forehead against the door between her palms in an attitude of abject despair. Slowly she sank down to her knees, her shoulders heaving with sobs. Nearby the cart had drawn up and Augustin signalled to the carter that he should wait. Then he went up the few steps to where the girl knelt and touched her shoulder.

"Mademoiselle Dremont?"

She raised a tear-stained face that stunned him with its extraordinary charm. In spite of the flowing eyes, the mouth awry with anguish, she had the most fascinating looks, ugly until one realised at the same instant it was a rare beauty of the most sensual kind, her alarmingly white skin pure alabaster, her thin brows winged to a point as if for flight from lashes as thick as a fringe on a bed's drapes. As she blinked to gain sight of him through the dazzle of her tears, she gave an indrawn gasp of recognition. Immediately she flung her arms about his knees, frantic in her appeal.

"Help my mother, I implore you, Monsieur Roussier! She didn't know what she was saying to the King. My father's death has unhinged her mind."

"You know me?" He had an almost irresistible urge to bury his fingers in the glorious mass of her unruly hair.

"I've seen you many times." She pressed her face against

the edge of his brocade coat, her wet cheeks making patches on it. "I've no one else to ask for aid. For mercy's sake, hear my plea."

Two of the Swiss Guards, who by long tradition guarded the Kings of France, had come onto the scene in their blue and gold uniforms, prepared to drag her from him and be rid of her, but he shook his head and indicated they should be about other duties. Then he stooped down to take her by the arm and bring her to her feet, aware of the trembling of shock in her. She was taller than he had realised, reaching his shoulder, and he liked it that she did not hang her head but let her chin rise high.

"I know what happened and I understand your mother would not have acted as she did if it was not as you say. However, there is little I can do as yet. The King will have his guests with him until the end of the day, which will be my first chance to speak to him. In any case it will be as well to let his anger ebb."

"But my mother's flogging?" The girl's strongly arched nostrils, indicative of a passionate temperament, quivered in her dread.

"It won't be carried out here. I can assure you of that." He knew that Louis did not allow any sort of sordid punishment to take place on a site he revered. It was an old tradition that the Kings of France could not stay in a place of death, and to save inconvenience nobody, other than a member of the royal family, was even allowed to die at the Château. Those taken by a fit of apoplexy or some other illness of a possibly fatal nature were hastened away immediately. "I should think it would be tomorrow at the earliest and then at some appointed time at whichever prison she is to be taken."

"Where will that be?"

"I shall find out and do whatever lies in my power to abort the sentence she has received. Remember I can promise you nothing."

"Nevertheless, I thank you with all my heart, sir." She snatched hold of his hand and kissed it in a rush of gratitude.

"My advice to you now is that you should go home with the cart and do everything that has to be done for your father."

She nodded bravely, unaware that her courage touched him. "How shall I know about my mother?"

The obvious reply was to say a message would be sent. Instead, inviting untold complications, he heard himself say what he had least intended. "I'll bring you the news myself, whether it be good or bad."

Leaving him, she went to the cart and clambered up beside the carter to be driven under the same archway through which they had come with such speed only a short while before. She looked ahead unseeingly. There must be no more tears, for there was much to do before her mother was released, which she hoped would be in time for the funeral. She could not believe the King would not relent once everything was explained to him, and there was no one she would trust more to put her mother's case forward than Augustin Roussier. Oddly enough, all her youthful infatuation for him had evaporated completely, swirled away in grief and fright and, curiously, thankfulness for his timely presence. She did not know why. He had loomed above her in all his handsomeness as she knelt on that step and he could have been any Good Samaritan. Perhaps all along fate had had another reason as to why he should come back into her life that day. It was not so much for her sake but that Jeanne should be saved from imprisonment, a reward for keeping faith over such a long period and wishing in vain for what in reality would never be.

As soon as the cart was gone, Augustin rapped authoritatively with his tall cane on the door that had been barred to Marguerite. It opened at once and he entered to be taken through to the Chief of Police.

From that officer he learned that the prisoner would be kept there overnight and transferred to the fortress of Pignerol shortly after dawn where the flogging would be carried out.

"Why Pignerol?" he asked, surprised.

"She has offended personally against the King."

So that was it. How many others were incarcerated there for slights real or imaginary? He knew one. When he himself was newly come to Court the finance minister had been Nicolas Fouquet, who had just built a marvellous château, Vaux-le-Vicomte, which had been grander at that time than anything the King owned. Proud of his new residence, Fouquet had been reckless enough to give a

great ball for six hundred people in its gilded magnificence
with lavish gifts of diamonds for the women and thoroughbred horses for the men. Louis, who had been the guest of
honour, had been furious that any subject should set himself above the Throne. Fouquet had been imprisoned, his
treasures annexed, and it was said it was at that ball Louis
first thought of enlarging the lodge at Versailles. It was
certainly true that very soon afterwards, Le Vau, Le Brun
and Le Nôtre, who had been responsible for the architecture, the interior decoration and the gardens of Vaux-le-
Vicomte, were brought to Versailles to transform the lodge
into the Château that now far surpassed in size and gran-
deur anything else in France and, it was beginning to be
said, in the world.

As Augustin left the police headquarters he thought how
his trust in the King had waned since he had once spoken
of it in his father's house. Gradually he had become aware
of the deviousness in Louis's character. Today had been
another prime example of Louis's unpredictability in the
matter of justice. Out of the blue it could take a devastating twist after months of carefully considered and reasonable judgements.

Setting off up the Cour Royale, Augustin hoped that
Jeanne Dremont was not to be subjected to the long imprisonment that Fouquet had already endured. There
were several ways of petitioning the King that he had
never tried. He had always previously secured an audience
by appointment, for it was known by now that he never
approached on any trivial matter. But that took time,
which was running out for Jeanne Dremont. The most
obvious alternative was to approach the King's chair during supper, but with many courtiers hovering around like
birds of paradise in full court dress, it was sometimes an
undignified case of elbowing in front of others to gain
Louis's attention. In any case, his appeal for clemency for
the unfortunate woman was a difficult subject to present
during Louis's munching of game in wine sauce or his
spooning of a compôte.

Augustin finally decided to wait instead by the door of
the King's bedchamber. It was generally considered that
to delay Louis when his thoughts were directing themselves towards his mistress for the night was not the best of
times, but he had no other choice.

When the supper reached its closing stage, Augustin left the anteroom and took up his station. He had only been waiting a few minutes when a comte whom he knew quite well came looking about as if in search of someone. Spotting Augustin, he hurried across.

"There you are! You are to attend the King's *coucher* tonight. I was afraid I wouldn't find you in time."

It was a summons that could not have been more opportune, an honour sought after by every man at Court, but the highest nobles were always in attendance and the few others invited were usually there for some special reason or other. Augustin could only conclude that in his case his recent successful journey as envoy and his swift return that morning had pleased Louis more than the haughty, autocratic face had shown.

As always, there was a stir among those present when the King appeared. He passed through the doors of his bedchamber and Augustin, observing the tight protocol that prevailed on all these occasions, followed last of those entering the royal sanctum and the doors closed behind him.

It was a spectacular room, almost entirely gold, which was fitting for it was here that the Sun King laid his head. Interwoven crimson in the lustrous patterns of the Lyonnaise silk added to the fiery splendour of the walls, furnishings and the great bed itself, its huge canopy topped at all four corners by gilded trophies holding snowy ostrich plumes that almost reached the ceiling. A gold-encrusted balustrade divided off the bed from the rest of the room and no one followed the King into this royal sanctuary.

Although it was the first time Augustin had been in attendance at a *coucher*, he had been present many mornings among other courtiers and members of the royal family to see the King dressed, lifting no finger himself. There had also been state occasions when Louis, sitting on the end of the glorious bed, had received ambassadors and other important personages, for there was no higher compliment to be paid by the King than to grant an audience in the royal bedchamber.

Everything was laid out in readiness. A gold and lace robe lay across one chair with matching slippers beside it, a nightshirt of Lyonnaise silk exquisitely embroidered lay across another and on the balustrade was a cloth of gold cushion supporting a nightcap and handkerchief.

Louis, who took almost no part in his own undressing any more than in his dressing at the *lever,* glanced across to where Augustin stood at the back of the room. "You may hold the candle, Monsieur Roussier."

Honour upon honour! Why it should have evolved that holding the special gold candlestick at the *coucher* should be such a privilege nobody knew, but it was one more sought-after favour by which Louis kept his nobles in thrall. Augustin made a deep obeisance before removing his glove and taking the candlestick from the head valet who brought it to him. He recalled a tale that he had heard. Such was the terror Louis could inspire that a page had once fainted simply because he thought he had singed the royal periwig with the candle. Holding the candlestick high, Augustin seized the privileged moment to speak instead of waiting until the end of the *coucher* as he would have done otherwise.

"May I put an important matter to you, sire?"

Louis gave a nod as his *Cordon Bleu* sash was released. He was used to being petitioned until the last moment of the day was over, everyone always wanting personal advancement, or promotion of some kind for relatives, sometimes even a dispensation of the tax that Colbert was demanding. "Come forward, Monsieur Roussier. What is it you want to ask me?"

Augustin began his appeal for clemency for Jeanne Dremont. Those present thought he would have made a good advocate in the law courts, for he put the facts forward succinctly. Louis listened impassively as he submitted to his undressing. His hooded lids made it easy for him to disguise his thoughts and the glint of his eyes gave nothing away of the implacable hatred he felt towards the creature who had railed at him that day. When he was ready for his nightshirt, he nodded to the duc who held it, the honour of presenting it going always to the man of highest rank in the room. When it was slipped over his head and the silken cords tied, he looked with eyes of ice beyond where Augustin stood waiting, almost as if he could see beyond the walls into some cold and frozen place.

"Your petition cannot be granted, Monsieur Roussier." That was the end to it. Louis had listened and given his verdict, polite as always, but obviously disliking what had been put to him.

Nobody else in the room cared in the least what happened to the peasant woman and several of them began to put requests of a minor nature, coming forward in turn. It added to Augustin's frustration that each was granted.

Being lowest in rank, he was the first to bow out of the room. The bedchamber was held in such esteem that those of highest rank stayed longest in it instead of being the first to leave as happened elsewhere. As Augustin had left its threshold he realised the only course that was open to him now was to bribe those taking Jeanne Dremont to Pignerol and ensure that she only received a token flogging of a stroke or two. As for her future, she must serve her sentence until some special occasion, such as a victory in the field or a royal wedding of one of the Princes of the Blood, when the King sometimes granted amnesty to a few harmless prisoners.

As instructed, Augustin's valet awakened him just before dawn. He decided to be barbered upon his return and as soon as he was dressed he left the room, which was in the enormous new wing that had been specially built for housing the courtiers and was large enough to have been a palace in its own right elsewhere. Cleaning women and floor polishers, not normally seen by any except the early-risen servants, were busy everywhere, some engaged in cleaning of a special nature.

With the only privies located behind a wing flanking the Cour Royale, although there were plenty there, it was not always possible, due to the size of the Château, for people to reach them, or a *chaise percée* in their own rooms, in time. Visitors not in residence were frequently at a loss. The result was that those caught in desperate straits urinated, defecated and vomited in any private corner of a deserted corridor or staircase or even in a window embrasure. Those who were drunk behaved even more carelessly. It was an achievement by the cleaning staff that the Château should be as clean as it was, particularly as in addition to all else thousands of feet trod dust or dirt or mud in and out of it every day.

With some unpleasant stenches not yet dispersed, it was a relief to get out into the fresh morning air. It promised to be a splendid day and the big square cobbles of the Cour

Royale and those of the Place d'Armes beyond the shining gates were bathed in the pink glow of the rising sun. When Augustin reached the door against which Marguerite had hammered in vain the previous day, it stood open and the prisoners' wagon was drawn up in front of it, the whole area well out of sight of the central and main windows of the Château. Apart from the money for bribes, he had a purse of gold louis in his pocket to give to Jeanne, which would enable her to buy a few comforts for herself, gaolers being obliging to those with money.

He entered the police quarters and surprised the Chief of Police at his desk in the middle of a huge yawn. The man swallowed it hastily and stood to doff his hat and bow.

"I want to see the prisoner Dremont," Augustin informed him with the air of command that came naturally with his wealth and rank. "I'd like a few minutes alone with her."

"Certainly, sir. Some food is just about to be taken along to her cell."

Augustin followed one of the Chief of Police's subordinates who carried a mug of watered wine and some slices of bread, keys jangling on a ring. Judging by the unlocked cell doors Jeanne was the only prisoner. The key was inserted in a lock stout enough to have kept in a score of strong men instead of one slightly built woman.

"I'll take the food," Augustin said and it was handed to him. He stepped into the gloomy cell and the door was locked after him. Putting the victuals on a table, he announced himself at once. "Don't be alarmed, Madame Dremont. You know me. I'm—" His voice trailed away. She was slumped against the wall in a sitting position on the narrow bed below the high grating that let in a mere glimmer of light. To his horror he saw she was soaked in blood and that it was everywhere. *"Mon Dieu!"* he exclaimed despairingly under his breath. She had slashed her wrists.

He rushed across to her but she had been dead for several hours. Lying on the floor by her foot was a small knife such as housewives used for paring vegetables. Picking it up, he saw a few carrot scrapings dried on the handle. He sighed and shook his head sadly, his thoughts going to Marguerite who would have this double bereavement to bear. Immediately he made up his mind what to do. He tapped on the door and it was opened. Making sure he blocked the view into the cell, he asked that the Chief of Police should come there.

As soon as the officer had entered, Augustin, standing between him and the body, instructed him to send his subordinate in the passageway well out of earshot. When this had been done the Chief of Police turned back into the cell, the ring of keys in his hand.

"Well, sir?" he asked inquiringly. It was then that Augustin drew aside. The man's eyes, adjusting to the gloom, registered his dismay at the sight that met him. "I never thought she was the type to do anything like this!"

Augustin exploded in fury. "You neglected your duty! She must have had this knife in her apron pocket. Why didn't you make sure she had nothing with which to harm herself?"

"If she had been hysterical I might have had her apron and stockings taken from her, but she became quiet as a mouse as soon as she was brought in here." He began to bluster, throwing his hands about. "In any case, nothing like this has ever happened here before to my knowledge. We only get thieves to take in charge temporarily, or the occasional drunken peasant being rowdy in the park. I looked in on this woman before I went off duty and she was sitting quietly with her hands in her lap, staring at the wall."

"You fool! Now I will tell you what you are to do. Send for a reliable woman, one you can trust to keep her mouth shut, to lay out the body and clean this cell without anyone else knowing what has happened. I will arrange for a coffin to come in a closed baggage wagon at eleven o'clock to collect the body for a joint funeral with the late husband."

"I can't allow that! It's unconsecrated ground for this woman outside a prison yard somewhere. I'll have to look up the nearest one."

Augustin's face was already livid with rage and his lips drew thin. "Jeanne Dremont lost her reason. She didn't know what she was doing. Her soul had nothing to do with her self-destruction. Now do as I say. Enter the death as being from natural causes and close your book on the case."

"I can't do that!"

"I think you can." Augustin's tone was dangerous. "Consider for a moment. As far as everyone at the Château is concerned the matter has been settled, because the sole responsibility for custody here in these quarters is yours." There was a pause that was a threat in itself. "If you don't do exactly as I say, I shall take the matter of your neglect to the King himself. Have you forgotten that nobody other than a royal personage is allowed to die at this Château, even in this part of it?"

The officer blanched. He had not forgotten. "What if the woman's priest should come to question me?"

"You can say truthfully that it was to spare the King's inconvenience through death at the Château that the body was taken away discreetly after heart failure."

"Very well, sir." The officer knew his whole future was at stake. "It shall be as you say. I'll send my squad out on routine duties and be alone here."

"One more precaution. Make sure you nail the coffin lid down securely. That will finally ensure that nothing more is ever heard or said about this terrible tragedy."

Augustin sent his servant to hire a baggage wagon and entrusted him both to drive it and to assist the Chief of Police in carrying out the coffin and loading it when they could be certain of being unobserved. If any of the policemen asked about the prisoner they would be told she had died suddenly and it had been expedient to have the body removed as quickly as possible. They would understand the necessity for haste, for they were jealous of their good reputation and would not want their section to fall into disfavour with the King.

Augustin set out in plenty of time for the Dremont cottage, planning his arrival to be well ahead of the coffin. He was full of pity for the girl to whom he had to break the news of this second bereavement and pondered how he might ease the pain of it for her.

Marguerite must have been watching out for him, because as he dismounted she opened the door and stood waiting. She was in black with her hair drawn back under a white cap, tendrils escaping all around as if nothing could control it. Her beautiful eyes, which impressed him again with their luminous blue, were bruised with grief and she looked as if she had slept little during the night.

"What news of my mother?" she asked at once, although her voice faltered at the gravity of his face.

Before replying, he entered the cottage and she closed the door after him, staying where she was as if any movement on her part might make what he had to tell all the worse. Her father's coffin was on the table, a candle burning beside it and some wildflowers picked from the hedgerows in a little bunch on the lid. He had removed his wide-brimmed hat upon arrival and he put it aside as he turned to face her.

"Summon up your courage, Marguerite," he urged gently. "I have sad tidings. I failed to get any kind of reprieve for your mother, but shock can wreak havoc on the heart and release came to her by another way."

He saw comprehension dawn agonisingly in her eyes. She did not faint as he half expected, although her pallor increased. "My mother is dead," she whispered in anguish. "Were those ravings of hers a kind of death throes?"

"I believe they were."

She gulped painfully. "Where is she?"

"Her body has been released by the authorities and is on the way here. You will find the lid fastened down. Leave it that way. Remember her as she was in life."

"That is what she would have wanted." Her mouth began to quiver uncontrollably and she flung up the back of her hand against it in a desperate effort to restrain it. Then he did, as he told himself afterwards, what anyone of compassion would have done in the circumstances. Almost of their own volition his arms went out to her. With a choked cry she hurled her face in his shoulder, clinging to him as if she would never let go.

As he held her he became aware of a great warmth of feeling that he had not experienced since Susanne had first stirred his heart. Almost with incredulity he considered what he had already done for this girl whom he hardly knew. He had risked the King's displeasure and incurred it by his appeal for clemency; he had threatened a chief of the police and contrived in smuggling a body out of the Château; lastly he had taken action against all the rules of the Church, Catholic and Protestant, to ensure a suicide would receive Christian burial and be laid to rest in hallowed ground. He regretted none of it.

Turning his head slightly, he rested his cheek against her hair. His hand, leaving her back, went up under her cap to

dive into her luxuriant curls. She took it as an added gesture of comfort and sank still deeper into the haven of his
arms until the shadow of an arriving baggage wagon fell
across the window.

Four

If it had been anyone but Augustin who had interceded on the peasant woman's behalf it was likely that Louis would have ignored his existence from that time onwards. The incident in the park, followed closely by the appeal for clemency, had upset him more than even those who knew him well would have estimated. As it was, he knew this courtier to be the champion of the distressed and on those grounds he pardoned him in his own mind. He showed his magnanimity by inviting Augustin to play billiards with him one evening in the Diana Salon. It was a fair contest, both of them excellent players, and Louis was gratified to win by a marginal point.

Augustin did not attend the Dremont funerals, which would have been out of place, and waited three weeks before he called on Marguerite. When he knocked on the cottage door there was no reply. Then a neighbour appeared, bobbing a dozen curtsies as if he were the King himself.

"Marguerite has gone to despatch a box of fans with a

carrier going to Paris," she informed him. "If she has to wait for the man she'll be some time."

He thanked her for telling him and was about to go in search of Marguerite when he saw her appear at the end of the lane. She had a swift, light step and he thought to himself that if trained she would have every chance of matching the dancers in the evening ballets. When she drew near he could see the effect her double bereavement had had on her, for her eyes appeared sunken and her face looked pinched.

"Good day, Monsieur Roussier," she answered to his greeting. "It is kind of you to come and see me."

"I wanted to know how you were." He had hoped she would be pleased to see him and he believed she was, even though her attitude was extremely reserved in contrast to their last meeting.

"Please pardon the disorder of my home," she said, leading the way indoors. "I'm packing up to leave. This cottage is soon to be demolished."

"So this area is to be changed now, is it? The town is unrecognisable these days from the time when I first came to Versailles."

"Was it a pleasant village in the past? I can't remember it without construction work going on somewhere." She skirted two wooden boxes filled with possessions to reach a shelf on which stood a flagon. "May I offer you a glass of wine?"

"I thank you. As for the village, I don't recall anything to commend it."

She poured the wine for him and another glass for herself, making no apology for its rough quality, for although he was a nobleman, as was every courtier, he would also have served as a soldier and had surely sampled a wide range of wines in his time. It surprised her that she should be so down-to-earth with him, treating him as the equal she had once resolved she would be, although that was to have been within the bargain her mother had struck with him on her behalf. Everything was on a different footing now. Somehow the romantic figure whom she had admired from a distance across the King's supper room bore no connection with the splendid physical presence of the man raising his glass in homage to her across the table.

If it had not been for the tragedies that had occurred her

head would have been completely turned by his attention. It was terrible that the deaths of the two people dearest to her in all the world should have been instrumental in clearing away every foolish fancy with which she had regarded him. She had been thrown forward into common sense and reality, the last of her mother's dreams dispersed. She had become her own person as she would never have done if she had merely exchanged a protective parental wing for that of a lover's as had been planned for her.

"Whereabouts are you going to live?" he inquired. "I should like to call on you."

"It's a small apartment above a hatter's shop not far from the Place d'Armes. The entrance is through an archway with a ribbon shop on the other side of the street. There I'm going to start my own fan-making business. Now that I have completed and sent off the outstanding orders that were in hand, I'm free to do as I wish. I always thought my mother wasted her talents making fans for someone else to sell at enormous profit, but she was content with things as they were. I'm not of the same temperament and I'm not afraid to take my chance."

He could believe that. "I have a Dremont fan with your name on it."

She showed no surprise. "My mother told me she gave you one as a keepsake. It was the purse of gold she received from you that gave me some education and is enabling me to start out alone in fan-making."

He was astounded that the money had been harboured so carefully. That past gesture of munificence on his part undermined the financial help he would have given now. The way she had answered him about the keepsake fan led him to believe she had also been told exactly what had been said during the giving and receiving. He could still remember the shock of feeling bonded by the gift and his attempt to cut himself free of it with money. "How shall you dispose of your wares?"

"First of all I shall build up some stock. Then I shall take a selection with me to the vestibule of the Queen's Staircase at the Château where goods may be offered for sale."

He knew it was a good place for those wanting to sell goods of special appeal to the nobility. If he had not been certain of rebuff he would have offered her an alternative future, for he was finding it impossible not to view her speculatively in the light for which Jeanne Dremont had originally prepared him. Nothing would have pleased him more than to have taken this girl as his mistress to live in a stylish apartment in Paris for as long as his fancy lasted. Then, when it was over, she should receive a handsome dowry such as her mother would have expected of him. Long experience told him that she would be quick to learn the arts of love, for there was a sensuality in her fascinating looks and in the suppleness of her figure with the unconsciously provocative swing of the hips that made her every movement a delight to his appreciative eye. He decided to test how the land might lie in the weeks to come.

"If you know about the fan I took away with me from this cottage and of the gold left behind, it means you must also know of what was planned to be between us."

"You can't hold me to that," she countered defensively. "Now that my mother is gone any agreement she made is invalid."

"I realise that. I want nothing from the past. Only what you would be willing to grant me in the future." His tone was designed to melt and to disarm.

She chose not to look at him, her lashes lowered. With all infatuation for him gone, her heart was drained and empty, bereavement making her still more vulnerable. It was the first time in her life that she had been without a close bond of affection to anchor her and she must not let a feeling of being alone run away with her. No doubt it would be easy to care deeply for this man of strength and compassion. There might even come a time when she could let in the love that she would not have been able to cope with before. But she wanted more in return than to be merely desired.

She raised her eyes challengingly to his. "Ask me again when you have learned to love me."

He regarded her steadily. No woman could obliterate Susanne for him, but it was possible that Marguerite's unusual beauty and tantalising spirit of independence would create some kind of antidote that might last longer with him than he had found with anyone else. He had not been taken aback by her answer, for he had begun to anticipate the unexpected from this girl of strong character. Leaning an arm on the table, he thrust his face towards her.

"I'll take my cue from you and make no promises. I suggest we await developments."

She nodded contemplatively. "Do you want to see me often?"

"Whenever I am at Versailles."

"What of the ladies in your circle?"

"I have no attachments."

"Why haven't you married yet?"

He had no intention of disclosing that the woman he would have married was the wife of his closest friend. "A marriage of convenience is not an inviting prospect. It curtails a man's freedom and hampers his enjoyment of life at Court. I shall marry sooner or later. It has to be done. Just remember that it would make no difference to any established relationship between us."

She thought that over carefully. Not being in love with him she could reason rationally and she decided that she should be able to share him with a woman who only claimed his duty. But there was a more unsettling aspect. "What if you should marry for love?" She warmed to her subject. "There must be beautiful daughters joining parents at Court all the time. You may suddenly see one of them and everything would change."

"What makes you think a man can't love two women?" He caught her startled glance and hastened to reassure. "If I should come to care for you nobody else could change that. You would always have your own place with me."

"But circumstances would be completely altered." She was adamant, her eyes direct and clear. "I could never share a man's love on that basis. It would be the end."

He inclined his head in acceptance. "I'll remember that. I can see that you mean what you say. As it happens, I'm not in the least perturbed, because I would wager my life against any new love crossing my path now. I have you and I'm prepared to go on from there. Remember that your destiny and mine have been linked too long for anything to sever us now."

She realised that they were both talking as if they knew underneath that they were already committed to each other and these were practicalities to be discussed openly, and then put aside completely. "How shall I know for certain if and when you love me?"

"I'll find a way of showing you that will leave you in no

doubt." His gaze on her was compelling. "That's when I'll ask you for your love in return."

Her voice was calm and purposeful in reply. "I wouldn't wish for it to be any other way."

He lifted his glass to her again and she responded in settlement of their curious agreement. As they set down their drained glasses he smiled slowly at her, drawing a reciprocal smile from her. They were in harmony together and, for the moment, at peace. It was like an amicable truce before a battle. Neither knew what the outcome would be, but for the time being they shared a roseate anticipation of the future.

Marguerite moved into her apartment above the hatter's shop a week later, taking all the furniture from the cottage with her. The accommodation consisted of three rooms with the use of the privy in the courtyard. The largest room became her workshop where the table from her old home was well placed to get the light from the good-sized windows that enhanced all property built since the new town of Versailles had risen out of the village.

From the first day of having everything to rights, she sat down to work with the materials she had ordered and stayed at the table from early morning until late in the night. Quick and efficient, she soon had several boxes of finished fans. Each one had to be different, for if she hoped to sell to Court ladies she must offer a variation of design. Augustin came to see her once during this time, mounting the outer flight of steps to appear through the door that she had left open to catch whatever wisp of breeze was there.

"It's a glorious June morning!" he announced, grinning at her. "Leave all that you're doing and spend the day with me."

She shook her head decisively, resisting a strong temptation to leap up and go with him. Too much was at stake with her project and she had resolved to let nothing stand in the way of preparing plenty of stock. "I must work. I have set myself a quota of fans for each day."

"Do you never break rules?" he demanded in exasperation, hands on his hips, elbows jutting.

"Not those that common sense dictates." She thought to herself that he could take that reply any way he chose. He did not like it, seeming to fill her whole apartment with his annoyance. Her guess was that he hated to be thwarted in any matter, however trivial, and when he left in the same state of mind she wondered with a pang if he would want to see her again. Surely no man and woman had ever been such worlds apart in social status and in outlook. She would yearn for him if he did not return, but she dare not let the situation become one-sided. Their agreement had to be kept.

He sent a messenger with a posy of flowers for her a few days later, a red rosebud at its centre. There was no written word with it, but she understood the silent message of the flowers and her spirits, which had been cast down, rose again.

When enough boxes of fans were stacked to ensure that she was well supplied for a while, she knew the day had come to launch her new venture. She did not expect anything to be easy, particularly since she was sure that established vendors would want to crowd out a newcomer. Many of them had probably served the Court through two or three generations and most of them moved with it from palace to palace and château to château, setting up their stalls and stands in whatever regular places were allotted to them.

Wanting to avoid her competitors' attention as much as possible until she had established her right to be there with her wares, she decided to wear a large cap, for she knew her hair to be her most striking asset. Men always looked after her as if their heads had been jerked by a string whenever she tied up her thousands of curls with a ribbon. Today not a tendril must hang free. Putting all her fans into a flat basket lined with a piece of white linen, she set off for the Château. At the gates the guards let her through when they heard she was aiming to sell in the vestibule of the Queen's Staircase and not in the park where voices had to be subdued and the hawking of wares was forbidden.

She walked briskly up the slight rise of the Cour Royale. The original hill on which the old lodge had once stood unenveloped had been enlarged years ago to support the massive wings. As she approached the rose marble and gilt face of the East Front, which had been so carefully preserved, she came to triple arches enclosing gilded grilles at her left hand. These led into the vestibule where she intended to sell, and it was here that the King and the royal

family alighted from their coaches. Three corresponding
arches with grilles on the opposite side of the court led to
the Ambassadors' Staircase, the entrance for those for
whom it was named and others of noble rank.

Marguerite entered the spacious vestibule with its black
and white chequered marble floor. From it rose the
Queen's Staircase, balustraded in dark green marble. At
the head of the staircase, gleaming like a golden medallion,
was a symbolisation of the marriage of the King and
Queen. Since this was the staircase to the Queen's Apartment, as well as a main area, it was a busy thoroughfare,
while the vestibule itself presented an intensely busy
scene.

It was familiar to her from previous visits with her
mother when they had been there to gaze and admire.
The stalls were elegantly canopied in green, blue and rose.
The vendors, whether men or women, were extremely
well dressed, for this was no ordinary market scene. Here,
and in some other shops on this floor, they were all ca-
tering to the nobility, although there were some cheaper
things too for the general public who called in while visiting the park. There were silks and filmy laces, good wines,
grand paintings, fashionable canes, jewellery and the best
that the goldsmiths' craft could produce. Aids to beauty
were there in plenty, creams and lotions, patches of every
shape for the cheek or chin and crystal flagons of fragrant
perfume, but only orange blossom since the King, who had
a strong sense of smell, had forbidden the wearing of all
other scents in the Château. As he detested the stink of
smoke or snuff on a woman, there were none of the pretty
porcelain snuff boxes or ornamented pipes aimed at feminine taste such as could be obtained elsewhere.

Those with flat baskets, like Marguerite's own, had them
similarly lined for the small goods they offered, such as
herbs and sweetmeats, handkerchiefs, hand mirrors and
purses, as well as maps of the Château and guides to the
park. She was relieved that these basket-holders, who
were more her competitors for custom than the stall-holders, did not have a fan-seller among them. There were
some extremely costly fans displayed with other items on a
stall, but Marguerite felt her designs put her fans in a class
of their own and was optimistic she would do well. She
took up a good position near the gilded gates at the side of

a portly sword-seller, who had his gleaming-handled wares in a tall, cone-shaped leather holder, which he held propped vertically in front of him, his protruding stomach a buttress.

He eyed her suspiciously. "I haven't seen you before. In any case you're encroaching on my pitch." He spread out his elbows to make her draw a step aside. "Have you a permit?"

She felt a qualm. A permit? She knew nothing of having to gain permission to sell here. Perhaps he was bluffing to get rid of her. It would take more than that to shake her confidence. "I'm here in my citizen's right to sell to the King if he should want to buy. None can deny me that." She flicked open one of her loveliest fans, a design of jasmine and tuberoses. A lady, followed by her page with a little dog on a leash, glanced towards it with a flicker of interest, but passed on. The sword-seller, who had lost two sales just prior to Marguerite's arrival, which he blamed on lack of space for display, a daily grumble of his, became more belligerent.

"Oh, is that so? Can't be denied, eh? You impertinent chit! Get out! Clear off and leave room for those with a long-established right to sell here!" He gave her basket a vicious shove, spilling her fans, which went scattering under people's feet. She saw her hours of work wasted as they were trodden on and cracked. Swinging round on him in a fury, she kicked the tapered base of his sword holder and it fell with a clatter, some of its shining blades jerked out of their scabbards by the impact, their razor-sharp edges skimming about on the marble floor. There was immediate commotion; women squealing and men bellowing at the sword-seller's carelessness. Marguerite snatched up as many of her undamaged fans as she could retrieve and slipped away quickly to be swallowed up in the crowd near the staircase.

Luck was with her there. She found a space and sold three fans in little more than as many minutes to well-to-do bourgeois with printed guides to the park in their hands. A young man in the sober clothes of a scholar was her next customer, his sentimental smile causing her to guess that his purchase was for his sweetheart. After that a woman keeping a stall of exquisite shawls beckoned her over, not to question her presence as she had feared, but to buy a fan painted like peacock feathers that she had been displaying.

"I've never seen one like this before," the woman commented after paying for it. "It's your own design, you say? Well, I've just bought a bargain. Put your prices up. The customers you should be aiming for scorn anything cheap."

"I appreciate your advice."

The woman looked kindly at her. "I've been watching you. You see, I started out like you once, stepping in where I had no right to be." She leaned forward and lowered her voice confidentially. "It's not generally known, but if a newcomer such as yourself makes a sale to one of the nobility before being turfed out it ensures a right to stay, providing certain standards are met. Usually we stall-holders keep that information to ourselves, but your work is good and deserves a chance."

Marguerite expressed her thanks and in resuming her place she glimpsed the sword-seller protesting heatedly to a black-coated official-looking man in a white periwig. She did not doubt but that she was the subject of their conversation and it was only a matter of time before she would be evicted on the strength of his complaint. Quickly she moved still nearer the stairs where a stream of nobility was going up and down, but she made no sales. Usually they were talking to one another, having no eyes for the fans she opened and closed, or else hurried by intent on some duty ahead. Suddenly, catching her off guard, the sword-seller pounced on her, grabbing her by the arm.

"Now you'll not get away a second time! I've reported you! You're going to be thrown out and there'll be no coming back!" Then he jerked away, releasing her with a yelp, as a sword aimed with a musketeer's flourish flashed across the balustrade to point downwards at the knot of his neckcloth.

"I think not!" Augustin's voice said drily. "This young woman is doing no harm that I can see."

The sword-seller's flushed face grew sweaty. "She has no permit, sir! And you did not witness how she threw my swords all over the floor."

Marguerite, grateful though she was for Augustin's intervention, feared it had come too late. The black-coated official had been following after the sword-seller and was almost through the crowd. Seizing the first fan that came to hand, she spun round to reach up on tiptoe to where Augustin was leaning an arm on the balustrade.

"Buy this from me! Quickly!"

Augustin, giving her a smile, dived into his pocket and tossed a gold louis down into her basket. "Will that meet the cost?"

"Most adequately," she exclaimed joyfully. "Now I can lodge my own complaint about the tilting of my basket and the loss of goods."

It did not take long for matters to be sorted out between the sword-seller and her, the official deciding that one complaint cancelled out the other, and he reprimanded both of them. Then he took Marguerite with him to an office where she had to wait while her fans were taken away and inspected for quality and workmanship. When eventually they were returned with a nod of approval, her name was registered and a list of regulations handed to her. Able to leave the office at once and start selling again, she found Augustin waiting for her.

"Did all go well?"

"Yes, it did, I'm thankful to say."

"May I call on you later? There's somewhere I'd like to take you."

She was intrigued. "Yes, indeed."

He arrived at her apartment in a calèche for two. As soon as he had helped her into it they went off down the street at a good speed and she was given no hint as to their destination. She was able to tell him she had done quite well with sales after he had left her again in the vestibule.

"No more trouble from that fellow?"

"None at all. We have an unspoken agreement to keep a distance from each other," she declared with relief.

"How are you going to maintain your supplies and do the selling?" he asked.

"If my sales keep up I'll soon be able to take on an assistant fan-maker, although she will have to be good, because I'm only selling the best I can produce and every fan has to be unique. Later on I want to specialise in really spectacular fans, but I have to take a step at a time."

He took a turning off the main avenue and drove through the outskirts of Versailles until they were in the countryside. As they went along he told her of his home in

Normandy, of his mother who had died in his childhood, of his father who had never married again and of his late aunt who had been like a mother to him. He could see he had her full attention, for she listened keenly, asking questions now and again, showing she wanted to know as much about him as possible. For himself, he did not intend to lose her to some young oaf who might come into her life. It was almost like netting a little bird, bait and skill needed and delicate handling. She was becoming more important to him with every meeting. Her intense youth, her vitality and even her stubbornness made her refreshingly different from any other woman he had desired. He looked forward to the time when all her fan-making ambitions would be forgotten in the sole aim to pleasure him. It was a wry thought that he had shared a mistress often enough with an unsuspecting or uncaring husband, but never before with a money-making project.

She was full of excitement as to where they might be going. It was obviously a surprise of some significance. As yet she was still wary about her feelings for Augustin, his attraction having to compete with her cool common sense. She would have to know him much better before she committed herself and she believed he realised that he would have to court her for a long while to come.

The town had been lost from sight, but they had not gone more than a short way when some brand-new gates appeared as the road curved ahead. Painted green and tipped with gilt, they stood open to reveal an arrow-straight drive. She sat bolt upright in alarm as the calèche went bowling in through the gates towards a large mansion in the distance.

"Are we visiting?" she questioned in alarm. She was wearing a new bodice and skirt she had made in printed calico, a French fabric that had recently come within range of everyone's pocket. Although it was pretty enough with its conventional rose pattern, she was not gowned to be presented to nobility at any kind of social level.

Augustin pressed her hand briefly and reassuringly as if guessing her thoughts.

"This is my new home, the Château Satory. I've not moved in yet and the only person we're going to meet there is the architect, Laurent Picard, with whom I'll be discussing a few outstanding details. He is a baron by birth and comes from a family impoverished by gaming. The family estates and everything else went when his father finally staked it all during a single last desperate evening at the tables. Picard has put his talents into designing property of distinction, so recouping his lost fortunes. I admire him for it."

She thought to herself that it was thanks to her teacher, Marie Printemps, that she knew how to conduct herself and if Augustin did not think it important that she was not wearing silk or satin there was nothing to worry about. Relaxed again, she glanced about observantly as they drove along. Much of the new ground was raw as yet, parterres dug but not planted, paths laid out for gravelling and a marble fountain awaiting a centrepiece. When everything was finished it would be a fitting setting for the imposing residence they were fast approaching. Built of ivory sandstone, it had many tall windows and a balustraded roof that rose gracefully in the classic French style.

"What made you decide to build here?" she asked, full of admiration for the newly finished edifice, which she could see now had a grand entrance framed by columns of pale green marble, the double doors standing wide for the owner's coming.

"That's easy to explain. I wanted more room for myself."

She raised her eyebrows incredulously. "But that gigantic new wing was added to the Château specially to house the Court whenever the King is there."

"Oh, it's vast, I agree, but it's crowded and parts of it are unfinished as yet. Sometimes it's almost impossible to get along the corridors when sedan chairs carrying people to some distant part of the Château get jammed up in the wing. There are over two thousand of us courtiers housed there. Some of the highest nobles have large apartments, but the rest of us have accommodation too small to swing a cat in. Any number of rooms have no windows. Mine does at least look into an inner court, but I've lived in discomfort far too long during my service to the King. Now I shall have a spacious abode whenever I'm at Versailles."

"The King does seem to be spending longer and longer periods at the Château. I should think you have made a sensible decision."

"Many others have built already. I was lucky to get this

land when I did, because favourable areas are greatly
sought after."

He drew up at the entrance near a waiting barouche,
which she guessed belonged to the architect. Together
they went up the steps and entered the spacious hall. She
moved away to the central green star that patterned the
marble floor and rotated as she looked about her. He came
and stood close to her, bringing her to a standstill by capturing her wrists.

"You're going to bring great happiness to this place,
Marguerite."

It was a moment of awakening for her, creating a sudden, unexpected stir to her heart at his words, which combined with the way he was looking at her to bring her with
a rush to the brink of love. It lay before her in this château,
which had been planned and built long before their meeting, but it was to become her domain. His eyes were telling
her that it was here he would love her, under this roof they
would discover each other when the terms of their curious
agreement had been met. She almost trembled for what
would have been lost if she had not escaped from her early
infatuation for him.

"I hope for that," she replied huskily, able to see that he
was about to kiss her. But she wanted to postpone the
sweet contact as long as possible, for it was far too soon to
have fires ignited in her that might race away beyond
control. "Now let me see the château."

A voice spoke from a salon doorway. "May I have the
honour of acting as guide to you both?"

Full of interest, she saw a squarely built young man with
a somewhat unruly mane of thick fairish hair that curled
down onto his shoulders, framing a broad face that was
pleasing without being the least good-looking. The jaw was
wide and prominent, the nose aquiline and the dark grey
eyes had a kindly crinkle at the corners. As for his age, she
judged him to be in his mid-twenties. Augustin greeted
him. "Good evening to you, Monsieur le Baron. Have you
been waiting long?"

"Not at all, sir," he replied courteously, his voice deep
enough to suggest that he could produce some good bari-
tone singing out of his broad chest. "The concierge let me
in only a few minutes ago." He came forward to be presented to Marguerite, giving her as much deference as if

she were high-born, although her plain attire must have given her away.

"You have designed a beautiful house here," she said sincerely. There was something about him that made her feel immediately at ease. "I'm sure the rest of the interior I've yet to view is going to match the exterior and what I see here." She indicated the sweep of the gilded staircase and the arched ceiling painted like a summer sky with birds in flight.

His answering smile showed that her praise had pleased him. "I was fortunate in having a splendid site to start with and a patron whose ideas ran parallel with my own."

She thought he seemed lacking in any airs except those that custom demanded of a nobleman. "How soon will it be furnished here?" As far as she could see through whatever doors were open there was not as much as a chair anywhere.

"Very soon now. Everything from the draperies to the furnishings will be of the best French craftsmanship. Just as it is at Versailles."

"At least you've built more quickly than the King," she joked.

The architect's smile widened. "That doesn't mean to say that this building went up without a hitch. Even the King knew what it meant for doors of the wrong size to be delivered and to have a chain of workmen held up through the incompetence of others. At least it has ended well."

She had liked him from what she had heard about him from Augustin and now for being without conceit in his achievement, for this country house was no ordinary edifice. Perhaps hard times had not only brought out resourcefulness in him, but had made him as realistic in his outlook as she. Maybe that was why she felt curiously akin to him; as if they were two of a kind. At her side Augustin nodded amicably at him.

"Why not lead the way now for us? We can discuss our business afterwards."

The tour was more enjoyable than anything she could remember. The salons were all of fine proportions, high and spacious, each hung with Lyonnaise silk, the predominant colour different in every room. Upstairs there were many bedchambers, each with a marble bathroom or an anteroom for bathing facilities. She remembered her fa-

ther telling her that there were two hundred and fifty
baths at the Château, which had impressed her and her
mother enormously, but since hearing of the crowded conditions she could tell the number was woefully inadequate
for those who were as fastidious about cleanliness as the
King was known to be.

When Augustin and the architect went downstairs again
to have their business talk she returned to the bedchamber
that had enchanted her at first sight. It was a feminine
room with panels of soft rose and silver-threaded silk. The
view from the south-facing windows was of lawns and the
circular marble summer pavilion with trees beyond. For
whom had this room been created? Had Augustin expected it to be for a bride when the plans had been first
discussed? She never wanted him to bring any other
woman to this place!

Pushing open the window, she inhaled the soft scents of
early evening. The setting sun had laid a rich patina over
everything. If she could have wished for anything on this
magical evening it would be to find herself married here.
It was an impossible dream, pleasant to think about for a
few moments and then to be put away forever. She was not
going to waste a minute of her life hankering after what
could never be. Far better to make the most of whatever
came her way and be thankful that when she was certain
Augustin truly loved her she could come to this château
and live with him. Let him marry one day if he must, a
plain noblewoman left in Le Havre to breed. She alone
would hold his love.

Deciding that the business discussion must have reached
a conclusion by now, she went downstairs in search of
Augustin and Laurent Picard. Eerily she could hear no
sound of their voices or see any sign of them as she went
from salon to salon, all of which opened one into another.
Then, unexpectedly, she heard them in the small anteroom through which she had just passed, and they had not
entered by the doors. They were talking in low and confi-
dential tones that reached her clearly in the stillness.

"As you have seen," Laurent Picard was saying, "I followed exactly the same plan as in your father's house. You
have my word as a gentleman that none shall learn from
me what lies behind this wall."

"I thank you," Augustin said. "It is vital for security that it remain secret." He did not know that Marguerite, who had been on the point of making her presence known, promptly changed her mind.

"It was for that reason I did not use local labour," the architect went on, "and I fitted the mechanism myself."

In the neighbouring salon Marguerite slipped away into the next one, drawing the doors closed silently behind her. She did not want either of the men to think she had been eavesdropping deliberately. At some time in the future she would confess to Augustin what she had heard, for by then he would know she could be trusted to keep whatever was there to herself.

Several minutes passed before Augustin, coming in his turn to search for her, found her four salons away in the library, the shelves still empty of books. "There you are!" he exclaimed. "Baron Picard wants to say his farewells."

She went with him back through to the hall, passing through the anteroom on the way. Although she gave a sideways glance to the left and then the right there was no sign of the hidden aperture through which they must have come. The architect was waiting by the door.

"I didn't want to go without seeing you again, Mademoiselle Dremont."

"Farewell, sir," she replied as he bowed over her hand. "Perhaps we shall meet again one day."

"I should be honoured."

She watched him take his leave of Augustin. He must have assumed that she was his patron's mistress already and he had been quite taken with her himself. How transparent men were! A woman could always tell even when they tried to hide that flare of attraction as the Baron had done.

"I've another surprise for you," Augustin announced as soon as they were on their own. "It should be ready by now."

She thought he was going to show her the hidden door and was pleased that he was to take her into his confidence already. Instead he led her in the opposite direction to the Crimson Salon into which she had looked earlier. When she saw what was there she gave a soft laugh of sheer delight. Where there had been an empty room before, a table of portable construction had been set up and laid for supper with damask and crystal and silver, candelabra lit to counteract the fading light outside. The two seats were folding tabourets with velvet cushions.

"Did invisible hands prepare this?" she suggested merrily, guessing it was the concierge. Yet it would not have been hard to believe that magic was at work, for it seemed like an extension of the mystical mood that had come upon her upstairs.

"So you've guessed," he replied in similar vein. "Sprites come at sunset to do service here."

It was a happy meal. He lifted the silver covers to reveal dish after dish of cold meats and game and fish. There were salads and sauces and compôtes and preserves. The wines were unlike any she had tasted before, running like nectar down her throat. The rest of the evening became hazy. She was to remember dancing for him in the empty ballroom by the light of a pair of candelabra he had carried in from the table and set down on the rose marble mantel of the fireplace. In her exhilarated mood she whirled around in the swift steps of country dances she had known since childhood, her shadow thrown high on the brocade panels, dimming momentarily the glittering golden threads as it passed over them. Augustin clapped the rhythm, and her singing of the tunes echoed in the empty space like the notes of a caged lark. Then, suddenly dizzy, she came to a standstill in the middle of the floor, her petticoats and her soft calico skirt swirling about her legs before falling into place again.

"Are you all right?" he asked, looming up at her in a mist of candlelight.

She looked at him through her lashes and sensed the power she was gaining over him. A few more paces and he would meet her along the path of love. It was in the burning glow of his eyes. Surely no other man had ever had such a potent gaze. Tantalisingly, not answering him, she spun away before he could reach her and swept into the steps of a Slow Courante that Marie Printemps had taught her, humming in accompaniment. He watched her for a few enthralled minutes and then he entered into the dance with her, right shoulder following right foot and then again with the left in a lovely curving movement and the graceful set of slightly extended arms. They partnered each other perfectly, their dual shadows, sometimes together and at others apart, now crossing and recrossing in a constantly changing pattern over the floor, walls and ceiling. In her final curtsey she sank to the floor, slid a leg under her and sat down all in one swooping movement. She looked up at him laughing.

"The wine has finally melted my bones. I don't think I shall ever be able to move from this spot again."

Amused, he sat on the floor beside her, resting an arm on an updrawn knee. "Nothing would suit me better. That you should remain here, I mean."

She teased him with a sideways glance, evasive and alluring. "Let's not talk about that now."

"Who taught you to dance?"

"The teacher I told you about."

"She did well. How would you like to dance in the gardens of Versailles with me? There are several royal galas and events planned for the weeks ahead." Then, forestalling a refusal for the most obvious of reasons, he added, "But you would have to allow me to buy you a gown that was suitable or else we should both be asked to leave."

He had judged it better to put her under an obligation to accept a gown for his sake rather than offer an outright gift which she might have refused. The phrasing was immaterial since the result was the same, but she was well flown with wine and he could see that his words had lulled her.

"I would never want to cause you any embarrassment," she exclaimed anxiously.

"It's settled, then. I'll ask one of the women at Court to recommend a dressmaker and send her to you."

She felt vaguely that she was slipping out of her depths but somehow it didn't seem to matter. It was an evening in which wonderful things were happening and her veins were full of golden bubbles from a source of happiness she could not locate. As if she had been gently pushed by invisible hands, she raised her arms above her head and sank backwards to lie stretched out on the floor gazing up at the ceiling.

"There can't be another house to match this one's magic in all of France."

"No woman either to compare with you." He leaned over her, looking down into her face. Nothing would have been easier than to seduce her now, but he wanted her spirited and loving and aware, not in this dreamy, bemused state. "It's late. I'm taking you home."

He scooped her to her feet. Briefly she rested against him and her eyes went to his mouth as if magnetised, but she turned her face away. With a last burst of energy, she twirled once more around the floor like a child extending a special treat for a few more minutes and then skipped before him in dancing steps out through the hall and down the steps to the waiting calèche. She sang softly, as much to herself as to him, all the way back to her apartment.

She parted from him at the stone flight that led up to her door out of the flagged court at the back of the hatter's shop. "Good night, Augustin. This has been an evening I shall always remember."

"It is the first of many."

With a lingering smile she began to mount the flight, but on the third step she flung herself back again to press her soft lips on his. He clasped her to him, not letting her draw away again, and her girlish kiss underwent a change as the warm cavern of his mouth showed her how kissing should be. She clung to him, her soaring response something previously unknown to her, all that had been smashed inside her over long weeks healed and made whole again by love.

She breathed deeply as he released her, gazing at him. He cupped the side of her face gently in his hand. "Go to bed now, Marguerite," he advised softly, "or else I shall have to take you there myself."

With a gulp she started from him, bunching up her skirts as she bolted up the steps. Slamming the door and locking it, she ran into her bedchamber and threw herself on the bed. Her heart was pounding and her body was burning in its most intimate parts. His words had set off a reflex action of panic in her yearning to feel his hands on her naked flesh and to know his caresses. Too soon! He did not love her yet. She must not let her own desire jeopardise everything they had agreed between them. If he possessed her before his heart was entirely lost, how could she ever be sure of holding him always? Love and sexual intercourse could be worlds apart but shared love and tenderness in a complete union must surely form a bastion against anything that fate might hurl against them.

She fell asleep just as she was. In the morning she woke astounded to find herself fully dressed. It was a rush to get ready and be off with her basketful of fans for another profitable day in the vestibule of the Queen's Staircase.

During the day she saw several members of the royal family as they passed up and down the staircase and through the vestibule, sometimes getting into a coach that had arrived there for them. She had seen most of them, including the Princes of the Blood and various princesses, many times before, but it was interesting to view them at close hand as well as the rival ladies, Mesdames de Montespan and de Maintenon. The former was quite overweight and always brightly dressed, the latter possessed a formidable smile and dressed elegantly in sombre colours, usually with no adornment except a simple gold cross. The King's only legitimate son, whose splendid height had caused him to become known as the Grand Dauphin, exuded good humour, his plump face rosy with good health, his curly, shoulder-length hair bright as the Château's gold leaf. The Dauphine, wife of the Grand Dauphin, was lumpish and plain, disadvantages he did not seem to be aware of, for he showed her the greatest devotion.

The most colourful personage was the King's younger brother, who was always addressed as Monsieur. He tripped past on his high heels, painted like a doll, a married man with children in spite of being the very opposite to Louis in his sexual preferences.

Although the Queen could pass through the vestibule without busy sellers and buyers paying much attention unless they flanked her path, Marguerite noticed that whenever Louis appeared it was entirely different. It was as if suddenly there was a sunburst for all present. Even those at the very back of the vestibule were compelled by the force of his personality to look in his direction, straining their necks, and the bowing and scraping amounted to a positive commotion.

Every time, abhorrence for him rose in her as she recalled painfully his lack of mercy to her poor mother. She struggled to understand why he, the most courteous of kings, inclining his head graciously to all in the vestibule however many times he passed through, should have hardened his heart so completely against an unfortunate woman obviously out of her wits. She observed how he always doffed his hat to any noblewoman he recognised and how he lifted it to varying degrees according to the rank of any courtier who happened to bow in his path. It was astonishing that he could remember whether a man

was a duc, marquis, comte or baron considering how many
there were, but he did and never made an error.

She arrived home that evening to find a dressmaker
waiting to see her. Madame Dreux had taken a seat in the
hatter's shop to rest her limbs and she came hurrying out
to follow Marguerite through into the courtyard at the
rear. She was a large, domineering woman and had a brow-
beaten apprentice with her, who held her pincushion and
tape measure.

"I number many ladies at Court among my clientele,"
she informed Marguerite as soon as they were indoors,
"and I pride myself that no other dressmaker can compete
with my gowns."

She glanced about her as she spoke, taking in everything. It was poor, neat and clean. She had sewn many a
garment for the humbler paramours of courtiers but this
was the first time she had to measure one of them above a
hatter's shop. Nevertheless, this girl would pay for dressing. Even in her working attire of striped cotton there was
an air about her, a certain thin-boned look that marked the
Frenchwoman of elegance, taking no account of age. Why
such a quality should have reared itself in these drab quarters was beyond Madame Dreux's comprehension, but she
did not question it, for it was all to her personal advantage
when her gowns were attractively displayed in public.

"Please sit down," Marguerite invited, indicating a
chair.

Madame Dreux settled herself, but a snap of her fingers
stopped her apprentice following suit on a nearby stool.
Advice on the latest fashions poured from her. Out of a
velvet-lined box, which she opened on the table, she produced a range of small dolls, all dressed to illustrate her
suggestions in style, fabric and colour. She tugged gently at
the froth of silk on one of them.

"As you can see, the simple overskirt is now almost unrecognisable from its origins." Neatly she balanced the doll
on her left palm and kept it steady with the tip of her right
forefinger on its head. "Note how the fullness is drawn
back into abundant gathers over the posterior, to be secured by a handsome bow or brooch, or even suspended
over a loop of ribbon from behind the shoulders. Whatever
you choose, the skirt must flow out into a slight train. As for
the underskirt itself, that hangs straight down in front

from the tight-fitting bodice. Is that not charming? Breasts almost bare with a wisp of veiling to intrigue as to whether or not the aureole is showing like a rising sun. This is the ultimate in seduction."

"I think not for me, Madame Dreux," Marguerite countered. "I don't intend to reveal that much to the world at large. Low-cut by all means and the square neckline. As for colour—"

"Rich blues or emerald green or jade for you, my dear!" Madame Dreux was already picturing her creation, closing her eyes as if almost swooning at the image she had conjured up.

Marguerite agreed that she would favour those colours, but for this gown she was not to be swayed. She had given it a great deal of thought and the fabrics she had been shown decided her. "Gold gauze for the overskirt, I think. Glittering over the lovely taffeta the third doll is wearing. It's paper fine and quite delicate in texture."

Madame Dreux looked at her with new respect. Nothing would suit those crimson-dark curls better than the sparkle and sheen of gold. This young woman had taste and was right to dismiss the exaggerated décolletage, for only the vulgar showed all they possessed. Quickly she made her notes.

"That's one ensemble settled," she said with satisfaction, setting aside her notebook for the moment. "Now we can discuss the rest."

"The rest?" Marguerite echoed in surprise.

Madame Dreux nodded. "Monsieur Roussier said you were to have whatever you wished. Two score and more of gowns if needs be, capes and hats and hose and all else to go with them. He has put no limit on your spending. I can advise you with everything."

Marguerite brushed her fingertips across her forehead as if to adjust her thoughts. This was what her mother had dreamed of for her; every luxury and clothes beyond her utmost needs, but it was all too much and too soon. Like the feelings that had almost run away with her the previous evening, Augustin's generosity had to be held in check until the time was right for her and also for him.

"One gown is enough for now," she insisted, her tone brooking no argument, "although I like all the designs you have shown me. You may take my measurements now,

Madame Dreux. Just deliver the finished garment to me as soon as possible."

The dressmaker opened her mouth as if to speak and then appeared to decide against it, whipping the tape measure from her assistant's hand. As soon as the two women had gone, the list of measurements written down, Marguerite gave them no more thought and counted up her takings for the day. Even allowing for the rising heat of summer aiding her sales, she had done exceptionally well. Most important of all was the promise of her success being maintained in special orders she had received from two noblewomen, both of them young and fashionable, who had wanted a fan each in special colours. She would have to start work on those immediately. Perhaps the time was coming sooner than she had expected for her to draw in another pair of skilled hands.

She worked late into the night and was up at dawn the next morning to continue. It was as if she had done a full day's work already when she took up her basket to set off for the Château, but she felt satisfied by what she had accomplished.

By chance she met Augustin crossing the Cour Royale. He quickened his pace at the sight of her and they stopped amid the passing coaches and calèches and sedan chairs, the riders on horseback, the marching squad of the Swiss Guards and the countless number of people on foot coming and going at the Château.

"I was on my way to look for you," he said as they stood smiling at each other in the unexpected pleasure of meeting, particularly on such a brilliant morning, the sky a shimmering stretch of cobalt blue silk. Although it was not yet ten o'clock, warmth was thrown up by the big square cobbles from heat stored the previous day.

"The dressmaker came, if that is what you wish to know."

"Yes, I have already heard. Madame Dreux informed me that you chose only one gown." His eyelids closed slightly as if that had not been to his liking. "Do you intend to accompany me to only one gala?"

"Why, no."

"That's all I wanted to know." He gave a broad smile as if somehow all was well and a way had been cleared. "In the meantime, would you care to have a picnic supper with me somewhere out in the country this evening?"

"Oh, yes. But what of the King's supper?" She was remembering that he had missed one already during their evening at Château Satory.

He flicked his hand dismissively. "This evening there's a state banquet for foreign dignitaries to which I'm thankful to say I'm not invited. So you and I can escape the heat of the town to the coolest surroundings we can find."

In the vestibule the marble floor and staircase kept the outside temperature at bay, but people were hot as they came and went, willing enough to buy a fan if they were without one. Marguerite sold to both men and women, having made some in plain vellum and also in dark silk that were suited to masculine taste. In spite of having brought more fans with her that day, she was sold out by noon and had to fetch a fresh supply. Her basket was almost empty again when she went home early to finish the work on her commissioned fans before Augustin arrived to take her on the picnic. The two fans were wrapped and ready when she heard wheels in the courtyard and ran downstairs in joyful anticipation of the evening ahead.

The heat was still intense. He drove her to a leafy dell by a stream with a view of the hills. As soon as they arrived he asked permission to remove his periwig and she gave it, welcoming the informality between them. The youthful habit he and his friends had enjoyed of wearing their own hair long to the shoulders, scorning a wig, had long since given way to adult formality. Marguerite was always full of sympathy for men having to cover their heads so abundantly whatever the temperature, and although periwigs were much lighter in weight than appearance suggested, they had become the size of small blankets and reached halfway down the back at the highest mode. Relieved, he tugged the shining spread of the periwig from his head and tossed it with his hat to the ground before divesting himself of his coat. In his billowing white shirtsleeves and long silk waistcoat, he flung his hands wide in a questioning gesture.

"Well? Do you still like me when I'm scalped?"

He was handsome before, the periwig giving him a most dashing air, but she thought him twice as handsome now. His cropped black hair was as curly as her own, covering his head like a cap. In fun she pretended to consider, her eyes dancing, and with a finger tapping the side of her face in assumed concentration she circled him as if he were a statue.

"You look quite fine," she admitted, laughing as she came face to face with him again. "You should start a fashion for going wigless."

He threw back his head in mirth. "And put the wigmakers out of business? They would rise up against me!" He reached out and gripped a handful of her curls to bring her merry face close to his, becoming slightly more serious. "Thank God the follies of fashion haven't tried to smother your crowning glory."

He kissed her lingeringly, in contrast to the force of the previous evening, and she slid her arms about his neck, eyes closed, lost in wonder at this new tenderness that was no less devastating to her emotions. In her heart she cried out to him to say the words she wanted to hear above all else, but when their kiss ended he merely smiled at her, tapped the end of her nose with a fingertip and suggested they see what the picnic hamper contained.

The sun set and the stars came out, but no breeze came to stir the grass or the leaves. When the picnic was done they sat and talked, each wanting to delve back still more into the other's life, to learn and savour and put together a whole background as a setting for this growing bond between them. A nightingale sang in a tree nearby and she rose to her feet to go down to the bank of the stream and stand listening, bathed in the moonlight. When he went to her he saw there were tears in her eyes and he kissed them away.

Marguerite soon learned that the noblewomen had been pleased with their fans when others made a point of coming to see her wares, sorting them over and then ordering one with jasmine, or lilac, or whatever happened to be their favourite flower. Originally she had planned to make up stocks during her evenings, never supposing she would sell as well as she had, but she could not refuse to see Augustin when he was free even if she had wished it. Their time together had become all-important to her. It did not matter that Madame Dreux was taking longer than expected to complete the gold gown, because Augustin seemed to be as content to be alone with her as she was with him, taking drives, finding new beauty spots in which to picnic and eating supper by candlelight in the summer pavilion at his château, moths dancing about the sconces on the walls like little ghosts.

One Sunday he took her to Paris in his coach, it being more convenient to have a coachman drive the longer distance. It was her first visit to the city and she was greatly excited. For the occasion she had expended some of the profits from her fan-making on a length of blue silk and made herself a simple gown. She had not felt she could travel in Augustin's coach and possibly meet acquaintances of his while wearing her village calico skirt and blouse. Not everyone was like Laurent Picard. On the way she told Augustin of some plans she had made for her work and to her relief he smiled indulgently, not objecting as she had feared.

"Why not let me invest in this scheme of yours?" he suggested. "My father and I have always backed ventures that showed promise."

"Later, perhaps," she conceded, pleased by his offer, "but I want to advance on my own first."

He did not know when he had met a less predictable woman and it was all to her credit in this instance. Better for her to have the building up of her fan-making business to occupy her time than to be at leisure to notice that there were other men younger than he who would be more than ready to take her from him. It had long been established that royal mistresses conducted a business of their own in taking money and gifts in exchange for a timely word with the King or the exertion of a little influence on behalf of a courtier. He happened to know that Mesdames de Montespan and de Maintenon were rivals in this exchange as in everything else. He thought fan-making far more commendable.

"Shall we soon reach Paris?" she asked eagerly.

"It won't be long now."

When they reached the city they first went on a tour to enable her to see some of the famous buildings: the ancient Île Saint-Louis, cradle of Paris, and the great Cathedral of Notre Dame; Sainte-Chapelle with the jewel colours of its stained-glass windows; the Palais Royale, home of the Ducs d'Orléans for generations, and many more great mediaeval edifices that still predominated in spite of changes and rebuilding in the past twenty years. As they drove past the Louvre, Marguerite's gaze followed it, scaffolding encasing one part of the palace as if the King could never be satisfied to see a building without workmen all over it. In the autumn, when the Court returned to this seat of government, she would not see Augustin as often as she did now. Suddenly it was as if Paris held some threat to her happiness, but as she turned to Augustin and was kissed, the thought went and did not return.

They spent the rest of the day wandering like countless other couples out to enjoy a summer Sunday. Everywhere there was a feast of entertainment laid on by tumblers, jugglers, singers, dancers, musicians and strolling players. Every moment was a joy to her. Gradually she became aware that he was looking at her more than at any of the troupes in vivid colours that they stopped to watch.

"You can see me any time," she teased at last. "Don't miss this splendid show."

His worldly, rather wry expression brought home painfully to her the nineteen years between them. Never before had she thought of his age or hers. Now she realised how gauche she must appear to this man who had seen and experienced everything. Then he, noticing her flush, put an arm about her and lowered his lips to her ear.

"How can I look at anything else with you making a spring morning out of every event of this day?"

She thought no sweeter reassurance could ever have been given by a man to a woman. The incident, which had threatened to mar the day, had only added to its perfection.

They left the city as dusk fell and his pockets were full of ribbons and small gewgaws he had bought for her from the pedlars. In the coach she fed him and herself with sticky sweetmeats until neither could eat any more. When she ran up the steps to her door, her little gifts fluttering in her arms, he would have followed after if she had made it clear that his waiting for her was at an end.

Two days later, after a particularly good day of selling, Marguerite went to see a young widow a few years older than herself who did fan-making for the same shop in Paris that she and her mother had supplied. When she arrived at the garret room that Lucille Sologne occupied she was warmly welcomed although she saw at once she had interrupted the gumming of fan-sticks to vellum leaves on the table.

"Have I come at an awkward time?" she asked.

"Not at all." Lucille, her hair dark above a face of careworn prettiness, gave a little shrug of apology. "Forgive me if I carry on while we talk. I don't want the gum to set."

Marguerite had known Lucille for a long time, but they had never been close friends. She could guess the reason for the extended working hours, for Lucille had nursed her late husband through a long illness and had been left in poverty-stricken straits. From this garret she was struggling to get back on her feet again. She had shown courage and resilience and Marguerite felt she was just the woman to provide the extra skill and labour needed in her venture. After they had talked for a while, exchanging news, Marguerite broached the subject that had brought her there.

"I'm working on my own now and have established myself at the Château." She went on to give more details and stated the rates she was prepared to pay, which were higher than those Lucille was presently receiving. Selling had given her an insight into the vast profits that others made out of peasants' piecework and she intended to be meticulously fair in all her dealings.

Lucille looked eager but uncertain. "There is nothing I should like more than to work for you. As for the rates you're offering, they are more than I could ever hope to earn elsewhere. But I have heard that a rich protector calls on you. It is common knowledge that he came to your parents' home after the tragedy and you have been seen riding in his calèche. Suppose he forbids you to work any longer? I should find myself destitute with my previous contacts gone." She blushed with embarrassment. "I'm sorry to have to speak of this matter in view of your generous offer, but in spite of all the changes Versailles is still a village at heart and gossip abounds as it always did."

Marguerite was taken aback to hear how much was known of her association with Augustin, but Lucille had not put anything to her that she hadn't thought out carefully already.

"What you have heard is true to an extent. Yet I'm free

to make my own decisions. Remember, I can never be part of Court life, which is for the nobility only—"

Lucille interrupted her. "Madame de Maintenon isn't noble. She was little more than foster mother to Athénaïs de Montespan's bastards by the King until he took a fancy to her."

"So it is said. But she has moved in society always and is the widow of a famous poet. Her position is quite different from mine. Unlike that lady, I can't travel socially with the Court and pass my time in its entertainments when Augustin's envoy duties take him to distant places." Leaving the chair where she was sitting, she leaned both hands on the table as she looked urgently across to Lucille, who had paused in her task, the brush poised in the air. "I've worked hard for as long as I can remember and I could no more sit idly waiting for his return than fly to the moon. I'm aiming for a stall in the vestibule, and a shop in the town. My mother wore herself out working for a pittance just as you are doing now and hundreds of women like you in the same position. I could give good employment to many of them once I have established myself. Take a chance with me, Lucille. You'll not regret it, I promise you."

Lucille put down her brush and sat back thoughtfully in her chair. "I'll do it!" she declared at last. "I can finish the work I have in hand within the week and start work for you next Monday."

Marguerite released a satisfied sigh. She had taken another step towards achieving her ambition and she could have no one better at her side than Lucille Sologne.

When she arrived home again there was a message from Madame Dreux to say the finished gown would be delivered on the day of the Gala.

The furnishing of Château Satory was completed and Augustin moved in. Some records which he had stored at the Manoir for safekeeping now came into his possession. Ever since he had first taken a copy from his home of an account of injustice against some fellow Huguenots he had gathered reports on many incidents, investigated wherever he could, made appeals to the King and over the years gradually built up a network of Huguenot contacts until it covered France like a stretched cobweb. He had devised a code for correspondence and messages, for Louis's secret service had eyes and ears everywhere, and Huguenots came to consult him, to look to him as a keeper of their interests at Court. Through these representatives of Protestant communities he had built up a chain of safe houses and places of refuge where occasionally those in extreme trouble could find sanctuary from their tormentors.

It was on Huguenot business one morning that he had an audience with the King. In one southern area of France there had been a disturbing new move against young Huguenot men. They were being convicted on trumpery charges such as drunken singing in the street or some outburst of tomfoolery common to young males of any nationality or creed, and their fate was to be sent to man the oars in the galley ships, which was virtually a death sentence, for only the strongest survived for any length of time in the terrible conditions that existed, their shackles never removed by day or night. Augustin made a strong protest as soon as he was in the King's Cabinet.

"The galleys are in need of oarsmen," Louis replied. "Those convicted of serious crimes have always filled the thwarts of our fighting ships."

"But these men are not criminals, sire. For the same deed those of the Catholic faith are merely reprimanded, fined or put to cool their heels in a cell overnight. The Huguenots are being discriminated against for no other cause than their Protestant beliefs. The Edict of Nantes was passed to prevent such a state of affairs. The act is being flouted as never before."

Louis already had some knowledge of these arrests. Never liking to be challenged when not entirely sure of his conscience, he decided there was only one way to silence this petition effectively, and that was with a veiled threat. "Then perhaps the Edict of Nantes is outdated and should be reassessed."

"Sire!"

Louis, seeing that his outraged courtier was about to worry this statement instead of being silenced by it, held up his hand quickly. "Don't be alarmed. I'm simply pointing out that if loopholes exist they should be closed. This matter you have brought to my notice shall be investigated." He stood up, putting an end to the audience, and glanced at a clock. "Come along, Monsieur Roussier. It's

time to view the new statuary that is to be set up by the
Tapis Vert. Dismiss your worries. The sunshine and some
new works of art await."

Augustin could only bow and follow the King out of the
Cabinet. Louis, who allowed nothing to slip his mind,
would ask for a report. It was only to be hoped some good
would come out of it, but a new source had been found to
supply the ever-demanding galleys. Augustin suspected it
to be the devilish idea of the soldier War Minister, the
Marquis de Louvois, for it was the kind of merciless move
that bore his stamp. As for the threat about the Edict of
Nantes, that had been extremely significant. Even if it had
been uttered on the spur of the moment, it must have
been lurking in Louis's mind, however deeply buried.
Therein lay a hint of danger of devastating proportions.

With other courtiers he went in the King's wake in the
direction of the Queen's Staircase. Marguerite, selling by
the foot of the flight, was able to tell by the clearing of the
way on the stairs that the King was coming. There was
always the chance that Augustin was with him, for it had
happened a number of times before. Knowing Augustin
would have a smile for her and in her hope of seeing him,
she hesitated longer than she did normally in drawing
back with everyone else to make a path. For the first time
she found herself at the forefront of the vendors and buyers as the King stepped from the last wide marble stair.
Like the rest of the women close at hand, she dropped
swiftly into a curtsey, she alone in her thoughts rejecting
homage to him personally and allotting her respect to the
Throne of France. To her dismay, her head still bowed, she
saw his silver-buckled shoes pause and come to a standstill
squarely in front of her.

"Good day, mademoiselle. What is your name?"

She straightened slowly, her gaze travelling up the crimson silk hose, the full-cut breeches of gold-patterned silk,
the long brocade waistcoat and matching coat sashed
across the chest with the *Cordon Bleu* and the sparkling
diamond star of the Order of Saint Esprit, then to the lace
neckcloth and finally, framed by his black periwig and
swooping hat with crimson plumes, the haughty, middle-
aged face of the most autocratic monarch in all the world.

"Marguerite Dremont, sire." She stood very straight out
of tenseness, her chin higher than she realised. Those dan-

gerous, hooded eyes were boring into her from his imposing height. No wonder those new to Court accustomed
themselves to his fearsome majesty before approaching
him. Even she, who knew the sight of him well and with
hatred of him sustaining her, felt dominated by his powerful presence, her heart hammering under her ribs and a
dryness in her throat.

"How long have you been selling in the vestibule?"

So her surname had meant nothing to him, but then it
was ordinary enough to be without significance. After all,
that clash between her mother and him had been over in a
matter of minutes. In no way did he connect her with the
woman whom he had ordered into custody to die of terror
and a broken heart. "Several weeks, sire."

"Indeed?" He took one of her fans from the basket, rings
flashing ruby and emerald fire from his gloved fingers, and
opened it with a graceful flourish. It showed a flight of his
own hummingbirds against the gilded bars of the Cour des
Oiseaux. "Charming. Your own work?"

"Yes, sire, it is."

He looked over his shoulder and addressed the courtiers
clustered behind him. "I have discovered a new artist right
here in the vestibule. Monsieur Le Brun will have to look
to his laurels." There were polite smiles, for nobody failed
to respond whenever he made a little joke. He returned
his attention to Marguerite, not seeming to notice her
stony expression, and replaced the fan in her basket. "In
my opinion you would benefit from a guided visit to the
Cabinet of Paintings." He beckoned for a courtier to come
forward and Augustin seized the chance to shoulder the
duty. "Let Mademoiselle Dremont have access at a suitable time."

"Yes, sire."

Louis, turning to leave, inclined his head graciously to
Marguerite, his well-shaped mouth curving in a smile that
lifted the neat ends of his thin moustache. For a telling
moment his gaze hung on her. Then he passed on, his
courtiers following after, only Augustin staying behind to
speak to her.

"Don't be upset," he urged, drawing her aside where
they could not be overheard. "The King has honoured you,
however much you may resent it. I'll let you know when
arrangements are made."

She shook her head distractedly. "I'll accept no favours from the King."

His expression was compassionate, for he understood her distress. "Nobody spurns a favour from the King. Suppose he should question you one day about which paintings you like best?"

"He will forget he ever gave me the chance."

"No. He has an indelible memory for such things." He looped his fingers about her arm with a caressing touch. "But you can forget him when you see the paintings with me. Enjoy them. They are part of our country's heritage. After all, the Kings of France are only the custodians."

She looked at him gratefully. He was surely the most understanding of men.

Five

Augustin suggested to Marguerite that there could be no better time to visit the Cabinet of Paintings than on the evening of the Gala. Although the State Apartment was open to all, there came an hour when the general public had to vacate the Château, gently herded out by the Swiss Guards. Only the anteroom in another part of the palace became available at a later hour, solely for those who wished to see the King eat his supper. Frequently ordinary folk did escape the net in their curiosity to look at everything and blundered in on a private party, or appeared wide-eyed at an exclusive ball. They were always requested to leave with such courtesy that they felt honoured by it, for the King would let none suffer through innocent trespass.

"If you are in formal attire," Augustin explained to Marguerite, "there will be no question of your having to leave the Cabinet of Paintings earlier than you wish. Would that suit you?"

Marguerite agreed. Deliberately, as he had advised earlier, she was going to concentrate on the paintings, divorc- ing the visit entirely from any other association.

Early on the Gala evening Madame Dreux arrived with the gown looped across her arms. The apprentice carried two boxes, one containing luxurious undergarments trimmed with lace, the other fine hose and a pair of satin shoes with gilded heels. In the wake of the women came a male hairdresser as painted and powdered as the King's brother. Between them he and Madame Dreux fussed over Marguerite until she felt she must scream. When finally the apprentice held up a silver-framed mirror, which had been sent by Augustin to Marguerite that day, for her to view her reflection she scarcely recognised her- self. A rose of cream silk interwoven with golden threads topped her curls that had been drawn back to set off the contours of her face. The neckline of the gown plunged, the gold silk taffeta moulding her breasts and narrow waist, and then the skirt hung like a narrow bell with the glit- tering sumptuousness of the overskirt giving the required fullness into the charge of a flat bow. She blushed with excitement.

"Distinguée!" Madame Dreux breathed. There was no other word to describe this lovely, elegant girl.

The hairdresser nodded. "Now for the final touch." He reached out for a patch-box and popped a tiny crescent moon on Marguerite's left cheek near the eye just as there came a knock on the door.

"Monsieur Roussier is here!" Hastily Madame Dreux be- gan gathering together the boxes and the rest of her pos- sessions. The hairdresser did likewise. Neither allowed Marguerite to open the door, for her nobleman must see their handiwork first with full effect. Both stood well back while the apprentice, also keeping out of sight, pulled the door wide. Augustin, a gleaming figure in an embroidered silk coat, responded instantly to the spirit of the occasion, his eyes alert with pleasure at the sight of Marguerite. He bowed to her as deeply as if she were the Queen herself. When he came towards her, neither of them noticed the dressmaker and her companions slip away, closing the door quietly behind them.

"Is this my little meadow flower?" There was a fondly teasing note in his voice. "I misnamed you. This evening you are the ultimate, a lily of France."

She gave a smile at his gentle jest that was the peak of compliments, scarcely able to bear the intensity of his gaze, a kind of senseless rapture coursing through her veins. "I'll not change names now."

"I wouldn't let you," he replied softly. "My beautiful Marguerite."

She knew then that the waiting was over. Tonight he would put into words what she had yearned to hear ever since she had faced the realisation that her love for him had been reborn. As the more mature person she had become, she accepted that what she felt for him bore no relation to the infatuation of her young girlhood, but she wanted to believe that the roots of her passion were buried in those dreams, strengthened and enriched by them just as a long friendship is doubly blessed by memories of the past. To retain her composure, there being such a turmoil of joy in her, she turned back to the mirror to check her final appearance.

"I'm ready now," she said, giving a last unnecessary touch to her hair.

"Not quite."

There was a sudden sparkle as the facets of a jewel caught the candlelight. Spellbound, she saw in the mirror's reflection his hands reach forward over her shoulders to rest a pendant against her cleavage and to fasten its gold chain behind her neck. It was a huge sapphire set in diamonds and gold, its blue as strong in hue as her dilated irises. Slowly she raised her eyes to his in the mirror. If she had needed any seal on the uniqueness of the evening it was in this glorious jewel. But there was more to come in the shape of two matching eardrops. When she had fastened them herself, she continued to gaze into the mirror as if trying to adjust to her own appearance.

"This is the most wonderful gift of my life," she breathed.

He lowered his head and kissed the side of her neck, his hands resting lightly on her bare shoulders, and she shivered deliciously, her pulse leaping. Gently he swivelled her around towards him and looked down into her upturned face. "The jewels can't compete with your eyes."

He was overwhelming her. She knew that if he said anything more there would be no Gala, no use for the gown that had been made for her, no chance to display the love-jewel he had given her, for passion beyond his control and hers would sweep them away. Almost in confusion she took up her fan from the table.

"I mustn't forget this."

"Don't take that one." He drew another from his pocket. With a questioning glance she took the new fan and let it slide open. There on its silk leaf was the Château as it had been in days past and her own name was written as if in satin ribbons, entwined into garlands of flowers. Instinctively she knew it held some significance unknown to her.

"Surely I recognise my mother's work? Is this the fan she gave you?"

"That's correct. There's a little story to it that I'll tell you later."

Intrigued, she left the apartment with him. His carriage took them to the gilded entrance of the Ambassadors' Staircase. Together they joined the flow of people going up the central flight to where it branched off on either side like jewelled wings. The whole staircase blazed in rich marbles and Le Brun paintings of exotic scenes. Many a foreign ambassador had caught his breath at the sight of it upon his first visit to the most elegant and brilliant Court in Europe.

"Here we go," Augustin said with a grin as they reached the head of the flight. It was on this first floor on the north side that the King lived, whereas the Queen was on the south side, the staircase there more familiar to Marguerite than the one she and Augustin had just ascended. She had been holding her skirt up slightly to avoid treading on it and she let it fall into place, putting her hand lightly on his raised wrist as Marie Printemps had once instructed her. She exchanged a sparkling glance of anticipation with Augustin and then they sailed forward through wide-open doors into the huge Salon of Diana with its golden walls and ceiling paintings of the goddess. A handsome bust of Louis by Bernini stared haughtily from its marble plinth.

With the doors of the State Apartment aligned and all standing open to the enormous rooms it was possible to see a great distance through to the far salon, and the effect was of a vast sea of people teeming about. There were Swiss Guards and musketeers; foreign dignitaries with escorts; clerks scurrying on their business; tradesmen who had delivered or were seeking payment of a bill; ordinary bourgeois and humbler peasants gaping about, some with over-awed children clinging to their hands; footmen in their blue livery; cardinals in their scarlet soutanes and humbler clergy in black and, predominating, the nobility like swarming peacocks in full Court dress, which they wore with many changes from morning until night, and their magnificent jewellery giving an allover multihued dazzle to everything.

Marguerite could see why the furniture was compara-tively sparse and kept back by the walls. With all the curt-seying and bowing that was constantly taking place, skirts sweeping out and coattails swinging, every courtier and male visitor wearing a sword, maximum space would have been required by even a small number of people and un-der this roof, whenever the Court was in sojourn, there were thousands.

She had asked Augustin to tell her everything of interest. He obliged her by describing first the *Appartement* eve-nings and telling her where the various entertainments were held.

"Billiard tables are always set up here." He indicated the room in which they stood. "The King much prefers the game to cards, which make him impatient. In the neighbouring Salon of Mars," he continued, leading her into the vast room with its lavish decorations of war tro-phies and walls of crimson brocade, "the concerts are held."

Moving on into the sumptuous Apollo Salon she found it was also the Throne room, an appropriate choice. The crimson-canopied throne, crafted ornately from solid sil-ver and nine feet high, stood shining on a dais spread with a gold Persian carpet. The most precious marbles in the Château gave an added glory to this room, and above the fireplace was a life-size portrait of the King in his blue and gold coronation robes. Here as everywhere there were bowls of fresh flowers and orange trees in silver tubs, while overhead each ceiling was a masterpiece of decorative painting in fresh, lively colours, of gods and goddesses ca-vorting or battling or drifting across azure skies, all set within gilded mouldings and in keeping with the mythical theme that ran throughout the whole Château and the park.

Much of the furniture throughout was of silver, and she

felt dazzled by so much magnificence. In the Cornucopia
Salon with its green silk walls, Augustin told her, chocolate
and coffee, liqueurs and juices were served in silver containers from buffets on the evenings of the *Appartements,*
while in the glowing Salon of Venus light suppers were
served, the dishes cradled in silver baskets. He amused her
with his account of the behaviour of those courtiers who
lost at gaming in the splendid Mercury Salon.

"There are such scenes! They weep and shout and curse,
hammer their fists, and tear off their wigs to stamp on
them. It's no wonder that the ladies prefer their own gaming tables."

"What do you do when you lose?" she teased.

"I go white at the gills and play for still higher stakes.
And I don't cheat."

"Cheat! Don't tell me the nobility cheat!"

He nodded, thoroughly amused by her shocked expression. "Worse than ragamuffins pitching stones in a gutter."
Then he gave a shrug of his broad shoulders. "It's generally
accepted, although it's a practice I personally abhor. Quarrels do break out from time to time, and usually unbeknown to the King, who frowns on duelling, they get
settled with swords somewhere at dawn."

It was at that point they found their way blocked by a
barred door. Some structural alterations were taking place
behind it. It was not only in new extensions and satellite
buildings that the Sun King's Château was always in a state
of flux; interior improvements and enlargements were forever taking place and even the Chapel was in its fourth
location.

"I think I should be selling printed guides to the Château
instead of fans in the vestibule," Marguerite remarked
jokingly as Augustin led her on the detour to which a
footman directed them. "New ones are always being produced and are out of date in no time at all."

"I always thought the guide-sellers must do a roaring
trade." He stepped aside with her as one of the royal sedan
chairs in blue and gold came through. Only the royal family had their own sedan chairs within the Château and
anybody else wanting transport had to hire from the man
that held the franchise there. As this one went past, Marguerite recognised the self-important eleven-year-old Duc
du Maine, the King's greatly spoiled elder son by Athénaïs

de Montespan, the offspring of double adultery since her husband still lived and, exceptionally, never failed to rail publicly against her infidelity, a well-known source of embarrassment to Louis. Since titles had been given to all his bastards, they shared many of the privileges enjoyed by the Princes of the Blood and riding in an Apollo-emblazoned chair was one of them.

"Are you envious?" Augustin jested, seeing how her gaze had followed the spoiled young Duc on his imperious way. "Would you have liked to ride on this tour we're taking?"

She made a mischievous face. "Not at all! I could outwalk anyone in the Château and still be ready to dance till dawn."

"Do you know," he remarked drily, "I believe you."

They had taken the detour to a salon where a number of people were gathered in conversational groups and ahead lay the double doors into the Cabinet of Paintings. They were about to cross the threshold into it when a woman's voice, soft and melodious, followed after them.

"Have I changed so much in the months I have been away from Court that you fail to recognise me, sir?"

Although Marguerite's touch was light on Augustin's wrist, she felt him tense. As she withdrew her hand, turning about with him, she saw a fine-looking woman in a shimmering gown of buttercup yellow detaching herself from a group chatting together.

"Susanne! You're the last person I expected to see!"

Something in the way this woman and Augustin were looking at each other sent alarm signals ringing through Marguerite. There was a quality in their expressions that came from long acquaintance of the fondest kind and even of faraway secrets shared. As Augustin presented her he explained that Susanne was the wife of Jacques de Fresnay of whom he had spoken many times.

"You have a charming companion this evening," Susanne observed as her dazzling smile went from him to Marguerite. "Have you been long at Court, Mademoiselle Dremont?"

"This is my first evening as a guest here."

"You come from far afield perhaps?"

Marguerite was conscious of being weighed up, not from any malicious intent, but because this woman was keenly interested in anything Augustin said or did and whatever female company he kept. In view of the lengthy acquaintanceship it was quite natural, but it was odd that in all her long hours of talk with Augustin he had never spoken this woman's name before.

"I live in the town of Versailles," she replied. It had become customary for local inhabitants to make the clear distinction, for references to Versailles had long since come to mean only the Château, just as other royal residences were known as Chambord or Saint-Germain or whatever the location.

"Is that so?" Susanne gave a nod. "Well, many families have built an additional abode in this district to make life more convenient."

"Oh, I haven't moved here. The house where I was born was recently demolished, but it stood north of the village pond."

Susanne looked faintly incredulous. "The pond? Where was that?"

Augustin took over. "It was where the new Lake of the Swiss Guards lies now."

"Oh, was it there? I remember how sorry I felt for those guards excavating the earth in all weathers. Personally I thought the gardens of Versailles had water enough." She tapped Augustin's chest with her closed fan. "I hear that Château Satory is finished now. I look forward to seeing it."

"It goes without saying that you and Jacques will be the first to visit. But tell me, why are you here? Jacques didn't disclose that you were coming back from Orléans."

"I wanted to surprise you!"

"You've succeeded admirably!"

Somehow their shared amusement seemed to bind them closer together. Yet it was not their intention to shut Marguerite out and Susanne smiled at her while giving an explanation for her return.

"When Jacques was away at the wars I was well occupied with the children in the country and, although France has enjoyed peace for a while now, I'm afraid I clung selfishly to my retreat in the countryside. Jacques spent more time with me there, away from the Court, than he should have. Fortunately it has not hindered his promotion in the musketeers, but when this recent trouble reared in the blockading of Luxembourg, I began to think of returning to

Court, even though the children must remain presently where they are for their health's sake. As yet Jacques has had no orders to indicate his regiment of musketeers will be sent to the developing affray, but he has long wanted me to come back to our Paris residence and now, as you can see, I'm here to stay. If he does have to fight at least we'll have had every possible minute together."

"I thought Jacques had been in excellent spirits lately," Augustin commented. "I should have guessed that your return was imminent. I drove past your house when Marguerite and I were in Paris recently."

"Next time you must both come to dine. I insist. Where are you bound for now?"

"The King invited Marguerite to view the masterpieces in the Cabinet."

"Then I'll delay you no longer. We shall meet later at the Gala, I'm sure."

Susanne rejoined those with whom she had been passing the time until Jacques, who had had some business to complete before the entertainment, came back to her. She let the conversation flow over her, no longer taking part and busy with her own love-torn thoughts. How had she ever supposed that her love for Augustin could be lessened by absence, or children, or even the unfailing devotion of a husband whom she betrayed in their most intimate moments in fantasies about the man she could not have?

"Is that not so, Madame de Fresnay?"

The query directed at her brought her back to the moment with a start. Blankly she looked at the half-circle of faces waiting for her reply, trying desperately to recall what was being discussed. Fortunately it came to her and she was able to make a moderately intelligent reply.

In the Cabinet the Keeper of the Paintings awaited. He was a quiet, courteous man with intense pride in his position and nothing pleased him more than to talk of the paintings to an interested party. Marguerite could have spent hours listening to him as she gazed at masterpieces almost beyond belief in their beauty. The artists' names, all new to her, rang through her head like bells. Titian and Leonardo, Raphael, Guercino and Bassano, Rubens and Mantegna, Giorgione and many more.

"The King is a great collector," the Keeper informed her, "and drawn in particular to the Bolognese and Venetian schools." They had moved on from Veronese's *Virgin* to a portrait of extraordinary tranquillity.

"Who's this?" she asked.

"That is Leonardo's portrait of the wife of a Florentine named del Giocondo. The Mona Lisa."

She stood fascinated by the beautiful painting, which was small in comparison with most of the others in the room. There was something about the secret look across the eyes and the enigmatic smile that reminded her of Susanne de Fresnay. Did they both hide a secret love? She felt she was close to the truth.

They were such a length of time with the Keeper that eventually the evening candles took over from the last of the daylight and in the park the Gala was in full swing. They left the Château by the way they had come and went out into the warm darkness. It would have saved time and distance to have gone out through the West Front where some part of the scaffolding had been cleared away for the Gala evening, but Augustin wanted to spare her setting foot on the place where Théo Dremont had fallen to his death. He knew it must be in her mind because she did not glance in that direction as he escorted her forward in the direction of the Water Parterres and then down the wide steps to the cascading Latona fountain, which threw a faint mist in their faces. Music matched the perfume of the flowers in filling the warm air as they went to the Ballroom Grove and, from the terrace, looked down at the central marble platform that was encircled by walls of shimmering water. The dancers in their gem-hued silks and satins formed ever-changing patterns, creating a pretty sight.

Augustin led her onto the floor and swept her into the measure. Her pendant flashed blue fire in the glow of the hundreds of candles as if competing with the starlight overhead. She felt she could have danced all night in that magical place. Seventeen sparkling cascades tumbled gloriously down over the gilded rocks and scrollwork to meet the fountains soaring arrow-straight from the waiting pools. It was a marvellously cool place in which to be active on a warm summer night.

Between dances they sat on silk-upholstered couches along the sumptuously furnished terrace. When it became excessively crowded they left for the quieter leafy grove where they had a little orchestra almost to themselves, they and half a dozen other couples requesting their favourite tunes and measures in turn. Augustin took advantage of the lack of spectators to kiss her sometimes as they danced, her hand, her wrist, her cheek and her lips all subject to the romance of the evening. Neither of them noticed new arrivals until addressed by Susanne.

"Oh, you're here, too! There were so many people everywhere we came in search of space to dance."

Jacques was with her. He was prompt to partner Marguerite while Augustin took Susanne forward. Marguerite, trying not to glance too frequently in their direction, noticed when she did look that they both appeared immensely happy and were conversing closely. There was no lack of talk with Jacques, who was openly curious about her and where Augustin had found her.

"I can't think why we haven't met before," he said persistently.

She decided that the time had come for the moment of truth. "We have met, although you may not remember the occasion."

"How could that be?" He was at his most flirtatious, making her feel as exalted as the goddess Diana whose statue gleamed opaquely from her plinth as they rotated by.

"Cast your mind back over seventeen years to the King's first grand fête at the Château when you and Augustin and two of your comrades from musketeer days stayed in an artisan's cottage. That was when I was born."

He stared at her, his mouth widening, and began to laugh quietly, she smiling at his mirth. "Who would have thought it! However did it come about that Augustin found you again?"

Her expression changed subtly. "Don't ask me that. Not this evening. It's the sad part of the story and too recent for me to relate it to anyone as yet."

He pressed her fingers reassuringly in his, all amusement gone from his face. "Forgive me. I blundered."

She thought him the nicest of men, and if he had not been returning her to Augustin at the end of the dance she would have gladly stayed longer as his partner. The four of them went on together down the tree-lined Avenue of Bacchus and Saturn to watch the fireworks over the Grand Canal where the King was sailing in his barque and leading the small flotilla. By now the hour was late and they made their way to one of the groves where supper was being served.

"There'll be nectar and ambrosia for you, Marguerite," Augustin said with laughter in which she joined, half believing it was possible to find the food of the gods awaiting here.

There was plenty of chatter from those helping themselves from the candle-lit buffet tables set up in a circle around a glimmering pool, everything served on silver dishes. Augustin, Jacques and Susanne met many people whom they knew, her return to Paris a favourite topic of conversation. Marguerite was presented to them, not always catching their titles or their names in the merry buzz of noise backed by the music of an orchestra. She found herself being lavishly complimented by the men, who eyed her lasciviously and at times were startlingly outspoken about her attractions. She was learning fast that talk was extraordinarily open at Court, sexual matters discussed freely and the latest scandal seized upon with relish like a bone among dogs.

Not for the first time she thought how Versailles could be compared with Mount Olympus, with the Court moving in its charmed, hedonistic circles like mythical creatures, their lives bearing no relation to those of ordinary folk. Because they lived entirely for pleasure, the welfare of those socially beneath them never entered their thoughts except when it was connected in any way with their own personal comfort. Their arrogance and conceit were supreme, their satisfaction with themselves unassailable. No matter how much she chose to think of Augustin as the exception, he was as much part of the life of Versailles as the rest, bound by its rules and etiquette, held securely in a sphere into which she could never penetrate.

But this was no night for sober thoughts. It was a time to enjoy the enchanted atmosphere, to let the gaiety of the moment drive all else away. She fluttered her fan, threw back her head to laugh at all that amused her, and dazzled in her own right those who thought themselves to be competing for her.

Augustin, finding her drawn a distance from him by two or three courtiers and sometimes more whenever he turned his head, finally rounded her up by putting an arm firmly about her waist and drawing her possessively to his side.

"What have they been saying to you?" he enquired with wicked amusement, guessing full well.

"Nothing I intend to repeat," she gave back provocatively, spreading her fan, her eyes dancing at him.

"All your innocence is slipping away from you this evening, is it not?" His voice had become charged with a sensual warmth that matched the look in his eyes, ravishing her.

"So it seems," she whispered, resisting a reaction to cover herself with her hands as if she stood quite naked before him in this crowded place. The curve of his arm tightened about her, raising her up against him as he kissed her cheek and spoke against her ear, his breath soft, ensuring that no one else could overhear.

"Let us leave. I want to be alone with you."

They made no partings with anyone, simply breaking away and threading their way to go back together under the archway through which they had come. Their eyes were only for each other as they went on down the dark tree-bordered lane.

Susanne was alone in seeing them leave. Her heart contracted as if struck by a knife. Hastily she put down her plate with its half-eaten slice of a delicious wine-soaked sponge, unable to face another mouthful of it and not far from vomiting at the thought of Augustin making love to that witchlike beauty. It was foolish to agonise. The love he gave to other women was without depth, nothing compared to his feelings for her, which had remained the same, something she read in his face whenever they met, however long the interval between. It had been there a thousandfold this evening when he had turned from the threshold of the Cabinet of Paintings at the sound of her voice. She knew herself to be the reason why he had not married. He could not endure the thought of tying himself to anyone else, not even in a *mariage de convenance*. Nobody else could take her place with him, least of all this peasant girl whose origins Jacques had just revealed to her.

She straightened her shoulders and drew breath, answering as somebody spoke to her. That girl could have her moment. Better by far that Augustin should continue to pleasure himself with mistresses than be lost to her in the arms of a clever wife. She was sustained by her secret that he was still hers and always would be.

Augustin and Marguerite wandered back through the park, delayed once when a crowd of young courtiers and their ladies surged forward from a side path to capture them individually in loops of wide satin ribbon, hilariously demanding forfeits for release. They took it in good part, Marguerite agreeing to kiss the courtiers in turn and Augustin willing enough as each pretty female face was upturned to his with lips pouting readily.

Laughing together about it, he took Marguerite's hand again into his as they continued on their way. The Gala would continue until dawn by which time much of the splendour and charm would be tarnished, and he was glad he was taking her away now. The accusation by moralists that Versailles was no more than a brothel set in gold was an exaggeration, but neither was it a place for prudes or those who wished to live an abstemious life.

Ahead of them loomed the great edifice. Not for the first time Augustin was struck by its beauty at night, every window glowing, its sandstone walls pale as moonlight. Marguerite's attention had been drawn elsewhere. She stopped, inhaling the aromatic scent of the orange trees that came wafting on a gentle breeze.

"Surely their aroma has never been more fragrant. There must be something special about every moment of this night."

"I'm sure there is," he said huskily, drawing her into his arms to kiss her lingeringly. It was the bouquet of her skin and hair that was intoxicating him, making him impatient for the hours to come. When they reached the Cour Royale his carriage was brought forward. As they were driven in the direction of his new home the wheels did not turn swiftly enough for him.

She had been several times to Château Satory since it had been furnished, but it was the first time since he had moved in. The servant, who had opened the door to them, melted away and they might have been alone there as they went into the Ivory Salon where glass doors stood open to the terrace and the newly-laid-out gardens beyond. In a patch of moonlight that was defying the candlelight as it fell into the room, he took her by the arms and pulled her close to his chest. He spoke tenderly to her.

"I love you, Marguerite. I have loved you for a long while, but I've waited until I could tell you here in this house where you belong. I also had to be sure that you were ready to keep your side of our agreement." His eyes searched hers as if for confirmation of his hopes. "Reveal your feelings to me. Show me I haven't spoken too soon. Say you care for me."

She cupped his beloved face gently between her hands, love flowing from her to him in the harmony of that special moment. "I love you with my whole heart. I'll always love you. I, more than any woman who has ever lived, was born destined for one man and you are he."

His arms went about her and he kissed her long and hard. They smiled at each other in perfect understanding when he loosened his embrace. Turning to the wine that had been put ready for their coming, he poured a crystal goblet for each of them, handing one to her.

"To our happiness together," he said, raising his goblet to her.

"May it last forever." There was rapture in her face.

When they had drunk their toast he spoke more about the fan bearing her name. "It was meant to be a reminder of the vow I had made to return and to keep before me a name I was not to forget. Behind that was the understanding that it should be given to you on the day I intended to make you mine." He moved closer to her and took the goblet from her hand to set it aside with his own, his gaze holding hers. "That time has come, my love."

They went upstairs together. She had not been on the upper floor since her first visit here and when they entered the bedchamber with the rose and silver brocade she saw that dominating the new furnishings was a four-poster bed hung with silken drapes and silver-fringed canopy. He closed the double doors and stood watching her. She unclipped the ornament from her hair and put it aside. That was all she had to do for herself, for he unfastened every hook and set free every ribbon bow as he removed the fine layers of silk and lawn from her body until all that remained were her satin shoes and her white silken hose. He dropped to one knee to take her shoes from her feet. Then he untied her garter ribbons and peeled off her stockings, pausing only to kiss her toes. Still on one knee, one arm resting across it, he absorbed her with his gaze.

"You are beautiful." His green eyes were as dark with desire as the depth of a lake.

Raising her arms slowly, she combed her fingers through her hair, making the last pins fall to the ground around her with little tinkling sounds. She felt no shame in his open adoration of her nakedness. Gone completely was the shyness that had affected her momentarily at times in the past. There was only a rising joy in her that he was looking at her as if she were the most beautiful creature ever formed. Yet an involuntary little gasp escaped from her when, from where he knelt, he seized her by the hips and pressed an ardent kiss into the silky red-gold triangle that glowed at her loins. Then, fired through, she reached down her hands and clasped him to her, eyes closed, her head falling back, and felt herself lifted up as he rose to his feet in one swift movement. He laid her on the bed and kissed her again.

Against the lacy pillows she watched and waited. He was like a lion in the strength and power of his movements as he divested himself of his clothes. Only a terrible scar across his shoulder, long since healed to a puckered line, marred the muscled perfection of his body as he came to her in the wide bed. Her arms received him, her mouth welcomed him and her nipples leapt at the first touch of his palm.

"I love you," they whispered to each other as if their words were fresh every time. There seemed to be no part of her body that did not tremble joyously under his passionate caresses and exploring kisses, he exulting in the pleasure he was giving her. Her awakening was that of a deeply sensual woman and he encouraged the instinctive response of her loving hands towards his manhood. His final tenderness at the moment of possession fulfilled all that he had wished for her. It enabled her to lose her virginity with the minimum of pain and achieve a crescendo of ecstasy that she felt afterwards would have thrown her from him by its force if he had not held her in his adoring embrace.

"Oh, my darling," he murmured as the mists of passion cleared. "My love. My Marguerite."

They made love through the remaining hours of the night, only sleeping when dawn broke. Later they awoke to love again, insatiable for each other. Then they bathed together, a tug on the bellpull having brought the delivery of hot water to the adjoining bathroom. The bath was of green marble, far too small for two people, but it taught her a new way of being loved and of loving that was exquisitely pleasurable, enhanced by the warm water and the steam-filled atmosphere.

They put on the silk robes that had been laid out for them and returned to the bedchamber where a table had been set up with food. Both of them ate ravenously, laughing at themselves, linking fingers across the table and loving each other with their eyes. He stayed with her until mid-afternoon when duties at Versailles took him away from the love-rumpled bed.

She dozed for a while and then bathed again, luxuriating in the scented water, a maid now in attendance. When asked what she wished to wear, she was astonished to learn she had an abundance of clothes and shoes in an adjoining dressing room she had not discovered. Entering it, she found her gown from the previous evening set on a wicker frame to let the creases drop out, and on others, in the designs she had approved, were the rich blues and greens that Madame Dreux had thought the most admirable colours for her hair. Lifting a chest lid, more gowns came to light and in a clothespress were embroidered and lace-trimmed undergarments that seemed enough to last her for the rest of her life. No wonder the dressmaker had taken such a time with the golden gown. She had had this mammoth order to contend with at the same time.

The mirror in the dressing room's recess reflected Marguerite in many different gowns, a thoroughly enjoyable way of passing time, before she settled on one of lily-green and tied matching ribbons in her hair.

She ran to meet Augustin when he came home late after the King's supper, flinging herself in his arms. To them both it was as if they had been parted for years instead of hours and they made up for loss of time in passionate loving.

If he could have stayed away from Court completely to be with her at least until the first madness between them had subsided a little, he would have done so, but she was not his bride and his duties at Court could not be set aside for the cementing of a relationship with a new mistress. Instead they both went daily to the Château, travelling separately, for he could not arrive with a fan-seller any more than she could be seen with him. She was always dropped a distance from the gates in a hired calèche that collected and delivered her with more anonymity than would have been possible in any carriage of his.

But at Versailles few secrets could be kept. Despite the certainty that they could rely on the discretion of Jacques and Susanne, Marguerite knew that sooner or later her flaming head of hair would cause somebody to recognise her as the fan-seller from the vestibule. Out of deference to him, she asked Lucille to take her place at the Château while she herself stayed at the workshop employed in designing and making the fans. At the same time she offered Lucille the accommodation above the hatter's shop since she no longer needed it herself. Lucille accepted the accommodation gladly, but she declined to sell in the vestibule, being quite shy by nature.

"I do have a suggestion. My niece, Clarisse, is a pretty girl, bright, intelligent and honest. She would be a credit to your fans."

"Would her parents consent?"

Lucille threw up her hands to show there was no problem there. "Her late mother was my sister and now Clarisse is an unwanted presence in the house of a second marriage where she is treated abominably. I would have taken her to live with me if I had had more than my garret room."

"Well, you will have the space now. Since you recommend her I know she will please me. Let her come to the apartment. She will be company for you."

It turned out to be an excellent arrangement. Clarisse was black-haired and dark-eyed, neat in her appearance and with a friendly smile.

"I know all about fans," she told Marguerite. "I have helped Aunt Lucille with her work many times. I can continue to do that whenever I'm not in the vestibule."

Marguerite went there with Clarisse on her first day. She wanted to make sure there would be no trouble about her sending a deputy and that the girl did not receive the same rough treatment she herself had faced on her first appearance. But all went well. Clarisse was her employee and had a perfect right to take up her stand by the foot of the Queen's Staircase.

Augustin took Marguerite to every evening event in the park: masked balls, concerts, galas and plays. Once they viewed a Molière play performed on the old Cour de Marbre, which being two steps higher than the Cour Royale and enclosed on three sides by the East Front, made a charming stage. The actors and actresses made their entrances and exits through the glass doors under the gilded balcony and the rose pillars were perfect to be leaned against nonchalantly or for a heroine to hide behind.

By rights Marguerite should not have been at any of these events, which were intended only for the Court and notable guests, but since the bourgeoisie infiltrated these open-air festivities, the ever-open gates an invitation to the bold and the curious, she was not the only one lacking noble blood who happened to be there. He could not take her to any formal occasions inside the Château and had to leave her three evenings a week for the *Appartements*. She knew he met Susanne and Jacques there, for he always recounted anything that he thought would be of interest to her.

The Fresnays had become frequent visitors at the Château Satory. Marguerite found them good company, witty and lively, never showing that they were in any way aware of the social difference between their status and hers. She knew their attitude towards her sprang primarily from their long friendship with Augustin, but Jacques at least was an exceptionally kind man and Susanne never uttered a careless word to make her feel an outsider in their charmed circle of wealth and position. Yet with that intuition that women have about each other, Marguerite's first twinges of suspicion were soon confirmed. Susanne was in love with Augustin.

Once the situation came close to being spoken about. Susanne and she had left the two men looking over some thoroughbred horses that had been delivered to Augustin's stables, and with the friendly familiarity that had evolved between them, they strolled side by side through a bower of roses to a goldfish pond. At its centre a pyramid fountain cascaded down. They seated themselves, facing each other, on the stone surroundings, Susanne trailing her fingers in the water.

"It means much to Jacques and to me to see how happy

Augustin is these days. You have made a great difference to his life, Marguerite."

"Have you never seen him so content before?"

"Never. I answer you truthfully."

Marguerite judged her moment. "Not even in the days before you had any thought of marrying Jacques?"

Susanne's serene composure did not change. "I did not know him then. When I first spoke to Augustin my marriage to Jacques had already been arranged." She flicked the shining droplets of water from her hand and rested it on the sun-warmed stone to dry. "All I would advise is that you give him no cause for jealousy. He has suffered torments from it in his time and his toleration of it must be at a low ebb."

"I want no other man." Marguerite spoke softly and emphatically, her heart in her voice. "I love him."

"That's not hard to see and I commit you to that declaration." Susanne's gaze drifted away from Marguerite as she looked down at her own reflection rippling across the water. "Just remember it is an old saying that faithfulness, once broken, resists recall."

Marguerite thought over that conversation several times afterwards. It had been both poignant and significant. With the confidence of youth she could foresee no danger. Whatever had been between Susanne and Augustin in the past was over.

In the evenings when Augustin was absent at Court, Marguerite was never idle. She did her accounts or jotted down ideas for her work the next day. She had kept her workshop and it was a pleasure to share the table with Lucille, who was as industrious as she was herself, and sometimes they sang at their tasks. Lucille had a flair with lace and produced the prettiest ribbon-laced fans of her own invention, which found a ready sale from Clarisse's basket. Marguerite allowed Lucille a bonus on these, which was greatly appreciated.

Sometimes they discussed between them the designs they would launch when Marguerite's finances allowed. In a drawer in her bedchamber was a purse of gold that Augustin had given her for personal expenses, but she would not take a coin from it for her own enterprise. She had to prove herself and her own efforts, and only then would she consider his offer of investment and expand fully along the lines she wanted to follow.

Having been brought up to make one coin do the work of several whenever possible, she decided it was time to stop bringing in her raw materials from Paris and cut expenses by tapping local sources. These days the town had an abundance of craftsmen in every trade, drawn there by an endless demand for skilled hands in the service of the King's constant building projects, not only at Versailles, but also at Marly, which was not far away.

There he was erecting a miniature palace and at nearby Clagny a new château had replaced the one built for Athénaïs de Montespan at the height of her favour and which she had rejected as being fit only for an actress. There was also the little porcelain palace at Trianon that was expanding beyond its original purpose as a place for summer picnics and gaining gaming salons and bedchambers. Marguerite, passing it one day, noticed that tilers were as busy replacing its wall-tiles cracked by the weather as the gardeners were in relaying several parterres to suit some latest whim of the King.

It was not long before she found a weaver able to supply just the kind of silk she wanted at a reasonable price, far less than she had been charged by the Paris supplier. He worked by himself at his own loom in one room, his name Pierre Ouinville, and he came from a district where the looms had been silenced by competition from Lyons.

"All I have to find now is a fan-stick maker," she said to him as she was on the point of leaving.

"I think I may be able to help you there, mademoiselle. A fellow of that trade, with the name of Taraire, is living in the cellar of this house. He's found work cleaning and polishing the hundreds of coaches and carriages in the Great Stables, but it's a waste of a skilled man."

Taraire arranged to meet her the next day. He came from the Great Stables in the wake of the King's coach to which he had given a final polish. It had been driven inside to the vestibule of the Queen's Staircase as Marguerite came into the Cour Royale to talk business with him for the few minutes he could spare.

"I mustn't stay long, mademoiselle, but I couldn't risk anyone else offering you his labour before me."

"I understand. Show me your samples."

He produced them from a leather bag slung over one shoulder and she saw at once that his work was of the high quality she wanted. The previous day she had received a first shipment of ivory and fine woods ready for fan-stick work from an importer in Marseilles, cutting out any middleman, and this craftsman would do full justice to them. She stated what she was prepared to pay and he accepted readily.

"When can you start, Monsieur Taraire?"

His long, thin face, not unlike the shape of a fan-stick with its cadaverous cheeks, broke into a wide grin. "Next week. I'd start today if I could."

"Next Monday will do well enough. Collect some materials from me at my workshop beforehand and then you can set to work without delay."

They parted company, he to return to the Great Stables with his loping stride while she drew to one side, able to see from the parting of people by the grille that a royal equipage was about to come through.

Within the vestibule of the Queen's Staircase Louis had stepped into his coach, which was set with mirrors within and upholstered in satin. The reflected sunshine threw sparks from the jewelled buttons on his cinnamon silk coat and from the brooch adorning the single orange plume of his hat. He was on his way to see how work was progressing at his new palace at Marly and to view the thousands of replanted trees that had been brought the far distance from Compiègne to forest the slopes around it.

He was looking forward to the day ahead. It would refresh him to get away from Versailles for a while. Athénaïs's temper, ever quick, had become a torment to him. If it had not been for darling Françoise de Maintenon acting as a gentle buffer between them, as she had done again only an hour ago, he would not have known how to go on enduring the scenes and tantrums.

In the coaches that followed him down the Cour Royale towards the gates were a number of courtiers. It was his policy to avoid having any of them on a journey, because invariably they began making requests for promotion or some other tedious matter. Nothing annoyed him more than to have his attention trapped. Women were far better company in any case, vivacious and smiling and full of inconsequential chatter to divert him, but today the drive to Marly was too short for him to become bored.

He heaved a slight sigh on his thoughts of Athénaïs and Françoise. It was a great trial for a man to have two favoured women under the same roof; one his mistress of long standing and of whom he was still fond whatever her faults, and one who chastely continued to withhold her delights, increasing his passion. Both had luxurious accommodation on the same floor as his own and within as easy distance of his bedchamber as was that of the Queen, which meant he should have all that any man could need for the gratification of his desires. He realised that Françoise was aiming to have Athénaïs dislodged from her twenty-two-room apartment, larger by far than the Queen's own eleven rooms, but he was not ready yet to rid himself of the woman who had borne him seven children.

How well he knew Athénaïs. Much of her fear of losing him lay in the dread of having to return to her ill-tempered husband who still waited to claim her back. Poor darling. Once in a panic she had put love potions in his food and drink, giving him terrible pains in the head and stomach, he who was never ill and did not know what it was to catch cold. It was the only time in his life that his gargantuan appetite had been affected, causing him to vomit excruciatingly. And he had forgiven her.

Recently he had upset all three women over his passionate affair with Marie Angélique de Fontanges, a quite gorgeous young noblewoman with the thighs of a goddess. He had made her a Duchesse and then she had miscarried his child, since which time his interest had waned completely. It had been a traumatic time. The Queen had wept, although she tried not to displease him by showing her feelings. Athénaïs had raged, which was normal at these times, although she tolerated without reproof those frequent occasions when he took a woman, high- or low-born, to bed or to a day-couch for a few hours or minutes of carnal pleasure.

Hardest to bear had been Françoise withdrawing her shell-like ear from the troubles he liked to confide in her. She was forty-four, three years older than he, and her sympathetic attitude and her solicitous care of his favourite bastard, the young Duc du Maine, had won her to him and melted away his initial dislike. How could he ever have not liked that amiable, witty and clever woman who had become his beloved confidante? Perhaps he had sensed her crusading spirit from the start and had resisted what had now come about in a certain submission to her good influence. He was spending more evenings with the Queen, who liked Françoise immensely as a result, a feeling that had never been extended to Athénaïs. Inevitably Françoise's spiritual saintliness had also turned his thoughts more to the duty his mother had bequeathed to him, which was that he should rid France of heresy, a task he had allowed to simmer with the minimum of pressure on the Protestants to mend their ways.

His abstracted gaze turned to the window at his right hand. The guards presented arms but he paid them no attention. Then suddenly his hooded eyes snapped alert as a young woman of fascinating countenance came into view, her hair bright as rubies. He remembered her. The little fan-seller with the artistic talent. She was not looking at him, although bobbing a curtsey as women did whenever he drove by, her lashes lowered. Her young beauty fired the familiar surge in his loins. He watched her until the edge of the window sliced her away from his sight.

He smiled to himself. The priests said that his erasing of heresy would atone for his lechery, although they were wise enough not to state his sins quite as bluntly. But he was not ready yet to devote himself entirely to the righteous path along which Françoise had pointed him. That young woman had been as heart-lifting as a lovely flower, in more ways than one.

His red coach, drawn by six bays, headed by mounted musketeers and flanked by his escort and equerries, bowled out of the Cour Royale into the Place d'Armes. As usual, beggars were thick at the gates that they were not supposed to enter, although a guard sometimes took pity on them and looked away. Louis's profile passed them by. He never tossed a coin or deigned to notice them, unable to comprehend their plight. The poor were completely beyond his ken, a subterranean flow of misery that he chose to ignore in spite of petitions on their behalf that appeared frequently on the anteroom table on Monday mornings, when people from any walk of life could set down a written request. He read them all later in the day and granted whatever was possible, but those appeals for the poor he passed over completely. It suited him to block them out and not to acknowledge their existence. To have done so would have irked his supreme conceit that he, the all-powerful Sun King, had an enemy in poverty that would never lie down before him in defeat.

At Marly he had the most enjoyable day, viewing first the final stages of the great machine, a masterpiece of engineering, that would keep an aqueduct filled with water from the Seine and feed the site of his new château as well as the fountains of Clagny and Versailles. To ensure still greater supplies of water he was turning over another possible source in his mind, but that he would discuss with his engineers at a later date.

In the meantime he had the building of Marly to inspect. It stood at the apex of a horseshoe made up of six pavilions on either side, eleven with accommodation for two married couples each, and the twelfth given over to bathrooms.

As he strode round looking at everything, his sharp ears caught the comments the noblemen made among themselves. They had seen how exclusive invitations would be to this place and how desirous all would be to receive them. For the second time in a few hours he smiled to himself with satisfaction. This was where he intended to enjoy the company of his friends on about three visits a year. Any spare pavilions should be allotted to those among his courtiers who deserved a reward. His inner smile spread to his lips and almost induced a chuckle. It would be like throwing titbits to his red setters. He could foresee many a nobleman being brought smartly to heel on the hope of an invitation to Marly.

It was late when he arrived back at Versailles, but he was in good time for his public supper. The ladies joined him and he seated himself in his red brocade chair, looking about keenly as he always did, seeing who was there and making a mental note of persistent absentees. No invitation to Marly for them.

He took the napkin from the ledge of the gold *cadenas* in front of him and lifted its ornately embossed lid to take a spoon that lay within beside a knife and fork. It was a signal for the ladies to follow suit with their spoons. As he took the first taste of the soup served to him, he looked across at a group of common folk who stood, as always, a little apart from the grandly dressed. He thought wryly that the expression on these honest faces was always the same. They were gazing at him with the same kind of fascination that children showed when watching the wild animals being fed in their dens in the park's menagerie. The fan-seller was not among them. There was no reason why she should be, but he would have liked the pretty sight of her once more at the end of the day.

Jacques was not posted to the minor war centred at Casal as Susanne had feared, but remained at Court. The couple visited Orléans from time to time, attended functions at Versailles and entertained at their Paris mansion where Augustin and Marguerite were fairly frequent guests to dinner or to supper after a performance at the Comédie-Française. No matter where they met the Fresnays, it became increasingly noticeable to Marguerite that Susanne was becoming more strained, her cheekbones a little sharper, an almost haunted look in her velvety eyes. Having no one with whom to discuss these changes, Augustin least of all, and with only her instincts to go by, Marguerite grew quite convinced that Susanne's love for him had increased to a violent torment. Full of compassion, she tried to find ways by which to lessen it for her and the most obvious one was to avoid meeting the couple too often.

"Do we have to dine with the Fresnays again on Sunday?" she asked one day when Augustin had accepted in her absence on their joint behalf. "It would be fun to picnic on our own somewhere before the summer comes to an end."

He frowned impatiently. "Why have you started to make excuses about going to their house or to their coming here? I've accepted for Sunday and it would be discourteous to make a trumped-up excuse."

"It wasn't that. I love a picnic with you on our own."

He hated to deny her anything and put his arms around her, holding her close. "We'll go for a picnic tomorrow morning. Just as we used to. On one condition."

"What's that?"

"You don't keep me at bay as you did before."

She laughed. "I let you kiss me."

He squeezed her waist. "Do you think that was enough? You had me permanently on the rack."

The moment passed without the least discord between them, but Marguerite could tell she must not try again to keep him from his friends. She was such a new part of his life whereas his roots with them went deep. But that did not prevent her deciding that it was time at last to tell him that she knew of the existence of the secret door at Château Satory.

She chose her moment when they had come together from the library where she had been selecting a book on his recommendation. As they came back into the anteroom where she knew the door to be concealed she stopped and turned to him, holding the book she had chosen close to her with folded arms.

"I would trust you with my life," she began, having thought out beforehand what she should say. "Would you trust me with yours?"

"What's all this about?" he asked in surprise. "You know I would."

"Well, then I think you should not be afraid to tell me why you have a hidden door in this room. I was in the next salon when you and Baron Picard came from there the day I first came here."

He was taken aback, but shrugged and gave a grin. "Lots of houses have hidden places. Versailles is full of them."

"What is yours? A room? A passageway?"

"You shall see for yourself." He went first to lock the door of the anteroom against intrusion. Then he went to the fireplace where he twisted a piece of carving in the woodwork above and a door swung inward in the least-expected corner, for she had amused herself several times by trying to find its location. After lighting one of the candles in the anteroom, he led her through the aperture and in the small space beyond was a massive door that he unlocked. Beyond there was simply a room of moderate size with stacks of papers and leather binders holding more. There were several stout boxes of the kind in which money and valuables were kept, a table, two chairs and a supply of candles. On one wall several good swords were racked and there were muskets on another. "I store family papers here and other items of importance," he explained. "There is a similar vault at the Manoir and it has kept the

family heirlooms secure during times of war and rebellion.
In time I should have told you about this place."

"You've satisfied my curiosity," she said with a smile.
"Why didn't you ask me before?"

"I had to be sure that you knew me well enough to
disclose the secret door to me with confidence."

He gave one of her curls an affectionate tug. "You should
have had no doubt about that."

As she preceded him back into the anteroom, he locking
up after them, she rubbed her arms. Yet it had not been
cold in there. Vaguely she was reminded of some moment
in her life when she had had a similar sensation, but did not
try to isolate it. The vault was only a place of storage and of
no significance for her. Yet when she had picked up the
book from the chair where she had left it, she moved
quickly into the sunshine coming through the windows
while waiting for Augustin to open again the anteroom
doors.

Towards the end of August, Augustin made a visit home
to Le Havre. Marguerite yearned to go with him, but without any mention on his part or hers she knew it was impossible. As his mistress she would never be received in his
father's house.

During his sojourn of a few days at the Manoir, Augustin
discussed with his father the new and sinister shift against
the Huguenots. More and more children were being forc-
ibly removed from their homes to be given a Catholic
upbringing, the distraught parents having no knowledge
of their whereabouts. Protestant churches were being
closed on some pretext or another and Catholics encouraged to shun the shops of tradesmen not of their faith.

"How have you progressed with outlets into Holland?"
Gérard asked him. Augustin had decided some time ago
that, as a precaution, escape routes should be established
for those in danger of their lives. The Manoir itself was
ideally suited as a stopover for anyone wishing to get to
England, which was like Holland in being a Protestant
realm.

"I have begun to thread up contacts. It's a slow business,
but I now have a number of Dutch who, living along the
frontier, are willing to assist anyone in flight. My own
house has already sheltered a youth escaping from service

in the galleys. He was in the attic for three days before he left in the guise of valet to a friend of mine travelling to London."

"What of your mistress?" Gérard knew of her presence in his son's house.

"She suspects nothing. As for the servants, every one of them is a Huguenot and a staunch member of our Church."

"Well done. Here it is the same. In the cellars of the Manoir one could keep a whole congregation and no sound would penetrate the thick stone walls to reach the main floors. We are ready to receive whomever you send to us."

"If ever Louis should revoke the Edict of Nantes, I fear there would be a flood tide."

Augustin inspected the cellars before he left. As in those of his own house there was a special door well hidden from outside by shrubs that would facilitate secret comings and goings. When he returned to Versailles his only worry was that his father was not as robust in health as he had always been. For the first time Augustin realised that Gérard, far from being ageless as parents generally seemed to be, had become an old man.

With the full onslaught of autumn the Court prepared for its great exodus to Fontainebleau. An increase of wolves in the forest there promised excellent sport and many of the courtiers, who were good shots like the King, looked forward as well to bringing down plenty of wild duck and partridge. Marguerite was well prepared for this upheaval. To her joy Augustin had insisted she accompany him and had promised to find her comfortable accommodation not too far from the palace.

She outlined her plans to him over supper one evening when she was wearing a diamond necklace he had given her, the pear-shaped briolettes dancing with fire against her white skin. "I am having some boxes of fan-making material packed to take with me, so that I have something with which to occupy myself while you are attending to your duties at Court. But before I leave I'm taking on two more hands at the workshop, women known to Lucille who are desperately in need of employment. She can vouch for their skills." Marguerite had a succulent morsel of chicken on her fork halfway to her mouth and she put it down again. "They can help swell stock in my absence together with such fans as I can send back to Lucille from Fontainebleau."

"Won't two more hands mean overproduction? There must be a limit to what Clarisse can sell."

"That's the whole point. I intend to expand my fan-selling when you and I return with the Court in the spring."

"There's no certainty the King will come back to Versailles then. The Court may follow him to Paris or Chambord."

She struggled against her own ambition. "Then it would mean a slight postponement to my plans, that's all. Nothing shall deter me, although I know I'll be taking a chance."

"Is it to be a stall manned by Clarisse in the vestibule?" He knew she would have to seek his influence there. Those concessions were hard to come by. Her answer surprised him.

"No. Not yet anyway. I'm going to rent a little shop."

"Wait a moment," he warned gently. "Remember I have first call on your time. I'm not playing second fiddle to anything that would keep you away from me."

"That will never happen." Her reassurance was intense. She had not needed Susanne to tell her to be wary of his jealousy. She had seen it flare whenever other men had made advances to her, his veneer of smiling politeness towards them very thin. Until now he had been remarkably tolerant towards her work, which puzzled her at times, and on no account did she want him to begin resenting it. "Am I not always here whenever you come home? I shall keep it that way by taking on an assistant to be behind the counter at all times."

"I am relieved to hear it." He smiled to banish the anxiety in her face. It was not his intention to dispel her enthusiasm. On the contrary, he admired her for wanting to strive ahead and give employment to women whose hard circumstances she must know only too well. "What put the idea of a shop into your head?"

"More can be sold from a counter than from a basket. In any case I want to expand my range. There's a profit to be made in cheaper fans, too." She had finished the chicken and put down her fork.

He had finished, too. Two footmen stepped forward to remove the plates. Two more set a fresh course in front of each of them, following the custom of announcing it aloud at the same time.

"I am hoping to find a shop with a back room where I can do my accounts and designing while at the same time be aware of what goes on at the counter."

"You said, 'not yet' about a stall in the vestibule. Where does that come into your plans?" he asked when the footmen had withdrawn again.

She suddenly beamed at him. "When I'm successful enough to be able to stock it with fans gleaming with pearls and glittering with jewels!"

"I'd wager my last louis on your achieving that goal." His warm gaze approved her spirit. Not for the first time he experienced the sharpest regret that birth and lineage made it impossible for him to marry her. His father would have found in her a daughter-in-law after his own heart. Gérard Roussier would have been won over completely by her keenness to launch a new venture, her determination to make money through her own initiative and her bright spark of independence that made her choose the harder path towards success rather than the easier one that could have been paved for her. In her own way she had all the qualities that a banker looked for when faced with a request for financial backing. "I'm asking again when I'll be allowed to invest in this enterprise of yours. I fancy having a slice of this cake that you are baking for yourself!"

She gave back his grin. "In time, sir. Be patient. I have yet to see how the business continues to flourish in my absence."

"Not much doubt of that, I'd say. Well, now"—he pretended to ponder some great decision—"it's only about seven hours' journey from Versailles, but it would be an uncomfortable ride for you in a hired calèche to Fontainebleau. I had better buy you one for your own use."

She sprang up from her chair and threw herself across his lap, hugging him. "You're too good to me! You've given me so much already and now a calèche of my own!"

It was the first time he had ever had a mistress who had not taken everything for granted. Her honest appreciation was as refreshing as everything else about her. He chucked her chin playfully. "You'll never want for anything all the time it lies in my power to care for you."

She clasped him tightly round his neck, her arms buried in the curls of his periwig, and pressed her cheek to his. "Material things don't matter. If ever you should be poor and lose everything, I'd still be able to earn a living for both of us."

He was both amused and touched by her outburst. Yet she had revealed more of herself than she knew. Fanmaking represented stability to her, an anchor she could be sure of in the midst of all the swift changes that had taken place in her life. Balancing the romantic side of her nature, her peasant origins demanded a foot on the ground, practicality set against dreams that could vanish at a turn of fate.

"What if some handsome lad should offer you something I can't give you?" he asked, hiding his dread of such a catastrophe behind a careless smile.

She leaned her head back to look into his face. "Do you mean a wedding ring?"

"Yes. It could happen."

She shook her head vigorously and tightened her clasp again. "Never! I want only you with your man's mind, your man's body and your man's love!"

Such a declaration was invitation enough. Heedless of their unfinished supper, he slid an arm under her legs and carried her upstairs to bed.

A few weeks later he commissioned a fashionable artist to paint Marguerite's portrait. His own, painted when he was younger, hung above the fireplace in the Crimson Salon, set deep in a gilded frame. To please him, Marguerite wore her golden gown for the sittings and held the Versailles fan in her left hand, the leaf spread wide enough to reveal her name on it. When the portrait was finished Augustin had it placed above the fireplace in the Ivory Salon where it drew the attention of anyone entering the room.

As he regarded the excellent likeness it occurred to him that sooner or later he must make some provision for her in case anything untoward should happen to him. Yet he did nothing about it then and was only reminded much later when danger began to play a part in his life.

Six

The winter was exceptionally cold. Hooves struck ice-splinters from the ground in glittering showers. Marguerite had plenty of time to work on her fans in the little house Augustin had rented for her in the village of Fontainebleau. She kept in constant touch with Lucille, for although the widow was unable to read or write, a letter-writer bridged her share of the correspondence and read every communication from her employer to her.

With no business taking place in the vestibule at Versailles during the Court's absence, Clarisse was helping Lucille in the workshop. Yet she was keeping her hand in selling to townsfolk who were drawn to buy direct from the workshop, attracted by the notice Marguerite had nailed up in the archway prior to leaving. Lucille reported excellent sales.

Since winter was the time when wars stopped due to the difficulties of terrain and the securing of supplies, many courtiers, who served with the regiments presently engaged in the skirmish that had moved on to Strasbourg, returned to the Court to be reunited with wives and paramours until spring should take them back again. For Jacques the situation was reversed. He had not been long at Fontainebleau before he was sent to replace a colonel who had been left in command but fallen ill. Susanne went with him.

"I hope we're not long away," she said to Marguerite as they bade each other farewell. "Jacques says it's only a matter of tidying up when spring comes because our forces are fully in control."

Then she turned to Augustin, and if she clung to him for a few seconds more than was necessary when they kissed each other's cheeks in their parting, it was not unduly noticeable. Yet Marguerite experienced a faint sense of relief at the Fresnays' departure. She did not wish to be uncharitable, but she had found the atmosphere increasingly oppressive whenever Susanne was in the same room as Augustin.

Unaware that she was showing a wisdom beyond her years, she had never attempted to test Augustin's feelings towards Susanne. Her down-to-earth common sense told her that to peck at him with hints and questions like a hen with corn would only send his thoughts spinning and awaken memories that he was prepared to let lie. Instead, whenever she spoke of love it was only of hers for him. Throughout those winter months their passion for each other deepened and matured and took a hold on their hearts that each knew could never be dislodged; there were such moments between them that she was at a loss to know why she did not conceive, for their lovemaking was without the least restraint. When month after month went by she thought no more about it, content to accept the joy of carrying his child whenever the time should come.

Apart from the hunting and shooting, all entertainments at Fontainebleau arranged for the nobility were, through the very nature of the weather, held indoors, formal or private occasions to which Augustin could not take her. She missed none of this, for he spent every evening he was free from Court attendances with her. It was a time that neither would ever forget—of glowing fires on a flagged hearth, snowy walks in the forest, drives to another village where they would eat at some rough hostelry with as much enjoyment as at a palace, and the crisp mornings when he taught her to ride.

Unless he had to remain at Court for some reason beyond his control, he spent every night with her in the ancient four-poster that must have been carved by some local peasant craftsman in the long-ago days of Charles V. Its timbers creaked to an extent that caused her to fear the heavy canopy would give way. One night to reassure her, Augustin rose naked from the bedclothes to climb up onto the canopy to prove its solid structure, only to roll off it again sneezing and begrimed with dust. Her hilarity brought him leaping back to her and not for the first time he possessed her with laughter and with love.

"I never knew it was possible to be so happy," she whispered to him in the gentle aftermath as she lay with her head on his shoulder.

"Nor I, my love," he murmured, pressing his lips softly to her brow.

During the sojourn at Fontainebleau he left her several times on envoy duties for the King into which she did not enquire beyond asking his destination. It was during one of his absences that she had the most frightening experience. She had gone to the village market to get provisions for his homecoming, a servant carrying the basket, when there was a sudden commotion in the most crowded part. She always purchased her herbs from an old woman with a stall set for shelter within an archway leading to a derelict stable at the end of a street. With a bunch of dried rosemary in her hand she turned in alarmed astonishment at the sudden stampede, knowing that her servant, collecting some meat, was in the midst of it.

"Mad dog! Look out!" The shout of warning was taken up on all sides. Women screamed and snatched up their children while bawling men seized bludgeons of any kind. Pandemonium reigned. In a sudden clearance Marguerite saw a large dog, its mouth foaming, its fangs bared. She and the herb-seller were directly in its path as it came loping along, its maddened eyes on them.

"Quick!" she shrieked, rushing round the stall to pull the old woman to her feet. "Into the stable!"

"Those doors don't open!"

Marguerite threw her weight against them in vain and saw with horror that the snarling animal was gathering itself to leap. In the same instant a young man, who had thrust himself through the scattering crowd, raised a field-piece to his shoulder. There was an explosion of shot and the dog gave a terrible howl, its back legs collapsing. Then, as calmly as if he were in a gathering of fellow sportsmen shooting partridge, the young man exchanged the field-piece for another ready-loaded by his servant and ran forward to aim again at closer range. This time the head of the writhing animal received the full blast and after a few jerks it lay still. Everybody's sigh of relief had the sound of a sudden gusty breeze and there were cheers and applause. Two men came with sacks to carry the dead animal away. Marguerite helped the old woman back to her stall, for she was badly shaken.

"Are you all right, mademoiselle?"

She turned about to meet the young man's dark brown eyes, which had a certain deep look to them that she found attractive. He had a broad forehead, presently concentrated in a frown of anxiety on her behalf, prominent cheekbones and a square, resolute jaw. His nose was slightly hooked, the nostrils compressed, and his lips well-cut but thin. She recognised his speech and inflexible air as that of the nobility and his age was no more than her own.

"We are unharmed," she replied on behalf of the herb-seller and herself, returning to the customers' side of the stall where he stood. "I thank you most sincerely for your timely action."

"I'm only too glad that I happened to be in the vicinity. Allow me to present myself: Stefane Le Pelletier, your servant, mademoiselle."

She gave her name in return, able to see that it was what he wanted and it was a small return for what he had done for her. It was no surprise that he should invite her to take some refreshment with him at the nearby hostelry in order for her to be calmed and rested after her ordeal. He had ignored the herb-seller as if she did not exist.

"I've recovered completely," Marguerite assured him, "although the moment of seeing that maddened animal ready to leap will stay with me for a long time. So I accept your offer of refreshment."

She finished her purchase of the herbs and then went with him through the stalls to the hostelry. People called out their praise and their thanks as he went by, but he ignored them. The hostelry was crammed but the inn-keeper showed them into a parlour kept for his more supe-rior customers.

"Are you shooting with the King today, Monsieur Le Pelletier?" she asked when hot chocolate had been served.

He gave a half-smile which showed the boyishness be-neath the mask of the gallant. "I'm too newly come to Court to be in his exalted company. In truth, I've hardly seen him yet and I'm following the advice given to all newcomers in that respect."

"That you should get used to his awesome presence in small doses first?"

His smile widened. "That's correct. In spite of his being an old man who has entered his forties, he exudes majesty on a scale that has surely never existed before among mor-tal men."

"You would find no one to disagree with you there. Is your home far away?"

"I'm from Avignon. And you, mademoiselle. Have you been long at Court?"

She thought how he was judging her entirely on her rich velvet clothes and fur-lined cloak. He would be surprised if he knew that the old woman selling herbs and the younger one whom he had set out to charm were from the same peasant stock. "I'm not at Court. I'm only staying here in the village of Fontainebleau. My home is near Versailles."

His face lit up. "That's most interesting. I have yet to see the grand Château."

"Then a pleasure awaits you. As for the gardens, there's surely no finer sight anywhere than when the fountains are playing in the sun."

It had not been her intention to stay long with him, but as they talked she forgot the time. It was refreshing to be with someone of her own age. In truth, Augustin was only seven years younger than the King, but she never thought of him as being older than herself, for she had lost the outlook of extreme youth that Stefane Le Pelletier still held, which viewed those out of their twenties as being quite ancient. Nevertheless, suddenly she was finding it fun to have young company. Everyone she met through Augustin was far closer to his years than to her own.

As they continued talking, she learned that the Marquis de Louvois was his cousin, a powerful noble much disliked by Augustin and others, but that was no fault of Stefane's. Naturally he would benefit from his relative's influence, but he struck her as being independent and even solitary, not one to mingle much with others, although along with the rest of the Court he held an enthusiasm for hunting and shooting that almost reached an excess in his case. She had no stomach for it herself, and could never have followed the hunt as some of the women of the Court did on occasions, driving themselves in small calèches specially built for speed. The sight of a soaring bird shot from the skies, the squeals of a stuck boar and the terror of a pursued stag upset her sensibilities. She could not condemn Stefane's enthusiasm for the shoot since it was natural to the nobility, but the peasant blood in her argued for a kill only to eat and not for pleasure. In her enjoyment of his company she dismissed completely the niggling suspicion that he might have a strong streak of cruelty in him.

Perhaps he sensed her aversion for hunting after a few minutes, for he changed the subject, seeming anxious to engage her time for as long as possible. He found that she liked to read books on history, an interest he shared, and another hour and a second pot of chocolate kept them still longer in each other's company.

Eventually she had to close this agreeable interlude. He wanted to escort her home and she declined the offer politely. "I wouldn't dream of interrupting your day's sport any longer."

"May I see you again?"

"Not here, but it's likely we shall see each other at Versailles. Thank you again for what you did today."

"I look forward to our next meeting."

When Augustin returned from his journey she told him about the incident. He was alarmed at how near she had come to danger, but at her insistence that she wanted to forget about it, he fell in with her wishes and did not mention it again. Unbeknown to her he sought out Stefane Le Pelletier to commend him on his swift action in saving Marguerite's life, for there was no death more agonising than that which resulted from the bite of a mad dog. Le Pelletier answered him in a most mannerly fashion but Augustin did not like the young courtier. It had nothing to do with hearing that he was related to the Marquis de Louvois. There was simply something about Le Pelletier that set his teeth on edge. Nevertheless he was grateful to this newcomer to Court and was glad he had said so to him.

In early spring the Court made ready to transfer itself with the usual upheaval to Saint-Germain for a period of pre-Lenten festivities before moving on to Paris for Easter. A few days before their departure from Fontainebleau, Marguerite received a letter from Lucille. The ribbon shop, which was located conveniently on the opposite side of the street to the hatter's shop, was up for rent.

"You mustn't lose this chance to get it," Augustin said when she had explained the situation.

"Are you sure?" She appreciated his encouragement.

"Indeed I am," he insisted. When she was at work with much to keep her busy, she was not being rescued from mad dogs by young whippersnappers or drinking hot chocolate with them or any others of the same calibre.

When the cavalcade of the Court passed the fork in the road that led in the direction of Versailles, Marguerite branched away in her calèche. She waved au revoir to Augustin on horseback and he missed her as soon as she was out of sight. He would be visiting Château Satory in order to see her and check on matters there, but he never liked her to be far from him.

Marguerite found everything going well at the workshop. The fan-stick maker had produced some charming new patterns and one of the hands taken on at the beginning of winter had a knack of threading feathers to give the effect of a bird's wing. Lucille wished Marguerite good luck when she left to cross the road to the ribbon shop.

Arrangements were soon settled. She had to buy the stock, but the price was not unreasonable and the quality good. She settled for it, paid a month's rent in advance and received the key the same day. The ribbon-seller had been elderly and the place was much neglected, but a coat of fresh paint inside and out soon brightened the premises. She polished the counter and shelves to a good shine and cheerfully washed the floors, an apron on and her sleeves rolled up, just as she had scrubbed the flags of her old home countless times when her parents had been alive.

She thought it was as well that Augustin was too far away to walk in and find her with her arms in the suds of a bucket. Privately he would think it absurd that she should

keep to her close budget instead of paying someone out of
the funds he allowed her, and yet at the same time he
might understand she needed to retain the freedom to
solve her own problems that were no part of her life with
him. In all, there were many reasons why she loved Augustin Roussier.

It took her less than a week from the time the redecorat-
ing was finished to hire an assistant and to move in stock
from the workshop. As soon as her pretty wares were displayed in the multipaned windows of the shop, would-be
customers began trying to open the door and she had to
unlock it to begin selling sooner than she had anticipated.
In her opinion it was folly ever to allow business to be
turned away. She was desperate to make a success of her
shop. On it depended the next step she could take as well
as the livelihood of the people she employed.

On May 6th, the day after Marguerite's eighteenth natal
day, the King made an announcement that reverberated
throughout France and far beyond.

"From this time forward the seat of government shall no
longer be at Paris but at Versailles."

The nobility was in an uproar. It was inconceivable that
France should be ruled from a country seat instead of their
beloved Paris, the most cultured and civilised capital in
the world, the true hub of the nation. All the old complaints about the climate at Versailles, its scenery and its
inconveniences were revived with vitriolic fury. Was the
Louvre, that palace of Kings wherein so much glory had
been reenacted, so many rich traditions laid down, to become nothing more than the shell of a town house for the
Monarch who had always despised its environs? The courtiers felt tricked that all the handsome extensions to the
Louvre, its magnificent reembellishment and the restoration of time-worn ornamentation had never been intended for the Court's habitation, but were merely
building whims of the King in his constant beautification of
Paris and the Île-de-France through bricks and mortar.

Ministers approached Louis, imploring him to recon-
sider. A line of nobles waited daily in the hope that some
word of theirs would sway the dreadful decision. The King
was courteous, gracious and smiling, but immune to any
persuasion. Who could tell how long he had had this aim in
mind? Had it sprung roots twenty-one years ago when he

had first taken Louise de La Vallière and a little party of close friends to enjoy the seclusion of Louis XIII's retreat in the countryside? Or had it been the year before in 1660 when he had introduced it to his young bride, fresh from Spain and already besotted by him? Yet it may have dawned long before when, as a twelve-year-old, he had first hunted in the forests of Versailles with Mazarin, the great statesman who had moulded him into the all-powerful ruler he had become. Most likely it had evolved over past years when the Château had begun to outshine any other palace in Europe. Whatever the truth of it all, this masterstroke eliminated Paris with all its taint of treachery and betrayal, while at the same time it made Louis and Versailles one and the same, indivisible and, to many, the new centre of the world.

Like every tradesman and -woman in Versailles, Marguerite welcomed the news of the King's decision to reign from Versailles. It meant that never again would the whole Court depart together, leaving trade to slump in the town and causing many of those not linked to building to find themselves financially hard-pressed. From this time onwards, there would always be life at the Château, the ministerial offices in the south wing forever busy, courtiers in permanent residence in the north wing and never-ending traffic passing in and out of the gates even when the King absented himself for a change of hunting fields or went off to war.

When Louis made his grand homecoming to Versailles, it brought crowds into the town from far afield to watch his triumphant entry into this new seat of government. Cannons boomed in salute, trumpets gave forth fanfares and in the Cour Royale the Swiss Regiment formed a guard of honour as, preceded by his escort of musketeers, he rode past in his red coach.

Marguerite gave Lucille and the fan-making hands time off to witness this spectacular event in France's history. She herself only went to see Augustin ride by with a number of courtiers on horseback in the wake of the Queen's grey and gilded coach drawn by six white horses. She was overjoyed to have him home again, for it was almost three weeks since she had seen him, when he had returned for her natal day and given her a necklace of eighteen beautiful pearls.

There was still scaffolding at Versailles and would be for months and years to come. Every facility for government and administration must be of the best in this new heart of France. The new gallery in the West Front was far from completed and workmen were as much a part of the scene as the nobility themselves. With many apartments allotted to married courtiers it was to be expected that some of the wives, faced with permanent residence, should want to change the decor or make some other cosmetic alterations essential to their settling down there.

Patiently Louis allotted funds for these requirements, seeing every expenditure as further investment into this great casket of French craftsmanship that was Versailles. It had created a constant demand abroad for the luxury goods of France. Trade with foreign lands was at a peak. All over the country workshops were busy producing jewellery, silks, tapestries and carpets and furniture, crystal, mirrors and masterpieces in gold and silver to be exported to every corner of the globe. Louis, knowing his courtiers as he did, was well aware that the smaller projects for carpenters, gilders and decorators in the enhancement of individual accommodation at Versailles would soon grow to proportions where there would be rivalry among all resident at Court to have the most elegant apartments or, in the case of bachelors, the most handsome rooms. His private campaign was to win them over with splendour, to dazzle them with increasing sumptuousness, to intoxicate their senses with the beauty of their surroundings until it became inconceivable for any one of them to want to live anywhere else. It would be a hard fight, but nobody could withstand his will once he had made up his mind.

Louis never noticed the smell of paint and plaster, which were as pleasing to him in their own way as the flowers that he loved. Many of the disgruntled courtiers, eager at this stage to find fault, declared themselves to be permanently nauseous through the building odours and dust. Well out of the King's hearing, still more of them groaned aloud or feigned a swoon when they heard the news that he had conceived the idea of creating a great new apartment for himself, causing more internal disorder.

The new apartment was to be at the very heart of the Château in the rooms that his father had occupied long ago in the old East Front. There the windows looked out over

the original Cour de Marbre to the Cour Royale and the
Place d'Armes beyond the gates. Louis, delighted with this
notion, wondered why he had not thought of it before and
called for plans to be drawn up. He wanted his new apartment to shine like a great gem with an exquisite central
salon adjoining a gilded bedchamber fit for Apollo, to face
out through glass doors opening onto the gilded balcony
supported by the lovely old pillars of rose marble. All the
comings and goings of Versailles, which had virtually become a city of the rich with seven thousand people under
its roof at any time of the day or night, would be spread out
before him.

The allegorical significance of the new apartment's central location was plain to everyone. Just as the planets were
subject to the sun, so should Versailles, and thus France
herself, revolve around Louis's daily risings and retirings,
his *levers* and his *couchers,* his dawns and his sunsets. The
Sun King was finally to reach his full zenith.

Louis had much more to please him. The flurry of the
war he had evoked some months before was being settled
to his complete satisfaction. He welcomed his returning
courtiers who had acquitted themselves well and among
them was Jacques. Marguerite happened to be calling in at
the vestibule the same day as his return. She had come
especially to check that all was well with Clarisse, for the
girl had gone back to work that morning after a bout of
fever. But everything was running smoothly and it was as
Marguerite was about to leave again that she came face to
face with the Fresnays.

"Say you came here specially to welcome us!" Jacques
greeted her jovially.

Susanne looked pleased to see her. "I trust we find you
well. How is Augustin?"

Marguerite noticed that Susanne appeared relaxed and
happy, no sign of the tensions apparent before she went
away. After a brief exchange of news, Jacques had to leave
but Susanne was eager to talk longer. Upon Marguerite
finally saying she must return to her shop, they were about
to part at the foot of the staircase when they were witness
to an extraordinary scene.

Athénaïs de Montespan was descending the flight, chattering to the ladies with her, a little lapdog in her arms. She
was still beautiful and continued to wear the flamboyant

fashionable colours with flair. Approaching the foot of the staircase was Françoise de Maintenon, elegant in dark blue with touches of white lace. She paused briefly as she saw who was on the stairs. Once she and Athénaïs had been great friends, which was why the royal bastards had been entrusted to her care, but all warmer feelings between them had been dispersed long since through rivalry over the King.

Neatly Françoise began to ascend the staircase. As she met Athénaïs, she smiled sweetly. "I see you are well on the way down, Athénaïs. As you may observe, I'm on the way up."

She sailed on, leaving Athénaïs gasping. By the staircase Susanne gripped Marguerite's arm. It was obvious to all who had overheard that it had been a direct and savage thrust at Athénaïs's decline in the King's favour and Françoise's own soaring ascent.

Athénaïs's eyes were bright with tears of temper as she bustled through the vestibule to her waiting carriage. Susanne looked serious and showed none of the amusement that was on the faces of others who had overheard the barbed exchange.

"You must tell Augustin what we have just heard," she said urgently to Marguerite. "It's most important."

"Why? I don't understand."

Susanne regarded her incredulously. "Has he not discussed anything with you, then? Madame de Maintenon is no friend of the Huguenots. If she is confident enough to address her rival in such a way in public, it bodes ill for Augustin and those of the Protestant faith."

Marguerite felt a chill of fear run down her spine. "Do you mean he's in danger?"

"Not directly." Susanne felt only impatience with such a question when Augustin and his well-being were forever in her thoughts. What did this girl know of lasting love or what it meant to follow closely every turn of events that might help or hinder such a man. "Perhaps he never will be. We can only hope."

"Tell me more," Marguerite implored.

"That's up to Augustin, not to me."

Susanne left her to follow up the stairs in the wake of Madame de Maintenon. Marguerite emerged into the sunshine of the Cour Royale with little heart to return to the shop that day. If Augustin had been at home she would have gone straight there and forced a confrontation. She wanted a full explanation of what was known to Susanne and Jacques, and no doubt to many more people in his confidence, while she, who loved him more than life itself, had been left in the dark. The incredulity she had seen in Susanne's eyes at her ignorance had been like a slap in the face. She felt humiliated and denied, completely shut out. Her cheeks flamed with sudden anger.

It quickened her pace, which was as well, as she had been dawdling in the path of one of the ice-wagons that delivered huge amounts to Versailles each day, bringing it from underground stores of winter-cut lake and river ice that was packed in straw in specially built ice-houses. Every courtier demanded a silver bucketful for his requirements. The cold air swept over her and restored her to a more levelheaded assessment of the situation. Anger was pointless. Augustin must have a good reason why he had kept from talking over with her what he had obviously discussed at length with the Fresnays.

It was not that she did not keep abreast of current affairs. On the contrary, she took a keen interest and read any pamphlet that came her way. Yet as she pondered over the warning that Susanne had urged, it came to her how adroitly Augustin always avoided any talk with her that bordered on his being a Protestant. She had always supposed that he considered their opposing religions to be a gulf between them that could be bridged by love but not by discussion. There was even the time last summer when she had mentioned to him she had heard that in the south of the country a large number of heretics were being put to the gibbet and the rack, a scrap of information she had overheard from the workshop window when two gentlemen had emerged from the hatter's shop and had stood engaged in conversation below where she sat.

Knowing that many Huguenots lived in the Cévennes and Languedoc she had expected Augustin to be highly alarmed, but he had made some quiet remark about rumours, leaving her with the impression that he had known more about it than he was prepared to admit. Why then had he not been open with her? Then there had been times when visitors had called after dark. He always received them on his own and saw them out himself. Until this moment she had given them no thought, but suddenly everything had begun to take on a sinister significance.

There was an *Appartement* that evening and he was later than usual coming home. Her anxiety had reached a peak where she could do nothing but watch from the window and pace the floor until she heard his carriage wheels. He was surprised to find she was still up, for usually he found her reading in bed when the hour was exceptionally late. She stood clasping and unclasping her hands.

"What's the matter?" he exclaimed with concern, seeing how distressed she was.

She flung herself into his arms. "I heard something today that has made me afraid for your safety. I feel so stupid and foolish that I haven't grasped what the Fresnays and many more must have been aware of for ages."

He laughed softly to soothe her, wondering what she had heard and from whom. Sitting down in a wing chair, he drew her onto his lap. "I think you had better start from the beginning and tell what is troubling you."

It poured out of her and included all she had put together that evening to add to her fears. "I've heard of the mission to convert all Protestants, but now that I've put together different little bits of hearsay I'm terribly afraid. Where will it all end?" She caught hold of the richly embroidered edges of his silk coat in an impassioned plea. "Please tell me all I should know. Why is Madame de Maintenon such a threat?"

"I don't know that she is," he replied calmly, "although it's interesting to learn she is growing so confident. However, her rival isn't ousted yet by any means. I can understand Susanne being alarmed on my behalf but she shouldn't have upset you unnecessarily. You see, everyone at Court knows that Françoise de Maintenon's one aim is the salvation of the King's soul. She wants to rid him of his mistresses, Athénaïs in particular, and reunite him with the Queen in matrimonial fidelity—a Herculean task in itself."

"Is Madame de Maintenon not his mistress too?"

"Nobody knows, but the general consensus is that she is not. In any case, she has more than physical attractions for him because, being both clever and devout, she is able to debate spiritual matters with him at an intellectual level as no other woman has done before. Think how enjoyable it must be for him, a man with an insatiable appetite for female company, to be able to talk to her of his deeply religious feelings instead of with his priests, who only want to upbraid him for his sexual indulgences. It's well known that they tell him he can only atone for his past by making France an entirely Catholic state."

"With no freedom of choice for any individual?"

"None at all."

"Then Susanne thinks that Madame de Maintenon's influence on him will be towards the same goal?"

"That's right."

"Then you are under threat!" She gasped in despair, snatching up his hand to cradle the back of it to her cheek. "You'd never submit to pressure, I know!"

"It may never come to that. Recently I went to see Colbert and I asked him to intercede on behalf of the Protestants as he has always done in the past. He's an old man now and far from well, but he made a special effort to see the King and urge restraint. Louis listened to him and there's every reason to believe he will follow that advice."

Marguerite was considerably comforted. "But who are those visitors who come by night?"

"That's easily explained, but you must keep your knowledge of those callers to yourself." He tapped a forefinger gently against her lips. "In a way I have become a Court banker, the link with the Roussier bank of which my father is still the head. Many courtiers are less rich than others, but they struggle to match everyone else in the extravagance of dress that the King expects of them and their wives, and many more get into financial difficulties through gaming. Not wanting it to be general knowledge, they come to me by night for loans, or even to make repayment when their fortunes change."

"Oh, I see."

He cupped her face fondly. Although he had told her the truth about some of those night visitors, he had withheld the fact that not all were noblemen on monetary business. There were many more who came on more secret matters, some from the very part of France about which she had sought to alert him. He could have shared everything with her, but for her own safety it was best she know as little as possible about his involvements. "Put your fears away, Marguerite. Remember there are a number of Huguenots at Court besides myself, and all of us go about our duties without invoking the King's frown. On the contrary, he actually smiled at me the other day and said I should be invited to Marly soon."

Again he did not tell her everything. Louis had asked him jovially if he would have a wife to bring with him then, for the charming surroundings at Marly would be particularly conducive to wedded bliss. But it was not only the King who was urging marriage on him. His father mentioned it more insistently at every visit. Among his friends Susanne was the only one who never said, jokingly or otherwise, that he should take a wife. She knew that if she were free she would still be his first choice. Again he regretted that he could never marry Marguerite. At least he would never let her wed anyone else, for she had become an integral part of his life.

For a while Marguerite's anxieties were lulled. Then one evening a few weeks later she came out onto the landing in time to see Augustin bidding farewell to one of his night visitors. She did not see the man's face, but something about him was familiar as he went off into the darkness.

"Still awake, my love?" Augustin said smiling as he came up the stairs. "I'm afraid my visitor's business took longer than I had expected."

"Another nobleman in debt?"

"There's a particularly dangerous game that is all the rage at Court at the moment. It's called *Hocca* and fortunes are being won and lost at little more than the turn of a wheel. I can see it bringing many men to their ruin."

As she led the way into their bedchamber she did not show that she had seen through his evasive answer. At least he had not lied to her, but it had not been a nobleman who had called that night. She had recognised that cloaked figure as her own weaver, Pierre Ouinville, and she knew him to be a Huguenot. All her disquiet swept back again. It seemed that Augustin was playing some game of his own that was far more dangerous than *Hocca*. At the same time it came to her that she was the only Catholic in the house. Every one of the servants was of the Protestant faith.

When Jacques arrived one evening he was announced, welcomed and seated to be poured a glass of wine. But he was not the bearer of good news as far as he and Susanne were concerned.

"I have just received the worst posting of my life," he informed them, unable to contain his gloom.

It had all come about through the need for extra water to supply the fountains of Versailles, which did dry up occasionally in long spells of hot weather. This requirement, combined with Louis's liking his regiments to be kept busy when not at war or on almost interminable manoeuvres, brought about the royal decision that the course of the river Eure should be changed to bring a new source of water to Versailles. It was a mammoth task, involving the need for thousands of men, and just as the Swiss Guards had had to dig the great lake that enhanced the view from the South Front of the Château, so should regiments of infantry be assigned to this excavation work. Jacques was one of the officers posted to go with them.

"What of Susanne?" Marguerite asked. "Can she be with you?"

"There's nowhere for her to stay," he fumed. "All the army personnel are to be concentrated on a vast campsite. The nearest town is Chartres and Susanne knows no one there. We have decided that she shall spend most of her time in Paris where at least she has a wide circle of friends and those at Versailles are not far away."

"We'll see her often," Marguerite promised, "and you'll be home at frequent intervals."

"How long do you suppose this river project will take?" Augustin asked.

Jacques shrugged grimly. "Years, I should say. I just hope that my posting is not a permanent one. I've no wish to end my army career as a disciplinarian in command of mudslingers."

They were sorry to see him go when the time for departure came. It was a dismal reward for a soldier who had done good service and his promotion to brigadier was small consolation. For a while they saw little of Susanne, for she spent weeks with her twins at Orléans. Her son, Jean-Paul, would soon be at the age when he could become a Court page, for both she and Jacques had the necessary noble lineage going back two hundred years that qualified him for training and the education he would receive. But he was a studious boy and she could foresee him developing intellectual interests, possibly in one of the new sciences, and so decided to let him continue his studies with his excellent tutor. She did bring both children to Paris for a little while, and took them on a visit to Chartres to see their father.

Marguerite's business continued to flourish. She took on another hand in the workshop. On her nineteenth natal day she believed herself to be pregnant at last, but once again she suffered a disappointment. She had begun to yearn for a child to complete the fulfillment of her deeply loving relationship with Augustin, even though it was by no means without its tensions and quarrels. They were like any other couple in having their differences, but after the sparks had flown high and the angry words been spoken, they fell into each other's arms again, she always slightly frantic in their making up. It was at these times she was haunted more than ever by the unseen threat she felt to be hanging over them.

Then there came a quarrel worse than any before, caused, as some had been on previous occasions, by his unremitting jealousy. She had met Stefane Le Pelletier again during a *divertissement* in the park. Afterwards he had begun to seek her out to chat and to ask her to dance. Augustin became almost demonic in his jealousy when she refused to cut off what was an entirely innocent association. Her new friend had not blended into the life at Versailles and was lonely, being of a serious mien and still somewhat out of place with the courtiers of his own age group, most of whom simply wanted to enjoy themselves.

"I won't snub him! Why should I?" She clenched her fists in her fury as their quarrelling over the friendship reached a crescendo. "He's the first person I have felt able to be friendly with at the Court apart from Jacques and Susanne."

"It's becoming noticeable how he is always hanging around you. I won't have it. You'll put an end to it the next time you see him."

With this final ultimatum he stamped out of the room. She rushed to the door and shouted after him, "If you can't trust me, it's best I go!"

He did not believe she really intended to leave and thought she would simmer down into an acceptance of his will. She went down the stairs carrying one small valise containing the few things he had not given her and was out of the house and far down the lane before he realised she had gone. He threw himself into a saddle and rode after her, overtaking her to block her way, his horse rearing as if a madman held the reins.

"I apologise!" he shouted furiously, his anger stemming from a different cause. "I have no right to dictate to you."

She came to a standstill, white-faced and unforgiving. "Neither have you any right to mistrust me. Never, even in my thoughts, have I been untrue to you."

He dismounted and patted his horse to quieten it, still barring her way. "I believe you and I beg you to forgive me. It's the deviousness of others that makes me wary and my dread that one day you might fall in love with someone else."

She saw that his rage had subdued to regret at his anger. Suddenly she realised that she held him in the palm of her hand. If she should bargain with him now, offering to return with him to the house in exchange for a wedding ring, she knew she would have gained him as a husband. His lack of legal right to her was a torment to him and lay at the root of all his jealousy.

Temptation reared in her. It would have been so easy. She could almost feel the gold band on her finger, but as so often happened in her life her sound levelheadedness came to the fore. It would be a selfish trick, and the cost inestimable, for no courtier could wed without the King's approval of the match. To go against that ruling and be discovered would mean the loss of everything from his father's respect and possibly his inheritance to banishment from Court. It was permissible for a nobleman to take a mistress from the gutter if it pleased him, but he could not marry beneath him with the possible exception of a rich heiress of reasonable stock. Never, to her mind, had it been more important for Augustin to remain securely in the King's favour, for every month she seemed to hear more disquieting news of rough justice being handed out to Protestants refusing to convert.

"I'll never love anyone else." There was a catch in her voice. "It's always been you for me and always will be."

He took two steps forward and held out his hands to her in appeal. "Then forgive me and come home." His face was agonised. "I could not sleep one night in that house without you."

It was impossible to hold out against him any longer. The handle of the valise dropped from her fingers and she left it in the dust as she met his enveloping embrace. Their desperate kissing was not enough to assuage their desire for each other. He gave his horse a slap across its rump to send it home and took her there and then into a neighbouring meadow. They made love amid the waist-high buttercups as if he were the country lad she might have married if their paths had not crossed. Afterwards they both felt the repairing of their quarrel had brought them closer in their relationship than ever before.

There followed untroubled weeks, although Stefane continued to be a thorn in Augustin's side. With effort he forced himself to be polite to the dark-eyed young man of the granite good looks, for Marguerite drew them both into conversation at every opportunity and had cut down her dances with her admirer to one or two an evening. Augustin found it easy to understand Le Pelletier's attitude, for it would have been his own at that age. The stiff-necked young sprig saw him as being too old at thirty-eight to be all that a young girl desired.

"Do you still hunt, sir?" was a deliberately tactless question delivered by Stefane one evening on the terrace of the Ballroom Grove while Marguerite danced below with someone else. Then, seeing the furious flash in the older man's eyes, he added with a condescension that did not lift the barb from his words: "I have heard of the wound you sustained in courageous battle and wondered if it hampered the enjoyment of sport."

"I have a disadvantaged left arm due to a damaged shoulder, but it is of minor importance in civilian life," Augustin replied icily. "My sword-arm in a duel would be unimpaired."

The underlying threat went home. A savage glint of naked hostility showed in Stefane's glance, setting the two of them silently at each other's throats before they turned to speak to Marguerite as she rejoined them. She was oblivious of any friction in the atmosphere, only happy that Augustin was being amiable and reasonable now about a friendship that seemed to be filling a gap in her life. She did not recognise that a natural need for youthful company had taken a powerful hold on her.

Augustin continued to remain firmly in the King's favour. This was in spite of his constant petitions on behalf of those Protestants being cruelly pressured. Again and again he requested an audience to put forward yet another case of a Huguenot church being closed or another heartrending case of parents having their children taken away, for only a few families could escape in time together, as those he had sheltered in his house before finding them a safe route to Holland. The King heard him out every time, bland, attentive and benign.

"I daresay the church was in disrepair," Louis would say, or, "The children will be kindly treated. Reassure the parents on that point, Monsieur Roussier."

It was like beating against a glass wall behind which Louis sat detached from all that was happening at a human level. At times Augustin did not know how to control his anger. The infuriating aspect was that he believed Louis knew it and out of a curiously perverse kindness pitied him for his frustration. If only he could direct a little of that compassion into the right channels he would have felt some good was being done. In the meantime he would continue to do whatever lay in his own power to help the persecuted. It was a highly dangerous business, for the King had the most efficient secret service who worked effectively, even to the point of opening every letter that went in and out of Court, presenting those of particular interest to him. It was no wonder that to those unaware of this system it seemed that Louis had uncanny powers that enabled him to see into hearts and minds and even through bedroom doors.

Susanne returned to Paris. Others found her singularly restless as if her sojourn in the country had built up a force of energy in her that had to expand. In her own mind she knew that her love for Augustin had built up once more. There had been times when her longing to be possessed by him again had almost made her a nervous wreck, but always she had fought and overcome it. She had never been in the least jealous of Marguerite, whom she had always liked and would have enjoyed having as a close friend if circumstances had been different. The reason for her tolerance was that she knew if it had not been Marguerite it would have been another woman, for since Augustin could not have her he had to have someone else. She had even been unselfishly pleased that he was happy in this relationship, but gradually those finer feelings had worn thin, exacerbated by Jacques's infrequent leaves and too much time to herself. Since she would never take a lover other than Augustin, she must seek the only outlet left to her, which was in an extensive social whirl.

She began to give lavish parties and banquets, appeared at every function at Court and although Jacques discouraged her from going to Chartres, she darted off to visit there whenever possible simply on the chance of seeing him. Having no accommodation at Versailles, she often stayed at the Château Satory, sometimes for a week, at others for a day or two. Marguerite gave her a special bedchamber, which looked towards the hills, and she left her possessions there in between visits, almost making it her own.

Marguerite was puzzled by the brittleness about Susanne, similar to times before, but combined now with this almost frenetic desire for pleasure. All of it was directed away from Augustin, which was some consolation, but she was convinced that Susanne was facing some crisis in her life and was attempting to ward it off.

She even mentioned her anxiety to Augustin one evening after Susanne had just departed again after another short and hectic sojourn.

"Jacques gets so rarely to Paris," he commented, "one could almost be tempted to think something secret was being built at the Eure instead of a simple excavation being dug. Susanne may be very tired of being on her own so much."

A few nights later, Marguerite dreamed she was rocking a baby in her arms but it would not stop crying. Filled with concern, she awoke with a start and sat bolt upright in bed, her heart hammering and the baby's cries lingering in her ears. Yet the house was silent. Then she saw she was alone in the bed. She felt the place where Augustin had lain and it was cold. An eerie sensation swept down her spine. What was happening in this house in the early hours of the morning?

Reaching for her robe, she slipped it on as she slid from the bed. Some faint noise drew her to the window and she looked down in time to see a small procession of people filing out of the house from where she had not known a door existed. There was enough moonlight for her to pick out a couple, the angle of the woman's arm showing that she held a baby, and with them were five young children, Augustin leading the way with a sixth child riding on his shoulders. They all disappeared silently in the direction of the stables.

She leaned back weakly against the wall. Had those people come to the house that night or had they been secluded somewhere in this spacious place? For days, perhaps. She did not doubt they were Protestants being moved to a sanctuary away from the efforts of some priest to convert them against their will.

With trembling hands, she lit a candle and, protecting the flame with her cupped hand, went down to the cellars from which the party had left. But there was no sign of anybody having been there. The only other place was the attics, for the hidden room would have been too small for so many people. Going upstairs again she ran along the landing and down a corridor to reach a staircase approached through a low door. It stood open and she mounted the long twisting flight to the attic rooms. The candlelight showed her all the proof she needed. Truckle beds were lined up in one room, all the bedclothes folded as if the mother had had good time to tidy everything before the nocturnal departure. In the neighbouring room a table held the remains of a meal. In this maze of rooms under the eaves of the château many people could be secluded for days, even weeks, providing nobody betrayed them.

She was on the point of leaving again when she trod on something soft. It was a rag doll, dropped in flight. She stooped to pick it up. Had it been the owner's cries upon discovering its loss that had penetrated her sleep? Or maybe the baby had chosen to utter a wail at an inopportune moment. She held the rag doll to her briefly and then laid it down on one of the truckle beds. If Augustin should have further contact with that family, he could return the battered and obviously well-loved toy.

Silently she returned to her bedchamber and after removing her robe she blew out the candle. About an hour later Augustin came back to her side and was soon asleep. She lay looking towards the window until the dawn came. Then, fortunately, she slept and he had to awaken her at the hour when they usually arose for the day.

That evening, when he was at an *Appartement,* she stole up to the attics again. Nothing remained to show that they had been occupied. All the truckle beds were stacked as if they had never been disturbed. Who among the servants in the château shared his or her master's secret? By the state of order prevailing she hoped it meant that no more Huguenots would be coming to endanger the security of the man she loved.

Seven

Two months after Versailles's rise to be the seat of government, the Queen died at the age of forty-five. She had been with the King and Madame de Maintenon to view army manoeuvres, something that she did not enjoy. Just as they returned to Versailles she discovered a small abscess under her arm which was treated by her doctors, and in a matter of days she was dead. Augustin, who happened to be among those waiting anxiously outside the Queen's bedchamber, saw the King emerge when it was all over. Louis's eyes bore evidence of copious tears, his face still sad but resigned.

"Never before this day has that poor woman caused me the least inconvenience," he remarked to those courtiers with him, his words overheard by all. It was a scant epitaph for a wife who had loved him devotedly throughout his innumerable infidelities.

Outside the Château, word of the Queen's death flew to every street and habitation. Marguerite closed her shop immediately as well as the workroom and went as a mark of respect to the gates of Versailles. She was remembering the woman who had washed her feet as a child on a Holy Thursday, the gentle hands and the sweet smile.

The Place d'Armes was already a sea of people when within less than an hour of his wife's death the King departed, following the royal custom of vacating a place of death as soon as possible and not attending the funeral. Already he had put his bereavement behind him, planning that Françoise de Maintenon should have the late Queen's apartments when she joined him at Fontainebleau in a few days' time.

The coach with its galloping escort bowled quite close to Marguerite. Louis glimpsed her dark red curls and knew her again. It must be two years ago at least since he had spoken to her in the vestibule. Although she had stopped selling fans there since Monsieur Roussier had made her his mistress, he had glimpsed her several times dancing and supping at Versailles. She had a face that lingered on in the mind for its unusual beauty.

Augustin had to follow the King to Fontainebleau. Marguerite did not go with him this time, for he planned to make quite a lengthy visit home during the sojourn, which would have left her on her own. His father ailed and needed him there to take charge until a more permanent arrangement could be made. It was a pleasant surprise for her when Stefane Le Pelletier, who had been visiting his estate at the time of the Queen's death, returned to Versailles and did not go on to Fontainebleau.

"Come for a drive with me this evening," he invited after appearing at her fan-shop on the first morning. He had long since found out all about her and was congratulating himself on Roussier's absence. "We'll have supper afterwards at the best place in the town."

She hesitated. "It's difficult. I have Madame de Fresnay staying with me."

"I invite her, too."

She accepted for two reasons. Having won her case with Augustin to continue this platonic friendship she saw no cause to avoid Stefane in his absence. And secondly if all outings were restricted to the times when Susanne was on her visits to Château Satory, that would ensure peace all round.

The next morning after a thoroughly enjoyable evening

she wrote to Augustin of this arrangement and, judging
from his reply, he was satisfied.

But somehow after Susanne left again it seemed ludicrous not to keep on with the harmless expeditions. She
and Stefane went out several times in one of the little boats
for two on the Grand Canal and had many strolls in the
park amid the parterres glorious with blossoms and talked
for hours in leafy corners. All the gardens were remarkably
deserted in the Court's absence. On one occasion the fountains were being tested, as they were sometimes when the
King was away to make sure they were in order. Stefane,
who was in a particularly lighthearted mood, took her into
the Ballroom Grove where they danced together on the
marble floor with no one else present and the cascading
water the only music. He would have kissed her then, but
she avoided the contact and he did not persist, almost as if
carefully biding his time.

The weeks passed quickly. Susanne returned with the
first signs of autumn and raised her eyebrows disapprovingly at hearing Marguerite had continued to see Stefane.
"I think that's most unwise," she said censoriously. "I'm
older than you and I can see danger where you cannot."

Marguerite held back an impatient retort. It would be
tactless to point out that it was precisely because she and
Stefane were not of Susanne's age group that she found
being with him particularly enjoyable. It was a change to
be with someone young and that was the beginning and
end of it all.

"If you're worried about Augustin's disapproval," she
said carelessly, "that matter was cleared up between us
before he went away. He knows it's only friendship."

"Have you reported every meeting to him?"

Marguerite shrugged. "I don't think of it always when I
write. There's so much to put in my letters."

"That sounds to me as if at the back of your mind you
think he would forbid you if he knew the details."

"Augustin can forbid me nothing!" Marguerite retaliated sharply. "I have a successful business that's growing
every day and, whatever you may think, I'm not his kept
woman! He and I share our lives because we love each
other. I'm not dependent on him for my livelihood."

Susanne spoke in forthright tones. "Sometimes a woman
can be too independent. I warned you a long time ago

never to give Augustin the slightest cause for jealousy."
She wagged an admonishing finger, the strength of her
feelings on the matter having brought a rush of heated
colour to her cheeks, showing she was quite angry. "If you
should fail him now because it turns your head to have a
young gallant dancing after you, I warn you I would immediately take up cudgels on his behalf!"

Marguerite, although caught off guard by finding this
normally gracious and amiable woman prepared to attack
like a tigress, answered sharply, "You have no cause to
lecture me. Stefane is taking me to a play in the town this
evening. Come with us. You are welcome as you were
before and you may see for yourself that your concern is
without foundation."

If Stefane would have preferred to have had Marguerite
on his own, he was too well-mannered to show it. The play,
a comedy, put all three of them in excellent humour and
he had secured a table for supper afterwards. When the
evening was over and he had departed after bringing
them home, Marguerite danced triumphantly round and
round the entrance hall, her skirt swinging out.

"There!" she exclaimed. "Now you are reassured, I'm
certain! Tell me your worries have been well and truly put
to rest."

Susanne, about to mount the stairs, gave her a long wise
look. "You were a different person this evening. Stefane
has worked his spell on you. He has made a thoughtless girl
of you again."

Marguerite stopped her twirling. "You started out in a
biased mood," she accused hotly. "You saw what you had
made up your mind to see."

"Not at all. I was determined to keep an open mind."

"Augustin could not have faulted Stefane's behaviour
towards me."

"No, I agree. But he would have seen what I have seen
all along."

"What's that?"

"Stefane is head over heels in love with you." Susanne
gave a sharp nod of emphasis and continued up the stairs.
"Good night to you. Sleep well."

Marguerite, left alone, looped her arms around the
newel and rested her forehead against the gilded wood. It
was the truth and she should have faced it long ago. In the

past she had shouldered so many responsibilities all at once, even that of loving a demanding man to the height and depth of her being, and if Stefane had given some carefree days back to her, had it been so wrong to accept them?

Susanne did not refer to the matter again and neither did she join Marguerite and Stefane on any more outings. She had friends residing in the town with whom she spent most of her time. The couple had a daughter whom Susanne was prepared to sponsor at Court and she liked to be present at the course of instruction on protocol and general etiquette that the girl was receiving.

The time came to within a few days of the Court's return. "Am I to continue to have the pleasure of seeing you?" Stefane said to Marguerite one evening at the end of a concert they had attended. Musicians who did not follow the Court frequently gave recitals to local townsfolk. Now he had brought her home again.

She shook her head firmly. "I made that clear from the start."

The repressive reserve, which normally made it difficult for him to express his innermost feelings, finally broke like a dam. "I'm in love with you!"

Never once had she expected it to come bursting out into the open. His face was so tense that the skin was stretched over the still boyish bones of his face. "We agreed to friendship," she reminded him hastily. "Nothing more."

"I know that. I've been glad of every hour I've had with you. But since you can't attend the *Appartements* at Versailles or any of the *divertissements* held indoors it will be a long winter for me without seeing you." There was a slight pause before his voice rushed on again, throbbing with urgency. "I could give you everything that Roussier gives you and more. You would have your own apartment instead of living in his house. Leave him and come to me. He could never love you as I love you, dearest Marguerite."

"Hush!" she whispered. "You must not say such things to me. You know where my loyalties lie."

"But Roussier is years older than you!" he protested vehemently. "You'll still be young when he is in his dotage."

She could not tolerate any attack from this quarter. "Although Augustin was the same age when I was born as you are now," she said, "nineteen years are easily spanned when two people love each other."

"But it's better to be young together as we are!"

"Not always," she answered confidently. "In any case when one partner is older and the other younger they can meet halfway."

"But you like being with me."

"Of course I do. But when it comes to love that is in another category altogether and takes no account of age or wealth or colour or creed."

"Will you promise me one thing?"

"What's that?"

"If ever you and Roussier part from each other, you will let me take his place."

"If that should happen I'd never want anyone else," she stated firmly.

He did not believe her. Roussier had a hold over her that he was determined to break. Never in his life had he been denied anything he wanted. From childhood upwards he had only to point at anything that took his fancy and it had always gone ill with anyone who had tried to cross him. The icy fury that had filled him at her rejection was not directed against her but at the man who possessed what should be his. At least she should not guess at the hatred he felt for Roussier.

"You say that now, but you and I have all our lives before us."

She knew she had disappointed him and appreeiated his moderate contradiction. Some men would have been angry. It was as well, because she had more bad news to break to him.

"I think this should be our last evening together."

"No! Don't deny me what little time I have left with you. Let me go on seeing you until Roussier returns."

She had told him, unwisely it seemed to her now, that Augustin did not expect to return until a week after the Court, coming straight from Le Havre. It was hard to refuse his request, but she had to do what was best. "I can't agree to that, but if you like I will put someone in charge of my shop on the day the King comes back to Versailles and spend it entirely with you."

It was small consolation for him but better than nothing. The Court returned as the first days of October began to

lay gold on the trees, as bright as anything within the
Château itself. Louis, arriving in the late afternoon, went
almost at once to the Queen's Apartment, which was now
stripped of his late wife's personal possessions. It was almost as if she had never been, and no one would ever
speak of her actual passing, for it was forbidden to talk of
death at Versailles.

The King viewed the rooms without sentiment, merely
considering whether he could incorporate some of the
space into his own new centralised apartment that was not
yet completed. The windows here had a pleasing southern
aspect, an allegoric choice for a Queen's abode with its link
with fecundity and warmth by which all nature thrived.
Admittedly she had only given him the Grand Dauphin,
five other infants failing to survive, but fortunately the heir
to the Throne was strong and healthy, like himself in never
being ill and, also following in paternal footsteps, he was a
collector of paintings and other precious objets d'art. Only
the young man's preference for ugly women was beyond
his father's comprehension.

"I need beauty in all its forms as other men need air,"
Louis muttered aloud to himself as if suddenly compelled
to keep back any encroaching shadows in these lovely,
peaceful rooms. And a beautiful woman would have been a
benediction to his love-starved body at that moment. Still
in full and lusty prime, he had known as soon as he was
widowed he would have to marry again and soon. He was
well aware of the speculation that buzzed about him. He
would be a prize to many foreign princesses and there was
jealousy already among the young women at Court as each
hoped to be the next Queen of France. But he had made
his decision. None knew it except three people whom he
could trust completely and the lady herself. During the last
weeks at Fontainebleau he had entered a state of celibacy
at her insistence in preparation for the entirely new phase
of his life that he was to share with her. It meant a commitment to fidelity at last, a prospect that did not enchant
him, particularly in his present physically deprived state,
even though he loved Françoise de Maintenon whom he
was to marry secretly and morganatically in the Chapel in
a few days' time.

Restlessly he wandered across to one of the windows and
looked out over the South Parterre towards the site where

the architect Mansart was to commence building a huge
Orangery in the spring. A courtier and a young woman
were strolling along one of the paths together and he saw
them stop as they made their farewells. Although no kiss
was exchanged, apart from the man's conventional lifting
of her hand to his lips, they stood quite close. There was
something poignant about this parting as if an end was
being made to a love affair.

Louis continued to watch as the man turned away reluctantly and then quickened his pace to take the archway
through to the Cour Royale. The young woman remained
where she was as if in mingled regret and relief, looking
after him. Once she lifted her hand to wave as the courtier
paused for a last exchange before vanishing from her sight.

The young woman herself seemed in no hurry to leave.
She stayed by the fountain looking down into the water,
but Louis's guess was that her thoughts had little to do with
her reflection. Suddenly there was a shift in the cloudy sky
that let the late afternoon sun sweep over the South Parterre and made her curly hair blaze like a peony. Marguerite Dremont. The fan-seller. He felt his whole body
tremble at a violent thrust of desire for her. A scrap of
conversation, overheard at Fontainebleau, and not intended for his hearing, came flashing into his mind. It had
been Athénaïs who had uttered it in ill-tempered exasperation.

"If a suitable wife isn't found soon for the King he's liable
to wed the nearest pretty face, be its owner a laundry-maid
or a fan-seller!"

Well, he had made his choice of a bride, but there were
four nights left before his marriage and the chains of conscience it would clamp on him for the rest of his days.

Marguerite walked slowly in the direction of the steps
that led out of the South Parterre. Never again would she
encourage a friendship destined to end in sadness. Men
seemed to find it impossible to keep desire out of friendship. Her affection for Stefane was deep and warm, but
nothing more, whereas he had allowed himself to become
torn apart by his feeling for her.

He had wanted to drive her home but she intended to
visit the shop to see that all had gone well there during the
day and had arranged that a coachman from Château
Satory should collect her there. Stefane would willingly

have driven her that short distance, but she had thought it more fitting that they should part in the park where they had spent many pleasant hours together.

She shivered as she mounted the steps. A chill breeze was rising and the clouds had closed together again, darkening as if for rain. She pulled the hood of her cloak up over her head and quickened her pace to leave by the way of the Cour Royale. Somehow she had the feeling that Stefane was watching her from one of the windows and she resisted the temptation to turn her head. She had not gone far when somebody came hurrying after her, feet clacking lightly on the cobbles.

"Mademoiselle Dremont!"

She turned and saw one of the "blue boys," as the pages were called from the livery they wore. "Yes?" It was half in her mind that Stefane had sent her a final love-note with the lad, but that was not the case.

"His Majesty the King wishes your attendance. Follow me, if you please."

Her reaction was one of astonishment and dismay. It must have been the King whose eyes she had felt on her from a window. This summons was most surely connected with his letting her view the masterpieces in the Cabinet of Paintings all that time ago. Augustin had warned her that the King would probably question her about them one day, but after a lapse of two years she had never expected it to come about. Yet as everyone knew, the King never forgot anything and so she should not be surprised. It was as well that the paintings had made such an impression on her that she would be able to answer anything he cared to put to her.

The page did not lead her through the State Apartment as she had expected, but took her into a part of Versailles where she had never been before, opening a door that appeared to be part of the décor. They went on through narrow corridors and up spiralling staircases with scarcely room enough for anyone to pass. Not that they met a single person on their route. They might easily have been on their own in a maze. Finally they reached another door which the page opened for her before standing aside for her to enter.

"Please wait in here, mademoiselle."

She entered a charming salon in green and white that

offset the rich colours of a superb Savonnerie carpet, while a bright fire burned in the grey marble fireplace. Its warmth was welcome and she held out her hands to it after giving her cloak to the page, who took it away. She supposed she was in an anteroom and at any moment she would be summoned to the royal presence beyond the double doors in the opposite wall. There was dread in the pit of her stomach. She never saw the King without recalling his inhumanity to her mother and hoped the interview would soon be over.

As daylight faded, a footman came to light the candles and close the shutters on the view of an inner court unfamiliar to her. Another servant replenished the fire and then she was left alone. Needing to answer a call of nature, she went to the only other door in the salon, which was half covered by drapes. Beyond it was a small gilded room with, as she had hoped, a velvet-topped *chaise percée* with an attendant supply of soft, square linen napkins on a gold salver. She rang a little hand-bell before returning to the salon. A few moments later, back by the fireside, she heard a maidservant putting everything to rights again.

By now she was seething with impatience. The coachman would have given up waiting at the shop for her, for it had become customary that if she should decide to drive with Stefane the calèche would go home without her. As soon as she was out of here she must get a hackney cab at the gates.

Footsteps were coming. She sprang up in relief. But again it was a footman and with him two others, all in identical black periwigs, who spread a damask cloth on the table and proceeded to lay out a supper for her.

"Does the King usually keep his subjects waiting as long as this?" she enquired angrily.

The footman did not blink an eyelid, drawing out a chair at the table for her to sit down. "Quite often, mademoiselle. Affairs of state take precedence at all times."

She sighed heavily as she seated herself. To her relief the footmen, after pouring her wine and removing silver dish covers, left her to eat alone. The clock in the corner of the salon showed her that by now the King would be at supper and surely for him all mundane matters, such as being gracious to a fan-seller, would be over for the day. She would leave as soon as someone returned who would be able to guide her out again, for she would never be able to find the way by herself.

But when the table was cleared the footmen were unable to leave their duties and once more she was on her own. She was pacing about impatiently when a middle-aged waiting woman arrived.

"At last!" Marguerite exclaimed, her patience at an end. "Please fetch my cloak for me. I've been kept waiting for hours and I must go home now."

The woman looked shocked. "You can't leave, mademoiselle. It would not be etiquette. His Majesty will not have forgotten that you are here. You must wait all night and all tomorrow if needs be, but I doubt it will come to that." She went sailing on to the double doors which she opened to reveal, not some official chamber such as Marguerite had supposed to be there, but a bedchamber of blue and gold. "I will help you prepare for bed, mademoiselle."

"This is ridiculous!" Marguerite let her arms rise and fall to her sides in exasperation. No wonder Augustin talked of courtiers kicking their heels for days when trying to seek an audience with the King. No doubt foreign envoys were accommodated in these luxurious rooms until their turn came.

There was an embroidered silk nightgown, as pretty as any she had at home, satin slippers that fitted well enough and a silver-backed brush for her curls. When she was ready for bed, the woman folded back the bedcovers for her. Marguerite propped herself against the pillows and took up a book from a side table.

"Don't snuff the candles," she instructed. "I'm going to read for a while."

"I wasn't intending to, mademoiselle," the woman replied with a lift of her eyebrows and closed the doors after her.

It was a book of poetry with the love poems of François Villon and she lost track of time, enchanted by their passion and tenderness. Beginning to feel drowsy, she glanced up from a page when the door opened. It was not the waiting woman. Her mood shattered as though it were glass splintering. Louis stood smiling at her, clad in a robe of scarlet and gold, a nightcap of silk with a golden tassel at quite a rakish angle on his head.

The colour drained from her face with painful swiftness.

Comprehension crashed into her brain and she was appalled by her own naïvety. Why had she not guessed? The book dropped from her hand to the coverlets and she sprang from the bed to drop into a low curtsey in which she stayed as she tried to overcome her panic. Was it treason to spurn the King? People who offended him disappeared forever. Oh, why had it seemed such a good idea to come to the gardens with Stefane today when any other place would have saved her from this catastrophe!

"Good evening, my dear. I think we may dispense with formality now." Louis had come across to her and he cupped her elbow to bring her to her feet before him. Even without the heels he wore during the day he was of daunting height and the terrible power of his presence made her feel faint. She shuddered inwardly with revulsion of him, afraid that at any moment her teeth would begin to chatter from the shock she had received.

"Sire, I feel I could not please you," she burst out.

"It seems to me you have the ability to please any man of discernment. It was not Monsieur Roussier with you in the gardens today."

"A friend, sire."

"It looked more than friendship to me," he remarked sagely, taking her chin between his finger and thumb to tilt her face to his. Her unusual wild-witch looks had attracted him from his first sighting of her in the vestibule and she was even more alluring with the shape of her breasts showing through the fine silk of the nightgown that had moulded itself against her hips and thighs. "I know your lover is at Le Havre. Your secret is safe with me."

"What of the secret of this night, sire?"

"Your protector will be honoured that his King has found his lady pleasing. Just as any husband would be. But that is as far as our secret goes. Is that understood?"

"Yes, sire." She wondered with an almost hysterical urge to laugh if he supposed she would wish to boast of this dreadful honour paid to Augustin.

"Come now, my dear. It is time for us to become better acquainted." He spread his firm hand at the back of her waist and she arched as he drew her to him and enfolded her in his embrace to kiss her with mounting passion. She was utterly dumb and unresponsive, able to observe in her state of detachment that he knew how to kiss a woman to homage and arouse her. Oddly her only anger was against herself for having become trapped in this situation. Yet even if she had comprehended from the start she would have had to obey his summons. Recently a lady of the Court was sent to the Bastille for displeasing the King and nobody knew why. Had she found herself in the same dilemma and refused to comply? Nobody crossed Louis's pride without the most dire consequences. Marguerite checked the scream of refusal rising in her throat. Her instinct for survival was strong. She could endure anything that would not shut her away from Augustin forever.

Louis brought his kiss to a tender close and smiled at her again, letting a hand slide down caressingly over her buttocks. Her lack of response did not deter him. He was used to women having last-minute nerves when finally finding themselves alone with him, for even in his nightrobe they continued to see him as the King and not as a man. That soon changed. No man knew better than he how to delight a woman throughout the night hours.

"Could we not talk for a little while?" she suggested, trying to appear composed. She had some faint hope he might fall asleep, for he had travelled all the way from Fontainebleau that day and the hour was late.

"You shall have all the love-talk your heart desires, my dear," he promised with a twinkle in his eye. Then he lifted her effortlessly up in his arms and bore her to the bed where he deposited her gently against the pillows. As he went around the end of the bed to get in the other side, he pulled his nightcap from his head and pushed it into the pocket of his robe. His cropped dark hair was without the least trace of grey.

"The candles!" she implored, half rising from the pillows. This ordeal could only be endured in darkness.

He had met this request before and knew where the snuffer lay. It was his custom always to leave two flames that gave a romantic glow at the most strategic angle, for there was no point in having a beautiful woman in the bed and not being able to appreciate her charms to the full.

"You've overlooked two candles, sire."

He was removing his robe and pretended not to hear. Usually there was no protest. Women seemed obliged to make some token wish for darkness and then were well satisfied to have it otherwise. This young woman must still be in awe of him, but he would soon put that right. In bed they would be just a man and a woman, albeit that even naked he was still fully possessed of the power of a Sun King.

Seeing him loom in silhouette towards her as he entered the bed she knew complete and utter aversion that made her feel her heart would stop if he possessed her. She had heard that in times of mortal danger both men and women sometimes uttered an involuntary cry for their mothers. Hers had come leaping into her mind with a clarity of image that almost took her breath away.

"My mother was Jeanne Dremont, sire!"

He propped himself on an elbow to look at her with amusement, drawing the covers over him. "And mine was Anne of Austria. Now that's settled."

"You don't understand!" She scrambled into a kneeling position as she faced him. "I'm telling you something of the utmost importance."

"There have been many Jeannes in my life, my dear," he answered patiently, still somewhat amused. Had he once coupled with her mother among the housemaids and waiting maids that had crossed his path throughout the years?

"But there was only one Jeanne Dremont! You never forget anything! Are you playing a game with me, sire?"

He felt suddenly uneasy. Was she trying to tell him she was his own bastard? He had a horror of incest that was unmatched by anything else. He saw it as the sin for which there was no atonement. "Where did I meet her?"

"On the terrace the day my father fell from the scaffolding of the West Front. She abused you out of her crazed grief and you condemned her to prison where she died. You cannot want to make love to her daughter!"

He froze. All desire for her left him. Rage began to pound through his veins and his complexion became congested by it. He could see again that madwoman's hate-twisted visage and the gaping mouth spewing forth those unforgivable insults. Once again he seemed enveloped in the cold vapours of the past she had summoned up for him.

Without a word he flung himself out of bed, beside himself with fury that he should have been brought face to face with that humiliating incident again. His robe swirled and lashed against the double doors as he jerked them open and departed. In the salon the other door slammed behind him and silence reigned.

Marguerite stayed where she was, dropping her face into her hands as she began to tremble with relief. He had gone. Never again would she have to face such a situation.

It was easy to find her clothes. Her gown and cloak were in a closet and her undergarments had been laid in the drawers of the clothespress. She was soon dressed and after tying up her hair with its ribbons again, she went to the door of the salon and looked out, hoping to sight a servant on duty, but the corridor was deserted and in darkness. Louis must have brought a candle with him to light the way and see him back again.

She rang the little bell in the gilded room of the *chaise percée* but this time nobody came. Perhaps the servants had orders not to come near until dawn when the King would have returned to his state bedchamber in good time for his *lever*. Deciding it would be sensible to wait where she was until someone turned up to direct her, she tucked into a wing chair by the embers of the salon fire in the warmest corner and hoped to sleep. But she only dozed and awoke constantly on a sensation of alarm as if she might find Louis standing in front of her again.

In the end she could endure it no longer. She would find her way out somehow. On this thought she took a three-branched candlestick and set off, having no idea where she might be, for the windows of the room she had occupied, looking down on an inner courtyard as they did, gave her no guide. Here, in the corridor, there were no windows at all. Reaching a turning she went confidently onwards, hoping to come across some landmark to help her get her bearings. With relief she came to a narrow staircase and hurried down its twisting route, only to be met by a locked glass-panelled door that made her retrace her steps up again. Her candles, spilling wax and burning swiftly in the constant draughts that met her around corners, were getting lower every minute and to save their light she pinched out the wicks of two of them and went on by a single flickering flame.

Eventually, at the end of a passageway, she came to a door that opened at her touch. Cautiously she widened its gap and was able to see she was looking into a large room. On the far side were unshuttered windows through which she would be able to tell if she was north, south, east or west in the Château, for there were always some flambeaux burning at night and the glint of water would be a guide. She pushed the door wider and it creaked. Immediately there was a rustle of movement and to her alarm she glimpsed one of the tentlike beds in which guards slept at night in the staterooms.

"Who's there?" came the demand.

Swiftly she drew the door shut and held her breath, her heart hammering. Suppose she had entered and the guard had taken her for a thief on the prowl? The King would never vouch for her presence and nobody else would dare. She had escaped one danger only to put herself into another. It was too late to wish she had stayed in the suite and she would never be able to find her way back there. She must keep going and open no more doors until she came to one she could be sure led outside.

At that moment she thought she heard the guard approaching the door by which she stood and she spun about to run blindly in the direction from which she had come, taking one corner and then another until she could be certain there was no pursuit behind her. Even as she paused for breath and looked back fearfully over her shoulder, her candle went out. In her fright she had failed to notice it had reached the point of drowning in its own wax.

She sank down to the floor in the darkness and sobbed. It was a welcome relief after all she had been through. After a little while she felt better again and dried her eyes on her petticoat, afraid of spilling the contents of her purse if she fumbled in it for a handkerchief. She stood up and began to feel her way along the wall in the inky blackness. Surely she was the only woman ever to be in this unhappy predicament, trying to grope her way out of Versailles like a little mole in the bowels of the earth.

At dawn a floor-polisher found her curled up asleep at the halfway turn of some stairs. He prodded her with his foot and she awoke with a start. "You'd best be moving from there," he advised drily, forming his own opinion as to how she had passed the night. "It will soon be busy along here."

She sprang up. "Please show me the way out. I am lost."

"Come on then." He turned back down the narrow flight and she followed. In spite of her cloak she was chilled to the bone and she hugged her arms, trying to rub some warmth into them as she followed him. It was quite a distance before finally he opened the same door through which the page had shown her the previous day. She gave him a tip from her purse and then rushed out into the early morning daylight as thankfully as if she had been released from prison.

On she ran down the cobbles of the Cour Royale, her cloak billowing about her. She met the fife and drum band marching to take up their position to play beneath the King's window as they did every morning. By the gilded entrance to the vestibule of the Queen's Staircase a horseman, about to set off on a ride before breakfast, swung himself into the saddle and cantered after her.

"Marguerite! What on earth are you doing here at this hour?"

She stopped her headlong flight at the sound of Stefane's voice and looked towards him with such relief that hope rose in him again. "I've never been so thankful to see anyone in my whole life," she exclaimed emotionally. "Can you take me home?"

"Willingly! Whatever has happened?" He dismounted swiftly and took hold of her by the arms. It pleased him that she did not draw away but seemed thankful for his nearness. His glance had shown him that her clothes, which were the same as those she had worn the previous day, were badly crumpled and there were dusty cobwebs clinging to one side of her cloak. As for her hair, he had never seen it in such disarray before. Grimly he gripped the handle of his sword, looking ready to fight a dozen duels on her behalf, his jaw set, his thick brows frowning. "Has someone offended you?"

She could almost believe he would call out the King if she told him the whole truth and not just what was permissible for him to hear. "I'll tell you on the way. Let's not delay."

He turned and summoned from a distance the groom who had brought him his horse. It was not long before it had been returned to the stables and a *calèche à deux* was brought in its place. Emboldened by her relaxed attitude, he put his left arm about her as he drove down the Avenue de Paris.

"Now tell me what happened," he said.

Her own inventiveness amazed her. She said she'd been asked to take some fans to one of the royal ladies and been told to wait. When she finally realised she had been forgotten it was dark and she became hopelessly lost in the labyrinth of corridors. By including her fright at the chance of being taken for a thief, he had been given a logical reason for her state of mind when they met.

"I slept eventually on one of the small staircases," she concluded, able to see he had swallowed her lies. It gave her no satisfaction, for she hated to deviate from the truth even in these circumstances.

"What appalling ill manners of anyone to treat you so!" He was outraged on her behalf. "If only I had known of your predicament!"

It was as well that he had not, she thought thankfully. Nobody must ever know of what took place. It was a mercy that Augustin was away and need not be told anything at all. Susanne was the only hurdle, for she would be harder to convince than Stefane, but fortunately she always slept late and, as her bedchamber was at the far side of the château, she would know nothing of this early morning return. Neither would Susanne have missed her the previous evening, for with their individual social engagements they sometimes did not see each other. There did not seem to be anything to worry about. Nothing at all.

Stefane smiled when he saw Marguerite had slipped into sleep against his shoulder and he slowed the pace of the horses as much to prolong the contact as not to disturb her. When they reached the gates of the Château Satory she awoke to look at him again with such melting gratitude that he felt it must be the luckiest day of his life. At the steps of the château he jumped out to hold out his arms and help her alight. It seemed natural to both of them that it should become an embrace and she let him kiss her for the first time, kissing him back out of her heartfelt thankfulness that he should have appeared just when he did.

"May I see you later today?" he asked eagerly as they drew apart.

"I shall be at the shop. Call this afternoon at closing time. By then I shall be myself again and able to express my thanks in full."

"I'm ever your servant, Marguerite."

She waited as he drove away and waved to him once

before turning into the house. A shadow moved away from the glass in an upper window.

A bath revived her. A breakfast of hot twisted bread and steaming coffee made her ready for the day. She arrived at the shop only a few minutes later than her usual time. Lucille, who had a second key to the shop, had opened it for Marguerite's assistant who had finished the early morning dusting and was already behind the counter.

"How did sales go yesterday?" Marguerite asked as she removed her cloak and hung it on a peg.

"I was quite busy, mademoiselle. And Clarisse did well with the new batch of designs."

The shop was busy again that morning. Marguerite had never dispensed with selling ribbons, which had been the shop's original trade, and recently she had begun to stock some unusual and more expensive ribbons, which were proving popular with the bourgeoisie. She hardly seemed to have turned round before Stefane arrived as arranged. When the day's business was at an end and after locking the shop door when the assistant had left, she took him into the room at the back of the shop.

"Thank you for appearing again at the right moment this morning. Just as you did at Fontainebleau."

"All I hope is that you've recovered from the indignities of last night." He took hold of a chair by its back to swing it round and sit by her at her desk.

She shrugged cheerfully, wanting to avoid further discussion about the incident. "That is over and done with now."

"I have something for you." He took a pretty little casket from his pocket and put it in front of her on the desk.

"La! How kind of you." As she had made it clear on a previous occasion that she would never accept jewellery from him, which he had wanted to give her, she fully expected it to contain a choice selection of sweetmeats. Instead, on a bed of velvet, a magnificent emerald ring released its sparkle. She slammed the lid shut quickly and thrust the casket back at him along the desk.

"You know that's an impossible gift!"

"Not when it's a betrothal ring. I'm asking you to marry me."

"Have you lost your wits?" she exclaimed, aghast.

"No. You showed me this morning how your feelings had changed towards me."

"That was only appreciation of your appearing when you did." She sprang up from her chair and faced him, entwining her fingers agitatedly. "It was also a kiss of adieu. I'm fond of you, Stefane. Very fond. But everything is just as it was when we parted in the gardens yesterday afternoon."

He rose slowly to his feet. "I don't believe that. I want you to be my wife."

"How can you think of such a thing?" she declared, sounding angry because she was upset by his folly. If he was prepared to go this far with her, he was likely to ask someone equally unsuited to his rank. "You're a nobleman! You're at Court! Think of your family."

"My parents are dead as you know, and as I am the only son, already come into my inheritance, none can gainsay me. As for being at Court, that's only temporary as far as I'm concerned. Being a popinjay at the City of the Rich for the rest of my life is not for me. I've no liking for Court life. I don't fit in and I've made enemies and no friends."

"Why did you come to Versailles in the first place?"

"Simply because it is expected, and rightly so, that every nobleman should serve the King as a courtier for a year or two as well as take service in a regiment for an allotted span of time. I'm fulfilling the former now and will join the dragoons next spring. All I ask is that you become betrothed to me and wait until my spell of service is finished. I shall then return to my estate and not even the King is able to stop me marrying there the woman I've chosen for my bride." He opened the casket and took the ring from it, trying to coax her with love in his voice. "Let me put this on your finger."

She put her hands behind her, shaking her head defensively. Last night she had been thankful that Augustin was far away in Le Havre. Today she wished he could be here to see her put his fears to rest that one day she would accept marriage from a younger man.

"No, Stefane. You've made a great mistake."

He changed his tone to one of urgency. "If you won't become my betrothed for any other reason, at least in God's name do so for your own safety!"

It was an impassioned plea and she regarded him warily. "Why should you say that?"

"Roussier may contaminate you with his Huguenot beliefs and then you would be classed as a heretic with him. Haven't you heard the news yet? Stricter measures are to be introduced against Protestants who do not convert. There are to be no marriages between Catholics and Protestants and the children of those unions already in existence are no longer legitimate. Protestant judges are barred from the bench. In fact, all public offices under the crown are to be withheld from those not of your faith and mine."

"That's monstrous!"

"Guard your tongue, Marguerite! What you have just said to me must not be overheard by others. All I have mentioned is only the tip of the iceberg."

"What more?"

He told her and she listened in distress. There was to be complete segregation in all areas of daily life, even to a Catholic midwife being forbidden to attend a Protestant woman and vice versa.

"So you see," he concluded, "you are inviting danger simply by living under the same roof as Roussier. My ring would remind you daily to be vigilant and with time you would also see it as a symbol of betrothal to me. Move out of the Château Satory before Roussier returns."

"I'd never do that."

He leapt from his chair. "Damnation! How can you be so stubborn?"

"Augustin and I have respected each other's beliefs from the start. I have nothing to fear. Even if I had, I'd still stay with him."

"How can you respect anything about him? He's a Huguenot! He's destined for hellfire!"

She smiled faintly. "I'm in a state of sin myself."

"Nothing that could not be absolved if you leave him."

"For you?"

"Yes!"

She shook her head. "I've given you my answer."

He heaved a great gust of a sigh and turned away to pick up his plumed hat from the table. "There's no point in talking on this matter any more today."

"Or on any other day. Goodbye, Stefane."

As he left her he was not unusually cast down. Roussier would not always stand between them. On that he was resolved.

When Marguerite arrived home that evening she learned that Susanne had departed again. It had happened before when Susanne needed to go to Paris, or an urgent message from Orléans had informed her that one of the children was unwell, when always she flew off in a rush. Marguerite thought it might have been the case this time, for it was always on these occasions that Susanne forgot to leave a note of thanks for hospitality and also of explanation. An apologetic letter was likely to arrive in two or three weeks' time.

For a while, apart from business mail, Marguerite did not receive communications from anyone. When Augustin's day of return came and went without any sign of him, she feared that his father, who had been almost well again when she last heard, had had a relapse. When another ten days went by she had begun to be extremely worried and it was with relief that she finally received a letter. It was brief, but deeply loving, telling her he would be home the following day.

It was the longest time they had ever been apart and when he returned their reunion was more passionate than ever before. To her relief, and somewhat to her surprise, he did not ask her about Stefane. As for the night at the Château, it remained a closed secret between her and the King.

Eight

Susanne had made an appointment to see the King. Nearly four months had passed since she had gone to Le Havre to break the news to Augustin that Marguerite was no longer faithful to him. He had been shattered. She knew if it had been anyone else reporting the young woman's early morning return and fond parting from Stefane Le Pelletier he would have struck down the bearer of the news. But he knew she would never lie to him.

"It was sheer chance I happened to witness the scene that morning," she had said. "I had awakened much earlier with a bad headache and, unable to bear it any longer, I went to Marguerite's bedchamber to ask if she had any potion that would be of help to me. I found her bed had not been slept in and it was then I heard the carriage wheels."

"Oh, my God."

There was such hurt in his voice that she had hardly known how to bear it. She could tell his mind was floundering, disillusionment and despair mingling with incredulity. Yet she could not have taken back her words even if it had been possible. It would have been far worse for him to be betrayed, perhaps time and time again, and then deserted without warning. There was no shame in her through having comforted him as she had done.

She tapped her fingers impatiently on the arm of the chair where she was sitting as she awaited her turn to see the King. One of his ministers had been with him a considerable time and there were a number of courtiers waiting to see him after her. She had no idea how the King would receive her request, but he could be lenient towards a beautiful woman and to this end she had spent a long time on her appearance. The one real hazard to her petition was the King's new moral attitude. Everybody knew that he slept only with Madame de Maintenon and the belief was that he had married her. Yet it would be more than anyone's position at Court was worth to ask him outright. He, who knew everything, must be laughing up his sleeve at the speculation, gossip and whispers, but then there was nothing the Court liked more than to have something about which to wag tongues and nobody knew that better than Louis himself.

She straightened in the chair as the doors opened and the War Minister emerged. It was the Marquis de Louvois, a sinister wolf of a man. He recognised her and bowed, which she acknowledged by inclining her head, dislike in her eyes. Under her lashes she watched him saunter past and disappear out of the room.

In his Cabinet, Louis sat at the brocade-draped table looking through the reports that Louvois had left him. The Protestants were presenting a stubborn front to conversion that must be changed. Aside from political reasons for not having a divided country and his own abhorrence of any defiance against his will, it was only through the achievements of a purely Roman Catholic France that he would be granted atonement for his past sins. The priests had been saying it for years and Françoise's endorsement had removed any last doubt, like drops of water wearing away a stone. Gone were the days when he had thought that the Almighty's variegated colouring of the flowers and leaves might also mean He was prepared to accept different shades of worship from men.

Colbert, aged and dying, had always urged religious tolerance towards the Protestants and had done so again not all that long ago, seeing their skills and wealth as an enrichment of the nation. Well, it was natural he should have thought that way since they were one of the many sources of the huge taxes he drew out of the people. Now there were others in power to gather those monies, but no one to be heeded any longer on how to deal with the Huguenots.

In Louis's carefully considered opinion all that was needed to adjust the situation was sterner enforcement of the measures already in operation, and it had been the subject of his discussion with Louvois. These measures already ruled were just and fair, for they bypassed massacres and banishments, the ultimate attack on heresy, and thus cleverly retained without disruption the very assets that Colbert had prized. Louvois, who would probably have preferred the sword and the burning pyre for the obdurate, being notorious for his bloodlust when out to punish or defeat, was to take on this duty.

Louis closed the velvet-covered binder over the papers. He was confident that this new disciplined pressure compelling Protestants to search their hearts for the truth would bring the desired conversions while, at the same time, effectively restricting Louvois and keeping him within bounds. There was no denying it was a strategically brilliant move. Louis felt well pleased with the resolutions of the day so far.

In the anteroom Susanne rose from her chair and smoothed her skirt to be ready when announced. As her name rang out she swept forward into the King's presence and dipped into a deep curtsey.

Louis looked up from where he sat, charmed by the sight of this alluring woman, her smooth chestnut hair topped by the new headdress known as a *fontange,* no more than a wisp of lace starched or wired to stand high like a half-open fan, the filmy lappets floating down over the shoulders.

"Bonjour, Madame de Fresnay. Pray sit down." He rose from his own chair until she had taken the seat he had indicated. After inquiring about her health and that of her husband and children, he made it known he was ready to hear the purpose of her request for an audience.

"I'm in great need of your help, sire," she began, hoping she would not break down. This was the climax to weeks of worry that she had kept to herself, not disclosing it to anyone. Now, speaking of it for the first time, she could not keep an involuntary catch from her voice. "Only you have the power to save one of your loyal officers from a most unhappy future."

"Your husband?"

"Yes, sire." The long-suppressed tears gave her eyes such a lustre that even her lids and lashes seemed to shimmer. "As you know, he is at the Eure in command of a division of the troops engaged in the excavation work. We do not see each other often. Had he been home the catastrophe that has overtaken me would not have occurred."

"I believe I'm beginning to understand." Louis's tone was sympathetic. "Are you telling me you have been indiscreet?"

"Yes, sire." She spoke the truth without losing her dignity. "I am with child by a lover."

"You are neither the first nor the last, madame," he remarked drily, observing how the skilful arrangement of her shawl and the bows ornamenting the fashionably elongated point of her bodice artfully concealed her pregnant state. "But I fail to see how I may be of assistance to you."

The plea burst from her. "Let my husband stay at the Eure for another five months without leave to come home. Spells of leave from there are infrequent in any case, and by that time I shall have found a good foster home for the infant and my husband will not be destroyed by my unfaithfulness!" She pressed fingertips to her lips as sobs threatened. If tears came they would not be of regret for what had passed between her and Augustin, but for what the outcome would do to Jacques whom she had once vowed never to hurt.

Louis's glance went to the reports on his desk. One of them contained further disturbing news on conditions at the excavation site. Strange fevers were taking a toll on the soldiers' lives. As with the digging of Versailles, the vapours of the ground were blamed, but whatever the cause sometimes the lists of men succumbing resembled that of battle losses. It would suit him well to keep Fresnay and the rest of the officers bottled up there without bringing the risk of infection home. They had been under orders not to talk of conditions there, for it did no good to panic people unnecessarily. As a result things had been kept quiet, the garrulous soldiery having been confined to camp from the start. Not once had it occurred to Louis to abandon the project in view of the epidemics. Since the soldiers were not needed for war they must be usefully employed and although the losses were lamentable, the glories of Versailles took precedence.

"I think your request could be arranged," he said benevolently.

Overwhelmed by relief, she flung herself on her knees in a rustle of azure taffeta and kissed his hand. "I thank you with all my heart, sire!"

He smiled, pleased to have won her gratitude, and invited her to be seated again. "How do you propose to keep your condition secret from others? Shall you retire to the country?"

"No, although I must let society think I'm at Orléans while I stay in seclusion at our Paris house. In that way I can deal with all correspondence and domestic matters without anything being out of order. All along Jacques has discouraged my visits to Chartres, concerned always for my health in new surroundings, so he will not question a cessation of my occasional visits."

Louis nodded, knowing full well why her husband had been anxious for her not to be there. "To make it still easier for you I will forbid visits from officers' wives and families as has already been the rule for the ranks. The excavation work is not progressing as well as I had expected and privileges will only be resumed when schedules are met."

"Your kindness to me is beyond bounds, sire."

The interview was at an end. As she was about to leave he asked her one more question. "Does your lover know of your predicament?"

"No, sire. Nor shall he."

Susanne's letter arrived one morning. "She has left Paris again for Orléans to be with the children," Augustin said when he had read it, handing it over to Marguerite. "It means we shall not be seeing her for a while."

There was no word of greeting for her in the letter, which struck her as odd when she read it through, especially as there had been no communication between them since Susanne's hasty departure and no meeting during her sojourn in Paris this time. But she soon forgot about it. Life was full and busy. She had four hands in the workshop now apart from Lucille, the shop doing well and the vestibule sales high. If there was any cloud on her horizon it was in an indefinable change in her relationship with Augustin. He loved her more than ever, of that she was in no doubt, and yet there was a barrier of unspoken thoughts between them that had never been there before. Where previously they had been completely open with each other the ease of communication had gone. She blamed herself entirely. The night at Versailles still weighed on her mind and somehow she must have conveyed to him that something crucial had happened in his absence.

She saw Stefane more than she wished. He was persistent in calling in at the shop when he knew she would be there and nothing pleased him better than to meet her by chance in the street where he could stroll along with her to her destination. She began to dread seeing him, which was ludicrous, for he was always agreeable and never tried to press her into any kind of social engagement. Yet at the same time, underlying everything he said, there was the message that he meant to have her in the end. What disturbed her most was that if ever Augustin's name came into the conversation an almost fanatical gleam of hatred came into his eyes. It was as if his desire for her was matched only by his loathing of Augustin, whom he seemed to consider to be the one barrier between them.

It was a relief when his time for military service drew near. She did not refuse his request to dine with him before he left, for it would have been churlish. They met at one of the cafés that catered for the nobility and where they had had supper on previous occasions before Augustin's return had put an end to their meetings. He was in the uniform of the dragoons, which suited him well and gave him a dashing appearance, deep blue plumes on the sweeping upturned brim of his hat, which he doffed at her approach.

"I've been looking forward to seeing you today," he said in welcome. "I wanted to be able to talk to you once more away from the trappings of your daily life."

"When do you leave?" She could understand that he should wish this final farewell to be in more amenable surroundings and they were in a room of their own that looked out on the street.

"Early tomorrow morning. It may be a long while before I return to Versailles."

"That's to be expected."

"I shall miss you."

She gave a slight shake of her head to discourage this line of conversation. "Tell me where you are going."

"To keep order wherever it is needed." He leaned across the table to her. "Give me a kerchief of yours or some other favour as a keepsake to carry on my person until I return."

She did not want to do that and turned his request aside lightly. "That would not be appropriate. After all, it's not as though you're off to war."

"Isn't it?" His eyes narrowed. "The Huguenots are as dangerous to France as any foreign enemy."

His words sent a chill running down her spine. "What are you saying?"

He shrugged as if to allay any alarm. "Only that my regiment is being posted to one of the Huguenot cities in Gascony where there has been some trouble. Weapons have been used and several buildings fired. That's akin to war, I should say."

Her words came in a rush. "I hope you will take on the rôle of peacemaker and heal the disquiet there!"

"That's my intention."

They talked about many things after that, but when their time together had almost run out he returned again to the subject of her giving him a keepsake.

"Say no more about that," she insisted. "It would seem like a love-token and there is nothing between us on that score."

"Not anything you're prepared to admit. But one day you'll grow tired of being tied to a man twice your age. I'm coming back for you, Marguerite. Never think otherwise."

It was as if he were throwing chains about her and she made a move to leave as if mentally throwing them off. "We're parting as friends. Let's not spoil the time we've had together with any arguments."

"I agree. It's been such a pleasure for me to have you to myself for a little while. Let me kiss you in farewell. It will be something to remember until we meet again."

Before she could answer, he reached out his arm and pulled her close to kiss her ardently. Several moments passed before he let her go with a smile of triumph. "That shall be my keepsake."

She had not minded the kiss, for it was impossible to dismiss entirely the fondness she had for him. In spite of his protestations that he would come back to her he was going to be away from Versailles for a long time, seeing new faces and new scenes. The memory of her would fade. Had he been older it might have been different, but he was a youth yet and could fall in love a dozen times before his military service was over.

Much encouraged by this thought she parted from him. In her bedchamber back at the Château Satory she realised the buoyancy of her mood was due to his departure from Versailles. It therefore came as a greater shock when she found the emerald betrothal ring in her purse. She had loosened the drawstrings to take out a sample of ribbon she had brought home with her from the shop and there was the green fire of the gold-set ring winking at her. He must have slipped it into her purse, which she remembered putting down on the seat between them, at some moment when her attention was diverted. Slowly she reached out and picked it up. It was his keepsake for her, intended as an emblem of love and safekeeping, but she saw it more as a possible bone of contention between Augustin and her, for she would not conceal it from him.

Holding it in her hand, she went downstairs to the library where he was writing a letter at the table there. Without a word she put the ring down by his hand. His gaze went to it immediately and his pen became still.

"What's that?"

"It's a betrothal ring. I have refused it twice."

His face went ashen and he sat back in the chair. "Who offered it to you?"

"Stefane Le Pelletier."

He spoke with steely restraint. "I want no mention of his name in this house."

There was something about his rigid attitude that unnerved her. She found herself summoning up her courage to go on with what she had to say. "Nevertheless, I have to tell you about the ring."

"Very well. If you refused it why do you still have it in your possession?"

"I met him to say farewell before his departure to serve with the dragoons. When I came home I found he had put the ring in my purse without my knowledge."

His hand clenched on the pen and then he threw it from him. "When did Le Pelletier first want you to become betrothed to him?" he questioned in the same hard tones. "Was it when you went to his bed while I was away and made your homecomings in the early hours before the house was fully astir?"

She thought her knees would buckle and she clutched the edge of the table for support. "Did you set a spy on me in your absence?"

"No!" He leapt out of the chair with such abruptness that it toppled and fell backwards. "I was told in my father's house by someone who came to me there from the highest motives."

Putting her fingers to her temples, she rocked in her anguish. There was only one person who would have gone running to him. Hadn't Susanne warned that she would take up cudgels on his behalf? "It's true I spent a night away from my bed when you were away and Stefane brought me home. But nothing is as it must have appeared. I had met him shortly before in the Cour Royale when he was going for a morning ride."

"In the Cour Royale? Where had you been then?"

"Lost in the corridors of Versailles. After I had spurned the King!"

The whole story poured out of her. When he came from where he stood and put his arms about her she knew he believed her. For him, the way she had described the King's reaction to hearing she was Jeanne Dremont's daughter tallied exactly with the haunted, glacial look he had seen in Louis's eyes when he had appealed for clemency on the woman's behalf. He did not know how he could have doubted Marguerite, she who had always been frank and honest with him, but he had been blinded by jealousy. He had even expected to find her gone when he arrived home and he would never forget his overwhelming relief that she was still there. He had done his best to win her back, not knowing then that he had never lost her.

"Promise me one thing," she implored when their reconciliation was complete.

"What's that?" He was ready to grant her anything in his power.

"Next time you have to go away for a long period at your

father's house, let me come with you. I can stay in Le Havre and not intrude in any way."

"That shall be done."

It was too soon to tell her what he had in mind for his next visit there, for he did not want any unexpected hitches to cause her disappointment. Certain arrangements would have to be made first and his father well prepared. The idea of making her his wife had taken hold during his lengthy absence from her, shattered only when Susanne had arrived with her well-meaning but erroneous report. He had long wanted to marry Marguerite and the King's almost certain morganatic marriage offered the solution. He would find a Huguenot priest to perform the ceremony and they would be husband and wife even though the world should remain in ignorance of their union.

One morning early in May Augustin received a summons from the King. He had been trying to gain an audience for weeks over an urgent cause and thought his luck had changed, but no sooner had he entered the Cabinet than Louis made it plain he had a matter of his own to discuss.

"You and Brigadier de Fresnay have been friends for many years, have you not?" he asked solemnly.

"Since our musketeer days, sire."

"Then I have to give you a painful duty to perform." Louis picked up a list of names from his table and flicked it with his fingers. "This morning I received the names of those who have died recently of fever at the Eure excavations. I regret to have to tell you that Fresnay's name is among them."

He saw the terrible effect his words had had on Roussier. The courtier stood stricken, scarcely able to believe what he had heard. To give him time to recover, Louis drew away to the window and looked out.

"Is there any chance of a mistake being made, sire?" Shock made the query come on a harsh note.

Louis turned back to him. "None. He fell sick yesterday morning and before the day was out he had succumbed. It is God's will."

"Does Madame de Fresnay know this news yet, sire?"

"No. I was sure you would be prepared to break the news to her as gently as possible."

"I'll leave for Orléans immediately."

"She's not there. You will find her at her residence in Paris."

Augustin was surprised. "But I have received correspondence from the family château."

"Nevertheless you will find her in Paris."

Puzzled, Augustin left to tell Marguerite the news in the room at the back of the shop. As he had expected, she was deeply upset.

"Do you want to come with me to Paris?" he asked her.

"It may not be the best time for me to go now. Susanne and I have not met since you wrote to tell her of the error she had made. I wouldn't want her to see me as an intruder at this time of sorrow. Ask her if I may come. Then I will go to her immediately."

He rode fast to Paris and just before noon arrived at the great mansion where he knocked on the door. "I have come to see Madame de Fresnay," he said, entering at once.

"Madame de Fresnay is not here, monsieur. She is in the country," the manservant replied.

Augustin answered brusquely. "I know she is here. Tell her the King has sent me."

This announcement had the effect he had anticipated. His name was asked for and then he was kept waiting about a quarter of an hour before being told the Madame de Fresnay awaited him in her bedchamber. It was quite customary for ladies to receive important visitors from their beds while refreshment was served. Often a dozen or more people would be gathered there.

To his relief nobody else was present when he was shown into the bedchamber where Susanne sat against the beribboned pillows, grandly attired, her jewellery sparkling. The folded sheet over the embroidered coverlet came to her armpits, almost concealing the richness of the robe that she wore. He thought at once that there was something different about her, a puffiness to her face, dark shadows under her eyes that her paint and powder could not hide. Grief at his mission kept him from any thought of their last encounter.

"I'm having a few days in Paris to see my dressmaker before I return to the country," she lied. "Sit down, Augustin." Then the gravity of his expression made her hand flutter to her throat in a flash of rings. "Oh, dear God! What is wrong?"

He sat down on the bed, facing her, and took her hand into both of his. Then he broke the news to her. For a few seconds she was dumb, staring at him with dilating pupils. Then she uttered a heartrending cry.

"I killed him!"

She threw herself across the bed in her abandonment to grief and the coverlet slipped away to reveal that she was at least in the seventh month of pregnancy. He tried to find words to comfort her, but each time she shrieked out that she was a murderess or that Jacques would still be alive if it were not for her. Finally he began to fear for her condition and drew her back onto the pillows where she lay with the tears running pitiably down her face.

"You're in no way responsible for what happened to Jacques," he said consolingly. "Even if you had been notified immediately of his illness there is nothing you could have done to save him."

"You don't understand," she said tremulously. "I asked the King not to let Jacques come home until after this baby was born. If he had had leave when it was due he might have escaped the fever that struck him down."

"Why should you have made such a request? Did Jacques not know? But he would have welcomed another child."

"Not this one." Her voice was almost inaudible, thick with sorrow. She watched the comprehension dawn painfully in his eyes. With no further need of concealment she turned back the coverlet completely and left the bed, her robe falling into place over her many petticoats. "I wanted to spare him misery! I didn't intend that you should know either, but Fate can be devious at times."

"What were you planning to do when the baby was born?"

Her expression was tragic. "Foster the infant out in a good home. That is the usual procedure for women of the Court when they find themselves faced with this dilemma."

"Could you really have parted with my child?" He spoke out of the love that each had held for the other over so many years. It had nothing to do with his feelings for Marguerite, had no bearing on preference, or even on whether he would have wished the clock back to that evening when he first saw Susanne at Fontainebleau and might still have won her. What he had shared with this woman, culminating yet again after many years of denial in an outburst of uncontrolled passion, had its own value, not to be belittled or ignored.

She drew a little flower out of a bowl of blossoms and held it against her cheek, the tears continuing to trickle down the sides of her face. "Part of my heart would have died at the separation. Now at least I can come out into the open, although the cost is terrible to me."

"There's no proof that Jacques would have escaped the fever if he had come home for a week or two and there never could be."

"My guilt will never leave me."

"What of mine in having brought you to this pass?"

She turned about to face him. "You have punishment enough in seeing your son brought up as another man's child."

"How can you be certain it's a boy?" He was already half convinced, for she looked so sure.

She placed her palms flat on the rise of her body. "I know by the way I'm carrying him." Suddenly her whole face registered remorse and shame, even a kind of angry desolation as an explosion of self-hatred burst from her. "I hope I die in childbirth!"

"No!" he shouted in protest that she should have passed such a sentence upon herself, and went across to put his arms protectively about her. Immediately she broke down completely, sobbing against his shoulder. There were no more words to be said then. All he could do was to see her through her immediate grief and help her face the time ahead. It meant sharing the burden of conscience with her, for he could not let her bear it alone. As she wept out her sorrow against him he saw all he had planned for Marguerite and himself vanishing like a dream.

He returned home later that day. Marguerite was saddened, but not surprised to hear that Susanne did not wish to see her. She wrote a letter of sympathy that same evening, letting her know at the same time that she held no grudge over the error that had been made and hoped their friendship would continue unimpaired. Augustin took the letter with him when he returned to Paris; Marguerite

knew he had to organise the funeral since Susanne was
expecting another child and was more or less indisposed.
The Duchesse de Valmy, although elderly, arrived in Paris
to be with her niece and the day after the burial travelled
with her to Orléans. Two months later Susanne gave birth
there to a son. He was named Edmund after her father.

In that same year of Edmund's birth Louis finally hardened his heart against Athénaïs de Montespan. She was
turned out of her huge apartment and virtually dismissed
to another far less roomy on a less exalted floor. Her reign
was finally over and it was said that she wept for days in her
new abode. Françoise did not gloat, for that was not her
way, but now at last she had everything as she wanted.
Except, perhaps, for her marital duties, which she considered excessive, for she was not a passionate woman and the
King, at forty-five, was still as virile as a man half his age.

Two marvellous additions to Versailles were completed
in that year of 1684. The first was the King's new suite of
rooms at the East Front with a beautiful central salon
where double doors opened for the royal presence to go
forth into what was the crowning glory of Versailles,
the spectacular and glorious Hall of Mirrors, flanked at the
north end by the War Salon and at the south end by the
Salon of Peace.

Nobody entered that long gallery of gold and glass, statues, marble pilasters and solid silver furniture for the first
time without a widening of the eyes. Augustin took Marguerite to see it, overcoming by persuasion her aversion to
going anywhere near Versailles since her unhappy experience there. Now she was glad she had come as she stood on
the threshold of that great Hall of Mirrors that was more
wonderful than she could have imagined.

It exploded upon the vision in golden opulence, filled
with dazzling light from the seventeen tall windows that
corresponded in height and design with the seventeen
mirrored alcoves on the opposite wall. Gilded life-size figures held cascading crystal candelabra and from the high
curved ceiling, painted brilliantly with scenes from Louis's
eventful life, were suspended by cream silken ropes a
double row of huge chandeliers. The floor, over eleven
yards wide and stretching the vast distance of one hundred
nine yards from end to end, was patterned in wood pol-

ished to the hue of gold, further enhanced by a magnificent, specially woven carpet from the Savonnerie workshops in the richest of hues. This Hall of Mirrors, created to glorify a Sun King, harnessed the sun itself as it bathed the West Front, the rays becoming trapped in the mirrors. The sun and Apollo were made one with the Château and thus subject to Louis himself.

Marguerite looked about her as Augustin drew her by the hand past one mirror after another until they reached the central window in the long row that looked out over the terrace and the Latona fountain in a direct line to the Tapis Vert and the Grand Canal beyond, which lay swallowed up in sun-diamonds. It was a last hurdle for her to stand at this viewpoint, for it must have been her father's many times before he plunged to his death from this height to the stone flags below. Augustin had never seen her turn her gaze directly on the terrace, but she did now without faltering and then on to take in the rest of the vista. It was what he had hoped for when he had first asked her to come here with him after the decoration of the Hall of Mirrors was finally finished.

"Is all well now?" he asked her.

She gave him a smile, turning to link her hands about his arm. "I'm at ease again here. I never thought I would be."

From the windows of the Peace Salon Marguerite could see across the South Parterre to the great ramp under which the new Orangery was being constructed, advantage being taken of the lower level of the land there. It was impossible to see anything of it except by going down over a hundred steps to reach that level and it left the view of the Swiss Lake unimpaired. When completed the Orangery would add another dimension of beauty to this great palace, which still retained the humbler title of Château and seemed destined never to be elevated from it.

"Is the King ever going to stop building?" she queried as together they retraced their steps through the sunny brilliance of the Hall of Mirrors.

"I doubt it. If Louis had not been born a king, I daresay he would have been a mason."

"I can only picture him being that in his state robes with a trowel in his hand."

They exchanged amused glances at the absurdity of the image. Augustin was more serious these days and she val-

ued their lighthearted moments. She knew he had much
on his mind that he did not confide to her. He was no
longer sent anywhere as the King's envoy and neither was
he entrusted with other duties. Hope was fading that Louis
would listen to him ever again on a compassionate cause
and thus the purpose of his being at Court was virtually at
an end. She believed that if his château had not become a
place of refuge in transit for many Huguenots in flight, he
would have sold it and gone fully into banking at Le Havre.

She had begun to know the signs whenever someone
was being hidden in the attics. Finally she had asked to be
allowed to help.

"I knew I couldn't keep it from you forever," he had said
with a sigh. "Now that you do know it's best if I find you an
apartment in town."

"No! I'll not leave. When women and children are here
there must be much that I could do."

"These people are not of your faith," he reminded her.

"They are in trouble. That is enough for me."

Thoughtfully he traced a finger down the side of her
upturned face. "Would that all men and women shared
your Good Samaritan attitude. Very well. I'll be glad of
your help at times, but if ever extreme danger threat-
ens, you will leave at once."

She nodded to show she understood his wishes, although
she had not the least intention of leaving his side in any
crisis.

Whenever he did go away, usually for no more than a
week or two at the most, she knew it was always on Huguenot business and too dangerous for her to go with him. She
was always on tenterhooks until his safe return, for violence against Protestants had come into the open under
the Marquis de Louvois's command, particularly in the
south and southwest of the country. What was personally
upsetting her was that she had heard Stefane's name mentioned in connection with some strife against the Huguenots in one district.

Once when Augustin was away on a Huguenot rescue
bid, which was the other side of the coin to Louvois's campaign, he called on Susanne at Orléans. He did not bring a
message of reconciliation back to Marguerite as she had
hoped. It seemed that Susanne had made a decision not to
renew their friendship and was prepared to stick by it.

There was no doubt that Augustin had been greatly taken with little Edmund, praising him as a bright and sturdy child. It made Marguerite yearn more than ever to give him a son of his own, but she had begun to fear with great sadness that she was barren.

Then in the July of 1685 she knew for certain that she was pregnant at last. Her joy was beyond bounds, but by September it was at an end. One afternoon, being in haste to get back to her shop counter, she missed her footing on the flight down from the workshop and took a tumble of two or three steps. She did not hurt herself beyond bruising her arm and even made a joke about her own clumsiness, but within an hour she had suffered a miscarriage. It was devastating to her. During the following weeks she took no interest in anything, unable to be cheered by assurances from a doctor and by friends, even by Augustin himself, that next time all should go well.

There was no telling how long her lassitude would have lasted if in October the King had not signed, in a full council of his ministers, the Revocation of the Edict of Nantes. On his ornate silver throne he took his pen and set his signature to the document. It removed all protection from the Protestant minority and denied them the freedom of worship according to their own consciences. Louis saw it as the only way to finally bring them to heel since all other attempts had failed to result in the desired conversions.

The effects were almost immediate as far as Marguerite was concerned. Augustin met her at the shop one day at closing time with an urgent request.

"I need your help. There's a sick child in the attic, and no woman in the party of Huguenot refugees to care for him."

She went to the child at once. His father, three brothers and an uncle were with him, but his mother had been drowned in a well for heresy by the Marquis de Louvois. They were bound for England by way of Le Havre and the small sailing ship that Gérard kept in a creek near the Manoir, but could not travel until the boy was strong enough for the journey. Marguerite devoted herself to winning him back to health, her own trouble forgotten.

When eventually she was able to see them safely on their way, two more refugees from the south arrived. Where previously there had been the occasional trickle of people, it now became almost a floodtide. Marguerite comforted a widow who had seen her husband roasted on a spit and another whose son had suffered an equally terrible death, broken on the wheel and then hanged. Over and over again she redressed ghastly wounds that had been received while defending families and property from attack or during torture. More times than she cared to hear, Stefane had been connected with the proceedings, for he had been quickly promoted by Louvois and become an avid follower of his cousin's ugly methods.

From what she was able to see and hear for herself, she realised the awful persecution inflicted by the Marquis de Louvois on those who clung to their own beliefs. The dragoons had been billeted in Huguenot homes, ostensibly to keep a defiant section of the population in order, but in reality to torment the unconverted now that mere harassment and subtle pressure were at an end.

As if going into battle, Louvois had struck out first at those least able to defend themselves before moving on to the more powerful members of the communities. With his encouragement, the dragoons had begun to rampage as if in a conquered foreign land instead of on their own French soil. They pillaged and looted as they wished, helping themselves to whatever took their fancy, and vented their lust on the wives, daughters and women servants of the households. The men were tortured, no account taken of age, and it had become a cruel sport to devise some new way to humiliate and torment. Inevitably there were conversions out of terror, expediency or to save children being taken away, although often these last-minute changes of faith were considered too late for punishment to be spared. It was Augustin's guess that when Louvois put his lists of new converts before the King he gave no true account as to how they had been gained or subsequently treated. Before long the atrocities were no longer confined to the south, but were erupting in various parts of the country, these acts of terrible persecution becoming known as *dragonnades*.

Judging his time, Augustin made another determined effort to catch the King's ear, wanting to present the gruesome facts. Refused an audience once more, he waited to waylay Louis as he came from morning Mass, the time when he should be in his most charitable mood.

"Sire! A word on the brutal treatment of the Huguenots by the Marquis de Louvois!"

Louis paused and smiled wearily. "Not again, Monsieur Roussier. As I said to you before, where is the proof of these rumours that you repeat to me? Are you yourself being persecuted? Have you been banished from Court? Are Protestants in the Château or in the town of Versailles itself being whipped or tortured in the park or in the streets?"

"It is happening elsewhere. Parts of the southwest are little more than charnel houses. Ride with me and see for yourself, sire."

A glazed look had come over Louis's eyes. It was the same when the plight of the poor and starving was put to him. It was as if his understanding deliberately rejected what his ears received. "The conversions are coming about through the wise counselling of the priests and nothing else. In their compassion they even take dying Protestants into their care and save those souls at the last moment, sparing them the contagion of their own families' false faith at the end. I have the personal assurance of the Marquis de Louvois that this campaign for conversion is being conducted with patient firmness as I would wish it to be. So no more on this matter from you, Monsieur Roussier."

It was an ultimatum, but not given with any personal hostility. Augustin bowed after him, wondering what Louis would have said if he had known that in the attics of Château Satory another group of Huguenots were resting on their flight from France.

At her country estate Susanne was not cut off from what was happening in the rest of the country. She kept up an energetic correspondence with friends at Court and elsewhere. Not long after the Revocation she moved with the three children back to Paris, taking a tutor with her in order not to disrupt her elder son's education. Her one aim was to be at hand should it seem likely that the Marquis de Louvois's barbaric methods were about to stretch towards the Château Satory. For that purpose she managed to get a small one-room apartment in the Château, which enabled her to appear again at Court, where she was constantly on the alert for any whisper that might warn her of a plot afoot. It meant leaving the children in Paris, but she visited them frequently. She met Augustin again at an *Appartement*.

"I've missed you," she admitted with some emotion, careful not to be overheard by anyone nearby.

He gave her the special smile she desired and it went right to her heart. "How is Edmund?"

"Strong and well. Come and see him in Paris when next I'm there."

"That's not wise at the moment. Although I still attend Court it is simply to find out daily how the land lies. All the time I'm here as a kind of bastion there's some hope for others that Louvois's methods will not reach as far as Paris or Versailles. But it could be dangerous for you to receive a Huguenot in your home."

She concealed her disappointment, loving him more than she had ever done. "I will arrange for Edmund to be taken to a park or someplace where you may meet as if by chance and spend a little while with him."

"I look forward to that. Now I fear we have talked as long as we should."

She watched him stroll away to the gaming table where he was greeted enthusiastically and invited to join in. As yet he appeared to be facing no ostracism from fellow courtiers and she knew the King still played billiards with him on occasions. Her hope was that as Louis had never taken any action against sodomites because of his brother, he would take none against those Huguenots like Augustin whom he knew personally and who had served him faithfully over many years. But this hope proved to be short-lived when the King sent for her one day. The audience was short and to the point. She came away from it full of trepidation.

When Augustin was next in Paris to see his son, which he did once or twice a month unbeknown to Marguerite, Susanne was waiting for him with the child in a carriage instead of the nursemaid who was usually in charge. Edmund held out his arms to his father immediately and Augustin scooped him up fondly before taking the seat beside Susanne.

"What brings you here today?" he asked her after they had kissed in greeting.

"I had an audience with the King. He wants me to use

my influence through friendship to convert you away from Protestantism."

He raised an eyebrow. "Well?"

"I know it's no use."

"Did you tell him we have discussed the issue before?"

"Yes, I did."

He pressed her hand reassuringly. "When he questions you again, you may say that you said your piece without result. Some good can come out of this. Since Louis approves of you associating with a Huguenot, you can come with Edmund and me to see the tumblers near the Pont de Neuf."

After that day she always went with Edmund to meet him. At Versailles they were able to be seen in each other's company, sit together in the Mars Salon for concerts on the *Appartement* evenings or dance in the great Hercules Salon with its rose marble and gilt bronzes under one of the most beautiful decorated ceilings in the world. Yet he never visited her at her Paris residence, which he could have done quite easily, because of Marguerite. Many times in private she wept over this, knowing that if it had not been for Marguerite he would have been with her all the time. In spite of having borne Augustin a child and in the knowledge that he had committed himself to his responsibilities, Susanne had had to accept that she could not keep him at her side. She was resolved that one day she would find a way of making him accept that his place was with her and no one else. How she would do it she did not know, but sooner or later the chance would come and she would seize it.

Augustin had had no need of Susanne's warning about the King's intention towards him. It was logical that eventually Louis must turn his attention to those Protestants still at Court. All he could do was carry on as if nothing was amiss and try to bring about as many rescues as was possible in the time that was left. As for his relationship with Marguerite, his feelings towards her were more intense than ever in view of the side of his life involving his son that he was keeping from her. She had never been more precious to him, adored or desired, and he would never have believed it possible to find such deep happiness as he had found with her.

More than three months went by. Marguerite was thankful for every day that went by without disruption, for Augustin had told her of the task that Susanne had been given. She was wary at first.

"Does she attempt it?"

"No. In any case she has no chance. We are never alone."

That was reassuring to know. She herself rarely saw Susanne and then only from a distance. The pleasures of Versailles were not the same as before, for she had no wish to see the King and only attended when she could be sure of not crossing his path. As a result, she and Augustin went more to Paris for their entertainment and they particularly enjoyed the plays at the Comédie-Française. They spent many hours on horseback in the surrounding countryside and picnics on their own never ceased to appeal to them.

The dark clouds created by Louvois were coming nearer all the time. Only Versailles and its vicinity remained virtually undisturbed as if Louvois chose not to bring the stench of blood and tortured flesh within range of the King's nostrils. Marguerite shuddered as much at his name as she did at Stefane's. Who would ever have supposed that what she had taken for reserve in him had been arrogance? Or that his feelings for her, genuine though she had believed them to be, were rooted in savagery that a Huguenot should have the love of the woman he wanted for himself? She hoped to be spared ever seeing him again.

Then early one morning Augustin arrived at the shop, not dressed for a day's hunting as she had seen him at breakfast, but for travelling well-armed. She took him into her office out of earshot of her assistant and he broke the bad news to her.

"A messenger failed to find me at home and was directed to the meet. The dragoons have been billeted in my father's house. In spite of his having armed his servants they took over and he is being brutally treated, a prisoner in his home. At the time the messenger left yesterday two of the menservants were dead. I have to leave at once."

"You're not going alone!"

"Be reassured. I have Georges, Charles and Eric with me, all good Huguenot swordsmen with military experience like myself."

She knew their names, for they had been involved in

previous sorties with him. "Shall you bring your father back with you?"

"That's unlikely. Things are no longer safe enough here. As soon as I've assessed the situation there I'll know what to do."

"Take care," she implored when he had kissed her. It was the hardest parting she had ever known. She went out into the street to watch him ride off and a terrible premonition settled on her.

At Versailles Susanne was entering the Council Chamber, having been summoned there by the King. He greeted her in a friendly manner, although he became grave when she admitted she had made no progress in winning Augustin into becoming a convert.

"I have been in no haste," he pointed out, severe but benign. "You have had plenty of time to use gentle persuasion." He thought how effectively Françoise had won him round to fidelity and atonement. There were several Huguenot waiting women in his wife's apartment, but they were of no consequence at all, having no influence, and doubtless Françoise would bring them round in her own good time. She had shown an intense dislike of the Marquis de Louvois, listening but not commenting whenever he was praised for the great number of conversions he had achieved.

"Perhaps you will grant me another month or two, sire," Susanne requested urgently. "I may not have used the right approach."

"Surely you could have achieved anything you wished in the time you've already been allowed."

His eyes were like those of an eagle on her, penetrating and unblinking. Her cheeks hollowed. There had been something in his tone that made her realise that somehow he had surmised that Augustin was the father of her second son. All the old tales of the King having supernatural powers came to her, but she dismissed them. Augustin had told her that Louis had spies everywhere and never to write in a letter anything that she did not want known.

"Monsieur Roussier may be persuaded yet," she said, trying to gain another respite for him. "Another good talk could easily tip the balance."

"I agree. You have paved the way and it is up to me to lend my weight to save this otherwise excellent courtier from his heretical beliefs. If he fails to heed my wisdom he shall be confined to a seminary until such time as enlightenment dawns."

She was aghast. "You are having him arrested?"

Louis looked displeased. "Not at all. His freedom would be curtailed to give him the maximum benefit of lectures and instruction. You see, madame, to gain Monsieur Roussier as a convert would be a great influence for good. Where he leads others would follow. I only need his assurance that he will obey my wishes. I do not wish to see him deprived of his liberty."

"You're making an example of him!"

Louis frowned ominously. "Not yet. If the seminary should fail, the Bastille would do that."

She left with but one thought in her head, which was to warn Augustin immediately. Louis, guessing this, was not disturbed. Roussier had never struck him as being particularly religious, far more a man of the flesh than of the spirit, and unlikely to cling to the remnants of heresy when faced with the alternative of defying his King. With such a nobleman, loyalty would always come first. Louis was complacent as he waited for the next person to be shown in to him. He had chosen to believe that the conversions pouring in on the lists Louvois sent him were coming about by the moderate methods he was using towards Roussier. He had perfected to the full the ability to ignore whatever he did not want to know.

Susanne searched everywhere in the Château where she thought Augustin might be. She even went down the flight of more than a hundred steps to the site of the new Orangery, knowing that the courtiers often went to see how the work was progressing. Eventually she arrived at Marguerite's shop. It was the first time they had come face to face for a long time, the meeting a traumatic experience for both of them.

"I've been trying to find Augustin," Susanne explained quickly. "He has to be warned. If he doesn't convert, he'll be under arrest."

"He isn't here." Marguerite was seized by a new alarm to add to her existing worry about his safety. "He's gone to his father at Le Havre. The dragoons are there."

"When do you expect him back?"

"Not for three days at least." Marguerite gestured nervously. "How urgent is the situation?"

"Nothing can be done until he returns. Then the King has to speak to him before any steps are taken."

Marguerite gave a faint sigh of relief. "That will give him a respite in which to decide what to do. Can we not be friends again now, Susanne?"

Susanne blanched and drew away to the door. "No, Marguerite. Never." Abruptly she turned and went out, almost at a run as if it had hurt her to reject a generous attempt to heal the breach. As the coach bore her to Paris she worked out all she must do in the hours ahead. She would make a brief halt at her residence and then set off with an escort of armed menservants for Le Havre to warn Augustin not to return to Versailles. She had no fear of the dragoons, who were in the service of the King and indirectly for her protection, however much she and many other Catholics abhorred their brutal methods. Her only fear was the highwaymen that lurked to waylay travellers on the road by night.

No sooner had Susanne left the shop than Marguerite went from it herself to the workshop of Pierre Ouinville. When Augustin's rescue work had first been discussed between them she had learned that Pierre was an active agent and one whom she could trust at any time of crisis. She found him at his loom and he stood up at once, able to see by her expression that something was gravely wrong.

"What has happened, mademoiselle?"

Quickly she explained the situation. "Can you ride after Monsieur Roussier?" she asked urgently. "He should be warned."

He had already reached for his jacket. "Monsieur Roussier and his companions have a head start, but I have the use of a fast horse and I'll follow one of the routes across country that I know well and waylay them at some point."

Without even bidding her farewell he was gone and she returned to her shop. Throughout the rest of the day she found it hard to concentrate on the work in hand and it was a relief to her when closing time came and she was able to go home. She had not been long indoors when there was a clatter of hooves in the drive and Pierre was shown into the salon where she sat. She sprang up from her chair, her question in her anxious eyes. He smiled reassuringly and she released a thankful sigh.

"I delivered the warning, mademoiselle. I have a message for you in return. In view of this new development the time has come for you and Monsieur Roussier to leave France. I'm to escort you without delay to a meeting place on the coast near Le Havre. It's a hostelry known as the Lys d'Or. Monsieur Roussier will be there with his father by the time you arrive and there will be a ship to England."

She nodded composedly. Augustin had prepared her for any emergency and she knew exactly what she had to do. "If you are to ride with me you must have some food and rest. Meanwhile I shall pay off the servants and close the house. Every one of them has an escape route already arranged by Monsieur Roussier as you probably know, and it will not take me long to be ready."

The servants gathered in the kitchen to receive the purses of money that Augustin had kept ready in the vault from which Marguerite had taken them. Some of the women shed a few tears that the time for flight had come, but they wasted no time in taking out the dustsheets to cover the furniture while the men went to secure doors and shutters. Only the two cooks remained in the kitchen, making up packages of food for the individual journeys. Marguerite returned to the vault where she burned certain papers as Augustin had instructed her and took others to pack in her saddlebags. Then she locked the vault and closed it away again behind its panel. Everything was ready. Previously she had prepared Lucille for taking over the shop in an emergency and it would be in good hands.

Farewells were said and the servants departed, taking the dogs and the horses with them, only the two fastest mounts being left for Marguerite and Pierre. He was sleeping soundly and the château was strangely silent as she paused in the hall, thinking it was not unlike her first visit when she had broken the silence of the new house with her excited talk and laughter. She supposed this was the last time she would ever be under this roof, for even when Louis was gone the Dauphin was too unimaginative to do anything but follow the path that his father had laid down. She and Augustin would be exiles forever from France and this house where they had known such happiness. Deep in her heart, not to be acknowledged until the time came, was the belief that in their country of refuge Augustin would marry her, for there would be nothing from their old life to keep them apart any longer.

Sustained by this thought she was better able to leave the Château Satory that was the home she would always love. Side by side she and Pierre rode away down the drive and out through the gates on the start of their long journey to the coast.

Augustin and his companions arrived at the outskirts of the Manoir when it was still night. They left their tired horses, which they had changed regularly along the route, and went with swords in hand to scout out the lay of the land. He led the way through a hidden entrance into the grounds that he had used often as a boy. As he had expected, the dragonnade guards were dozing at their posts by the main gates and these were swiftly and silently despatched by Charles and Georges. The same act took place by the stable gates and the danger of any alarm being raised was safely removed. There was no way of knowing how many dragoons were in the area outside the boundary walls, but with luck these would not be alerted. It was unlikely that they were encamped anywhere near, for it was customary for them to be billeted wherever they could cause the maximum distress to the Protestant inhabitants.

With anger Augustin saw that the pavilion where all financial matters had been conducted was burnt out, a still-smoking shell. He did not doubt that it had been looted first. Ahead lay the Manoir, standing high against the fast-fading stars. His guess was that he would find it occupied by the officer in charge and those nearest him in rank, for it was the custom for the best mansion in the district to be commandeered for this purpose.

Augustin had no need of light as he led the way, every inch of the gardens familiar to him, and when they reached the Manoir he guided his companions through thick bushes to a secluded door that led down into a passageway through the cellars. The key was hidden in a crevice in the wall and the lock turned easily, being always kept oiled for any Huguenot agent to come or go. Inside the passage he took a lantern from a hook and lit it, the rays

leaping over the grey stone walls with doorways and archways leading into the cellars.

With swords ready they looked into every room as they
passed, for if Gérard was being kept prisoner he could be
in this part of the house as well as anywhere else. The wine
cellars had been ransacked and in places the flagstones
glistened with spilt wine.

They came to one of the heavy doors which, unlike the
rest, was locked. Hopeful of finding his father inside, Augustin turned the large key that had been left in place and
pushed the door wide. Immediately there came a strange
whimpering and scurrying as if the place was full of mice.
As he stepped forward through the door, lantern in one
hand and sword in the other, a demented screaming broke
out. The lantern revealed a pathetic sight. At least a dozen
women, all of them household servants, were huddled together in a corner, clinging to one another in what they
believed to be the face of death. Their clothes were torn
and bloodstained from assault, bruises on their faces and
half-exposed breasts. One young kitchen-maid, no more
than twelve years old, appeared to have lost her wits in her
distress, for she sat laughing hysterically.

"Quiet!" he urged. "Don't be afraid! You know me as
well as you know my father!"

They were like madwomen in an asylum, scattering as
he approached them and it took several minutes before he
and his companions could convince the women that they
were not the dragoons returning to rape again and then
murder them. Then the scene went almost as wild, for the
women clung to Augustin like limpets, sobbing and beg-
ging that he should take them away to safety. Finally he
managed to calm them, a slap on the face by Charles silencing the little kitchen-maid, who then began to suck
her thumb, curled up by one of the women.

"I can do nothing for you unless you help as well," he
said to them. "Where is my father being held prisoner?
And how many dragoons are there in the house?"

Several began to weep. It was like a prescience of doom.
He felt the colour in his face recede. One woman an-
swered him tearfully. "He is dead, sir. Late yesterday.
They threw his body out by the midden."

Grief ran like ice through his veins. Charles pressed his

hand sympathetically on Augustin's shoulder and spoke for him to the woman. "Who was responsible?"

"The officer in command."

"His name?"

"Capitaine Le Pelletier. He that hates Huguenots. The menservants were tortured before being put to the sword. Some who recanted were locked in the stable loft, but not before the dragoons had had their obscene sport with them." Her throat became choked. "We were made to watch."

Augustin clenched his jaw. His voice was rigid and without expression. "Is Le Pelletier in the house?"

"Yes, sir. He is sleeping in your father's bedchamber."

He then established there were four other officers in the house and in which rooms they would be found. Telling the women to stay where they were, he led his men along to some steps up to the great kitchens and on towards the door into the central hall. He could guess at Stefane Le Pelletier's satisfaction in wreaking this vengeance on the father of the man who stood between him and the woman he wanted.

The flicker of a candle running along the floor beneath the hall door warned that a guard might be stationed in the hall. Using the element of surprise, he thrust the door wide and all four of them rushed forward. Two guards were present, the one awake sprang up from a bench with a yell, rousing his comrade. Both were run through in a matter of minutes, but overhead there was a rush of movement and doors crashed open as the four dragonnade officers, breeches pulled on and shirts awry, appeared from different directions, swords in hand. Stefane, standing at the head of the stairs, grinned malevolently as he recognised Augustin at the foot of the flight.

"So it's you, Roussier! Let's see what your sword-arm can do now. I've had plenty of experience running my sword through Huguenot guts since I left Versailles. You'll find me more than a match for you!"

"We'll see!"

Augustin led the charge up the stairs. The dragoons had the advantage at first, but then the Huguenot swordsmen fought their way onto the gallery. Curses and grunts of effort and the clash of steel resounded as the fighting surged relentlessly to and fro along the gallery. Augustin and Stefane, fighting with fury and hatred, lunged and parried and sidestepped, their swords ringing out and flashing back the first pink flush of dawn penetrating the windows. Augustin could feel himself tiring. With a sleepless night in the saddle, he was fighting a much younger man refreshed by a sound sleep, but the frenzied outrage he felt at the ignominious death of a dignified and devout man conquered the aching in his arm and shoulder muscles as he plunged on, fighting as he had done on many previous clashes with the enemy and on the battlefields of his youth. Suddenly Stefane gave a kind of strangled gasp and fell clumsily to his knees.

"You have me!"

He was mortally wounded, blood spouting from his chest. Even as Augustin drew back a step Stefane fell forward on his face and life went from him.

Augustin spun round to join in the rest of the fighting only to find it ending. Three of the dragonnade officers were dead and the fourth had surrendered. There were some minor wounds but nothing that some quick binding up would not suffice for the time being. The surviving dragoon had his wrists tied with a cord from bedhangings and was left gagged and roped to the post. The women, who had crept into the hall to watch, clustered forward as Augustin came down the stairs.

"Go to your quarters and find clothes to make yourselves decent. Then wait for me here. Those of you who are able, I ask that you find clean linen and lay out my father. I have learned from the captive officer that it is another two hours before the guards change. In that time I shall get away any of you who wish to leave France for refuge in England. The rest shall have a purse of gold to go home to their families or wherever they believe they will be safe."

He left Charles and Georges to open the stable gates in readiness for the general exodus and to unlock the door of the stable loft, releasing those who were imprisoned there. At the midden he and Eric found the body of Gérard Roussier lying face down in the mud. Gently Augustin turned him over. The curiously twisted expression on the face made him hope that a sudden stroke had spared his father the greater part of pain. Both hands had crushed fingers and an arm appeared to be broken. Lifting his father's body up he carried him into the Manoir. While the women did their work, Augustin went to the secret vault in the house where he filled his saddlebags with gold and the family jewellery. There was gold in plenty for his comrades-in-arms and a purse for every servant as he had promised.

Then the late master of the Manoir was borne out to where a grave had been dug near a rose arbour by the released menservants, who were themselves a pitiable sight. The burial took place, prayers were said and leaves scattered over the grave to protect it from possible desecration when the rest of the dragonnade troops discovered what had happened during the last hours of darkness.

Every one of the menservants and the two stableboys opted for escape, their temporary conversions revoked, but only two women wished to leave France, one of them prepared to take the kitchen-maid with her since the child had no family. The rest left, going home to the outlying farms from which they had come originally.

In the stables, those ready for escape saddled horses, the men taking the women pillion, Georges in charge. Eric and Charles were keeping watch at the front and back of the Manoir respectively. Augustin, taking a last look around his childhood home, was about to leave to join those at the stables when Charles entered the hall to give the alarm, the opened door letting a ray of early sunlight slant across the slain guards.

"There's a coach approaching!"

Rushing to the nearest window, Augustin recognised the coach coming from the shelter of the plane trees that lined the long drive. "It's Madame de Fresnay! I'll not let her into the house. Leave by the back way and ride with the refugee party. Georges knows where the ship is waiting."

"I'll do that. Good luck!"

"And to you."

Augustin waited until the coach was almost at the steps. Then he withdrew the key from the door and went outside to lock it after him. Susanne alighted as soon as the wheels stopped. To his astonishment he saw that the twins and his son were asleep in the coach.

"I've been travelling through the night," she greeted him before turning to supervise the helping out of her children.

"Wait!" He held up his hand. "I'm afraid I can't offer you

any hospitality. I've just closed the Manoir and all the servants have been sent away."

She looked bewildered. "But my servants are tired. They must have food and rest. Where—" She was about to ask the whereabouts of his father, who had been so gracious and welcoming to her when she had visited before, but fierceness in Augustin's glance alerted her to something being thoroughly amiss. She amended her question. "Where can refreshment be had?"

"Well, there's nothing in the Manoir," he lied, ushering her back into the coach, "but there's an excellent hostelry a few miles along the road. We'll all take refreshment there."

He gave the coachman instructions and took a seat beside Susanne. Edmund, rubbing his eyes sleepily, climbed onto his knees.

"What's happening?" Susanne wanted to know. "I came to tell you not to return to Versailles. The King is planning your arrest."

"Certain events have taken place that prevent my return in any case," Augustin replied, keeping a wary eye as the coach approached the main gates. As yet there was no sign of the new guard. "My father is dead. Murdered by the dragoons. My life will be next on the list."

"Oh, how dreadful!" She was doubly distressed. Her daughter snuggled close to her as if to comfort.

"Did you fight them, sir?" Jean-Paul asked from the corner seat.

Augustin looked questioningly at the boy. "Why do you ask?"

"There's blood on your cuff."

Then he saw an emergency bandage had soaked through, allowing a trickle of blood to seep under his cuff. Susanne promptly tore a strip from her petticoat and rebound it, asking no questions in front of the children. "I'll do better when we get to the hostelry," she promised.

The coach left the grounds of the Manoir and turned away down the road. The new guards had not appeared when the gates were lost to sight. Augustin judged there were still a few minutes in hand.

Marguerite and Pierre rode through the night. She found him to be a cheerful and very efficient companion.

Horses were changed regularly and although she wanted to go on without stopping he insisted that she snatch some rest at a Huguenot house where they were given food. She only dozed for half an hour, but it refreshed her.

It was noon when they came to a little fishing village near Le Havre. A fresh salty wind was blowing off the sea and it flapped her cape like a sail as she and Pierre approached the ancient Lys d'Or. Augustin was in the forecourt watching for her and they waved to each other as she quickened her horse to cover the remaining distance. He ran to help her dismount and she almost fell into his arms.

"Are you exhausted?" he asked with concern.

She shook her head happily, holding on to him. "I was well looked after, although I begrudged the resting time. I wanted to get to you as soon as possible. I'm so thankful you're safe."

"Come inside. I've much to tell you."

He took her up the stairs to a bedchamber with low black beams under which he had to dodge his head. She wanted nothing to eat, but coffee was brought to them. Over it he told her all that had happened and broke the news that Stefane was dead.

"So we must leave France as soon as possible," she said meditatively. "My greatest sadness is for your father."

"My darling." His voice was full of grief. "You can't come with me."

She stared at him in disbelief. "I'm not afraid to go. I've nothing to leave behind. I only want to be with you. Am I to follow later?"

He shook his head, despair wrenching at his face. "No. Although I intended that we should be together when I asked Ouinville to bring you here. But now—now Susanne is coming with me. She is in this village at another inn. When she came to warn me that the King planned my arrest, she brought the children with her in readiness to leave for England with me."

Marguerite rose slowly from the oaken table at which they were sitting. It was as if her limbs had suddenly stiffened, for she went jerkily across to gaze unseeingly out of the window in the direction of the sea. "Why have you made this choice?"

He came to stand behind her, holding her arms in a

gentle caress. "Edmund is my son. I wanted him to bear
my name. With mixed marriages forbidden, I married Susanne secretly a few hours after Jacques was buried."

It was as if madness possessed her then. She spun about
and lashed out at him, shrieking and crying. He tried to
contain her blows and hit his head on a beam as he dodged
them. After that he seized her wrists while she still tried to
pummel her fists against his chest. He kept holding her
until eventually the spasm passed and she sank hopelessly
against him.

"Why didn't you tell me before?"

"And lose you? You told me long ago in your parents'
cottage that you would never share me with a wife I cared
anything about. Susanne has always been dear to me and
you have known it. What I felt for her has never touched
my love for you, but you would never have stayed with me
if you had known I had married her."

"You're losing me now by your own will," she accused
spiritedly.

"If Susanne had not wanted to come with me I would
have taken you as we always planned. But she is my wife,
the mother of my son, and wants to go with me into exile."

"How was she able to tolerate sharing you with me?"

"There was never any sharing." He drew her forward by
the shoulders to bury his lips in her rich red hair, his face
contorted with the agony of having to leave her, this
woman who was the other half of himself and always
would be. "Since those few days with Susanne when I
thought I had lost you to Le Pelletier, there has been
nothing between us. She accepted that you were the mainstay of my very existence."

She leaned back to look into his sad eyes. "You knew that
eventually the truth would come out."

"I had hoped it to be a long way off, and that by then I
should have made it impossible for you to be able to leave
me."

She closed her eyes wearily, resting her head against his
shoulders. They had been together for less than five years
and must face the rest of their lives without each other. He
began to talk of the provision he had made for her future,
but she could not concentrate, her thoughts running along
their own hurt and shattered path. No matter how much
time might have elapsed, it would have made no differ-

ence to her original decision. Once she had thought she could share him in a loveless marriage but now, as then, she knew she could not stay in the background of a wife for whom he had genuine fondness. Susanne loved him too much herself, and if this flight to England had never come about she would have found some way to exert her rights.

"How long have we left together?" she asked almost inaudibly.

"The ship leaves with the tide. There's an hour to go."

With trembling fingers she reached up and loosened his cravat. Then she began to unhook her own gown. "Once more," she whispered yearningly.

He made love to her for the last time and with worshipping passion that let no part of her escape his caresses or his kisses as he absorbed her into his memory to retain her there forever. At the climax of their final ultimate ecstasy she hoped that out of those precious moments she would gain the child she had always wanted by him.

From the bed she watched him dress again, his movements slow with sorrow. When he was ready she pulled the sheet about her naked body and left the bed for his farewell embrace. Once more their kisses were both tempestuous and tender.

"I love you, Marguerite," he declared again in a blurred voice, "as I've never loved any other woman or ever will. You are and always will be my own, the first in my heart."

Footsteps had come running up the staircase and a fist banged on the door. "Monsieur Roussier!" Pierre Ouinville's voice urged. "You should come now. It's almost sailing time."

Augustin went to the door and opened it slightly. "I'm leaving now. Wait downstairs to escort Mademoiselle Dremont back home again."

"Yes, sir."

As the man's footsteps clattered down again Augustin turned back to Marguerite, leaving the door ajar. She had gone to the table on which lay her drawstring purse containing her jewellery and other valuables. Out of it she took the Versailles fan that bore her name and pressed it into his hand.

"Take this memento once again. It kept me in your mind before and it will do so again. Maybe one day you'll have a granddaughter. Give it to her as a keepsake of France.

That will not hurt anybody and it will ever be a link between us." She saw he was too full in the throat to answer her, all his adoration in his eyes, and she took his beloved face gently between her hands and kissed him again, he responding with passion and despair. Each knew it was the last kiss they would ever share.

"Farewell, my darling Marguerite," he said brokenly.

At the door he turned to gaze tormentedly at her as if to hold this final image of her ever more. It was all she could do not to throw herself at his feet in a final bid to stay him. Then he closed the door and she remained standing exactly where she was, quite motionless, long after his footsteps had gone from her hearing. At last she sat down slowly on the edge of the bed and rested her head back against its carved post in deepest desolation, having no will to move and heedless of time.

On board Susanne waited with the children in the cramped and crowded quarters below deck. The ship was full of Huguenot refugees, not only those from the Manoir, but others fleeing to sanctuary on English shores. She began to be afraid he was not coming, that somehow Marguerite had found a way to keep him, but as the sails billowed and the ship began to surge away from the quayside he came down the companionway. Almost at once she saw that some irrevocable change had taken place in him. It was as if he had become a completely different man. Then she knew it was she and not Marguerite who had lost him. The only bond left between them was through their son. Out of his love for the child he would be kind to her, would take care of her, but his heart had been left behind in France.

Nine

Afterwards Marguerite could remember nothing of the journey back to Versailles. It was as if from the moment of parting with Augustin she was in a terrible nightmare from which there was no awakening. Pierre was again her escort. When he had seen her into the Château Satory he went to fetch Lucille as Augustin had instructed him, for he had not wanted her to be long on her own there.

Alone in the silent house Marguerite moved as if in a daze into the Ivory Salon where she opened the shutters before sinking down into one of the shrouded chairs. Augustin had told her to read the documents she would find left in the saddlebags after he had taken what he wanted with him. It gave her some purpose in the midst of her shattered existence, almost as though she were clinging to a lifeline to save herself from going under, and she had taken them from the saddlebags that Pierre had deposited in the hall. Unfolding the documents she began to read them. By the time she reached the end of them her state of shock had not abated, but her blood began to stir again.

When Lucille arrived she found Marguerite, still pale and somehow a mere wraith of herself, going from room to room removing the dustsheets.

"Help me," Marguerite exclaimed at once. "As a precaution I have to make it appear as if I haven't been away from here. By now Augustin will have been missed from Court, especially if the King has summoned him, and that means the soldiers may come at any time."

Lucille did not waste time in any questioning. She moved swiftly into action, folding dustsheets, opening shutters and windows and unlocking doors. When all was done Marguerite changed out of her travelling clothes, dashed rose water into her face and tied back her hair with a fresh ribbon. Then she went in search of Lucille and found her in the kitchen. In the hasty departure some food had been left and Lucille had prepared a simple meal out of what she had found in the pantries. Wearily Marguerite sat down at the long wooden table and took a sip of the wine that had been poured.

"Augustin has given me Château Satory." Her voice was jerky as if it were an effort to speak. "Unbeknown to me he signed it over as a deed of gift some while ago when he made provision for my future in case anything happened to him. I suppose Pierre told you that he has gone to England with his wife."

Lucille's face was full of compassion. "Yes, he did."

"There are monies to go with the property, enough to keep me in style here until I make a good marriage." Still her voice was toneless. "That is in keeping with a bargain struck between Augustin and my mother when I was born. Neither of them counted on one thing, which is that I shall never marry."

Lucille refrained from any advice that time could heal. The loneliness of being without the man she had loved had never left her. "The upkeep of this château must be enormous. Shall you be able to manage financially as time goes by?"

"I'll shut up part of it and live modestly. On the way back from the coast Pierre and I reclaimed my horses from the hostelry where we first changed mounts and they will draw my calèche. One maidservant should suffice and I'll hire daily women to cook and scrub and do the laundry."

Lucille felt obliged to offer good counsel. "This place

would fetch a fortune if you put it up for sale. Surely a smaller dwelling would be better for you?"

The waxen immobility of Marguerite's face gave way to a fervent, almost angry expression and she shook her head vigorously. "No! Never, I tell you! I loved this château from the moment I set foot in it and I've known happiness here such as I shall never experience again, however long I may live. It was Augustin's gift to me and under this roof I'll draw my last breath. Nobody shall ever take Château Satory from me!"

Swiftly Lucille held up a hand to show that she intended no more argument. "Did you make all these plans on the way home from the coast?"

Marguerite's strength seemed to ebb again and she gave a deep sigh. "No. I didn't know the place was mine until I returned here. Was it only little more than an hour ago? It seems like years already." She broke off as a bell jangled and a distant knocking could be heard, demanding swift admittance. She jumped up from the bench. "It must be the soldiers! Quick! Go into the Ivory Salon and sit there. Light the fire. Find a book. Anything to look as if our peaceful domesticity is being interrupted by these unwanted callers."

Lucille did as she was bidden. Marguerite, glancing about to reassure herself that all was in order, set her shoulders and went to fling the entrance door wide. On the steps stood an officer of the musketeers, a small band of his men waiting in the forecourt.

"Good day, mademoiselle. I'm here to see Monsieur Augustin Roussier. The King summons him to his presence."

"He is not here."

"Where is he to be found?"

"To the best of my knowledge, not in France. He left Versailles in great haste for the coast. By my reckoning he should be in England by now."

"That is your tale. I'm here to search for him. Stand aside."

She did not move, continuing to block his way. "I'm a Catholic. This is my property. Nobody may enter the Château Satory without my permission."

The officer eyed her cynically. "Have you proof of ownership?"

"Wait here." She was gone only a matter of minutes to

fetch the appropriate documents out of Augustin's desk where she had put them for the time being.

After the officer had perused them he handed the documents back to her. He had to be careful in this sort of case. The King did not care to hear of Catholics being offended or arrested by mistake. Amending his tone to one of extreme politeness, he turned his previous order into a request. "I ask your permission, Mademoiselle Dremont, to search Château Satory in order to make a full and satisfactory report."

"I am alone here with a woman companion. If you enter, it must be without violence or damage."

"You have my word."

The musketeers made their search, tramping everywhere upstairs and down. Marguerite and Lucille sat on either side of the fire in the Ivory Salon and waited for the intruders to leave. When the officer finally came to find her before departure Marguerite was well prepared for his question.

"Why do you have no servants here?"

"They were Monsieur Roussier's servants before this house became mine. When he left they were all dismissed. I'm a law-abiding citizen and could not employ Protestant staff."

He gave a nod, not disputing her words. It was logical that with her lover gone she would make a clean sweep. The fact that she had not attempted to go with him showed that her private loyalties remained steadfastly with the King. "I thank you for granting us admission. The search is being continued in the grounds as a matter of routine, but you will not be disturbed again, mademoiselle."

She shut the door after him and his men. When she failed to reappear in the Ivory Salon Lucille went to look for her. She found Marguerite standing pressed against the door she had closed as if suddenly all physical strength had drained from her. As Lucille approached, Marguerite turned around, her expression blended of triumph and despair.

"I hope I'm with child, Lucille! I want to bear Augustin's son in this house!"

There was no child. When disappointment dawned and the last rays of hope faded Marguerite turned to her business as never before. With nothing else to distract her, she began to channel all her energies towards her fans and her ribbons, working long hours by day and by night. She showed no interest in anything else. It had long been a source of pride to her that her business had given her a modest income on which she could have lived independently if she had wished and now it was almost as if she wanted to compete with the Château Satory itself. Having sought financial advice from a reliable banker she had set aside an amount to cover the household expenses and used no more. Her existence became a strange one, for she lived in a part of the château that had the least association with her memories of Augustin. Her bedchamber had been one of the minor guest rooms and her drawing room one of the smaller salons. Few business callers came to the château, but those who did were received in the Ivory Salon. As soon as it had become known that Augustin had gone to England, a number of courtiers called in turn to proposition her, thinking to take his place, and were all shown the door immediately. It did not take long before she was left in peace again.

Until the word spread among the Huguenot community that Château Satory had changed hands she sheltered a number of refugees. They announced their presence by tapping at her lighted window when she was downstairs and giving the persistent hoot of an owl by night. She was familiar with the signals since the time Augustin had taken her into his confidence and she followed the same procedure of guiding the refugees through the cellars and up to the attics. She had no problem with security, for although the maidservant was a good worker, she was not very intelligent and snored her nights away at the far end of the château. The local women only came in for a few hours a day and Marguerite cooked for the refugees herself.

The atrocities had not eased. Some people who came to the château had *H* for *Huguenot* branded into their flesh or had had other red-hot irons applied to their bodies. One man died of his wounds in the attics and had to be buried by his fellow refugees in a wooded part of the grounds where the gardener never went. When those in flight were in need of fresh clothes Marguerite drew on Augustin's wardrobe or gave from her own. She kept a supply of small toys on hand for the children and would willingly have given a home to several little ones who were orphaned if it had been possible. Then, although the Huguenots' exodus from France did not cease, fewer came to Château Satory until eventually the flow ceased altogether.

The Revocation of the Edict of Nantes had far-reaching effects that Louis had not foreseen. His action was condemned abroad, several Catholic nations coming out against him. Elsewhere in Europe Protestant countries and states joined in a treaty against him and before long France was surrounded by enemies. Louis, confident that his armies were supreme, lost no sleep over it. He had another building project on his mind.

"I built Versailles for the Court," he said to Françoise, "and Marly for my friends. Now I need a retreat for myself."

"Where is that to be?" she enquired, looking up from her sewing of an altar cloth. All France knew now that she was the King's wife, for it had distressed her to learn that she was being regarded as his new mistress and to please her he had duly let it be known that their marriage had taken place.

"On the site of the Porcelain Trianon. There shall be another Trianon of marble for my use alone. There you and I will spend tranquil hours together."

She bent her head over her work again. There could never be any real peace in the company of this vigorous, demanding man with his delight in the open air, always wanting to be out in it or else throwing windows wide, even in the most bitter winter weather. It never occurred to him that she or anyone else might be vulnerable to draughts, or travel-weary, or unwell. If he wanted company everyone had to be up and go to suit his wishes. Yet she could understand his wish for a retreat from Court. It had only to be whispered that he was considering going to Marly for the corridors to be lined with courtiers all anxious to accompany him there. "Marly, sire?" each would say as he went by. If he nodded they knew the coveted invitation was theirs; if ignored, they suffered keen disappointment.

The lovely little Trianon palace, with its pink marble pilasters and a graceful colonnade, was finished just three years after the signing of the Revocation. In September the following year Louis took France into a war that put an end to the excavations at the Eure River. The troops left the dangers of fevers there to face perils to which they were more accustomed under Louvois's command.

Marguerite's range of cheaper fans sold well as departing soldiers bought keepsakes for their wives and sweethearts. When Clarisse reported that courtiers, also off to war, showed that they were looking for something more costly than her fans, however pretty they might be, Marguerite knew the time had come to invest in a new line of fans.

Within the next few days she consulted her financial adviser, talked with a number of jewellers and goldsmiths, and examined Lille and Valenciennes and Flemish laces, looking for the best that money could buy. When everything was settled and designs for these new and expensive fans began to be made under Lucille's expert direction, Marguerite went into the Crimson Salon where Augustin's portrait hung above the fireplace. It was in this salon that they had first sat down to a meal together and had joked about being served by invisible hands. She had not entered it since the day after her return from the coast when she had replaced the dustsheets and locked it up in her dividing off of the house.

She went first to fold back the shutters and let the light pour into the beautiful room. It was with effort that she turned her head from where she stood and, rimmed with light from the window behind her, looked towards the portrait. In the same instant she clapped a hand over her mouth to keep back the huge choking sob that threatened to break from her throat and trigger off the tears that after the first few empty days she had resolved never to shed again. Although she had been prepared for anguish, she thought that work and more work had dulled her sensibilities and during these four years without him she had become resigned to her solitary state. The force of her love racked her. Almost without being aware of it she was drawn to stand in front of the portrait and gaze on the face of the man gone from her life. Through a trick of the artist's brush he appeared to be looking directly at her.

"I know you are in London." Her whisper sounded loud in the shrouded room. Only a few days ago her financial adviser had given her this scrap of news. "You are now a prosperous banker in Lombard Street. Here I have given you the chance at last to invest in my venture as you always wanted, although I had never expected it to come in these circumstances when you first asked me. I'm going to make the bejewelled and bepearled fans that I have been designing in readiness over a long period, hoping that the day would come. Your gold has opened the way for me. Just as it changed my life when you paid for a keepsake fan that bore my name on it."

Her voice faltered and failed her, but she straightened her shoulders as she turned away and left the room. After that the double doors were never locked and the Crimson Salon was kept in order. With time she would be able to take her meals there without dying a little whenever her eyes met those in the portrait. But that was a long way ahead.

Launching into such a costly new line presented a number of difficulties. Marguerite applied in writing for a stall in the vestibule and was told no names were being taken at the present time. These fans could not be sold from Clarisse's basket, for it would belittle their value and importance; in any case she had no wish to interrupt the steady flow of Clarisse's sales with a still-uncertain product. She displayed a few in her shop window, but the clientele for whom she aimed did not look for items of such value in a little fan and ribbon shop. Disaster struck when a pane was smashed and a thief grabbed the fans and fled. They were found later in a broken state with the jewels prised out of them.

After several months of outlay and disappointment, she drew further on her Château Satory funds and took a fat purse with her when she called on the official in charge of the vestibule. He greeted her and enquired after her business, expecting it to be a minor matter connected with her fan-seller. When she said she was prepared to pay a fee to get her name on the list for a stall he understood her immediately and all went well for them both. She secured her name at the top of the waiting list and he had the purse to put in his pocket, one of the perks that had long since benefited the post that he held.

Yet still she had to wait. He could not work miracles and produce space in the vestibule where none existed. Many months went by during which the shop kept her busy and her designing went well. With nothing else in life to distract her she laid up a full file of designs in readiness for the day when the birds and flowers and garlands, even scenes of balls and masques in the gardens of Versailles, could be carried out with the delicate use of pearls and rubies, sapphires and diamonds and emeralds.

Exactly two years after she had displayed her first jewelled fan in her shop window she was notified that stall space was now available. When she went to claim it she was delighted to find it was in a most advantageous position where it would be in full view of anyone going up or down the Queen's Staircase. When the stall was erected she had it dressed in a rose velvet cloth, the canopy lined with tinted silk.

The time of getting her stall could not have been more opportune. It coincided with news of a forthcoming marriage between the King's second bastard daughter by Athénaïs de Montespan and the young Duc de Chartres, it being Louis's policy that all his bastards should make a good match. Although the Court was grandly dressed from morning until night as etiquette decreed, this would be one of the great occasions when all would vie with one another more than ever to be the most elegantly clad and adorned with a whole fortune in jewels. On Marguerite's first morning in the vestibule her fans, sparkling out from a space previously occupied by a seller of rather dull paintings, were destined to draw the attention of those on the lookout for unique accessories. She had arrived early to make sure she had everything just as she wanted it.

"I do feel nervous," she admitted to Clarisse.

"Please don't be," the young woman said encouragingly. "I know exactly what to say and do when you give me the signal."

At that moment some early morning riders, returning from a canter, paused to view her wares with marked interest and said they would come back later. It seemed like the promise of success.

As soon as the Court was fully astir the busiest did not even give a glance from the stairway, but when the more leisurely began to appear there was a sudden cluster in front of the stall. It was then that Marguerite staked everything on the gamble she had planned. As arranged, before any sales were made, she beckoned Clarisse over to take her place. The young woman slipped her basket under the stall out of sight and began to answer the questions of would-be buyers.

"Yes, madame. That design could be made up with sapphires instead of rubies. Indeed, sir. Here is another with pearls."

Marguerite slipped away. She collected her jeweller in her carriage and went straight home to Château Satory. There she installed him in the Ivory Salon and went behind a locked door into the vault where she kept her stock of jewelled fans for security. Back in the Ivory Salon she made an arrangement of some of them on a side table and put the rest out of sight. Then she settled to wait. The minutes ticked by. The jeweller, who had put on his best coat, was a presentable man in his mid-thirties, untroubled by the waiting since he was being paid for the time away from his bench and also it could lead to much more of the fan-work that he particularly liked. He had opened the box he had brought with him and had a variety of precious and semiprecious stones laid out on silk-lined trays in front of him.

"Have I made a mistake, Monsieur Doignel?" Marguerite asked on a note of anxiety when an hour had gone by without result. She was banking on what Augustin had told her about the Court's ability to take up a whim of fashion and make it de rigueur.

"Allow them time, mademoiselle."

Hardly had Doignel given this advice when from the window she glimpsed a barouche bowling through the distant gates. She spun round in triumph. "At least one has come!"

"Then let's hope the rest will follow."

The first couple to be admitted by the young footman, whom Marguerite had employed recently with this occasion in mind, were a young marquis and his wife. Marguerite had seen them at the stall before she left. She received them as graciously as any well-bred hostess welcoming distinguished guests to her home. Immediately they were at ease, not having been quite sure what to expect, and they expressed surprise that the fans on display in the vestibule at the Château of Versailles were only samples and not for sale.

"What better than to select a fan in comfortable surroundings?" Marguerite replied, leading the way to the Ivory Salon. "This is my jeweller, Monsieur Doignel, who is here to show you a choice of stones for any special requirements."

The marquise went straight to the fans on display, delighted to have first choice. Marguerite nodded to the footman that it was time to bring in refreshments. No sooner had they been served than a second coach arrived and then a third. Since all those present happened to know one another, it became quite a conversational occasion. More people arrived and took the seats of those who had left, none departing without having purchased or given an order.

Marguerite took on extra hands to meet the demand and Doignel with his assistants worked all hours to get through the orders before the State Ball at the start of Shrovetide with the wedding the following day. By that time it had become the height of fashion to flutter a fan chosen amid the luxurious surroundings of the Château Satory.

Marguerite had soon found it necessary to open up all the ground-floor salons. Members of the Court made their visits a social event, not always buying, but that was not expected of them. They strolled about at leisure or sat together while sipping hot chocolate or coffee or some of the château's best wines. Since it was risky for women to smoke at Versailles, for somehow the King always seemed to find out about their secret smoking parties, they requested a salon at Château Satory where they might indulge their pleasure. Marguerite gave them the Garden Room, which could be shut away from the rest of the house. There amid the orange trees and palms and potted shrubs they puffed their long-stemmed pipes and gossiped to their hearts' content, the lacy *fontanges* they wore on their heads nodding like so many starched petals among the foliage.

There were gallants who came hoping to find a convenient place of assignation, but they soon realised that this was a handsome château in which business was conducted on elegant terms and nothing untoward was allowed. If people made private arrangements to meet among themselves that was entirely their own affair, but whatever the outcome it did not take place at Château Satory.

Marguerite began to hold concerts, entrée by invitation

only. Then she introduced a monthly salon where poems were read, new books discussed and lectures given on the new sciences. Before long it was almost as important to be seen at the Château Satory as it was at Marly. For this reason people settled their accounts for purchases and whatever refreshment they had imbibed on their visits without delay, for there was something about Mademoiselle Dremont that told them she would not tolerate debtors under her roof.

Those who remembered her in the company of Augustin Roussier thought how changed she was. There was a sober, tight-laced air about her, a withdrawn quality that put her at a distance even when she was smiling and at her most welcoming. She had become adept at turning aside amorous advances, and courtiers were neatly put in their places. Between themselves the gallants joked that either Roussier had locked her into a mediaeval chastity belt before his departure or her stays were so knotted as a precaution as to make them impossible for any male to untie. Yet behind their jokes there was pique, and often angry resentment, that this intriguing, fascinating woman, moving gracefully amid her patron-guests, should be impervious to their swashbuckling attractions.

Yet in reality she was not as immune as she would have had them believe. She was twenty-eight, had once experienced to the full the ardour of a passionate man and had made work a substitute for love ever since. There were times when her flesh cried out to be embraced, to know again the kisses and tender caresses of a lover, but although there were men who had interested her the encounters had been brief and without fulfilment. She was too wary and unhealed. Sometimes she wondered if she would ever be whole again.

Plenty of invitations came her way and she accepted those at which she could be sure the King would not be present. In gambling on the Court's obsession of being à la mode she had never expected to find herself an acceptable figure in society. It had happened to her just as it had to Françoise de Maintenon in the days when she had been the humbly born wife of the poet Scarron and had carved her own niche in the elitest circles. For her it had ended in marriage to a great king. Marguerite saw no marriage ahead for herself, for as she seemed to be incapable of bearing children even that benefit could not weigh the scales in making a match.

She devised a new line of portrait fans. These were painted on silk with the same techniques that her mother and her grandmother had used before her, but each one was unique in depicting the purchaser of the fan in some scene at Court. The first had not been commissioned. Marguerite painted a scene of the King riding off to his Flanders campaign in the company of several ladies honoured by his invitation to accompany him, and several of them recognised their own likeness on the leaf. As she had anticipated, this led to orders for a purchaser to be portrayed at a State Ball or at the hunt or, in the case of younger women new to Court, at their own weddings. This new line was catching on like wildfire when her fortune increased from an entirely unexpected source.

Her lawyer called to see her with the news that monies from the sale of the Manoir, which had once belonged to the Roussier family, together with its land and properties had been directed to her according to instructions laid down by Augustin over two years before his departure.

She protested strongly. "But he made those arrangements then in case anything should happen to him, such as imprisonment or some other fate. His father was getting old and since the property would have been Augustin's eventually, he simply included it at the same time. This money is his and must go to him in London!"

"Even if we were not at war with England that would not be possible," the lawyer replied. "Monies from Huguenot properties are forfeit to the Crown if there is no other legal claimant who is not, I hasten to add, of the Protestant faith. It is yours, mademoiselle." His face became grimmer than the severe expression normal to him. "Waste no pity on the Huguenots, mademoiselle. Most of them took the greater part of their fortunes with them and are thriving wherever they have settled."

She knew that apart from England and Holland they had settled in Geneva among other places, including several Catholic states, such as Genoa in Italy, which was among many that had voiced abhorrence of Louis's treatment of fellow Christians. It was said that nearly a quarter of a million Huguenots had fled the country. One of them had made her a very rich woman. The least she could do was to see that others benefited as well, and that meant giving as much employment as was possible to those in desperate need of work.

When the hatter's shop came up for sale she bought it and the buildings of the court behind, where she installed three jewellers in a workshop of their own, gave two large areas over to ribbon-making and the rest of the space to an increased number of fan-makers. Where once hats had been purchased there was a new décor and her fans were displayed to advantage. The old shop and the floors above it were altered to provide accommodation for some of her workers, many of them young country girls, thus giving them a homelike atmosphere in which to live. Whenever the Court was at Fontainebleau or elsewhere, she sent stock and reliable saleswomen to be on the spot. In Paris she opened a shop facing the wide avenue of the Champs-Élysées.

In 1697 there was another wedding of supreme importance when the son of the Grand Dauphin, the Duc de Bourgogne, married the captivating and mischievous Princesse Marie Adélaïde of Savoy. To Louis and Françoise she became a beloved granddaughter, bringing laughter into their private apartment where they spent more and more time together, he with his work, she with her sewing. Louis was beginning to show his age, and his waistcoat bulged as it had never done before. Although he continued to dominate the Court with his awe-inspiring presence and his code of etiquette that kept them all like puppets on strings, he was content that the young and lively among the nobility should set the social scene. The Court gave itself up to new heights of frivolity and debauchery, fostered its club for sodomites and danced into every kind of exciting and time-passing diversion that could be devised.

It did not please Louis when the war came to a somewhat indecisive end with the Treaty of Ryswick. Fortunately a source of consolation to him was the new chapel that Mansart was to build at Versailles. It was to be the final addition to his great Château, a glorious place of worship that would be a hymn of praise in itself with its huge proportions. In white and gold with multicoloured marble pavings, there would be beauty in every line, its graceful arches supporting a gallery with white columns soaring to a vaulted ceiling enhanced by paintings to the glory of God.

Work began. As if the clock had been turned back once again, there was a great confusion of scaffolding and winches, blocks of marble, earth from the vast foundations, stacks of slates and other materials, and a flock of workmen numbering hundreds. Mansart had as his assistant on this new project a fellow architect whose work he had long respected. One afternoon, when all was going well and they could take a little time to themselves, Mansart suggested that they visit Château Satory where there was always amiable company.

Marguerite, chatting with guests in the Ivory Salon, turned her head as the footman announced the new arrivals. She knew Jules Hardouin-Mansart from previous visits. His companion was instantly recognisable, although seventeen years had passed since their first and only meeting.

"Baron Picard!" She greeted him with an overwhelming sense of pleasure, associating him with Augustin and the happy time when she had first entered Château Satory and fallen in love twice over, once with the house and yet again with the man who owned it. "What a marvellous surprise! Welcome back to this house that you designed and built!"

"You remember me?" He was equally delighted, thinking her more beautiful as a mature woman in her mid-thirties than as the girl who had dazzled him on that summer evening, spinning around on the central star of the marble floor with the sun setting fire to her hair.

"I'd have known you anywhere, but it gladdens me that we should meet again here in this same place." She spoke the truth. He looked much older, the golden locks of the past replaced by a periwig of similar hue and, if anything, he had put on weight and was fuller in the face, but his smile was as friendly as ever and there was still the same kindness in the eyes. "Are you visiting Versailles?"

"I'm here for as long as it takes to build the new chapel for the King."

Her eyes widened. "So once again you are at work in this district. Is your wife with you? I'd be pleased if you would bring her to take supper here—"

He interrupted her. "I'm a widower."

"Oh, forgive me. My condolences." She was afraid she

had touched a raw nerve and showed it by the compassion in her face.

"I should be honoured to accept your kind invitation," he said quickly to ease the situation for her. She brightened and, still talking about her pleasure at their reunion, she led him to a group of people where presentations took place. She no longer charged for refreshments and the selling and buying of fans took place only once a week in the Ivory Salon. She found that she sold just as many and business was kept apart from the social routine that she had come to enjoy, for loneliness with its memories and heartache had to be kept at bay.

On the evening he was to take supper at Château Satory, Laurent Picard was aware of high expectation such as he had not experienced for a long time. Since he specialised in building country residences he had done a great deal of travelling over the years and it was his work on many fine private chapels that had resulted in Mansart's invitation to assist at Versailles. As soon as Marguerite's name had arisen in connection with Château Satory he had questioned Mansart about her and learned of her business success, that she was a rich woman and that her Huguenot lover was long gone.

Laurent had known sorrow himself, for he was a widower twice over, both his wives having died in childbirth, their infants expiring with them. From that time he had put marriage from him once and for all. He had an apartment in Lyons, which was his base more than a home, for he had no real interest in any place since his ancestral château had gone into other hands through his father's folly and been lost beyond recall. He had been faithful to both wives whom he had loved each in her own right, and these days he took a mistress wherever he happened to be for any length of time.

It was certain that the Royal Chapel would take at least ten years to complete down to the final gilding and the last stroke of an artist's brush. This meant he could expect to be in Versailles for a long span and then at intermittent intervals until the day of consecration. So it was not without hope of an amorous nature that he set off in his yellow periwig and a new brocade coat to have supper with Marguerite.

By the time he returned home he knew this was to be no

passing fancy on his part. He was already on the brink of falling in love with her at a far more serious level than he had anticipated. Marriage had taken the place of mere seduction in his mind.

Ten

At first Marguerite did not realise that Laurent was court-
ing her seriously. For her it was only friendship, a pleasant
state of affairs to enjoy when away from work and the
harassment of business. They had much in common, liking
the same kind of witty plays, never missing a concert of
Lully's music, and he appreciated the countryside as much
as she, a good companion whenever they went riding together. Most of all, it was his association with the happiest
time of her life and the man she had loved that gradually
began to break down her reserve. In addition he had built
the home that meant so much to her and that in itself gave
him an advantage over all other men who had tried in vain
to win her.

She found it increasingly pleasurable to be kissed by
him, long-dormant feelings set astir. She judged him to be
a passionate man keeping himself under tight restraint, not
wanting to ruin everything between them by making a
move too bold or too soon. He knew all about Augustin's
departure; she had told him enough to let him understand

that she could never love again in the same way. Fourteen years had gone by since she and Augustin had parted at the Lys d'Or, but it could have been yesterday, the pain healed, although not the aching in her heart.

At a realistic level, away from all the tender memories of Augustin, she began to see that she and Laurent, who was a mere eight years her senior, could enrich each other's lives in a physical relationship. She was only thirty-four, an active, healthy woman with all the natural desires that he had reawakened, and since they had both lost partners whom they had loved, it was possible that they could find consolation in each other's arms.

What she had not expected was Laurent's proposal of marriage on her thirty-fifth natal day. All along she had supposed that he had been looking for no more than to share her bed as soon as she felt so inclined.

"We can't marry!" she exclaimed, much put out by this unexpected turn of events. "The King would never approve such a match, and you would lose any chance of establishing yourself at Court!"

"I've told you before. The King sees me as Mansart's assistant architect and general overseer. I have no entrée at Court. There are thousands of noblemen like me all over the country who have neither the prestige nor the right connections to get a foothold there. Look at me!" He flung out his arms in display. "I'm a free man, able to come and go, unlike those poor popinjays at Versailles who must almost ask the King's permission before they can sneeze."

That made her smile and he saw he had made some progress. She was less rigid when she put her next question to him. "If you have no ambition at Court, would you still be agreeable to living near Versailles?"

"Yes, if that is what you wish." He could guess what she had in mind and spoke out. "I should be content to make Château Satory my home with you, if that is what you wanted to know."

The last barrier had gone. "Dear Laurent." She moved into his loving embrace. "I will marry you." They kissed and then she added almost wonderingly, "You've made a long-ago dream of mine come true. On the evening I first came here I wished I could be a bride within these walls. You were downstairs at the time."

"So you see, darling Marguerite, it was meant to be."

He knew well enough that she had not had him in her dreams at the time, but he did not let that spoil the moment for him.

As they had both anticipated their marriage proved to be a good one in that they were friends as well as husband and wife. Yet they had their problems, for it was in his nature to spoil the woman he loved, to cosset and protect her, whereas Marguerite was far too independent on that score. A placid man, amiable and tolerant, he did not lose his temper easily and although his feelings were often hurt by his wife's self-reliance, her tossing away some gesture he would have made, he did not quarrel with her for a long while. Then it came devastatingly to them both.

He had had his portrait painted on his fiftieth birthday. It showed him in a new green velvet coat and all agreed it was an excellent likeness. But when he wanted it to hang above the fireplace in the Crimson Salon, finally ousting Augustin Roussier from that place of honour, Marguerite seemed to lose her head.

"No, it can't go there! It would look just as well in the Blue Salon or the library. As for hanging the Roussier portrait in that upper corridor, I won't allow it."

His temper exploded. "I'll remind you that I'm master in this house and the removal of that portrait is long overdue!"

"And I'm mistress here!" she flashed at him. "Augustin was your patron. He built this château and was driven from it to a foreign land by the cruelties of the King. I will not let him be chased from this Crimson Salon where he chose to let his likeness hang."

"I have let you have your will in all matters up until now, but on this I shall not budge!"

After more heated words that would have been better left unsaid, revealing to him all too painfully how much the Huguenot still meant to her, they reached a compromise. His portrait was hung where he wanted it to be and the Roussier portrait rehung in a deep alcove in the Ivory Salon. Afterwards Laurent wondered if he should not have chosen that alternative himself, for the eyes of Augustin Roussier were now directed towards the portrait of Marguerite in her golden gown, which had hung above the fireplace in the Ivory Salon ever since it was painted.

Marguerite's newest shop locally was on the Avenue de

Paris. It was a grand mansion that had taken the place of Château Satory for fan-buying on an elegant scale. She had felt she owed it to Laurent that he should not always come home to find the château full of people. By playing hostess in the same way at the new site she gradually weaned away from her home all except those who had become their friends. Laurent made one floor of the new house his offices and another became an apartment rented to a courtier. In all it was a most satisfactory arrangement.

When Marguerite was forty-three and had been married to Laurent for eight years she discovered she was pregnant. Her joy at this late blessing was matched by Laurent's fear of losing her. She did her best to reassure him.

"I'm strong and well and nothing will happen to me. Don't be afraid, my dear. Let's look forward to this child of ours. There's every chance of arrival on my forty-fourth natal day. What could be better than that?"

Nothing she could say put his mind at rest. His past bereavements returned to haunt him and he fussed over her, seeing that she was waited on, urging her to put her feet up and generally harassing her with the best of intentions until finally she made a stand.

"No more! I'll expire beforehand if I'm treated like a hothouse flower any longer. Remember I'm of strong peasant stock and I shall take the birthing in my stride. Tomorrow I'm going to visit my workshops—and yes! I will be careful not to trip over anything."

She had once told him of the miscarriage she had suffered through slipping on the old workshop's flight of stairs. There were no secrets between them. Those she had not spoken of were known to him anyway, for he was too intelligent a man not to know her almost as well as she knew herself.

She went into labour on the first day of May in the hot spring of 1708. It did not go easily for her. At the height of her torment she arched up from the bed, her tousled curls dark with sweat, and screamed out involuntarily.

"Augustin! My love!"

The midwife, thinking she had been privy to a dark secret with regard to the unborn child's fathering, hushed her quickly, mindful that the bedchamber was not soundproof. Marguerite, collapsing back on her pillows, the pains tearing her asunder, was barely aware of the heart-cry she had uttered, except that her agony was akin in some way to what she had suffered mentally on the day when he had left her.

Some hours later she gave birth to a daughter. The baby's wail was lusty and Marguerite smiled in her exhaustion. Jasmin. A flower name like her own. That was what Augustin would have chosen. Symbol of beauty. It had come to her on the spur of the moment, for all along she and Laurent had expected a boy who was to have been named after him.

Laurent was beyond speech on being told all was well. He was more grateful for his wife's safe delivery than for anything else he had ever known. He worshipped his daughter from the moment of setting eyes on her. Marguerite, watching from the pillows, was touched by the way he gazed as if spellbound into the crib. She did not realise then that he was going to treat their child as indulgently as he would have done her if her character had been different. Already he had resolved to give Jasmin, whose second name was to be Marie after his mother, everything her heart desired. He would do all in his power to ensure a cushioned path for her in life.

His attitude began to manifest itself when Jasmin took her first tumbles as she toddled about. He would rush to pick her up, to soothe her tears with sugar comfits and upbraid whoever was in charge of her.

"Couldn't you see Jasmin was going to trip? Suppose she had hit her head! I will not tolerate neglect."

Marguerite, who needed a reliable nursemaid in order to be free for her business commitments, despaired as he dismissed one after another perfectly capable young woman when he imagined they had failed in their duties. Finally he appointed Berthe Clemont, a thin-faced woman in her mid-thirties, who kept constant vigil over the chestnut-haired little girl with the deep violet-blue eyes and intelligent brow.

Since 1702, six years before Jasmin's birth, France had been engaged in the War of the Spanish Succession, many nations ranged against the French cause. Apart from some minor victories there had been defeats at the hands of the English commander, Marlborough, at Venloo and Liége and Blenheim. Again he defeated French forces at Ramillies when Louis, outraged at Heaven's desertion in his hour of need, shouted out his frustration.

"After all I have done for God!"

There were defeats elsewhere, including Spain, and the situation became desperate, the drain on the treasury never-ending. Difficulties were made manifold when a terrible winter brought starvation to thousands of French people. Eventually, frantic for money, Louis made a direct appeal to the patriotism of the nobility and the well-to-do bourgeoisie, asking that they should surrender their gold and silver plate to be melted down to raise urgently needed funds.

"To think that things should come to this," Marguerite said resentfully. "This war would never have come about in the first place if the King had not made up his mind that his grandson should rule Spain."

Laurent knew that the King could never do anything right in Marguerite's eyes and held back from pointing out once again that ultimately it would strengthen France against her enemies to have a Frenchman on the Spanish throne. He also guessed how hard it was for her to consider handing over the Roussier silver that had come to her with the château.

"Let us give everything in silver and gold that we ourselves have added to this house since it became yours," he suggested. "We could donate a large sum of money to compensate for what we shall be keeping back."

She gave him a grateful smile. "That's a splendid idea."

Two large crates were filled and duly delivered to the nearest collecting point together with the donation. People lined up to hand over many beautiful items that abroad would have fetched small fortunes for the craftsmanship involved. It saddened Marguerite to think of France's treasures being lost to furnaces in the cause of war. Nearly all the exquisite silver furniture that had graced Versailles, each item a masterpiece in its own right, went to join the flood of precious metal that carried much of the nation's heritage with it.

There was one article that was Laurent's, which Marguerite insisted should be kept. It was a charmingly decorated porringer from which Jasmin ate every day. Her cheerfully banging spoon added more tiny indentations to

those made by her father in infanthood and his forebears
before him.

Marguerite loved her daughter and considered herself
to be a good parent, but with the passing of time she began
to realise that there would never be the same bond between Jasmin and her as that which she had shared with
her own mother. She often pondered over it. Maybe hard
times created stronger relationships. Yet the argument
against that was the devotion of Jasmin and Laurent for
each other.

First and foremost Jasmin was her father's child. It was
to him that she would run with squeals of delight whenever he returned from a prolonged absence. The gifts he
brought her were secondary, for she was used to being
lavished with them. It was his company, his reading to her
and his participation in her childish games that she valued
most. Marguerite did her best to counteract Laurent's
spoiling, anxious that Jasmin should not be ruined by it. It
was her hope that her firm discipline would eventually
balance the child's headstrong but loving nature. In this
aim she was given support by Berthe.

"I'll not have an unruly brat in my nursery," the woman
was fond of saying whenever she corrected her charge.
Loyal to her employers, thankful to have more comfort
and privileges than she had ever known before, there was
a lack in Berthe that went unnoticed by either Marguerite
or Laurent. She had lost whatever maternal affection that
she had had in the past, soured out of her by life's experiences. She did not harbour the least fondness for Jasmin,
but neither would she have ever deliberately failed in her
duties towards her. In fact, she was conscientious to a degree. Her punishments were basic; a sharp tug on the
bright brown locks was always effective and the mere
threat of ten minutes in a dark cupboard was enough to
bring instant obedience after Jasmin had suffered its ter-
rors.

"The child has too much," Berthe would mutter to herself when Jasmin received yet another plaything from her
father. At first chance she would take it away from the
child, ignoring the tearful protests, and then give it back as
a reward later for good behaviour. Jasmin weathered the
petty tyrannies of the nursery and never bore a grudge, for

there was too much happiness in her days for her to be troubled by anything.

Those at Versailles were not so fortunate. Tragedy struck unexpectedly when the Grand Dauphin, Louis's only legitimate son, who had always enjoyed the best of health, caught smallpox and died. Marguerite's compassion went out to the whole royal household, even to her old enemy in the hour of his grief.

Two years later when a particularly virulent epidemic of measles swept through Versailles and its environs, the new Dauphin's young wife, who had brought such joy to the King and Françoise ever since she had come there as a bride, fell fatally ill with the disease and died in a matter of days.

Marguerite, who had recently nursed Jasmin successfully through the disease, was grief-stricken when Laurent brought home more bad news. The Dauphin himself had been struck down and with his elder son lay at death's door.

The young man died the same day. Marguerite sat with Laurent by the library fire, both finding it difficult to concentrate on reading in their saddened mood. Neither of them was expecting a visitor and it came as a surprise to them both when a servant announced that the Duchesse de Ventadour had called and wished to see them urgently. They knew her well. She had come first to Château Satory to buy a fan and over the years had become a close acquaintance.

"Show the Duchesse in at once," Laurent said, rising from his chair to receive her while Marguerite hastily returned a book to the shelves before coming to his side.

To their astonishment when the Duchesse swept into the room she carried in her arms the two-year-old younger son of the late Dauphin, his head lying sleepily against her shoulder. She halted a few feet from them and indicated with a shake of her head that they should not come forward to greet her.

"Wait! Don't come near me yet. I know Jasmin has safely recovered from the measles, but is there a chance I might be bringing fresh infection to either of you?"

"Very little indeed," Laurent replied. "Both my wife and I suffered the disease in childhood and a second attack is most unlikely."

The Duchesse closed her eyes briefly in relief. "Thank God! I did not know where else to take little Louis." She addressed herself to Marguerite. "As yet he has no sign of the measles, but if he should succumb would you help me to nurse him? I remembered you said once you trusted in nature's healing and good nursing, which you have proved by Jasmin's return to health. I took this child from his bed to bring him here, because at the first sign of fever he would be at the mercy of those doctors with their emetics and their bloodletting. It always seems to me the weaker their patients become the more barbarous their attempted cures. I need hardly say that these are comments I would not care to utter in other company."

Marguerite exchanged a swift glance with Laurent. When Jasmin had fallen sick he had wanted to call in the royal doctors, only the best being considered good enough for his child, but she had refused to let him summon them, remembering that Augustin had said once he believed the Queen would not have died if the doctors had not used their knives on her. Her distrust of them had deepened, all her peasant blood outraged, when she learned that they sometimes had a sheep flayed alive in a birthing room to lessen the agony of a difficult delivery. Perhaps the poor expectant mother simply fainted away before being wrapped in the bloody fleece.

"You are welcome here," she said to the Duchesse, "and I'll do everything in my power to ensure that the little prince gets well again if the measles should appear." She held out her arms. "Let me take him from you and put him to bed. You look exhausted."

The Duchesse surrendered her burden and sank down in a chair, putting her hands to her face. "It's terrible! Three heirs to the Throne dead within two years."

In sadness, Marguerite held the sleepy child closer to her. "Is there then no hope for this boy's brother?"

"None at all."

Laurent opened the door for Marguerite and she carried the child up the stairs. How strange was fate. In her arms she held the great-grandson of her old enemy, Louis XIV's last direct legitimate heir, a fragile, sickly-looking child whose chances of surviving an illness as severe as measles were slim indeed. But she would fight for this boy as if he were her own. His limbs were like little sticks. He needed

building up like a baby and that should start immediately.
She had the solution at hand. The wife of one of the gardeners had recently had a baby and was troubled by an
abundance of milk. She should be brought into the château
to act as a wet nurse and the breast milk would be the basis
of the nourishment required to build up his resistance.

Little Louis did not develop measles. Jasmin, who was
two years older save for a matter of weeks, was well
pleased to have a playmate, even though he was so delicate
she was expected to let him have any of her toys when he
wanted them, no matter what game she was playing. He
was not unlike a doll himself with his frail appearance and
soft brown hair.

"Louis likes you," he said to her once, but it made no
impression.

Such was the distress of the King and the Court over the
deaths that had occurred that nobody questioned the
whereabouts of the child, for the Duchesse had been appointed to have him in her charge. He stayed at Château
Satory for a considerable time until the epidemic had
waned and the Duchesse felt it safe to return him to Versailles.

Eventually she told the King she had kept the boy from
infection in her rooms, not letting it be known that she had
taken him elsewhere. Neither did she confess to her fear of
the doctors, for the King had complete faith in them as
everybody else apparently did. Little Louis continued to
be delicate for a long while, but the Duchesse followed
Marguerite's advice in seeing that he had plenty of goat's
milk, vegetables, and meat free from any spices, which
often disguised a lack of freshness even at the royal table.

Jasmin cried when Louis left her home. Marguerite tried
to comfort her in her loss of a playmate, but she pulled
away, unconsoled.

"I liked Louis being here," she sobbed, the tears gushing.

Laurent swept her up in his arms and bore her away to
distract her. "Some day you'll have your choice of princes,
my beauty. That's Papa's promise to you."

Marguerite, stooping to collect some scattered toys,
smiled and shook her head. Laurent had been speaking
figuratively, for he wanted a love-match for their daughter
as much as she did.

Long after little Louis's departure his presence remained, first in his name which Jasmin gave to a favourite soldier-doll, and later when she invented an invisible companion, as an only child often does, calling him Louis and talking about him as if he sat in the next chair or wished to share her supper. It became quite a joke in the household that the new young Dauphin was residing at Château Satory and not at Versailles at all. But it went over Jasmin's head, for gradually she had forgotten that there was any connection between her Louis and the future King of France.

When little Louis was four, the long War of the Spanish Succession finally came to an end. It had almost brought France to her knees, but in her most dangerous hour her forces had rallied with a surge of strength and the tide had turned. The peace treaty had its disappointing aspects but a Bourbon had been set firmly on the throne of Spain, which had been the King's primary aim in taking his country to war over the matter. The cost in lives was a subject everyone at Court put aside in his hearing. Hymns of praise and thanksgiving rang out in the newly consecrated Royal Chapel until every beautiful corner of it absorbed the *Te Deums* from many hundreds of voices.

The end of the war was far more of a relief to Louis than anyone suspected. He felt his years at last and would have preferred to spend all his time peacefully with Françoise at the Trianon rather than at mighty Versailles. Yet his sense of duty had not waned and neither had his hold on the Court, trapped as it was in a spiderweb of etiquette centred on the Throne. But he lacked the energy to attend balls or masques or even the *Appartements* and he no longer cared what went on in his absence. Inevitably the entertainments thinned out and once again after several decades Paris regained her place as the hub of the social scene.

Such matters were beyond the little Dauphin's understanding. He was a shy, serious child who might have been expected to be overwhelmed by the bustle of the Court, which was still an intensely busy place, but he was cosseted by kindness, adored by the Duchesse whose sole aim, next to keeping him alive, was to ensure he had a happy childhood. He did not share the Court's knee-shaking awe of his great-grandfather, which was as strong as ever. To him the King was ever-smiling and affable, lifting him up on his knee whenever the occasion permitted, and there was always a sweetmeat for him from one of the jewelled comfit boxes.

The only time the King seemed at all distant from him was on state occasions. It was hard not to blink at the magnificence of his great-grandfather in a coat encrusted with gold embroidery, the Order of Saint Esprit dazzling all eyes, and a magnificently plumed hat seated like a giant on the high, ornate silver throne in the Hall of Mirrors, to which it was brought from the Throne room on such days. It was no wonder that visiting dignitaries often looked overawed as they approached the royal dais in that glorious gallery while the Court, laden with jewels, gleaming in silks and satins, stood back to make a path through to the Sun King, who dominated the whole vibrating scene.

Whenever little Louis was well enough, the Duchesse took him along in the mornings to be present with the rest of the royal family at the King's *lever*. The royal bedchamber had changed its location again and been set once and for all in the very centre of the East Front. The child never failed to be fascinated by the way every gilded cornice and garland and frieze competed for brilliance with the morning sun pouring onto his great-grandfather's massive bed in its holy of holies beyond the balustrade, the crimson and gold winter hangings changed to flower-patterned damask of gold and silver when summer came.

To the little boy the ostrich plumes topping the canopy seemed high as a house. His gaze was always drawn to the relief in gold on the wall above the bed, depicting France watching over the sleeping King. He liked that. He thought it must give his great-grandfather a safe feeling to know she was keeping guard over his head. Yet he did not think he would care to sleep in this bedchamber himself. It would be like sleeping in a vast gilded box. And all these people crowding in every morning to watch one dress must be very tiring because they all talked and never stood quietly. Yet it would be his fate one day when he was a grown man and King in his great-grandfather's place. He hoped that time was a long way off.

There was one morning at the *lever* when a disturbance occurred in the Cour Royale and little Louis was as curious as his great-grandfather to see what was afoot. The King, fully dressed even to the ribbon of the *Cordon Bleu* sash across his chest, went out onto the balcony of the bed-chamber and little Louis slipped away from the Duchesse to follow him. An ice-wagon had overturned and the slabs of ice lay like huge glittering diamonds on the cobbles. In the warm sunshine, apart from the fun of seeing the com-motion, which was bringing people at a run to right the wagon again, the balcony was a splendid place to stand with the Avenue de Paris stretching in a direct line to-wards the horizon beyond the open gates and the Place d'Armes. It was almost possible to believe that Paris itself could be seen from this strategic spot. Even all France, which was not inconceivable since Versailles was its very apex.

A shout went up. Someone had spotted the King and the Dauphin standing side by side on the balcony. A spontane-ous burst of cheering broke out and suddenly it seemed as if all the busy Cour Royale had left whatever they were doing to rush towards the balcony and clap and cheer.

"Long live the King! Long live the Dauphin!"

Proudly and graciously the King acknowledged the ap-probation, but little Louis drew back in his shyness. He was momentarily overcome by the number of faces turned up to him. Then his great-grandfather set a hand firmly on his shoulder, reassuring him, and he gave the obligatory little wave that was met with a renewed burst of cheering.

"Well done," the King said to him with a smile as they turned back into the room.

It was not long afterwards that the King fell ill. As he lay in his magnificent red and gold bed submitting trustfully to the doctor's bloodletting and emetics and the strange lo-tions they applied to the black patches on his leg he knew wearily that if he departed this life now he would be leav-ing France in a sorry state. Many wars had drained her once handsome resources and her national debts were enormous. He did not blame his own extravagances in any way, for through them he had given work to thousands and made the world look to France as the centre of culture and fine arts and elegance. His beloved Versailles would always stand as a monument to beauty and his own sun-god reign.

As the mood of the Court became solemn and people began to talk in low voices as if fearful of creating even the slightest disturbance, it became apparent to little Louis that some great calamity was about to fall on the House of Bourbon. The Duchesse tried to prepare him.

"Your great-grandfather and our most Christian King, Louis XIV, will soon be taking leave of us all. You must be brave. When he sends for you there must be no tears. You must show him that you have a heart as stout as his and that will give him peace of mind."

Little Louis dreaded the summons. Snatches of unguarded conversation reached his ears.

"The King's leg is rotting away and the asses' milk has brought no benefit."

"Another purge and still the King gets weaker."

"He bears his agony stoically and without a word of complaint. His fortitude and his will are as strong as ever."

The day finally came. The Duchesse gave little Louis a kiss and led him by the hand into the golden bedchamber. For the first time the room smelt unpleasant and the shrunken, wigless old man in the great bed bore little resemblance to the imposing face and figure familiar to him. Yet the voice was his great-grandfather's. It came with extraordinary strength and a thin graceful hand extended towards him.

"Come here to the bedside."

He obeyed, entering the sanctum beyond the gilt balustrade where he had never stepped before and stood close to the bed. The King's pain-racked eyes were fond on him.

"Dearest child, it is your destiny to become a great King. Don't imitate me in the passion for building that was mine or in my constant engagement in warfare . . ."

These words were to stay with young Louis throughout the years ahead. He was never to forget the advice to keep France at peace with her neighbours, to keep true to his duty and to God, always to try to improve the lot of his subjects—a point on which the King admitted that he had failed—and keep them close to the Faith. It was then that the King expressed a desire to kiss him and the Duchesse lifted him up. The thin, dry lips pressed briefly against his cheek and when he was set down again the King gave him his blessing.

Little Louis bowed as he had been taught. Then the Duchesse led him away. The King had told him never to forget what he owed her, moving her to the tears she had forbidden him to shed. He was conscious of being greatly loved. It made up for knowing his parents and his brother only by their portraits. He hoped he would always be loved as he was this day.

A few days later, on the first day of September in that year of 1715, Louis XIV died peacefully and with majesty, bringing his long reign of seventy-two years to an end. Jasmin remembered it as the time when shades were drawn and the maidservants went about mopping their tears with the corners of their aprons. She went into the Ivory Salon where her parents were talking, not at first aware of her presence. Her father sat in a chair and her mother stood by the glass doors that led out onto the terrace, looking towards her favourite view of the lawns and the marble summerhouse as she held aside the drawn curtains, letting light into the dim room. She was almost in silhouette, softer in outline since the *fontange* had begun to be outmoded and skirts had taken on more fullness all around instead of being confined to the back.

"It seems strange to recall now how much I hated the King when I was younger. I had not realised until now how mellow I've grown with the years."

Jasmin, ever curious, ran forward. "Why did you hate him, Maman?"

Marguerite turned with a start and then held the child to her. "He did much wrong to my mother when I was a girl. She was imprisoned for shouting at him when her mind was disturbed."

"Have you forgiven him?"

Marguerite looked back again at the view of the garden, her eyes distant as if she saw beyond it. "I suppose I did long ago, although without knowing it at the time. We should always forgive those who wrong us." In her own mind she was adding that forgiveness did not necessarily mean that forgetting went with it. It was through that same man's actions that she had lost the love of her life, and even though she was thankful for the compensations that had come her way, there was no question of forgetting. The thought of Augustin still stabbed at her heart and his portrait still regarded her with that direct look into which she sometimes read messages of the past. It was a long time since she had had news of him. His children were married with children of their own and she wondered if there was a little girl old enough to receive that Versailles fan.

Laurent had brought the news of the King's death home with him. He had seen it announced from the balcony by the Duc de Bouillon with a black plume billowing in his hat that in turn had been changed to a white plume immediately afterwards for the trumpeting shout, "Long live the King!"

Already the Regent, the Duc d'Orléans, who had been appointed by the late King himself, had whisked the new King away to Vincennes, the Duchesse de Ventadour accompanying her beloved charge. Laurent foresaw an immediate decline in the glory of Versailles and gave his views as Marguerite let Jasmin go skipping off to Berthe, who had come in search of her.

"The Court will leave for Paris as soon as everyone knows the new King is not coming back. Official business won't continue at Versailles. I consider a stall for the display of your fans will be a needless expense."

"I realise that." Marguerite took the chair opposite him. "My shops are outlets enough for my products and my clientele always order from me wherever they happen to be."

He leaned forward, hoping this was the time for which he had been patiently waiting over the past few years. "Should you not think of selling the business now, my dear? This could be the right moment to be rid of it."

She stiffened. "No. I wouldn't consider it. In any case I have Jasmin to think about. I want her to learn to make fans as I did and my mother and grandmother before me. It's good discipline, teaches patience and brings out any latent artistic abilities."

An uncomfortable suspicion brought a deep frown to his brows. "You're not thinking of giving her a turn at the workbench?"

"Yes, I am. I will not let her grow up in a cosseted existence without having an insight into what it means to work for a living."

"She has you as an example, for mercy's sake!"

"She sees only my success and knows nothing of my beginnings."

"Are you planning to dispense with her education?" he exploded. "And what of her dancing lessons, her singing and musical instruction? You'll make a fan-maker of her over my dead body!"

"Calm yourself." Marguerite held up her hands in a soothing gesture. "There'll be time for everything. I shall teach her at home first and then when she is older she shall spend a little time in each section of fan-making in my workshops, including the jewellers' department. I want her to gain a broad spectrum of life, to keep her head from being turned by luxury and to make sure she keeps her feet on the ground." She moved from her chair to sit on the floor beside him and put her hand on his arm, her whole expression softening. "You want to protect her too much, Laurent. And you give her too much and excuse her too often. I love her as much as you do, but I will not let her grow up unprepared for the hardships of life."

His hand cupped her upturned face. He never liked to be stern or angry with her. "Jasmin will never know poverty as we knew it. If anything should happen to us she would be rich enough to snap her fingers at the world."

"That's just it." She gave his arm a little shake. "She's basically a good child, warm-hearted and affectionate, not given to quick temper. But already your praise has made her enchanted with her appearance in the mirror, and she must not become vain and self-centred with no thought for others, which too much indulgence could do. I've seen many such women at Versailles. Don't argue with me that Jasmin has your noble blood in her veins and must not soil her hands. She also has mine, which has equal right."

He sighed deeply, a sign she recognised as acquiesence. "Very well. But use your discretion. I don't want anything to hamper the social life that will be hers in time to come."

"You have my promise."

Jasmin could never understand why her mother was always so strict with her when everyone else fell in with her wishes. Berthe could be sharp-tongued and nasty at times, quick to give her a slap, but on the whole the woman was more tolerant than she used to be and sometimes it was possible to get round her by persistent persuasion. It was not a pleasant surprise when she was ten to be put to her first lessons in fan-making at her mother's side when she could have been playing or riding or generally enjoying herself. Life was such fun, for she had plenty of friends and even her daily lessons gave her no trouble, and now here was her mother ruining everything by giving her useless instruction in fan-making.

"But I shall always buy my fans or have them given to me," she protested. Then she saw a look in her mother's eyes, half anger, half pain, that touched her and she did not know why. Never liking anyone or anything to be hurt, she had flung her arms around her mother's waist. "What is it, Maman?"

"Nothing, except that we never know what lies ahead of us." Marguerite gently withdrew her daughter's arms and began to name the parts of fans on the table at which they sat. Jasmin felt snubbed and there was a pain in her as sharp as any that her mother had known. There was a need in her for harmony at all times. Severe rejection of any kind made her feel physically sick. Fortunately that played little part in her normally joyous existence. A determined streak in her rose to the surface. Perhaps if she did badly enough at her fan-making her mother would give up in despair.

The ploy did not work. Marguerite's will matched her daughter's. She recognised tricks she had played herself during a rebellious period in her own youth and sometimes hid a smile at the transparency of them, thinking how her own mother must have also seen through them.

The tussle lasted several weeks. Eventually, in spite of herself, Jasmin became interested and this was cemented when Marguerite suggested that she should make her own fan to match a new dress she was to wear to a party. After that there were few problems. Marguerite gave her instruction regularly and Jasmin's enjoyment of painting and drawing with her tutor also helped her in making simple designs for the leaves of her fan.

Then this happier time was ruined again for Jasmin by a period of instruction in household management that she saw as an infliction being forced on her by her mother. She raised protests similar to those before.

"I'm going to marry well. Papa has promised me that. Rich ladies don't have to know about such things. There are always others to arrange matters for them." She voiced the secret dream that her father's constant admiration had sown in her. "I may even marry a prince." There was a challenge in her sideways glance, daring her mother to dispute it.

"If you should gain so grand a husband," Marguerite replied drily, "at least you will know what it is like for the humblest scullion in your kitchens to work at washing pots."

And it had come to that. Jasmin found herself put to a stint of pot-washing. Admittedly it was when the servants had time off to spare her their gaping, but that did not stop her shedding tears of humiliation while her mother stood over her, unmoved. Her father was furious about it when she wept out her woes to him, but in that part of her upbringing her mother had the upper hand and there was no getting out of bread-making and sweeping and silver-polishing as well as the other menial tasks that she viewed as a great punishment and injustice. It came as an enormous relief when Marguerite considered her to be sufficiently drilled in domestic skills and let her revert to an easy life again.

During this period, which she looked upon as a dreary time, although her instruction had never taken up more than an hour or two in a week otherwise crowded with interest and enjoyment, she made visits to the workshops with her mother and loved to see the variety of fans in production. At times she was allowed to take some small part in the professional work in hand and was proud of what she produced. Some of the talk between the women that she inadvertently overheard gave her information that she never expected to need, but nevertheless opened her eyes to a side of marriage other than the romanticism in which she held it. A special joy in her life was being allowed to go with her father to houses of his design or where he was supervising extensions or alterations. Best of all she liked accompanying him to Versailles. With the completion of the beautiful Chapel and its consecration five years before Louis XIV's death, the last of the great architects had departed Versailles, the palace finally to be left in peace after almost a hundred years of building and rebuilding and countless alterations. Laurent, who had supervised work on the Chapel, first with Mansart and afterwards with Robert de Cotte, had been appointed the permanent architect in charge of any necessary maintenance and it was surprising how often he was required to go there and give his authority to some task.

With the Court in permanent absence, it had become a

quiet place with the exception of the governmental wing where a few offices were used for civic matters, ministerial affairs conducted once again in Paris. Jasmin often skipped and ran through the silent staterooms, but she liked best to dance in the Hall of Mirrors, humming to herself and watching her reflection in every one of the seventeen floor-to-ceiling mirrors from one end of the gallery to the other. Her father was full of exciting tales of Versailles in the days of the late King and more and more she became enthralled by its magic and beauty.

When she was fourteen three quite major events took place. The first was that a rich nobleman, thrice her age, and an acquaintance of her father, asked him for her hand. There was no question of his proposal being considered, but she giggled about it and took a fresh look at herself in the mirror. Tallish, with a slender neck, she carried her head well, her patrician nose and chin almost tilted as if her mass of chestnut hair had weight to it. Her lashes had grown thick and long and if her eyes had not been large and sparkling they would have darkened the violet irises of which she was proud. She wished her pink mouth was better shaped, but her teeth were pearly-white and her creamy skin without a blemish, except for some quite deep scars at the back of her neck, easily hidden by her coiffure, and another on her right cheek, disguised on special occasions with a beauty patch, all of which were the result of a mild attack of smallpox through which her mother had nursed her tirelessly. She had been prone to infectious diseases in her childhood but now those days were behind her. As for her figure, that was promising and she was resolved somehow to retain her tiny waist even after she was married and had babies.

Berthe was forever upbraiding her for vanity, but she was not unduly conceited about her looks. Anyway Berthe always did find something to complain about! The woman's only virtue in Jasmin's opinion was that she liked to take a snooze with her feet up more often than in the past, and these times gave some leeway in which to escape those penetrating, watchful eyes. Yet there was a weapon that Berthe had always held over Jasmin's head, which was a threat to tell her adored father of any of her more serious misdemeanours. This curtailed more effectively than anything else the mischievous escapades into which she would otherwise have entered, carefree and thoughtless.

The second major dramatic event to occur was a sad one and filled Jasmin with panic. She and her father had returned from Versailles one afternoon in high spirits, laughing together as they entered the château, only to be told that Madame had received bad news from England. They rushed to the library where Marguerite had received the messenger and they found her alone there, sitting drooped in the wide-backed chair by the hearth.

"My dearest! What has happened?" Laurent exclaimed, guessing even as he asked.

"Maman! Tell us!"

Slowly Marguerite raised her head as if her whole spine pained her and her face was ashen, pulled into the age she was, which somehow had never shown before. Without answering, almost as if shock had silenced her vocal cords, she just gazed at Laurent, her huge eyes shimmering, and he gave a compassionate nod of understanding, reaching out his hands for hers. But she did not take them. Instead, she seemed to be fighting to gain control of her emotions by herself and gripped the ends of the chair arms to lever herself up to her feet. Jasmin was terrified. She had never witnessed such anguish and that it should be wrought on the face of her dear mother was almost beyond her endurance. A whimper escaped her, but neither of her parents heard, intent only on each other, he ready to offer comfort to the wife who was not able as yet to respond.

Marguerite released the support of the chair and clasped her trembling hands together in front of her. She was aware of shaking from head to foot, conscious of feeling icy-cold, and for a moment she thought her jaw had become detached, there was such an odd sensation to it, until she realised her teeth were still chattering from the emotional blow she had received. Her words came with difficulty.

"He has gone," she managed to say, knowing there was no need for explanation to this kindly man who knew her almost better than she knew herself. "He died at his home in London three weeks ago. A full twenty-one days and I didn't know." Her mouth went awry and she pressed her fingertips to the corners of it as if there were no other way to control her facial muscles. "In his last breath he called to me." Then grief finally tore her asunder and she half-threw herself forward with arms outflung on a terrible cry: "Augustin is dead!"

Laurent caught her as she fell in her deep faint. Jasmin screamed, thinking her mother as dead as the man whose name she had uttered, but her father quickly reassured her. Tearfully she followed behind when he carried Marguerite upstairs. It was evening before Marguerite recovered consciousness and afterwards she stayed bedridden for a long time, almost as if she had to find the will to go on with her life again. Jasmin did everything she could to revive her mother's spirits, but Marguerite remained withdrawn during what was virtually a convalescence from bereavement.

Before his wife came downstairs again Laurent removed the portrait of Augustin Roussier from the Ivory Salon. It was wrapped in canvas and put into storage in the secret vault and another painting hung in its place. By now Laurent had explained to Jasmin that Marguerite had once been fond of the sitter in the portrait, which was why his death was such a shock to her.

Marguerite knew the portrait would be gone and that there was no jealousy or malice behind its removal. Laurent had understood that the sight of it would bring a constant renewal of grief until there would have been no healing. Since Augustin had been much older it was to be expected that he should die first, but she had been able to bear his absence all the time he was alive, perhaps because hope had remained that somehow they might yet meet again. She wrote a letter to his widow thanking Susanne for her compassion, not only in sending the news by word of mouth instead of by letter, but for letting it be known that Augustin's last thought was of her. She did not expect a reply and none came. It could not have been easy for Susanne to live with the knowledge that Augustin's love was centred far across the Channel, but at the end she had shown the generosity of spirit that had always been hers.

Life was hardly back to normal at Château Satory, at least on the surface, when the third important event of Jasmin's fifteenth year took place. There had been rumours that the King, now twelve years old, was about to return to Versailles. For several weeks there had been polishing and dusting and cleaning on an extensive scale.

Beds were made ready and special care taken with the great royal bedchamber for its new occupant. Man-high orange trees, neatly clipped, were brought from the Orangery to be set in silver tubs and all the vases filled with choice flowers just as the late King had always liked to see them. But when nothing happened the excess of energy began to wane, although the flowers were continually replaced with fresh blooms and the orange trees kept moist just in case.

Jasmin was with Laurent at Versailles one day and as usual had passed through the Hall of Mirrors, too grown up to dance for her own delight now, but not above eyeing her reflected appearance all the way. In the Peace Salon at the south end of the wing, she passed time looking out of one of the windows at the gardeners replanting the South Parterre. Then there came a commotion from the direction of the War Salon. She spun round and saw that a boy had entered there with clacking footsteps and, not noticing her at such a distance away, advanced into the Hall of Mirrors, gaping about with a grin on his face as if well pleased to be there. He was a good-looking, sturdily built lad with curly brown hair and peaked brows over clear brown eyes, a high square forehead and a firmly cast chin. Hardly had he entered when he stopped, setting his hands on his hips with elbows jutting as he tipped his head back to gaze at the decorated ceiling. To her surprise, he suddenly flung himself down on his back the better to view the paintings depicting the life of Louis XIV, edging himself along the polished floor like a caterpillar, propelled by his heels and the rise and fall of his knees. He presented such a comical sight that she had to stand back out of sight at the side of an archway and smother her laughter. It was certainly the most sensible way to view the magnificent ceilings throughout Versailles without getting a crick in the neck. Just as she was wondering if he had done all his sightseeing in a similar manner throughout the staterooms she observed a sparkling on his chest and realised he was wearing the Order of Saint Esprit. He was the King!

She did not think he would have wanted her to see his undignified progress. Perhaps if she stayed where she was, he would get to his feet and not see her.

It did not work out that way. Boylike, he gave himself a final impetus with his heels and came sailing feet-first into

the Peace Salon close to where she stood. Immediately he
flushed with embarrassment, springing up and dusting off
his velvet coat as he did so.

"I didn't know anyone else was here."

She dipped into a curtsey. "May I welcome you back to
Versailles, sire? Be assured there's no better way to view
the ceilings. I only wish I had thought of it myself."

He bowed in a courtly manner. Then their eyes met, his
look solemn, hers quite serious in her effort to make him
feel at ease, and simultaneously they both smiled. "I thank
you, mademoiselle. Since you know my identity please
reveal yours."

"I'm Jasmin, daughter of Baron Picard."

"Why are you here alone?"

She explained that when her father was busy in some
part of the Château she invariably wandered about on her
own looking at everything. Then she added, "We have met
before. It was a long time ago and you won't remember."

"Test me, Mademoiselle Picard. I pride myself on my
memory."

It was obvious he planned to follow his great-grandfather's example in that respect. She shook her head. "It's
too far back. You came to our château in the company of
the Duchesse de Ventadour. I'm told we played together."

He did not recall the time personally, but he knew how
the Duchesse, who had loved him as her own child, had
whisked him out of danger. Even his great-grandfather at
the point of dying had spoken of her solicitude. Yet when
he was only seven the Regent had removed him from her
care, forbidden her to see him again and given him over to
harsh tutors. That had been the end of any gentleness and
loving in his life. He had lived with loneliness and learned
to draw on his own resources to become the guarded,
private person he was. Yet there was something about this
girl that made him feel comfortable in her presence. If
anyone else had seen him lying on his back like an urchin
in a gutter he would have been angry that his exuberant
pleasure in returning to Versailles had been marred by
some inquisitive witness. But with Jasmin Picard he felt in
tune and it reinforced his delight in his return to the place
he associated with the only happiness he had ever known.

"I know of that time. It would please me to take up those

threads again. I trust you will continue to come often to
Versailles after the Court returns to residence here."

"I'm honoured, sire." She curtsied again. Drawing back,
she made it clear she would no longer intrude on his reunion with the place of his birth. But as she retraced her
footsteps through the Hall of Mirrors she met his attendant
courtiers hurrying in search of him and she knew his time
of peaceful contemplation was over. Laurent, when he
heard of her meeting with the King, was pleased and
proud.

The Court returned to Versailles as if it had never been
away. There were still those who would have preferred to
remain in Paris, but wherever the King was there were
opportunities for favours, advancement and everything
else that benefited a courtier's life. Laurent and Marguerite found that their names and that of their daughter had
been put on the guest list. Invitations began to come regularly to concerts, plays and balls. Although much of the
festivity went on without Louis's presence, he was always
there whenever the Picards attended. The friendship between Jasmin and Louis grew steadily, insomuch as it was
possible for him to have friends, watched and guarded as
he was from morning to night, his days regulated by the
clock as his great-grandfather's had been, his very existence as much a public affair. There were many times
when he longed for privacy and resolved that when he was
no longer under the control of the Regent he would secure
a haven somewhere in Versailles for himself.

Jasmin was more enchanted than ever by Versailles. She
revelled in the balls to which she wore increasingly bouf-
fant gowns in satin or taffeta in pastel shades, ribbons and
flowers in her hair. Fashion was changing. Soldiers had
always worn their periwigs tied back for convenience and
that had set the new style for men. The gallants were
wearing wigs neater and lighter, tied back with bows, and
only the elderly and the more conservative clung to the
old style.

By the time she was sixteen Jasmin was one of the beau-
ties at Court and had brushed against love more than once,
only to butterfly on to another handsome face and there
were plenty of those at Versailles. Laurent had already
turned down a number of offers for her. He was a good
judge of character and was well able to discern those suit-

ors to whom Jasmin was merely the more than pretty daughter of a nobleman backed by a large fortune. For it, they were prepared to overlook the distaff side of her origins which, in spite of the distinguished company received at the Château Satory, had links with commerce, albeit in a jewelled and elegant line.

He also refused, as he had done when first approached for her hand, older men, almost without exception widowers who had already lost two and even three young wives in childbirth. Although he himself had been in that position when he had courted Marguerite, they were both mature adults at the time with comparatively little age difference between them. Jasmin must love and be loved by the man she would marry and experience the ecstasy that comes from the mating of youth with youth, the growing together in wisdom and companionship towards later years which, as he had observed from his own life and that of others equally fortunate, could be the most contented and even the best time of all.

Marguerite was his at last. He no longer had to share her with a distant dream, a memory that had lain like a shadow between them even in their most intimate moments. If her feelings for him were still far from the heights for which he had once hoped, it no longer mattered. They shared a good life together and their bond was their beloved daughter.

Had Louis been two years older instead of younger than she, Jasmin might easily have fallen in love with him. At fourteen he was already taller than she was and his broadening shoulders were giving him the graceful, majestic bearing that she was told resembled his great-grandfather's. It was a delight to dance with him, for he had been as well taught as she had and they both enjoyed an innate sense of rhythm. He always partnered her at least once in an evening and more when he was able. At a masque they let each other know beforehand what disguises they would be wearing and these were occasions when they could enjoy each other's company without restraint. If they met by day in the park it was not necessarily by chance, although Jasmin was never unchaperoned, Berthe ever her watchful guardian. Louis ignored as much as possible the five-year-old Spanish Infanta to whom he had been betrothed and who, to his chagrin, frequently trotted after him if a door was not shut in time. One afternoon in the Hall of Mirrors, with Berthe waiting patiently on a velvet seat in the War Salon, he spoke to Jasmin about his forthcoming marriage in ten years' time.

"If I had my way they'd send her back to Spain," he said grumpily, his hands shoved into his pockets like any disgruntled schoolboy, his shoulders hunched with displeasure. Two years ago he had wept when he had been told what had been decided on his behalf, but he had become a man since then. "I should have some voice in my choice of a bride when the time comes."

She sympathised with him. It was the first time he had spoken of any personal matter to her, for he was at all times intensely reserved. She gauged it to be the measure of his pent-up despair over the situation. "I must say I could never tolerate having someone chosen for me," she admitted.

He sighed heavily and turned his gaze on her just as she looked towards him. The words came from him in a rush of exasperation at his fate. "I wish you were a princess, Jasmin."

She blushed, putting up a hand to hide her cheek from Berthe's eagle gaze. Louis, knowing he should not have made such an unguarded, impulsive statement, flushed to the roots of his hair. For once all his training, his self-discipline and his own natural reticence had broken down before her lovely spring-morning face and her glorious, understanding eyes. She rescued him quickly.

"It's lucky I'm not or else I should have been sent away from here to make a marriage in a foreign land. Then we wouldn't be walking along together here today."

"I agree. You're right, of course."

She had spared him embarrassment and he was grateful for it. The subject of his marriage was not mentioned between them again. Yet the thought remained with him, mixed up with the trumpeting urges of his strong young body, that if they had given him a bride like her he would have considered himself fortunate indeed; also there would have been no waiting for the marriage to be consummated. She began to figure in his dreams. As a result he sought her out more than ever. How old would he have to be before they allowed him a mistress? There were nights when he thought he would die of physical frustration.

Marguerite, whenever she looked on the well-built young King, was always thankful he had grown from the sickly infant he had once been. She also saw what others were beginning to notice, which was that he was not far off from being in love with Jasmin, whether he knew it or not.

"You're worrying unnecessarily," Laurent said, tossing the matter aside. "He's a Bourbon, remember. They are attracted to women like bees to honey and you can be sure he has eyes for all the prettiest girls at Court."

"Nevertheless, I think we should keep Jasmin away from Versailles for a while."

Laurent would not hear of it. "Don't let it trouble you. Nothing can come of it and nobody knows that better than Jasmin or Louis himself. She is a sensible girl. Did we both not talk seriously to her of the dangers to be wary of at Versailles? What's more, you and I always attend with her, or else I take her on my own. At other times Berthe guards over her."

Marguerite thought wryly how once he had declared he would never have any part in the Court life of Versailles, but that had all changed since he had set himself to give Jasmin every enjoyment and to see that she made a match brilliant in love and social position. "I'm not asking for her to stay away from Versailles altogether. Just for the time being."

But for once Laurent was adamant. He was unable to see that their daughter's charmed existence might be threatened by her previously harmless friendship with the King now that it was moving onto more dangerous ground. Marguerite listened in silence as, patiently, he pointed out that she had had her way in teaching Jasmin fan-making when the time could have been better spent in additional music lessons or other rewarding instructions. He had also been tolerant in not stopping Jasmin from visiting the workshops once a week in the rôle that her mother had created for her.

"I've been thinking," he said in conclusion, "those visits must end now. Before long Jasmin will be ready to marry and I want nothing to hamper the approval of the young man's family, whoever he may happen to be."

She saw the sense of his argument on that point. The nobility were extremely finicky when it came to the antecedents and background of a prospective bride or groom, and it was unlikely that Jasmin, moving in high social circles as she did, would fall in love with any ordinary man. The last thing Marguerite wished to do was to ruin anything for her daughter.

"Very well," she agreed, "Jasmin's round of social engagements has been making it difficult to allot the necessary hours to the workshops." In a way it was a task completed on her part. She had shown Jasmin what it meant to work long hours for a living, albeit her workers were better off than many, but there had been personal hardships and domestic difficulties among the women which had opened the girl's eyes and ears to the conditions of those who lived close to the breadline.

It was odd that none of those workshop visits had brought her any closer to her daughter, even though she and Jasmin had tried to solve many of the problems together. Neither had those hours shared in fan-making bridged the gap, nor the time when Jasmin had attended her when grief for Augustin had laid her low. Always the barrier, the slight unbridgeable distance. Marguerite did not doubt that when eventually Jasmin found herself in love Laurent would be the first to know.

Yet in that she was mistaken. The news reached her first from an unexpected and totally unwelcome source. She happened to be in her shop in Paris for the day when one of her long-standing customers in the city arrived. Madame Poisson was a Parisian beauty, the wife of a wealthy bourgeois, and she purchased all her fans at Marguerite's establishment. Although neither she nor her husband had ever been to Court they had high connections, the King's own banker being godfather to their dainty little daughter. Madame Poisson's looks, figure and charm ensured her a place in elite circles and she was said to have had several lovers among the nobility. She greeted Marguerite effusively, long lashes fluttering over sharp dark eyes, gauzy shawls floating about her, red-striped taffeta skirts rustling.

"Madame la Baronne! What good fortune that I should find you here today! I'm desperate for a new fan to match an oyster silk ballgown. I have brought a swatch of the fabric with me."

"Step into my salon, Madame Poisson, and we can discuss your requirements."

Marguerite led the way out of the shop into the luxuriously furnished salon kept for such occasions. The procedure took the best part of an hour before Madame Poisson was satisfied and throughout she had chatted incessantly. Then, as was usual, hot chocolate was served as refreshment and she began talking about her daughter.

"She has earned the nickname of Reinette in the family," she revealed with proud amusement, "because in a game of fortunes she was told that one day she will hold sway over the King."

"Anything is possible," Marguerite conceded, for the child was as pretty as a picture and was surely destined to be a fine-looking woman as her mother was when grown.

"What of your lovely daughter?" Madame Poisson smiled roguishly over the chocolate cup she held. "What made her desert the King for the Marquis de Grange?"

Marguerite felt a warning chill run down her spine, but she answered composedly. "Jasmin's friendship with the King, rooted as it is in a childhood meeting, is unchanged. I don't understand what you mean about the Marquis. He is a married man."

"Precisely!" Madame Poisson's wickedly alert eyes revealed an inner satisfaction at being the first to let the girl's mother know what was afoot. "I can hear from your tone that the association is not to your liking. There is no need to pretend with me, madame. I know how wayward girls can be, although fortunately little Reinette is still at the stage of playing with dolls."

"I fear you have been listening to groundless gossip." Marguerite spoke sharply. "To my knowledge my daughter has never even spoken to the Marquis. The Baron and I are careful that Jasmin should be chaperoned at all times. He would never have had the chance to get near her."

Madame Poisson sat back in her chair with feigned astonishment. "La! Since you are her mother you should know. Yet my eyes did not deceive me when I witnessed her exchanging amorous glances with Fernand de Grange when they danced together at a ball given by a family friend of ours, Monsieur Pâris-Duverney, at his residence in the new faubourgs of Paris."

Marguerite felt her stomach lurch. The Marquis de Grange mixed with the worst element at Versailles. He was a notorious womaniser whose marriage had long since gone awry, he and his wife going their separate ways.

"Jasmin did visit Paris recently," she admitted, "as a guest of the Tourtain family. My husband has long been acquainted with Monsieur Tourtain, although I know his wife less well. Their daughter, Isabelle, and Jasmin are of the same age and have been close friends for some years. They often exchange visits. Yet I heard no account of any ball from this sojourn in the city."

"Well, the Tourtains were there and Jasmin with them. I know that couple by sight."

Marguerite suppressed any visible sigh of relief. Then all would have been well with that straightforward couple in charge. This woman was mischief-making for the pleasure of it. "One dance is no cause for scandal, Madame Poisson," she pointed out severely, "even though on this occasion Jasmin should have known better than to take the floor with the Marquis."

"It was more than that, as I said before. As for one dance, that was not the case." Madame Poisson put down her cup and saucer in readiness to leave. "Jasmin danced far more times with him than you would have allowed. I will say that Madame Tourtain did her best to advise Jasmin on her folly, because I was sitting not far from them and could see that lady's stern expression and discreetly wagging finger. But I fear that a wilful streak in your daughter came to the fore that evening because she seemed to see nothing except the Marquis's face and to hear only what he was saying to her. In the end the Tourtains took her home early with them, much to the annoyance of their own daughter who had behaved perfectly, yet was being penalised for Jasmin's headstrong behaviour."

Marguerite was remembering Jasmin's earlier than expected return from that visit to Paris. There had been some vague excuse about becoming tired of Isabelle's company and that they had fallen out. The cause of the quarrel was now clear.

"Mercy me!" she said with a little laugh, trying to make it appear that she was making light of the matter. "Jasmin's high spirits must have run away with her for once."

Madame Poisson was undeceived and in any case she had more to tell. "I have heard that prior to the ball Jasmin rode with the Marquis in the Bois and, according to my reliable informant, there have been trysts at Versailles in the gardens and anywhere else they could whisper together, whenever that maidservant of hers may have dozed off in the sunshine."

She had the satisfaction of seeing the brave smile on the Baronne's lips freeze away. Rising from her chair she made an affable farewell. "Good day to you. I shall look forward to the delivery of my fan. Now I'll see myself out."

Marguerite, left alone, threw back her head in the chair where she sat, there being such rage in her against Jasmin that it was all she could do not to dash the porcelain cups to the floor. However much she wanted to dismiss the woman's tales, the incidents had rung true. Foolish, empty-headed, gullible Jasmin! With all the young men from whom she could choose she should finally fasten her affections on one she could not marry and also jeopardise her good name in the process. This was the result of Laurent's spoiling of her! He had led her to believe she could have the moon if she wanted and no retribution would come her way from plucking it out of the sky.

Furiously Marguerite sprang to her feet. From her office she snatched her hat, gloves and cape. Five minutes later she was being driven at top speed towards the Tourtain residence.

Eleven

In a secluded grove in woodland a safe distance from Château Satory, Jasmin lay half-naked in her lover's arms, their heartbeats subsiding together after the passion-racked minutes that had just passed. He had spread his coat for her on their bed of new-fallen, coppery leaves, and the dappled sunlight played over them through the thinning branches. Her riding hat had been cast aside with his, the grey plumes and the yellow mingling together in the bracken.

There was a glow from beyond her closed eyelids that came from the brilliance of the trees above, and the melted-jewel hues of autumn seemed to flow through her veins in these perfect moments and on this perfect day. Until she had surrendered to Fernand some weeks ago she had never suspected the degree of desire lying unawakened within her, never known that she would be totally abandoned in love, all modesty flown, all her secrets open to this man who now knew her more intimately than she knew herself. She felt gloriously wicked and free and at

last wholly a woman with none to gainsay her slightest
whim.

She smiled blissfully as he removed his weight from her
and she ran her hands adoringly over his chest. "Darling,
darling Fernand."

"My sweet Jasmin," he replied, a trace automatically,
but well pleased with her. She had a delicious body and her
beauty was a constant delight to his jaded eye. Since he
knew how a woman liked to be treated after lovemaking as
well as before, he murmured all she wanted to hear and
cradled her tenderly, giving her little kisses.

She gazed into his face, never able to have her fill of the
sight of him. Not as handsome as many men at Court, there
was nevertheless a lean, foxy look to his features that she
found irresistible. It had been his heavy-lidded, brilliantly
blue eyes that had won her heart and there had been no
going back.

She had no fear of pregnancy for he used what was
called a preventative machine. Such were made from
sheep's bladders and imported from England, which apparently carried on a large underground trade with Catholic countries in this commodity. Fortunately he had not
told her with what he was ensheathing himself at their first
wild coming together, or else that knowledge might have
had an adverse effect, but now she gave no thought to it,
only glad that they could enjoy their lovemaking without
anything to trouble them.

"I'll give you all the babies you want one day," he had
promised when they had talked seriously of their future
together. It was a vow she hugged to herself, knowing that
as soon as the annulment of his marriage came through
from Rome all this secrecy would come to an end and she
could go proudly to Versailles as his bride. He was twenty-
five with every chance of advancement at Court, for the
King, being young himself, would promote first those with
advanced ideas when he took the reins of power into his
hands and all those dreary old men presently on the Council of Ministers would have to take a backseat.

"I must go," she sighed reluctantly, wriggling provocatively on the slippery satin lining of coat beneath her. As
she had hoped, he guessed she still had time to spare and
began to make love to her all over again.

They parted in the woodland to avoid being seen together, he riding one way and she the other. Within a short distance of home she carefully rechecked her appearance in a gold pocket mirror. Did her lips look swollen from his kisses? Were there any telltale pieces of grass or dried leaves in her hair? Fernand had assured her there was not, having plucked out whatever had been entangled there, but her sense of guilt was such that whenever she came near Château Satory after being with him she felt that what she had been doing must be radiating out of her. It angered her that her conscience should not be clear, for Fernand's wife actively disliked him and there were no children from the union, nor would there be now. Nevertheless, until her love for him could come out in the open, she feared that the necessary deceit would continue to trouble her.

Reassured that all was well with her looks, she rode the rest of the way and left her horse with a groom in the stableyard. Humming a merry little tune, she entered her home with her quick, light tread, carelessly switching her riding whip against her blue skirt as she went. She reached the hall and was halfway up the graceful staircase when Berthe, who must have been watching out for her, appeared at the head of it, her face grim.

"Your parents wish to see you in the Music Salon. I don't know why, but the Baronne came back from Paris in quite a state about two hours ago."

Jasmin experienced a qualm. Had her mother seen Madame Tourtain and heard that she had behaved a little recklessly at that ball? Well, she would make the excuse that the company was all middle-aged while Fernand had been the only young man present able to dance well. But she must remember to call him the Marquis de Grange or there would be more awkward questions and she did not want that. Quickly she removed her hat and gave it to Berthe with her whip and gloves before she turned and went back down the stairs, feeling more confident.

The Music Salon lay three rooms beyond the Crimson Salon and as the double doors of each were all aligned she was able to see her parents from a distance away, illumined by the sunshine diffused to an amber tint by the flaming trees outside. Her mother had turned at the first sound of her step and stood with hands clasped, while her father sat on a sofa at an angle in profile to her, his gaze steadily set at some point beyond the windows. But when she reached the threshold of the Music Salon he did twist round towards her with a stunned, baffled expression that was linked in its own way to her mother's furious glare. She felt herself begin to tremble. It appeared that more was amiss here than she had expected.

"You wished to see me?" she said enquiringly, glancing at each of her parents in turn and hoping her trepidation did not show.

Marguerite gave a sharp nod and her question lashed out. "Is it true what I heard today? Have you been secretly meeting the Marquis de Grange?"

In spite of being half prepared Jasmin felt as if her knees would give way. Then her love for Fernand strengthened her and she set her shoulders, answering defiantly. "I have and I'm not ashamed of it!"

"How dare you speak to me in such a wanton manner!"

"Would you have preferred that I lied!" Jasmin retorted wildly.

Laurent intervened quickly from where he sat. "Come now. Let us try to discuss this matter rationally. The first step is to sit down."

Marguerite tossed her chin, too angry to comply. It was all she could do not to pace up and down. Jasmin did take the chair nearest him and perched on the edge of it, flinging him a loving, anguished glance. "I'm sorry it all had to come out like this. I suppose Madame Tourtain's tongue has been wagging."

He frowned, displeased by the suggestion. "You should know better than to accuse that good woman. Your mother has spoken to her, hoping to have the gossip proved false. Madame Tourtain was unaware of anything except your behaviour at the ball and thought that after her severe reprimand you would never be so foolish again, otherwise she would have spoken to us privately. However, when she called Isabelle into the room to question her, all your other misdoings came to light."

Jasmin, although outraged by her former friend's betrayal, was only thankful that not even Isabelle had had any inkling as to what lengths her love for Fernand had taken her. For a while Isabelle, swayed by the romanticism of the situation, had been an ally in distracting the attention of whoever was chaperoning them in order to give her those snatched minutes, and sometimes an hour or more, alone with him. But pique, boredom, even a trace of jealousy, had finally built up in Isabelle to erupt in the quarrel that had followed from their having to leave the ball early.

"Fernand has had little joy in his life." Jasmin gestured in what was an appeal for understanding. "He was betrothed to that plain and disagreeable wife of his when they were children and they never cared for each other. I admit he has gained a reputation for himself, but since he has met me he is a changed man."

Marguerite groaned and threw up her hands. "How can you be so naïve? Did he give any thought to you or your good name at the ball or when he drew you aside at Versailles and in Paris as soon as backs were turned?"

Jasmin was instantly defensive on his behalf. "Don't blame him alone! I wanted to be with him. I made the choice freely and without coercion to slip away with him whenever an opportunity presented itself."

"Your own sense should have told you he had no right to ask you in the first place!" Marguerite flung back at her. "What would a married man have to say to you, a young single girl, that he could not say before others?"

"That he loved me!" Jasmin exclaimed proudly. "Just as I love him!" Out of the corner of her eye she saw her father prop an elbow on his knee and drop his brow into his hand. She was speared through by his deep disappointment in her, which was far harder to bear than her mother's fury. They had never been estranged before, never known what it was to be at loggerheads.

Marguerite issued her ultimatum. "Never again must you speak to the Marquis de Grange. Should he attempt to engage you in conversation your father would be forced to call him out."

"No!" Jasmin was panic-stricken. She sprang to her feet. "Father is more than twice his age. At the very least Fernand would be compelled to wound him in a duel."

"Then you are fully aware of the consequences of any more foolhardiness on your part. Your dalliance with the Marquis is over."

Jasmin drew back a pace and clutched at the back of the chair in which she had sat as if needing some support to save herself from collapse. "Don't ask that of me," she implored in a small voice. "I'll die if you part us."

"Has he already seduced you?" Marguerite demanded crisply.

"No more!" Laurent had risen to his feet, white-faced and shaken. He did not want to hear what he feared might be a terrible answer to that question. He addressed his daughter with deliberate calmness. "Try not to be too distressed. Together the three of us as a united family will resolve this situation. You shall have the full support of your mother and myself in whatever this break will cost you."

"But I tell you again that Fernand loves me!" Jasmin burst out distractedly. "He wants his marriage annulled in order to marry me." Then seeing from their faces that neither of her parents was prepared to relent, she burst into helpless, noisy sobbing, throwing her arms over her bowed head in her abject misery. "He's everything to me and I to him."

Laurent, suffering at the sight of his daughter's dreadful despair, went and put his arms about her. "It can't be, my beauty, however many tears you shed. Try to adjust to that."

She clung to him as if drowning, her face buried in his shoulder. Marguerite stood a little distance from them, full of sadness. Why did parents always imagine their young would follow the path that had been set from birth and never be waylaid by predators or their own folly? She and Laurent had been like all the rest in thinking that their child would be different.

Silently she turned and went from the room, neither of them noticing her departure as she went back through the quiet salons. Without a single angry word Laurent would probably accomplish more than she had been able to do with her whole tempest of rage. No matter what problems still lay ahead the bond between father and daughter would remain unbroken whereas she had seen something close to hatred in Jasmin's eyes. It was not to be wondered at. The girl had no way of knowing that she herself had been through the indescribable agony of being parted from love. The relationship between Jasmin and herself, if not completely severed, had been damaged beyond recall.

For a long time Laurent and Jasmin remained together in the Music Salon. When eventually Jasmin came from it to hasten up the stairs to her own room, Marguerite went from where she had been waiting to find Laurent again. He had returned to his seat on the sofa near the harpsichord where he remained deep in thought, arms across his knees and his hands loosely linked. As she sat down beside him he turned almost in surprise at seeing her there.

"How is Jasmin now?" she asked, her voice weary with anxiety. "What is to happen?"

He comprehended how long the waiting must have been to her and when he extended an arm she sank against him into the haven of it. "Well, we reached a compromise. She accepts that she must stay out of the public eye until the gossip has died down and I have given her permission to write to the Marquis. She is sure he will come at once to see me and appeal to be allowed to wed her when he is free."

Marguerite drew back to look searchingly into his face. "You don't believe he will, do you?"

"My dear, he is like many such womanisers at Court. He has a rich wife. Why should he cast her aside for an immature girl who is about to cause him trouble and harassment and, most likely, at the end of it come penniless to him through parental opposition? He is a rich man in his own right, but you know as well as I do the constant competition and rivalry at Court to be grander and finer than everyone else, quite apart from the drain of gaming debts and the extravagant whims for faster horses, new carriages and still more sumptuous jewels. Jasmin, lovely though she is, is neither the first nor the last beautiful young face at Court."

"But suppose he really loves her?" Marguerite persisted, feeling she must present such a possibility even though her own opinion was against it.

"Marriages are not easily annulled. The procedure always takes many months and even years sometimes. I'm not a cynic, but I'm realistic and my guess is that the affections of the Marquis would not last that long. The same applies to Jasmin. This is her first love, which is never fatal and rarely lasts forever."

Marguerite sank back into his arm, her face turned away from his. It had lasted with her, right through to this very day. She prayed that Jasmin should not be similarly affected. "Is she to have no punishment?"

"For falling in love? How should I penalise her for that when all along you and I have each had our individual reasons for bringing her up in the knowledge that she would never be pressed into a *mariage de convenance.*"

Never before had he referred to his own reasons or hers. Outwardly Jasmin's happiness had been their joint aim, but inwardly they had both wanted her to find a depth of love in marriage that they had failed to find together.

"What of the gossip she has brought down on herself?"

He flicked his hand dismissively. "Chocolate-cup gossip, nothing more. It will soon be forgotten. The Court has far more salacious topics to enjoy than anything as mild as that. There will be no more scandal unless an application for the annulment of the Marquis's marriage should go ahead and I don't think you need lose any sleep over that."

His sensible words soothed her worries. "You're a wise man," she said with a catch in her voice. She could see that her condemnation of the Marquis and her furious ultimatum would have driven Jasmin recklessly into his arms, heedless of the consequences, whereas Laurent's lack of anger, his patience and farsightedness, had won a degree of compliance from her and would enable her to discover the truth about the man she loved, whether it be good or bad. "Jasmin is greatly blessed in having you for a father."

He responded by pressing a little kiss on her brow. She slid an arm about his neck and lay across his chest in his embrace, aware of being equally blessed.

No reply came to Jasmin's letter. A week and then another went by. She ran to the window at the sound of every carriage wheel and, if she happened to be upstairs, to the balustrade at the ring of the doorbell, always expecting Fernand to arrive. Soon she was convinced that her father's messenger had delivered her letter into the wrong hands and wrote again, a still more impassioned plea that the situation should be resolved with no more time lost. She had only agreed to her father's compromise in the first place because she had been certain that Fernand would come to Château Satory at once to convince her parents that all would be well. At times she raged privately against him for failing to appear and then with equal fervour invented dozens of reasons for his delay, yearning romantically for the sight of him. Had her emotions been balanced at either end of a seesaw she could not have been in a greater rise and fall of spirit.

When once again no reply came she voiced the cause most logical to her. "He must be in Paris again and not at Versailles," she declared to Laurent, her confidence still unshaken. "My letter will be waiting for his return."

"Oh, no," Laurent said, shaking his head. "I saw him in the Hall of Mirrors only yesterday."

"Did he speak to you?" she asked on a rush of hope.

"No. He was with jovial company and otherwise engaged."

"You ignored him!" she accused, heartsick that Fernand could find anything to laugh about when deprived of meetings with her.

"Indeed I did not. He saw me and had ample opportunity to approach." He took his daughter by the shoulders and looked her steadily in the eyes. "I'm being fair, my child. As I told you, if he comes to see me with honourable intent I shall receive him. How matters go after that depends on the case he presents."

She leaned towards him eagerly, her weight against his hands. "Let me go and see him just once. I know what's amiss. He is shy of coming and fears being refused by you on my behalf."

He set her back from him. "You know what the old adage says. Only the brave deserve the fair. Let him prove his courage. In the meantime you'll stick to your side of the bargain as I'll keep to mine."

She left him to go to her room and pen another letter. This time she set down as never before all the passionate outpourings of her love and she closed by asking that Fernand send back a reply with the deliverer of the letter, because she could go on no longer without hearing from him. She entrusted it to Berthe and despatched her in the fastest carriage. It seemed hours before the woman returned, but when she did she had a reply in her hand. Joyfully Jasmin snatched it from her and ran to a deserted salon in which to read it on her own. There were only a few lines and they were addressed formally to her:

An apology is long overdue from me for the gossip that resulted from my thoughtless behaviour in dancing too often with you at the Pâris-Duverney Ball. Since my concern is only for your good name it is best that all past

meetings be forgotten and no more future arrangements
made. I remain, your servant, Fernand de Grange.

She began to shiver as if the temperature of the room
had plummeted. Berthe, entering the room, saw how
stricken she was and felt little sympathy. People who had
everything had to learn that fate would not always bend in
their favour. The girl had been lucky through not being
married off quickly to some elderly widower, which was
what any father other than Baron Picard would have done
with a wayward daughter.

"You'd best forget the Marquis," she advised brusquely.
"He has all but forgotten you."

Jasmin seemed to have difficulty in speaking, her throat
choked. "That can't be. He's thinking only of me and that I
should be protected from further gossip."

Berthe gave a snort. "I doubt if the likes of him have
ever thought of any except themselves. I delivered the
letter to his room. I heard a woman's voice in there before
he opened the door in a robe over his nakedness."

For a matter of moments Jasmin stared at her, pupils
dilating. Then, white as paper, she slumped forward from
her chair to the floor in a faint. It took a long time to bring
her round.

To those at Château Satory it seemed that Jasmin lost
weight and all her liveliness in one stroke. She had no
interest in anything, her actions listless, her voice dull, and
she sat staring into space for hours. Marguerite watched
helplessly, for her daughter refused any comforting and
was positively hostile towards her. Laurent did take Jasmin
riding with him and she would return with her cheeks rosy
from the increasing nip of winter in the air, giving an
illusion of being back to normal. But once indoors again
the pale, wan look returned and she would shut herself
away in her room once more.

"Does she talk to you?" Marguerite asked Laurent.

"Hardly at all," he replied. "Let's be patient. It is still
early days for her."

The weeks passed and Christmas came. Talk at Court
was of the hunting at Fontainebleau soon to come. The
usual autumnal exodus had been cancelled through the
King having gone down with a serious illness. The Picard
family and many others like them were concerned only for
the King's recovery, but it was common knowledge that

the new Deputy Ruler, the Duc de Bourbon, had been close to panic throughout the days of crisis, for there was no heir other than an unsuitable claimant, which had portended trouble and upheaval for France. Fortunately Louis was now fast regaining his health.

It was the first day of February when the King sent word from Versailles that he wished to see Jasmin before his departure for Fontainebleau the following morning.

"I shall escort you," Laurent said to her. It had been his hope as well as Marguerite's that their daughter would not have to set foot in Versailles for a long while yet. Their opinion was that in keeping her away from that place, she would have plenty of time to recover from the whole dismal affair by the time spring came again.

It was with some misgivings that Laurent set off with his daughter, who was warmly wrapped in a fur-lined cape, on a crisp, cold afternoon with some pale sunshine filtering through. He did not ask Jasmin what her feelings were as she sat beside him in the coach withdrawn and quiet, offering no conversation.

When they arrived it was to be informed that the King, long starved of fresh air during his illness and convalescence, awaited them on the terrace of the West Front. They found him surrounded by courtiers and he turned at their approach with his shy, handsome smile.

On the brink of his fifteenth natal day he was fully mature and could have passed for being older. He was wearing his curly brown hair looped back and tied with a bow in the fashionable mode. If he had not yet regained his full weight after the fever that had laid him low, the leanness suited him and there was nothing of the invalid in his restored colour and vigorous stance. Jasmin, not having seen him for many weeks, was struck anew by the regal bearing that came naturally to him. The thought occurred to her that if the centuries could have been turned back, Jeanne d'Arc would have nominated him as the King among that cluster of well-dressed men as easily as she had once picked out his predecessor from a similar gathering.

"I trust I find you completely back to health, sire," she said when greetings were done.

"Yes, I am myself again. I thank you for your letter of good wishes. It was one of the few I chose to read for myself. Is it too cold for you if we remain here for a few minutes before taking a stroll in the park? We are on the very spot where Louis XIV always advised beholders to stand in order to view the gardens and the park itself to best advantage."

She knew that. It was something that was oft repeated, but she also knew it was being said today solely for her benefit. That same King's sensitive, considerate great-grandson was smoothing away any reference he might have been expected to make about her absence. He would have been one of the first to have heard the gossip about her and his aim was to put her at ease, rightly surmising this was a difficult visit for her.

"Whatever the season the vista from here is always beautiful," she said, letting her gaze rove with his to the Orangery and Swiss Lake to the south and then north to the Neptune fountain. They were standing on the terrace at an exact distance between the two huge War and Peace vases, which corresponded to the salons dedicated to those aims that flanked the Hall of Mirrors in the West Front behind them. There had been a light fall of snow that morning and it lay piled on the vases like wreaths of icy flowers. Today everything was brilliant in the clean, cold air. The Latona fountain threw only diamonds in its spray and beyond the snow-carpeted Tapis Vert the glitter of the Apollo fountain was almost lost in that of the Grand Canal. The perspective was perfect, the design faultless. None could fail to be moved by it.

Louis glanced at her as they went down the steps. There was excitement in him today that came from two causes; the first he could hardly wait to tell her outright and the second would have to be disclosed with diplomacy.

"I've had good news," he began happily, "although that's not the only reason why I wanted to see you before I leave for Fontainebleau. The Duc de Bourbon and the Council of Ministers have finally made the decision I thought would never come about. They're sending the Infanta back to Spain. I'm to have a new betrothed closer to my own age." He was no fool and knew why the decision had been made. His illness had made them realise how risky it was to keep him from marrying until the Infanta was nubile. The sooner he had an heir the better. Yet he had not let them see how much the news meant to him. It was unlikely they had expected him to leap about with joy, but they had probably thought to see a smile of relief. He had taught them on that day he was a boy no longer but a King able to keep his distance from them on every plane. His nod had been majestic as if the decision had been his and not theirs. His great-grandfather would have been proud of him.

"I'm so glad for you, Louis," Jasmin exclaimed with pleasure, able to be on informal terms now that they were out of earshot of those following behind. "Do you know yet who your bride will be?"

"A number of princesses have been listed." He did not add that the choice would depend on which of them was the most likely to prove fecund, but she would know that. "The arrangements always take time. That does not matter now that I'm free of that prattling infant."

She thought it was no wonder there was such a spring in his step. He must have loathed, more than could be estimated, the indignity of having that little girl always at his side on formal occasions. At best his feelings for her when grown could never have been anything but brotherly and now he had escaped what could only have been a disastrous marriage.

"You will be able to enjoy the hunting at Fontainebleau without anything to spoil it," Jasmin declared jubilantly. "Your health is restored, the Infanta is departing and you are King of all you survey."

He appreciated the little joke, chuckling with her. As always she was the only one with whom he was completely at ease. It was as if that meeting nigh on three years ago in the Hall of Mirrors had set up a rapport between them that only recently he had come to fully comprehend. All other relationships in his life since the age of seven had been bleak, barren of affection, and yet there was stored up in him a huge capacity to love. It was as if he were waiting for a door to open. During his convalescence he had had plenty of time to think and it had gradually become clear that it was Jasmin who held the key to releasing all the emotions in him that others should never know or see.

They reached the Apollo fountain in companionable talk and strolled around to the far side of it, leaving her father and the courtiers to stand waiting in conversation with one another, a colourful group in their vivid cloaks against the backcloth of the distant Château. Not knowing why, for she had seen Tuby's magnificent sun-god more times than she could remember, her attention became riveted by it, perhaps because of the curious luminosity of its gilding in the wintery sun. She felt herself awed by the power of Apollo, the reins taut in his masterful hand as he urged his team of four plunging horses, their nostrils flaring, their eyes bulging with their efforts to lift his chariot wheels free of the forceful fountain water and carry him high into his rightful place across the Versailles sky. She was suddenly gripped by a new relevance in the symbolism of the Apollo fountain, bringing home to her with painful intensity the need to shake herself free of what was holding her back, not in her case a plinth hidden beneath the spouting jets of water, but a love that had never been shared as she had foolishly believed. Abruptly aware that Louis was speaking to her she turned to him with a start.

"—when I return," he concluded, mistaking her quick reaction to surprise at what he had said. At least there had been no rejection in her expression, which his pride could not have borne.

The noise of the gushing waters had half-drowned his words and her thoughts had been elsewhere, but the meaning of what he had just said, however he might have cloaked it, showed in his eyes and in the amorous note she had caught at the tail end of that sentence. Her colour, always quick to come and go, flooded roses into her cheeks, which increased the ardour in his gaze.

"Do I understand you correctly?" she asked cautiously. How could one admit to not having listened fully at such a time? She could tell he had never been more serious than in what he had voiced to her, his face tense.

"I think you do." His tone was urgent. "I have cared for you ever since you managed to hide your laughter when I came sailing through on my back into the Peace Salon on the day of my return to Versailles." His smile answered hers on the memory he had evoked, taking away the strain in his features. "That's why I particularly wanted to speak to you today. While I'm away from Versailles you'll have a breathing space in which to accustom yourself to what my request will mean to you."

"And what of you in the interim period?" she asked, playing for a little time in which to deal with this new twist of events.

"I'll be looking forward every day to returning to you in the light of this conversation. For the first time ever, hunting will have lost its magnetic hold on me."

It was a charming statement from a boy unused to making romantic speeches. Her thoughts were in a whirl. Contrary to her father's hopes and in keeping with her mother's misgivings, it was easy to deduce that the gossip about her had damaged her good name as thoroughly as Berthe had predicted from the start. As a result Louis thought her more available now. Previously he would never have considered approaching her with an immoral aim. The King's mistress. Her parents would be the only people not to see her honoured by his proposition. There were thousands of women who would willingly be in her shoes and even more if they knew as she did that Louis was more than a little in love with her. It was enough to turn any girl's head, but hers was entirely stable, sobered out of frivolity and lightheartedness by the first harsh blow that life had ever dealt her.

"I've always been fond of you, Louis," she admitted. It was true, even though it had come to no more than that. Perhaps with time it would. Since the initial shock of losing Fernand had worn off, her ripe young body had a craving to be loved and cuddled and caressed as if for a short period she had become addicted to a delicious wine only to have it dashed away from her. Louis was clean and healthy and fastidious in his appearance, grave and serious and not inclined to any flippancy of thought or feeling. Even at this age he would commit himself to her, of that she was sure, for she had come to know his temperament well. If she wished it she could draw him into loving her always. Then she would reside grandly at Versailles until the end of her days. And why not?

Another aspect tempted her. Fernand would see what he had lost! And he was nothing compared to the King! She would have beautiful gowns and glorious jewels and snub her faithless lover whenever he asked her to dance or paid court to her in any way. Better still, she could stem any advancement for him. The chance of vengeance was being put into her hands, an opportunity that would never have come her way by any other means.

"You agree then?" Louis pressed eagerly.

She still hesitated. How to ask the King of France

whether those still governing the country on his behalf would agree to his having a titular mistress at so young an age. "I may meet opposition. So may you."

"None that I can't overcome," he insisted with emphasis. "This is my will on the matter."

Then she knew that the days of the Duc de Bourbon's control over him were drawing towards their close. Soon Louis would take over the rôle for which he had been trained since childhood. She could help him to be a good king, to avoid the extravagances of Louis XIV and then the Regent and currently the Duc de Bourbon, none of whom had set him an example in thrift. She had heard her father say often that France's finances had never been in a sorrier state and there was no denying the vast numbers of hungry beggars in the streets. Love, as she had known it briefly, was unlikely ever to come again and neither would she desire it. There was a limit to how much hurt one could endure. With Louis she could have a loving friendship in which her heart need never be involved.

"I need the time you have allowed me, Louis. When you return to Versailles we'll talk again."

"Only for you to tell me what I want to hear," he insisted anxiously.

She smiled and gave him her hand. It was the promise that he wanted. He caressed her fingers as he raised them to his lips. She observed to herself that he was learning fast the ways of a lover.

They both thought that the fountain spray had been a screen for them, which was why he had drawn her there to converse with her unobserved. But one courtier had shifted his position slightly from the start in order to watch them covertly out of the corner of his eye. He had seen the expression on Louis's face, love-sick as that of any country lad, and caught the surreptitious caress of hands before the lingering kiss on the fingertips that had been more than courtliness. The nobleman was one of the Duc de Bourbon's ministers and he had recently been entrusted by him to start negotiations for a marriage between Louis and a Polish princess. The last thing wanted at the moment was any side distraction for the King that might complicate matters.

As soon as steps were retraced to the Château and the King had parted from his visitors, the courtier hastened to the Duc de Bourbon and reported what he had seen. Monsieur le Duc went to his writing desk, drew a list towards him and added Jasmin's name to it.

Louis, unaware that anything might be moving against his newfound happiness, went off to Fontainebleau where he spent many hours on horseback. He noticed the absence of several young courtiers of ducal rank whose company he had begun to rely on for their wit and often extremely entertaining if caustic remarks about the Court. He asked where they were.

"They are in disgrace," he was told, "which is why the Duc de Bourbon has banished them to their estates."

"What kind of disgrace?" Louis asked, having a good idea. Although he lacked any kind of sexual experience his tutor had taken on the duty of informing him of the pitfalls of human behaviour to be avoided at all costs. He could see that the courtier was racking his brains to know what to say. The answer came on a rush of words and on a flash of inspiration.

"They went on an orgy of destruction in the gardens of Versailles and pulled up palisades."

If Louis had not had the gift of hiding his thoughts he would have laughed out loud. Whatever had been indulged in at the orgy it was unlikely to have been the pulling up of railings.

"Indeed," he replied drily, "they must have been very drunk or else they are all extremely strong."

"Oh, yes, sire," the courtier replied vaguely, needing to mop his brow, for the sweat was trickling down his temples.

The joke flew round the Court. Louis was aware of it and kept his amusement to himself. Then he began to take note that certain other noblemen were either being summoned back to Versailles by the Duc de Bourbon or being called away by urgent matters on their estates. Since he knew that the majority of courtiers cared nothing about their properties, except as a source of funds, he suddenly realised what was afoot. Those who might have had an adverse influence over him were being weeded out and he understood why. At least two of his famous forebears had had no liking for women and the Duc de Bourbon, guessing at his increasingly lustful state, normal to any well-developed youth, was taking what he believed to be sensible precautions.

Louis thought it unnecessary interference in the lives of others and quite pointless. If he had been consulted he would have let it be known that in many ways he was his great-grandfather all over again, except that unlike Louis XIV he would never tire of Jasmin and cast her aside as Louise de La Vallière and then Athénaïs de Montespan had been. It was in him to be loyal and faithful insomuch as it was possible to be true to a mistress with a marriage looming on the horizon.

He particularly missed the company of an older man, the Duc de Valverde. As a huntsman Sabatin de Valverde was unsurpassed, as a drinker he could stay on his feet when those all around were under the table and as a source of information about the Court he was as valuable as any spy. Through him Louis had learned a great deal about whom to trust and of whom to be wary. Admittedly Sabatin himself was a scandalous character, known to indulge in orgies in which he was not particular about the gender of his partners, but Louis had been prepared to ignore the nobleman's private life for the use that Valverde could be to him with his keen insight into the ways of the Court. He hoped that Valverde's absence was only temporary, but he did not make any more enquiries. No courtier was indispensable.

The days at Fontainebleau passed pleasantly. Whenever his thoughts turned to Versailles excitement surged through his veins. Jasmin would be there when he returned. Winning her would be a joy. In spite of her modest hesitation she of all the people he knew would never fail him. His heart was full of love for her.

Sabatin de Valverde had not been unduly worried when he received the summons from the Duc de Bourbon to return to Versailles for an audience, but he was irritated by the inconvenience. However, one did not refuse an order by the King's Deputy Regent and, although he delayed his departure for several days, not wishing to miss a number of social events that were among the highlights of any sojourn at Fontainebleau, he eventually entered his handsome gilded coach with its scarlet velvet-upholstered seats and the journey commenced. He had brought his current mistress for company and some good wine to quench the thirst the dust of travel could create.

"How long do you expect to be at Versailles before we return?" the woman asked from the seat beside him, although the length of time was unimportant to her. Their liaison was new, no more than a few nights shared to date, and she was still full of curiosity about this square, heavily built man with his horseman's hands and ugly saturnine features that both thrilled and frightened her. It was why she had come. He was a brutal lover, a deep savagery in him, but since he had the ability to fire her again and again until she was sated with ecstasy, she could put up with his rough handling and the bruises that resulted.

He glanced at her sideways, his long nostrils flaring at the pleasing scent she wore. His eyes, close-set, raked her as she settled herself more comfortably, smoothing her skirt with a pretty flick of her fingers. She was one of those thin, pale women that turn out to be full of surprises, the twenty-year-old wife of an old nobleman who was unlikely to have been her tutor in the pleasurable sexual tricks at which she excelled.

"A day at the most," he replied. "I know what to expect. Monsieur le Duc intends to reprimand me for giving my new hunter to the King. It's a spirited beast and didn't take kindly to a change of rider, which means that exaggerated reports of how the King was nearly thrown will have reached his ears. Since he hates me as much as the Devil himself it has given him the opportunity to submit me to this tedious journey and lay down the law to me at the end of it. Until there's a legitimate heir to the Throne I fear Bourbon will continue to be like a cat on hot coals at the slightest risk of any danger to the King."

"Did you warn the King that the horse was frisky?" She knew that Sabatin was also a practical joker of the worst kind, for there was no pity in him.

"As it happens, I did. Why should I not when he could do so much for me? I've no wish to see Louis with a broken neck. After all, the next in line of succession is Orléans and he is no friend of mine. But the King could be. I'm gaining his confidence and I intend to see that he is served according to his wishes. I'm thinking of offering you to him when we return unless he should prefer my page."

She jerked forward in the seat, tears of outrage springing to her eyes. "I'm not a horse to be given away!"

He burst out laughing and spread his hand across her thigh, squeezing it through the layers of silk and lace. "I've paid you a compliment. Only the best is good enough to be a gift for the King."

She was slightly mollified. "You're teasing me," she pouted.

His laughter died away and his grip on her thigh tightened like a vise until she could have shrieked out with the pain. "I never tease. Don't ever accuse me of that nonsense again." With his free hand he began to loosen his breeches.

She let him pull her over to him. He wrenched up her skirts and cupped her buttocks, bringing her down on him, her knees spread. A gasp escaped her as he thrust into her without the least caress. Fontainebleau was hardly out of sight. However was this journey to be?

At Château Satory, Laurent had also received a summons from the Duc de Bourbon and deduced as easily the reason for it. They had earlier discussed some minor extension to Monsieur le Duc's apartment and if that nobleman was shortly to rejoin the Court at Fontainebleau it would be an admirable time for the work to be carried out. He had the plan ready and it was simply a matter of final approval. He put on a new coat for the audience. It was of dove-grey velvet with the wider flare to the coattails. Louis XIV had never liked the colour of grey and had objected to it being worn at Court, but now it was in favour again. Wide-brimmed hats had gone out of mode and Laurent picked up his new-shaped tricorn hat to set it on his formal white wig, which had three rolled curls over each ear and was adorned with a black bow at the back of his neck. A final adjustment to his lace shirt cuffs and he was ready. He had always taken a pride in his appearance, never the dandy, but well tailored and at the moderate edge of fashion. Wigs were a blessing for men who had become as bald as himself, projecting the illusion of youthfulness, provided that the face was not too wrinkled and the figure had not gone to pot.

He took up his leather folder and went down the stairs to his waiting carriage. Marguerite was at her salon on the

Avenue de Paris and Jasmin was at the dressmaker's. The girl's spirits had revived just as he had foreseen. Although by no means her former self she had begun to take an interest in everything again and new clothes had become important to her once more. Now and then he had thought she was on the point of confiding something to him, for she had made oblique references to the King and the Court that had left him puzzled. It seemed to him that she must be feeling her way as to whether, when the Court returned to Versailles, he would allow her to reenter the social scene, which was not an unreasonable request if she should be able to convince him that she had fully recovered from her infatuation for the Marquis. On those grounds he would be willing enough, although it would be on a more restricted level than before. Maybe he should retire Berthe and engage a younger woman with sharper eyes. Then he felt a pang that his trust in his daughter should have diminished to that point and he dismissed any thought of change from his mind.

It was a glorious May morning. Everything was in blossom and the parterres were carpets of bloom. Yesterday had been Jasmin's seventeenth natal day and he felt no older than when she was born. As he sat back to be driven the pleasant route to Versailles, he smiled to himself that he should have thought of retiring Berthe, who was barely fifty, when he himself was in his late sixties still with commissioned designs and drawings and plans mounting up in his offices above Marguerite's salon where she, only a few years behind him, was as busy as she had ever been.

At Versailles he puffed a bit as he went up the Ambassadors' Staircase, reminded that his waistcoat was not as flat in the front as he would have wished, and set off on the long walk to the Council Chamber. He did not have many minutes to wait and he entered briskly to bow from the waist towards the Duc de Bourbon, who sat on the far side of the council table with its draperies of blue and silver brocade. Sliding the plan from the leather folder under his arm, he advanced to the table and made ready to unfold it for inspection. To his surprise it was waved aside.

"It is not about the alterations to my apartment that I wished to see you today, Monsieur le Baron. You may sit down. I have another matter entirely to reveal to you."

Laurent was never able to remember how long that

audience in the chamber lasted, but if anyone had taken particular notice of his going in and coming out they would have thought he had aged twenty years in the interim. He emerged with a stunned expression and shuffled to the nearest chair where he sat down and began meticulously to refold the plan he had drawn up with such precision and return it to the folder. His trembling hands made the paper rustle to the extent where one of the Swiss Guards by the double doors of the Council Chamber glanced in his direction.

It seemed to Laurent to take an interminable time to fasten the buckles of the folder, but when it was done he moved slowly to his feet and began to drag himself back the way he had come. He felt hot and sweaty and nauseous, but he had to hurry. There was no time to lose. He, one of Louis XV's most loyal subjects, was about to commit treason by breaking all the commands given to him by Monsieur le Duc in the King's name. He had to get Jasmin away in time. They would all flee; he, Marguerite and Jasmin. But where? Holland or the German states or England?

With relief he reached the Ambassadors' Staircase where a cold draught met him from the open arched grilles below. He tore at his neckcloth to loosen it, needing to get some air into his lungs, for a tight band was closing about his chest. Heedless of the disarray of linen and lace at his throat, he began his descent, clinging for support to the marble balustrade. Those passing him in both directions were busy about their own affairs and the few that glanced at him, none of them acquaintances, thought he was dead drunk.

He reached the place where the branched flights met for the last section of the staircase. By now his shirt was soaked and clinging to his body while beads of sweat rolled down from his forehead and dripped from the corner of his mouth onto the velvet of his coat. There were still many more marble stairs to descend when his heart exploded into such pain in his chest that he collapsed with a shuddering groan, slithering on his back down the rest of the flight, arms and legs askew and sheer horror in his staring eyes at what was happening to him.

There was nothing that made men-at-arms and lackeys move faster than the prospect of imminent and forbidden

death within the confines of Versailles. Three "blue boys"
and two soldiers rushed to pick him up and race with him
out of doors. His throat was gurgling and his unsupported
head hanging. In his wake his wig and hat and folder were
snatched up from where they had fallen and carried by a
lackey who ran behind. They would have borne Laurent
all the way down the Cour Royale and out beyond the
gates if his coachman, watching out for his return from the
audience, had not recognised him by his new grey coat
with the silver-braided pockets.

"In here!" he yelled, whipping open the carriage door.
Then he took charge as his master was lifted in onto the
seat. "Careful now. Gently does it."

"Get going!" the Swiss Guard ordered when the task was
done.

Glowering at the unseemly haste with which the Baron
had been treated, the coachman drove with care the short
distance to the Picards' business house on the Avenue de
Paris, not wanting to shake the sick man from the seat. As
the footman on duty came to open the carriage door he
leapt down from his box.

"Leave that! You race back indoors and tell the Baronne
that her husband is out here and has had a seizure."

As he had expected, the Baronne came white-faced out
of the house at a run without cape or hat. He held the door
for her and she leapt in to fall to her knees at her husband's
side, putting a gentle hand to his face. Then she glanced
back over her shoulder. "He's still alive," she said in a
choked voice. "Drive us home as quickly as you can."

Laurent was paralysed down his left side. Marguerite
undressed him with Berthe's help and put him into a clean
nightshirt. For the first time she felt she should send for a
doctor, for the bleeding of a patient in a case of seizure was
generally acknowledged to be beneficial, but she would
not have any of those monsters at Versailles to his bedside.
Instead she sent for a young doctor who had just established a practice in the town, and her hope was that he
would prove to be more enlightened in his treatments.

Thin and serious with clean, capable hands, he bled Laurent, who was barely conscious, and gave Marguerite some
powders that were to be administered to the patient in
milk. "These will help your husband to sleep, because he
needs rest more than anything else. Have you any idea

what brought on the attack? Has he complained recently of feeling unwell?"

In her own mind Marguerite wondered if prolonged worry about Jasmin had taken its toll, but she would not reveal that to anyone. "No, he has not. This morning he was in good spirits. When I left here he was shortly to depart for Versailles on a business mission that he was looking forward to."

"Well, the heart is an unpredictable organ. I'll call tomorrow and see if he needs to be bled again."

When Jasmin came home Marguerite met her in the hall to break the news. She became nearly hysterical at hearing of the serious nature of her father's attack. "He's not going to die, is he, Maman? I couldn't bear it. Nothing in this world matters except to see him well again."

"Go and see him," Marguerite advised, "but be prepared for a change in his appearance."

Although she had been warned, Jasmin was still shocked by the droop of his features on the left side, which even in sleep gave him a look of torment. She sat by his bedside and would not leave, her face pale and distraught. Marguerite kept vigil that night, but had a bed made up for Jasmin in the room, for if Laurent drew his last breath it was only right that they should both be with him. He seemed to her to have become much weaker since the bleeding, and the powders had made him vomit in a most distressful manner. She resolved that if he lived through the night she would nurse him in her own way and dispense with medical men entirely.

She held Laurent's right hand all through the hours of darkness, wanting him to know she was there. Once he opened his eyes with a kind of restless start, making her fear the worst, but when he saw her face in the candleglow, he became quiet again and slept once more. Her thoughts ranged back over their time together. If the hours of happiness she had known with Augustin could be weighed against those given her by Laurent the scales would have dipped in her husband's favour, simply because they had had many more years together. Admittedly it had been joy of a different kind, but it had had its own qualities that had brought contentment to them both. She loved him, never with the passion of her youth, but age had taught her that even with Augustin that would have settled in time to much the same loving companionship she had shared with Laurent, albeit on a deeper level.

"Don't die, my dear Laurent," she whispered, linking his fingers with hers to raise and kiss them. "Let me dedicate myself to caring for you from now on as you have always cared for me."

In the morning his condition was unchanged. The young doctor arrived, prepared to bleed him again, and was sent away without having reached the bedchamber door. Marguerite spooned a little nourishing liquid into Laurent's mouth at intervals during the day and he kept it down. His sleep became less restless, which she took to be an encouraging sign. The next day he rallied considerably and tried to talk to her, panic coming into his eyes at finding his speech slurred. She reassured him quickly.

"There's nothing to worry about. You've been ill, my dear, and soon your speech and your strength will return."

"Jasssss . . ." he brought out with effort.

"Jasmin has been here all the time. I've just persuaded her to take a turn in the fresh air. She'll soon be back."

He became agitated. "Jasss . . . 'way." Then exhaustion overcame him and against his will he could only lie with his eyes closed.

Jasmin was joyful at hearing he had asked for her and resumed her seat at his bedside, eager for his waking. When he did open his eyes to find her sitting there he tried to shout as if better to enunciate and was completely incomprehensible. She caught up his good hand and pressed it to her cheek.

"Don't get upset, Papa," she implored, reverting to the appellation of childhood. "I'll stay with you all the time until you're well again."

To her dismay he pulled his hand from her and gave every sign that he wanted her to go from him, getting into such a frenzy that she fled in tears from the room. Only then did he become quieter, looking to Marguerite with such a plea to be understood that she almost broke down herself.

"What is it, my dearest?"

He repeated what he had said at the start. "Jasss . . . 'way."

"You want Jasmin to be kept away?" She saw that she had made progress but still had not defined what it was he wished her to grasp. "Should she stay out of here until you're well again?"

A slurred affirmation came from him. Then he said almost distinctly, "My . . . sister-in-law . . . in Florence."

"You want Jasmin to go to Italy?" she exclaimed. "My dear, there is no need for that. She can simply be in the house until you wish to see her." It was immediately obvious she had blundered there and she tried again, for it did not seem that his mind was wandering. "Very well. I will try to guess why. You think she is threatened by whatever feelings she still has for the Marquis de Grange, and since you yourself will not be in a position to guard her for a while you wish her to be safely away in Florence."

Wearily he closed his eyes as if she had come as near as he could expect her to get with this terrible affliction holding back all he would have said. "Jasss . . ." he murmured.

Seeing that he slept she let Berthe stay with him and went in search of Jasmin, who was still sobbing. At Marguerite's approach she sat up on the sofa where she had sprawled, her eyes wet and glistening. "Will he let me sit with him now?"

With a sigh Marguerite sat down and explained the situation. "We may have to appear to comply with his wishes or else he is going to continue to worry and that will hamper any chance of recovery."

Jasmin stared in disbelief. "But there's nothing to fear from Fernand any more as far as I'm concerned. I wanted to tell Father many times that my future is now destined to be with someone else." Eagerness came into her voice. "It is the King, Maman. My Louis from childhood. He wants me to be at Versailles when he returns."

For a matter of seconds Marguerite stared incredulously at her, eyes wide with dismay. "You little fool!" she gasped. "Are you going to spend your days dancing from one folly to another? How long do you think the Duc de Bourbon would let you stay at Versailles? Everyone knows that the Infanta was sent away to leave the King free to marry soon. No woman who loves a man with all her heart could ever share him with another!"

Jasmin slid her feet to the floor and stood up, her attitude one of bravado. "I never said I loved Louis. It's no good loving a man in the way you describe, because that brings nothing but misery. I'm fond of him. He's kind and good and cares for me. You're wrong about the Duc de Bourbon having the power to turn me away. Louis would never allow it. He'll accept whatever royal bride is chosen for him because that is a political matter and has nothing to do with his personal feelings. But he'll want me with him always and I intend to stay."

Marguerite turned her face away, wanting to cry out in desolation, filled with a sickening sense of futility. Since Jasmin's birth all she had wanted was that her daughter should know as she had known the kind of enduring love that was the enrichment of life, the ultimate experience. To hear such words of disillusionment made her wonder where along the way she herself had failed. The girl was weak, too easily influenced, too quick to take whatever pleased her at the moment. Marguerite blamed herself entirely. She had not done enough to counteract the endless cherishing and cosseting and indulgence of every whim. Jasmin's life seemed destined to end in shreds and she could not see what could be done to avert disaster.

"You mustn't burden your father with this new waywardness," she said despairingly. "He will stop asking that you be sent away if you reassure him, as you have me, that the Marquis de Grange no longer means anything to you."

Jasmin lifted her chin. "I didn't say exactly that. Do you think me so shallow that I can forget already what Fernand meant and still means to me? The difference is that love and hate are mixed together now, making it impossible for me to decide which is the stronger and at times they even seem the same. But I'll never look in his direction again, that I swear. It's why I need Louis's gentleness now. With him to care for me that will be all the love that I'll ever need."

Marguerite pressed her hands together in her sadness and let them rise and fall distractedly. Worse and worse. "Maybe I should send you to Florence. There you would be out of harm's way from the King and everyone else. Even though Laurent is ill he shows more wisdom than any of us."

Jasmin's expression softened and she came to stoop by the sofa and look into her mother's face. "Do you think Louis wouldn't send for me at once? How could you or my father or I go against the wishes of the King of France?"

A shuddering sigh racked Marguerite's whole frame.

What Jasmin had said was true. "Then let us at least try to remove all anxiety about you from your father's mind. When he has recovered some strength he will be better able to accept what you have told me."

Although Marguerite prepared Laurent for some reassuring information from his daughter and he did hear Jasmin's assurance that Fernand would never again be part of her life, his agitation about her going away started up again immediately afterwards, even to the point that tears ran from his eyes and sobs rose in his throat. Marguerite cradled him in her arms.

"Don't weep any more, my dearest," she implored, full of tears herself. "Jasmin shall go away. I'll make arrangements without delay."

He was immediately comforted, trusting her to keep her word, and as she held his head against her breast she thought this was the first time she had ever lied to him. Her plan was that Jasmin should simply stay out of the bedchamber and away from that part of the château to ensure he had no hint of her continued presence, for ill as he was his brain had not been affected except for this delusion that Jasmin would still be safer far from Versailles. Any possibility of his having heard about the King's arrangement with Jasmin was ruled out, for she had spoken of it to no one and knew that Louis, reticent in all matters, would not have breathed a word. In fact, her being at Versailles upon his return was to be a fait accompli against any move that the Duc de Bourbon might otherwise have made.

Then on the eve of the day when Jasmin was to go through the masquerade of departure, a letter was delivered from the Duc de Bourbon that lifted away the need of pretence to a certain degree. It was addressed to Laurent. Marguerite, opening it on his behalf even as she was dealing with all other communications that came for him, read that she and Laurent were to present themselves with their daughter, as previously arranged, at the hour of eleven o'clock the following day. The reason was in the single sentence that stated Jasmin should bring all the possessions that she would need with her.

Marguerite let her hand sink with the letter into her lap, feeling herself sag with it. It meant only one thing. As Jasmin had said, Louis would not be thwarted in taking her as his mistress and this was proof that Bourbon had agreed to install her at Versailles in readiness for the royal return. Laurent must have been informed when he had had his audience with Bourbon that day. It gave an explanation at last for the stroke and for his desperation that his daughter should leave the country while there was time. If he had been truly in his right mind he would have realised that Louis, even putting aside all regal powers, would only have had to beckon with his finger for Jasmin to follow her own headstrong way and come running back to him.

"You see!" Jasmin exclaimed excitedly when she was told. "I knew Louis would not be overruled in anything to do with me. He must be returning with the Court late tomorrow afternoon at the usual hour, and by that time I'll be installed in my own apartment waiting for him." Then she saw the anguish in her mother's face and became subdued. "Don't be sad, I beg you. It may be that through Louis's love for me I'll be able in time to do much for France. At Versailles he lives in a crystal bowl, seen by all but never seeing out himself. I'll change that. I'll let him know what it means to be a peasant worker living on a pittance just as you showed me. He needs me, Maman. More than he is aware of yet."

Marguerite's voice was heavy with sadness. "Have you thought what your fate will be when he tires of you? You'll be given the choice of marriage with someone else or retirement to a convent."

"You don't know Louis as I do. But if what you fear should ever come about I'd spurn both those alternatives and come home to Château Satory. That would always be my haven."

"Oh, my dear child!" It was a throbbing cry. Marguerite held out her arms and Jasmin flew into them. They hugged each other tightly, coming closer in spirit at that poignant moment than they had ever been. Marguerite, her eyes tightly closed against tears, thought how Château Satory had been her refuge when all else had gone. Leaning back, she took her daughter's face between her hands and kissed her on both cheeks and then again. "I find no pride in your being chosen for this rôle and I never will, but you've given me hope for your future. Here under this roof you would always be able to find a meaning to life again."

Jasmin spent the rest of the day deciding what should be

taken in travelling boxes to Versailles and what should be
left behind. Marguerite could take no part in advising her,
for Laurent would not endure her being away from his
bedside. Whenever he opened his eyes he wanted to see
her there, lifting his good hand for her to hold, his fears
soothed immediately by her presence. While he slept for a
little she wrote to the Duc de Bourbon, explaining that
neither she nor her husband could in these special circumstances attend at Versailles, but their daughter would be
there at the appointed time. As she sealed the letter, making the imprint in wax of the Picard crest, she wondered
how Berthe would feel about her days of chaperonage
being at an end. Jasmin would be taking Josette, her
personal maid, with her, a quick, skilful young woman,
talented at dressing hair and sewing, who had been appointed on Jasmin's twelfth natal day when Laurent
thought it high time she was treated more as if she were
grown up and less like a child. Although Berthe's status as
chaperone had been inviolate, she had been savagely jealous of Josette, seeing her as an usurper, which led to friction, and it would be a relief to have that running battle
over at last.

That evening Jasmin sat a long time at her father's bedside. He believed she was departing for Italy at dawn the
next morning and was content that she should be there for
their last few hours together. She guessed he doubted
whether he would ever see her again and she was thankful
that she would not be far away if the day she dreaded
should come. Emotion made him more incomprehensible
than ever and after several heartrending attempts to talk
to her he gave up, sinking deeper into his pillows, his eyes
tormented.

"One day we'll be together again, Papa," she promised
when the hour became too late for her to stay with him any
longer. Her tears were running profusely as she kissed him
good night and farewell. After she had gone from the room
he began to have breathing difficulties, making Marguerite
fear that grief would stop his weakened heart, but after she
had held him propped in her arms for a little while, the
spasm passed and he slept without waking until dawn
when he supposed his daughter to be well on the way to his
sister-in-law in Florence.

He was sleeping when Marguerite slipped away from

the bedchamber to see Jasmin leave in good time for the appointed hour at Versailles, Josette having departed already with the baggage. Jasmin was in full Court dress and to her mother's eyes had never looked more beautiful. Her gleaming chestnut hair was dressed straight back from her forehead, curled at the sides and arranged in longer locks at the back. Her gown, low-cut with sleeves that reached to the elbows where they burst into frills of fine lace, was of summer-sky blue over one of the new cone-shaped hoops and so thickly embroidered with silver and pearls that it twinkled and shone from waist to ankle and showed the diamond buckles on her satin shoes at every step. Pearl eardrops and a single strand worn high around her pretty neck completed a picture of style and elegance.

"How is Papa now?" she asked anxiously.

Marguerite was quick to reassure her. "Tranquil and at ease in his mind. I'm full of hope that now he will begin to improve, although it will be a long, slow progress."

"We'll keep in close touch. When he is well enough to have visitors you must warn them to say no word of my presence at Versailles."

"Have no fear. Somehow we must keep up our pretence until we are certain that to reveal the truth would not bring on another attack."

Marguerite had no chance to stand in the doorway and watch Jasmin drive away, for Berthe came at a run to say that the Baron had awakened. He had begun to gasp for breath upon failing to find his wife at his bedside.

In spite of Jasmin's brave appearance there was no gladness in her as every beat of the horses' hooves took her away from home. She felt it was her rightful place at the present time where she should be helping to nurse her father, even though circumstances had made that impossible. With effort she forced herself to look forward with the reminder that the most powerful Duc in the land was being compelled by his sovereign to arrange everything for her comfort at the greatest palace in the world. Soon she would see the grand apartment selected for her and there within a few hours Louis would arrive to take her shyly into his arms. He would be sympathetic about her father, but he would not consider himself to be in any way responsible for what happened, however indirectly. In

fact, she did not think he would ever want to be burdened
with her troubles. Her task would be to lighten his.

Bejewelled and perfumed, dainty as a doll in her finery,
Jasmin was driven through the gilded gates of Versailles on
the first stage of the new life ahead of her.

Twelve

For three days Sabatin de Valverde was kept waiting for his audience with the Duc de Bourbon. His annoyance at the time wasted showed in his expression when he finally entered the Council Chamber. It was to be the most stormy and violent encounter ever known there. Both men lost their tempers and at one point only the damask-draped table between them prevented a furious grappling with each other. Sabatin, well aware that he was dicing with the Bastille itself, was nevertheless unable to restrain his fury.

"The risk of the King taking a fall was minimal!"

"I'm aware of that."

"So you're using that minor incident to gain your own ends!" Sabatin's forbidding, angular face was blazing. "You've long wanted to be rid of me at Court."

"I don't deny it. Since only you and I are within this chamber I'll tell you that it's why I'm taking this action against you!"

"But this sentence you've passed on me is insupportable." Sabatin's voice was close to a shriek in his wrath.

"I want you as far from the King as possible," Bourbon ground out between his teeth, his colour almost purple. "He shall not be contaminated by lecherous influences all the time it lies in my power to prevent it."

"Nevertheless you would never have made a move against me if you had not seen the chance of killing two birds with one stone. This wretched female you would thrust onto me is some silly creature who pursued the Marquis de Grange until he could stomach no more of her. I heard it from him myself. You have no right to inflict such unwarranted punishment on me!"

"You dare to speak to me of *right!*" Bourbon looked as if he might explode. "Watch your words, Valverde. Do you wish to add treasonable utterances to all else marked up against you?"

"A tally kept by you alone!"

"You're wrong. The whole Council of Ministers is for your removal from Court."

"Only because you have most surely spoken against me! Has the young woman been similarly condemned or is that a private move on your part?"

"Enough!"

"So I come too close to the truth for you, do I? It would be disastrous if the romanticism in the King's character should lead him to think along the lines of Louis XIV towards Madame de Maintenon. That would interfere with your plans for his marriage. Damnation!" Sabatin raised his arms and shook his fists in the consuming fury that possessed him. "I will not be a scapegoat to take the threat off your hands!"

"You have no choice! I've made my decision!"

It had been said inexorably. Sabatin took a step back under the impact. Gulping, he switched his tone abruptly to an impassioned plea. "If banishment from Court is to be my fate then at least confine me to Paris. Not to my estate. I haven't been there for years!"

"In Paris you would worm your way back to the King somehow."

Sabatin's lips drew back grotesquely over his bad teeth. "How you fear me, Bourbon!" he taunted viciously. "You were able to foresee yourself being supplanted by me as adviser to the King when he begins to reign as he should. Already he is showing signs of asserting himself, of using his own mind as to whom he wishes to have around him. Your days are numbered."

"I think not. But if by some unlucky chance they should be, the decree I've given in this chamber on this day in the King's name, with the authority of the Council of Ministers, will hold until you draw your last breath. I hearby banish you from the Court forever, and you will depart as soon as your marriage has taken place!"

Sabatin gave a terrible roar as if he were already in his death throes, raising his fists high and crashing them down on the table with a force that would have split asunder anything less well constructed. He looked crazed, his close-set black eyes narrowed, his heavy brows drawn together until the natural peak of his sleek hair seemed almost to touch them. Bourbon, thoroughly alarmed, shouted for the guards, who burst into the room.

"Escort the Duc de Valverde to his apartment," he ordered. "He is to remain there until noon when he is to attend the Royal Chapel to await his bride."

Sabatin shot him such a virulent look of hatred that the guards tightened their clasp on their pikes, ready to leap forward in the Regent's defence if need be. But Sabatin made no move against him. Instead he spat contemptuously, leaving a glob of spittle darkening a spot on the blue and silver damask of the table's drapery. Then he strode from the room with his features still congested with rage, and although the guards followed him, they hoped there would be no altercation. He looked ready to strangle with his bare hands.

It was a long walk through many rooms and down long corridors to reach his apartment. Although wrath kept his blood boiling there rose in him such desolation at his fate that his normally ruddy skin turned patchy and grey, drawing taut until his nose was bone-white, his eyes hollowed. By the time he reached his apartment his brain felt dazed as if the blow dealt him had been a physical battering. His mistress, sitting curled on a sofa with a box of sweetmeats, bored with Versailles in the Court's absence, turned her head lazily towards him as he came slamming in through the door. Then she saw his racked face, the stare of unadulterated misery in his eyes, and could think of only one explanation for such grief. She sprang to her feet, pressing a hand to her heart and heedless of the sweetmeats that she sent scattering to the floor.

"*Mon Dieu!* The King is dead!"

He shook his head from side to side as did the caged lions in the royal menagerie and his voice broke from him hoarsely. "No. Worse than that."

Compassion swept over her and she moved swiftly to him. "Then you have lost your father? Your mother? A brother, perhaps?"

He brushed her queries aside with a sweep of his hand. "My parents died long ago and I have no brother. I have been banished from Court. It is my own death you should be proclaiming, because to leave Versailles and everything appertaining to it is to enter hell." He gave a crazed laugh. "Mourn for me, my sweeting. My grave is my estate in the Périgord."

She drew back several paces from him, all sympathy gone. In a matter of seconds he had become a pariah before her eyes, one of the despised nobles who had no political influence and no entrée at Court through lack of favour or finance, through banishment or their own preference for a quiet life. Whatever the reason they were all figures of fun to be ridiculed by those whose sumptuous lives were centred on the Throne.

"Such punishment!" she exclaimed faintly. "For letting the King ride too spirited a horse."

"That's only the peg on which Bourbon is hanging his vengeance. He has found a way to settle old scores by the deadliest means in his power, simply because he is desperate to get rid of a young woman who has caught the King's fancy." His temper soared again until his face became grotesque with it, his hatred divided evenly between his enemy and his bride-to-be. "I'm to be wed to a creature of no standing or importance. She is the basic cause of my being thrown into exile and I'm to drag her along there with me."

She felt a pang of pity for whoever was to marry this man set with such loathing against her. "Who is she?"

"The daughter of Baron Picard, a fellow who exists on the very fringes of Court. But my marriage need not spoil anything for us." He came forward and took her by the arms, his tone becoming savage in defiance. "We'll create our own Court at Château Valverde! Enough noblemen have been banished over the years to form a social circle of some grace and you shall reign as queen over it."

She gaped at him incredulously. "You expect me to go with you?"

"Why not? Your husband is too senile to miss you."

She pulled away from him, disgust in her face. "Do you imagine I would ever leave the Court of my own free will to bury myself in some God-forsaken abode? This is your disgrace, not mine! I've had enough of you anyway with your strange desires and your brutal ways. I pity the poor creature who is to marry you."

She made to flounce away into the bedchamber to collect her cape, for his baggage and hers stood ready for the departure he had expected to make after that morning's audience, but he grabbed her, struck her twice across the face, his rings drawing blood, and then threw her to the floor. As she struggled to her feet, shrieking and crying, he pulled open the door into the corridor before seizing her again and hurling her out into it with such force that she hit the wall opposite, breaking a wrist in the process. Then he slammed the door on her, leaving it to the two guards to help her to her feet and send for assistance.

He was familiar enough with the layout of Versailles to be able to allot the exact amount of time he would need to reach the Royal Chapel on time. His pride compelled him to array himself as grandly as he could for the marriage ceremony, however detestable his bride, and his valet took one coat and then another from his wardrobe that previously had been kept permanently at Versailles but must now follow Sabatin to his château. He finally decided on a handsome coat of purple satin with a dashing flair to it and deeply turned-back cuffs, the whole so encrusted with gold embroidery that it could have stood on its own. An equally modish waistcoat went with it, and knee breeches in a lighter shade with cream hose. Rubies, sapphires and diamonds flashed from his fingers and from his buttons and his shoe-buckles. Lastly he took a purple tricorn hat with ostrich feathers ornamenting the brim and stood to regard his appearance in the mirror that his valet held for him.

"What a waste," he remarked bitterly, full of admiration for himself. "There's not a soul in Versailles, man or woman, that I can't put in the shade. May the Devil rot

Bourbon and leave his bones to lie in a rustic setting even more remote than mine will be in Périgord."

The valet looked away. There was something decidedly satanic about his master and it was easy enough to believe that the chilling curse would come to pass.

In another part of Versailles Jasmin sat straight-backed and ashen-faced, her feet neatly together, her hands clutching the folded fan in her lap. She had not fainted when the Duc de Bourbon, who was under the delusion she knew exactly why she was there, had let fall the reason for her presence. Somehow the horror of what she was hearing seemed beyond belief. She was to be married to the Duc de Valverde, who was being banished from Court and was in need of a wife. Suddenly everything was clear to her. This was the explanation for the seizure her father had suffered, his panic that she should be sent out of France beyond harm's way and, most significant of all, that by some means Bourbon had caught wind of Louis's intention of installing her at Versailles and was acting swiftly to get her out of range while there was still time.

"I will not go through with this marriage." Those at Château Satory would have recognised that headstrong note. Force would never budge her from her stand; only gentle persuasion from her father had ever worked on her. "I know the Duc de Valverde only by sight and that is the end of it. I'm here to await the King's return."

Bourbon had a smooth voice and silky manners. He sat back in the huge gilded chair in the Council Chamber where he had received her and smiled quite graciously. "I would not force you into anything, mademoiselle. I gave your father full choice. You could either be bride to the Duc de Valverde or spend the rest of your days in the Bastille."

Her reaction was a resurgence of spirit and her face flashed triumph at him. "The King would not allow it! He would have me released immediately."

"Your whereabouts would be unknown to him. There are deep dungeons in the Bastille where prisoners soon lose their identity."

"My father would go to him at once!"

Bourbon sighed regretfully. "Ah, but your parents would be with you in the Bastille. I would not dream of separating a family in such circumstances. Not that I think

Baron Picard would survive long in his present state of
health, but you would have the comfort of your mother's
presence until the end of her days."

She knew she was beaten and dipped her head under
the weight of the sentence passed on her, biting deep into
her lower lip to retain her composure before this awful
man with his sweeping powers. Her father had had no
more choice than she, each of them faced with harm to
those they loved that stemmed any personal show of defiance. There were no tears in her. She was dry-eyed with
fright and aversion at what lay ahead for her, but it had to
be faced. Slowly she lifted her head again and met Bourbon's confident, awaiting gaze.

"I should like pen and paper in order to write to my
parents."

"You may have it."

She wrote them a long letter in the quarter of an hour
she was allowed, sealing it just as the Duc returned to
escort her to her bridegroom. She had made no reference
to the Bastille, for she was certain it would be read by
Bourbon before delivery and she did not want to risk it
being torn up. Her father would not know her fate for
many months to come, but she still wanted to include him
in this loving farewell that would be delivered into her
mother's hands.

"You are ready, Mademoiselle Picard?"

She nodded, noting somewhat incredulously that Bourbon had changed into garments of cloth of gold for the
ceremony. That such a farce should be enacted with all the
pomp accorded to the marriage of any high nobleman of
the land seemed bizarre to her. He held out his arm to her
and she settled her fingers lightly on his wrist. Dread lay
like a stone in the pit of her stomach as they began the long
and stately walk through the staterooms to the Royal
Chapel.

A paean thundered forth from the organ as she entered,
a tiny figure dwarfed to the size of a chess piece by the
great height and beautiful proportions of that jewel-like
place of worship. There were a surprising number of people gathered there, the wives of government officials,
drawn as women are to weddings, courtiers who happened
not to be at Fontainebleau for some reason or other, and
quite a number of the public interrupting their tours to

stay and watch the ceremony. She glimpsed her maid, who looked towards her pitiably, eyes streaming. Josette had been looking forward excitedly to being at Versailles and was taking her disappointment hard. Only farm girls liked to live in the country.

Jasmin felt that the music must be bearing her along, for how else could she keep moving one foot in front of the other. She had attended Mass here many times in the past, days that now shone out in her memory in the fullness of the happiness she had known in her friendship with Louis and before Fernand had come into her life, and, with the aid of her own folly, had reduced it to ashes.

Sabatin de Valverde stood waiting with his back towards her, ready to take her the rest of the way. In the depth of her own despair she was able to feel some sympathy for him, because he must be as wretched as she over this whole matter. It was always said that such was the grief of a courtier banished from Versailles in the old King's time that suicides were not uncommon. The feeling of Sabatin and others in the same situation would be no less now with a new young King on the Throne and fresh glory bursting forth at Court.

With a whisper of her skirts she reached his side. Then he turned his head and looked at her with such vicious contempt and loathing in his eyes that she almost collapsed. She must have swayed on her feet, for he grabbed her hand, slapped it onto his wrist and held it there until she had recovered herself.

Together they advanced to where the priest awaited them. Afterwards she could remember nothing of the ceremony and supposed she made the right responses or else there would have been some hitch to the proceedings. Sabatin was aware of every minute of it, every word like another nail being hammered into the coffin of his banishment, and all because this scheming bitch kneeling beside him had set her cap at the King. Well, she should live to regret it for the rest of her miserable life.

The ceremony was over. He turned with his bride to lead her back down the geometrical-patterned marble floor, the organ filling the air with its music. Like most palatine chapels built with two storeys, a gallery ran all round, on a level in this case with the State Apartment. Jasmin, holding her head high, let her gaze rise for the last

time to the section of the gallery facing the altar where the
King and the royal family always sat unless a cardinal, or
some other high dignitary of the Church, conducted the
service, when they would come down to the main floor.
Many times she had looked up to see Louis there, sitting
where his great-grandfather had once sat before him,
young and regal and acutely aware of her presence in the
congregation.

She was just about to lower her saddened eyes to the
open doors ahead, when there was a slight commotion in
the salon beyond the gallery. Then Louis burst into view,
rushing forward to the balustrade where he stared down at
her. For several long moments their eyes held bleakly before he turned abruptly and strode away. She felt a choking sob rise in her throat. He had come just too late to
intervene.

Louis went despairingly to his own apartment, waving
aside the courtiers who sprang in his path with some request or another as they seized an unexpected chance to
waylay him. Even when he reached his Council Chamber
there were two ministers sorting papers, and in the red
and gold royal bedchamber beyond, servants were scurrying, put into a flurry by his arrival two days before expected. Although they backed out immediately he was to
have no peace, for one of the ministers had followed on his
heels to discuss some matter on which he could not concentrate in his present upset state.

"Later," he said. "Not now."

But others were waiting to see him, urgent matters having cropped up that Bourbon had said he should see. He
knew why. It was to foster the illusion of his governing
while Monsieur le Duc continued to hold the reins. It was
the same cunning that had whisked Jasmin away from him.
A word of warning that something was afoot had been
whispered in his ear, causing him to leave Fontainebleau
immediately. He had ridden fast with escort but still had
not arrived in time to spike Bourbon's plot. In the future
he would guard his secrets still closer and judgements on
all matters should be his and no one else's.

Opening the glass doors he went out onto the balcony
where once he had stood with Louis XIV when the ice-
wagon had overturned. He could see the coaches about to
depart from the Royal Chapel. It was in his power to halt

that departure, to take Jasmin from Valverde's side and install her in an apartment on this same floor, but the resulting scandal would reach beyond the borders of France. He did not intend to sully his reign from the start and lose the respect of his people, because he knew they loved him already and his duty came before all else.

The coaches were on the move, bowling down the Cour Royale to the gates. Jasmin and her husband would be in the first one. Following them in the other ten were personal servants and after them came the Duc's riding horses and the baggage vehicles. His guess was that Jasmin could see him on the balcony even though he could not see her. He wanted to put a hand on his heart as a final gesture of the love he had never voiced to her, but always there were eyes on him and even at this moment he could not let his private feelings show.

As soon as Jasmin's coach was through the gates he went back inside. Voices buzzed beyond the doors that led into an adjoining salon where more people were waiting to see him. It was becoming intolerable never to be anywhere wholly by himself. Even at night when he lay in the Sun King's bed, which was now his own, a bodyguard slept by ancient custom on a portable couch beyond the gilded balustrade. He had never felt this lack of privacy more than at this time when there was a heaviness of pain and sorrow in him that was hard to keep from showing in his face. The truth was that there was nowhere in this great labyrinth of Versailles where he could be truly alone. That should be changed. His great-grandfather had advised against too much building, but a simple alteration to give him space and solitude was another matter entirely. It would need careful thought but it should be done.

He glanced once more through the still-open glass doors. The Valverde coaches were far down the Avenue de Paris and almost out of sight. With a sigh he pulled the bell-rope and sat down on a gilt-fringed tabouret with his legs stretched out in readiness to have his boots pulled off. It had been a long hard ride from Fontainebleau. He needed a bath and a change of clothing. If he were wise he would teach himself never to think of Jasmin again.

In the coach Jasmin and Sabatin sat side by side, lost in their own thoughts. As yet since the responses made in the Chapel they had not spoken to each other. She had seen

Louis on the balcony and in a last little flare of hope had
wondered if he had sent someone after her to bring her
back. But as the wheels rolled on even that flickered and
faded away. He was simply following her in his thoughts
and conveying his feelings just by being there. After he
was lost from her view she concentrated on the bustle of
the passing street, storing everything up in her memory.
She took a long head-turning look at the mansion whence
her mother's lovely fans went out to high places and at the
windows of the office floor where her father would never
again sit at his drawing board. When would she see the
town of Versailles once more? Perhaps in a few months'
time Sabatin would allow her to visit her home for a short
sojourn. Surely by then she could reassure her father about
her marriage, whatever the truth might be, and help to
cheer him towards steady improvement if not full recovery.

The houses were thinning out. The trees prevented any
chance glimpse of Château Satory and the first stage of the
journey south had begun. A full hour of unbroken silence
went by before Jasmin summoned up enough strength in
her voice to be ready to address her husband for the first
time. Half-turning in her seat, she looked towards him,
wishing she did not feel repelled by his arrogant features
and thick-shouldered frame. It was a hard face without the
least kindliness in it and the glare he had given her in the
Chapel still chilled her. She decided to open their conversation by referring to it.

"I know from your expression in the Royal Chapel that
this marriage was not of your choosing any more than it
was mine. We have both lost everything that meant most
to us. For you the pleasures of Court life and the chance of
advancement, for me the company of my parents and
friends, my home and even the affection of the King." She
paused, awaiting some response from him, but he continued to stare out of the window at the passing countryside
as if it were his personal enemy. Drawing breath, she continued with effort. "Since we have to live under the same
roof in a place that is probably almost as unfamiliar to you
as it will be to me, let us try to sustain each other in our
troubles and let friendship result."

Had he given a nod then, or by some small gesture
shown that he was in agreement with all she had said, it

would have helped her at this most desolate time of her life, but he continued to ignore her. She sank back in her seat, closing her eyes, and the journey went on.

In woodland he stopped the coach to get out and relieve himself among the trees, giving the servants time to scatter elsewhere in the bushes. Josette came running to her with the silver receptacle used by women on journeys and she had barely settled her clothing again when he flung himself back into his seat. Still he spoke no word to her.

They dined alfresco with two footmen to wait on them and with almost as much pomp as if they were at Versailles. A portable table was unfolded and put up under trees and set with damask, silver and crystal. Two folding stools embroidered with silver thread were placed on either side and she sat facing Sabatin as they were served a cold collation on silver dishes; salads, cheese and fruit. *Vin de Champagne* was poured, that beautiful and delicious wine that was all the Sun King would drink in the latter years of his life.

Sabatin had brought all his personal servants from Versailles, averting the panic that always arose among those suddenly left without a master. Eating a humbler meal out of sight were his valet, his clerk, his chefs, footmen, grooms and a page as well as all the coachmen, making at least forty in all apart from those waiting at table. It was unlikely that any of them liked moving to the country, but it had saved them the humiliation of having to jostle with one another in the vestibules and the Cour Royale while pestering other noblemen to employ them. Josette, who was the only woman among them, was heard to laugh once or twice and Jasmin hoped that it meant her maid was becoming more cheerful again.

She and Sabatin ate their repast in silence. She would have spoken but feared to be snubbed in front of those waiting on them. He ate heartily, enjoying the pheasant, the chicken, the slices of tongue, lamb and beef. She managed to eat a little and finished with fruit. He also quaffed a considerable amount of *vin de Champagne* and fell asleep as soon as the journey recommenced.

When he stirred and yawned, she tried again to draw him into conversation, hoping that by now he would be in a better frame of mind.

"Please let us talk, Sabatin. Tell me something about

where we are going and what it is like there. Is it your birthplace and the family seat? Shall we be near a city or town? I know nothing of your background or of your interests, except that I have heard you are a keen huntsman. That was told me by the Marquis de Grange with whom I know you are acquainted." She waited for a reply, but still he remained silent. "If you don't wish to talk about yourself yet, would you like me to tell you about myself?"

He sighed heavily, taking up his cane and rapping for the coach to stop. A footman sprang to open the door for him, but he did not alight, merely giving him some instruction. After a short wait the footman returned with a travelling writing desk. Sabatin took it onto his knees and she watched in amazement that he should choose this moment to pen a letter. But he was very brief, handed back the desk, folded the piece of paper and handed it to her. On it were written two words: *Be silent.*

Furiously she crumpled the paper and threw it down, turning sharply away from him. Then as the hours continued to drag by it dawned on her how terrible it would be if he continued to maintain the silence between them for any great length of time.

The night was spent at a hostelry that was neither clean nor comfortable, but that was not unusual. She had her own room, but whereas Sabatin had his bed made up with linen packed in readiness, she had to make do with what was there. Josette, sulky and irritable, grumbling all the time under her breath about leaving Versailles, did manage to get her some clean straw for the bed and a large pitcher of hot water with which she bathed herself. She had travelled all day in full Court dress and although fortunately the day had been cool and overcast, she was thankful to be free of the elaborate garments. Josette unpacked a lighter gown for the next day, a simple silk that would be comfortable for travel. Seeing no reason why she should join Sabatin for supper, she had it served in her room and had a better appetite away from his icy company. She thought she would find it hard to sleep that night with so much to trouble her, but no sooner had she shut her eyes than she was away, worn out by the day's events, and slept soundly until a knocking on her door awakened her with a start to bright sunshine.

She blinked, sitting up and bewildered by the knocking.

It would not be Josette and where was her maid anyway, for there was no hot water ready or tray of coffee and rolls by her bed. "Who's there?"

"A message from the master, madame. He is waiting to depart."

She sprang from the bed and opened the door wide enough to look out. One of the footmen was about to go downstairs again, his message delivered. "What time is it?" she gasped.

"Nine o'clock, madame."

"My maid should have been here long ago. Find her and send her to me at once."

The footman had come back across the landing to her. "I was told by the innkeeper that your maid left here at dawn. A wagon came by on its way to Paris and she went with it."

So even Josette had deserted her! What a way to start another dreadful day. "Very well. Send one of the hostelry's maidservants to attend me and I'll take breakfast downstairs."

"I'll do what I can, madame, but all of them are running about serving food to arriving passengers at the present time."

She was in no mood for prevarication. "Send one! Also inform the Duc de Valverde that I shall be at least an hour yet."

She closed the door and went across to the window. Horses were being changed on two coaches that had just arrived and the Valverde coach stood in another part of the forecourt ready to leave. She could see Sabatin strolling about wearing a light brown coat and cream silk knee breeches, far better attire for travel than the wedding garments of the previous day. Let him wait! It was a fine morning and would do him no harm to kick his heels at her convenience in the sunshine for a while. Perhaps it would give him time to think over his ill manners towards her and decide to amend them when she eventually appeared.

Propping up her own handglass, there being no mirror in the room, she proceeded to dress her hair, expecting nothing from whoever came to wait on her. Well-brushed from the night before, it needed only clever use of her comb to bring the glossy mass into curls at the back of her head. By the time she had pinned them into place and coaxed a few tendrils across her brow the maid had arrived.

They had sent up the kitchen slut, a thin sickly-looking girl in greasy clothes, her soiled apron still wet from washing pots. In addition she looked scared stiff. Jasmin, in spite of her annoyance, spoke kindly to the girl, her mother's training coming to the fore.

"Is someone else bringing up the hot water for me?"

The girl shook her head slowly, plucking nervously at her apron. "Nothin' was said about water. When I came through the hall I was given this for you."

She held out a folded piece of paper. Jasmin recognised it as being from Sabatin's travelling desk and she took it with a qualm. It was slightly longer than the message she had received from him the previous day, but it was equally terse. *You have delayed my departure by a quarter of an hour already. I allow you another five minutes and then, whether you are dressed or not, I shall fetch you out to the coach myself.*

She did not doubt that he meant it. With a little moan she fled to the pitcher that Josette had left the night before and found enough water left to rinse her teeth. After splashing her face with rose water from her own crystal flask, she called on the kitchen maid to help her with her petticoats, but the girl fumbled so much in her nervousness that Jasmin became increasingly desperate and sent her away, more hindered than helped by her presence. She pulled her gown over her head. Never in her life before had she dressed herself, for there had always been Berthe and then Josette with her nimble fingers. The treacherous wretch! But, oh, how she would welcome her if she should reappear again at this minute.

Struggling with the blue satin ribbons that laced the back of the silk gown, Jasmin kept an eye on Sabatin through the window. Now he looked at his fob watch and snapped it shut. He was on his way! She darted about the room, thrusting her feet into her diamond-buckled shoes from the day before, there being no time to search for another pair. All her possessions about the room she scooped up and thrust into the open travelling-box. She slammed the lid down, locked it, snatched her hat from a peg and was out on the landing below as Sabatin put his foot on the first tread of the staircase.

"Good morning," she said, giving him a chance to be agreeable even though his message rankled with her. He merely glanced up at her with the same fierce glare of hatred that she had met in the Chapel and she realised that this day was to be no different from the one before.

He stood aside to let her precede him out of the hostelry, probably to ensure she did not linger and delay him further. There was an appetising smell of new-baked bread and soup and coffee and other delights drifting through an archway beyond which people were eating; it made her realise how hollow she felt. A maidservant went by with a laden tray and it was all she could do not to snatch a roll from it, but she retained her dignity and went out into the sun. There she had to lose it a little, seeing how his nostrils flared in supercilious disgust at her somewhat dishevelled appearance, and her temper rose.

"I'm without a maid to attend me. Mine has run away!"

She bounded into the coach ahead of him and took her seat. For the rest of the day her gown slipped about on her shoulders from its loose lacing and added discomfort to the tedium of the journey. He spent the first half hour reading a newssheet that had probably been obtained from one of the passengers in the hostelry. When he had finished reading he did not offer it to her, but she took it from the opposite seat where he had tossed it and it helped to pass the time, boring though it was with complaints about taxes and the price of bread with nothing on fashion or anything in the least entertaining. But it turned her thoughts towards her mother's fan-makers who were far better off than those employed in similar trades. Would her mother sell the business at long last? She thought it highly likely with her father needing attention every minute and she herself prevented from taking any weight from her mother's shoulders. Suddenly she felt physically ill with homesickness. It had set in from the moment of leaving Versailles and threatened to get worse as the distance between her and Château Satory stretched longer and longer.

The day passed in much the same way as before, but that night she was spared the discomfort of a hostelry as they stayed with one of Sabatin's uncles, a bucolic old widower, eccentric enough to prefer retirement on his estate to ending his days in the vicinity of Versailles.

"I'm going to die in my own bed," he said as he must have said many times before, judging from the contemptuous boredom in Sabatin's face. "No lackey is going to toss me out as I begin to draw my last breath, which would happen at Versailles."

Deaf and garrulous, he talked most of the time of the past, telling scandalous tales of the Sun King's Court that made Jasmin realise that then things were no different than they were now. Intrigue, gossip, jostling for favours from the King, concealed pregnancies, secret orgies and all the rest that made up the sensual, throbbing, exotic and dangerous atmosphere that pervaded Versailles to that day. Sabatin listened as grim-faced as if he were at a funeral, for all the time the old nobleman was unwittingly rubbing salt into a raw wound. Intermittently there was some family talk enabling Jasmin to learn that Château Valverde had been run by a skeleton staff ever since the death of Sabatin's parents and, as so often happened in these cases, an impoverished relative, Henriette de Valverde, had lived there in charge over the years.

Jasmin would have liked to be cheered by the knowledge that there was to be another woman in her new home, but since she found the old nobleman to be as unpleasant as Sabatin she had little hope that anyone else related to him would be any better. It was not that the uncle did not talk to her, for he shouted at her across the supper table as much as he did to Sabatin, but he was one of those men who even in old age did not lose their lecherous ways. He was forever trying to fondle her, his rheumy eyes drawn constantly to her cleavage, and as she went up to bed she heard him trying to bargain with Sabatin for the night with her. There was no question of straining her ears to hear, for like many deaf people he had no idea of the volume of his voice.

"What do you want, nephew? A new hunter? Your gaming debts paid? You've always liked that porcelain clock that was your aunt's. You can have it."

On the stairs Jasmin paused in fear, a hand at her throat. Out of his hatred for her would Sabatin agree? She was conscious of the terrified thumping of her heart as she awaited his reply. It was shouted sardonically.

"I have a price for her, but you couldn't meet it."

"What is it?"

"A letter from Versailles to end my banishment."

His uncle spoke peevishly. "You know that's beyond anybody's power. You and that pretty piece have to live out your banishment together, because what applies to you also applies to her." His voice became persuasive again. "One night is not too much to ask."

Sabatin answered mockingly. "It is for you, you diseased old goat."

"So that's it!" The old man, accepting defeat, took it in good part. "Frightened of her giving you the clap afterwards, are you? It hasn't killed me yet and I'd take a wager that won't be the trouble that will put me in my coffin. It's more likely to be a surfeit of maidservants!"

Both men burst into loud guffaws. Jasmin hurried up the stairs, nauseated by what she had heard and devastated by the information that the uncle had let fall. Why had she not grasped from the start that as Sabatin's wife she was as much subject to the banishment as he! It meant that if she were widowed within the next minute she still could not go home.

In the candle-glow she stumbled into the old-fashioned bedchamber that was hers for the overnight stay. She was just seventeen and everything she valued in life had been taken from her. With her father destined to be an invalid to the end of his days her mother would not be able to make the long journey to visit her and she was alone as she had never been before, the gentle, loving relationship that had sheltered her gone forever. She had not expected in those carefree days that fate would exact full payment for the recklessness into which her vigorous and sensual nature had led her. All that was young in her was draining away in that ugly, overpowering room with its massive oak furniture and gloomy paintings. An ancient mirror, constructed before the glass-makers of France found the secret of perfect reflection, held her image in its flawed depth as she let her hands fall listlessly to her sides and looked towards it. The distortion of her youthful appearance was apt, for inside she had become old and withered from the weight of despair. Never again would she know lightness of heart or the bliss of running free.

"Oh, Maman," she whispered in the quiet room, "why did you instill some element of strength in me? It would have been so much easier for me to put an end to my life."

She moved a step nearer the mirror. "I don't want to go on with what I have to face, but through that silent battle between you and my father for my good you've left me with hell when I could have known oblivion."

That night she slept as deeply and soundly as at the hostelry. It was as if her need for sleep came as much from exhaustion of the spirit as from the journeying. But this time there was no oversleeping. The maidservant designated to attend her awoke her in good time and she was bathed, dressed and at the breakfast table before either Sabatin or his old uncle appeared. They looked as though they had been drinking together far into the night, a certain heaviness about their movements showing that the effects of the wine had not quite worn off. Sabatin winced visibly when plates were clattered.

The departure came shortly after breakfast. Jasmin managed to avoid being kissed by the old man, but did not quite escape the grab he made for her breast. Sabatin did not appear to notice or to care, although she suspected he was as glad as she that the stay was over. Her guess was that he had expectations from his uncle. Fortunately for him the old man had not taken his disgrace at Court very seriously.

She had learned at the previous night's supper that there were another two or three nights to be spent en route, but at least she had a maid again to attend her. The girl, named Lenore, countrified in her speech and manner, newly come to the household, had been selected to wait on her through an intuitive ability to dress hair. This skill had made the girl popular among the other maids whose tresses she had curled and primped and made more flattering to the caps that they wore. Jasmin, not wanting to face another night, let alone two or three, without the services of a personal attendant, had sent for the housekeeper to ask if Lenore could be spared to accompany her. Domestic matters were not the concern of the master of the house and the housekeeper might do as she pleased.

"Take her by all means, madame. She is a good girl, quick to learn, clean and modest in her ways. If you should find her completely satisfactory there would be no need to send her back."

So Lenore had been installed with various instructions in one of the servants' coaches. She was as excited about this turn of events as her predecessor had been at the prospect of Versailles and was eager to serve well her beautiful mistress with the sad, unsmiling face. How could any woman be downcast when she possessed such fashionable gowns and so many delicious undergarments?

That night her former master sent for her. He had caught a glimpse of her twice about the place and was ready to take her to his bed. The housekeeper, dour and strict in her appearance, took enormous satisfaction in telling him that the girl had gone into the service of the Duchesse de Valverde. She hated him as much as did the young women he abused, but all of them were subject to his aristocratic power and none dared cross him. Only the fact that his nephew's wife was responsible for Lenore's departure saved her from being struck across the face by his cane.

Lenore, too shy as yet to open her mouth, inadvertently added to the conspiracy of silence that Sabatin had instigated. Yet her natural intelligence and amiable little face helped Jasmin through the discomforts of the remainder of the journey. Jasmin could not help but be struck by the grand scenery that prevailed the nearer they came to their destination. Tumbling rivers swept through rich, luxuriant valleys that were guarded by high plateaux with dark outcrops of rock and soaring cliffs. Every now and again the turrets of isolated châteaux showed against the sky and the villages with their romanesque churches were of brown stone with rust-red roofs. Mules and sometimes yoked oxen made it difficult for the coaches to get past on narrow, dusty ways. Sabatin looked out of the window at it all with increasing disgust. During the last stages of the journey he drank continually from the bottles of wine brought to him at every halt, discarding the crystal goblet with which he had been provided as the day wore on.

Château Valverde came into view as the sun was setting. It was as fiercely turreted as many others seen along the way, standing on a strategic site that gave it splendid views in every direction, essential in the past in defence against marauders and foreign invaders. Some of the upper windows held a chequered look of red-gold and black where a few absent panes gave no reflection of the glowing sunset, which warned of some neglect in sections that were unused. Its obvious age was neither more nor less than Jasmin had expected, for there had been enough talk on architecture in her home for her to know that it would not be a mansion built in the past hundred years. Whereas the Île-de-France had become bejewelled with magnificent mansions from the time the Sun King had first begun to enlarge Versailles, the rest of France had been left forgotten by those at Court, the neglected husbandry of rich lands dragging the agricultural workers and their families down to the dregs of existence. At least here, with Sabatin's homecoming, his tenants and workers would benefit from the renewed interest that would surely be his once he had settled to his return.

Sabatin showed no haste to alight and still took his time after the footman had sprung down from the coach to pull on the iron handle of the doorbell, bringing someone to open the heavy door of the Château Valverde. Jasmin, watching her husband out of the corner of her eye, observed how loathsome this homecoming was to him. There was a twitch in his temple and a clenching to his heavy jaw. He uttered a curse under his breath as he finally swung himself up from the seat and out of the coach in an upsurge of energy. Before she could follow him he was up the wide steps and had disappeared into the entrance hall where candles had begun to flicker. As she went up the flight in his wake she noticed the thickness of the ivy that had climbed, unkempt and unpruned, up the amber stone walls as if in a race against time for possession.

She found Sabatin shouting orders in the high-beamed hall, his stamping entry having stirred dust up from the unswept floor. Already he had snatched up a candlestick to take a shooting glance into the rooms that led off on either side. Servants had come scurrying from all directions like mice out of their holes, their candles showing the cobwebs festooned like drapery everywhere, and some of them actually bumped into one another as they turned about to carry out a bawled bidding from their returned master. In the midst of the commotion a woman in her late sixties appeared on the gallery by the massive staircase. She was thin and frail, her hair almost white and topped with a *fontange*, a whim of fashion that had become virtually outmoded when Jasmin was still a young child. As for her gown, that belonged to some more distant decade in its style and was faded and shabby. She was staring at Sabatin as if he were the Devil himself who had come bursting into the château. Her jaw, hanging open, shook slightly as did her hands.

"Damnation, Henriette!" he roared at her. "Come down here, you stupid crone! What have you done to this place? It's like a pigsty!"

"How you have grown, Sabatin," she stammered foolishly. "You left home a youth of seventeen and have come back a man. Yet I still know you."

He gave a bellow of exasperation. "Twenty years does not alter a man beyond recognition, but it does take toll on his patience when he meets blatant idiocy instead of a civil answer to a question."

Jasmin, although afraid he might turn and strike her, intervened. "Stop frightening her! Can't you see that your appearing out of nowhere has shattered her nerves?"

He rounded on her, his face livid, his large hands balled, but even then he did not speak, letting his eyes bore his fury into her. Henriette, vaguely aware of an ally somewhere down in the hall, rallied. "If it's not as you like it, you should have come back on a visit before now."

"I'm not here on a visit!" he answered her in a roar, striding to the foot of the staircase. "I've been banished from Court! From Versailles! From civilisation itself to come back with a wife to this place that you've turned into a hovel. I'm home to stay!"

A curious silence fell. Every servant turned his or her head with varying expressions of dismay, unlike their counterparts from more sophisticated abodes who learned never to reveal their thoughts whatever they might hear. At the top of the stairs, Henriette gave a long, low whimper.

"Oh, dear. Not all over again." She pressed a hand to her quivering mouth and turned about, disappearing into the shadows as quietly as she had come.

"Come back!" he exploded, but when she failed to obey he went thundering up the stairs after her, his shouts echoing everywhere from the oak-panelled walls.

In the hall Jasmin beckoned one of the maids forward. "Show me to the rooms reserved for the lady of the house if they are not already occupied by Mademoiselle Henriette."

"She has her own suite on the floor above them, madame."

A manservant presented himself at the maid's side. "The windows have been closed in your rooms for a long time, madame. They may prove difficult for one person to open."

"Come with us then."

Lenore, her mistress's jewel box in one hand and a shawl in the other, was still staring round in disbelief at the cobwebs. She recovered herself to spring forward as the manservant began to lead the way and managed to get right behind her mistress, exerting her right to precede the housemaid coming up in the rear. She had already learned much about the hierarchy of the servants' world.

Jasmin looked about searchingly as she went up the massive staircase. Beyond the landing, which was large enough itself to have held a ball in, doors were unlocked for her and she entered through an anteroom to the smell of dust and decay. The manservant had sprung ahead to start opening shutters and send them clattering back, letting the last of the sunset's glow aid the candelabrum he had set down. Jasmin halted on the threshold in dismay. The condition of this spacious room was far worse than anything else she had seen on her way there. The maid gave the explanation.

"This bedchamber was closed up the day after the master's mother died here more than thirty-five years ago, madame. Nothing has been touched since."

She did not berate either of the servants for not having forewarned her and shown her into another room used more recently than this one. It was understandable that they were in a condition of shock similar to that of Henriette at the unexpected turmoil after years of living in quiet and lazy idleness. She began to look around, knowing that to establish her authority from the start these rooms would have to be hers. Lenore, opening the drawers of a clothespress, showed her under-linen yellowed by time, and she signalled for it to be closed. As the door of a side room was held wide for her inspection, she saw chests for holding gowns and one of blue velvet in a mode long gone by lay draped across a chair, its lace turned brown with age.

In the bedchamber itself silver toilet articles, tarnished black, lay on a handsome ebony commode, the centre section deep-set to allow a woman to sit in comfort to apply cosmetics, something that was unusual in such a piece and Jasmin guessed it had been specially made to the woman's instructions. It suggested both vanity and common sense. Again Lenore, unable to contain her curiosity, pulled open the top drawer in the commode to reveal porcelain pots of paint and powder, patch-boxes, combs, pins and an assortment of crystal flasks, a stale perfume arising from them.

Jasmin turned towards the bed. It was enormous, matching the high proportions of the room and marvellously carved, the bedhead embellished with a whole scene of the triumph of Aphrodite. She had glimpsed enough of the château already to be able to tell that the bulk of the furniture, tapestries and paintings were from that particularly rewarding period when Francis I relinquished his dream of conquering Italy to allow a peaceful invasion of Italian Renaissance glory to blend with and finally overcome French Gothic. She had recognised in the hall the work of the Italian artists Primaticcio and Rosso, for she had seen other paintings by them on a visit she had made once with her parents to Fontainebleau. Here the bed alone was a masterpiece of craftsmanship, although nothing whatever would have induced her to sleep on its ancient mattress amid its spider-infested draperies.

"For tonight I want a bed made up for me in a habitable room," she said to the two servants who had finished struggling together to open the last of the windows. "Tomorrow all the late Duchesse's possessions must be taken away from here and the whole apartment washed, cleaned and polished throughout. Those are winter bed-hangings in any case and somewhere there will be summer ones folded away in linen and lavender. Even the mattress must be destroyed with all the pillows, and others with fresh goose feathers put in their place. That procedure must also be followed in the Duc's bedchamber."

"That room has been looked after, madame."

"Not to the extent the Duc will require, I can be sure of that. You shall do as I say. Where is his apartment located?"

"His bedchamber is on the other side of that door, madame." The manservant and the maid were taking turns in answering her and she guessed they were trying to sum her up for a report belowstairs.

She had hoped the distance from Sabatin's apartment

would be greater. As yet she had resolutely kept from her mind the marital duties that would normally be expected from a wife; instead she had allowed the certainty to grow that Sabatin's distaste for her was such that he might never be able to touch her. Since there was nothing in the least romantic in his nature, it was not the unpleasantness of the hostelry bedchambers that had kept him from her, or he could easily have taken the chance to come to her in the accommodation she had been given at his uncle's château. If this state of affairs continued the proximity of his room would not be important, and she could look for her nights to remain undisturbed.

"I assume that supper is being prepared. Afterwards I will speak to the housekeeper." She intended that the whole château should be scrubbed throughout and every cobweb swept away.

"There is no housekeeper, madame. Mademoiselle Henriette manages everything."

Jasmin refrained from making any comment on Henriette's incompetence. She had seen for herself that the woman was old and timid, just the sort of person of whom servants would be quick to take advantage. They would find they had a different mistress in her. In the foolishness of her young girlhood she had resented being taught how to run a household, and if her mother had had second sight in preparing her, that instruction was certainly going to come to fruition now. She could have put on an apron and cooked the supper herself if the need had arisen; instead tomorrow she would begin to ferret out all the faults, errors and general laziness that had brought this fine mansion to its present chaos and put matters to rights.

"In future you will take your orders from me. Tomorrow, in addition to putting this bedchamber to good order a start will be made on the rest of the château. It is to shine like a new pin. Is that understood?"

"Yes, madame."

The maid bobbed and the servant bowed, both of them with the same look of wariness on their faces. They could see she was going to make her own mark on the château and their lives in it as much as that terrifying man with a voice like a whiplash.

Jasmin went for a little exploratory walk about the château before supper. There did not appear to be a room that had not been treated in a slovenly manner, although here and there a swathe showed where a duster had been carelessly wiped over. Yet the layers of dirt could not hide the wonderful carving and she traced a forefinger over incised fruit and flowers, foliage and scrollwork. Now and again she stood back to admire caryatids through their festoons of cobwebs. There were a large number of ebony cabinets, proof of the wealth of Sabatin's forebears, who had been able to order these ornate pieces from French *ébénistes* in the most expensive of all woods at that time. She noted observantly that in far too many places there were signs of deterioration, far more serious than surface neglect, in damp patches on walls, stained ceilings where rain had dripped through and cracked windowpanes. For these defects she blamed Sabatin, who should have visited at least once a year to ensure the structure of the château was being kept intact.

Henriette did not appear at suppertime and neither was a place laid for her. Jasmin made up her mind to seek her out in the morning. She and Sabatin ate in the same silence that had prevailed at all their previous meals, he at one end of the table and she at the other. Here at Château Valverde there was a slight difference of custom in comparison with meals taken at Versailles, Château Satory and other such noble houses. There, as in the homes of the bourgeoisie, day rooms were multipurposed and none set aside especially for eating. Tables were set up as required, a number placed end to end according to how many were to sit down to eat. In Sabatin's château, due to the weight of the carved oaken furniture, the old style of having one great massive board permanently in place still applied and she and Sabatin were as far removed from each other as if they were in separate rooms. Candelabra, standing lighted at intervals between them, added a screen of light and tarnished silver to increase their isolation from each other. The food was better than she had expected and she guessed they were sharing the servants' supper unless Henriette insisted on keeping a good table for herself, which seemed unlikely in view of her fragile appearance.

Sabatin grumbled a great deal at his end of the table. He was receiving the usual faultless service from his own footmen who, in their white gloves and the livery they had hastily unpacked, looked somewhat incongruous in that dusty setting, one unaware of a thick cobweb caught on the back of his wig and another with a smudge of grime on his sleeve. It was the lack of choice in the dishes that annoyed Sabatin, used as he was to a good spread even when travelling, and he drank heavily to make up for it and maybe to forget where he was and why he was there.

When the supper ended, Jasmin bade him good night, intending to leave him to his imbibing, but he crashed his fist on the table so demandingly that she slowly resumed the seat from which she had risen, not wanting any kind of scene. The footmen, obeying his irritable command, set a full decanter at his right hand after drawing the cloth and removing everything else to carry it all away. This gave her the chance she had been waiting for with nobody to witness any further display of his temper against her. She rose to her feet again, determined this time to follow her own will.

"You may retain your silence towards me for as long as you wish and I shall spare you the sound of my voice whenever possible. But you shall never again thump your fist at me. You brought me here as your wife and as mistress of this house I intend to make it the place it should be. Your own comfort in it is at stake, because if you should continue to show ill manners towards me I'll not be able to maintain the servants' respect and they'll listen to me no more than they have listened to Henriette in the past. Your Versailles servants, with their snobbery and their airs, lording it over their country counterparts, will be the worst. Think it over. You will see that I am right. Otherwise you will find yourself the main loser in the end. I bid you good night again, Sabatin."

All the time she had been speaking he had been watching her with a lowered, bull-like thrust to his head, his eyes glittering through narrowed lids, his ruddy colour heightened by the wine and a sneer of contempt to his nostrils. Yet what she said went home to him, making his bile rise as he was forced to acknowledge to himself the sense of her crisply stated words. If he had dared he would have had her murdered and be rid of all encumbrance, getting a capable steward instead to keep the château to rights. He could have cut her throat with his own hand and with no more feeling than if he were slicing an apple, merely thankful not to have to look any more upon the creature responsible for his downfall. Moreover it would have been easy enough to dispose of her remains in these lonely parts, some excuse of sending her away covering her absence. But there was always the King. If Louis should take it into his head to write to her at some time in the future and failed to get a reply, there was every likelihood he would send someone to investigate.

His gaze followed her as she went from the room. His silence was simply his hatred, impossible to break down since one was the expression of the other. Yet he would give her the respect by day that she demanded. He took up his glass, tilted back his neck and emptied it at a gulp. Then he pushed back his chair. The nights were a different matter.

She heard him coming behind her when she was halfway up the stairs and did not look round, hoping that his pace meant he was going to overtake her and pass her. But when he reached her side he slowed his step to hers and fastened his hand on her wrist like a clamp. Instantly she knew what was to happen that night. She fought down an impulse to scream and run, revolted by the prospect of his hands on her, his body joined to hers. Had she been a virgin still steeped in ignorance, perhaps this moment would have been easier to bear. His merciless grip told her there would be no evasion for her. Nothing she could say or do would stop him making her his wife sometime in the hours ahead.

They reached the door of her temporary bedchamber, behind which Lenore would be waiting to help her to bed and there should be a short respite from his company in which to steel herself for his touch. But she was not to be allowed that. He drew her onwards with a sharp jerk of the arm when she could have paused to enter there and led her to his own great bedchamber that neighboured the one that was to be hers the following day. Had she come into it with a man she loved it would have been a welcoming place. Servants had been at work during the supper hour and it was newly swept and polished, ebony gleaming in dark corners and the massive bed-hangings of emerald silk moving slightly in a mild draught from the open windows. Bedcovers had been folded back to reveal the snowy linen and the flickering candles competed with the moonlight.

He released her wrist to turn the key in the lock and she went across to the nearest window to look out. It was a night full of stars and the mountains lay like a ridge of curiously fashioned silver. A floorboard creaked as he came towards her.

Taking her by the waist, he swivelled her round towards him and her heart quailed at his elated, lustful expression. She would have lifted her reluctant hands to unfasten the rope of pearls around her neck if he had given her time, but he did not. He slid the back of his fingers under her neckline at the shoulders on either side and with a single fierce movement fastened his hold and tore the garment from her.

In the middle of the night, wanting to ease herself away from contact with his sweaty flesh, her wide-awake eyes still dilated with horror at all he had subjected her to, she thought to leave the bed and let the cleansing air of the night fall on her. But he was not sleeping as deeply as she had supposed and even as she sat up, swinging her legs cautiously to the floor, he reached out and grabbed her by the hair, yanking her back onto the pillow beside him.

It began all over again. The indignities and the humiliation, the violation and the unremitting brutality conducted to the noise of his gratification, the creaking of the ancient bed, and her own helpless sobbing when there was nothing but pain. Twice in the night she had screamed out but each time he had continued to ride her mercilessly, her straddled form pale in the moonlight, her face covered by her tumbled hair.

At dawn when he snored she did manage to leave the bed. She had nothing with which to cover herself, for her clothes lay torn on the floor where he had flung them. Taking up a ragged petticoat she draped it about her as best she could and went as soundlessly as possible from the room. There was a moment of panic when she thought she could not remember the location of her bedchamber and her relief was doubled when she opened a door and found it was the right room. Lenore was still waiting for her, fast asleep upon a stool at the end of the bed, her head resting on the coverlet. Jasmin spoke to her.

Lenore was one of those rare people who always awaken with a smile, but as she lifted her head, blinking away sleep, it faded at the sight her mistress presented. "Madame! Whatever in the world—" Then she broke off, turning scarlet as realisation dawned, and sprang to her feet. "I'll go down to the kitchen myself and heat some water for your bath. It will soothe those bruises—" Again she floundered, knowing from her initial training at the other house that the first rule was never to appear to notice anything unusual about one's employers and absolutely never to make any comment. But her mistress only nodded at her gratefully and said, "Thank you. I should appreciate that."

Jasmin remembered hearing once that the first instinct of a victim of rape was to bathe, a reaction she now completely understood. She immersed herself completely, doubling her knees in the short bath to lower herself until even her hair swam about her head in the cleansing water that Lenore had scented with rose water. She was thankful to slip between the white sheets of the bed that had been turned down for her, but it still took a long time to get to sleep.

When she awoke around noon Lenore brought her hot chocolate which she sipped as best she could, for her lower lip had been cut through by the brutal force of Sabatin's mouth. A bustle of activity beyond her door told her that in spite of her nonappearance that morning the cleaning of the château was going ahead with energy. She could only suppose that in giving her orders she had adopted unconsciously the authoritative note that Marguerite always used when she wanted people to jump to her commands.

She closed her eyes yearningly on the thought of her mother. If she had become a little child again she could not have needed her more. She longed for Marguerite's presence, her comforting arms and the rock of her strength in this terrible situation. For the first time Jasmin failed to see her father as the protector, which had nothing to do with the sickness that had laid him low. It was the revelation that all along it had been her mother who had been the driving force in her upbringing, trying to fit her for whatever life might bring, to dispel the illusions about a soft and easy existence, the virtual bed of roses that her father had imagined for her.

Today she would write Marguerite a long letter, the first of many that would be written in the years ahead. She would not add to her mother's worries by letting her suspect how bad the relationship was with her husband, but she would describe the journey and the scenery, the layout of Château Valverde and its splendid views. She would also mention Henriette, but could add no more on her until there was a proper meeting. Most important of all, the letter would be a link with home. She had thought herself homesick on the journey, but it was nothing to that which assailed her now and that went to the very core of her heart.

She spent three days shut away in her room during which proof came that she was not pregnant from that dreadful night. Such a possibility should not arise again. A chance overhearing of conversation between two fan-makers once when visiting the workshops had been of extreme interest to her in her innocence; now that simple precaution should protect her in the future, for it would take more than a locked door to keep Sabatin out when he was resolved to enter. She knew that she could never love a child that he had fathered.

Lenore gave out that her mistress was tired from the journey and needed to rest. It aroused no speculation, although some of the maidservants wondered among themselves if she could be pregnant already. Lenore also inspected the apartment that had been made ready and said it looked splendid, but Jasmin did not emerge from her retreat until her cut lip had subsided and her facial appearance was once more as it should be. Since most of her gowns had the fashionably low-cut neckline, she had to make use of her lacy shawls to hide the bruises that still stained her breasts.

She went first to inspect the salons that had been cleaned, for the size of the château was such that it would be a long time before every part of it met with her approval. Unaware that she was already getting a name for herself as a Tartar she wore a pair of white gloves to run a fingertip along forgotten rims and was furious to find the library was considered finished when not one book had been taken down from the shelves. She left the servants responsible with their ears smarting from all she said to them.

Her next sortie was to go out into the grounds where a greensward lay thick with weeds to the south of the château. Once there had been a formally laid-out parterre to greet those looking out of the windows on the west side, but little remained of it. Behind unclipped hedges a kitchen garden was in good order, showing that skills were there, and she looked for the one gardener she knew to be present. She soon found a makeshift hut, a hideous eyesore, that the old man had built for himself as a permanent residence on what was a wide terrace by a dry hollow that had once been an ornamental pool. When she entered the gloomy interior the stench almost took her head off.

"Move your belongings into the stable loft and sleep there," she told him irately. "Then make a fire of this place. I'll send someone into town to bring back some young men you can train to gardening if no qualified ones are available."

He was gaping at her. Did this whirlwind mean there would be money spent again on plants and garden tools and all else that was needed? It looked as if he was about to get wages again. Enthusiasm for the land, long crushed by tasks too numerous for one elderly man, soared anew. "You'd better get me some weeding boys as well. I'll train them up too."

She went back indoors and sent one of the Versailles footmen into town to carry out the errand, to advertise for extra staff and, in particular, a housekeeper. There was still one more important thing to do and that was to make herself known to Henriette. According to Lenore, the old lady had barricaded herself away in her rooms after running from the gallery upon their arrival and the Duc had not been able to get her to come out again. Jasmin was not surprised about this, considering how he had bullied the poor woman.

As she went to the upper floor, which she had not yet inspected, most of the rooms there having been out of use for a number of years, she was reminded of the elderly widow of a nobleman who had lived as a recluse in a top room in a wing of Versailles for years without anyone remembering she was there. It could easily have happened here in Château Valverde, for it was doubtful whether Sabatin would have troubled any more about Henriette and the servants would have taken trays to her out of habit until the day she died. A tray with the remains of a meal was on a table beside her door. Jasmin tapped twice.

"Who is it?" came from within.

Jasmin hesitated as to how she should answer. To say she was Sabatin's wife might cause Henriette to expect the same bullying treatment. She tried another way that in reality was no different but avoided the direct use of his Christian name with its possible effect on her. "Jasmin-Marie, Duchesse de Valverde."

There was a lengthy pause. Then a bolt was shot back, a key turned and the door opened a crack and Henriette's suspicious eye regarded her. Jasmin curtsied, pale lilac silk skirts billowing softly. The gap in the doorway widened. It was a long time since Henriette had been accorded such respect from a fellow noblewoman.

"Sabatin is not with you, is he? Then come in."

It was even more like stepping back into the past than entering that reopened bedchamber had been. There was an anteroom, a salon and a bedchamber, all crammed with a lifetime collection that ranged from the wooden dolls of Henriette's childhood to the early fans of her girlhood and a large number of family portraits, some so discoloured as to make it almost impossible to discern the features painted on wood. Old Venetian glass, full of rainbow colours, jostled for space with porcelain vases, charming but worthless fairings, bunches of faded ribbons such as women wore in their hair decades ago, jade pieces of inestimable value, little caskets of mother-of-pearl set in gold and many other curiosities. On a large scale there were intarsia panels with perspective decoration in a variety of woods that were at least two centuries old, a stone relief of figures that were Roman, and a bishop's throne in ivory that looked decidedly Byzantine.

Jasmin thought how fascinated her father would have been by all that was here, for on the days when she had gone with him to great houses and churches where his advice had been sought, he had always pointed out what was old and beautiful, waxing almost lyrical about the craftsmen of the past. Infatuated by Versailles as she always was, she had been unable to see that anything surpassed what was displayed there, but coming upon this strangest of treasure houses she found herself delighting in all she saw.

"I believe you have more articles of interest here than there are in the whole of the rest of the château," she declared.

Henriette looked alarmed. "Don't tell Sabatin! He will want to sell them. His father did. That's why I had to get items of value hidden away up in my apartment where he never came, well out of sight. There were so many things that needed to be kept. One of Sabatin's ancestors brought some of them back from the Crusades."

"Put your fears at rest. Whatever is here is yours to safeguard. I'm merely charmed by it all. Those fans particularly interest me. I was taught how to make fans by my mother."

Henriette looked at her eagerly. "Would you make me a fan? I haven't had a new one since I was young."

Jasmin was momentarily taken aback. In her present homesick condition the last task she wanted was to make a fan. "One day," she promised, meaning what she said, "when I have had time to settle down."

The old lady beamed like a child promised a treat and clapped her thin hands together. "I'll have all you need. Lace and silk and ribbons. You may have to search the drawers and chests for them because I don't remember where everything is." She sat down and patted a chair next to her. "Sit down. How old are you? Seventeen? With your lovely face surely your father could have arranged a better *mariage de convenance* for you than with Sabatin. He's the wicked son of an evil father and it's no wonder she sent for me to come and live here. She had no one else."

"You mean Sabatin's mother?"

"That's right. Sabatin was conceived during their time at Versailles, but the Sun King never liked the sight of pregnant women and her husband sent her home. That's when I came to keep her company. It was obvious by that time I was never going to marry and my parents wished to get me off their hands, so there was no going home again for me after that poor dear woman died in my arms." She had an expressive little face, its wrinkles expanding and contracting according to what she was relating and at this point those around her mouth drew down quiveringly as she fought against tears even though so much time had passed since that tragic day. "Sabatin was two years old then. His father never came back to see him when he was born, nor did he come home for the funeral. He only returned later when he was short of money through gaming to sell what he could from here. He didn't live long after that. Years of dissipation and debauchery had taken its toll on him."

"But if that man had lost all he had, how is it that Sabatin is a rich man?"

"Oh, family money came back into the coffers again as various Valverdes died. He inherited a huge fortune from one great-uncle alone and there'll be more to come."

"Did you raise Sabatin?"

"As far as anybody could. He was wild and wayward from the time he could walk. By the age of seven he was uncontrollable. Tutors never stayed and servants left. He used to hit and kick me if I tried in any way to restrain him from getting his own way. There was nothing I could do."

Jasmin could imagine how ineffectual this weak, unpractical woman must have been in trying to discipline a strong-willed child. "Did no one else in the family step in to help you?"

"Those that could have were all at Court and far away. When Sabatin was nine his mother's brother came after I wrote a letter of appeal. He was a sea captain and was back in France to retire after many years abroad. He moved in and lived here as if he were still afloat, treating Sabatin like an insubordinate midshipman. In that way some discipline was instilled into the boy and he finally settled to lessons and learning. The Capitaine was a bluff, good-hearted man who had lost two sons in naval battles and aimed to be a father to Sabatin, but the boy hated him. To cross Sabatin in any way is to build up such ire in him that he becomes almost crazed." She shook her grey curls anxiously at Jasmin. "Always do what he says. It's the only way. That's why I daren't leave my rooms now. I didn't obey him the day he arrived with you."

"I should think he's not troubled by that any more. I've taken charge and the château is being put in order."

"I did what I could, you know. But servants won't work when they have to wait for their wages."

Jasmin looked incredulous. "Didn't you receive a regular allowance?"

"Oh, he never sent money here. Those at Court always expect funds to be sent to them from their estates and that's all the interest they take. A certain sum had to reach Sabatin regularly at Versailles and I had to manage on what was left for another year. I used up my own money long ago and although the Capitaine bequeathed some to me I've had to use it to keep everyone fed. I couldn't bring myself to dismiss servants with nowhere else to go."

"You can rest assured your worries are over now." Jasmin took the old woman's bony fingers into her hand and patted them before rising to leave. "There'll be money coming back into the household and more staff indoors and out."

Henriette stood up to see her out. "It's such a joy for me to have someone to talk to again," she said wonderingly. "Nobody ever comes here any more. Not since Sabatin's last year at home before he went to do his year's service in the King's army prior to being at Court."

"Did you and the Capitaine act as host and hostess?" Jasmin asked, supposing the old lady's outmoded clothes must date from that time.

"No, the Capitaine died tragically when Sabatin was sixteen. It was he who gave a year of parties for other young bucks like himself. They brought in women of the town and all that went on does not bear repeating. I kept to my rooms."

"Those days have gone, too. Come down and dine with us today."

Henriette's nervousness returned. "No, I think not. It's best if he just sees me about the place two or three times first."

"Very well." Jasmin opened the door and paused by it. "How did the Capitaine die?"

"It was a shooting accident. He must have been inspecting a pistol and before he realised it was loaded it went off." Henriette's eyes slid away and fastened on a patch of carpet. "Sabatin found him. He was nearby at the time. They had been talking together only a few minutes before."

Jasmin caught her breath. "Talking or quarrelling?"

The old woman raised terrified eyes to hers. "I'm telling you what Sabatin said at the time. For mercy's sake never question him about it. Maybe I shouldn't have told you."

"I promise you I'll never mention it."

Outside the door Jasmin released a shaky sigh. She had learned much more about her husband in the past hour. It was hard to sustain any pity for his muddled upbringing in

view of the treatment he had dealt out to the only two
people who had shown affection and concern for him.

When she reached the hall Sabatin had just come in
from riding. It was the first time she had seen him since she
had fled from his room at dawn. With a new aversion
added to that which she already felt she would have passed
him by without a glance as she fully expected him to do.
But there were servants present. To her surprise what she
had said to him on that first night after supper had had
effect in spite of what had followed. He bowed to her as
courteously as if he were the most devoted of husbands. It
was to be his well-mannered attentions to her by day, such
as his bows, his rising to his feet whenever she entered a
room, and his standing aside with some gesture of consideration to allow her to precede him at all times that were
to win the servants over into thinking that it was *she* who
was not speaking to *him*.

That same night Jasmin moved into her refurbished
apartment. No sooner was she in bed than the door between their bedchambers opened and he came to her. He
used her silently and selfishly in all the ways that pleased
him, setting a pattern for their nights together, but sparing
her the extreme brutality he had shown the first time.
Having wreaked his full vengeance on her by debasing her
to the limits, his pride was satisfied. Yet the unspoken
threat was always there between them, fully understood
by her, that he would not hesitate to abuse her by those
means again if ever she should baulk her marital duties
towards him.

Every day Jasmin became more and more obsessive
about the cleaning of the château. It was the only way she
was able to shut out her dread of Sabatin, her anxiety about
her parents, her homesickness and her sadness that all her
friends should have abandoned her in her banishment, for
no letters came. The resentment of the long-established
servants rose steadily against her, the seeds of irritation
having been sown from the start by her new-broom attitude towards them and their work. Only the Versailles
servants remained detached, keeping to themselves and
their own opinions like some noble circle among yokels
and ignoring the grumbling that went on.

"The Duchesse made me take down those tapestries and
brush them for the third time!"

"She climbed the library steps to look at the top of the oak cupboard again. I hoped she'd fall and break her neck."

"What about Jacques then? She said if he couldn't take the trouble to wear a clean neck-stock every day and keep his wig tidy he might as well work in the stables and that's where she sent him!"

None of them liked the Duc either. He would bellow like a bull when displeased, think nothing of using his boot in a servant's backside and he was harder on the horses than any rider they had seen before. But there was a certain grudging respect for the way he held his drink, for even after several hours and any number of emptied bottles he could still reel to his feet and make his own way upstairs. By the same token they resented the fact that he had no drinking companions to bring some liveliness to the château, but his conceit was such that he could not bring himself to associate with the rustic nobles he had always despised. For that reason he refused all the invitations that had begun to come trickling in and was scathing about them to his clerk.

"How do such people expect to engage the presence of one used to the company of Princes of the Blood and the King himself at their dreary social affairs!"

The clerk continued to pen the refusals. Then one day, in presenting the latest invitation that had arrived, he dared to make a suggestion. "Perhaps Madame la Duchesse would like to attend this musical evening."

Sabatin answered him with a glare and snatched the card from him to tear it in two. Jasmin never knew of these invitations, for all letters delivered to the château were the responsibility of the clerk, who in turn took them to his master. Sabatin burned all correspondence that came for her after glancing through it, prepared to tell her if her father was dead, but nothing more. In the same way not a letter that she wrote got beyond him. Every one was destroyed. Had he been speaking to her he would have given his reasons, which were perfectly logical to him, but since he was not he let matters be. He certainly did not intend to waste his time writing notes as he had done on the journey or else it would go on ad infinitum, for nothing would induce him ever to utter a word to that strumpet responsible for bringing him to such straits.

In August when Jasmin had been at Château Valverde for three months, which had been more like three years for her, the news came that the King was to be married to Princesse Marie Leszczyńska, daughter of the exiled King of Poland. She went to an isolated corner of the old terraced garden where restoration work had not yet begun and sat there quietly for half an hour. She shed no tears at the memories evoked. Self-pity had dried up in her as had everything else except her longing for home and a desperate need of some word from there. The fear had grown steadily that her mother had finally washed her hands of her as if this marriage to Sabatin had been the final betrayal of the hopes that had been held for her.

Whenever such thoughts came upon her she did not know how to hold herself back from screaming out her despair. Springing to her feet, she seized once more on the only antidote she knew and went to inspect the attics to see how clean that morning's scrubbing had made them. She further occupied her mind with plans for a celebration of some kind for the servants and tenants on the fifth day of September, which was to be the King's wedding day.

Thirteen

Due to Marguerite's devoted nursing Laurent showed much improvement, and there was less permanent damage than had first appeared. His speech was still impaired and not all visitors who came to see him could fully grasp his words, which allowed them to do most of the talking. Everyone was primed beforehand by Marguerite not to reveal Jasmin's marriage.

"It could cause a relapse if he knew," she explained truthfully, recalling how she herself had almost collapsed when she had received her daughter's sad farewell letter written at Versailles. "The Baron thinks she is in Italy."

She always left him alone with his callers, for they helped to ease him into an acceptance of her being absent from him for short periods. How she would have managed without Berthe to assist her she did not know.

At first he had been too ill to have any conception of the passage of time, but with the betterment of his condition he began asking about correspondence from Jasmin. Marguerite made excuses, hoping that the next day would

359

bring one, already sick with worry herself that nothing had come. Eventually when he started to fret she was left with no alternative.

"A letter from Jasmin!" she exclaimed one morning, unfolding what she herself had written the evening before. That day began for her the endless pretence that letters were coming at regular if lengthy intervals. Fortunately in the past Laurent had spoken several times of his sister-in-law and her home that he had visited on two occasions, and it enabled Marguerite to be considerably inventive. It would have been natural for Jasmin to chatter on about balls and fêtes, parties and concerts and the latest fashions, and often these took up the greater part of the fake letters. The good side of Laurent's face always creased into an indulgent smile, his delight unchanging in the picture of beauty and grace he supposed his daughter to be making at these functions, and he was always more content afterwards.

Eventually, unable to bear the lack of communication with Jasmin any longer, Marguerite wrote direct to her son-in-law. She had never spoken to him, but she remembered seeing him on occasions at Versailles when snippets of salacious gossip about him had been exchanged within her hearing, enough to convey to her that if even a tenth of it were based on fact he was a man violent, lewd and dissipated. That her daughter should be his wife made her start from sleep at night, horrors tumbling in her mind, and her only hope was that Jasmin would arouse some love in him to make him at least kind towards her.

Marguerite received her reply quite promptly from him, showing there was no problem over the conveyance of mail by messenger from that distant region of the country. His opening sentence was one of regret that he had been troubled over this matter. Jasmin was his wife with no further commitment to anyone other than himself and he wished it to remain that way. Moreover, he would remind Baron and Baronne Picard that he had taken their daughter without a dowry, that Jasmin's social status was woefully inadequate for a nobleman of his rank, and that she was entirely responsible for his banishment. As a result he could suffer no contact of any kind to exist between his house and theirs. All letters to Jasmin had been destroyed and that would continue without reprieve. The parental duties of an architect and a fan-maker towards the Duchesse de Valverde were at an end.

At first Marguerite was so aghast at the arrogance and callousness of the letter that it shook in her hands. With a stroke of his pen Valverde had severed the bond between her and her child. Her fears about his treatment of Jasmin increased a thousandfold. She did not know what she could do and, putting trembling fingertips to her head, she could hardly think. Remorse had long been heavy on her that she had not listened to Laurent when he had wanted to send Jasmin to Florence. The fault was all hers for misinterpreting his reasons. If she had acted promptly her daughter would have been spared. As for Valverde's accusation against Jasmin, whatever he might believe, she had heard from Laurent's visitors that the Duc de Bourbon had worked systematically through a blacklist to rid the Court of those presenting any kind of moral danger to the King. That Jasmin must also have been on that list was something that Marguerite kept to herself. Others thought Jasmin had simply suffered the same unfortunate fate as several young noblewomen who had been cruelly married off to those "pullers-up of the palisades" and sent with them into banishment, a more than vicious trick played on each one of them by the Duc de Bourbon.

It was through the King that Marguerite saw the only ray of hope. He could order Valverde to allow correspondence to pass between her and her daughter. Yet she did not have enough liberty at present to wait here and there at Versailles to waylay him with her petition, knowing that Laurent would become distressed during her absence. Augustin's warning long ago about the censorship of everything written that went in and out of Versailles held her back from penning an appeal. It was likely Bourbon would see that Louis never received it. She would simply have to wait until an opportunity presented itself. In the meantime she must carry on fabricating correspondence from Jasmin, which had become such a sad task for her.

September came and with it the dawn of the royal wedding day. Louis had fallen head over heels in love at first sight of his betrothed when she arrived at Versailles. A cruel whisper or two beforehand had warned him that she was plain, and perhaps she was to other men, but her

piquant face and clear dark eyes had captivated him from
the start. He did not care that Marie Leszczyńska was
seven years older than he. Jasmin had been his senior by
two years bar a month or two, and that had made no
difference. Not that he gave her more than a passing
thought these days. Excitement about his marriage had
taken over, for Jasmin's going away had left a painful void
in which he had waited, ripe for love. And it had come
with his bride-to-be! Inwardly smiling, outwardly cool and
composed, he was dressed for his wedding in white silk,
and when the long, ermine-lined cloak of sapphire velvet
with the gold fleur-de-lys was put about his shoulders it felt
like a caress.

In the Cour Royale a military band played. People had
been flocking through the ever-open gates since early daylight, everyone in a festive mood, and the sellers of goods
in the vestibules were doing a roaring trade, many in
favours specially made for the wedding day. All were hoping to get a glimpse of the King and his new Queen on the
balcony when the ceremony in the Royal Chapel was over.
In the midst of the crowd Marguerite had to leave her
carriage, there being no way for the coachman to get
through, and she threaded her way towards the triple
arches with their open gilded grilles and entered the vestibule of the Queen's Staircase, so familiar to her from the
time when a glimpse of Augustin had been such a bonus to
her fan-selling days.

The anxieties of the past months, concern for the two
people dearest to her clawing at her constantly, had taken
their toll on her. She was much thinner, lines that had been
faint on her face more deeply incised, and her once glorious ruby-red hair had faded to a softly tinted grey, only a
few gleaming threads remaining to hint at what had been.
Yet at sixty-one she still walked with the same straight back
and graceful swing of the hips that often made younger
men turn and look at her. But today there was no room in
the seething throng for anyone to take notice of her as she
ascended the Queen's Staircase against a tide of humanity
going up and down. On and on she went to reach the
Peace Salon that led into the Hall of Mirrors from the south
end.

She had heard on good authority that the King would be
coming from his apartment by this route on his way to the

Royal Chapel in order to let as many people see him as was possible. She had not expected to find such a mass of people already gathered in that long, glittering gallery where even the seventeen window alcoves were filled, every seat taken on the tiered velvet seats that were placed there on grand occasions. She did not enter but took up a position ignored by everybody else, which was with her back against the green and white pilaster of the archway dividing off the Peace Salon, the sweep of the arch itself curving upwards above her head.

There should not be long to wait. She glanced towards the grey marble fireplace in the Peace Salon, but there was no clock on it to tell her how time was passing. Not until this very morning had she known whether or not she could come today. Everything had depended on whether it was a good or a bad day for Laurent, but fortunately he had seemed quite well and had smiled when she had expressed a wish to see the royal bride.

"Go, my . . . dear. Berthe . . . will . . . be . . . with . . . me."

She had flown around to get ready, putting on a Court gown and her emeralds. Lastly she had taken up one of the jewelled fans and set off. At such a time of joyousness and celebration the King would grant many requests that day and she wanted hers to be one of them.

"The King is coming!"

The call was being taken up by people either in courtly whispers or the louder tones of the bourgeois, who had managed to cram themselves into every space as far as the second antechamber with the lovely oval window in a gilded frieze of children into which the King's bedchamber opened. In her mind's eye she pictured his stately progress and found herself holding her breath when he finally came into sight, this youth who had loved her daughter, never more a King than on this day. There was a rustling on all sides as courtiers and their ladies to the forefront bowed and curtsied low. Others applauded and there was a spontaneous burst of cheering from those at the back, which was picked up immediately by many in the Hall of Mirrors.

Marguerite saw the flicker of recognition in Louis's gaze as she moved further into his path under the archway to drop her own deep curtsey to him and then hand him a late summer cream rose from the parterres of Château Satory. He took it graciously.

"I thank you, Madame la Baronne."

"It symbolises joy, sire."

"What a charming thought. How is your husband? Better, I trust."

She was touched that he should remember to enquire after Laurent on this auspicious day and relieved that Louis had unwittingly aided her in putting forth her request.

"He has improved, sire." Her voice throbbed eagerly. "But his prospects would be much brighter if he could receive a letter from Jasmin in her own hand. The Duc de Valverde has forbidden her to write. Only you can counter that cruel stipulation. I beg you to intervene, sire!"

He had not caught her words in the increasing tumult of approbation rising in the Hall of Mirrors into which he had glanced with a smile. Courtiers, clustered behind him, were creating a furor of their own, trying to keep back those crowding after them. He thought he knew what she had said and her strained expression was natural to a mother deprived of her daughter on such an emotional occasion.

"Thank Jasmin for conveying her good wishes through her letter to you. I wish her happiness in turn."

People shoved her aside as he moved on and she was lost helplessly in the crush. Extricating herself, she drew aside to a window and looked out abstractedly, letting the throng sweep on by her in his wake. Her last hope had gone. At the mention of Jasmin's name she had seen in his gaze that particular blank look that always came into a man's eyes when a woman no longer interested him. Although it had never been directed at her, she had seen it in the case of other women. It was invariably accompanied by the polite smile, the glancing about for escape and the overenthusiastic welcome of whatever diversion presented itself. With Louis there had been no deliberate spurn, but she had seen enough to know that if she should approach him again at any time he would say that he could not intervene between husband and wife.

Disconsolately she left Versailles. When she arrived home Laurent had visitors, a fellow architect and his wife. Although she was in no mood herself to be sociable she felt obliged to join them, for the architect's wife had recently come to live in the area with him after staying behind to sell their house in Chartres. Before she could reach the door of Laurent's bedchamber it burst open and the woman rushed out.

"Quick! Your husband! I fear he's dying!"

Marguerite rushed to him. She saw at once he was having one of his attacks brought on by nervous agitation that racked him for breath and caused him pain. She did what she always did at these times, which was to prop him higher and hold him to her in reassurance until the spasm passed, never knowing whether he would pull through once again. The architect and his wife hovered helplessly.

"What did you say to him?" Marguerite demanded of the couple.

The woman answered tearfully, wringing her hands. "I only spoke of his daughter's marriage to the Duc de Valverde."

Marguerite closed her eyes wearily for a moment. After all her efforts the sustained pretence had broken down. "Did Berthe not warn you?"

The architect answered. "I suppose she saw no need since I have been here several times before. I had forgotten to forewarn my wife. Is there anything we can do?"

"No. Don't blame yourselves. It couldn't be helped. Please leave us."

Berthe came to assist as soon as they were gone. There was always the opening of the windows wider if they were not closed, the pouring out of cognac, for sips were beneficial to him, and the dampening of clouts in cold water for soothing his brow, which ran with sweat at these times. Marguerite gave her no reproof for the slip that had been made. The truth had a way of coming out, however hard one tried to suppress it. That would have happened sooner or later.

That night at Versailles was the happiest Louis had ever known. In the morning his dazed and delighted bride informed her eagerly attentive ladies that the King had made love to her seven times. They were thrilled and quick to spread the good news, which flew round the Court causing immense rejoicing. It promised well in the important matter of heirs and before long it was obvious to all that the Queen had conceived on her wedding night.

With the King deeply in love and the Queen smiling and gracious, if a trifle pious, there had never been a more joyous time for everyone at Versailles. The cynics declared it could not last, while the romantics were equally sure it would, talking of how all the world loved a lover and how the whole nation had taken the King to their hearts. Just nine months after the wedding day, and by long tradition before a full audience of courtiers and noblewomen, as well as a few ordinary bourgeois who had managed to squeeze into the bedchamber, Queen Marie gave birth to twin daughters, the first of several public performances she was to give at intervals in her magnificently beplumed bed.

At Château Satory the blunder made on the royal wedding day had set Laurent back almost to his original state after the seizure. For weeks afterwards Marguerite was spared having to face him with an explanation for having falsified letters from Jasmin. Since she had also forgotten to wait and see Marie Leszczyńska as a bride, she did not have to make excuses about that either. When after many months Laurent finally made up the ground he had lost, she was able to tell him the whole truth and after that there were no more lies or evasions, for she had given him their son-in-law's reason for the lack of correspondence with the daughter now lost to them. For the first time since Laurent's illness had struck him down Marguerite was unable to hold back tears in front of him and they wept together.

For Jasmin the day of Louis's marriage had also been a traumatic one. In spite of her fears, it was impossible to believe that her mother, however displeased with her, would not have let her have reports on her father's condition and an unpleasant suspicion that had long been with her began to take hold. To confirm it she needed proof first. Her chance came when she was outside in the gardens watching the housekeeper supervising the arrangements for the wedding day feast. She happened to spot a letter-carrier loitering to watch the scene of excitement, for all the servants were eagerly carrying stools and trays of platters and mugs.

"I'll take those," she said, holding out her hand to take the two letters he held in his clasp. One was addressed to Sabatin and the other to her in a handwriting she did not recognise. She took them to her apartment and, careful not to crack the seal, she managed with the aid of a paperknife to prise open the one addressed to her. It was from a local noblewoman inviting her to a ladies' card party. She resealed the letter and took it back to the carrier whom she had told to wait. He had been willing enough, especially as one of the maids had begun talking to him as she set the nearest table. Jasmin, after telling him to take the letters on to the château, strolled back to where she had been standing. Whether he thought it odd that she had removed the letters from his hand for a short while she did not know or care. She had set a trap and would await results.

Sabatin did not deign to appear at the festivities, his thoughts at Versailles and the sophisticated pleasures he was missing there. He took refuge with a number of bottles and wished it was as easy for him to become insensible as it was for other men. Henriette was as excited as a child over the whole celebration and she and Jasmin, although they left the crowd of merrymakers to themselves most of the time, distributed bowls of sweetmeats to the children and watched the fireworks together from one of the windows.

Jasmin had been struck that day by the poor condition of the tenants. They did not look ill fed for it was the time of year when the fruits of the earth were in sufficient supply for even the poverty-stricken of the countryside to eat moderately well, but they would have put on their best clothes for such a day and many of them were in rags. She questioned Henriette about it and was answered vaguely.

"I don't know any of them. They pay their dues to Sabatin for the land they farm and he owns every acre for leagues around. Even the village is built on his land. It is the walnut crop that is most important in this area."

Walnut oil was the essential ingredient of a good salad and Jasmin recalled how often it had enhanced a dish for her in the past without her ever giving a thought to those who toiled to produce it. But that side of the Valverde properties was not her concern. Her domain was the château as well as the gardens, which should be transformed by the time spring came.

She excused the resealed letter not being delivered to her by the close of the wedding day celebrations, for the routine of the whole household had been disrupted, but she did look for it next morning. She waited three days. Then she challenged the clerk about it.

"Why has there been such a delay, Monsieur Dupons?"

He regarded her uncomfortably. Quiet and retiring, he was a sallow-faced, hollow-chested man, who knew his place and wrote in a beautiful hand. Unlike the humbler staff he bore her no malice, but his first loyalty was to the Duc. Moreover, he had welcomed the move to the countryside, hoping that it would help the irritating cough that troubled him at times, and he would do nothing that might jeopardise his situation.

"The Duc instructed me to decline the invitation, madame," he said uneasily. "I did not know it had already passed through your hands."

"What of other letters that have come for me, Monsieur Dupons?"

He became thoroughly flustered. "Everything goes first to your husband, madame."

"I shall speak to him without delay. In future all my letters come direct to me. That is an order."

Sabatin heard her out in the library, standing with his back towards her, staring stonily out the window. He was rarely entirely sober these days, often starting his day's drinking with *vin de champagne* at breakfast, shades of Versailles in which he found balm. She made a civil request for the letters she knew him to have kept back from her, not wanting to rile him and thus lose all chance of recovering what was hers.

"They are my property. I have no idea why you should have kept them from me unless it was to further your initial punishment of me for the events for which you erroneously hold me to blame. Let that be over and done with now. Out of mercy let me know whether my dear father is alive or dead!" Her voice cracked and without being aware of it she had flung out her hands towards him in a gesture of appeal.

He sighed to show that she bored him, but swung away from the window to open the door into the side room where the clerk did his work. She felt weak with relief. The letters were to be brought to her! How many would there be? In a matter of seconds they would be in her hands.

"Monsieur Dupons," Sabatin drawled on a wearied note, "have I overlooked news of any bereavements?"

The clerk turned his head, pen in hand, and was able to see Jasmin beyond his master through the half-open door. He was careful to avoid her gaze.

"Not that I know of, sir."

"Then there have been none. What of letters from inferior personages? Have there been some more recently?"

"Only those I have handed to you."

"Good. With time this pestering should cease. I have never had to tolerate correspondence from inferiors on such a scale before. In future you will relieve me of the tiresome task of tearing them up by putting to a candle-flame anything not addressed to me."

"Yes, sir."

Sabatin closed the door and without a glance in her direction resumed his seat at the library table with an open volume before him where she had found him upon entering the room. She remained where she was, staring at him with such hatred that she shook with the revulsion she felt. In the most callous way he had let her know that her father was still alive and at the same time made it plain that she could never hope to hear from her parents or anyone else who chose to write to her. She also understood that none of her letters would have reached them. Worse than any of the humiliations that he had inflicted on her was that he was causing constant hurt to those dearest to her. Something snapped in her. She flew at him, clawing and lashing out.

"You cruel, heartless devil!" she shrieked. "You belong in hell!"

Being seated and completely taken by surprise, he was for a few seconds at a disadvantage. As her fingernails made scarlet grooves down one side of his face, he sprang to his feet with a roar, knocking back his chair and throwing her from him. She careened backwards to fall heavily against a bookcase and slide sprawling to the floor. Before she could move he had plunged forward to grab her by the throat and with one foot on either side of her he jerked her into a sitting position. His face hung over her, congested with rage and purple as a ripe plum, blood trickling down from her scratches. There was murder in his eyes and she knew he was going to strangle her. She struggled but the pressure on her throat was increasing. Just as she was almost at choking point he released his hold, letting her drop, and her head struck the floorboards, adding a fresh explosion of pain to what she was already suffering. Then he went charging out of the library, the door crashing after him.

She did not lose consciousness although her thoughts seemed to come and go as she lay helpless, coughing and gasping for air, unable to move. The door of the side room opened as the clerk looked in and then was closed hastily, showing he did not intend to become involved. But he must have sent for her maid, because after some timeless lapse she found Lenore supporting her head and then helping her to her feet. She was left alone again when Lenore rushed to fetch a gauzy scarf, which was then wrapped about her neck to hide the bruising. After a little while she was able to walk upstairs unaided to her apartment. Once behind her own door she collapsed and Lenore put her to bed.

As she recovered she spent many hours weighing up this new situation. She was and always would be the reason in Sabatin's eyes as to why he had been forced to leave Versailles, no matter that the Duc de Bourbon must have made it plain to him there were other good causes for his banishment. What they could be she was only able to guess, for no explanation had been given to her, but Sabatin was like many people of supreme conceit in being unable to accept any measure of blame himself. He was also such an egotist that his pride would not allow for his own wife to keep contact with her kin whom he saw as his inferiors. From now on she would have to find a means of smuggling out letters and she was considering how that was to be done.

As yet she had not been to the town of Périgueux, although it was no great distance away. Lenore had been two or three times to make purchases on her behalf, travelling with the housekeeper on marketing sorties. She herself could call a carriage and drive there any day but, as if under a spell, she had neither the curiosity nor the interest to break away from the sprucing up of the château, something in herself she did not want to question. Lenore should take a letter the next time the housekeeper set out and it could be despatched from Périgueux.

During the next few days Jasmin covered a long sheet of paper as she wrote down all she could think of that would please her parents but making no secret of Sabatin's ruling which, with their knowledge of the arrogance of those of high rank, they would completely understand. On the morning that it was sealed, Jasmin handed it to Lenore with a purse and told her to let nobody, not even the housekeeper, know what she was about.

It was the usual hour of late afternoon when the housekeeper returned. Jasmin, sitting with some embroidery on a window seat, rested her needle as she looked out, watching for Lenore to alight in the housekeeper's wake, but the girl did not appear and the carriage rolled on out of sight to the stables. Puzzled, she rang for the housekeeper who came at once.

"Where is Lenore?" Jasmin asked.

"Dismissed, madame."

Jasmin stared incredulously. "For what reason and by whom?"

"Monsieur le Duc, madame. He told me to search Lenore before we left as he believed she might be smuggling out a secret letter from his desk. I found it on her and gave it to him, whereupon he instructed me to take her with me as far as Périgueux and leave her there."

It was all Jasmin could do not to break down. She had lost her only trustworthy companion and friend in her isolation. There was a glint of satisfaction in the housekeeper's eyes that spurred her into keeping control. The woman liked her no more than did the rest of the household staff and should not glimpse the full effect that this blow was having on her. She spoke stiffly.

"You had better select the best maid suited to take Lenore's place until someone well trained can be appointed."

The woman bobbed and left. Jasmin pressed the back of her hand to her tremulous lips, choking back a sob and letting the embroidery slip unheeded from her lap. At least Lenore had a purse of money with her that would keep her in board and lodging until she found some new employment. She was thankful she received a regular allowance, although fully aware it was only due to Sabatin's pride, which could not permit his wife appearing to be penniless. Tomorrow she would go to Périgueux herself and send a letter. With any luck she might see Lenore and arrange for her to receive mail from Château Satory as soon as she was in a settled abode.

The following morning when Jasmin was ready to depart she was informed that no carriages were available as all were being repainted and reupholstered. Only the Duc's was in use and that was being kept for him alone.

"Then I'll ride," she said determinedly. But she knew the answer almost before it was uttered. Since the day when the King had almost taken a fall, the Duc had given orders that none other than himself or the grooms were to ride any of his horses. She went back indoors, pulling off her hat. To all intents and purposes she had become a prisoner at Château Valverde. Her loathing of Sabatin had reached such a peak that she feared for her own sanity. To allay all thought she kept on her white gloves and began one of her inspections for dust that the servants dreaded.

There was a chapel in the château where once a month the village priest held Mass for the household, although the days when a large family had gathered there were long since gone. It was a tradition that went back in time, probably instigated when the village church was first built on Valverde land, and it had enabled Henriette to remain within the gates of the château away from the outside world. After the service on the Sunday following Lenore's dismissal, Jasmin spoke to the priest. She and Henriette had been the only communicants, for Sabatin rarely attended and the servants were permitted to attend an earlier service in the village church which they preferred. As Henriette went from the chapel, Jasmin produced a new letter she had written and asked the priest if he would send it on her behalf, explaining the situation.

He was sympathetic, but he was as poor as many of his flock and the Duc de Valverde had recently sent him a generous donation for essential roof repairs to the village church without which the beams would have collapsed. It had probably been given to ensure there should be no derelict and abandoned church on ducal land, but that was not important if it could be instrumental in bringing a prodigal son back into the fold from the taint of the gilded den of vice that was Versailles.

"My dear child," he said gently to Jasmin, "your first duty after that to God is to obey your husband at all times. If he does not wish you to correspond with your parents he must have a good reason."

"Nothing but arrogance, Father! And what of my honouring my father and my mother?"

"Do that by your prayers and by loving them in your heart. Just remember you are a wife first and a daughter second now."

She could see that nothing would persuade him to take sides with her against Sabatin. "Then help me by writing to my parents yourself, I beg you. Tell them I'm well and think of them all the time. That's all I ask!"

"I tell you what I will do. I shall seek your husband's permission in the matter and if he raises no objection I'll do as you request."

"That's useless! He'll never grant it."

"Then, my child, I fear the subject is closed."

As the months went by invitations no longer came to Château Valverde. Sabatin would never have admitted, even to himself, that he was piqued by this falling off of social approach, but in refusing the hospitality offered he had kept up his spirits to a degree, for it had enabled him to continue to feel completely aloof from the long-despised. For the same reason he never did more than cast a supercilious glance to the left or right of him as he drove himself in a light calèche around his estates, leaving everything to his bailiff, who had to ensure that the required amount of income was produced each year, which was the limit of his ducal interest. It was as if he could not bear that even the dust from the soil he owned should fall on him with some contaminating effect.

Yet in spite of himself he was becoming avid for company other than that of his bleak-faced wife with whom he sometimes played a silent game of chess or backgammon, or that stupid old woman, Henriette, who, although finally persuaded to join them for the evening meal, rarely opened her mouth. His only other pastimes were to ride, to hunt with a few grooms in attendance and to drink to excess when gloom overcame him. Whereas at Court his drinking bouts had always been merry times in gatherings of friends, the occasions now were lonely ones, usually starting when he sat on alone after supper. If he fell asleep none of the servants, not even his valet, dared to wake him, for he had become savagely ill-tempered these days and worse when he was in his cups.

Jasmin spent much of her time with Henriette. After making the old lady the promised fan she amused herself for many hours making others in varying styles and fabrics until she had quite a collection. Although Jasmin never went anywhere to use a single one of them, this did not trouble her unduly, for she had developed a curious reluctance to go outside, although she would venture into the grounds to take a walk if she were sure the gates were closed. If they stood open for any reason she would not emerge. It was not related to the timidity and shyness that had turned Henriette into a virtual recluse, but seemed to come from some growing unnamed fear deep within her that added to the rest of the anxieties that continually gave her sleepless nights. She could date it from her abortive attempts to get a letter out herself. It was as if that failure had had some indefinable effect on her.

As far as she knew she had had no success in getting a letter home. Once she had bribed a pedlar at the gates to take one with him, but he had a sly face and she feared he had only pocketed the money and thrown the letter away. There was not a single servant she could bribe. Apart from the deep-rooted hostility against her, even Lenore's replacement being put out by her strict ways and standards of perfection, none would wish to risk dismissal. She was sure that the Versailles group would have accepted money for anything, except risking the Duc's temper on her behalf. She had even tried to persuade Henriette to journey to Périgueux and despatch a letter, but the woman almost fainted at the prospect of crossing Sabatin and had shut herself away in her apartment, not emerging again for two weeks.

Belowstairs there was now no one who did not know that the Duc and Duchesse lived in deepest animosity with each other. To the more worldly Versailles servants there was nothing unusual about this sort of marriage, but normally each partner found consolation elsewhere. With these two there was none of that. It was not that the Duc did not have an eye for other women. There were several good-looking young maids in the château who, out of awe or curiosity, had allowed themselves to be kissed and fondled by him, but all agreed that his wife must have some kind of fascination for him, for, even when thoroughly aroused, he would thrust them aside and go to her wherever she happened to be.

The truth was that after two years of marriage, Jasmin, with her listless submission, was no real pleasure to him, but he wanted an heir. By now she should have been pregnant twice over and on the way to a third child. At the back of his mind as he forced himself into her there was ever the thought that she was the daughter of elderly parents and perhaps her fecundity was impaired. If she should take as long as her mother had done to conceive, he would be old himself before an offspring was born.

He had cause for celebration one day and that had nothing to do with his wife. A cousin of his, who was his heir, kept him informed of events at Court and sent jubilant word that the Duc de Bourbon had not only fallen from power but had been sent to live on his estate at Chantilly, well away from Versailles. Sabatin laughed long and loud, rejoicing in the downfall of his enemy. It was a good omen. His own day would surely come again before long.

The year of 1728 was drawing to a close. Jasmin returned from a stroll in the part of the grounds where the woodland was a continuation of the forest of birch, aspen, pine and ash that clung like a robe to the slopes of the prominence on which the château stood. As she paused to look down at the valley where the stretches of cultivated walnut trees grew amid the scattered farmhouses, she heard carriage wheels. With the quirk of alarm that always plagued her, she realised the gates had been opened and she had not known. Immediately she hurried along the path, intent on getting back indoors, and saw a travel-stained coach and six tired horses at the steps of the entrance. Mounting the flight was a portly figure she recognised instantly.

"Berthe!"

She must have shrieked her nurse's name, but the woman merely stopped and looked in her direction. Being solid, undemonstrative Berthe, there was no wave of greeting or any move to meet her former charge now running towards her. Jasmin plunged up the steps and flung both arms about her, laughing and sobbing. Then, almost in the same instant, she was filled with dread as to why Berthe had come and jerked back to look into her face.

"Is my father—?" She could not bring herself to finish the sentence.

Berthe shook her head and actually smiled, warmed more by the welcome she had received than she would have ever acknowledged. "No, the Baron has not gone from us, but your mother spends all her time with him, which is why I'm here to see you in her place."

"All that long journey on your own! Come indoors!" Her eyes still full of happy tears, Jasmin led her through the entrance hall and up the stairs out of earshot of the attendant footman. "I can't wait to hear all the news," she said eagerly as soon as Berthe was seated in her apartment.

"Firstly your father. He is considerably improved. Some power has returned to the paralysed side and now with help he can walk a short distance and sit in his chair. Speech is almost normal and he can converse clearly, if a little slowly, with visitors."

"But how is Maman managing without you? You were surely another right hand to her in dealing with my father's illness."

"Lenore has taken my place. The Baron likes her because she can talk of you and the time she spent in your service, short though it was."

"You mean Lenore went all the way there after she was sent away from here?"

Berthe nodded. "It took her many months. She was penniless and had to walk and work for long periods and get wagon-lifts when she could."

"Was that when my mother first knew why she had not heard from me?"

"Oh, no. Your husband had written long before."

Jasmin listened to an account of what Sabatin had written, but she was beyond anger over that. In a way it was a relief to know they had been spared further worry over why they were not hearing from her. "Then Lenore filled in all the details, I hope."

"She did as soon as she was well enough. You see, when she reached Château Satory early this year, she collapsed upon arrival. We thought at one point the girl was not going to pull through, but your mother's care saved her."

"But Lenore had a purse of money I gave her. It should have helped her to reach Versailles without all the hardships she went through."

"Your housekeeper claimed it with the letter you had sent her to post. She had nothing."

Jasmin's eyes narrowed into the fierce look that many in the household would have recognised. "That's most interesting. I'll see about that later." Then her face became bright again and she took Berthe by the hand. "You shall have a bedchamber near mine and as soon as you've tidied yourself from your travelling I'll have refreshments served here."

"I'd be able to eat the food off the floor if the whole place shines like those parts I've seen already," Berthe remarked smiling. "I never thought a château this old could smell of anything but age. Here it's all beeswax and lavender."

"I won't tolerate anything else."

Berthe gave her a piercing look but said no more until they had entered the room that Jasmin had allotted to her. She viewed its brocades and fine oak and velvet cushions with disapproval. "This is too grand for me. Noble folk stay here."

"We never have any guests. Nobody visits us. You are the first."

Berthe frowned at her. "I'm not visiting. I've come to stay."

For a few moments Jasmin stood speechless with joy, her radiant expression saying everything. Then she flung her arms around Berthe again. "I had forgotten what it was to feel happy. Oh, Berthe! This is the best day I've had since I left home."

A much smaller room had to be found for Berthe, for with her old stubbornness she would consider nothing else. She would have chosen to be in the servants' quarters if Jasmin had not made a stand, knowing that Berthe's legs must be older than they were in happier days.

When Berthe took from the pocket of her cloak a long letter from Marguerite, it seemed to Jasmin that her cup of happiness was running over.

Opening it, she saw that her father had also signed his name in a shaky hand and she kissed both signatures. There were other letters, too, all from friends, who upon hearing that Berthe was to see her were eager to commu-

nicate in spite of what to them had been grievous neglect
on her part. She read her mother's epistle first. A full report on Laurent's progress was followed by the news that
Picard fans were being made under another name. Marguerite had sold the whole fan-making business, from the
mansion on the Avenue de Paris and the Champs-Élysées
shop to all the workshops. Then there followed all the little
items of news that make a letter from home such pleasure
to a member of the family far away. Marguerite did not
refrain from mentioning Versailles, telling her of the
younger people she knew there, their marriages and their
babies, the promotion of husbands and the latest betroth-
als, also adding that all said it was enchanting to see how
devoted the King was to his wife and twin daughters.

She was pleased on Louis's behalf and her mother would
have known that. He was not yet eighteen and had already
created a little family circle in which he would be most
content, making up for what he had lost early in his own
life. Yet remembering the laughter in him, his keen appreciation of his own strength and vitality after his sickly
childhood and the huge enjoyment he had of any merry
occasion, she hoped that the Queen would always be wife
and mistress to him, for she herself would never be there
to fill that second rôle he had once thought essential to his
happiness.

The following day Jasmin dismissed her personal maid
and replaced her with Berthe, who could sew and mend
and press lace as well as anybody. As for dressing hair the
current mode was simple enough, brushed back as it was
from the brow into curls at the sides and back of the head.
The fashion prints her mother had thoughtfully sent along
with a collection of gifts showed that styles had not
changed to any degree during the time she had been away,
although they were becoming flatter to the front and back
while widening at the sides.

She would have dismissed the housekeeper as well, but
it turned out that the woman had only been obeying Sabatin's instructions regarding anything Lenore was carrying
and had returned the purse to him intact. At first the
woman was truly afraid, thinking she would not be believed, and Jasmin observed to herself that as well as disliking her the domestic staff feared her power, for in no way
did Sabatin interfere with her running of the château.

When she gave a nod to show that the interview was over, the woman positively scurried away. She did wonder if her husband would raise any objection to Berthe moving in, for Henriette was their go-between, letting each of them know anything of importance, but he accepted the situation without the least interest. He would know that Berthe's immediate aim would be to get a letter on its way from Jasmin to her parents, but probably he no longer cared since the process would be secret from him as well as everybody else, and even he knew the ban would not remain undefied forever.

Jasmin still did not take the risk of having post come to the château.

Berthe, who became friendly with the village dress-maker, arranged for everything to be delivered there. Marguerite had sent her daughter three new gowns, in-cluding one with the new hoops, and Madame L'Haire, the dressmaker, coming to the château to make some small alterations to them, began to do sewing work at regular intervals, bringing or taking letters in her sewing-box. Since she and Berthe were two of a kind, able to hold their tongues, it would have hardly needed the extra payment she received for this service that she did willingly. There was little other excitement in the dull routine of her life.

Berthe had come in one of Laurent's own carriages with coachman and groom, which had been his gift to his daughter. It gave Jasmin the freedom to drive out when-ever she wished without facing the endless restrictions imposed by Sabatin, but she took no advantage of it, still continuing as before, obsessed by the château, and want-ing to go no farther than a daily walk in the grounds when the gates were closed. Sabatin did not exert himself to look at the six new horses that drew the coach, although he must have heard they were matched thoroughbreds and he was an admirer of splendid horseflesh. His wits were dulled by his daily drinking and he was less particular about his appearance now, his waistcoat often wine-stained and his breath permanently soured.

Berthe watching Jasmin snapping at the maids over a cobweb that had appeared overnight or complaining she could not see her reflection through a faint smear on a mirror, thought how changed she was, even her face hav-ing taken on a sharp look. Yet the warmth of heart was still there. It had shown itself on the day of her arrival and then been clamped down again.

"Why haven't you any babies?" Berthe asked her outright one day when they sat by the fire.

"I don't intend to have any," Jasmin replied crisply with equal bluntness.

"Oh? Like that, is it? I tell you that a child would give you something to think about other than house dust and it would melt that steel in your eyes."

Jasmin tossed her chin. "Three and a half years of marriage have made a different person of me. As for a child, I believe I'm barren in any case. In that at least fate has relented towards me."

"How can you be sure?"

The reply came icily. "I am, that's all. A wife cannot be forewarned and prepared against a husband like mine at any hour of the day or night. Had I loved him that would have been another matter and I would have welcomed children of my own. But never by him! So don't speak to me any more about having a family."

"I understand better than you think. I was married to a brute of a man once."

"You!" Jasmin looked astonished. "Maman never knew that, did she?"

"Not for a long while. When I came to Château Satory to be nurse to you I'd left my husband, taken another name and made a new beginning to my life."

"Did you have any children?"

"One son. He died when he was three. That was when I left. It had been my husband's ill-treatment that had killed him."

"Oh, my poor Berthe." Jasmin let her hands rise and fall in her lap, intense sympathy in her voice.

"I suppose that was why I could never take to you in those days." Berthe drew in her chin, regarding Jasmin reflectively. "You see, you had everything and I thought it would always be so, whereas my little son had had nothing. By rights you should have become a substitute for the child I had lost, but it didn't happen that way. If anything, I resented you still more because of it."

Jasmin smiled wryly. "You had no need. Look at me now. I have nothing and must live here for the rest of my life. Are you able to like me better in my misfortune?"

"I knew I had become as fond of you as my own when that Josette stepped in to take over much of my care of you with her primping irons and her advice on which lip rouge you should use."

"I know you hated her, but you never showed me any affection during the time when I was eating my heart out for Fernand."

Berthe shrugged phlegmatically. "I was as furious with you as your own mother and for the same reasons. In fact, if you had been my daughter I'd have boxed your ears."

"Yet you still asked my mother to let you come here to me."

"I'd have set out the very day we learned of your circumstances from Lenore if it had been possible, but your mother had more need of me than ever then."

"I thank God you're here now." Jasmin left her chair to slip to her knees beside Berthe and rest her head in the ample lap, gazing into the flames. "It won't be too lonely for you, will it?"

"Bless you! What a thought! After your father was taken ill there wasn't a quieter place than Château Satory. A peaceful existence suits me well."

Jasmin raised her face in the firelight. "Then you'll not tire of this gloomy place?"

"Never." Berthe patted her cheek reassuringly. "I'll be with you until the end of my days."

The months went by, brightened now for Jasmin by post from home. The announcement that the Queen had given birth to a future King of France reached Château Valverde before Marguerite's letter could let Jasmin know, but the additional information in the written word was that the new Dauphin had been baptised with the name of Louis. Jasmin could foresee French kings of that name reigning from Versailles forever.

Ever since the fall of the Duc de Bourbon from power, Sabatin had been awaiting the right moment to make an appeal to the King against his banishment. He thought the birth of the Dauphin the right time to seek a dispensation. As he awaited the decision he was optimistic and in a better mood than at any time since the day he had heard that the Duchesse de Bourbon had committed suicide, unable to bear the wretchedness of country life away from the pleasures of the Court.

The reply from Versailles was prompt and brought by special messenger. Alone in the library Sabatin broke the royal seal eagerly. When he read that his appeal had been turned down by the King he uttered a great bellow of disappointment and misery, crushing the parchment in his fist and hurling it from him. He could only see Jasmin as the reason. Naturally the King did not want her back there and he himself was the innocent sufferer. He leaned a forearm against the panelled wall and pressed his forehead against his wrist, fighting for self-control. If he had caught sight of his wife at that moment he would have killed her, for he had nearly strangled her once before and a longing to crush her out of his life was overwhelming him.

Growling with desperation, he jerked on the bell-rope and had cognac brought to him. Snatching a bottle from the footman's tray, he took two or three hefty gulps from it before wiping his mouth with the back of his hand and slumping down into a wing chair. He sat there all day and steadily drank himself into a stupor. His servants, confident for once that he was beyond retaliation, finally carried him upstairs and put him to bed.

For a few nights Jasmin was spared his relentless visits, but her heart sank when she heard the handle of the door between their rooms turn once more. Yet that night there was an unexpected development, which he blamed savagely on her for never opening her arms to him or trying spontaneously to please him as a wife should. Recently he had had some difficulty in achieving intercourse with her, but on this night he found himself to be completely unmanned. Devastated, he could not get away from her quickly enough and flung himself back into his room where he tossed down more cognac to follow what he had swallowed earlier and fell asleep on his own bed. A few nights afterwards when with her he sweated again with anxiety at his slowness and knew several moments of panic but all eventually went well. Then, in spite of everything he made her do for him, he failed again. This time he punched her in the breasts with his fists and she almost fainted.

The next night he found the door locked when he went to open it. A heavy thrust from his shoulder broke the old lock and sent it crashing wide. He entered in a fury to find her crouched in the bed, a knife in her hand, her expression desperate.

"If you hit me again I'll kill you!"

He merely struck her wrist and the knife went flying. The spurt of erotic excitement that her defiance had given him was of no avail. He dragged her from the bed by her hair and beat her until she was black and blue.

It was his triumphant belief that he had finally broken her spirit because the following night she lay waiting for him with tears running soundlessly down her cheeks, the pillow already damp. Yet when he failed again he saw the glitter of scorn come into her eyes and knew she had finished him with her once and for all. Before he could retaliate, the drink with which he had fortified himself gushed up in his throat and engulfed them both in a sea of vomit.

For many nights the door with its repaired lock remained closed. Then the hour came when Jasmin heard the low rumble of his laughter and a woman's responding giggle in his room. She turned her head sideways into the pillow and sobbed with relief. It was over. There was little likelihood he would ever return to her bed again.

In the morning she had breakfast in her apartment as she always did, Berthe bringing it to her these days. Then when she went into dinner that same day she found that there were places set only for Sabatin and Henriette while hers was left bare. The footmen watched her warily, wondering if she was going to make a fuss, for however the Duc treated her she was such a force to be reckoned with on the domestic side that they wanted no repercussions directed at them. But after one glance at the table she merely turned about and went from the room, liberation in her step.

The change in her was eventually noticed by everybody, the first being Berthe. She stopped being forever on the lookout for cobwebs and although she remained fastidious in her person she no longer took unnecessarily frequent baths. Her spates of depression lifted and the pinched look gradually eased from her face. It all took time and there were relapses, but when eventually she expressed a wish to Berthe that they should ride out into the village and the countryside, it was proof that Jasmin was really on the mend from all she had endured since first coming to the Château Valverde.

It was an overcast morning and Jasmin felt her old fears return as the carriage went down the winding drive and approached the gates. Blindly she reached for Berthe's hand and clutched it. It was extraordinary to her that the place where she had known such unhappiness should have also become a kind of refuge. She was on the point of hysterically demanding they must turn back when Berthe turned to her, gaining her attention with a tug on the hand and keeping her from the sight of the gates going by.

"I can't tell you what a treat this is for me! I wouldn't have wanted to miss a nice drive today for anything."

"Wouldn't you? But I can't—"

"Do you remember the times I accompanied you to Versailles? You in your silks and satins and I in that fine blue taffeta that was ruined when a drunken courtier fell over my feet and spilt his wine down the skirt."

Struggling out of the nameless terror of being beyond the gates, but not wanting to spoil Berthe's outing, Jasmin forced herself to reply. "I wonder you didn't box his ears!"

Berthe burst out laughing and did not seem able to stop, wiping her mirthful eyes. It was infectious. Jasmin began to smile. At that moment by lucky chance sunshine broke through the clouds and swept across the grass and trees and the rising slopes like a giant paintbrush, bringing everything leaping into colour.

"What a lovely day!" Berthe exclaimed happily. She did not press then for the windows to be opened, for although the day had been balmy, even without the sun, Jasmin had insisted on them remaining closed. After the village had been left behind and they were once more in the open country, Berthe let down the window on her side without saying a word.

"Do you realise that it's nearly three years now since I came," she said casually, her quick flow of words designed to stem any protest from Jasmin. "How time flies! I admit at first I thought it would be difficult to settle down, but that hasn't been the case."

She prattled on and the moment when Jasmin might have spoken out was safely past.

It took Jasmin a full six months to recover completely. Although at first in her nervousness much was a blur to her beyond the carriage windows, she became slightly better with each new outing. When the morning came when she found herself looking forward to the drive ahead she knew that the misery of self-isolation was behind her.

Now during drives she noticed the poor state of the little farmhouses. Most of them were little more than broken-down hovels, unsightly in the lush countryside.

"Who lives there?" she asked Berthe, her sympathy going out to the ragged children who ran to watch the carriage go spinning by. Often the mothers, gaunt, thin women, would come fearfully to draw them back, afraid of them running under the wheels.

"Your husband's tenants," Berthe replied in a matter-of-fact tone.

Jasmin had said nothing more at the time, but resolved that when she was able she would investigate their conditions. It was this aim that helped her to overcome her qualms more quickly than she might otherwise have done. She had seen whole families toiling in the fields and working on the walnut harvests, many of the women carrying the heavy baskets that the men swung into the waiting wagons. As the days grew shorter she saw them gathering firewood and digging their own vegetable patches, and much of what her mother had told her of the poverty-stricken conditions endured by many came back to her as she drove by.

Jasmin discovered from Henriette that part of the peasants' labour was given to Sabatin's long-established seigniorial rights and without wages since they lived on his land; the patches they farmed themselves and the hovels that were their homes had to be paid for at rents that kept them in penury.

Berthe was horrified when Jasmin announced she was going to investigate the tenants' housing. "You keep away from those people!" she ordered as if Jasmin were a child again. "You'll pick up fleas and infection and goodness knows what else."

"Nevertheless, I'm going and I want some baskets of food made ready in the kitchen. In this winter weather there'll be need of it."

"You'd do better to make contact with some of the noble families in this area and then you might begin to enjoy life again."

Jasmin gave her a humourless smile. "Sabatin would never permit it. You should know that by now."

"Need he know?" Berthe's face took on a cunning look.

"He'd find out. And what if those nobles returned my calls and had the door slammed in their faces? I should never forgive myself. Stop thinking I'll ever be the same as I was. The years have gone by and I've become a different person. Cease your dreaming that I can ever be again the girl I was long ago."

"You're still young!"

"My age has nothing to do with it. I became old the day I married six years ago. Now see about those baskets for me."

It was a day Berthe would long remember. In Jasmin's wake, fearful of leaving her unprotected, she plodded into one wretched stinking hovel after another. Some were better than others, but all were in a dismal, even derelict condition. There were bedridden old folk in crowded family quarters, many sick adults and children suffering from a fever that had swept through the community. In Berthe's eyes Jasmin seemed to take on a new stature as she went to the bedsides, felt hot brows, gave sensible advice, left food such as had never been seen before in such quantities and became her own mother again. Berthe recalled how often Marguerite had taken her daughter with her to visit a fanmaker's home when there was trouble of some kind, she herself accompanying them, and although conditions, due to decent wages, were never like anything she was witnessing in these farming hovels, it had given Jasmin an insight into what happened when disaster struck a family of modest means.

The bailiff glowered when Jasmin summoned him and gave him a long list of repairs to be done to the properties. He went straight to his master and laid his complaint. "Madame says that infection is rife and it could get worse if these places are not improved. But things are the same as they always were. The peasants are used to it."

Sabatin listened in boredom, but after a few moments realised that Jasmin's interference might benefit him, and the matter was worth consideration.

"Do whatever the Duchesse says. Those scum know the land and it would be deucedly inconvenient if a serious epidemic should wipe most of them out when the walnut trees are ready or at some similar time. So carry out the repairs and put up the rents to pay for them."

"They'll starve, master." The bailiff was alarmed. It was in neither his master's interest nor his own if that should happen, for he regularly lined his own pockets from the peasants' labours. "It's always hard on them in winter-time."

Sabatin shrugged. "Very well. Leave the increase in abeyance until the spring."

But when spring came the bailiff did nothing to remind his master. He had enough trouble with the Duchesse examining the rent records and questioning him about figures that did not tally. It was through her that he was dismissed for dishonesty and another bailiff, better suited to her standards, took his place.

All of this was conducted without any direct communication between Jasmin and Sabatin. She had written everything down and left it for him, much as people left petitions to the King on Monday mornings at Versailles, and the results were forthcoming. Since the day when there had been no place for her at his table, he had ignored her completely and put an end to his play-acting of courtesy towards her in the presence of the servants. It did her no harm, for the changes she had made for the tenants and the dismissal of the bailiff went home to all the staff and she continued to receive the respect due her. The mood was slightly less hostile than in the days when she was chasing them to scrub and clean all the time and newcomers to the staff considered her pleasant and easy to serve.

To Jasmin it was almost a relief to be ignored completely by Sabatin. She might have been invisible for all the notice he took of her and at times she knew herself to be so when he staggered past her, dead drunk and unable to focus.

Inevitably maidservants had become pregnant as a result of his philandering. They were automatically dismissed by the housekeeper as soon as their condition became apparent. Although it was the custom to send away such unfortunate girls without reference or wages, Jasmin always made sure they had both, seeing that extra money was added to save them being without a roof over their heads when their babies were born.

"I used to hope my husband would die in his cups," Berthe remarked one day during a conversation with Jasmin. "But not long before I left your home to come here I met someone who told me he is still alive and kicking and drinking as heavily as ever."

"If you suppose I'm wishing the same for Sabatin then you're mistaken," Jasmin replied, thinking how transparent Berthe was at times. "Now that he and I lead our own lives I no longer fear him as I did before. Neither he nor I can ever leave this place, no matter which of us goes first. In my case, should I be widowed, the only difference would be if Sabatin's heir allowed me to stay on in the château itself or wished me to move into one of the lodges."

"Who is his heir?"

"His cousin at Court, the Comte Armand de Valverde. Henriette told me about him when I first came here."

As so often happens when someone has been mentioned for the first time in years there is an unexpected appearance of that person soon afterwards. Henriette brought the news to Jasmin that Armand de Valverde was to visit Château Valverde and stay for several weeks.

"You are to have some new gowns," Henriette exclaimed excitedly, "and to take your place at table again for the duration of his visit."

"And if I should refuse?"

"Oh, please don't, I beg you!" Henriette was like a frantic little bird, her hands beating the air. "Sabatin has been so affable since the letter arrived. This will be the first guest the château has received since long before you came as a bride and it will be Sabatin's first contact with the Court again. He'll be like a madman if you cross him and likely take his ill temper out on me."

Berthe muttered to Jasmin out of the side of her mouth. "Or you. Use your sense and agree."

Jasmin, not at all pleased at being prompted, gave a nod. "Very well, Henriette."

"You never know," Berthe said after Henriette had left again, "some good may come out of this visit."

It was to be an understatement as far as Sabatin was concerned. He ordered new clothes from Paris, drank slightly less and looked forward immensely to seeing Armand again. There was little difference in their ages and in their wild youth they had been for a while more than cousins and closer than friends, creating an amiability between them that had never been lost. Uppermost in his

mind was the hope that he could persuade Armand to
speak on his behalf to the King. There was no reason why
he should not be pardoned while Jasmin could remain
where she was.

When Armand arrived he was much impressed by the
outwardly splendid appearance of the château with every
pane winking, even in the highest turrets, and the parterres and lawns comparable to anything at Versailles, if on
a smaller scale. It had occurred to him that his cousin's
marriage was into its seventh year and there was still no
heir to supersede his claim to Château Valverde. He remembered it as a good property with abundant land,
which prompted him to look it over again since there was
every chance it was going to come to his branch of the
family after all. He knew for a fact that Sabatin had fathered several bastards in his musketeer days and so the
lack of offspring must be due to the woman he had married.

Armand was slightly shorter and much thinner than his
cousin, whom he greeted with genuine affection after
alighting at the steps of the château, hiding his shock at
Sabatin's grossly increased weight, the bloated complexion
and the telltale bloodshot eyes. It was not unusual for a
banished nobleman to drink himself to death, but somehow Armand had not been prepared to see his kinsman
going down the same path.

"It's good to see you again, Sabatin," he declared heartily.

"I appreciate your coming to visit me more than I can
say! It's been some comfort not to have been forgotten by
the nearest of my kin. Even your children have kept in
touch with me."

Armand, twice widowed with a grown family, had seen
no cause to marry again and had a charming mistress in
Paris whom he had left behind out of courtesy to his hostess. He remembered Jasmin as one of the loveliest young
girls at Court and was not surprised to see she had become
a truly beautiful woman, although in an austere and rather
chilly way.

"Welcome to Château Valverde, Cousin Armand," she
greeted him. "I trust your stay will be a pleasant one and
you will not let the spell of the Court entice you back too
soon."

"I thank you, Cousin Jasmin." His gallantry was ever to the fore. "Who could remember the Court in your delightful company? I can see you weave magic of your own here."

How well she remembered such compliments. It all came flooding back in a wave of nostalgia. Armand's presence had brought an all but forgotten elegance of manners and appearance into the château with his well-cut clothes, a new fashion note for gentlemen in the high clocks of his silk hose, no garters, but a jewelled buckle keeping his breeches smooth at the knee. That evening at supper he presented her with the gift of an emerald bracelet, to Henriette a pair of embroidered and scented gloves and to Sabatin a gold-headed cane. He lifted all strain from the atmosphere by being full of amusing, often risqué anecdotes and even though most of them were centred on Court life Sabatin laughed many times, enjoying them as much as Jasmin and Henriette. But all amusement went for Jasmin when he began to gossip about the King.

"The Queen gets increasingly pious. She won't let him come to her bed on the eve of saints' days. Unfortunately for him she's discovered more and more saints in the calendar than anyone else has ever heard about!"

Both men guffawed and even Henriette giggled. Jasmin looked sadly into the glass of wine she held. It sounded as if Louis's marriage was not going as well as she had hoped.

When supper ended she and Henriette left the two men to their pipes and heavier drinking. Sabatin was surprised when his cousin spread both hands over their glasses to prevent refills from the decanter he had picked up.

"No more yet," Armand said. "I want to talk seriously for a while. What's happened to you? And why did you not speak a word to that beautiful wife of yours throughout supper?"

Sabatin's thick-jowled face became sullen. "That bitch is responsible for my entire downfall. As a wife she's no good to me any more and there'll be no heir from our union, so you and yours will be fortunate. Damnation! I don't want lectures from you! Drink with me, man. I haven't had a drinking companion since I left Court."

Armand drank with him, but not too much to forget all the grievances that poured out of his cousin. He saw that much of Sabatin's misery was self-inflicted simply by his refusing to associate with rural noblemen and slighting them at any opportunity. Like everyone at Court, Armand shared the same opinion about them, but Sabatin himself was among that number and should be making the best of his lot, not cutting off his haughty, aquiline nose to spite his face. Armand knew that if ever he had the misfortune to land in his cousin's shoes he would not condemn himself to this lonely existence. No wonder the marriage had gone awry. Good God! The fellow did not even have a hunt to ride with and what it must have been like for Jasmin with only that idiotic old woman for company he did not know. If she had taken a footman for a lover to divert herself he would not have blamed her.

It was a bitter disappointment to Sabatin when Armand would make no promise to speak to the King, knowing from the rejection already received it would be useless. Sabatin would have taken refuge in drink, losing all further interest in the visit if Armand had allowed it. Instead he watched Sabatin like a hawk, took him riding in the forests all day, bestirred his slack muscles by handing him a rapier on the terrace and challenging him to a mock clash of blades, an exercise that became a daily event. After supper, when Sabatin normally drank out of depression and boredom, he diverted him with cards, gaming for high sums as if they were back at Versailles. After three weeks Armand came beaming to Jasmin.

"Sabatin has agreed to give a ball, inviting all the nobility for miles around. Your days of isolation are over. Welcome back into the land of the living!"

She threw her arms around his neck and kissed him on both cheeks.

When the invitations went out, not all were accepted. There were those who, still smarting from past snubs, were not to be won over by this unexpected move on the part of the arrogant Valverde, but curiosity swayed everyone else. The women were eager to see the elusive Duchesse and the men hoped it would prove to be an opening towards viewing at close hand the magnificent thoroughbreds in the Duc's stables. Most of those who came to the Valverde ball were rural landlords, noble by recognition of their blue-blooded lineage going back to 1400, but if they had no other income it went hard with them when their crops failed or their cattle were stricken. There were exceptions and the wealthy had sent to Paris for new clothes while the rest made themselves as grand as possible.

Jasmin wore white satin embroidered with gold thread. Sabatin was in black velvet with silver, which emphasised his saturnine looks. As the guests were announced he managed to receive each one with an air of acknowledging his wife at his side without ever directing a word to her. None noticed the omission. He had it to a fine art. There was an uncomfortable moment for her when she and Sabatin had to lead the opening dance and she almost shuddered as he took her hand, but it was soon over and they did not partner each other again.

The supper was superb, served on gold plate that had finally been unpacked from the Versailles crates for the occasion. If on the whole the gowns were sadly out of date by Court standards and the coats lacked a fashionable cut, the overall effect of the ball with its flower-garden hues was as festive as any scene at Versailles. A surprising amount of beautiful heirloom jewellery added to the glitter.

Armand did much to add to everybody's enjoyment of the evening. He had previously conducted his own preliminary enquiries into the local families and made sure that Jasmin became best acquainted with those most likely to benefit her existence, their financial status not important. He also danced with plain girls who might otherwise have lacked a partner, complimented the matrons and exuded bonhomie among the men. But he made one mistake.

He had managed to locate three banished nobles known to Sabatin and thought to help his return to society by getting them to come to the ball. They all lived within a reasonable distance, not more than a day's journey away. Two were ducs and one a marquis, their names Chavein, Oliveray and Gance respectively. One had been a "puller-up of the Versailles palisades," and the other two dated their banishment back to the Duc d'Orléans who had been the first Regent during the King's childhood. Chavein had brought his wife with him, a haughty creature who wanted everyone present to know she had been used to better social events, while the other two were widowers. Sabatin did not exactly greet them as brothers in exile, but it pleased him to have some company with an outlook comparable to his own. Before the ball was over he disappeared with them into the library where they sat down to play for high stakes, became uproariously drunk and caroused until morning.

Jasmin had to suffer the obnoxious presence of the Duchesse de Chavein for two weeks. It was that long before Sabatin's three companions left, their days having been made up of riding like madmen in the mornings and gaming and drinking and playing stupid practical jokes the rest of the time as if they were schoolboys instead of middle-aged men.

Their eventual departure left Jasmin free to take up the new friendships that had begun at the ball. Her only regret was that Armand decided to leave at the same time. He did not look as well as when he had come, having drunk too much with Sabatin and his guests, but the error he had made lay heavily on him as he bade Jasmin farewell.

"I'm afraid I have done you a disservice, Jasmin," he said gravely to her. "I should never have brought those nobles back into Sabatin's life. I foresee trouble."

"My husband's volatile nature will always attract disaster of one kind or another," she replied sagely. "Don't worry about it, Armand. Without your kind intervention I wouldn't be looking forward to enjoying social events again and Sabatin has accepted invitations to join two local hunts. It will mean more to him to be back in the hunting saddle than anyone can estimate." She tilted her head and smiled confidently at him. "There's no need for you to be unduly concerned. Nothing can be as bad as it was before."

Later she was to remember those words.

Fourteen

It was Laurent who requested a portrait of Jasmin. Twelve years had gone by since he had seen his daughter. The only likenesses of her at Château Satory had been painted when she was five years old and another just before her sixteenth birthday in those blissful days before all the troubles had started. She had been a girl when she had left home and he wanted to see her in her maturity.

In the intervening years he had recovered enough movement to be able to hobble around with a cane or with Marguerite's arm to support him and together they had built up a life between them once more. Yet the emptiness created by Jasmin's absence was always there. Had she been able to visit, however occasionally, it would have helped. Once he had suggested that Marguerite should go to Périgueux, although the prospect of being without her filled him with dread.

"Now that Jasmin is not confined to her home you could stay in the city and meet her there," he said bravely, trying to adopt a nonchalant air to hide his fear. Marguerite was his mainstay, his comforter, the preserver of his life and, above all else, his beloved companion. To his huge relief she refused.

"My place is with you. Jasmin is young and resilient. You and I are old and need each other." She gave him a kiss, hiding her yearning to see their daughter, but she could not leave him to make that long journey. She was anxious if she was away from him for more than an hour because he had suffered several minor strokes since his first attack, each setting him back for a while, and she never knew if the next one was going to be the worst of all. She welcomed the idea of a portrait. It would be the next best thing to seeing Jasmin again.

"I shall commission the best artist in Paris today," he said enthusiastically. "Who painted the latest portrait of the King that earned such praise?"

A preliminary letter was written, but before the artist could reply Laurent was dead. Marguerite awoke in their bed one morning to find that he had gone from her in his sleep.

"Oh, my dearest," she whispered, her tears flowing as she took up his hand to hold as she had done countless times in the past when he had been in need of reassurance. "I loved you far more than you ever knew."

At Versailles the King heard the news. The Baron had served Versailles well in his time. Louis wrote a letter to the widow in his own hand. Not a thought was given to Jasmin.

Louis had every reason to be preoccupied. Unlike his great-grandfather he had never resigned himself to being forever in the public gaze. He still went through the pantomine of the *lever* and the *coucher* in the State Bedchamber, but no longer slept there. He had a far more comfortable bedchamber near at hand in a private apartment he had created in which to escape constant attention. It enabled him to get up early to work on affairs of state in his study, a dressing-robe over his nightshirt, simply dashing along to the State Bedchamber to be in time for his official awakening by the First Valet of the Bedchamber. At night he often dressed again after the *coucher,* being a man who needed little sleep, and would slip out to go incognito to balls and other late-night entertainments locally or in Paris. He had had a warren of secret passageways installed, which hid his whereabouts. But, proud of his Kingship, he never behaved foolishly and disliked anything that tended towards debauchery.

Yet he had taken a mistress. It was not his wish and would never have come about if he had not finally lost his temper and his patience with Marie's pious excuses to keep him from being a husband to her. Admittedly she had given him ten children and was tired of being pregnant, but he was still fond of her, even though they had little in common any more. She had withdrawn into a circle of dull friends and no longer wanted to share with him the lively festivities of the Court which he found so entertaining. These days he enjoyed the company of younger women, no longer attracted to those older than himself as he had been to Marie and to Jasmin before her.

Jasmin. Her face leapt into his mind briefly and sweetly, held in the bloom of her youth. Then it had gone again as swiftly as a bird passing in flight.

At Château Valverde, Jasmin bore with courage her terrible grief at her father's passing. Had it come several years before when she was suffering from the depression and idiosyncrasies induced by her husband's persistent rape she was certain she would have lapsed permanently into melancholia, for her sorrow was beyond measure. Fortunately she was no longer that bewildered girl who had been precipitated into an abyss of hate, but a mature woman able to conduct herself with dignity and reason.

Although Sabatin never came near her, the door between their bedrooms permanently locked, the key on her side, a bolt on his, she had had much to put up with from him in other ways since the ball when he had renewed his acquaintanceship with the three nobles from his Versailles days. It was a relief when he went to stay with them, it having become customary for the three to meet in turn at one another's châteaux. He was often absent for weeks at a time, but that peaceful respite had to be paid for when the return visits were made. The Duchesse de Chavein had never come again. Even though Jasmin had not liked her, it was impossible not to extend sympathy towards her when the gathering was held at the Chavein residence, for it was her guess that the noblewoman shared her aversion for them.

It was as if these former gallants of Versailles had decided by unspoken consent to ignore their present situation and pretend they were still moving in the gilded circles of their youth. The fact that they were all much older
and should have long since reached the age of sobriety and
good sense completely escaped them. They were like vet-
eran soldiers in a reunion, reliving old battles and trying to
recapture through drinking the joie de vivre of their
youth.

But their behaviour did not stop there. As with all the
nobility, Chavein, Gance and Oliveray travelled with their
own retinue of servants, and theirs were without exception handsome young men and women. Three aligned salons were given over to the drinking bouts and the gaming
at which Sabatin and his guests often quarrelled and
shouted when they lost, just as if they were at an *Appartement* out of the King's hearing. Sabatin regularly ruined
his white-powdered wigs by snatching them off and kicking them across the room in his rage. Always he and the
guests were attended by the visiting servants who lorded it
over the resident staff. Only the Versailles servants guessed
from the start what the duties of these exalted beings included and they said nothing. The rest found out later
when on certain evenings during a visit the doors leading
into the three linked salons would be locked from inside,
the stranger servants remaining within to continue their
attendance on Sabatin and their masters in other ways.
Sometimes there was riotous noise with gales of laughter
and a great deal of thumping about. Then came sessions of
a more sinister kind, which had the effect of silencing the
rest of the château as here and there other doors were shut
to keep out the ugly echoes that came from the locked
salons.

Jasmin never invited anyone to Château Valverde when
the nobles were there, for in a drunken state they were
liable to play some cruel prank on whomever they came
across. Berthe and several servants of long standing had
already suffered. As yet she had been spared, perhaps because Sabatin wanted nothing to spoil his own exquisite
pleasure in his peculiar torment of her, for he knew her
outrage at the profligacy he had brought into their home.
She could tell that the nobles had adopted Sabatin's hatred
of her, seeing him the victim of circumstances induced by

her, and she reciprocated to the full, loathing them for
their haughtiness, their loud imperious voices and their
devious vices. As for Sabatin, she detested him more than
ever, if that was possible.

She was never idle and that helped her cope with the
heavy grief of her bereavement. It was not just seeing to
the welfare of the old, the sick and the young on the estate
that kept her busy. Having discovered a lack of employment in the village during many months of the year, especially in the winter, she had set up a little fan-making
workshop which had a good market in Périgueux and the
larger towns in the region. Henriette also took up her time,
for the old lady was fading and virtually an invalid, never
leaving her museumlike apartment where she was happiest, living in the past.

When another letter came from Château Satory soon
after the one that had brought the news of Laurent's demise, Jasmin expected it to be an account of the funeral. It
was, but there was more. She closed her eyes thankfully
and clutched the letter to her.

"My mother is coming to Périgueux," she exclaimed to
Berthe, whose face lit up instantly like a lamp. "I'm going
to see her again!"

By lucky chance the day before Marguerite was due to
arrive Sabatin set off for one of his lengthy reunions, this
time to be held at the residence of the Duc d'Oliveray. It
meant that Jasmin could safely entertain Marguerite at
Château Valverde for at least a month without any danger
of Sabatin returning.

Mother and daughter met again at the hotel in Périgueux. Jasmin had arrived in time to meet the coach as it
drew up in the forecourt. Even as Marguerite alighted,
straight-backed and purposeful in spite of tiredness from
the journey and the weight of her seventy-three years,
Jasmin was there with open arms.

"Maman!"

"My child!"

They embraced with joy and tears. When eventually
they drew apart to take a long and loving look at each
other, Marguerite inwardly lamented the change in her
daughter's appearance. Even at this moment of intense
happiness Jasmin no longer had the inner radiance that
had always added to her beauty. The lovely face had been

dulled by ordeal and there was a transparency to the thin cheeks that the dust of rouge could not disguise. Jasmin read her mother's thoughts.

"I know I'm not as you remembered me. Grieving for Father has also taken its toll. Your company will be a tonic to me in every way. Oh, Maman! It's so good that you are here!"

At first Marguerite hesitated about agreeing to stay at Château Valverde. "Won't you have to face repercussions? Your husband forbade your father and me ever to come to his house."

"He no longer cares about anything except his objectionable friends. I'll tell you about them another day. Come with me, Maman. Everything is prepared."

When they reached Château Valverde, Berthe was watching out for them and came waddling forward to curtsey and be greeted, overjoyed to see the Baronne again. Jasmin gave Marguerite the suite of rooms next to hers and it seemed as if they would never stop talking. There was so much Jasmin wanted to hear, first the details of her father's illness that had not come into her mother's letters, and after that news of home and everyone she knew. She heard that faithful Lenore was shortly to marry one of Château Satory's gardeners.

"Their marriage was only delayed through Lenore's loyal commitment to your father and myself. I'm giving them one of the cottages on the estate and they're getting it ready. She will still be on hand whenever I need her, at least until she starts a family. I've promised to be back for the wedding."

"When is that to be?" Jasmin asked anxiously, not wanting her mother's stay cut short.

"Not for six weeks. We have plenty of time and I can always come again."

Marguerite stayed for five weeks. It was a period of sunshine for Jasmin. In spite of everything it was the happiest time they had ever spent together, and a closeness was established that had never existed before. They could be heard laughing over humorous incidents remembered and old family jokes. Together they were invited to dine and sup at the homes of the friends that Jasmin had made, took strolls and drives and visited the fan-making workshop, which Marguerite found particularly interesting.

The range of fans was simple and charming, a far cry from the demands of Versailles but ideal for regional requirements. She was quite fascinated by the fans that Jasmin had made for herself over the years, her expert eye appreciating the delicacy of the work and the skilful setting of semiprecious stones.

"It was through you that I learned those skills," Jasmin replied with a chuckle to her mother's praise. "Remember how I fought against your instructions?"

"Indeed I do," Marguerite declared, equally amused.

They had their serious times. During one of them Marguerite told Jasmin of her love for Augustin, how it had come about and how it had ended. "I wanted you to know all this," she concluded, "because one day the deeds of Château Satory and certain documents might have come as a shock to you. Above all else I didn't want any element of doubt to arise in you about your parentage. Augustin was gone from my life many years before I met your father."

"I'm glad you've told me."

Marguerite absently twisted the rings on her fingers, her thoughts distant, a faint smile on her lips. "Augustin once said to me that a man could love two women. I discovered the truth of that in a different way from how he meant it. I loved your father just as much on a different plane. Yet I have to say Augustin remained the spark of fire in my life and the passage of time has not doused it."

Jasmin's throat was tight with emotion. Her mother had experienced love such as she herself would never know and it touched her in the coming bequest of Château Satory, which she prayed would be far off. Yet there was something that had to be said.

"You do realise that Château Satory can never be mine even from this far distance, don't you, Maman? As my husband, Sabatin would claim my inheritance and sell everything."

Marguerite became firm and direct again. "Not as I have worded my will. He can never touch it. But that's all in the future and I don't want to discuss it any more now."

It was easy to guess that this reluctance of Marguerite to refer again to her son-in-law was due to what she had been told about him. Jasmin had revealed as much as she felt able. The subject of the will was not mentioned between them again.

The golden days slipped by far too quickly, bringing Marguerite's stay towards its close. The day before her departure as she and Jasmin strolled arm in arm through the parterres, she mentioned the portrait that Laurent had wanted.

"I should like his last wish to be carried out and your portrait to hang near his in the Crimson Salon. He would have liked that so much. Would you wear that new gown I brought you? He helped me to choose the fabric for it a few days before he died."

"I'll do that." Jasmin did not relish the thought of long sittings for the portrait, but it would be done willingly for the memory of one parent and the solace of the other.

The morning of Marguerite's leaving dawned. She and Jasmin spoke little to each other at breakfast, the cheerful smiles with which they bridged the silences bearing no relation to their feelings at this time.

Marguerite was in her hat and cape, very fine in shades of deep jade green, and was coming from her suite with Jasmin when Berthe came panting up the stairs, her face alarmed.

"The Duc's carriage is coming up the drive!"

Jasmin answered her evenly. "Be calm, Berthe. Maman's visit is over and there is nothing he can do to spoil it now."

She and Marguerite set off down the stairs together, Berthe following behind. The footman on duty flung open the door as his master's carriage drew up outside. Sabatin alighted at once and entered the hall as Marguerite and Jasmin reached the last tread. He came to a standstill, able to deduce immediately from a certain similarity in the features of the two women that this tall, stately female was his mother-in-law. He stared at her, his eyes glittering with animosity in his bloated face, but spoke no word. Marguerite treated him to the same icy silence, sailing ahead of Jasmin out through the open door. Even as Marguerite crossed the threshold Sabatin acted. He slammed the door after her and thrust Jasmin backwards with the full force of his hand on her chest. She gasped, recovered and made for the door again. This time he seized her by the arm and struck her twice across the face with his free hand before casting her from him. She would have fallen if Berthe, who was strong in the arms, had not caught her. Regaining her balance, Jasmin spun around to rush away down the hall and through the room adjoining and then onwards until eventually she reached another way out of the château.

Breathlessly she raced along a path to reach the drive. As she had hoped, the Picard coach had waited by the gates. Her mother was watching for her with the door open and Jasmin scrambled in to sit down.

"Your face!" Marguerite exclaimed in horror. "What did he do to you?"

"It's nothing." The pain of parting was far worse than her bruised cheeks. "What matters is that I'm able to say au revoir to you."

"Come with me!" Marguerite urged frantically. "Now! Leave that monster! I'll go down on my knees to the King and plead for a dispensation of your banishment."

Jasmin gave a quick shake of the head. "It would never be granted to a wife and not to the husband. Even if Louis took pity on me for old times' sake he would have to respect Sabatin's legal claim to me. Sabatin would never let me go back to Versailles while he remained here. I think he would kill me first."

Marguerite went pale. "If he is that dangerous—"

"Not in normal circumstances," Jasmin hastened to add, not wanting her mother to go away with that anxiety on her mind. "Once I used to be afraid he would murder me and often I welcomed the prospect of an end to it all. But that danger is past. His satisfaction nowadays comes from tormenting me by whatever means are available. You have just been a witness to one example."

"I can't leave you like this!"

"You have to. I'll be all right. I have so much now— friends for amiable company, the fan-making workshop and the care of the sick and old on the farms to give a purpose to my life. I'm thinking of starting a little school for the children. In addition, I've had your visit and next time I'll stay with you in Périgueux. Just promise me that you'll come again soon."

"I will, my child."

They hugged and kissed each other. Then, holding her mother's hand, Jasmin stepped down out of the coach before contact was lost. The door was shut. Marguerite leaned from the window to wave until all that Jasmin could see of her was the jade green speck that was the plumes of her hat. Then trees shut away the departing coach and Jasmin turned to walk slowly back into the château. There was no sign of Sabatin and she sighed with relief, feeling she had escaped lightly for having had her mother to stay for such a time against his wishes. Suddenly she came across Berthe sobbing in a chair.

"What is it?" she asked, hastening to her.

"I didn't say adieu to Madame la Baronne. I knew my stiff legs would not get me there in time and I'm never going to see her again."

Jasmin felt a chill run down her spine. "Don't say that. She's coming back before long. That's been decided."

The artist, Michel Balaine, arrived at the Château Valverde two months later. He had not welcomed the commission, having work in plenty, and he had asked such an exorbitant sum to compensate for travelling time and the inconvenience of such a journey that he had expected it to be turned down. But the Baronne Picard had been set on his painting her daughter and had accepted his price without a quibble. So he had come. There was no one to meet him. The Duc was out riding and the Duchesse was visiting a school. The only other member of the family was an elderly old lady at present indisposed.

He stood impatiently in the hall while being given this information, a tall, passionate-looking man with frowning fair brows, fierce grey eyes, a proud nose and a powerful chin. His unruly hair, straw-coloured, was held in some semblance of order by a black silk bow that tied at the nape of his neck. Although relieved to be in the coolness indoors after the summer heat outside, he was offended by these country manners that had left him high and dry. His reputation as a master of portraiture had gained him a special entrée at Versailles and in many other great houses where at least one member of the resident family, however distinguished, would make sure he was received with the usual courtesies. Here there was nothing. Never again would he venture beyond Paris and the Île-de-France, or Versailles, for a commission. He had learned his lesson already. Heaven alone knew what he had let himself in for.

"Come this way, if you please, sir."

He followed the liveried, white-wigged steward up the magnificently carved staircase. At least the appointments of this château were of the best; there were many fine mirrors and rich silk hangings. As he reached the head of the flight there was a bustle of movement below. He turned about to look down and saw the entrance door being swung wide for a woman who had come hurrying in, muslin skirts swirling, and wearing a wide straw hat with pink-striped ribbons flowing from it. She was chatting to an old servant lumbering behind, amusement in her lilting voice. He spoke out from where he stood with his hand resting on the carved newel.

"Madame la Duchesse de Valverde?"

She looked up, the wide brim lifting to show him an oval face that shot straight home to his painter's eye. Superb bone structure, a high brow, creamy skin and a red mouth, all framed by shining chestnut hair full of coppery tints. More than that, there was the mysterious luminosity of her violet-blue gaze that stirred him to a strong excitement, dispelling the artist and leaving the man. It had always been his principle to keep business divorced from pleasure, but suddenly he was able to foresee a perilous situation he had not anticipated. All his regrets about coming to Château Valverde were forgotten as he and Jasmin took in fully the sight of each other.

"Monsieur Balaine!" She swept forward as he hurriedly retraced his steps down the flight to reach her. "My apologies that there was no one here to welcome you after your long journey from Paris."

He bowed over her hand, noticing with surprise that there was a smudge of ink on her fingers. Somehow he found it particularly endearing. There was still a girl in this alluring woman and he resolved to seek her out.

"I've only just arrived and have suffered no inconvenience."

She did not think any man had ever looked at her as Michel Balaine had done from the moment their eyes had met. It was as if he had been reborn and she was some whole new horizon that he had never viewed before. It was both flattering and disturbing, far more than an artist's first appraisal of his subject.

"After you have been shown your apartment," she said, "we shall dine. There is much to talk about. You are free to make your choice of location in which to set up your canvas."

"You are most kind."

Sabatin monopolised the conversation at dinner. Armand still kept him in touch with Court matters by regular correspondence and thus he knew Balaine to be a gentleman; otherwise he would not have sat down with a painter any more than he would have done with his wife on his own, her presence only tolerated as a necessity when guests had to be entertained, as in this case. Moreover, Armand had written that Balaine was lionised at Court since he had risen to fame and the King and Queen were delighted with their latest full-length portraits by him.

"I want you to paint me," Sabatin stated, taking it for granted that the commission would be accepted. "My last portrait dates back to my days at Court and there should be a more recent one to hang here." Under the influence of the wine he had imbibed, he gestured grandly towards a panelled wall ornamented only by a shield. "Full-length. Imposing. You know the sort of thing."

Jasmin was acutely embarrassed by Sabatin's highhanded attitude and fully expected Balaine to refuse, but the artist made an unexpected suggestion. "Why not on horseback, sir?"

"Capital!" Sabatin beamed and slapped the table with the flat of his hand in approval. "I've a handsome stallion that no one else can ride. Coal-black. Call your own price. You'll not find me close-fisted for a job well done."

Jasmin was amazed. Marguerite had written that Balaine was inundated with commissions and could scarcely spare the time to travel to Périgueux and yet he had volunteered to take on a piece of work that would surely take weeks. Then, catching her unaware, he turned his head and looked straight into her eyes as he had before. Then she knew that she herself was his reason and she experienced a curious sense of destiny. It was as if a net, fine as gossamer and strong as silk, had been thrown over her. How and when she would extricate herself was beyond anything she could visualise at the present time. It was at that moment that she began to think of him as Michel and no longer by his surname.

As was to be expected, Sabatin ordered that his portrait

should be painted before his wife's since in his eyes it was the more important. Michel set up his huge canvas in a north room with wide windows as well as with doors high enough to get the completed work through when it was finished. He spent many hours in the stableyard making sketches of the stallion. Jasmin did not always see him at meals, for she was often with friends, but somehow he always instigated a meeting to talk on the outside steps, on the staircase or in the gardens. One morning he turned up at the school, a small cottage given over to a middle-aged gentlewoman, previously without means, who taught those children that could be spared now and again from work by their parents.

He made individual sketches of the children at which they gaped, overawed when given them. A lightning drawing of Jasmin was done and she received it with amusement and pleasure.

"Is this how you are going to paint me?" He had sketched her making bracelets of straw and hay for some of the younger children to help them distinguish between their right and left hands. His drawing showed her that a long tendril of her hair had escaped from its pins and hung curling down the side of her face. She hastily tucked it back.

"That's how I see you," he said with a smile.

Something in his voice drew her to look at him and then away. He was in love with her. Perhaps he had been from the first moment he had stared down at her with those absorbing eyes of his. It was as well she felt nothing more for him than an admiration of his work in the beautiful sketches of the horse and now the children. The one of herself had been signed as if he hoped she would keep it. Deliberately she faced the children and waved it over her head.

"Who would like this one?"

There was a scamper for it and she gave it to the youngest. But Michel was already doing another, his weight perched on the edge of the table at which the gentlewoman sat. When they left the cottage he handed it to her. It showed her laughing with the same wayward tendril slipping forward again from where she had attempted to tidy it.

"Now this is how I should like to paint you."

"Come now," she said in mock reproof. "I'm sure you didn't say that to the Queen until she was perfectly gowned."

"I've never seen the Queen playing with children or with ink on her fingers or with her hair in disarray."

She caught her breath. Had he been describing her naked his voice could not have been more sensual, more tender. "Nevertheless, my portrait is to be a formal one that will hang in my mother's house."

"Your wish is my command." Now there was a chuckle in his tone.

That was better. She met his glance and chuckled with him. They talked of other matters as they went back to the château. She kept the sketch, putting it safely away in a drawer.

After that she saw less of him. He began the painting of Sabatin in earnest and the rich portrait began to leap out under his brushes. Sabatin was depicted in a green velvet hunting coat and gold-braided black tricorn, whip in hand, on the rearing stallion. It was as yet ghostlike in outline upon the canvas and set against the wooded and mountainous background with Château Valverde rising on its prominence at the top left-hand corner. Two students had accompanied Michel as well as his own servants, and these two youths mixed paint, cleaned brushes, and had prepared both canvases and filled in some of the extensive background of Sabatin's portrait. But after a special wooden block had come from Paris, which was saddled in order that some painting could be done in detail of the sitter on horseback without involving the restless stallion, Michel sent both students back to the city with it when its use was over. He explained why at supper the same evening as their departure. There were several guests at the table, for in the double life that Sabatin led he seemed to revel more and more in playing the genial host to the local nobility.

"As I'm going to be here far longer than I first anticipated," Michel said to his attentive neighbours at the board, "my students can be getting on with work in plenty during my absence. It's far better for them to be at my Paris studio than kicking their heels here for much of the time."

Jasmin alone was undeceived. She knew that when he came to paint her he wanted nobody else near at hand.

In his conceit, Sabatin had forgotten completely that Michel had come originally to paint Jasmin's portrait. He enjoyed boasting that he had the King's own artist in his house and that a masterpiece was being created in the north room. It annoyed him that Michel would allow no one to view it until it was finished, particularly as he had become intensely bored with the sittings and would be thankful when they were at an end. He would be going visiting again shortly, for a gathering at Oliveray's residence where courtesans, brought from Lyons, would provide a change of entertainment. The original quartet of banished nobles had increased to an exclusive circle of twenty, which meant he need never act as host any more, some venues proving particularly popular and everybody else contributing towards the not inconsiderable expense.

He never had the least concern about leaving Jasmin on her own. She had never shown any interest in another man. He had even seen her rebuff mild advances made at local affairs, which did not surprise him, for he knew she was aware that he would devise some terrible punishment for her if ever she made a fool of him, let alone a cuckold. He found her so unattractive himself that it never crossed his mind that he might be unwise to leave her virtually alone at the château with a personable man of her own age. She spent so much time looking after Henriette and running after the sick and needy that he saw her more as a drudge these days than anything else. Moreover he was intrigued to know from his cousin's letters that the artist had his pick of beautiful women at Court. Had anyone suggested to him that the portrait painter might see a rarer beauty in his wife, he would have guffawed as much as he did at obscene jokes.

He departed as usual, taking a few special servants of his own. Jasmin, nursing Henriette, did not know how he could leave at such a time, for the old lady was close to death. He did come to the bedside to take a look at her before he left, the first time he had entered her rooms since his youth, and saw for himself that the end was near. Without giving her a kiss of farewell, he turned on his heel and went again, his purposeful stride showing clearly enough that he wanted no part in the funeral when it came.

Henriette died three days later. Word was sent after him but, as was expected, he did not return. Jasmin's grief was acute. When she had first come to Château Valverde, Henriette had been her only friend and had always been kind to her. Michel was a tower of strength. He did whatever he could to help her and left his work completely until the funeral was over. It was well attended, for although few knew Henriette or remembered her, people came out of respect and were puzzled that Sabatin was not there.

"I'm going to miss her so much," Jasmin said as she and Michel strolled in the gardens one evening after supper. It was very warm and the sky was heavy with stars. "I think I must shut her apartment up for a while and see to everything later."

"That will enable me to start your portrait."

They had stopped by the pond where now a fountain played, a sound she loved, for it reminded her of Versailles.

"Have I delayed your work?" she asked anxiously. "How selfish of me to let my troubles drive all else from my mind. Naturally you want to get the portrait completed as soon as possible."

He put his fingertips lightly to either side of her chin, just on her jawline, and looked into her eyes. "Do you really imagine that is my true purpose? Time no longer matters to me all the while I can see you, hear you and be near you."

His gaze was so ardent that she could scarcely bear the joy it was bringing forth in her. She felt as if her heart might shatter with it, no longer able to contain the love that had been growing there steadily since the day she had begun to know the kind of man he was. This had been no headstrong rush into love as it had been with Fernand in her girlhood, no spell cast by a handsome face or a call to the waking sensuality of youth. This had been a steady advancement through knowledge of character, ideas and mutual interests. This was the love that had roots, the kind that struck deep and never shifted again.

"I never thought to hear such words," she whispered wonderingly. "I hoped it was as you felt, but that you should say them makes me so happy."

"I've more to say." With an enfolding arm he drew her

into a tight embrace and stroked her back caressingly. "I love you. I've wanted to hold you in my arms ever since I first saw you."

In the second or two before his eager mouth took hers, he saw panic flood her eyes and then her lids closed and she melted against him. Her response was intoxicating to him and neither he nor she could break the passionate kiss that was expressing their love and desire for each other. When eventually it did come to a conclusion in loving looks and smiles and more little kisses, he embraced her again and, with his cheek pressed against hers, his hand cupping her head, he asked her what any man would have requested of the woman he loved in such circumstances.

"Allow me to come to your room tonight."

She could not let him into that bed where she had known such degradation and horror. Instead she went to him, letting the moonlight guide her, a wraithlike figure in a floating nightgown and robe of sheerest lawn, her hair loosened and hanging down her back. He was waiting for her and she fell into his arms.

Yet at first she lay rigidly in the bed like a terrified virgin, her forearm across her eyes. He saw some scars on her lovely body and drew his own conclusions. Whereupon he began to make love to her with enormous tenderness as if it were the first time for both of them. There was a gentleness in every caress and worship in the touch of his lips and tongue. His long-limbed body was silky against hers and his loving whispers, heartfelt and heart-expressed, drove all shadows of the past away. She let her arm slide away from her eyes by her own volition and saw his beloved face rise over hers.

"My darling Jasmin. I've never loved any woman as I love you. All my life I've been waiting for this night and I never knew it until we met."

She gave herself up to him in ecstasy, no thought for anything else beyond their loving.

After that they were never apart at night. Only Berthe guessed what was happening and she was thankful Jasmin had found some happiness at last. By day Michel painted Jasmin's portrait. She sat on a gilded upholstered chair set on a dais, rich silk drapery drawn to one side behind her. In that space he would paint Château Satory, which was what Baronne Picard wanted, and he had made the necessary sketches there before setting out for Périgueux. Jasmin's gown of topaz satin was in the height of Parisian fashion with hoops spread out at the side over the hips to give lateral width, the bodice tightly laced at the back, the skirt opening like an inverted V to reveal a cream silk petticoat intricately embroidered as if pale yellow roses cascaded downwards over it to gather in thick clusters at the hem.

Before her first sitting Sabatin's finished portrait had been removed and carried downstairs by six men to be set in a frame previously ordered from a wood-carver and gilder. There was nothing in the north room, cool away from the heat outside, to remind either Michel or her that her husband had ever been there. They forgot him completely. It was as if he had never existed.

She did not care how long a sitting lasted, for she could feast her gaze on Michel's face with its concentrated expression every time he reappeared from behind the canvas to scrutinise her again, his brush in one hand, his palette in the other. Sometimes she would make a funny little grimace, making him grin, and he would wag his brush reprovingly at her. They were madly in love. Both knew their time together was limited and could not be extended, for parting was inevitable, but they did not waste a minute in foolish speculation or wishing for what might have been. The hour was theirs and they used it to the full.

Being apart for the sake of appearances elsewhere in the château was torment to them. He became almost crazed with impatience if she was a minute late coming to his room at night and when she arrived he would sweep her up in his arms, laughing with her and kissing her in celebration of their being together again.

One night she was considerably delayed. Berthe had slipped and strained her wrist and Jasmin bound it up for her, gave her a cognac, for she was in a great deal of pain, and saw her to her room. When Jasmin returned to her own bedchamber to snuff the candles before going to Michel, she found him waiting there for her.

"Not here!" she gasped when he would have taken her into his arms. "Not in this room."

She had turned her face away from him, but he took her chin between his finger and thumb and coaxed her into looking at him again. "Yes, here," he said softly. "Where I can finally drive your last nightmares away."

He did that for her. Every gruesome memory was banished from that bedchamber. Ever afterwards she associated it with one of the most exquisite nights that any woman could have experienced and rarely went to sleep on the pillows without a smile of blissful memory.

The portrait was finished. Michel was going to deliver it himself to Marguerite and it had been splendidly framed in gilt before being packed. Yet still he did not go. Jasmin was adamant that he should be gone before Sabatin returned, but he could not bring himself to leave her until the last possible minute.

"At least be packed and ready," she implored him. "You and I will never be able to hide our true feelings if we wait until he is here before we say goodbye."

Now that time was running out he began to put alternatives to her. "I'll give up my Paris studio. We can go to Geneva or Venice or Rome. I can paint as well there as anywhere else—"

"No. The scandal would follow us and destroy you. Your place is at Versailles. Don't make it harder for me by offering dreams that can never be fulfilled."

He knew she was right. He would have hated a self-imposed exile, even with her. Inevitably it would have affected their relationship and he wanted that no more than she.

They had one last stroke of good fortune in that they were given advance warning of Sabatin's return. The housekeeper, returning from an expedition to Périgueux, informed Jasmin that she had met the Duc, who was breaking his journey overnight and would be home on the morrow. Michel made that last night with Jasmin romantically and passionately memorable for them both. Early in the morning, when he was ready to leave, they shared a long and loving kiss of farewell.

"If ever—?" he said questioningly, pausing with his hand on the salon door that led out into the hall.

"If ever," she promised with a nod. But there was no real hope in either of them.

She did not go out to the steps to see him off, but watched from a salon window. He looked back at her from the coach seat before the wheels jerked forward and swept him away. Her face was made misty by the ancient glass as if the distance was already far between them.

In Paris he made a copy of Jasmin's portrait and hung it in his studio where he was to glance at it every morning for many years to come. When he delivered the original portrait to Marguerite he found she had had a fall and broken her hip.

"Such a foolish thing for me to have done," she said breathlessly from the daybed in the Ivory Salon.

"Does the Duchesse know?" he asked as the footman set up a display easel that had been carried in with the wrapped portrait from his coach.

"No, she doesn't and should you write to either her or her husband, please do not mention it. She will only worry unnecessarily and think I won't be able to journey to see her again."

He thought the possibility unlikely himself, for the Baronne looked far from well. Chest infections frequently followed falls in elderly people and she seemed to have some difficulty in breathing. It added to his longing for Jasmin that he would not be at hand when eventually she learned of her mother's condition.

"Come now," Marguerite urged him eagerly. "Take away that cover and let me see my daughter's face."

He took a corner of the silk wrapping and threw it back. Jasmin was revealed in her handsome gown, radiant and beautiful. Marguerite looked so long and hard at the portrait, coughing once behind her lace handkerchief, that Michel began to think she was not pleased with it, her expression impossible to read. Then she looked at him and spoke forthrightly.

"You've painted my daughter as a woman in love. I can see it in her face. What happened at Château Valverde?"

He answered her with equal frankness. "I fell in love with Jasmin as never before. I wanted her to leave France with me, but she refused."

She gave a firm nod. "Such decisions are heartbreaking, but it is better to part in love than to let circumstances tear down what was there." Her gaze returned to the portrait. "You made her happy. I can see that. You will always have my gratitude, Monsieur Balaine. Shall you see her again?"

"That is unlikely." He spoke sadly. "I'll never forget her.

All I hope for is that one day things will change and she can be with me."

"Don't pin your hopes on dreams," Marguerite advised in a practical manner. "Be thankful for what has been. I hope Jasmin will be sustained by the same outlook." She indicated a portable writing desk on a side table. "Pray pass that to me, I will settle your fee."

"I want no payment."

She raised her eyebrows at him. "But you were weeks away from your studio."

He smiled and took up her slim, age-mottled hand to put it to his lips. "I'm grateful to you, Madame la Baronne. Without your commission I should have missed the most rewarding time of my whole life."

"That's a very positive statement."

"Truly meant, I assure you."

She gave him her hand. "Come and see me again, Monsieur Balaine."

"I will indeed."

After he had gone she lay back against the cushions and wiped her lace handkerchief across her brow. She believed she was getting a fever and would have to admit it when the doctor came later to see her. But she would not let him bleed her. It only increased weakness and she had always fought against that condition, mentally or physically.

Her eyes rested on the portrait again with pleasure. How wonderful it was to see Jasmin looking happy again, an almost girlish look about her, the inner radiance shining forth from her. Naturally she would be lonely now without her love, cast down and full of yearning.

"Did I not go through all that myself, my dear child," she said aloud to the portrait. "But you have my strength and you will come through."

Women were not and never had been the weaker sex, she reflected. They could make sacrifices from which men would ever shy away. It was easy to deduce that Jasmin had given up everything she wanted most because she knew at heart Michel would never have settled in a foreign land away from the fame and fortune left behind. With Augustin it had been his overwhelming urge to live on through a son bearing his name. All of them had some citadel they would not leave for love.

Marguerite coughed again. Michel loved Jasmin now,

there was no doubt of that, but would he forget her? Not that it really mattered since there was no future for them. What was important was the reblooming he had brought about in Jasmin. Only good could come of that. She would write later and tell Jasmin how pleased she was with the portrait, but at the moment she felt extraordinarily tired. Her cough was giving her little rest.

When news of Marguerite's illness reached Jasmin, together with the information that there was no hope of recovery, she made up her mind immediately what to do.

"I'm going to her!" she exclaimed to Berthe. "I'll be with her at the end. Order the coach to be ready and outside in twenty minutes from now."

"But your banishment!"

"The King would forgive me in the circumstances if he should ever hear. But he won't. I can come and go like a stranger at Château Satory. My mother needs me!"

Berthe went to do her bidding. Sabatin, returning from hunting, was surprised to see a travelling-box being loaded onto Jasmin's coach. "What's this?" he asked the coachman, tapping the baggage with his riding whip.

"We're going to Versailles, sir. The mother of Madame is dying."

"Oh, is she?"

Sabatin went into the château and up the stairs. He reached Jasmin's door as she emerged ready to leave. Faced with him standing squarely in her path, she was compelled to give him an explanation. He just stared at her when she would have passed him and pushed her backwards into the room.

"Don't stop me going to her!" she implored frantically. "I beg you!"

He pushed her again, prodding her in the shoulder. Berthe, who had been ready to follow her down the stairs, set up a wailing. "Let her go, sir. It's her mother, for mercy's sake!"

He turned on her in fury. "Get out!"

Then, because she was slow in her movements, he struck her on the arm with his riding whip. Jasmin cried out in protest and flew forward, but he swept her aside with his arm, withdrew the key from the lock and before she could get back at him he had slammed the door and locked her in.

For Marguerite in her last days it seemed as though Jasmin was at her bedside throughout, for the portrait had been hung where she could see it with ease. Lenore held her hand and answered gently whenever addressed as if she were Jasmin sitting there. Marguerite finally gave up any attempt to speak in the painful struggle for breath. Yet in her last moments she smiled, looking towards the foot of the bed. Her words were faint but clear, heard by both Lenore and the priest at the bedside.

"I must leave you, Jasmin. Augustin has come for me."

Then she closed her eyes on a smile and life went from her.

Sabatin kept Jasmin a prisoner until after the funeral was over. He himself retained possession of the key and opened the door only to let Berthe go in and out with trays and to perform other necessary chores. Jasmin knew it was her punishment for having had Marguerite to stay, remembering how she thought she had got off lightly at the time.

On the day of Jasmin's release, Berthe had been given the key and for the first time in a month the grim figure of Sabatin was not standing at the door. Jasmin, wearing a black silk gown, sat by the open bedchamber window where she had spent many hours during her incarceration. Her arm was resting on the sill and she was watching a wagon lumbering along the lane in the valley below. Berthe inserted the key back on the inner side of the door of the anteroom before going through to her.

"We can go for a drive today, madame," she said encouragingly.

Jasmin did not turn her head. "I'd like to do that. Is my imprisonment finally over?"

"It is. Try to make a fresh start and not to feel too sad in your bereavement."

"I have something to help me of which I think in this case my mother would have approved."

"What could that be?"

Jasmin looked up over her shoulder at Berthe bending towards her, a deep glow in her eyes. "I'm pregnant. I'm going to have Michel's baby."

It took all Jasmin's ingenuity to disguise her state as the months advanced. She laced herself tightly until Berthe warned her that she might harm the child. After that she was helped by a new fashion that had spread from Paris of lace fichus that were worn gauzy and full round the neck to be looped to hang down past the waist. A further aid was a Watteau cape, named after the artist whose charming paintings, exquisitely hedonistic, of gallants and ladies had so reflected life at Versailles until his untimely death. The cape, draped with enormous fullness down the back, was all part of the wearer's gown, and could be held by wide ties at the front of the waist.

"It's going to be a small baby," Berthe said one day as she helped Jasmin into her bath, "which is a blessing in your case. I was three times the size at half your time. At this rate you should be able to go to the last day without anyone suspecting."

"I hope so." Jasmin settled herself in the warm water. "There'll be no problem if Sabatin is away on one of his visits. Then we can go to Périgueux several days before I'm brought to bed with no last-minute rush."

Her plans were carefully laid. A small house had been rented on the outskirts of the city where she would be attended by Berthe and a midwife to whom she had given a false name. Should Sabatin be at home her coach would return to take him the message that she had sprained her ankle while shopping and since a break in the bone was feared she would stay under the doctor's attention for two or three days. She had an alternative plan in case of emergency, but she hoped it would not come to that.

As Jasmin entered her eighth month, Sabatin, who had just returned from being away, let her know he wanted to give a costume ball in April. These functions were as popular in the provinces as they were at Versailles and the chance to be dressed up with a mask could not have been more opportune as far as she was concerned. As the ball was to be held three weeks before the birthdate in May, she foresaw no difficulties. It pleased her that her own baby should share her and her mother's natal month and she wondered if it portended the birth of a daughter.

"Do you think I'm going to have a girl?" she asked Berthe as she sat checking a list of the latest acceptances to the ball. "After all, I'm carrying the baby low and you said that with your boy you were high."

Berthe shrugged. "Nobody can foretell for any certainty, but I was looking at you in your petticoats this morning. You *are* lower than I would have expected at this stage. Would you like a girl?"

"I don't mind as long as he or she is strong and healthy."

Berthe did not know how Jasmin could be in such good spirits about the whole thing. Even from the start she had rejoiced that she was going to bear her lover's child. It had given her courage such as Berthe could never have raised herself against such odds. When born, the baby was to be fostered by a couple who lived out in the country, a journey of two days, but Jasmin planned to see the child whenever Sabatin was himself away from home. What Berthe feared most was Jasmin's distress when the baby was taken from her so soon after the birth. She hoped it would not give her any ideas of running away with the infant, for Sabatin would only hunt her down, and would ever be within his rights to call in the law to assist him. It was not as if Jasmin had any refuge. Her mother's will had left her nothing except personal jewellery. Château Satory was being held in trust for fifty years. If during that time Jasmin should be pardoned her banishment, the property would revert to her, or if this never happened the château and all its lands were to be sold and the proceeds given to charity. Sabatin had been outraged by the will, which denied the enormous wealth of the Picard estate even to any children of his marriage, however unlikely that possibility might be. There was no way he could get his hands on this elusive inheritance.

Jasmin chose a costume to completely disguise her figure. She would go as a lady of Venice, which meant that above a skirt of scarlet satin she would be enveloped in clouds of gossamer lace attached to her black velvet tricorn hat on either side of her face, swathed under her chin and falling in massive fullness almost to the ground. A sparkling sequined eye mask would complete the costume. Sabatin was going as Alexander the Great in a gold breastplate and a gilded Grecian helmet. They always had to let each other know their disguises for their partnering in the first dance. She often thought how she and the King had shared the same secret for far happier reasons.

Despite Jasmin's optimism that no one would suspect the truth, Berthe became apprehensive of the housekeeper's eagle eye. There was fever in the village and when

Jasmin caught a slight cold Berthe exaggerated the symptoms greatly, announcing that Madame la Duchesse must remain in the warmth of her bedchamber to ensure a complete recovery before the ball. Jasmin gave her housekeeper the necessary instructions while Berthe contacted the gardeners with orders for such flowers as were available. Only on the day of the ball did Jasmin leave her room, wrapped in many shawls, to ensure all was in order.

Bowers of spring flowers gave fragrance to the château. There were new candles in every chandelier and candlestick. Outside flambeaux would illuminate the drive and the forecourt and the gardens.

Jasmin was halfway up the stairs returning to her room when a sharp pain made her halt abruptly and rest a hand on a balustrade to steady herself. It couldn't be! Not today of all days! She had had strange little twinges since early morning, but had supposed them to be caused by nerves due to the evening ahead. It would inevitably be something of an ordeal for her, no matter how well her figure was disguised.

Upstairs she rang for Berthe. As soon as the woman saw Jasmin's face she threw up her hands in dismay.

"Are you sure, madame? It could be a false alarm."

"Let's hope so."

It was not a false alarm. By midday the pains were regular and getting worse all the time. Jasmin was ashen and frequently doubled over. It was time for her to go to the turret room that featured in their emergency plan.

"I'll keep watch and stop anyone coming along the corridor," Berthe said. "You'll have to climb those turret stairs by yourself. I'll come as soon as it's safe."

Jasmin waited until Berthe gave her the signal that the coast was clear and then left the room to hurry as fast as she was able in the direction of the archway that led to the south turret. On three levels there were huge circular rooms that had to be unlocked from the ring of keys she had brought with her. The ascent up the curving flights was as difficult as if she were dragging herself up a mountain. Frequently she paused by the narrow slits in the walls to gasp in the cool air as another pain seized her.

Eventually she reached the top room where an ancient bed had been made up in readiness and she lay down on it with relief. Everything was prepared. Under a cloth on the table were twine, scissors, clean linen and all else that would be needed. In the great stone hearth a charcoal burner glowed, lit by Berthe that morning at the first alarm to give heat without telltale smoke and ready to boil the water from the pitchers that had been filled at the same time. Nothing had been overlooked. Jasmin knew she could scream as much as she liked and no sound would reach the rest of the château.

A baby daughter was born as several floors away the guests were streaming into the château for the ball. Jasmin held the baby in her arms. Berthe attended to her, not a minute being wasted.

"I want her to be baptised Violette," she said softly, kissing the infant's wrinkled red brow. "It's only right to follow the precedent that her grandmother set and name her after a flower. Isn't she beautiful. Oh, how perfect she is!"

An hour later, when the first dance was long over, Berthe helped her from the bed to dress in the costume that had been fetched. Some paint and powder concealed her pallor.

"You're mad," Berthe grumbled, anxiety making her angry. "It would have been better to go back to your room and stay there until morning."

"That's impossible. I must get to the ballroom before the hour of unmasking. As it is I must make some excuse, a twisted ankle or an attack of faintness, to account for missing the opening dance."

"But suppose you should collapse."

"I won't. I daren't. In any case I'm only doing what other women in similar circumstances have had to do at Versailles to keep their secret from the Court. I'm not the first by any means to rise from a birthing to make an appearance as if nothing had happened."

Before she put on the mask she cradled Violette in her arms once more, stroking and kissing and whispering loving words, not knowing when she would see her again. Berthe, seeing how hard it was for Jasmin, finally took the infant into her own arms.

"You had better go, madame," she instructed brusquely, tortured herself by Jasmin's swimming eyes and anguished expression. "I must leave with her at once while the dancing is in full swing and the servants are all too busy to notice me."

Jasmin gave a nod, too choked for speech. She kissed her daughter once more and then, without looking back, went from the room and down the curving flight, weeping as she went.

She slipped into the ballroom by a side door and mingled with the crowd, joining in conversation with those whose masks could not hide certain distinctive features even as voices and stature gave them away. She declined invitations to dance. Once the golden-clad figure that was Sabatin jerked its Grecian head in her direction as if he had searched for her in vain. At midnight, the hour of unmasking, she had to stand by his side in the tradition that the host and hostess unmasked first as a signal to everyone else. She dreaded to think what he would have done if she had not been there in time.

Somehow she managed to stay on her feet until the early hours when the guests began to leave. Then she went up to her room and crossed to the window to look out at the moonlit scene and the lights of the departing carriages. Somewhere out there Berthe was being driven through the night in a hired hackney cab, her absence being accounted for by a sudden attack of the fever, while Violette was being suckled by the wet nurse collected on the way and who would have no idea whose infant she held to her breast.

At least Violette was safe! Had Sabatin discovered the truth Jasmin knew she would never have seen her daughter again.

Fifteen

Château Satory had been closed for fifteen years when Michel Balaine called while in the vicinity on the chance that it might have been put up for sale. The thought of living in Jasmin's childhood home appealed to him. The last time he had entered there the Baronne had been too ill to see him, confirming his worst fears on the day he had delivered the portrait. He had left the flowers he had brought with him and hoped she had been able to enjoy their fragrance.

Lenore opened the door to him. She had been appointed concierge upon her mistress's death, and lived with her husband and two sons in the servants' quarters.

"Good day, Monsieur Balaine," she said, recognising him immediately. Time had done little to change his striking although not handsome looks. She bobbed a curtsey as he stepped into the hall, its furniture shrouded in dustsheets. When she heard the purpose of his visit she shook her head. "This château won't be put up for sale for many years yet. It is my personal hope that one day the Duchesse de Valverde will come home to live here again."

"How is Madame la Duchesse?"

"Well, I thank you, sir. By all accounts she is busy from morning until night. The last I heard from her was that she had set up a fan-making workshop in a third village to give employment to local women where none existed before." Lenore broke off. He looked interested, but it was not for her to prattle about the Duchesse's affairs.

As Michel rode away he mused over the past. A fire had destroyed his old studio and Jasmin's portrait had been lost, which had saddened him at the time. Not long afterwards he had married a woman who had reminded him of her, or perhaps it was that men were usually attracted to the same type of feminine beauty. Whatever the reason the marriage had been a disaster. Recently they had finally gone their separate ways, which was why he was looking for a new residence, having allowed his wife to keep their Paris mansion in the faubourgs. He wished there had been children from the marriage, which would have been some compensation for their wasted years together, and he would have liked a son.

He had no financial problems. His late father had been a wealthy merchant and as the only child he had inherited everything. He had also made a fortune for himself in portraiture before proceeding to make another in enormous paintings teeming with people in battle, hunting and biblical scenes. Those depicting events in the King's life, such as Louis's triumphant victory over the enemies of France in the battle of Fontenoy, which had put an end to a long and dreary war, were hanging in the grand settings of Versailles, Fontainebleau, the Louvre and Compiègne. Some of them had been interpreted into tapestry at the Gobelins workshops and were in great demand. Yet portraiture on a smaller scale remained Michel's preference and his present commission by the King was to paint Madame de Pompadour.

It was not his first portrait of her. He had known the Poisson family for many years and the late Madame Poisson had given him one of his first commissions to paint the little Reinette, who even then had been infatuated with the King, although she had only seen him from a distance, riding by in his coach or waving from a balcony.

"He is the most beautiful man in all France," she had said during one of those early sittings, clasping her hands to her heart and making an altogether enchanting picture, for she was as pretty and dainty as a porcelain figurine with her huge brown eyes and dark wavy hair. "Did you know that a fortune-teller once told me when I was just a little child that one day I should influence a King?"

Nobody who had ever been five minutes in the Poisson household could escape knowing that, for it was her favourite topic on all occasions. He had never imagined then, any more than anyone else, that the fortune-teller's prophecy would come true with a vengeance, or that he himself would be instrumental in bringing it about.

He had always enjoyed visiting the Poisson household. There was plenty of good conversation, stimulating company and lots of laughter. It was a natural outcome when Reinette married Monsieur Lenormand d'Étoiles that she, artistic, witty and intelligent, should create a salon at their Paris residence to which came philosophers, writers, artists and scientists. Her husband loved her as did almost everyone else with whom she came in contact. She was full of gaiety and charm, thoughtful, kind and considerate, as well as being musically talented, able to sing and play the clavichord to please all who heard her. Had she wished it, she could have made her debut as a professional actress at any time, having a flair for comedy as well as an ability to run the full gamut of emotions in heavy drama. Yet in spite of the adulation she received, her father and all her relatives devoted to her, she had given her heart to the King and never made any secret of it.

"You do realise, don't you, Michel," she said when he was painting her portrait at a later date, having been commissioned by her husband, "that I should leave everything, even my darling little daughter, Alexandrine, for the King?"

She was intensely serious, spoiling her expression for him just as he was capturing the sparkle of happiness normal to her eyes, and he tried to tease her out of her mood. "Come, my little bourgeoise, you need noble blood before you can even be presented to him. Do you want me to add a blue tint to your portrait? Would it help?"

Instead of winning a smile from her he gained a desperate look of appeal. "You could help me in a better way than that. You have an entrée at Court, which you have earned through your own merits." She sprang down from the chair on the dais in a rustle of carnation satin and lace ruffles to rush across to him. "Please, Michel! Speak to the King for me. I've done everything I can think of to draw his attention. I've driven my calèche to the royal hunt and changed its colour daily to match my outfit—white or pink or silver or blue—and always caught his eye. He knows who I am, I've been told that, and several times he has sent gifts of game to our château since his hunting lodge at Choisy makes him our neighbour there. He is attracted to me. I've seen the way he looks at me. A woman can always tell." She drew in her breath and released it in a gust. "He is without a mistress at the moment. The time is ripe."

Michel put aside his palette and brushes, seeing there would be no more work done that day. "I have to warn you. You have enemies at Court. People have seen what you are up to and are determined to keep you away from the King."

"Then they do think I present competition to those noblewomen with the same aim as mine!" She was excited and frantic at the same time. "Nobody loves the King as I do. When he nearly died during this past war I nearly died too. I wouldn't have wanted to go on living without him."

It was true. Her recovery had only come about with the rejoicing in Paris that Louis the Well-Beloved had recovered. Michel smiled indulgently, aware that he was like everybody else in allowing her to get her own way. He gave a sigh of resignation. "What is it you want me to do?"

With a joyous exclamation she threw her arms about him. Then she outlined her plan. It was all very simple. The sixteen-year-old Dauphin was about to marry and there were to be balls and parties in celebration every night for a month, festivities that the King enjoyed immensely. The climax would be a grand costume ball at Versailles. Reinette wanted Michel to let the King know that she would be there dressed as Diana in silver and white, her midnight blue mask covered with stars, and there would be a crescent moon in her hair.

"If he seeks me out," she exclaimed breathlessly, "then it will be the beginning of all I've ever wanted in life."

It was one of the most spectacular events ever staged at Versailles and one of the most famous. For once the King with his fine stature and warm, attractive voice was not recognised in his disguise. He and seven others came as clipped yew trees, such as were to be seen standing like soldiers along the parterres in the park, and none knew which was the King. Reinette waited in the crowded Hall of Mirrors, able to see the bobbing tops of the yew trees and trembling with suspense. Michel, whom she had insisted should be at her side, was dressed as Mars in a helmet and breastplate of red and gold. He had done as she requested and now the outcome was awaited.

"You are taller than I," she said to him, twisting her hands together agitatedly. "Is one of the yew trees coming this way? Can you see?"

He had no need to answer. The tallest had come edging through the crowd in search of her. She spun round as a silk-clad figure in green removed his headdress and she saw Louis smiling at her. With a burst of delighted laughter she whisked her own mask away.

"What a splendid disguise, sire!"

"It was not easy to see from within. Fortunately I had the moon to guide me." It was a reference to the crescent moon sparkling on her hair and his laughter joined with hers. In those few words much had been said and understood. Michel, seeing that he was no longer needed, slipped quietly away.

Since then Reinette had become the King's titular mistress. It had infuriated the Court that a bourgeoise should rise to such an important and influential position, although that had not stopped any number of them from attempting to ingratiate themselves at the first opportunity, for a courtier's whole future could depend on whether the titular mistress liked him or not. The King had given her the title of the Marquise de Pompadour with her own coat of arms and everyone could see that he adored her. A legal separation had severed her marriage to d'Étoiles, who had resigned himself to his loss.

It was typical of Reinette that she should not be late for her sitting when Michel arrived at Versailles still disappointed that there had been no chance to buy Château Satory. Her first question was an expression of concern for him.

"Have you found a house to suit you yet, Michel?"

He was on one knee, arranging a fold of her skirt where she sat on the dais. "No, I haven't, I'm sorry to say."

She rested a hand on his shoulder and leaned towards him, her heart-shaped face wreathed in smiles. "Then I have found just the place for you. A darling little château of some thirty rooms close to Versailles. I would have liked it myself, but your need is greater than mine."

He sat back on his heels and grinned at her, knowing that she had a passion for collecting houses as other women acquired jewels, and the King was generous to her every whim. "If you've set your heart on it, then I'll not take it from you."

"Nonsense! I'll be in your debt forever for what you did for me. I want you to have it, but on one condition." She wagged a finger roguishly.

"What's that?"

"Let me see to the décor for you. Please!" With her artistic trait she had a flair for interior decoration, her apartment the most delightful at Versailles, pastel-hued with elegant furnishings and exquisite objets d'art and always fragrant with an abundance of fresh flowers.

"If I decide on this house you have found for me you shall have carte blanche with the furnishings. Remember, I've taken only a few personal heirlooms from my previous residence and have to start from scratch."

"Perfect!" She clapped her hands together. "I promise not to be too extravagant."

He raised an eyebrow wryly, making her laugh. She had the ability to spend gloriously, a complete stranger to thrift, but everything she bought reflected her superb taste and he would not have the least qualm about the end result, even though the bills would be steep.

"When shall I see this château you have found?" he asked her, taking up his brushes by the half-finished canvas.

"We'll go there together as soon as this sitting is over."

He liked the château as soon as he saw it lying apricot-hued in the sun, a simple, unpretentious mansion with good lines in a spacious setting and situated halfway between Versailles and Paris, which was ideal for him. After an initial tour, Reinette left him to a closer inspection while she went to visit her daughter who lived nearby. Almost since birth Alexandrine had been in the charge of a responsible woman, this being the custom of many parents in society with little time to see to their own offspring. Since becoming the King's mistress she saw her child less frequently than before and could not miss this chance while in the vicinity.

A far distance away from Michel's new home of Château Montville, Jasmin was another who saw her daughter less than before, although for an entirely different reason. At first it had been easy with Sabatin away for long periods at a time. She was safe in spending three or four weeks at a stretch with Violette at the home of the foster parents, Monsieur and Madame Govin, a childless couple who owned a large farm. They knew her as Madame Picard, her own maiden name and the surname she had given Violette. The husband, resigned to never having a son, was training a young nephew to follow in his footsteps. His wife, who did not like the lad, became deeply attached to Violette, who was a bonny baby. Unlike most love-children, she bore no resemblance to her father, except in the colour of her hair, which was identical; her features were more like her mother's, although her eyes were deep brown and the long fair lashes darkened at the tips. It gave Jasmin great joy to care for her and by fortunate chance she was on a visit to the farm when Violette took her first steps.

Jasmin always came alone, hiring a local girl to act as her maid. Berthe's joints had become too painful for any travelling and in any case she was needed at the château with excuses should Sabatin ever return unexpectedly. Jasmin travelled in a hired carriage, changing transport and driver three times to leave no trail. As Violette grew there was always some initial shyness when Jasmin first arrived, but it soon passed and afterwards there was the excitement of the gifts that had been brought and the playing and romping and laughter until the visit was over and everything settled into routine for the child once again. Partings were always painful on both sides, Violette sobbing and clinging to her mother's skirts, Jasmin herself in tears.

"Don't go, Maman! Stay with me. Please!"

Since the pleas never worked, Violette began to resent these departures. She would add heartrending screams to punish her mother for leaving her. Then the woman she called Tante Govin would lift her up and cuddle her and give her a special treat of a sugar cake to silence her tears. She soon learned that both her mother and Tante Govin exercised some right to her and yet were resentful of each other, however polite they appeared to be on the surface. If her Maman told her she looked pretty, let her stay up late for a treat, or indulged her in any way, then her foster mother would have a sour face and shake her head disapprovingly. On the other hand, if Tante Govin gave in to her, then her Maman would object and speak in a strict voice. Soon it became easy to play one woman off against the other and became instinctive to throw an ugly tantrum if her demands were not immediately fulfilled.

Jasmin became increasingly worried about her daughter. She did not want to take her away from such a good home where she was safe from Sabatin and her foster parents cared for her, even her education provided by a retired tutor who lived in the neighbourhood. Yet it was becoming more apparent with every visit that Madame Govin hated her coming there. She could see that the woman was jealous of sharing Violette with her. It was also worrying that Madame Govin's discipline was lax and sometimes nonexistent. Jasmin could see that the child was turning into a selfish and self-centred individual, all gentler, loving ways swamped by the more strident side of her character.

"You really must be firmer, Madame Govin," Jasmin declared in exasperation after a particularly distressing scene in which she herself had sent Violette to bed in disgrace.

"The child only behaves badly when you're here," the woman replied coldly. "I never have any trouble with her on her own. You bring too many gifts and fine clothes for her instead of letting her be content with the everyday garments that it was agreed I should supply for her. She is a baby no longer, but an eight-year-old with a mind of her own, able to contrast the luxuries you provide with the mundane life she has to live with us after you've gone again. It's no wonder she's constantly confused and upset by your visits. It is you who are spoiling her to ruin, madame."

Jasmin could see there was some truth in what had been said, knowing that her conscience spurred her into being too generous, perhaps attempting some kind of compensation for her absences. She would continue to bring her daughter a fan every time because she made them herself and Violette was getting quite proud of her collection, but she would cut down on everything else.

On her next visit she took a single muslin gown instead of several more costly ones and was dismayed when Violette burst into tears of disappointment.

"You don't love me any more, Maman! You want me to look a dreadful sight." She flung down the new fan that had at first enchanted her.

"That's not true, my darling." Jasmin was kneeling beside the box that they had been unpacking and held up the muslin that was printed with bunches of violets. "This has your name-flower on it and you will find that the fan matches."

Violette flung her arms around Madame Govin's waist, huge tears flying. "You love me, don't you, Tante Govin? You'll never send me away from your home as Maman sent me away from hers."

"Never, little one." Madame Govin stooped and gathered the child to her, not quite hiding the flash of satisfaction in her eyes.

Jasmin rose slowly to her feet, letting her arms fall to her sides, the muslin gown trailing. "What have you been telling my daughter, Madame Govin?" she demanded sternly.

"Nothing but the truth. Just as I promised. Violette knows you are a busy lady and that daughters of such ladies often make their homes with lesser folk." She dried the child's eyes and gave her a loving kiss on the cheek. "No tears now that your Maman has come to stay again. You know how you've been looking forward to seeing her, haven't you?"

Violette nodded and retraced her steps hesitantly, a frown of concentration on her brow that was not anger but a genuine effort to make amends. "I do like the violets, Maman."

"That's good. Now shall we look at the rest?" Just for a second, as sometimes happened, Jasmin had caught a fleeting glimpse of Michel in the look across her daughter's eyes. She felt no pang. What had been between Michel and her had been wonderful and glorious and confined to those few short weeks. At no time had she looked to any future with him and the fact that he had inadvertently given her his child was a bonus for which she would always be grateful.

When Violette was eleven years old Berthe died. She had become old and feeble and in constant pain, her fingers curled like twigs. Jasmin was grief-stricken and mourned her deeply. During the latter years their rôles had been reversed, she becoming the comforter instead of the comforted, the old woman wholly dependent on her, which made the loss still more acute.

It was not many weeks after when Violette began asking questions about her future. She was maturing early, conscious of her looks and forever fussing with her hair. Toys no longer interested her and the gifts that pleased her best were hair ribbons, fans, necklaces and the pretty clothes she always craved.

"You must remain at the farm with Monsieur and Madame Govin until you are sixteen," Jasmin told her. They were taking a stroll together one spring morning along a cart-track. It had been raining earlier and now the sun had come out, the damp earth steaming, giving out the scent of grass and wildflowers. Violette halted and clutched her mother's arm.

"So long to wait! It's only my twelfth natal day soon. Why do you always leave without me? Why can't I come too?"

Jasmin cupped the child's hand with her own, holding it in the crook of her elbow as they continued on again. "As I told you on a previous occasion, your father was not my husband, who would only have ill will towards you if he knew of your existence. But by your sixteenth natal day I shall have arranged a good marriage for you through a lady of quality—that is a well-bred person who is not of the nobility. You will meet your betrothed under her roof and be married soon afterwards. It is my dearest hope that you and your future husband, whom I promise shall be young and kind and pleasing in appearance, will find love together in your marriage."

"Am I never to live with you, then?" The child's voice was thick with disappointment mixed with sullenness.

"That's not possible. I thought that had always been made clear to you."

"I know, but I've always hoped . . ." The words trailed away with a hung head.

Jasmin put her fingers under the girl's chin and tilted her face towards her. "Once you are married you may visit me often. None can gainsay that."

A cunning look glinted under the dark-tipped lashes. "Where is it that I shall visit you?"

Jasmin might have smiled at the artfulness of the question if it had not been such a poignant situation. She had never dared reveal her address even to Madame Govin. Reports on Violette's well-being had always gone to a banker in Périgueux where she had collected them herself when convenient.

"I shall tell you on your wedding day. Until then you must be patient, my darling."

She gave a still more evasive answer some months later when Violette asked her father's name. "I cannot tell you I have forgotten it, because that would not be true. I loved him truly. But he is leading his own life and you and I are no longer part of it. Just be content to know that he was a good man. He would have loved you as I do if he had ever known you."

Jasmin was resolved that father and daughter should never know each other's identity.

Violette could never be sure when she began to actively dislike her mother. She believed it started to take root with the knowledge that Jasmin stood between her and the father whom she was sure would have done everything for her. He would never have sent her to live on a farm with a country couple and an oafish youth. Her father would have taken her to live with him in a fine château and she would have worn pretty clothes every day of the week. He might be a Prince of the Blood for all she knew, because her mother often talked of Versailles with a dreamy note in her voice that showed it had been a happy time for her. Like many children adopted or fostered or otherwise unsure of their origins, she became convinced that her father was a romantic, unusual personage, and her dislike of her mother deepened.

The bond between them had never been strong on her side. Jasmin's visits had always been too brief and infrequent to make any lasting mark beyond the receiving of gifts. Whatever capacity Violette had had for love had been crushed by partings and the stifling possessiveness of her foster mother, who had never lost a chance to slide a wedge between mother and child. With the dawning of adolescence she had set her heart on becoming a part of her mother's life, unable to accept that the obstacles could not be overcome, for there was inherent in her a desire for what was rich and easy and as different from farm life as it could be. She had always resented the simple domestic chores that had been allotted to her, telling herself that one day servants would wait on her and she would be a lady like her mother. Now to all intents she was never to share that life: her husband would be a young gentleman but not of the rank or wealth she had anticipated. There grew in her a determination to outwit her mother and her Tante Govin and all the rest by making sure that somehow she achieved her aim.

For a considerable time Sabatin had been going away less and less, his absences no longer predictable, which made it increasingly difficult for Jasmin to arrange visits to her daughter, sometimes having to cancel at the last minute. When Violette was fourteen, probably her most vulnerable age when even the devoted Madame Govin was complaining of her moods and often ungovernable behaviour, Sabatin gave up going away altogether. His dissipations had finally taken their toll and he suffered badly from gout and dyspepsia. He was in his sixties and looked much older, his face bloated and crimson and hanging in heavy jowls; his stomach was grossly distended and beneath his wig he was bald.

His licentious friends had been decimated by disease, death, bankruptcy and in one case murder when two had quarrelled violently during some drunken debauchery. It had been passed off as an accident, but that particular nobleman had never been accepted back into the circle. Two more had duelled with rapiers, each in a matter of seconds fatally wounding the other and again there had been a certain amount of scandal. Sabatin no longer kept a retinue of elite servants and had turned once again to drink as his main consolation.

He and Jasmin had been married for more than twenty years and he had never once broken his silence towards her, his resentment having festered long since beyond any chance of a healing, and it had become so much a part of their existence that neither gave it any thought. She would write notes over anything important and he would either get his clerk to pen his reply or give her a sharp nod or shake of the head if no more were necessary when next they came face to face. His cousin Armand, who had tried to help and had succeeded in one way if not in another, had never been to see him after that one eventful visit, having died a year later from a hunting accident, but Armand's eldest son, Frédérick, who was a colonel in the army, did visit occasionally when on his way to manoeuvres or on some special business for the King. Sabatin always gave him the same greeting.

"Come to keep an eye on your inheritance, have you?" It was more of a joke than sarcasm, because Sabatin liked to keep contact with his relatives at Court.

"How did you guess, sir?" was always the jovial reply. Frédérick de Valverde was a big, bluff man with a hearty laugh and an even heartier appetite. Jasmin always enjoyed his company. Once he brought his wife, Gabrielle, with him and the two women struck up a friendship. It was from Gabrielle that Jasmin learned more details of Reinette's rise to be the titular mistress.

"I'm particularly interested in all you've told me," Jasmin remarked, "because when I was young I saw Reinette occasionally when her mother, Madame Poisson, brought her to my mother's fan-shop on the Champs-Élysées. She was like a little doll, dainty and petite with a pink and white porcelain complexion. Is she still as pretty?"

"Indeed she is," Gabrielle replied, throwing her hands wide expressively. She was an animated, talkative woman, almost as amply built as her husband, if in softer curves and proportions. "Madame de Pompadour has that rare kind of beauty that shines out of a happy face. She loves everybody —her friends, her enemies, her dreadful bourgeois relatives, her daughter, her pet animals and the King most of all. It is not an exaggeration to say she worships the ground he walks on. The Queen has grown quite fond of her, because Pompadour shows her every kindness and consideration instead of making her take a backseat as the other mistresses have done. Pompadour even persuaded the King to pay his wife's gambling debts with which he normally has no patience."

"It appears that a charming woman has grown from a delightful child."

"That's very true. Unfortunately there is one cloud on her horizon."

"Whatever is that?"

"Her health is not all that it should be. She is delicate in appearance and has a constitution to match. The whole Court knows she is often exhausted by the King's ardency." Gabrielle lowered her voice confidentially, although she and Jasmin were alone in the rose garden of Château Valverde with nobody near. "It is said she cannot respond to that side of their relationship."

Absently Jasmin picked a pink rosebud and inhaled its scent, thinking how the Court thrived on such intimate snippets. She could guess how Louis, a shy and private man at heart, must hate such open talk about matters personal to him. It was no wonder that he was showing little trust in even his own ministers. Frédérick had spoken of how frequently the King bypassed his Council and conducted treaties and settled other matters with foreign governments without consulting anyone else.

"I'm sorry to hear that about Reinette," she said thoughtfully, all her sympathy going out to the young woman incapable of physical passion, "especially when she loves the King so much."

"He adores her." Gabrielle released a romantic little sigh. Then she took the rosebud from her hostess and tucked it into her sash. "It's Pompadour's misfortune that she should be mistress to such a sensual man. He is first and foremost a Bourbon and all of that lineage have passion running perpetually in their veins."

Jasmin thought that was true of Louis but not necessarily of his family. Out of his seven surviving children only the Dauphin had married and all six daughters seemed more in love with Versailles than they could be with any man, which no doubt suited Louis, for according to Gabrielle he did not want them to marry. Perhaps he had seen too many disastrously unhappy royal marriages to wish such a fate on his daughters.

After her departure, Gabrielle proved to be an energetic correspondent and continued to keep Jasmin in touch with events at Court. It had the effect of making Jasmin yearn to be part of it again and it struck her that perhaps she had never really been any more resigned than Sabatin to being away from it all. Between answering Gabrielle's letters and dealing with those concerning the business of the fan-shops, she wrote often to Violette, hoping to bridge the gulf of separation to some extent. She had let both her daughter and Madame Govin know that circumstances beyond her control had put a stop to her visits for a while. Whenever she was in Périgueux she hoped to find a letter from her daughter with the banker, but whereas in the past there had sometimes been a little note, now there was nothing. Had it not been for Madame Govin's written assurance that all was well she would have begun to worry.

Eventually she did manage to get away for a week on the pretext of visiting a sick friend in Périgueux, although with two days' journey each way she would have little enough time with her daughter. Her fear was that if she made a habit of being absent Sabatin would suspect her of having a lover, for not only was she more than twenty years younger than he, but she had kept a good figure and, in spite of all her tribulations, she had not completely lost her looks. If he should put a clever spy on her trail at any time it would not be long before Violette's existence came to light. Had he simply confined himself to drinking for his pleasure she might have been absent without his noticing, but to compensate for his lost status at Court he liked to entertain the local nobility more than ever before and her presence was always expected.

There was no joyful reunion when she arrived at the farmhouse. Violette met her with undisguised hostility and pretended to show no interest in the gifts that had been brought.

"Why did you bother to come, Maman?" she jeered heartlessly. "There was no need to interrupt your splendid social round on my account. I'm perfectly all right here without your interference."

Jasmin regarded her steadily. "Don't be impertinent. You know perfectly well from my letters that I have longed to see you and be here again. Kindly leave my presence and don't come back until you're ready to apologise."

Violette flounced away upstairs and shut herself in her room. She did not emerge again that day or the next. Madame Govin made no attempt to intervene, well pleased with things as they were. Jasmin paced the floor, distressed that the precious hours were slipping away, but it was an impasse she did not know how to break. On the evening of the second day, with her departure looming on the morrow, she took Violette's supper tray from Madame Govin and went upstairs with it. When she entered the girl's bedchamber she saw that Violette's eyes were swollen with weeping and mistook the reason. She set down the tray and held out her arms, fully prepared to forgive.

"Let us never quarrel again, Violette. I know you didn't mean what you said."

Violette uncurled her legs from the bed and slid her feet to the floor. She would never have given in and gone downstairs to apologise. Her mother could have left again without their further sight of each other as far as she was concerned. Her tears had been for the gifts she had fully expected her mother to take away again as a punishment, several beautiful gowns of silk and velvet this time, and the prospect of that loss had gone hard with her. Suddenly she saw a chance to turn the situation to her advantage.

"Take me away with you tomorrow and then we'll never quarrel again," she implored, running forward to be embraced. "I can stay with that lady of quality you have mentioned! I'll be good and never cause the slightest trouble. Say you will, Maman! If you love me you'll do this for me."

Jasmin hugged the girl, kissing her forehead and smoothing her hair. "I can't, my child. Even when you are betrothed it will be risky enough to have you there until the marriage band is on your finger. That is why I've always impressed upon you that I shall choose just the bridegroom I know will be good to you, because there will be no time for a lengthy courtship. Even if it should be the eve of your wedding and my husband found out about it, he would not hesitate to devise a terrible future for you as his revenge on me."

The girl gasped fearfully. "What would that be?"

"Anything! He could have you driven publicly out of the city with a whipping or thrown into prison on some trumped-up charge. He could marry you off to one of his old and lecherous friends or have you shut away in a convent from which you would never get out and I should never see you again."

Shudder after shudder ran through the girl's frame and she drew back to stare with dilated eyes at Jasmin. "Could he really do those things?"

Jasmin nodded wretchedly. "I have to tell you all this for your own good, and that's why when you do leave here your marriage must be conducted as soon as possible without the least delay. My husband is the cruellest man it's ever been my misfortune to meet."

"Why didn't you leave him and go away with my father?" The girl's eyes were accusing. "Then I'd never have had to face that danger. My father would have protected me."

Jasmin blanched at the venom directed at her. For the first time she saw how wide the gulf had grown between them. "There comes a time in most people's lives," she said with a weariness that came from suffering, "when a decision has to be taken for the best, even though much heartache may follow in its wake. That was what I had to do when your father asked me to go away with him. It is my earnest hope that you will never be faced with such a dilemma. If ever you should be I pray you will make the right choice and be granted the strength to overcome the aftermath."

Violette withdrew another step and tossed her head, the smooth fair hair dressed close in a passable imitation of the current mode worn by Jasmin. "I intend to manage my life far better than you have done yours."

"That shouldn't be difficult," Jasmin remarked wryly, almost to herself. She held out a hand coaxingly, no longer caring that she was making all the effort to meet her daughter across the dividing gap. "Leave that tray and come down to eat supper with me. I have to go again in the morning."

Violette did not take the proffered hand, although she accompanied her mother downstairs. Now that she was confident the gifts would not be taken away it was worth the effort to hide her true dislike of this woman for a while longer. She blamed Jasmin for everything. It was a direct result of her mother's folly that she herself was exposed to the dreadful risk of vengeance by that unknown man. That was something she would never forget.

Jasmin was almost thankful when it was time to leave the next morning. There had been no real reconciliation, only politeness on her daughter's part, and the strained atmosphere had remained. She was well aware that Violette would not have given her a kiss of farewell if Madame

Govin, curiously triumphant and condescending, had not prompted the girl in a whispered aside.

"I don't know when I'll be able to get here again," Jasmin said from her seat in the hackney coach in the last moment before departure.

Madame Govin answered through the open coach window where she stood with her hand resting possessively on Violette's shoulder. "Don't worry, madame. I'll look after your daughter as I've always done. I think of her as my own."

It was a parting shot. Jasmin almost recoiled from the painful truth of it and all that was implied. She waved through the coach window, half expecting Violette to go back indoors, but the girl remained on her own by the gate to wave in return, perhaps once again on the instigation of her foster mother since her face was stony and dry-eyed. Jasmin went on waving until a bend in the lane hid away the slender figure with the silken skirt billowing in the wind and the fair hair dancing.

A year went by during which it would have been impossible to get away for more than two or three days, which made a visit to the Govins' far distant abode out of the question. Jasmin toyed with the idea of having Violette brought to Périgueux and meeting her there, but the danger was too great. There was nothing for it but to be as patient as she had once advised her daughter to be. In the meantime she could begin to take steps towards finding a husband for the girl. She had met several suitable candidates in the social circle centred at Périgueux into which she had been drawn long ago through card parties and entertainments provided by quality folk whom Sabatin considered too far below him to become involved. It had suited her to have a number of places where she could enjoy herself without his dampening presence.

Madame Gérard, who had acted as intermediary for many a *mariage de convenance,* was also a good friend. Yet even she did not know the truth and understood the future bride to be Jasmin's godchild. The simple deception would be easily maintained, Jasmin having no doubt that Violette's fear of a hitch to the ceremony, with its possible consequences, added to her quick wits, would enable her to carry it off then and afterwards. It was with Violette in the rôle of her godchild that Jasmin expected to welcome her and her husband to Château Valverde.

Eventually the young man most suited to the rôle was decided upon. He had pleasing looks, good height and a fine physique. A struggling lawyer, eager to branch out on his own, he was ripe to accept a personable bride with a handsome dowry, Jasmin having recently sold several of the less cherished pieces of jewellery inherited from Marguerite for this purpose. Discreet investigations had shown that the young man had all the qualities necessary to make a good husband, kindness being a special attribute in his favour. He was unattached, ambitious with excellent prospects. In particular he had greatly admired the specially painted likeness of Violette.

Madame Gérard had insisted that a portrait was essential. Fortunately a few months after receiving Jasmin's request, Madame Govin overheard two women in the local market praising a travelling artist then in the neighbourhood. She located the young man, commissioned him immediately and sent the surprisingly good resultant painting to Périgueux. In time the young lawyer would be able to provide Violette with the luxuries of life, something Jasmin knew to be essential to her daughter's happiness. All that remained was for Madame Gérard to make the right approach, and once the matter was agreed all the papers of the contract could be drawn up and the date set for Violette's sixteenth natal day.

Jasmin felt far more at ease in her mind with the investigations behind her and Violette's future all but settled. At Château Valverde she had her hands full, for preparations were going ahead for a grand ball to coincide with a visit from Frédérick, whose regiment was on eight weeks' manoeuvres, some taking place not all that far from the Govins' home. She wished it could be possible to find some excuse to travel back to the camp with him and see Violette. Then she could tell her that all was arranged, even deliver the ring of betrothment, for by then everything would be signed and sealed.

Finally she hit on a solution. She would simply confide in Frédérick. He was a man of honour and if she first asked him never to reveal her secret, he would die before he would betray her. What was more, she knew she had his sympathy. He was courteous to Sabatin at all times, but much about her husband was offensive to him, something she had deduced a long time ago. If Frédérick simply invited her to view some of the manoeuvres Sabatin would not be able to refuse without appearing ungracious; also there would be no question of his accompanying them, for his gout was too painful for jolting in a coach over rough roads.

Frédérick arrived on the eve of the ball. He was unusually tired from the long ride on horseback, quite a grey tinge to his complexion, and he retired early after supper much to Sabatin's disappointment. He had been looking forward to a drinking session. Next morning Frédérick appeared recovered and was in good spirits. Jasmin, busy supervising last-minute preparations, had almost no chance to talk to him except for a matter of minutes when they met by his bedchamber door.

"Tomorrow, when the festivities are over," she said, "I should like to talk to you on your own for a little while."

His dark eyes pierced into hers. "Are you in any trouble?"

She shook her head smilingly. "Not at all. I'm going to seek a favour."

"You know I am your servant at all times."

That evening as she took her place beside Sabatin to welcome their many guests, she felt excited and lighthearted. She was certain of Frédérick's support and with the happy arrangements that had been made to Violette's advantage, she was sure there would be no more adolescent animosity on her daughter's part. There was even the chance they could begin to become friends again, the natural transition that she had witnessed in the daughters of friends once all the youthful hysterics and rebellions were at an end.

Guests complimented her on her appearance. She supposed that some of her inner gaiety was showing through to give an added sparkle to her eyes. Her hair followed the style that Madame de Pompadour had made fashionable, dressed smoothly back with clusters of curls at the nape of the neck and powdered white, ribbons held there by a diamond clasp. Marguerite's magnificent sapphire pendant and matching eardrops glittered spectacularly at her cleavage and in her lobes, and her gown was of silver gauze with panniers puffing over the side hoops that had widened considerably during the past decade.

There was no dancing the opening measure with Sabatin any more, handicapped as he was by his painful foot. He, in his favourite black velvet, and leaning on a gold-headed cane, offered his arm to her at the right moment. Then they paraded slowly down the length of the ballroom floor to be applauded by their guests as if they were royalty at a public function, her suspicion being that Sabatin had stationed servants to start the clapping, although she had never managed to prove it. At the far end was a canopied chair on a dais, an innovation installed for these events since he had given up going away, giving the hint that he might be of royal descent. Jasmin found the charade embarrassing, but nobody else seemed to mind and Sabatin revelled in it, beaming and nodding as if he were the most benevolent of men. He had created his own Versailles at last and she alone suspected that he was in reality snubbing the King.

There was no chair on the dais for her, something for which she was thankful, and having seen him hobble into his thronelike seat of gilt and scarlet velvet she descended the two steps again to start the dancing with the guest of honour. This evening it should have been Frédérick who came forward to take her hand, but he was nowhere to be seen. Quickly she signalled with her eyes to a friend, Brigadier Cloquet, and he was at her side immediately to lead her onto the floor, having observed that something was amiss.

"Have you seen Colonel de Valverde?" she asked him, looking about her.

"Not this evening," he replied. "As a matter of fact, I was hoping to have a chat with him about the regiment. We once served together."

Just before supper when Frédérick had still not made an appearance, Jasmin became anxious remembering that he had not been all that well the day before. She left the ballroom and hurried upstairs to tap on his bedchamber door. His servant opened it.

"My master is unwell, madame," he said at once, his face worried. "He has a fever."

She went past him into the room and crossed to the bedside. Frédérick lay flushed on the pillows, sweat running in beads down his face. Swollen glands in his throat made talking difficult for him, but he croaked a protest.

"You shouldn't have left your guests."

"They'll not miss me for a little while." She took up a candlestick and brought it forward to let more light fall on his face. He blinked painfully and she set it back again, filled with dismay at the dreaded telltale rash that she recognised only too well. Smallpox!

"Is it what I fear, madame?" The servant had spoken behind her.

She spun round with a nod. He had a deeply pock-marked skin himself that was the result of a past attack of the disease and he would be immune, as she was, to any infection. She had treated many cases over the years and the age-old rule of isolation was the only effective way of controlling an outbreak. She beckoned him out of earshot of the man sweating in the bed.

"Attract the attention of one of the footmen in the hall, but don't go near. There may be infection on your clothes. Tell him to fetch Monsieur le Duc from the ballroom and then let me know as soon as my husband is at the foot of the stairs."

While the servant went to carry out the errand she hurried off in search of all she would need for nursing the patient. Clean linen, sheets to hang over the door to help keep the infection from seeping out, ointment for the blisters, potions to ease pain and induce sleep and various other lotions and medications that she kept ready in a large basket that she always took with her to the sick.

"Why the devil have I been called out here?" Sabatin's exasperated tones boomed up the stairs to Frédérick's servant standing at the top of the flight. "Where is your master? Fetch him at once!"

Jasmin went forward to the balustrade, sending the servant back to the bedchamber, and looked down at her irate husband. It was instinctive for him to jerk his face away from the sight of her, a habit formed over the years of their marriage, but her next words stilled him midway.

"Frédérick has smallpox."

He turned as white as paper, the mottled veining of his pendulous cheeks standing out against his pale skin as if inked and his eyes widened in horror. All the footmen on duty by every door in the great hall heard her words and exchanged nervous glances. Two stood as if transfixed when Sabatin swung round to them and gestured fiercely.

"Get my guest out of his bed and into a carriage! I want him gone from here!"

Jasmin had already descended a few steps. "No! Frédérick shall not be moved! God alone knows what his chances are, but I will not have him die on the road. This is not Versailles!"

Sabatin, ignoring her, mistook his servants' failing to jump to his orders, not realising immediately that their fear of infection was greater than their awe of him. "Take no notice of Madame la Duchesse! Obey me! Now! At once, damn you!"

He struck out at them with his cane and they scattered, not towards the stairs but in the direction of the kitchens, such panic in them that the rest of the footmen on duty bolted from their posts and followed suit, leaving him and Jasmin alone in the great hall. He stood leaning on his cane and glaring up at her, swearing under his breath. His colour had surged back on the force of his rage, reaching an ugly purple. From the ballroom several salons away there came the sounds of music and jollity, suddenly incongruous in view of the disaster that had befallen the château.

"Go and tell our guests to go home, Sabatin," she said evenly. "The longer they stay under our roof the greater their danger. Let them leave by the ballroom doors onto the terrace. I don't want anyone to come into this quarter of the house."

To her astonishment, instead of turning to make his way back to the ballroom he limped swiftly across the hall and wrenched the entrance door wide. As he went stamping out into the night she heard him shout for his carriage. He was losing no time in getting away from the infection himself, caring nothing for anyone else.

She ran back up to the landing and along to her bedchamber. In the anteroom she paused breathlessly. Her maid in attendance had sprung up from a chair in the bedchamber beyond and Jasmin indicated that a distance be kept between them.

"Don't come near me. I want you to go down to the ballroom and seek out Brigadier Cloquet. Tell him that Colonel de Valverde has smallpox and ask him to get the guests to leave without arousing panic. As a military man he should manage that well. Also let him advise the servants to stay where they are and not to leave. If any of them have been infected the disease will only be carried further afield, even to their families if they should go home."

Her maid, although scared, kept her head. "Yes, madame. Is there anything else I can do?"

"Yes. Throw one of the simple calico gowns I use for nursing out to me and later put out others. Then stay away from this floor and see that everybody else does. Trays can be left at the foot of the stairs."

In the sickroom she had to get Frédérick's valet to unlace the back of her gown and then she changed behind a screen. After donning a large apron she reemerged to begin her fight for Frédérick's life, thankful as she had been many times before that her mother's own good nursing had brought her through an attack of this awful disease in her childhood and given her the immunity to care for so many others. The odds were always against her, but she had been successful on many occasions and even those who could not be saved had their suffering eased by her constant watchfulness and gentle attention when even their closest kin would not come near. Already the blisters, which could leave such disfiguring scars, were beginning to cover Frédérick's face and body, making him groan with pain and fever.

"I always thought I should die in battle," he croaked with a brave attempt at humour, grateful for the soothing of the lotion she was dabbing on his scorching face.

She smiled at him. "So you shall," she said lightly in the same vein. "Just let me get you through this inconvenience first."

She fought hard for him, the first twenty-four hours being crucial. The château was strangely silent after all the guests had left. According to the valet, who talked over the balustrade with those brave enough to bring trays into the hall, many of the domestic staff had fled, spurning the advice that had been given. In her experience it would be a few days before it became apparent if Frédérick had infected anyone else during his sojourn, it being singularly fortunate that he had not mingled in the crowded ballroom.

In spite of all her efforts, Frédérick died before the week

was out. She had no chance to mourn him, for she was called to the stable loft where his sergeant, who had ridden to the château with him, was showing the first symptoms. In the days that followed, the disease scythed through the château's own coachmen, grooms and stable boys. Indoors, two maids and one of the chefs succumbed. News reached her that a laundry maid, daughter to one of the tenants, had gone home in fright and there were cases there.

The château became a hospital. She rounded up a few survivors of the disease in previous years on the estate, ordering them to carry all the sick into her home where in the staff sleeping quarters, cleared of everything except beds, she nursed and cared for them all. At the height of the epidemic, when she could hardly keep on her feet through tiredness, her helpers far too few in number, she was told that the master had returned on horseback. She hurried down a corridor to the great hall, intent on sending him away from the fresh infection that had occurred, but at her first sight of him she saw there was no need.

He had staggered into the house, leaving the door open, and stood swaying like a drunken man on his feet, lacking the strength to take another step on his own. His face was swollen with a terrible rash, which she recognised instantly as the most virulent form of smallpox. Then he spoke to her for the first time in the many years of their marriage, his plea utterly desperate.

"For mercy's sake, help me!"

She made no move, staring at him with loathing. If he had not spoken to her she would have gone forward and helped him to bed as she had many others she had nursed in the past weeks. But he had chosen to break his monstrous silence at last out of his own self-centred fear. Her thoughts went back to their wedding journey and his stony silence and cruel notes when she was as wretched as he, just a young girl alone and homesick and afraid. Then there was his endless brutality to her in their marriage bed, inflicted in that fiendish dumbness. All the slights, humiliations and needless malevolence began to drum in her brain, making her temples throb. He had kept her from her mother's deathbed and earlier destroyed the letters that would have eased her misery and which she would have treasured to this day, links with the parents who had loved her and the home where she had known nothing but kindness. Through him she had been denied the daily joy of watching her own child grow to womanhood. Something seemed to snap in her head.

"Get out!"

He glared at her and tried to assert himself, the sweat running down his disfigured face. "I'm master here!"

"Not any more."

With a surge of his old temper he clenched a fist and shook it at her, knowing the bell-rope was too far from him to be reached without crawling there. In a cracked, hoarse voice, he shouted for the hall servants and his valet. "Landelle! Froment! Allard!"

"They can't hear you. They're all dead, poor men." She saw that her rigid expression was beginning to alarm him.

"Jasmin! I beg you," he exclaimed beseechingly. "Forgive the past. I'll make up for everything if you'll only do your duty towards me now."

"My duty?" She looked scornful. "I owe you nothing."

He blustered, wishing he could get his hands about her throat and force her to do his will as he had done many times in the past. "Damnation! Have you no pity in you? It took my last strength to stay in the saddle to get here. See me up to bed. I can't get there alone."

"I give you a choice. Take the staircase or the door."

He groaned deeply and with effort reeled across to the foot of the flight, grabbing the newel in time to save himself from falling, his fevered colour reaching a dark crimson. With relief he saw her go to the door and close it. Watching her expectantly, he put out an arm in readiness to loop around her shoulders. Instead of coming to him, she turned in the direction of the corridor through which she had first appeared and set off down it at a brisk pace out of his sight. Panic seized him.

"Don't leave me! Come back, you bitch! Jasmin!"

She paused for a few moments to listen to him calling to her in terror and desperation. If he had whispered her name just once during the dark times she had known with him she would never have left him now. With a satisfied tilt of her head she continued on her way.

Half an hour later two able-bodied servants went at her orders to carry him up to bed. He had collapsed a third of the way up the flight and lay in a raging fever, not knowing where he was.

She nursed him herself. He was soon little more than a solid mass of suppurating pustules that overlapped and hardened into huge scabs. His body blackened, giving off a sickening stench, and he lay like a rotting corpse for ten days before death released him. As she pulled the sheet up to cover his unrecognisable features she had one thought in her head. She was free!

Her first move was to find a way of sending a letter to Violette that would hold no risk of contagion. Milk and other comestibles were delivered outside the gates and were collected when those who had brought them were a safe distance away. She stood well within the gates when the next delivery was made and asked the dairyman to fetch her a clerk from the village. This was done and she dictated her letter at a shout, for the clerk had been nervous about coming and stood far away. The message was brief, just explaining the situation and letting Violette know that as soon as the current epidemic was over her mother would be coming to take her away from the farm into a new life and that nothing should ever come between them again. As Jasmin returned to the house she pictured happily Violette's joy upon learning that all danger was past. The girl would be as impatient as she for the day of their special reunion to dawn.

Jasmin wore no black for Sabatin, apart from the day of the funeral, which she felt was his due. In her own mind she believed that with his inflated ideas of his own importance he would have preferred her to be predominantly in white, which was the colour of royal mourning in the House of Bourbon, a kind of magpie splendour prevailing at Versailles at such times. The village priest, although he had never had smallpox, conducted the service in the château's own chapel and saw Sabatin to rest in the family mausoleum. He had been equally fearless in praying by the bedsides of the sick and administering last rites to the dying. As there had been no more fresh cases she knew thankfully that he had come through the epidemic unscathed.

At last the château could become habitable for all to enter again. Linen, mattresses and clothing, including the handsome gown Jasmin had worn so briefly at the ball, were burnt together with the hangings and draperies from

Sabatin's bedchamber, its rugs and carpets. Everywhere was scrubbed and aired, all the windows standing wide to the soft scents of summer. It was then that Jasmin's energy was finally sapped. She fell into bed and slept for hours of heavy, dreamless sleep.

She awakened to a sensation of being reborn. A whole new lease on life was before her. Most wonderful of all was that soon Violette would be with her. She would entertain lavishly and give her daughter the happy time that should be every young girl's right. There would be no arranged marriage since the need for it had gone and due to the outbreak of smallpox the marriage contract with the young lawyer had not been signed. Violette could make her own choice and, if another plan went well, not in this locality.

Jasmin wrote that same day to the King, asking his permission to return in her widowhood to Château Satory. She knew from Frédérick that Sabatin had tried in vain to get back to Versailles, but she felt that in spite of all the years that had passed Louis would remember her and give her case special consideration. It was with high hopes that she despatched her appeal.

Sabatin had left her nothing in his will, but with his death she was able to draw at last on the money and investments that her mother had bequeathed her, even though Château Satory and its own supportive funds remained out of reach until the King showed clemency.

It was never to be clear how or where Frédérick had contracted smallpox, but neither had it been in Louis XIV's time when the Grand Dauphin had died of the same disease, the outbreaks always insidious and unexpected. There were certainly no cases among Frédérick's soldiers at camp, but he had done some visiting en route to Château Valverde and most likely had been infected somewhere along the way.

Sabatin's heir had notified Jasmin that he had no wish to live at his ancestral home. The young man was established at Court and wished to be nowhere else, which also meant that no visits from him need ever be expected. He was agreeable that Jasmin should live on at the château until the end of her days. All he asked in return was that the estate should continue to be run on the same satisfactory lines as before, and the seigniorial rights and income be paid into his coffers twice a year. Jasmin smiled to herself as she read the letter, thinking how he would have to settle for other arrangements once she had heard from the King.

Never had she prepared with greater joy for a journey to the Govins' farm and Violette. This time they would be coming home together! A bedchamber with one of the best views had been redecorated and rehung with new draperies and the girl's measurements given to a dressmaker for several new gowns to be delivered prior to her arrival. Already many pairs of bright-heeled shoes in silk, velvet and satin had come from Périgueux to make a multicoloured row by the wall of the dressing room.

Jasmin was never again to inhale the scent of honeysuckle without remembering the morning when she went light-footed into her carriage to leave for the farm. The blossoms had thrown forth their petals in abundance that day and were thick with bees. She had to brush a bee from her sleeve out through the open window, the sun as warm on her face as the radiance within her.

The hard dry roads enabled the coachman to keep up a good pace throughout the two days' journey, cutting a few hours off the normal time. When she arrived at the farmhouse Madame Govin did not come out into the sun to meet her with Violette at her side, which was usual, always depriving her of a reunion with her daughter on her own. Instead, the woman stood back in the shadows inside, holding the door which itself gave into the long living room cum kitchen of the farmhouse. There was no sign of Violette.

Jasmin swept over the threshold bursting into happy chatter of having come as her letter had promised to take Violette home with her. At first the interior seemed dark after the brilliance of the sunshine and, looking about for her daughter, she did not notice at first the agitated workings of the woman's face.

"Where's Violette?" she enquired buoyantly. "Is she on an errand? I suppose her boxes are packed? I want to leave with her without delay."

A snivelling sound from the woman made her turn sharply. Madame Govin had her apron pressed to her eyes, her head bowed as she pointed to the unopened letter lying on a side table. "Something terrible has happened, madame."

Jasmin felt as if her whole body had turned to ice. "What is it?" she demanded in a whisper, taut with dread. "Is my daughter ill?"

"No. Far from it. She has run away. Your letter came after she had gone."

At first Jasmin thought the scream of shock she uttered had been audible and then realised it had simply been trapped inside her. Her voice came out icy and expressionless. "How long ago?"

"Five weeks. Nearly six." Madame Govin was sobbing noisily, her words twisted on shrill, discordant notes. Jasmin wrenched the apron from the woman's clasp, forcing a face-to-face confrontation, her fury bursting forth.

"Why did you not send word to my banker? You know he would have made a personal visit to me in a dire emergency." In her stress she forgot there had still been smallpox at the château at that time when, even if there had been a message, it could not have been delivered.

"We kept expecting to find her. My husband and his nephew went far afield. They even searched among the camp followers of the army on manoeuvres not far from here, but nobody had seen her. It's been my hope every day that I'll look out the window and there she will be, coming up the path again." She wiped her eyes with the back of her hand. "I can't tell you the misery I've been through."

"What made her leave? There must have been a reason." Suspicion dawned. "Did anything untoward happen?"

Madame Govin flung up her head, taking refuge in defiance. "Nothing that wasn't your fault in the first place! You terrified her with your talk of incarceration in a convent and all the rest of it if your husband found out about her. It preyed on her mind. She had been difficult before, but that made her ten times as wilful. You drove her into running away."

"I think you are trying to find a scapegoat for the results of your lack of discipline and incompetence!"

"Don't abuse me! Do you think I hold any respect for a woman like you? I wonder if you realise just how long it is since you visited your own child? Naturally she felt abandoned and reached a point when she thought you were never coming again."

"She could never think that from the many letters I sent her."

"Excuses!" There was a sneer in Madame Govin's expression.

"Is that what you put into her mind?"

There was an uneasy shrug. "There was no telling what she was thinking about in these months gone by."

"You mean she changed in some way?"

"I've told you already that, due to you, she had become thoroughly unpredictable and wayward."

"I think you meant something more." Jasmin's earlier suspicions returned to become conviction.

"Very well. I'll tell you. I thought to save Violette from further fear of your husband with a plan of my own."

"What was that?"

The woman jerked back her shoulders in an aggressive stance. "Recently I put it to her that a marriage with my husband's nephew would solve everything."

Furious disbelief flooded Jasmin's face. "Then you would have had her under your roof for the rest of your life! And she has never liked that uncouth lad! No wonder she ran away!" Struggling for self-control, she dropped into the nearest chair and brushed her fingertips across her forehead as if to clear her head. "Sit down, Madame Govin. This dispute is not going to find Violette. Every minute that goes by is another that is probably taking her still farther away. I want you to tell me anything you can think of, no matter how irrelevant it may seem, that might give the slightest clue as to where I can start a full-scale search for her."

Jasmin's first move upon arriving home again was to contact Brigadier Cloquet. As once she had intended to confide in Frédérick she told him the whole story, knowing she could trust him. She gave him the little portrait of Violette that had hung in Madame Gérard's salon and he set out to organise a search for the girl, putting experienced individuals to the task, Jasmin having impressed on him to spare no expense. Her mention of the foster father making enquiries among the camp followers of the troops on manoeuvres led him to make his own investigations there. Officers and soldiers alike were questioned and shown the portrait. Nothing came to light.

At the height of these anxious days Jasmin received a communication from Versailles. It was sent by a Minister of the Council on the King's behalf and not only did it reject outright her application to leave Château Valverde, but it reminded her of the heavy penalties that befell those who broke the royal will. She broke down in her disappointment and despair, wondering if Louis had ever seen her letter or if he had never forgiven her for her marriage, even though it had been beyond her power to prevent it. At the present time this fresh blow was more than she knew how to bear.

In Violette's disappearance there was one clue that was overlooked by everybody. It was forgotten that a small band of Swiss halberdiers, who had been attached to the rest of the troops for the manoeuvres, had departed ahead to join the household guards at Versailles before Brigadier Cloquet began making his enquiries. Among them a certain dashing, onyx-eyed, black-haired captain in his mid-twenties could have told exactly what had happened to Violette and where she was now. Not that he would have said, for he was not a man troubled by conscience, and his fellow officers would also have kept their own counsel. They were clannish as foreign mercenaries of the same nationality were inclined to be; they were billeted together, drilled together and fought side by side whether in war or on manoeuvres. If Capitaine Léonard Vanneau chose to have a pretty girl in his quarters it was nobody else's business, least of all that of the French, for whom they had little liking beyond the pay received.

Léonard Vanneau had come across Violette when riding along a forest path one day. She was gathering kindling, wearing some fine cream leather gloves to protect her hands, which marked her out at once from an ordinary country girl. There was also a certain quality of looks, a refinement of features that could have come from breeding, and the fichu and sash that trimmed her calico gown were of silk. He judged her to be the daughter of some prosperous farmer and supposed she lived nearby. Most important of all he saw the chance of some sport, for he recognised unerringly a streak of recklessness in her comparable to that in his own nature, which had taken him from a small Swiss town and set him on the dangerous road to adventure.

"What's your name, mademoiselle?" he asked with a grin, wheeling his dappled horse about to block her path. She looked up at him provocatively under her curiously flecked lashes, ripe-mouthed with a slender, high-breasted figure, her waist no more than a handspan.

"Tell me yours first," she challenged.

He told her and then she still would not give her own, dodging away into the thickets where he had no choice but to dismount and chase after her on foot, stooping under low-slung branches and being lashed by bushes. She led him such a game that he became hopelessly lost and did not realise she had deliberately deserted him until he heard the hoofbeats of his horse being ridden away.

He had lost all sense of direction. As far as he could see there was nothing but gloomy forest on all sides, and he cursed and shouted as he tried in vain to find a path that would at least guide him somewhere. When the sun set he was resigning himself in angry exasperation to a night among the tree roots when he caught the glimmer of a lantern. With a yell of exhilaration he stumbled towards it in the darkness, shouting all the time to ensure the bearer of the light did not go away. Fortunately whoever it was remained stationary. Not until he came within a few feet of the lantern did he see that it had been hung on a branch and there was nobody there. The girl had fooled him yet again. Once more he let forth a stream of curses, thudding a fist against the trunk of the tree. Then he heard her giggle.

In spite of himself he began to laugh. "Where are you? You've played a good joke on me. Now show a little mercy."

She emerged into the lantern's glow wearing a gown of ruby velvet that must have come from Lyons or Paris. Her face was merry, her cheeks flushed with excitement. "Don't be so easily trapped another time, Capitaine Vanneau. Had I been an enemy agent you would not have left this forest alive!"

"Who are you?" His voice was low, for he was intrigued and fascinated by her.

"Violette Picard. Now I'll take you back to your horse. It's a fine mount. I enjoyed my ride."

"Not so fast." He caught her by the wrist and pulled her to him. "I deserve some compensation for the discomfort

I've endured." Then he released his hold with a yelp as she drove the point of a kitchen knife into the back of his hand, making a bead of blood appear as bright in the lantern light as her velvet gown. He sucked it, glaring at her. "You little vixen! Where did you learn that trick?"

She tilted her chin. "Through necessity. My foster parents have an oaf of a nephew they want me to marry. They think him such an innocent. They don't know I've had to keep him at bay for most of my life. Fortunately he's almost as scared of my foster mother as he is of me now and that has given me some protection."

"So your maidenhead is still your own?"

She gave him a deep look that fired him through. "I'm entirely my own person. People have talked to me, ordered me about, lavished gifts on me and thought always to mould me into a domestic creature to be wife to some man of their choice. I've always wanted more than that. Even when my mother spoke to me of a good marriage I knew it would be a kind of imprisonment. Oh, no! I want freedom. Not bonds to tie me for the rest of my life." She took the lantern from the branch. "Come along. Don't dawdle or you'll get lost again."

Grinning, he shook his head as he followed her. It would not be hard to believe she was a witch. Already she had cast a spell over him. When they reached his horse he saw that she had groomed it after her ride, its mane in braids and tied with ribbons as a final joke. He swung himself up into the saddle and looked down at her with amused eyes.

"You made a captive of me in the forest and a dandy of my war-horse. What more have you up your sleeve?"

Her smile, enigmatic and alluring, showed she was a born coquette, a natural enticer of men, making his blood race. "That remains to be discovered by anyone who dares to take the risk."

"I want to see you again."

She shrugged carelessly as if that was of no importance to her and then handed the lantern up to him. "Take this and follow the path in that direction." She pointed ahead. "You'll find yourself on the edge of the camp."

Without another word she began to disappear the other way into the darkness. He shouted after her: "Tomorrow! Meet me here by the oak. At the same time." When she did not even glance back to show she had heard, he stood in the stirrups and cupped a hand to his mouth. "Violette! Don't disappoint me!"

She had gone from sight. With a sigh, uncertain whether she would tease him again by not coming, he turned his horse about and retraced the route that took him back to where he had started out that morning. He was ravenously hungry.

Violette, running home through the darkness, clapped the palms of her hands together in a gesture of triumph, full of silent laughter. She had never supposed it would be as easy to put a ring through the nose of a man of the world as it was to tempt and reject the local country lads. And what a man! A hard face and restless eyes, heavy muscles in his thighs and shoulders like a rock. Of course she would be there tomorrow, but she would hide and wait until he was on the point of despair.

The next day she was there ahead of time and concealed herself behind the huge trunk of a tree. The wait was in reality as long for her as for him, she with her spine resting back against the bark, he pacing up and down the dusty path, his tethered horse cropping the grass nearby. Then, choosing her moment, she sidled around the trunk when his back was turned and when he looked up again she was there. She observed that momentarily he seemed quite drunk with relief, showing how effective her elusiveness had been. This time she made no protest when he pulled her into his arms, being as eager as he for their first kiss, and as their mouths fused she clawed into the side curls of his white wig and held his head hard until, gasping for breath, she pushed him away again. Her wickedly dancing eyes told him that she did not intend that he, or anyone else, should ever get the upper hand of her, not even in a kiss.

"Tell me more about yourself," he urged when she evaded his attempt to recapture her again. "Who are your foster parents? Where do you live? There's so much I want to know."

She took him by the hand and led him to a grassy grove thick with wildflowers. There she had set out a picnic on a cloth with little cakes, cheese, bread, some fruit and a bottle of wine.

"Sit down," she instructed, her imperious manner something he would never have tolerated in any other woman,

"I'm not going to let you starve all day as you did yesterday. It's your turn to talk first. Afterwards I may tell you more about myself. It depends on whether I think you've told me the truth or not. You're not French, at least not from these parts. I can judge that by your accent. Where are you from?" She settled herself on the grass, modestly arranging her skirt, which today was of costly silk patterned with rosebuds. "From Provence? Or perhaps the north on the borders of Holland?"

"I'm from Switzerland—from the city of Berne." He sat down opposite her, the picnic cloth between them, and watched her pour him a glass of wine. Then, all unwittingly, with his next breath he said the words that were to change the whole course of her life. "At the end of the month I leave with the rest of my countrymen for Versailles. We are to join the Royal Guard."

"Versailles!" Her voice trembled with excitement. "You are really going there!"

He saw he had impressed her at last and gestured boastfully. "We Swiss protect the two most powerful men in the world, the Pope and the French King."

She had recovered herself and made a little grimace. "It's only tradition. You're no braver as soldiers than anyone else."

He was outraged at the slight. "If you were a man . . ."

She laughed mischievously, holding out the glass of wine. "If I were, you wouldn't be picnicking with me in the first place. Taste the wine. It's good. I took the best in the cellar, one that my foster father has been saving for a feast day."

He could not hold out against her and with a grin he took the wine, raising it in salute to her before sipping it. Then he nodded approvingly and leaned back to rest on one elbow. "I think you would have made a splendid mercenary. You certainly know how to loot."

She appreciated the joke and their conversation continued in a similar vein, lighthearted and merry, while he told her of his home, his family, his travels and his past campaigns. She in her turn appeared to tell him a great deal while keeping back her dread of her mother's husband and the power he held. She did not want Léonard to suspect for an instant how desperately afraid she was of that unknown man. Tante Govin had made out that Jasmin was making excuses not to come and see her, but she knew it was far more than that. She could read between the lines. Fear was keeping Jasmin away. Her husband was with her all the time now, watching and listening and perhaps waiting to pounce. It was likely he was suspicious already. That was why it had been impossible to write to Jasmin about Tante Govin's mad idea that she should marry that clottish heir to the farm, because to set it down on paper was to invite the chance of it falling into that evil husband's hands.

The picnic was over. When she had packed what was left into the basket she let Léonard draw her down onto the grass beside him and kiss her again. She had put a brake on herself and kept detached, allowing him to caress her breasts through the silk of her bodice, but nothing more. Too much depended on her not losing her head. He had shown her a way of escape. When he left for Versailles she was determined to go with him. There was no more exciting place in the world, the centre of pleasure and fashion and romance. It was where she had longed to be ever since her mother had first talked of it and now the chance lay within her grasp.

She met him every day. Léonard could not understand why she should prove so difficult to seduce. He was wild for her. There were times when he felt desire vibrating through her and yet she continued to keep him at bay, tantalising him with small, sweet favours that made him groan with lust. Time was slipping away. When he was apart from her she filled his thoughts as if he were a love-sick boy, making him angry in his yearning and determined that at their next meeting he would have his way with her.

On the last evening he discovered why she had kept him on a string. Just when he had first caught sight of her white thighs and all he wanted from her she threw herself passionately across his chest, her petticoats billowing back into place.

"Take me with you tomorrow! Let me go with you to Versailles. You'll never regret it, I promise you."

He grabbed a handful of her fair curls and jerked her face back to look into her eyes. "So that's what you wanted all along. Why didn't you tell me before? I'd have struck the same bargain with you."

She hid her thoughts behind her glittering eyes. He was not to be trusted and would have promised anything to get his way and then leave her. Now she had him and she would keep him for as long as it suited her. Versailles would be full of handsome noblemen. "You can strike it now instead. Do I go with you, or don't I?"

"You know you do." Affection and admiration for her verve mingled in his voice. "Be ready at the end of the path at dawn tomorrow. I command the company and can arrange for you to travel in a wagon. That will also get you away unseen." He gave her a little kiss and then regarded her speculatively. "I'll expect a lot from you in return."

"You shall have it."

He crushed her to him, devouring her mouth, yet still she held out. Their treaty began on the morrow and until then he must wait. She was not going to be tricked at the last minute.

He never regretted his decision to take her with him. She was a revelation, such passion in her that she was like a wild cat in their lovemaking. He and his fellow officers, the manoeuvres and the camp behind them, were not expected to spend their nights in discomfort. The accommodation selected was always of the best, sometimes in a good hostelry and more often in a château where the host welcomed the diversion of offering hospitality to those gentlemen of Switzerland who were shortly to protect the King's life.

Léonard passed Violette off as his bride on these occasions and nobody suspected otherwise, for she had brought her best gowns with her and was given the services of a maid wherever they stayed. She knew she looked like a lady born, especially when escorted by their current host into supper, Léonard following with their hostess and the rest of the officers behind. If she was uncertain of anything at table, Léonard would always help her out with a signal or a glance and she soon accustomed herself to everything, getting a taste of the kind of luxurious living she had always craved.

She had been disappointed that the journey was not directly to Versailles, being impatient for her first sight of it, but Léonard had to keep three meeting points with other parties of Swiss halberdiers in order that they could march on Versailles together. Inevitably there were delays and what should have taken a week extended into two and finally into three. By that time they were only at Orléans and still a considerable distance away.

It was here that the accommodation was least to Violette's liking. They were in a busy, noisy hostelry with travellers coming and going all the time. Léonard, bored with waiting for the last party to catch up with them, took to gaming with some keen gamblers among his fellows. Occasionally travellers with time to spare would join the table. Violette knew he was losing money, the cards constantly against him, and one night when he came late to bed and the worse for drink she upbraided him for his stupidity, her reasons entirely selfish, for she had no money of her own and did not want him to become debt-ridden to her disadvantage.

He gave her a thunderous look. "Don't run the gauntlet with me," he warned dangerously. "You're not my wife."

"Nor do I ever intend to be!" she spat back. In that instant they realised how little they really liked each other, he having found her to be far more ill-tempered than he had ever suspected, she despising the weaker side of his character that led him into improvident ways. They had nothing in common. Yet her spell on him was such that he could not get enough of her and she kept her part of the bargain.

When the remaining band of Swiss halberdiers eventually arrived, there was carousing among the officers in celebration of the reunion. Later some of them, including Léonard, settled to cards, drawing in a prosperous middle-aged silk merchant on his way to Rouen and a couple of well-to-do younger men. Violette developed a headache from the drunken singing and became bored with watching the gaming. She was too inexperienced with cards herself to join in and the stakes were high. For once Léonard was winning and in jubilant spirits. She put a hand on his shoulder as she leaned forward behind his chair to tell him she was tired and going to bed. He caught her fingers in his and drew her hand to his lips and placed a kiss in the palm.

"I'll wake you by pouring my golden winnings on the bed, my sweeting," he boasted exuberantly.

As someone opened the door for her she looked back over her shoulder into the noisy low-beamed room thick with pipe smoke, bright with uniforms, the atmosphere heavy with the smell of ale and wine. She was well pleased with Léonard's turn of fortune, knowing he would be generous to her. His craggy features were planed and shadowed in the golden aura of the three-branched pewter candlestick set on the gaming table, his lace-edged cravat loosened around his strong neck for ease in the excitement of the game, and his ruby ring sparkling on the middle finger of his broad-backed hand as he cut the pack of cards. He must have sensed her female appreciation of his extreme maleness in that masculine setting, because he looked up sharply and gave her his old infectious grin, acknowledging her witchlike smile. In that moment good relations were entirely restored between them after the strain of the past days.

It was the last time she was ever to see him. Shortly before dawn she stirred, disturbed by whispering and what sounded like his baggage, which had been packed for departure, being dragged from the room. But she was half dreaming and would have lost herself in sleep again if memory had not risen to the surface with the click of the bolt on the door being shot home.

"Léonard," she murmured drowsily, "how much did you win?"

"He won nothing," replied a stranger's voice.

She sat bolt upright with a gasp, pushing her hair back out of her eyes, and stared aghast at the silk merchant from the gaming table downstairs, a thick-set, stern-faced man in a brown wig. "Get out!" she shrieked in outrage. He was already in his shirt-sleeves, his brocade coat cast across a chair. "How dare you come in here!"

"I have every right," he replied drily, unfastening the silver buttons of his silk waistcoat. "Luck turned against your Swiss officer. He lost everything to me. The last stake he put up was you. You're mine now, mademoiselle."

She gave a terrible wail like a wounded she-wolf, chilling his blood. Then she threshed wildly to and fro across the bed, sobbing hysterically and clawing the linen to shreds.

Sixteen

Jasmin never gave up hoping for news of Violette. Anxiety was a permanent ache within her that nothing could dispel, but no trace ever came to light. Her daughter's natal days were particularly poignant times and when five of these anniversaries had gone by she had an eerie experience. It happened when she was hurrying through one of the smaller salons, having forgotten the time while in the garden and in haste to change before going to visit her local fan-making workshop. One of the mirrors hanging by the double doors ahead reflected an image she registered immediately as being that of Henriette.

"Merciful Heaven!" she exclaimed, clapping a hand to her heart and coming to a halt before seeing that it was herself who stood there, the illusion having come and gone. Much shaken, she went slowly to the mirror. There was no physical likeness between her and the long-dead woman, but the experience brought home to her the realisation that in many ways she had become Henriette, a lonely woman without a man or child, the resident concierge of a property that would never be hers.

She regarded her reflection almost fearfully, depressed that she had slipped into the same ageing mould, which was what she had recognised in that chilling instant. Slowly she smoothed her fingers back over her face as women do when trying to recall the look of youth, lifting the contours of cheek and chin grown softer with the years. She had kept her figure but it was fuller than when she was young and whenever her hair was free of the white powder dusted on for social occasions, grey threads now predominated in her once brown tresses. Nothing could change a good facial structure, which was fortunate, and she was skilled in the use of cosmetics. Perhaps her deep violet eyes, shadowed with secret sorrow, revealed more than anything else what she had been through in her life.

Men still found her attractive. She had had several proposals of marriage from widowers, all pleasant, kindly men, and it was a measure of her tactfulness that she had not lost their friendship by turning them down. If she could have confided her innermost longings to any one of them, she would have said that all she wanted was to be reunited with her daughter and to go home again to her place of birth.

"Château Satory!" She breathed its name aloud. With it came a huge upsurge of homesickness that made her clench her fists and drive them into the sides of her waist. She threw back her head on the pain of yearning. It had always been with her, but she had deliberately subdued and crushed it down long ago, needing to eliminate one source of misery in order to cope with everything else. Now that a single unguarded thought had released it, letting it take wing, there would be no caging it again.

She swung herself wearily away from the mirror and leaned against the wall. If some miracle could have transported her home she would still have kept in close touch with the Govins on the slim chance that Violette might reappear at the farm. It was thoroughly unlikely unless she was married and secure against any schemes. Even then, had the girl ever been fond enough of her foster parents in the first place to want to see them again? Or her own mother for that matter? Had Violette ever really cared for anyone except herself? It was a bitter thought, but one that returned time and time again.

For several days afterwards Jasmin was restless and almost physically ill with her longing to go home. If only there was someone with influence at Court who could intercede personally with the King on her behalf. But she knew nobody, for she had been too long away. Then suddenly, in worrying the matter, a name came to her and with such impact that she could not understand why she had not considered it before. It was not that of a minister, not a courtier, not Michel even if he should still be painting royal portraits, but a woman who had won the King's heart completely. She was little Reinette, who had once skipped as a child into Marguerite's fan-shop on the Champs-Élysées, her dimples twinkling and as light on her feet as thistledown.

"Oh, Reinette!" Jasmin exclaimed aloud. "You could work this miracle for me!"

She ran at once to sit down and write to the Marquise de Pompadour. On the strength of that past acquaintance, which she could not expect the woman to remember, she made her plea, pouring out her longing to go home again and asking nothing more than that this should be granted to her after over three decades of exile. She sealed the letter and despatched it by personal messenger.

Three weeks later she returned from a visit to one of her fan-making workshops to find that two letters were waiting for her. Her heart began to pound when she picked up the top one and turned it over to see Madame de Pompadour's seal, her coat of arms depicting griffins and three castles. The second letter looked equally important and she caught her breath when she recognised the royal seal.

With violently shaking hands she opened it to discover that it was an official document revoking the banishment incurred automatically through her marriage to the late Duc de Valverde and restoring her in her widowhood to all rights as a free citizen of France. It bore Louis's own signature. She kissed it, wetting it with her tears and laughing softly with happiness at the same time. Home! She was going home to Château Satory and she would never leave it again. Never!

As soon as she had composed herself after reading the revocation through several times over, she wiped the moisture from her eyes and opened the other letter. The Marquise had written in a warm and friendly manner, saying how pleased she was to have been of help in the termination of Jasmin's banishment and that she well remembered her visits to the fan-shop owned by the late Baronne Picard. She closed by expressing a wish that Jasmin should call on her at Versailles at the earliest possible moment in order that they could renew their acquaintanceship.

It was more than Jasmin had dared hope for when she had sent off her appeal. Not only was she to return home, but she had been given an entrée to Versailles by the most influential woman at Court!

Although she set to work at once to organise everything for her leaving, it took well over a month before she could get away. She had to await the arrival of whoever was to take her place and, to her relief, a most amiable couple with five daughters arrived. They were the Comte and Comtesse de Valverde, grand in title but impoverished country relatives who had never been to Court and previously had eked out an existence with a small vineyard. As soon as the Comte viewed his new home he was able to see vast possibilities in the rich land of the estate. A closer inspection of the soil convinced him that large vineyards planted there would yield abundant crops, guaranteeing work for all the tenants for years to come. His wife had been used to looking after the sick and poor in their previous rural abode and was full of reassurance.

"Just let me have the names of those in need of extra food and care. As for the school, my second daughter had pupils of her own before coming here and will gladly take charge."

Jasmin sold the fan-making workshops. In each case she let them go reasonably and individually to her managers, knowing that in their hands working conditions would continue to the high standard she had always maintained. When all was done and the Govins had been informed of her change of address she left Château Valverde forever and set forth on the road to Versailles in the coach that had been her father's last gift to her.

As the long journey neared its end she could have bypassed the town of Versailles to reach her old home, but she told her coachman to drive by way of the Château.

This road approached it from the west and as her coach rolled over the cobbles of the Place d'Armes she saw again the great gilded seat of government, home of the King of France, its ever open gates seeming to emphasise the welcome back that had been expressed in the letter from Madame de Pompadour. As always, the vast spread of the Cour Royale thronged with people and the comings and goings of elegant carriages and humbler trade wagons. The sun picked out the rich garments of the courtiers and their ladies as if playing on the facets of scattered jewels. All about them the common folk scurried on errands of delivery or some other business while those with time to spare gaped about in their sightseeing and stared at the central balcony of the East Front behind which lay the King's own apartment, hoping for a glimpse of him. Everything was to Jasmin as if she had never been away, only the changes of fashion marking the length of her absence. Even from a distance she was able to see that at Court the women's side hoops, known as panniers, had spread out to an enormous lateral width, far wider than anything she possessed. She would have to call in a Parisian dressmaker before she could present herself to the Marquise.

Then she was being carried on down the Avenue de Paris in the direction of her home and she looked out for the shop and other familiar landmarks, memories springing from every one. The last stretch of road was to her the longest of the whole journey. She sat forward eagerly as the green, gilt-tipped gates went past and there, at last, at the head of the long straight drive, lay Château Satory, its sandstone walls pale as a woman's skin, its balustraded roof rising like a finely wrought crown and its windows reflecting the foliage and blossoms of the well-kept park. The entrance door had been set wide at the first sight of her approach and a host of new servants came pouring out to make double lines flanking the flight of steps. After them came Lenore, who had grown plumper with the years, and she descended quickly to be the first to curtsey as the coach stopped. Jasmin alighted without a moment's delay.

"Pray allow me to welcome you back to Château Satory, madame." Lenore's round cheeks were scarlet with pleasure.

"I thank you." Jasmin's voice was choked. "This is a day I've long awaited."

"Everything has been made ready for your coming. I've taken the liberty of preparing the apartment for you that Baronne Picard once mentioned as being the first she ever occupied when she came to live here in her youth."

"You have done well, Lenore."

Jasmin hardly saw the servants as she went up the steps, nodding automatically in acknowledgement of their bows and bobs, her attention fixed ahead. In the entrance hall she flung out her arms as if to embrace the château in her homecoming, her skirts swirling over the central green star in the marble floor, her gaze rising upwards to the azure ceiling overhead with its lovely swoop of painted birds. She knew so much more about her home now than before she went away, for her mother had told her many things on that one visit to Château Valverde. It was in this very hall that her parents first met and yet at the time Marguerite had been on the brink of her passionate affair with Augustin Roussier for whom Laurent had built this splendid place. It was here that Huguenots had come for refuge in those terrible times of persecution and Marguerite herself had sheltered many of them after Augustin had gone with his wife to England. There was also the secret vault about which Jasmin had known nothing until her mother had disclosed its whereabouts to her and given her a duplicate key in case the day should ever come when she could use it. It was in her purse now.

She went first into the Crimson Salon to see again the rather formal portrait of her father, his face ruddy against the whiteness of his wig with its tie-back and three formal horizontal curls over each ear, his linen neckcloth neatly tied. Yet in spite of the severe pose, the kindliness in his grey eyes seemed directed straight at her as she stood gazing up at him, her hands clasped against her chest.

"I'm home, Papa," she whispered, blowing him a kiss from her fingertips. Then she turned to the connecting doors into the Ivory Salon. There, in an ornate frame above the fireplace, a young Marguerite sat with a half-open fan depicting Versailles held gracefully across her gold gauze lap. Jasmin was thankful that nothing had been changed and everything was more or less as it had been before she went away. Then, remembering Marguerite's revelations about the past, she went to the shadowed alcove on the far side of the room to study the portrait of Augustin Roussier.

She recalled it being replaced after a long absence following his death. In her flippant youth it had been simply a
likeness of someone unknown to her and of no interest.
Now that had changed. This was the man for whom her
father had built Château Satory, never suspecting then
that he himself would draw his last breath in it. It was an
arresting face, chiselled and black-browed, set off by the
shoulder-length curls of the period, a passionate glitter in
the narrow green eyes. She could fully comprehend how
her mother had loved such a man and even though fate
had turned against them Château Satory remained as evidence of all he had felt for her.

Priorities over, Jasmin began a full tour of the château,
her pace increasing steadily in her exhilaration. She
paused here and there to touch a well-remembered piece
of porcelain or to stroke her fingers lightly along the surface of some item of furniture. Eventually she bunched
her skirts in her hands to raise her hems and allow her
speed to be unimpeded as she darted along. She had the
oddest sensation that somehow she was linked to a homecoming like this before. Then it came to her that it was
when the King as a twelve-year-old boy had run through
the salons of Versailles, joyfully reacquainting himself with
the place he loved, and had come to rest on his back at her
feet in the Peace Salon.

Upstairs she entered her new apartment. She must have
mentioned to Lenore during those first dark days at Château Valverde how she had always wanted this particular
suite for herself and the woman had remembered. The
bedchamber with its south-facing windows was one of the
most charming in the château, its décor having been kept
to its original soft rose shades with drapes and bed-hangings of silver-threaded Lyonnaise silk. In the light of the
knowledge she had acquired Jasmin was convinced that
this had been the love haven of Augustin and Marguerite.
It certainly explained why her mother had always been
adamant about not letting her have it for her own use and
it had become quite a bone of contention between them.
She felt regret at the way she had pestered Marguerite,
sulking when honoured guests had been accommodated
there. Looking back, she wondered why her ears were
never boxed over it. Her mother had been remarkably
tolerant.

Suddenly she found herself having second thoughts about moving in here, not through any past associations but simply because the bedchamber seemed to demand a younger occupant, one with high hopes and romantic dreams and blissful optimism, the very essence of youth itself. She would take her late parents' apartment instead.

It was there that she found Michel Balaine's portrait of her. It was hanging directly opposite the canopied bed and she could see how her mother would have viewed it from the pillows. She moved closer to her own likeness. Had she really looked like that? Young and radiant with happiness shining out of her eyes. It aroused no sentiment in her. The sight of Michel's signature did not inspire her to touch it with her fingertips as she had caressed various items downstairs in her nostalgia for the past. This was different altogether. Michel had given her the most ecstatic period in her whole life and her love for him had been whole and complete, deep-rooted in that time and bearing no relation to anything that had happened before or since. The fact that he was Violette's father no longer held any significance. It had ceased at the moment of her daughter's birth.

There was a rustle of a linen apron in the doorway and she turned to see Lenore standing there with a tray of hot chocolate and little cakes. "I thought you might like some refreshment, madame."

Jasmin indicated with a smile of approval that it was welcome. "I've changed my mind about the Rose Suite," she said as she took the cup that had been poured for her. "These are to be my rooms. However, I don't wish to gaze on my own portrait and some other spot shall be found for it."

Violette's betrothal portrait, which had never fulfilled its purpose, replaced Jasmin's, which was rehung in a reading alcove in the library where she never glanced at it and few people other than the servants ever saw it. Had she been in need of money she would have sold it without the least compunction, for anything with Michel Balaine's signature fetched a high price, but her long-delayed inheritance had made her enormously wealthy. For a few weeks she spent lavishly, replenishing her stables, having redecorations carried out and ordering many new garments and pairs of high-heeled shoes.

Busy though she was, she set herself a task to which she allotted time each day. She had decided she would make a beautiful fan as a gift for Madame de Pompadour, a token of appreciation for the woman's kindness. Design had not been her forte, but when searching among her mother's fan-patterns she had found several motifs that had never been executed. The one she chose was a garland of flowers entwined with ribbons and pearls. Her old skill in setting jewels came back to her and she finished the fan in good time for the audience with Madame de Pompadour that had been arranged by letter for the following week.

The morning came when she set off for Versailles in full Court dress. Her panniers were in the latest width; her low-necked gown of maize *lustrine*, a ribbed weave in fine silk embroidered in gold, and her hair was powdered white. She had chosen to wear Marguerite's sapphire pendant and eardrops, which scintillated gloriously. Inevitably she was reminded of the last time she had left Château Satory for Versailles, never suspecting that over three decades were to pass before she would see it again.

At Versailles she was taken aback to discover that the Ambassadors' Staircase had been taken down to make space for an apartment for the King's daughter Princesse Adélaïde, and a new flight, far less imposing, called the King's Staircase, had been erected. Jasmin had no need of the stairs that day, because Madame de Pompadour no longer occupied an apartment on the second floor, but for the past four years had been granted one on the ground floor, a privilege usually accorded only to Princes of the Blood, for locations at Versailles were still according to rank. No bourgeoise had ever risen so high in a King's favour as little Reinette.

Jasmin entered the most elegant of apartments, soft clear greens or blue or lemon or peachy-pink on the walls, superb furnishings blending with an artistic clutter of exquisite knickknacks. There were lacquer boxes with little scenes on them, seals set with rubies and diamonds, chocolate boxes in rock crystal, carvings in ivory, silver medallions and more than one table covered with engraved precious stones. In the window a bird sang in a gilded cage and everywhere there were either porcelain flowers or vases and bowls overflowing with a profusion of fresh blooms that filled the air with their perfume and made polished surfaces dusty with pollen.

There were a number of fine paintings and Jasmin's attention was caught by one painted by François Boucher. A group of young men and women were gathered around a swing on which sat the central figure, swooping high in the air with satin skirt and petticoats aswirl. There was a marked resemblance to Violette that tore at Jasmin's heartstrings, although the face was rounder and softer and sentimentalised, far from the wilful expression and darting greed of the beautiful eyes that she remembered so well. Then she heard the tap of heels and turned to curtsey low to her benefactress, the painting and the strange likeness to her daughter forgotten.

Madame de Pompadour came to greet her warmly, exuding the goodwill and friendliness that were natural to her, a little dog scampering alongside. Lovely in a shade known as Pompadour rose with ruffles of lace, she wore a garland of tiny silk flowers about her slender neck, a fashion she had set, and on her wrist was a cameo bracelet of the King's head in profile.

"My dear Duchesse de Valverde! What a pleasure to meet you again. I trust I find you well. I *do* remember you most distinctly. You once gave me a length of blue ribbon to tie up my hair because I had lost mine on the way to the fan-shop."

"Did I?" Jasmin gave a little laugh of surprise, finding it hard to think of Reinette by her title. "You have a better memory than I, madame."

"It meant a lot to me. You were a grown-up lady in my eyes then. Come and sit down. There's so much to talk about." She removed a sleeping kitten in order to make space for Jasmin and herself on a sofa side by side, scolding the little animal fondly for being there. As soon as they were settled, Jasmin held out to her the slim silver box that had been made to hold the presentation fan.

"Although I wrote my thanks to you, it was impossible to express in words all that your kind action has done for me. Please accept this token, madame. It comes with my heartfelt and everlasting gratitude." Reinette looked as delighted as a child at the surprise. "For me? Oh, I thank you. Whatever can it be?" She lifted the lid. "A fan! I have always loved fans." Taking it out, she flicked it open and

exclaimed with pleasure at the design in all its delicately
shaded colours with matched pearls that gleamed across
the ivory silk leaf. "It is perfect! What a gorgeous gift!"

"Even after all these years it is a true Picard fan—my
mother's design and my workmanship."

Reinette, who was fluttering the fan, exclaimed again
with shining eyes, "That makes it a still more special gift! I
count it as one of the best I've ever had."

It was impossible not to be drawn to such spontaneous
warmth. Because of the difference in their ages Jasmin felt
herself filled with a maternal affection for this Court
beauty, who showed herself to be quite unspoilt by her
prestigious position and all the power and splendour that
had come with it. For Reinette the rapport between them
sprang from the links with her childhood and the charm of
the fan-shop, and because of those nostalgic memories Jasmin's appeal had been impossible to refuse. But that was
not the only reason why she had interceded with Louis on
Jasmin's behalf, for she always tried to help any genuine
case when it lay within her capabilities and never looked
for any reward for herself. Yet she was beginning to hope
as she and Jasmin talked together that for once there was
to be an unexpected benefit for her. She still missed sorely
her adored mother and the hope was rising in her that she
would find a similar sympathetic ear in this older woman
from whom with time she could seek advice on personal
matters. It was impossible to confide in anyone at Court,
because it became common knowledge immediately. She
and Louis loved each other as much as ever, but in spite of
various diets that she had tried in order to strengthen her
constitution, it had been to no avail and finally her frail
health had defeated them both. He had wept in her arms
after the last time he had made love to her, knowing that if
she was to live it must not happen again, for she had virtually collapsed and for a few terrible moments he had
thought her dead.

It was then that she moved downstairs to this exalted,
semiroyal apartment and all the Court had guessed the
reason why. Her enemies among the nobility were legion,
none of them able to forgive her for being a bourgeoise,
and now they had begun to call her the Procuress and
other foul names, although it was the task of the concierge
of Versailles, and no responsibility of hers, to ensure that

attractive, clean young women were always available to satisfy Louis's sexual desires. They were housed in a modest mansion, the Parc aux Cerfs. Some were brought regularly to one of the upper rooms under the eaves to be available when required. None of them had any idea that their "nobleman" was the King, poor stupid little creatures, and they thought him to be one of the grand courtiers. They became pregnant at an alarming rate and new girls were ever having to be found.

Reinette knew the Court had expected she would fall from royal favour when the King no longer shared her bed and these other arrangements had to be made, but that was not the case. He sought her company more than ever. In many ways she had become a political aide to him and these days he discussed with her the progress and setbacks of the war that had broken out with England and Prussia. She marked the battles and skirmishes on a wall map. As he was likely to arrive at any time, she felt she should prepare Jasmin.

"It means much to me that you knew the King when you were little children together, and then onwards from adolescence until your unfortunate marriage," she said after questioning Jasmin about her young days at Court and her years in the country. "Did he get as easily bored in those days as he does now?"

Jasmin considered. "I remember he threw himself enthusiastically into all the entertainments. He loved to dance and never missed one measure during an evening. Hunting was his favourite sport and he was in the saddle at every opportunity."

"As he still is," Reinette interjected.

"I do recall that he was often restless and impatient were things not exactly to his liking."

"That's just the same!" Reinette clapped her hands together in emphasis. "Did he get liverish in colour?"

Jasmin's eyebrows shot up in surprise. "How strange that you should mention that! I haven't thought about it since, but I do recall he would turn quite pale."

"Nowadays his complexion takes on a yellowish tint. I watch for it always, because I will not let my darling Louis be bored, otherwise he is prone to dark moods of depression that are hard for him to shake off. My life is dedicated to his happiness."

Jasmin smiled. "He is a fortunate man . . . madame." She had been about to say "my child" but stopped herself in time.

"You may see him at any second. It will divert him so much to meet you again, my dear Duchesse!"

"Ah." Jasmin shook her head ruefully. "Will he recognise me after all these years."

"Oh, yes, madame!" Reinette was quite indignant on Jasmin's behalf. "You are a handsome woman and Louis never forgets a lovely face."

He came into the apartment almost before she had finished speaking. Swiftly she left her chair to curtsey and greet him vivaciously, chattering about Jasmin's arrival. Yet their eyes were only for each other as he kissed her hand and then her cheek. It gave Jasmin a few moments in which to assess his appearance and to note that there could be no doubt of the love of these two people for each other. Louis had put on a considerable amount of weight, having become broad and heavy, although retaining a good shape. Despite his forty-six years he was still attractive with the same enigmatic charm. Laughter had crinkled the corners of his eyes, but the burden of Kingship had scored his handsome features. He was as immaculate and fashionable in his dress as he had always been, his cravat and cuffs of pristine lace, and she had been told he had two baths in his bathroom, one in which he washed himself and another in which to rinse the soap away. She was able to recall vividly the extreme fondness she had once felt for him, but it was in its own compartment, divided off by the years, just as she had bracketed away her love for Michel. To her now, Louis was her King and nothing more. Any affection for him stemmed from that alone and from the great favour he had granted her. As he turned in her direction she dropped into a deep curtsey, her head low, and he took her hand to raise her up.

"I'm pleased to see you again, Jasmin." He was smiling at her, polite and gracious in his manner.

"You honour me, sire."

"I understand that you and Madame de Pompadour have an acquaintanceship of long standing."

"That is my good fortune."

Reinette spoke up. "It is mine, too." She reached out and

took Jasmin's hand into hers. "I hope we shall be good friends, madame."

Once again Jasmin's name was entered on the guest list at Versailles and at first she attended almost everything, feeling she had to make up for the time she had lost. Although the entertainments were still as lavish, plays and ballets performed by the best companies and the most talented musicians in Europe played at the concerts, she soon found that nothing was for her as it had been before. She no longer knew many people and several of those once counted as friends avoided her because of her years in the country. If she had come back to Versailles with straws in her hair and her knowledge of Court etiquette forgotten she could not have been more ostracised. Her friendship with Reinette gained her the same enemies and Louis was not sufficiently interested in her for any to try to curry favour with her on that account. Gabrielle de Valverde, whose company she would have appreciated, had left Versailles in her widowhood and gone abroad to live with a married daughter in Martinique.

It was not long before Jasmin, apart from attending an occasional concert or a play, confined her visits to events held in Reinette's apartment or otherwise supervised by her. On these occasions she was never left out, for there would always be many present who did not know or care how she had spent her past years. She met many members of the Poisson family, for Reinette adored all her relatives and her jolly brother spent most of his time at Court. It did not cross Reinette's mind that these bourgeois people might be out of place and never for a moment did the King give her any cause for doubt, enjoying the change of company and quite at ease with them.

He was less comfortable with the artists who came to her salons, finding some of them too eccentric for his taste, but there were always the writers, the scientists and the other intellectuals who flocked to attend her and on these occasions he was never bored. Jasmin found such stimulating company as heady as the sparkling *vin de Champagne* which was served with delicious food and she revelled in being present. Sooner or later she supposed Michel would appear, although she had been told that he came less to Court these days. Spiteful tongues said that it was since

Boucher had become the artist favoured by the King for
the latest portrait of Reinette while others declared he had
become virtually a recluse, absorbed in his painting to the
exclusion of all else. When any number of salons had gone
by without Michel making an appearance, Jasmin no
longer thought about him. He belonged to another part of
her life and had no bearing on the present. Only his paintings on the walls of Versailles occasionally reminded her of
him.

The time of Jasmin's return to Château Satory had coincided to a degree with the outbreak of the present war.
The streets were full of marching soldiers and many foreign mercenaries made brief and colourful appearances on
their way to battle. Having so much to absorb her, she gave
little thought to the war at first. In her nostalgia for her
youth she went to Paris and saw the shop on the Champs-
Élysées only to find it had become an exclusive milliner's.
She alighted from her carriage to look at the hats displayed
and was almost tempted to enter and purchase one just to
be within those walls again. Beyond the gauzy curtains
draping the back of the shop window her diffused reflection was caught in a mirror where a young woman sat
trying on a beribboned chapeau, enthralled by her own
appearance. Jasmin turned away to go back to her carriage, hesitated once more on the point of changing her
mind and with a shake of her head dismissed the idea.
Moments later she was driven away. A chance encounter
between a mother and daughter was lost beyond recall.

Shortly afterwards Violette emerged from the shop, a
little black boy in red livery following her with the striped
hatbox containing her purchase. She glanced up at her
coachman before stepping into her waiting equipage.

"Back to the Parc aux Cerfs," she said with a haughty tilt
of her head. She had come a long way from the misery of
being put up for stake in a card game by a soldier in a
rough inn.

On another day Jasmin went locally into the town of
Versailles to the fan-shop that had been Marguerite's near
the Place d'Armes. This time she entered. The fans were
pretty, but not to the same standard. Overcome by curiosity she went through the archway into the courtyard
around which workshops were situated on three floors,
noting the litter and general untidiness that had not ex-

isted when she had last been there. Nobody challenged her presence and she went into the entrance of one workshop to be met by the rattle of looms and the odours of dirt, decaying rubbish and urine. She looked through a glass panel and was dismayed to see how many looms were crammed into the area, the weavers sweating at their labours and little children crouched like monkeys under the looms to mend the threads as they broke.

Holding up her hems, she ascended the filthy staircase to the first floor. There another glass panel showed her the lace-makers at work, dozens of women crowded together where once her mother's jewellers had plied their craft with all the space they required.

It was on the top floor that she found the fan-makers. Again through glass her heart went out to the women and little girls crammed side by side at the large tables where previously only strictly limited numbers had been allowed. She opened the door, steering her wide panniers through the narrow aperture and all unconsciously presenting an image of high fashion and sunshine in her corn-coloured gown and wide straw hat. The workers looked up under their lashes and then gaped for a few moments before getting on with their tasks again. The woman in charge put aside her own work and came forward to bob. She was in her mid-forties, her hair greyish beneath her cap, and there was a strained look to her tired eyes behind her small spectacles.

"Good day, madame. The fan-shop facing the street sells the wares we produce here."

"I've come out of interest," Jasmin replied. "I remember when Picard fans were made on all the floors in this building."

The woman's face lit up. "I worked for the Baronne Picard here when I was a girl. Did you know her, madame?"

"I'm her daughter. What is your name?"

"Marie Frémont. I remember you, madame."

They talked for a while. It was as Jasmin had expected—the poor state of the buildings was due to the indifference of a wealthy landlord who leased the property to small businesses and was interested only in the rents. Marie Frémont's employer owned several fan-making workshops and conditions were equally cramped in each one. Before leaving, Jasmin had a word with each of the workers just as in the past, and afterwards asked Madame Frémont about one woman who had a persistent cough.

"Is she sick? She certainly looks thin and frail."

"She has chest trouble, but all the time she's able to work I'm keeping her on. Her husband died last year and she needs her money badly even though she has her two elder little girls working here, for there are two younger ones that I allow her to keep on a leash in the storeroom."

Jasmin shook her head slightly, conveying her compassion and despair. Taking some money from her purse, she handed it to Madame Frémont. "Buy her some physic and give her leave of absence. My mother always took care of any worker with a cough, having noticed how others could be infected. Tell me the woman's address and I'll see that she receives food and funds for herself and her family. If there is any trouble over it with your employer, refer him to the Duchesse de Valverde at Château Satory."

This incident opened gates as far as her helping the poor and needy were concerned. It shocked her that in such a prosperous town with wealth spilling into its shops, businesses and hotels, workers should slave on inadequate wages and that terrible poverty should exist on such a scale. In the country, where often a labourer's livelihood depended on the success or failure of the crops, it was more to be expected, but here she felt it to be inexcusable. Marguerite had opened her eyes to the hardship of others during her girlhood, but with the egotism of youth she had gained a mere inkling. Over the years she had come to view it as her mother had.

The winter proved to be exceptionally cold, great fires being banked up at Versailles and in the homes of the rich while the poor died of cold in their hovels. The price of bread shot up and many faced starvation. As if some invisible grapevine had stretched its tendrils halfway across France, Jasmin found the hungry gathering at her kitchen door as they had at Château Valverde when times were hard. It was her strict rule that nobody should ever be turned away. As the numbers increased she saw that cauldrons of thick, nourishing soup were always ready, stacks of bread sliced and pottery bowls and spoons always on hand. Those with families left at home were allowed to fill containers they had brought with them and she herself either visited the sick or placed them in the care of nuns.

At Versailles, Reinette shivered in spite of the glowing fires. She was easily feverish and felt the cold in summer and in winter, only at her best on really hot days. When unwell she was often cast down and it was at these times that she unburdened herself to Jasmin, seeking maternal comfort. Bad news of the war always upset her, causing her to lie awake at night. She still grieved for her little Alexandrine, who had died at the age of ten, and did not know that it gave her a close tie with Jasmin, who never spoke of Violette and was sometimes forced to wonder if she was still alive. Reinette lived constantly with her fear of the King's love turning elsewhere and Jasmin would reassure her time and time again, having no doubt at all that Louis was utterly devoted to her.

"You know the girls of the Parc aux Cerfs mean nothing to him. You hold his heart."

"But there are so many beautiful women at Court, all trying to take my place," Reinette declared, wringing her hands.

Jasmin knew this was true. The latest gossip was of a certain lady who had gone to his bed, only to be mistaken for a girl from the Parc aux Cerfs and to her humiliation had been told to come back another night when he was less tired from hunting all day.

"I tell you there is only love in the King's eyes when he looks at you." Jasmin shook her head firmly at the possibility of anyone winning him away. "Nobody else can hold a candle to you as far as he is concerned."

Reinette, comforted by this reassurance from someone she trusted, sighed gratefully. Yet there was one regret that never left her. It was that she had never had a baby by the King.

She spoke of this grief for the first time to Jasmin one warm May afternoon. It tired her to walk any distance after the untimely chill that had recently laid her low and Jasmin was driving her in a little phaeton around the gardens of Versailles to see at close hand the flowers that she loved. They were passing under bowers of purple and white lilac, the heavy blossoms weighing down the boughs, and the scent wafted deliciously into their nostrils.

"Is it not cruel of fate to deny me what is given to who

knows how many young women in the Parc aux Cerfs?"
she said sadly.

"What is that?"

"The supreme joy of bearing Louis's child."

Jasmin glanced at her and saw that her eyes were brim-
ming. "I realise what it must mean to you," she said sympathetically. Then, as the loss of Violette twisted in her as it
always did at any talk of children, she added gently, "Try to
console yourself with the happiness that has come to you
through him in other ways."

The huge silvery tears rolled down Reinette's cheeks
and she twisted her hands in her lap. "I think my lack of a
baby by him would be easier to bear if those young girls
that come from the Parc aux Cerfs did not become pregnant so easily."

It was a measure of her exceptionally low spirits that she
should have brought this out. The King's bastards were
always given good homes and an income for life, although
the mortality rate being what it was among children, there
were not many who lived to benefit from his generosity.
Normally Reinette was very bright and cheerful about a
new pregnancy; Jasmin had even heard her joking with
the King on one occasion, talking about how the father was
a well-beloved fellow and he answering her in the same
vein, which sent them into paroxysms of mirth. Was her
vivacity and merriment at these times a façade to spare
him her pain? All part of her endless efforts to keep him
content and in love with her? Jasmin made a suggestion.

"Why don't you tell the King what you have told me. He
would do anything to spare you heartache, although I myself feel it is all part of his deep affection which causes him
to share every aspect of his life with you."

Reinette looked a little uncertain. Nevertheless there
was hope in her voice as she said, "Probably you are right,
my dear friend."

Jasmin often felt she herself could never have led the
restless life that Madame de Pompadour shared with the
King. In his eternal fight against boredom he liked to be
constantly entertained and forever on the move, not only
between the royal palaces but also visiting the several
charming mansions and châteaux he had given Reinette.
There he expected all kinds of social events to be laid on

and arrangements made for the heavy gaming that he enjoyed.

Often Jasmin was a guest on these visits at Reinette's invitation and she liked best to stay at the château of Bellevue, which was well named with its splendid view of Paris and the glittering Seine in the distance. She even took part on a number of occasions in plays staged in Bellevue's own theatre, the standard of acting high and Reinette always surpassing the rest of the cast.

As with everything to which Reinette gave her touch, Bellevue was exquisitely furnished. It was almost as though beautiful things sprang up in her wake and flower gardens blossomed more profusely for her than others did for anyone else. In her own way she was giving much to France as well as sharing an interest with Louis, who also liked to collect objets d'art. It was due to her patronage that the arts and crafts flourished even in wartime, but the majority of the King's subjects saw only his extravagances and hers, resenting the burden of heavy taxes and grumbling constantly, every setback in the war another mark against those in power.

Jasmin was present at Bellevue when Reinette played a merry little joke on her guests and the King, who laughed as heartily as everyone else. On a winter's day she showed them a parterre of flowers in full bloom, taking in everybody until they discovered the flowers were made of porcelain, each with a scented sachet at the centre. It was because of her love of fine porcelain that Louis, who owned by royal right the great carpet factories of Aubusson and Savonnerie, as well as that of the Gobelin tapestries, gave her the factory and the entire village of Sèvres which lay close to Bellevue. Jasmin was exceptionally pleased when Reinette, who often used the fan of Marguerite's design, expressed a wish to have it copied onto Sèvres porcelain.

"I should be delighted!" Jasmin exclaimed. "How proud my mother would have been."

She went with Reinette to see the artists at work when the time came. Many beautiful pieces were being produced there to meet a market that had become worldwide, even though the war had interfered with the outflow. Not only were its artists of the best, but the sculptors as well, and the rich, newly invented colours made

Sèvres porcelain superior to all competitors. Jasmin watched in fascination as Marguerite's garland of cream and pink roses, yellow jasmine, lilac and orange blossom entwined with silvery ribbons spread from the artists' finely tipped brushes across the cups, saucers, plates, sugar vases and all the rest of the pieces that were making up the loveliest of tea sets for Reinette at Versailles. Jasmin did not know that a surprise had been planned for her until she was presented with a large flower vase with her mother's design entwined about it. Upon her return home she placed it in the Ivory Salon opposite the portrait of Marguerite.

Reinette held a sale of Sèvres porcelain at Versailles once a year. It was set up in the King's private apartment and Jasmin accepted the invitation to attend out of her own interest. She arrived to find the room crowded with courtiers, male and female, and it was a little while before she could get through the press of people to see what was on display. As usual, Louis was acting as salesman and thoroughly enjoying himself. This was a diversion for him, something different again, and not so unexpected that it should please him to play a humbler rôle, for he took every chance to be alone with Reinette in one of the many charming little country cottages which had been built close to Versailles and Fontainebleau and other palaces where they could pretend to be ordinary citizens and take turns in cooking supper for each other.

"Which of these handsome pieces of china tempts you most, Madame la Duchesse?" he jovially asked of Jasmin, always formal when others were present.

She had already picked out a charming biscuit figurine by the sculptor Pajou and, although the price was high as it was on every piece, she thought it well worth the thirty louis. "That is my choice," she said, indicating it.

At that moment a lace-cuffed hand stretched past her to take it up and a deep voice that struck bells from the past was close to her ear. "Allow me to buy this for you, just for old times' sake."

She turned her head abruptly and looked straight into the face of Michel. Taken so completely by surprise, she was rendered speechless and the transaction went ahead between the two men while she drew back out of the throng. Then Michel was putting his purchase into her hands, not having the slightest intimation that she had chosen this figurine of a young girl with flowing hair and uptilted chin because it had a look of their lost daughter. Yet she had been through enough in her life to be able to conceal her inner emotions as she looked from the figurine to him and expressed her thanks.

"That was most kind of you. I had no idea you were here."

"I saw you arrive." He smiled slowly at her. "You haven't changed, Jasmin. You're as beautiful as ever."

She saw he was not flattering her. It was that curious rapport between people who have known each other well that takes no account of the marks of age, each able to see the familiar essence of the other. He had the same penetrating eyes, the same smile, the same good teeth and the same proud carriage of the head that had once made her heart spin, and it took a few moments of readjustment to see the lines, a scar across one brow that had not been there before and the heavier jawline. He also wore the fashionable white wig with a black bow tie-back, his unruly hair no longer adding to the fierce, wild look that had first attracted her. Seeing him again was as she had always supposed it would be; she could remember their mutual passion as if it had been yesterday, but over two decades had gone by since then and that was where it remained, shut away in time with no trace to touch her feelings now.

"You look well, too, Michel. Have the years been kind to you?"

He gave her a long look before he replied and then said with a touch of wryness, "Good enough in some ways but not in others." He glanced about him. "It's too crowded in here to talk. Let's take a stroll outside in the park."

She fetched her cloak, left her figurine for delivery to her home and rejoined him again. On the way out into the cool autumnal evening air, she told him how she had been widowed and of her subsequent appeal to Madame de Pompadour with its welcome result. He in turn spoke of his unfortunate marriage, his work past and present and of his astonishment at seeing her at the sale.

"How long have you been back at Château Satory?" he asked. They had descended the wide flight of a hundred steps to the Sun King's Orangery on a level with the Swiss Lake, having chosen to leave the more-frequented paths

for the solitude they had known they would find here. All
the hundreds of orange trees, pomegranates and palm
trees, which were ranged in tubs like soldiers across the
vast area throughout the warm months of the year, had
been trundled by a special wheeled contraption into the
gigantic Orangery Greenhouse by which they strolled, the
foliage looming dark and ghostlike behind the large windows.

"Two years now."

"What!" He stopped and took her by the arms to jerk her
about to face him in the flickering light of the flambeaux.
"So long! Why didn't you let me know you had come
home?"

She had one good reason that she could never disclose to
him and others that came from sheer common sense. "I
knew we should meet again sooner or later. People like us
who have been lovers cannot pick up the threads again as
those who have been only acquaintances or friends. Your
path and mine crossed briefly and then went widely separate ways. I have heard at Court there is a woman in your
life these days to whom you are strongly attached and I'm
glad for you. It doesn't touch what was between us. Nothing can. But that ended the day we parted and cannot be
recalled."

He narrowed his eyes at her. "You're very sure."

"Totally."

He compressed his lips cynically, shrugged and let his
hands fall away from her. "I suppose I agree with you. We
were young then. The years have changed us both. Yet
seeing you again this evening made me remember clearly
how I once felt in those halcyon days when we were virtually alone at Château Valverde."

She hardly heard him, for she was staring at his hands.
For the first time she noticed the telltale swelling of his
finger joints that denoted the disease of aching bones from
which Berthe had suffered. She could only guess what it
meant to him as an artist to be thus afflicted. It explained
why he so seldom came to Court. Compassion gushed up in
her as it always did whenever she faced another's sickness
or handicap. Spontaneously she reached out both her
hands and caught his to bring them up to either side of her
face. She stared at him, her violet eyes opened wide in
dismay.

"My dear Michel! Your wonderful work! How do you paint now?"

"Slowly." His sardonic tone rejected pity.

She lowered her lids and kissed the fingers that she held. He drew his hands away only to cup her face towards him. If he had hoped to see in her eyes some rebirth of what had been before it was not there and maybe he had not expected it to be. His fingertips fell away from her.

"I love the woman who has thrown in her lot with me," he said frankly. "Not as I loved you, but then that kind of love rarely happens twice. Béatrice is ten years younger than I and remarkably good to me. She asks nothing in return. When I need a model she will sit patiently for weeks where once it took me only hours or days to set down my subject on canvas. She and I want to live out the rest of our lives together."

"Have you any children?" It seemed to Jasmin that her question came breathily and from a far distance.

"Two sons and a daughter."

A thought crashed through her brain. There would have been no room for Violette even if he had known, even if he had cared or even if their child had not seemingly vanished from the face of the earth. "Then you are greatly blessed in that respect. I've always thought fondly of you and wished you well. Would it be impertinent to say that Béatrice sounds just the woman I should have chosen to take my place with you?"

They were looking at each other steadily. Then suddenly, unbidden and unexpected, they found themselves reaching through their locked gaze to that plane of friendship that can come to a man and woman who have shared a loving, passionate intimacy with no bitter aftermath. On the crest of the revelation he smiled at her with deep affection and she responded warmly.

"Knowing Béatrice as I do," he said, "I think she would take that as a great compliment. I came here this evening to buy her a gift and I must return to the sale before it is all over. Come back with me and give me the benefit of your advice."

"Gladly."

He offered his arm and instead of taking it formally she linked her hands about his elbow, so that they were closely side by side as they went back up the hundred steps, the atmosphere comfortable and amiable between them as they talked all the way. At the sale they selected a pair of vases adorned with chased bronze mounts in the rich Sèvres colour known as King's blue.

Later she heard that Béatrice had been thrilled with them. That was when she met Michel by chance in the Champs-Élysées and dined with him. They never communicated in any way or sought each other out, but were pleased whenever they met by chance. Once, as her carriage passed the Château Montville, he was leaving on a trip and Béatrice and the children had come to the gates to wave him on his way. That was when she felt a pang that almost broke her heart, for all three children were like Violette in having the thick fair hair of their father's youth and there was something about the impish little girl that recalled Violette at that age. Nobody noticed her and she managed to snatch a glimpse of Béatrice. There had just been time to see that she was tallish with glossy black tresses and there was a look of vitality about her.

As they were lost from sight Jasmin gave way to tears, sobbing as she had not done for a long time. She knew she was weeping not only for Violette but also for love itself, which had gone from her life forever.

Jasmin's days followed the pattern that had been set. She had Reinette's friendship and the entertainments that resulted from it, once attending a special recital by the seven-year-old Wolfgang Mozart from Austria. It was held in the apartment of the King's daughter Princesse Adélaïde, and it was an evening long remembered. The child-musician's little fingers had flown about the keys of the harpsichord as he played his own sonatas and a concerto so difficult that only the most practised performer could master it.

Away from Versailles and in the environs of her own home, Jasmin continued her charitable work. She founded a hospice for unmarried mothers after springing out of her carriage one day to rescue a newborn baby boy mewing beside his young mother, who lay dead in a ditch at the roadside. Under her care orphans and those small children whose mothers were unable to support them were put into good foster homes where she personally kept an eye on their well-being and ensured that the boys were taught a trade and the little girls some skill with a needle and in domestic chores.

She had been back seven years at Château Satory when the war with England and Prussia came to an end. It had proved disastrous for France and through it colonial possessions in India and Canada were lost. The King found himself beset by political troubles, facing hostility among ministers and governors while France itself was restless and ridden by financial difficulties. Reinette worried about him and what he had to face, but he took it all in his stride. He continued to adore her and had begun to build a little palace for her close to the Sun King's rose marble Trianon, which was used far more by the Court nowadays than in his great-grandfather's time. She talked about the project to Jasmin, the excitement in her eyes giving her the look of a young girl again. Recently she had taken to wearing lacy caps which she thought befitted a woman who had turned forty.

"It will be like living in the country," she exclaimed happily, "and will be called the Petit Trianon. There Louis and I can be alone together while still close to Versailles." Her face clouded. Recently the King had had more lasting affairs with at least two beautiful young women, and the pregnancies of the girls of the Parc aux Cerfs were much as they had always been. She pressed her palms together and linked her graceful fingers, her face lighting up again. "I have known joy with him in all my dear houses and this is going to be a particularly happy place. I feel it in my bones."

She never saw it finished. Before the roof was on she was taken desperately ill while with the King at Choisy. As soon as it was possible to move her, he brought her back to Versailles with him and was with her constantly. A message was sent to Jasmin that Reinette wanted to see her. Jasmin found her seated in a chair with pillows, for she could not breathe in any other position, wearing a ruffled peach satin dressing-robe and with a touch of rouge on her sunken cheeks.

"I wanted to say farewell, my dear friend," she said as Jasmin sat by her and they held hands. "You have been like my own mother to me at times. Yet I was once told it was she who first revealed your indiscretion with Fernand de

Grange to your parents with all the distress it must have caused to them."

Jasmin, fighting to keep back tears at this parting, shook her head. "It would have made no difference to our being friends."

"I know that and I thank you for it." Reinette began to cough, only able to speak a few words at a time. As she recovered she beckoned Jasmin to her and they kissed each other on the cheek. "God keep you in his care."

At the door Jasmin looked back. Reinette gave her a sweet smile and half raised a limp hand in a final adieu. With her tears flowing Jasmin met the King on her way out and dipped a curtsey, but he, his face racked with anguish, did not see her as he made his way to the woman who was soon to leave him after more than twenty years.

He could not be with her when she died, for contact between them was prohibited after she had made her last confession. No sooner had life gone from her than she was placed on a stretcher, covered with a sheet and hurried from the apartment out into the damp spring night. The bearers rushed her through a side gate, the sheet flapping, and took her into her own residence, the Hôtel des Réservoirs, where she had rarely slept a night. The King had broken the strict rule that governed death at Versailles by letting one not of royal blood die there, and efforts were being made by others to make it appear that she had drawn her last breath elsewhere.

Jasmin attended the funeral. Her carriage joined the procession of the cortège as it went down the Avenue de Paris on its way to the capital, carrying Madame de Pompadour away from Versailles and all she had loved there. The King stood weeping openly for her on the balcony of his State Apartment.

Jasmin settled to a quieter life, devoting still more time to her charity work. With Reinette's salons being no more she found it hard to summon up interest in less stimulating gatherings. She had made some acquaintances at Versailles, but none was a friend as the Court beauty had been and she only saw them occasionally. From the terms of her late friend's will she received the bequest of a lovely lacquer box decorated with scenes of Bellevue, evoking happy memories, and a book of Reinette's own signed engravings, both mementoes to be treasured always.

The months went by and the King, lonely and grieving, sought what consolation he could find from the young women of the Parc aux Cerfs and other casual affairs. None took Reinette's place and he continued to mourn her. The death of the Dauphin, less than two years after hers, was a shattering blow to him and he saw history was going to repeat itself in that his grandson, a dull, serious boy, was destined to be the next King of France. How appropriate that his name should be Louis.

Jasmin continued to take an interest from a distance in the royal family. The young Dauphin had shouldered his new status for two years on the spring morning in 1768 when she sat reading in the Ivory Salon. The weather had been unseasonably cold and a cheerful glow radiated from the fireplace. She was absorbed in an essay by Voltaire, whom she had met many times at Reinette's salons, when a footman came to announce a visitor. She removed her spectacles and rested them across her open book as she gave him her attention.

"There is a lady to see you, madame. She declined to give her name but said you would know her well from her days at the Govins' farm."

Jasmin thought her heart stopped. The blood drained from her face with a speed that seemed to drag at her skin. "Show her in," she said faintly.

The footman went to do her bidding. As she rose to her feet she swayed and had to clutch the edge of the marble mantel for support, the glow of the fire leaping up to her face. She managed to move away and stand erect as Violette entered the room with a quick, light step and then came to a standstill, her chin high. For a few moments neither spoke. Mother and daughter gazed at each other across the expanse of Savonnerie carpet and the seventeen years that had separated them. Jasmin saw a handsome woman of thirty-three with a strongly self-possessed air, dressed richly in the height of fashion, clad from head to foot in King's-blue velvet. The huge brim of her creamy plumed hat turned up from her totally composed face, her jacket was double-breasted with silver buttons and her widely panniered skirt parted to show a self-striped satin underskirt in the same deep shade. Violette, in her turn, thought that her mother in old age looked extremely alert and poised, undiminished by the years that had drained the colour from her hair and left it snowy-white, abolishing any need for powder. Yet it was easy to see that she was shaken by this unexpected reunion, her face working convulsively. Violette spoke first.

"I hope I find you in good health, Maman," she said evenly.

Jasmin was struggling with her emotions. Absurdly there had risen in her the reaction normal to any mother who, after intense anguish, recovers a lost child and is unable to hold back from slapping it for running away. "Where have you been?" she exploded incongruously. Then with a sob she flung out her arms to her daughter. "My darling girl, I thought I had lost you forever." As Violette went forward to be embraced, Jasmin completely broke down and clung to her, sobbing helplessly.

Violette was quite detached as she accepted the smothering clasp. She felt no particular bond with this woman who had borne her, too much resentment having been built up in her in those early years, encouraged by Madame Govin, and the bitterness of always having been left behind when her mother had departed again. Yet she was not completely unmoved by this meeting after so many years.

Jasmin was drawing away from her, smiling and wiping away tears with a lace-trimmed handkerchief. "How foolish of me to cry, but happiness overwhelmed me. How well you look. Are you married?"

"I'm betrothed." Violette pulled off her white gloves and displayed a dazzling diamond ring set with rubies.

Jasmin bit her lip to hold back further tears of joy. "Does that mean you have come to be married from here? Oh, darling Violette, your boxes must be outside on your carriage!" Without waiting for a reply in her excitement she turned for the bellpull. "They shall be unloaded at once. I'll give you the boudoir that was mine when I was young; the rooms of that apartment are so pretty that even Madame de Pompadour would have been at home there."

Violette moved swiftly and slapped a hand against the brocade bellpull, holding it against the wall even as her mother would have tugged at it. "I'm not here to stay, Maman. I can dine with you and then I must go again."

Fighting against disappointment, Jasmin managed to go on smiling and put a hand to her brow. "I'm still dazed. You must excuse my jumping to conclusions. Try to remember that you were sixteen when I last saw you and for me the clock has been turned back. Remove your hat and jacket. The chef shall serve your favourite dishes."

Violette took off her hat and gestured impatiently with it. "I'll share whatever is being prepared for you." Her perfectly manicured almond nails shone as she unfastened her jacket to put it aside with her hat. "There's a great deal to talk about in the time we are to be together. I should like a cognac if it would not shock you to have one served to me and, by the way you look, I think one would do you good, too."

The cognac was served. It was a drink that Jasmin had taken only once and then for medicinal purposes. Violette, sitting back against the cushions on the opposite sofa, showed she had a real appreciation of it, cupping the bowl of the goblet in her hand and remarking after the first sip with the unselfconscious air of the true connoisseur that it was quite excellent.

"I had better begin at the beginning," she said, "and tell you why I left the Govins, or did you discover that?"

"Yes, I learned that a disagreeable marriage with the Govins' nephew was being forced upon you." Jasmin released a deep breath. "That was when I went to take you away with me. My husband had died and my letter telling you my news arrived a few days after you had run away."

Violette's face spasmed at this revelation and she leaned her head back briefly, closing her eyes as she tried to shut out how different her life would have been if she had not bolted just too soon. Then she showed no more emotion and began to recount her tale.

She told of the Swiss officer and of his treacherous betrayal by putting her up for stake at a card game. She had remained the mistress of the man who won her for two years, having her first taste of good living, although it was far from the luxury of which she dreamed. When he died of apoplexy in her arms, she rose from the bed, dressed, filled a purse with all the gold she could find and left. At the first hostelry where she stayed overnight she was arrested for theft by the police sent after her by the widow. She languished in prison for almost a year before the gov-

ernor's son, whose eye she caught in the prison yard, en-
veigled her release and kept her with him at his home in
Dijon until his wedding day dawned. Then, being fond of
her, he had given her a box of new clothes, a fat purse of
gold and a carriage and coachman to take her wherever
she wished to go. Her choice was Versailles, but when the
long journey was almost over the coachman robbed and
raped her, leaving her with only the garments she stood up
in. She sold two of her lacy petticoats and a pair of soft kid
gloves, which gave her some money, and managed to get a
lift with a carter driving his wagon to Paris. There she sang
and danced in the street to keep herself solvent and was
noticed by an artist. She did modelling work and was eventually seen by the Court painter, François Boucher, who
used her for several of his paintings.

"He said I had lovelier buttocks than Louise O'Murphy,"
she said with a satisfied twist of her mouth, "and she hated
me for it. I never had a civil word from her."

Jasmin, who had been listening to her daughter's colourful adventures almost in stupefaction, gasped at this latest
piece of information. The Irish girl had been a favourite of
the King at the Parc aux Cerfs until she had had the impudence to refer to Madame de Pompadour as "the old lady."
After that he had had nothing more to do with her.
"Where did you meet that creature?"

Violette raised a self-mocking eyebrow. "Where do you
think, Maman? Due to Monsieur Boucher's recommendation I finally achieved my lifelong ambition and came to
Versailles. I have been at the Parc aux Cerfs for several
years. I'm proud to say I supplanted O'Murphy in the
King's affections."

Jasmin looked down at her hands. "Oh," she said slowly,
"that place!"

"Come now, Maman," Violette chided cheerfully, "the
King is a charming lover and I have had every luxury. At
first I used to be in the attics at Versailles until I caught his
attention by addressing him as Your Majesty when none of
the others ever guessed who he was. After that I had the
best and prettiest apartment at the Parc aux Cerfs."

Jasmin raised her head again. "How did you know him?"

"The governor's son had a marble bust of him and I had
seen sketches and portraits in Boucher's studio. In any
case, the King sometimes forgot he was wearing his *Cor-*

don Bleu across his chest, and on one occasion he had failed to remove his diamond star of Saint Esprit." Tilting back her head, Violette drained the last drop of cognac from her goblet and set it down. "It is only a matter of weeks since I found out that you were here. There was some talk of Picard fans from an old woman attending me and a great deal of interesting gossip came to light about banishment through marriage to a notorious rake." She smiled wryly. "I remembered the little fans you made me and how you told me once that your mother had been an expert at the craft. I made further enquiries and began to put two and two together."

"You were more successful in finding me than I was in tracing you," Jasmin said with a note of bitterness. Then she recovered herself and set her shoulders back. "And you have had more resilience to your misfortunes than I would have had. Perhaps you inherited that from your grandmother." She gave a nod towards the portrait of Marguerite.

Violette left the sofa to study it with arms akimbo. "She was a beautiful woman," she remarked, "and if I did inherit that trait from her I'm thankful. It makes me think she would have understood me far better than you ever did, Maman." She seated herself again, smoothing out her wide skirts and continuing in matter-of-fact tones. "You were very foolish in all your handling of me, you know. You dumped me with the Govins, an ordinary peasant couple, albeit Madame Govin was a cut above her husband and kept some semblance of civilised manners and behaviour. Then you appeared at spasmodic intervals to play with me as if I were a doll, taking on none of the responsibilities involved."

"You misjudge me! I kept a constant check on your welfare."

Violette shrugged and continued. "If you had only come with a gift of a rag doll or a simple fairing it would have been more in keeping with my everyday life, but instead you lavished expensive presents on me and as I grew older you fed me tales of the magic of Versailles that awakened dreams in me to match yours."

"Mine?" Jasmin spread her fingers across her chest, her eyebrows raised.

"Oh, yes." Violette nodded sagely. "You had no one else

you could talk to about Versailles as you could to me. You made me yearn for the girlhood that had been yours, to dance with gallants in the Hall of Mirrors, to wear grander versions of the gowns you brought me that were almost always in the costliest of fabrics. Then, when I was primed to these great expectations, you told me I was eventually to make some quite ordinary marriage, which meant I should never come even to see Versailles."

Jasmin sighed as she looked into the fire. "You're only putting into words what I have come to realise over the years. Parents seem destined to make mistakes of one kind or another, no matter how hard they may try to do better than their parents before them. It is a cycle that goes on from one generation to another. I hope you will have learned from my faults when you have children of your own."

"I have a baby. She is ten days old."

Jasmin's gaze shot from the flames to her daughter and she swallowed hard. "May I see her?"

"That's why I came today." Violette sat forward. "A good marriage has been arranged for me with an Austrian nobleman. He is a widower with three young sons. The Court at Vienna is not like Versailles, but I shall live grandly and enjoy great wealth. I have met him twice, find him attractive and he is already besotted with me. There is only one flaw. I can't keep the baby since it is not his. A foster home awaits her where she will be brought up as a young lady, given an education and an income for life, but I want her to grow up with her own kin where she belongs. Will you take her, Maman?"

Jasmin was lifting her arms as if she already cradled the child. "Oh, yes," she exclaimed huskily. "Where is she and what is her name?"

Violette stood up. "What could I do but give her a flower name," she said with a half-smile. "Do you remember you told me once I was the third girl in the family to bear one? She is Rose. Her wet nurse brought her into the house with me and they are waiting in one of the other salons. Let's go and find them."

Jasmin rose from her chair to accompany her daughter. "How can you be sure that I'll bring her up without the mistakes I made with you?"

Violette looked amused. "You're her grandmother.

That's a different relationship altogether. In any case, she will be where she belongs. Come along, Maman. I want to know if you think she looks like her father." Deliberately she held her mother's eyes. Jasmin gave a nod to show that she had guessed his identity from the first mention of the baby.

They found the wet nurse by the fire in the library. Jasmin took the bundle from her and drew aside the shawl to look at the baby's sleeping face. For no more than a second, coming with that first sighting, she thought she caught a look of the King in the tiny features. Then she saw only the grandchild who was to give purpose to her existence again and bring life and laughter into Château Satory, which had been still and quiet for far too long.

Dinner was served at two o'clock and Jasmin and Violette talked freely together. The strain had dispersed between them from the moment she had accepted the child. Violette was free again to go her own way, but this time she was on a steady path and Jasmin had no more qualms about her.

"There is one thing you must tell me," Violette said firmly as they ate lamb cooked in cream and wine. "Who was my father?" Seeing her mother's hesitation, she added. "I don't intend to contact him if he is still alive. I just want to know."

Jasmin answered on a gush of love for him that she had not experienced for a long time. "The artist Michel Balaine."

Violette stared with widening eyes and then she smiled with pleasure. "That dear old man! I met him once when he came to Boucher's studio. His hands are so swollen he cannot paint any more, but from what I heard he lives a most elegant life and he is on the committee of the *Garde-Meuble de la Couronne* that supervises the decoration of the royal palaces and dates from the Sun King's time." Her face took on a look of urgent appeal. "Please tell me how you came to meet him and all you feel able to disclose."

For the rest of the time at table Jasmin talked about Michel, and all the happiness of those days came back to her, illumining her face as she recalled her memories. When they rose from their places she took Violette through to the library to show her the portrait that Michel had painted.

"Why is it in this dark corner?" Violette asked, peering at her father's signature.

"I have no interest in my own likeness."

Violette looked eagerly at her. "May I have it? It would give me both my parents within one frame."

"Take it! I'm delighted that you want it."

Violette kissed her spontaneously and they linked hands as they left the library, a servant taking the portrait down from the wall to get it packed. Time for Violette's departure was drawing near.

"I'll write to you regularly about Rose," Jasmin said as Violette put on her hat again in front of a mirror, her jacket already buttoned.

"No, I don't want that." Violette faced her. "I'm not in the least maternal. In fact, I never cared for the dolls you brought me, although I liked their pretty clothes. I have given Rose to you and my claim to her is severed." Her frown was severe. "Is that understood?"

Jasmin nodded sadly. "It's a hard decision you have made. Does it mean that you intend no correspondence with me?"

"Yes." Violette reached out and cupped her mother's shoulders. "I'm not being entirely selfish. If we write you'd be tempted to talk about me and Rose would start hoping I'd appear one day. Then history would start repeating itself and she would go through all the misery that was mine. I have to spare her that. Later when she is grown up you may tell her who her father was if ever the time should be right."

"But what if anything should happen to me? After all, I'm not young. Would you not take her then?"

Violette shook her head. "My future husband has forbidden it and I'm in agreement. Rose is your responsibility now. You must make whatever arrangements would be appropriate should such an unlikely event as your demise take place." She smiled again. "I've given you something to live for, Maman. I'm certain you'll see Rose married with children of her own."

"I shall pray for that," Jasmin replied huskily, unable to return her daughter's smile.

Rose was lying asleep in the crib that had been brought in earlier from the waiting carriage together with a box of garments. Completely composed and dry-eyed, Violette picked her up and kissed her.

"Goodbye, little one. You're in good hands. Love your *grand-mère* as you would have loved me." She laid the infant down again and then turned to her mother. "Don't weep, Maman," she said, wiping the tears from Jasmin's cheeks with her gloved fingertips. "I'm not worth it. Just be glad that at last I've found a man I think I'm going to love."

"I am, my dear."

There was one last tight embrace and then they broke from each other's arms. Violette swept out of Château Satory without a backward glance.

Two years later, married, lazy, rich and content, she watched from the windows of her grand home in Vienna as the fourteen-year-old Archiduchesse, Marie Antoinette, drove past accompanied by a cortège of fifty carriages on the start of the long journey that would culminate in her marriage to the Dauphin.

Violette wished the bride well and smiled to herself, remembering the promise the King had given her that one day Rose should be a lady-in-waiting to this future Queen of France.

Seventeen

"My late husband wanted a son so much that he refused to acknowledge the existence of a daughter," Jasmin lied to her social circle to explain the sudden appearance of a granddaughter to someone previously believed by all to be a childless widow. "So Violette was fostered out. Later there was an elopement and we became estranged. Now I have this orphaned infant in my care and it's the greatest blessing I've ever known."

The explanation was accepted without question. These things happened in the best of families, the importance of heirs paramount to any nobleman. Jasmin had never had any contact with the Valverdes at Court, but should they hear about Rose's arrival, Sabatin's evil temper was too well known in the family for them to doubt her story.

It had been Violette's decision that the child's surname should be Labonne, taken from a nickname given to Rose by the midwife, who had praised her for being a contented as well as a bonny baby. It continued to suit her as she grew to the toddling stage and onwards. There were tussles, for

498

she did not lack obstinacy or determination, but she was also naturally good-humoured, quick and bright and loving. As time went by she was never happier than when playing out of doors or riding her pony. If she escaped her nurse she was always to be found in the stables where there was forever a new litter of kittens or puppies, and the old groom, who had been in Jasmin's employ for many years, would lift her up to pat the horses and feed them apples or carrots from her outstretched palm.

When Rose reached her sixth natal year, an invitation came from the Château to a reception that included her with her grandmother for the first time. Jasmin read it with dismay. Her aim from the start had been that her granddaughter should have a natural, happy childhood well away from the spell of Versailles that had enthralled both herself and Violette, bringing them both to much misfortune.

She could count on the fingers of one hand the invitations she had accepted over the past six years. She had gone to the inauguration of the magnificent Opéra, which had been the last building for Versailles planned by the Sun King. The performance there was part of the festivities held to celebrate the marriage of the Dauphin and the Archiduchesse Marie Antoinette. The Opéra was as sumptuous as everything else conceived by Louis XIV, the auditorium a work of art and the stage of such exceptional dimensions that the most spectacular operas could be performed there, the acoustics superb. That evening the royal family had sat in the front row of the grand tier and she had seen them twice since. Jasmin had thought the bride with her oval face, large blue eyes and ash-blonde hair pretty and charming, her smiles for the audience and the performers alike showing nothing of the loneliness she must have been feeling surrounded on all sides by strangers, not least the lumpish unattractive young prince who was her bridegroom.

Now this latest invitation made it clear to Jasmin that her acceptance was expected and she had no choice but to take Rose to the reception. The child hated being dressed up, but children were expected to look like miniature adults on formal occasions. There would have to be a new gown for her since she only possessed garments that were light and comfortable in simple styles.

On the day the dressmaker came with fabrics and fashion dolls, Jasmin made her own selection of a suitable style before sending for Rose, believing the child should be allowed to state a preference for colour. She herself considered a pale blue satin to be the most attractive and was pleating the fabric between her fingers to see the general effect when there came the sound of running footsteps that heralded Rose's approach, which was normal for her, there never being enough hours in the day for her to do all she wanted. The dressmaker gave an involuntary gasp. Jasmin looked up and followed her gaze.

Rose had burst into the Crimson Salon cheerfully mud-spattered from head to foot, clutching one of the stable puppies in her arms. She had a mop of tangled and luxuriant golden curls that were impossible to control at the best of times and today were blackened with dust and draped with a trailing cobweb that was in keeping with a streak of dirt on her heart-shaped face. Jasmin could only remember seeing such curly hair on one other person before and that had been her own mother. Marguerite had mastered her tresses with careful dressing, aided by the fashion of the *fontanges,* and then the filmy caps she had worn, but when newly washed her hair had sprung as rebelliously about her head as did the permanent state of Rose's curls. There was no other likeness between them that Jasmin could see, and as yet Rose showed no sign of being a beauty, although she had a pretty tip-tilted little nose, a smile that brought dimples into play and amber eyes, long-lashed and expressive, which were more accustomed to amusement than to tears.

"You wanted to see me, Grand-mère?"

Jasmin sat back in her chair. "Not quite like that," she replied drily.

Rose looked puzzled and glanced down at herself. "I am a bit muddy. That must have been when I ran through a puddle in the stableyard." The puppy was trying to bite her curls and she laughed, scolding him with a kiss. "Isn't he a darling? I've been playing with him and his brothers and sisters in the stable loft."

"You had better take him back and then get changed and clean again. In the meantime tell me which of these fabrics you like best. It will be for your new gown for the reception."

Rose gave them an uninterested glance and pointed un-erringly to the self-striped cream satin. "I'll have that one. It's the colour of the new foal. May I go now?"

Jasmin nodded, trying to keep the corners of her mouth from twitching as she kept back a chuckle. The dressmaker was still gaping. Rose bobbed automatically and rushed away again. There was mud left on the Aubusson carpet where she had stood and a dark patch contributed by the puppy that had dripped from her skirt.

When Rose was being dressed for the reception there was such a commotion in her room that Jasmin hurried to investigate. From the start Rose had had the pink and silver bedchamber that had once been Marguerite's, first sleeping there in her crib, before that was replaced by a small bed. Recently she had demanded the big canopied bed for herself where she slept like a little princess. Jasmin found that her nurse, determined not to be defeated by the rebellious curls on this special occasion, had plastered them with a gumlike pomade by which the hair could be moulded high in the current fashion and dressed over a pad. Rose's shrieks came from being forced to hold a cone over her face while her hair was powdered for the finished effect.

"Hush!" Jasmin exclaimed. "You'll get powder down your throat."

"It's done," the nurse stated with satisfaction, standing back to view her handiwork.

Rose hurled the cone away from her. Her face was scar-let with temper, her eyes swimming with tears that came as much from the irritation of the white powder as with rage. "I look silly!" she stormed, stamping her foot.

Privately Jasmin was inclined to agree with her that this titivating was ridiculous, but Court etiquette demanded such attention to fashion even from one so young. "Wait until you have put on your pretty gown. Then you will get the full effect."

When the gown was on, the hooks fastened and the skirt smoothed into place over the specially made little pan-niers, Jasmin herself fastened a small cream plume to the rocklike hair and secured it with a pearl cluster. The result was that in spite of Rose's scowl she looked flowerlike. Regarding herself critically in the mirror, she made a gri-mace of disgust.

"I'd frighten my pony looking like this and none of the cats or dogs would know me."

"As long as you don't frighten the King," Jasmin remarked with laughter, "that's all that matters this evening."

In spite of herself, Rose's face cleared and she giggled, putting her thumbs to her temples and waggling her fingers as if they were horns. "Shall I say, 'Boo!' to him as well, Grand-mère?"

With her good spirits restored, Rose took Jasmin's hand as they set off together, chattering all the way. It was not through any excitement at what lay ahead, for she considered it something boring and adult to be endured, but because she loved her grandmother with all her heart and it was always exceptionally enjoyable to be together.

At Versailles they made their way through the State Apartment in the direction of the Hall of Mirrors. To a young child the magnificent rooms appeared no larger than the spacious proportions of those at Château Satory and without the advantage of being familiar territory. She only noticed the enormous number of people and had to remember her manners constantly when she found herself staring at ladies whose hair seemed as high as their skirts were wide, topped in every case by some ornamentation to give added height, such as a silver ship in full sail, a gilded basket of fruit, a gold château, miniature flower gardens and many more such fancies. It seemed to be the rage to be topical wherever possible and two or three overweight women, who had obviously never been hungry in their lives, had had their hair decorated with tiny beribboned loaves to mark the recent bread riots of the starving in Paris. At the sight of these, Rose was instinctively repelled, remembering the empty-bellied children brought to her grandmother's door. There were also plumes in abundance, hers no more than a sparrow's feather by comparison, and she watched in fascination as the wearers had to dip their extraordinary heads as they went through the high doorways from one salon into the next. She was glad that her grandmother kept to a simple style, albeit it was brushed over a pad as a token gesture to this weird quirk of fashion.

On the threshold of the Hall of Mirrors, she was hit by a wave of warmth from hundreds of candles and blinked at the crystal blaze of the chandeliers, reflected a thousand times over in the tall mirrors. A courtier, who must have been watching out for them, spoke in her grandmother's ear. There was an answering nod and her grandmother took her hand still more firmly and led her into the throng.

Jasmin acknowledged the greetings of people whom she knew and then stood where she had been asked to by the courtier. She was full of dread as to what the outcome of this evening was to be. It was obvious that the King wanted to see his child, and yet why he should be interested in her granddaughter when he had so many other bastards whose whereabouts he would neither know nor care about was more than Jasmin could understand. The Sun King had legitimized and raised to noble rank the children of Louise de La Vallière and Madame de Montespan, but those women had been his titular mistresses and no others born on the wrong side of the blanket had been similarly honoured. All Jasmin could hope for was that after one sighting of Rose the King would forget all about her.

He was being announced! Jasmin clutched her granddaughter's hand still tighter and managed to remain at the forefront as the courtiers parted to leave a clear aisle. "Here comes the King," she whispered unnecessarily to Rose, who was already looking in his direction.

Jasmin saw at once that Louis's dissolute way of life had finally caught up with him. He carried himself with the same majestic air, but his features had coarsened and aged, a world-weary look to his eyes, as if boredom, which had always been his enemy, had finally won him. If he had any regrets that he had not followed the Sun King's advice to rule more wisely than his predecessor as he had once intended, it was only partly revealed in the belated reforms he was attempting. It could not be sensitivity at his unpopularity with the French people that had anything to do with the reforms, or else he would have put those measures into force long ago. The days when he had been called Louis the Well-Beloved were a distant memory, buried under wars, famine, taxes and his own profligate ways.

He walked on his own, the Queen having died in the year of Rose's birth, and his hooded glance went as if by chance to where he knew the Comtesse du Barry would be. Beautiful, voluptuous and vulgar, she had been ennobled by marriage to a comte, who had been paid off to disappear by the King himself, enabling her to be installed at Court without any encumbrances. Now she curtsied deeply, giving him the full benefit of her cleavage.

Jasmin looked across at her with dislike. She felt that the King should have chosen a mistress similar in intellect and graciousness to Madame de Pompadour instead of this loud creature who wielded power over him and the Court to the benefit of her spendthrift ways.

After the King came the Dauphin, twenty years old, six feet tall and overweight, his receding forehead wide above a large, prominent nose. His lips were fleshy and bow-shaped. On any other man this would have been a sign of sensuality, but he was known to be of little passion, equable, shy and restrained. Social events were not to his taste, although his sense of duty compelled him to attend. He lived to hunt and when not in the saddle he devoted himself to his books and his hobbies—as a locksmith, his lathe installed in one of the upper rooms at Versailles, and as a blacksmith in his specially constructed forge. When any building was going on at Versailles, or any other royal palace where he happened to be, he would take off his coat to give a hand with the brick-laying and stone-heaving, the love of his forebears for raising up grand residences having taken a practical turn in him.

By his side his small and graceful wife looked almost as diminutive as was Rose in the gathering. The child's gaze had gone straight to her, this Dauphine with the pretty name of Marie Antoinette, whose ruched satin gown was in all the palest rainbow colours and hung about with little silver tassels, tinted plumes topping her high-dressed hair. Enthralled by this fairy-tale vision, Rose did not notice that the King had stopped in front of her until her grandmother gave her wrist a sharp shake. She looked up at him with startled eyes and dipped her best curtsey, which brought a smile to his lips as well as to those of others nearby, all much taken with her doll-like appearance.

"What is your name, mademoiselle?" the King asked.

"Rose Labonne, sire."

"How old are you?"

"Six, sire."

"A delightful age to be. I have had the honour of knowing your grandmother, Madame la Duchesse, for a long time." He patted the child's dimpled cheek. "How are you enjoying your first visit to Versailles?"

"Very well, sire. But I've had nothing to eat yet."

He threw back his head in laughter, those within earshot joining in. Rose blushed to her ears and hung her head, overcome by shyness and shame at having made herself look ridiculous and not knowing why.

"That should soon be amended, little one," he said with a chuckle still in his voice as he moved on, leaving Rose wanting to bury her face in her grandmother's skirts, but prevented by a sense of disgrace. Somehow she had not behaved properly. She thrust her knuckles into her eyes knowing she was about to cry.

Then suddenly there was a delicious scent like honeysuckle wafting about her and a crisp whisper of satin that made her raise her head to see the Dauphine crouching down in front of her. "I haven't had my supper either, Rose," she said quite seriously, putting arms around her in a relaxed embrace. "I'm hungry, too."

"Are you?"

She leaned forward and whispered into Rose's ear. All around wondered what had been said, because immediately both of them began to giggle as if there were no difference in age or rank between them. Eyebrows were raised among the staid, the jealous and the vindictive. Meaningful glances were exchanged. The nineteen-year-old Dauphine was far too frivolous and thoughtless in everything she did, too attracted to the dangerously flippant element at Court and ever heedless of criticism.

Marie Antoinette straightened up and held out a hand to Rose with her beautiful smile. "Shall we go in search of supper together?" Then she turned her head slightly to smile at Jasmin. "With your permission, madame."

Jasmin curtsied her acquiescence and then stood with an anxious expression as the Dauphine led her granddaughter away, ladies-in-waiting and others in attendance having waited to follow after. The whole procession had been delayed because of Rose's presence, and now everyone had seen her and might even question the interest of the King, made inadvertently more marked by the Dauphine's intervention. To top everything, the child was to be fêted by the first lady in the land.

Jasmin's troubles for the evening were not yet over. She

had glimpsed Michel in conversation when she and Rose had passed through the Mars Salon. To the best of her knowledge he had not noticed them, but whereas she had hoped to take Rose home as soon as the King had seen her, this prolonged stay meant it was highly likely he would soon learn the identity of the little belle of the evening.

She was sipping a glass of wine on a tabouret in the Peace Salon when he located her. "My dearest Jasmin, how glad I am to see you."

He took the tabouret next to her and sat with his hands clasped over the top of his cane which he held vertically in front of him. The aching disease had taken possession of one hip joint and he was obliged to use a cane at all times. They talked well as they always did, interested to know what each had been doing, and she was particularly animated, trying to keep the dreaded question at bay, but it came.

"I have been told that the little girl in the Dauphine's company is your granddaughter. Is that correct?"

She looked away from him and about the room, all she had prepared to say should such a moment arise flown away from her. The huge oval painting of Louis XV as the peacemaker of Europe gave her no inspiration. "Yes, it is," she answered without expression.

"Did you and Sabatin have a child, then?"

"No!" She flung up her head vehemently, appalled at such a thought even after so many years. "But I had a daughter."

There was a pause as he eyed her speculatively, her face turned slightly away from him. "How old would she be now?"

Her voice faltered. "Thirty-nine."

He reached out and put his hand gently over hers. "My dearest. Why did you never tell me?"

She turned to him, her eyelids quivering as she blinked back tears. "I had many reasons, Michel. In any case when we met again you had a new life with children of your own. There was no point. I had no idea then that one day I should be given my granddaughter to raise."

He lifted her hand and kissed it before lowering it again. "Tell me everything. I want to know."

* * *

Rose thoroughly enjoyed herself. The Dauphine fed her with all sorts of delicious things from the buffet table in the Venus Salon, mostly with the sweet cakes and jellies and candied fruits about which her grandmother was strict. The King himself popped a sweetmeat into her mouth and people clustered around all the time. If they were gallants being particularly attentive to the Dauphine she did not notice, content to be perched on a gilded chair close to her new friend while the marble statue of the Sun King stared out at the gathering from the shell-shaped alcove behind her.

It was getting late when she saw her grandmother coming towards her with an elderly gentleman, tall in spite of the limp that drew at his leg. She and the Dauphine had left their chairs by this time and she went forward to curtsey as she was presented to him, having lost count of the number of times she had curtsied that evening.

"I am honoured to make your acquaintance, Rose," Monsieur Balaine said to her. Then he asked her questions about her pony and her lessons, all the usual things that adults wanted to know, but she liked him. In spite of his fierce old face there was something nice about his eyes.

The King had already departed and the Dauphin and Dauphine were about to leave. Once more Marie Antoinette lowered herself to eye level with Rose.

"I look forward to seeing you at Versailles again, Rose."

"Yes, please, Madame la Dauphine." Rose saw nothing unusual in her new friend kissing her on the cheek, not seeing it as a sign of favour exceptional in every way. Strict Court etiquette governed whom royalty could kiss in public and Rose was not included in that exalted category.

In the State Bedchamber the King was going through the ritual of the *coucher*. There was a delay in the presentation of his nightshirt, which was always brought forward ceremoniously spread across the arms of the nobleman of highest rank in the room. At the last minute one wing of the double doors opened and there entered a nobleman of still higher rank than the one who already held the nightshirt. It then had to be handed over to him with formality and the allotted number of bows. Hardly was this done when a duc of royal blood arrived and the privilege passed automatically to him with the same ceremony. Louis sighed with relief when the nightshirt was finally

slipped over his head and he was able to release his
breeches and step out of them. Such delays were not uncommon and this was by no means the record. He slid his
arms into the brocade dressing-robe held for him, put his
feet into matching slippers and then took from a gilt-
threaded cushion his nightcap and a handkerchief embroidered with the royal cipher. After kneeling for his prayers
and a blessing by the priest, he made the token gesture of
lying down in the bed. Then as soon as everyone had
bowed out of the room, he threw back the bedclothes and
sprang out to leave by another door to go through to his
private apartment. There, in the Clock Salon, the marvellous astronomical clock, a gilded bronze masterpiece that
was the pride of his collection, chimed midnight as he
went through a concealed door and up a secret staircase to
the apartment of Madame du Barry, his thoughts with the
way the evening had gone.

He was more than pleased that Marie Antoinette had
taken to the child. Had she not it might have complicated
his promise to Violette, although he would have had to put
his foot down with his daughter-in-law much as he had
done when, new to Court and youthfully outraged and
moral, she had refused to speak to Madame du Barry. In
that she had been encouraged by his daughters, Victoire
and Adélaïde, who he had to admit had become sour in
their spinsterhood, and he knew they taught her to intrigue. But eventually she had heeded his wishes. In spite
of his annoyance with her obstinacy at the time, he
thought her attitude basically sound since it showed her
standards were high and that she would be a faithful wife.
With all her butterfly ways she was totally loyal to his son
and never allowed any gallant to be free with her or to
forget that she was the future Queen of France. It was
really no wonder that delightful little Rose had charmed
her that evening, for he had seen in both woman and child
the same kind of innocence that nothing could sully.

He had been exceptionally fond of Rose's mother, probably because Violette had been part of the most traumatic
time of his life when he had had to cease making love to
Reinette, and then later when he had lost her. Violette's
pregnancy brought a natural end to their relationship.
Wanting to give her a memento, he had asked her what she

would like, expecting a request for a ruby necklace or some other costly gewgaw, but she had surprised him.

"Be benevolent to my child when he or she is grown. If I have a son let him be schooled and trained to take some high ministerial post. If I should give birth to a daughter, raise her up to be a lady-in-waiting to whomever the Dauphin shall marry. Madame de Pompadour was bourgeois, but you gave her the title of marquise to overcome that barrier to her being a member of the Court. Surely your child deserves no less?"

He had refrained from saying that he had many such bastard children and if he ennobled them all it would be a long task. Nevertheless he could not go back on his offer to her. "Very well. I will see that the child, whether male or female, is guaranteed a position at Court."

She had burst into tears and kissed his hand, making him wonder if she was fulfilling vicariously her own dream of being at Court, something she had hinted at often, but which he had never contemplated. Perhaps becoming pregnant had been her last throw towards that aim and it had not come off. At a later date he had been astonished to learn that she was Jasmin's daughter. In the letter in which Violette sent him this information, she had added that her daughter had a further claim to a position of merit since she was also the granddaughter of a duchesse.

He opened the door into Madame du Barry's boudoir. Bosomy and loving, swathed in some garment of silk and lace, she hugged him, kissed him and then drew away to slip her arm through his.

"Come along, France," she said merrily, using her nickname for him, "make us some coffee."

It was a little task he enjoyed, considering himself an expert, and he had always made it for everyone on the evenings of Reinette's sales of Sèvres china. That was the only link this woman had with her predecessor.

Rose was asleep long before reaching home. She had told Jasmin what the Dauphine had whispered to her. "She said she was so hungry that her tummy was rumbling like a drum."

Cradling her granddaughter in the crook of her arm, Jasmin smiled at the remark made to put a child at ease. It was a great pity that the lovely young woman had no children of her own, but it was common knowledge that the Dauphin had a physical problem that made it virtually impossible for him to make love. Jasmin, remembering the days when she was young and healthy, but neither wife nor lover, could discern that the Dauphine's wayward frivolousness and her need of constant entertainment was an outlet for the frustration of natural desires. Jasmin herself had channelled her need to love into caring for others in her charity work, although it was only with the passing of the years that she had come to see that. With her ability to organise she was still able to supervise her extensive charitable interests without losing any time with her granddaughter.

"You've given me happiness in my old age that I never thought to find," she whispered to the sleeping child. Then the lines of her face grew deeper in a wave of anxiety. What had this evening portended for Rose? A shiver of apprehension ran down her spine.

It was not long after the reception that the King fell ill with a fever while staying a few days at the Petit Trianon with Madame du Barry. He was expected to recover quite quickly and there was no anxiety. Then overnight everything changed. Jasmin was in town when she met an acquaintance who told her the bad news.

"Have you heard? The King has smallpox!"

"How seriously?" Jasmin asked quickly. The previous year she had nursed Rose and several members of her household not previously afflicted through a mild form of the disease and she hoped to hear it was the same.

"He has been taken back to Versailles."

Jasmin turned pale and pressed a hand to her heart. That meant only one thing. Louis was going to die!

For eleven days he suffered, remaining fully conscious while becoming a mass of rotting putrefaction that made those who attended him retch and vomit. Jasmin, remembering how it had been for Sabatin, the infection being of the same virulent form, wept for Louis and prayed for him to be released from his decomposing body. As the end finally drew near and knowing her household was immune to contagion, she felt free to go to the Château to be near him in his last hours.

She was given a seat in the Bull's Eye Salon, so called after the oval window set horizontally high in the gilded frieze. It was adjacent to the King's State Bedchamber, but he was spared having to die in the room he had never liked and was in his own private apartment. In the time of waiting she had the opportunity as never before to study the carvings of little children dancing and playing that made up the beautiful frieze, reminding her of her childhood days when Louis had been brought to Château Satory to avoid catching measles.

Suddenly there came a rumbling in the distance like thunder. She sprang to her feet as did the others who were waiting there. The noise became louder. If Versailles had been crumbling it could not have been greater. She and everyone else knew what it meant. A reign of fifty-nine years had come to an end and courtiers were running at top speed to be among the first to pay homage to the new King.

She bowed her head in a moment of silent prayer for Louis's soul, crossed herself and went from the room and through the anteroom beyond. She was in time to see a swarm of several hundred noblemen and women charging down the Queen's Staircase to join up with many more coming from another direction into the vestibule below. Vendors were scattered and two of the stalls collapsed, with expensive wares being trampled underfoot.

At her own pace she followed slowly in the wake of this great charge towards the Dauphin's apartment on the ground floor. She did not expect to get near and found the way jammed solid from the vestibule. There she would have stayed if a courtier, who was the same man who had given her instructions where to stand with Rose in the Hall of Mirrors, had not spotted her and beckoned. He led her through a private door and onwards until she reached the salon where the new King of France waited with his Queen just before the doors were flung wide to those hammering to come in.

She was overcome with compassion at the sight of them. They had seen the snuffing of a candle in an upper window which had told them the news, and they were like frightened children, clinging to each other on their knees and in tears.

"We are too young for this huge responsibility," Marie Antoinette sobbed to her husband, her face in his shoulder. "It is far too soon!"

He clutched her still tighter to him, closing his eyes in urgent prayer. "Be with us, Lord! We are too young to reign!"

It was at that moment the courtiers burst in. Jasmin's quietly spoken "Amen" to Louis XVI's prayer was lost in the tumult as was her view of the young couple in the sudden crush.

No more invitations came to Château Satory from Versailles. Probably some official had decided that names of no importance on the guest list should be crossed off in this new reign where youth predominated and older people mattered less. It was only a relief to Jasmin. Once again she felt free to supervise her granddaughter's upbringing without outside interference. In keeping with the way of children, Rose was thoroughly occupied with the present and never referred to that evening at Versailles except when the chef produced a caramel soufflé that tasted the same as one she had eaten there.

Michel called one day with the gift of a small painting for Rose. He remembered meeting Violette, whose face still shone out of paintings by Boucher in various high places, but she had made no particular impression on him apart from the fact that her features were eminently paintable. Her daughter was a different matter. Although he had no intention of maintaining any close contact, he wanted to give Rose something to keep and he had selected a painting of his own pony done in his early adolescence which he thought would please her. It was also of considerable value, although that aspect would be immaterial to a child.

Rose was delighted with it, quite on tiptoe with excitement. "What was the pony's name? How old were you when you had him? Where did you ride him?"

The questions came in a stream and he took pleasure in answering her. When she had gone running off to show the picture to everyone from her nurse to the stable lads, Jasmin thanked him.

"That was very thoughtful, Michel. After all, you and Béatrice have grandchildren of your own who would have liked it."

"There are others for them. It was only right that since our daughter has my portrait of you, our granddaughter should also possess a piece of my work."

As he left he hoped Violette had not taken the portrait for its commercial value. He felt he had judged her a little better than her mother had.

Life at Château Satory followed a well-established comfortable and peaceful routine. Gradually Jasmin found she was slower getting upstairs and it took her longer to carry out small tasks, but she continued to lead an active life, enriched by the company of her granddaughter who was growing and thriving. There was much talk these days about France's dire financial straits and nobody knew more than she of the state of the poor. The millions of near-starving people who worked the land had her particular sympathy, burdened as they were by feudal seigniorial rights to absent landlords as well as by taxes. But one should always hope for the future.

"It's pointless to dwell on the past," she declared firmly in conversation, quoting the principle to which she had always adhered, "although one should learn from it. Our young King will put things right eventually. We have only to give him time."

She knew that as yet he was too indolent, weakly letting the Queen meddle too much in political affairs. Marie Antoinette was far too scatter-brained and influenced by her own personal likes and dislikes to be deciding who should be appointed to high ministerial positions or dismissed from them.

Since becoming Queen she had gathered a clique of the younger, wilder members of Court around her, forever chasing after amusements in which her royal spouse took no part. He went to bed while she danced every night away either at Versailles or incognito in Paris at the disreputable Opéra balls, unless she was gaming at the card tables until dawn in reckless company. She rode astride, a tomboy in breeches, her horses always lively and full of speed. When the snows came there were breakneck races in sleighs all the way to Paris, she shrieking her delight. There was also her avaricious passion for diamonds, unslated even by the Crown jewels and gifts from the late King and her own husband. Not only did diamonds constantly adorn her person, but frequently they covered the voluminous skirts of her Court gowns as if every star in the firmament had been plucked down to sparkle there.

Ever since she had come to Versailles she had been irritated by the rigid etiquette. With her new power she was able to flout and change many things, stepping on people's toes in the process. None could gainsay her, least of all the King since he was deeply in love with her.

Inevitably lurid tales had sprung up about her, fostered by those harbouring grudges and many newly offended for some reason or another. She was both a leader of fashion and simultaneously a source of scandal. There was widespread approval among the populace when the King gave her the Petit Trianon to be her own little retreat, but fury when it became known that she had redecorated and refurbished it lavishly with no heed of the cost; afterwards she caused pique among those at Court not invited to the exclusive and often riotous parties she held there for her own close circle of friends. It gave rise to more gossip of a scurrilous nature that was without foundation as far as she was concerned. Apart from her gaming debts and her diamond-buying, her extravagance in costly gowns was another bone of contention, but the silk-weavers of Lyon were the first to shout their indignation when they learned of the simple muslin gowns she always wore at the Petit Trianon, declaring that she was out to ruin them.

"I can do nothing right," she exclaimed merrily to her companions. "What a joke it is!"

Jasmin, whose own impetuous youth had been nipped in the bud, listened tolerantly to all accounts of the latest imprudence of the Queen. She believed that Marie Antoinette's youthful waywardness would run its course. Then surely with maturity the wisdom would come that should enable the Queen to be a true helpmate to guide the ineffectual King along the firm way that was needed.

Much of what she knew of the Queen's escapades came from her banker, Monsieur Darrac, an older man who was also Jasmin's friend. He was frequently at Versailles advising aristocratic clients and keeping his finger on the pulse of the Court. Whenever he came to Château Satory to dine or drink a glass of wine, he regaled her with snippets of gossip and more serious developments.

"I only wish I could have warned the Queen from the start that royalty is always the target of mud-slingers," she said to him on a stroll to her rose garden. He was a keen gardener and she had a new bloom to show him.

"How right you are, madame," Monsieur Darrac replied. "It should have been pointed out to the Queen that simply by having Austrian blood in her veins she was immediately open to suspicion and mistrust. Our nation and hers have been traditional enemies for too many years for Frenchmen to be much impressed by the alliance her marriage was supposed to seal. Her present behaviour confirms all our countrymen's worst fears. They see it as a lack of interest in France itself."

They had reached the rosebeds and the subject of the Queen was dropped. Later Jasmin's thoughts returned to Marie Antoinette again, full of compassion that she should remain unfulfilled.

"I suppose there are some people who see me as being old and doddery," she remarked to Rose, speaking as much to herself as to the child, "but I think I see many things clearly and not much goes past me."

"You're ageless, Grand-mère!" The young arms caught her off guard with an impulsive hug, making her wince, the protest of her old bones a denial of the compliment.

When the Emperor Joseph II of Austria, the Queen's brother, paid a visit to Versailles it was to speak strongly to both Louis and Marie Antoinette on the subject of an heir to the Throne of France. After he departed the King submitted to a long-delayed operation. It was simple enough but painful and dangerous. The result was a cause for rejoicing when a few months later the announcement came that the Queen was pregnant.

"Now all will be well," Jasmin remarked optimistically to those in her social circle who liked to criticize the Queen. "I guarantee we shall see a change in our royal lady."

It was true that Marie Antoinette had never been happier. She had written joyfully to her mother on becoming a true wife at last. Now she was to bear a child, fulfilling a yearning that had made her shed many secret tears.

There were those at Court who found it impossible to understand how she could be surrounded every day by handsome courtiers fascinated by her and still remain faithful to the plain and stodgy King. His looks had been a disappointment to her when she had first seen him upon her arrival in France for their marriage, and in his shyness he had almost shrunk away from her kiss. But he had touched a chord in her, albeit no more than pity for his awkwardness. Since she was as quick and alert in everything as he was slow-thinking and tardy, their interests totally at variance, it had been a long time before she had come to appreciate his good qualities such as his amiability, his kind heart and his unfailing consideration towards her. She regretted the times when she had exploded with exasperation on meeting him coming dirty and dusty from his forge or a building site, because he was hurt by her tone and he did try always to bathe and change before she saw him. It did not suit her to be the dominant partner in the marriage. She would have liked a husband who was her equal on all planes, but since she was tied to Louis and believed to the depth of her being that marriage vows should never be broken, he would remain the only man in her life.

She had been attracted to other men. There were times when she allowed flirtatious kisses in the shadows, but her will was such that she had never lost control of herself, her strict moral upbringing in a puritanical Court saving her from indiscretion. There was only one man for whom she had felt love. He was Count Axel von Fersen, a handsome young Swede. Four years earlier they had both been eighteen when she had danced, masked and incognito, with him at a ball in Paris. Although they had met before at Versailles it had amused them to pretend for a while that she was not the Dauphine of France, which had made the encounter highly romantic. After that the air seemed to crackle for her whenever he appeared at Court between travels, even to the point when, after she was Queen, just to look at him had made her tremble and her eyes swim with tears. Her retirement from public life through her pregnancy had given her a breathing space in which she had tried to recover and in future she should be diverted by motherhood.

It was the eighteenth day of December in 1778 when Jasmin heard the bells of the Royal Chapel ringing to announce that the Queen's labour had commenced and she wished her well. At Versailles, Marie Antoinette was still far from uncomfortable, the twinges merely repetitive as she lay in her State Bedchamber in the Queen's Apartment. The windows had been closed and caulked for several days in order to keep out any dangerous cold air during the time of birth and everything was ready.

It was a beautiful room in which her baby would be the sixteenth royal child to be born. The décor was of her own choosing, the wall panels of Lyonnaise silk in a floral design with roses predominating on a cream ground. The huge bed canopy was ornamented with carved birds about to take flight, delicate foliage and flowers, all gilded and topped by huge white ostrich plumes. In the gilded bedhead, against the silken backcloth with a central design of a profusion of flowers and peacock feathers, her initials were embroidered in blue curly-tailed letters. *M.A.*

Around her bed were screens, allowing space within for those attending her, and Louis himself was roping them together. She watched him, full of gratitude. It was an innovation of which many would not approve, believing that a royal birth should be fully open to view, but he knew how intensely modest she was, even to bathing under a linen cape and having towels held up in order that neither her ladies-in-waiting nor her bathing-women should look upon her nudity. His strong blacksmith muscles bulged through the satin sleeves of his coat as he secured knots that should be impossible to loosen. It was gloomy within the screens, shutting out much of the wintry light from the windows, but the two crystal candelabra were fully lit and there were extra candelabra on a cabinet if they should be needed.

"That's it!" he exclaimed as the last knot was tied. He turned towards the bed where his wife held out her hand and he took it between his own. She gave him an affectionate smile.

"I thank you, Louis."

He kissed her fondly, never ceasing to marvel that fate had brought this wonderful girl into his life. He felt he could never have reigned without her. Giving her a little rippling wave of his fingers, he left the seclusion of the screens by way of one of the two apertures left by the wall.

He came to see her several times during the day, telling her how many Princes of the Blood had arrived, they having been summoned from Paris and wherever else they happened to be staying in order to be witnesses at the birth.

It was three o'clock in the morning when the Queen's

agony, which had been increasing over past hours, reached the stage at which the King and the royal witnesses had to be summoned. From the pillows she saw the shadows of the arrivals leaping up across the ceiling, heard the tut-tutting at the screens and the noise of scraping chair legs and chatter as places were taken. Louis came through an aperture to stand at the bedside and ask her anxiously how she was.

"Well enough," she managed to reply, struggling to keep back a moan of pain that was close to the surface. The *accoucheur* could not tell the King to leave, although he wished it, but fortunately the Princesse de Lamballe, a kind and gentle friend of the Queen, who was one of the ladies-in-attendance, whispered to Louis.

"Yes," he agreed with a nod, "naturally the Queen must save all her breath for her ordeal."

Giving her a loving backwards glance which she did not notice, her eyes screwed up and her face contorted, he left the seclusion of the screens and was alarmed to find that the room was fast filling up. The Court had been on the alert for the entry of royalty into the State Bedchamber and now that the princes and princesses were all there, a rush had been made to get in before the doors were closed, the high-dressed hair of some of the ladies being knocked awry in the process. All manners appeared to have been forgotten in the crush. Some had brought their own tabourets to sit on and two servants at their masters' orders had hauled in one of the set of tiered benches that were placed in the windows of the Hall of Mirrors at large gatherings. As soon as it was put down, there was a scramble for the top seat, which would at least give a view of the heads of the *accoucheur* and the ladies-in-attendance above those annoying screens. The chatter, the excited laughter and the rising arguments over precedence for places were more like those of a fairground than a lying-in chamber. The double doors aligned to the entrance on the opposite side of the room had been mercifully locked or else the influx would have been twice the number.

Louis looked desperately for a footman to stem the flow and sighted one crushed against the jamb of the other doorway. The panniered skirts of two ladies had wedged, causing a hold-up, much to the annoyance of those behind. Louis gave a shout: "Close those doors. Let no more in!"

The footman wriggled free and slammed the double doors shut. With the pressure eased, people in the room settled down, but there were at least fifty present and having come they could not be turned out. Louis took the high-backed armchair that had been put ready for him and the long vigil began.

The room soon became stiflingly hot. When his wife could no longer hold back her shrieks and cries, Louis covered his eyes with his hand, his elbow propped on the chair arm, and never moved. His silent prayers were for her and the infant who was taking an uncommonly long time to be born.

Dawn came. Except for the odd creak of a stool and the occasional whisper the only sounds came from the excruciating torment of the woman in the bed. In the fireplace the fire had long since fallen into grey ash and still the temperature rose, people mopping their foreheads and their necks in the airless room. Close to mid-morning, after nearly seven hours, one of the ladies-in-attendance fainted, unable to endure the Queen's suffering any longer. It acted like a spark to tinder. Many leapt onto their seats to peer over the screens, which rocked and would have toppled if the ropes had not held, others shouldering one another to see through the cracks, all shouting or shrieking, and even some of the royalty caught up by the fever of excitement sweeping through the room. In the midst of the turmoil there came a newborn cry.

Louis, already on his feet in alarm at the unruliness that had developed, gave an exclamation of joy and darted to the bedside, others hauling the screens aside to push forward. It was a girl, but that did not stop the cheers and jubilation that rang to the ceiling and could be heard in the Hall of Mirrors and beyond where people were waiting.

Suddenly in the bed the Queen collapsed, struggling for breath. The *accoucheur* gave a warning shout. "She's suffocating! Stand back!"

Louis never remembered how he reached the nearest window in a matter of seconds or how many Princes of the Blood and others he threw out of his way. His powerful fist shattered the glass and the cool air rushed in. At the bedside the *accoucheur* thought it had come too late and the Queen was already on the brink of death. He yelled for hot water to bleed her, but even if he had been heard in the commotion the delay would have made it too late. In desperation he snatched up one of his instruments and drove the point into the sole of her small foot, making the blood spurt. She jerked violently on the impact, giving an enormous gasp that filled her lungs, and some colour rushed back into her cheeks. In relief, he wiped the moisture from his forehead with his sweat-sodden shirt-sleeve and nodded to the King.

"All is well, sire. May the room be cleared?"

It was done. In the Cour Royale the cannons commenced to thunder forth a salute. At Château Satory Jasmin stood counting aloud with Rose the number of volleys. When they stopped at twenty-one she raised her eyebrows with a smile at her granddaughter. "It's a little Princess."

"Let's celebrate, Grand-mère! I'm sure she's a dear baby."

They celebrated with ices, in spite of the weather, and the chef made an elaborate concoction with spun sugar, eggs and cream. Instead of watered wine Rose was allowed a little *vin de Champagne,* which she thought pretty in colour, but too tingly on her tongue. Jasmin always enjoyed her granddaughter's comments and this impromptu party for the two of them was as pleasurable for her as it was for Rose.

During their conversation at table it was almost inevitable that Rose's chatter should turn from the new Princess to her own beginnings and those of her parents. There had been similar questions before, dating from the time when she had begun to gather friends who had parents and not just a grandmother to take care of them. As yet all the child knew was what had been told to everyone at the time of her babyhood.

"Where was I born, Grand-mère?"

"In the country," Jasmin answered truthfully. There had been a small mansion at that time on the edge of Versailles where the girls from the Parc aux Cerfs had been accommodated for their confinements. "Your mother was staying with friends."

"Were you there at the time, Grand-mère?"

A tricky question, but not intended to be. "That was not possible. Everything happened so quickly. The first I knew was when you were brought to me. Then I was told you no longer had a mother or father."

"What was my father like?"

"A charming man." Jasmin spoke warmly, her thoughts going back in time.

"Where was his birthplace?"

"Not far from here." Impossible to add that it was the same bedchamber in which the new Princess had arrived. "Would you like to stay up and see the fireworks? There's bound to be some over Versailles later and we should have a good view from one of the upper windows."

"Oh, yes!" The delicate subject was forgotten in the diversion offered, but Jasmin knew it would come up again. It seemed heartless to deny Rose the knowledge of a living parent, but Violette had demanded it and to all intents and purposes she was dead to the child she had not wanted.

When Rose reached early womanhood there was less peace in the house as emotional outbursts took place and there were several rebellious incidents, such as riding a horse forbidden to her and covering her face with cosmetics that made her look like a young clown. Jasmin suffered it all with patience, knowing that eventually a light would show beyond the trees. It did, coinciding with a wedding to which they were both invited. Michel's wife had died some while ago and he was marrying Béatrice after their many years together.

It was a quiet ceremony, only the family and a few close friends at the church. Michel's limp was more pronounced, but otherwise he looked in good health and had retained his broad-shouldered, well-proportioned build. Béatrice regarded him devotedly.

"I'm never going to marry," Rose announced when she and Jasmin arrived home again.

"Oh, why is that?"

"Think how dreadful it would be if I had to go as far away as you did when you married."

"That's not to say you would have to do the same. It's more likely you will have a home in Paris or elsewhere in the Île-de-France." Jasmin took care never to refer to Versailles in the context of anything that might lead the girl's thoughts in that direction.

"I don't want to live anywhere except at Château Satory. I'm going to stay here and look after you when you're really old."

Rose was so intensely serious that Jasmin refrained from raising an amused eyebrow. The bridegroom that day was seventy-four and she herself was not far behind. "I'll not hold you to that promise, my dear. Some day you're going to fall in love. That will be when you discover there are young men in the world as well as horses and ponies."

"You're teasing me, Grand-mère." Rose's face remained resolute. "But I mean what I say. I love you. You've been father and mother to me. I'm never going to leave you. I'll care for you as you have cared for me."

She flung her arms about her grandmother and pressed her smooth young cheek against the wrinkled one. Jasmin closed her eyes in thankfulness that her granddaughter had such a loving heart. She hoped that whoever won it would appreciate what he had received and give back in the same measure.

By the time Rose was fifteen she had made the discovery that her grandmother had prophesied. Her interest in horses did not wane, but suddenly she noticed as never before the older brothers of her friends and was aware of male smiles and attention that was thoroughly pleasing. The first ball ever to be held at Château Satory since Marguerite's time seemed to her as much in celebration of what fun her life would be as of her actual natal day. She danced every dance and could have had her first kiss if shyness had not overcome her. She still had that experience to come, not through lack of opportunity but through an instinctive coquettishness.

Her carefree days proved to be numbered. Then the blow fell, shattering everything in which she had always felt secure and safe. It came exactly three months before she was to turn sixteen. A distinguished-looking nobleman called on her grandmother and they were closeted together in the Ivory Salon for an hour before she was sent for. She found them seated together at the Boulle table, documents spread over the marqueterie surface.

Jasmin looked towards her as soon as the door opened. Rose still made an entry whenever she came into a room. It was not done consciously any more than in the past when she had arrived in a state of dishevelment. There was something about her vivacious face, the sparkle of anticipation in her long-lashed eyes and her lively step that drew the full attention of whoever was in the room. Jasmin was often reminded of Madame de Pompadour, not that Rose bore any likeness to her, but the girl exuded the same goodwill and fascinating charm. Recently the Queen had tired of high, pomaded hair and had set a new fashion, turning to a coiffure of width instead of height, unpowdered and natural. Rose with her abundant curls was able to set off the new mode to its best, adding to her attractiveness.

"Be seated, Rose," Jasmin said when the presentations were over, and the Comte de Gramont waited for the girl to sit down first.

At first sight of him Rose had become nervous. The fact that her grandmother looked anxious added to her sense of foreboding. She was horribly afraid that this was a suitor who, for some reason, had not been shown the door. But it proved to be far from that. She sat in stunned silence as he proceeded to reveal the purpose of his visit.

"The late King, Louis XV, left instructions that on this day you should be given the title of the Marquise de Chuard with your own coat of arms, three golden griffins on a crimson ground. There is no longer any land or property to go with the title, this being an extinct marquisate that has been revived specially for you, but you will receive a suitable income."

Rose was staring at him in utter bewilderment. "I don't understand. Why should I be chosen for this? I only met Louis XV once and I was a child of six at the time."

He exchanged a glance with her grandmother before looking back at her. "Madame la Duchesse will explain the finer points to you later. That has been agreed between us. Prior to your coming to Court—"

"To Court! What should I do there? This is my home."

"It will still be your home. As I was saying it will be necessary for you to have a three months' course of instruction by a lady appointed by the Queen in the etiquette of Court life. Admittedly Her Majesty has made some alterations, but the basic principles remain and must be learned if you are not to make any solecisms that would embarrass you and all those around you. This will start tomorrow. On the eve of your sixteenth natal day you will go from here to Versailles where you will take up residence in an apartment already allotted."

Rose stood up. She was angry and indignant that this person should come without warning to change her life by some whim of the late King on the strength of his seeing a child who had amused him. "I can't accept this marquisate. I have no wish to live at Court. My place is with my grandmother." She moved to Jasmin's chair and stood by it protectively. "Nothing shall make me leave her."

"Admirable sentiments, but Madame la Duchesse has already agreed to your going." He ignored the look of betrayal that the girl shot at her grandmother. "The Queen is protective of her young ladies and keeps them, so to speak, under her wing."

"Are you saying that I am to attend the Queen?" Rose spoke on a note of disbelief.

"You have been thus honoured." He stood to make his departure and indicated the papers on the table. "I am sure you will want to study these documents at your leisure. I shall call again in a few days at a time convenient to you when I will answer any questions you may want to put to me." He made his farewells to Jasmin and then to her. "I shall look forward to our next meeting, Madame la Marquise."

Left on their own in the room together neither the old woman nor the girl spoke for several minutes. Jasmin, steeling herself for what was to come, moved to a more comfortable seat on a fireside sofa while Rose, still standing, picked up the documents and read them through. When she had finished she went across to the window and looked unseeing towards the summer pavilion where she and Jasmin had had many picnic suppers together on warm evenings.

"Am I a royal bastard, Grand-mère?"

Jasmin's chin jerked at the directness of the question. "Louis XV was your father. This royal honour automatically legitimises you."

"I always felt there was something mysterious about my origins. Lately I've been convinced that something was being kept from me and was sure you would tell me when I came of age. But I never dreamed it would be anything like this."

"I made a promise to your mother that I would only reveal your father's true identity when I was sure the time was right. I had planned it should be on your wedding eve."

Rose moved away from the window and came to face her, still standing, accusation in her eyes. "Did that conversation take place before or after my birth? How many lies have you told me?"

"None that were not forced on me by a promise made. I never wanted to withhold the truth from you, feeling that it would be better if you knew. If I had had any idea that this marquisate was intended for you, I would have prepared you long ago." It added to Jasmin's distress to see her granddaughter's expression was not only blended of hurt and bewilderment, but there was also something close to enmity. She had seen the same hostility in Violette's young face and it almost tore her apart to have it turned on her again where there had never been anything but love before. With a tentative hand she patted the sofa seat beside her. "Sit down. I will tell you everything."

Rose deliberately took a chair opposite and sat stony-faced as Jasmin revealed everything from the circumstances of Violette's birth and on through all that had followed.

"If I had not agreed to your mother's conditions she would not have let me keep you. That was made plain to me by her attitude." Jasmin's lips were quivering and her whole body was trembling as if she had been stricken by palsy, making her clasp her violently shaking hands together as though she feared they might fly off like birds. "One should never congratulate oneself on anything. I have always prided myself on making no errors in your upbringing. Instead, I made the gravest mistake of all by not keeping to what I knew in my conscience to be right."

"I'm afraid you did," Rose answered coldly. "I always trusted you. You were my anchor. Whenever I felt those sudden desperate longings to have parents of my own, I told myself that I had you and nobody could be dearer to me. All the time you were maintaining a lie and keeping up deceits that now make me feel blighted and lost. You say that my mother married an Austrian nobleman. She should not be difficult to trace."

"I don't know whether she is alive or dead!"

"I want to know either way. If she is still alive I shall write to her. At least she owes me one explanation. If she knew of the likelihood of the marquisate why did she not forewarn you?"

"I think I can answer that. During our conversation I told her that I would give you the happy, normal childhood that had never been hers. I promised that you should grow up carefree, secure in the knowledge of being loved in a stable home. Your mother, remembering how she had been filled with foolish dreams of Versailles, must have decided that whatever lay ahead for you should be kept secret until the time came."

Rose nodded restlessly, accepting the explanation, and threw herself up from the chair as if not knowing how to contain the misery she was suffering. "I'll not write, then. She wouldn't want to hear from me anyway. Let her go on believing that a stupid lie about her dying in childbirth is still keeping me in ignorance."

"Don't think too harshly of her. In her own way she did what she thought best for you."

"It should have been enough to leave me with you. I don't want this title and all it entails!" With a furious sweep of her hand she sent the documents flying from the table. "How shall I endure Court dress from morning until night and the endless formal occasions and the curtseying and all the shades of protocol that govern that gilded way of life?" She threw back her head in despair. "I shan't be able to breathe!"

"Oh, my dear child!" Jasmin was sharing her distress. "There's no way out for you. What a King has decreed, so shall it be. As I have told you, I was not much older than you are now when my world fell apart. You are strong and will face and conquer all the difficulties that await you. At least we shall not be far apart. We can see each other often."

"Is that so, Grand-mère?" Rose's gaze was icy. "I'm going into an existence as alien to me as if it were on another continent. I'll no longer be a person in my own right, but a vassal of the Queen, only able to come and go at her bidding."

"She was kind to you on the one occasion that you met her."

"I don't doubt her kindness. She is as much a prisoner of Versailles as I shall be and less fortunate, because she had to marry for political reasons. At least no one shall ever make me marry. Once I thought to stay here and care for you. Although I have been deprived of that chance it makes no difference for another reason. To marry means to bear children and that I will never do. I could never bring a child into the world to suffer the misfortunes that have fallen in different ways on you and my mother and me." She turned to face Marguerite's portrait and addressed it in a self-mocking tone. "Even you join us there, Arrière-grand-mère. I remember being told long ago how you lost the man you loved. We are not very fortunate, are we? We women with the flower names. At least there'll never be another to add to the bouquet!"

A huge sob rose up in her. Flinging the back of her hand across her mouth, she swirled about and rushed from the room, failing to hear what Jasmin called after her.

"But two of us have known a great love. Your mother was on the brink of it and it will come to you!"

The girl's running footsteps disappeared upstairs. Jasmin made to leave the sofa and found that a delayed reaction had set in to the shock of the Comte de Gramont's news and the subsequent scene with her granddaughter. All strength had gone from her legs. Unable to move, the bell-rope out of reach, she would have to wait until somebody came within earshot. Without panic, knowing that all she needed was a little time to recover, she fixed her thoughts firmly away from herself and on to the new society that Rose would be entering in three months' time.

There was no denying that the Queen was as extravagant and as set in her own ways as ever, but since the birth of Princesse Marie Thérèse, followed later by a miscarriage, the death of her own mother and then the arrival of a son, she had slowed her pace somewhat and become more level-headed. Jasmin could feel certain that her granddaughter would be in no moral danger at Versailles. Her assumption was not based solely on the Comte de Gramont's reassurance, but also on her knowledge of the kind of girl that Rose had grown up to be.

Eighteen

Rose had never known anything more tedious than the three months of preparation for Court. Her dancing master had taught her deportment, but her walk, which was neat enough, had to be changed entirely. She must only take tiny steps in order that her skirts appear to glide over the floor as if she were on wheels. There was also the manner of greeting those of rank, something she thought she had been taught already, but this was to differ between women who were better married than others, even if they should bear the same title, blood being bluer in their veins. This meant memorizing the relationships of all the great families, about which she had to take written tests, which made her feel as if she were a scholar at a university.

There were days at a stretch when she had to give a hundred versions of the same deep curtsey, depending on who her instructress was pretending to be. There were even lessons out of doors in her sedan chair when she was told to stop her bearers and get out to curtsey should royalty be approaching, but if she were in a carriage, on the other hand, she could halt her coachman and remain seated until royalty had gone by. At times her head spun with it all.

The Queen had sent the Duchesse de Noailles, the best instructress available. Madame Étiquette was her nickname, given to her by the Queen herself when newly arrived in France. This formidable lady had accompanied her everywhere, correcting, instructing and supervising her on formal occasions right through to the day she became Queen. Then Marie Antoinette had gladly rid herself of such depressing company.

"Cast off like an old glove," Madame Étiquette had grumbled to her friends. A sourness remained with her and she counted herself with the Queen's enemies, something she was careful not to reveal at Château Satory.

"Come now," she snapped at Rose. "Don't scowl. It is the height of discourtesy in pleasant company to be anything but smiling. Keep all ill humours to yourself. Neither must you ever mention death at Court, except in private condolence immediately after the event. Afterwards it must be as if it had never happened, even if it should be your own husband."

"That's heartless."

Madame Étiquette's eyes glinted. "Such manners have evolved over a long period to make life more agreeable for all and to show by small definitions how one nobleman or noblewoman has advanced in degree beyond the rest. It is not for you to question protocol but to obey, madame! Let us continue. Imagine you are a duc going to Mass in the Royal Chapel. How will you place your sitting and kneeling cushion on the marble floor?"

"At a definite angle."

"Why is this?"

"Because only Princes of the Blood may have theirs straight."

"Good. What notice would you like to see on the door of your apartment if you were away from Versailles with the Court on campaign or elsewhere?"

"The notice would read, *For the Marquise de Chuard*, if I were being given ultimate respect, but only my name if I was not."

"That's right. Many would cut off their ears to get a *For* on their door, but it is not as easy as that."

The questions went on and on. Madame Étiquette could be viciously sarcastic and Rose came to hate her, thinking it was no wonder she was never in the Queen's company.

Rose's feelings towards Jasmin were still in a turmoil. By reason of the lessons they spent far less time together. Mealtimes also became periods of instruction when Madame Étiquette pretended it was a banquet with a foreign dignitary or some such affair, until Rose longed to empty a plate of food over her supercilious head.

Jasmin herself was numb with sadness. Since the shock she had suffered, all strength seemed to have ebbed from her limbs. She took to using a cane, but followed Michel's example in keeping her back and neck as straight as possible. On the surface she and her granddaughter appeared to be as before, but laughter and ease were lacking. A great gulf had opened up between them and even when Rose bade her good night the kiss that was given seemed to come from leagues away.

Mademoiselle Bertin, the Queen's own dressmaker, came to organise and make a whole new wardrobe for Rose to cover every aspect of Court life. Fashion had banished panniers with the high-dressed coiffures, and now skirts fell straight and full, parting in the front to show embroidery or a contrasting pattern or colour. When finished Rose's new garments were delivered to her apartment at Versailles to await her arrival.

On the day she became sixteen Rose left Château Satory, Jasmin accompanying her just to see her into the apartment. Early that morning Rose's maid, Diane Arnaud, had gone ahead to unpack and get everything ready for her. Diane was the granddaughter of Jasmin's faithful maid, Lenore, and had been trained specially for her position. As Diane was three years older than Rose and as capable and reliable as her mother, Lenore's daughter-in-law, now housekeeper at Château Satory, Jasmin had no worries about new servants taking advantage of Rose's unfamiliarity with her new surroundings or stealing from her.

It was a silent journey to Versailles. Jasmin wanted to seize this last chance to reach out to the girl and try to mend their rift, but Rose's whole attitude was rigidly unapproachable, her gaze set out of the window although it was obvious she was seeing nothing that passed by.

Jasmin was dreading the stairs, for the apartment was on

the second floor, but upon arrival at Versailles they were told that the chair-lift was still in use. It had been installed to save Madame de Pompadour the effort of the stairs when she had first lived on the same floor before moving into her later, more regal accommodation. Jasmin was winched up in style, entertained by the short ride.

Rose's apartment was small, consisting of a tiny boudoir, a bedchamber and a bathroom with an ornate porcelain stove and a green marble bath from which the unplugged water would run away through a grating in the marble floor. The décor throughout was blueish-white and gold; all had been newly decorated and the silk hangings and furnishings were of the best. Rose went to the windows and looked down on the black and white court of the East Front. There was also a sideways view of the windows and balcony of the King's State Apartment on the floor below. So far she had said nothing.

"It's all most comfortable," Jasmin said to break the unhappy silence as she lowered herself onto the peach silk sofa.

Rose thumped a fist in frustration against a folded-back shutter. "It's my prison cell!" she exclaimed bitterly. Then she spun about, intending some other outcry of protest, but saw only the anguished face of her grandmother who, in this alien place, represented all the love and security she had ever known. Her own folly reared up at her. She darted forward to drop to her knees and throw herself across Jasmin's lap. "I've been cruel to you, Grand-mère! I know you only did what you had to do, but I haven't been able to forgive you. I see how wrong I was. It is you who should be forgiving me for these three long months in which I shut myself away from you."

Jasmin stroked the wayward curls. "Hush, my dear. Don't upset yourself. I understood, but it was more than I dared hope that you and I could be friends again."

Rose raised a tear-stained face. "Always! If ever you need me I'll come to you."

"I'm sure you will." Jasmin took a scented handkerchief from her purse to shake it from its folds and give it to Rose to dry her eyes. "Long ago I learned that when things cannot be changed, the only way is to seek out what is best. You will find much to enjoy in your new life. There will be compensations. Here, under this roof, you will meet some

of the most talented and interesting and exciting people in
the world and they will make up for all the rules and
regulations that you have to suffer. There's no reason to
lose your old ties. I think you will find yourself less of a
prisoner than you presently believe yourself to be." She
patted Rose's cheek. "Now I could drink a cup of delicious
Chinese tea. Jerk that extremely fancy bellpull and see
what happens."

Rose sat back on her heels and gave a watery grin, still
wielding the handkerchief. "I shall avenge myself on Madame Étiquette by slurping my tea out of a saucer," she
threatened mischievously.

Jasmin made a face of mock severity and shook her
folded fan reprovingly. "Not in my presence!"

She left soon after the tea was drunk, for Rose had to
meet her household, which consisted of ten servants—the
Queen had a hundred—and also change to present herself
in that lady's Petits Cabinets at six o'clock. Jasmin took
advantage of the chair-lift to descend while Rose hastened
down the stairs to meet her at the bottom of the silk-hung
shaft and see her into her carriage. They embraced each
other fondly. Jasmin was relieved that Rose appeared
slightly more cheerful. It enabled her to go home far more
comforted in her heart and mind than when she came.

Normally Marie Antoinette never received strangers in
her Petits Cabinets, which were a hideaway of small and
charming rooms for rest and seclusion that she entered by
way of a concealed door in her State Bedchamber, but she
had not forgotten how overpowering everything had appeared to her when she had first arrived at Versailles. She
had decided that an invitation to the intimate surrounds of
her little library would put the girl at ease. Unlike the
King, who even worked on affairs of state in his fine new
library, she was not an avid reader, but the books she liked
were arranged behind the glass doors of the green silk-
backed shelves together with a collection of small lacquer
objets d'art which she treasured. A tap came on the door.
"Enter."

Rose found Marie Antoinette turning from the window
to greet her with a smile. She had an immediate impression of the Queen's cream velvet elegance, ash-blonde hair
brushed smoothly into the fashionable width, before she

dipped into the deepest curtsey of all that was reserved for the King and Queen.

"Welcome to Versailles, Madame la Marquise. This is a reunion, is it not? I remember having supper with you in the Venus Salon a long time ago. Sit down and let us talk."

It was for Rose as it had been before. She was immediately aware of a rapport between the Queen and herself, although as a child she could not have identified the same feeling of trust and liking that flooded through her again without any expectation of it. They chatted for quite a while and laughed together several times. The depression that had afflicted Rose for the past three months, already lifted to a degree by her reconciliation with her grandmother, had receded a little further by the time she left the Queen's library, where emblems of the House of Hapsburg made it truly Marie Antoinette's own domain.

As Madame Étiquette had forewarned, Rose found that her days were long. She had to be present when the Queen was awakened in her State Bedchamber, although not always to rise immediately. If she had been dancing all night she would fling an arm across the lacy pillows and bury her face against the light in pretty dishevelment to fall asleep again. After a while she would be woken again, this time more persistently, and the Mistress of the Robes would present a peignoir for her to don. Rose, being the newest and therefore the humblest lady-in-attendance, had to stay in the background and was not allowed as much as to touch the little pair of satin slippers that the next in rank presented for the royal feet.

Yet Marie Antoinette never overlooked her. While eating a frugal breakfast of coffee and specially baked Austrian bread she would chatter away to her ladies and always included Rose. Then came the first of the Queen's big decisions for the day when she would glance through a pattern book of all the hundreds of gowns she possessed and make a selection, several changes being necessary before it was bedtime again. Next Monsieur Léonard arrived from Paris to dress the Queen's hair, combing the soft, fair hair back and away at the sides from her face with a cluster of ringlets at the back.

With the hairdresser's departure she sometimes received those wishing to see her on some matter and eventually, sumptuously gowned, she would emerge from her apartment to go to Mass with the King, Rose and the other ladies falling in behind. The rest of the day was taken up with official appointments, followed by any number of social events. Contrary to Jasmin's prediction, there was little or no change in Marie Antoinette's mad chase after pleasure. She was as resolute about keeping boredom at bay as Louis XV had been.

Inevitably Rose, healthy, energetic and in love with life, took to the endless round of entertainments as soon as she had overcome her homesickness. Within six months it was as natural to her as if she had been born to it. Since the Queen never at any time, no matter how high-spirited her mood or how riotous the gathering, behaved with the least impropriety, Rose knew the salacious gossip about her immorality to be untrue.

Admittedly when at public balls in Paris the Queen was the first to join in the country dancing, letting her petticoats fly, and she would shout as loudly as anyone else in the excited crowd when urging on the jockeys straining for the winning post at racing on the Plaine des Sablons. But these and other such minor matters were to Rose only the exuberances of youth in which she herself revelled. She could see how such a fun-loving Queen could offend many, but the tales of licentious behaviour at the Petit Trianon and secret assignations by night in the park were the lewd imaginings of the scandal-mongers. It enraged Rose that such a physically modest woman as Marie Antoinette should be so foully slandered.

She discussed the matter with Jasmin on one of her visits home. Since she was not among the privileged invited to the Petit Trianon, she was able to take trips to Château Satory more often than she had anticipated and could sometimes stay a night or two.

"There are those who say the Queen should never go to the Opéra Balls in Paris, but she and the rest of us in the party are always masked and incognito."

Jasmin smiled with a lift of her brows. "Do you really think she is not immediately recognised whatever her disguise? You all enter bright as dragonflies, the Queen in diamonds that few could match and her personality as sparkling. She may not mind that people from all walks of life, from the nobility to the lowest courtesan, rub shoulders in that dubious place, but there are a vast number of people who do object to her going there."

"But it is the diverse company that helps to make it such an exciting place, Grand-mère!"

"I trust you never dance with strangers."

"Never." Rose's lower lip came close to a protesting pout. "The Queen will not allow it."

"I'm relieved to hear it. She has more good sense beneath that flibberty-gibbet façade than anyone gives her credit for."

"You like her, don't you, Grand-mère?"

"I do, although I've had no contact with her since that evening when you were still a child."

"It's woe betide anyone *she* doesn't like, whatever their rank! She loathes Cardinal de Rohan and will never look in his direction. I heard her say privately that no lecher of his depravity should be allowed a cardinal's hat."

Jasmin nodded. "She would know all about him from her late mother. He once held a foreign minister's post at the Austrian Court and the Empress had him sent home to France because of his inexcusable behaviour."

"The Queen mentioned that once. To make matters worse, he's stupid as well as profligate, always fawning after the Queen in the hope of political advancement. He seems to think that his banishment is all she has against him, instead of having the wit to understand that she and the King know much more."

"Is he secretly her enemy, do you think?"

"No. He's too thick-headed and puffed up with his own conceit to seek power by any other way."

It had not taken Rose long to find out that just being the Queen's lady-in-waiting was enough to make her enemies of her own, something she kept from her grandmother to save her worry. Anyone showing loyalty to the Queen was immediately hated by those hostile to her. Rose received slights and glares on many occasions, but was only upset by a printed leaflet she found lying on her bed.

"What's this?" she asked Diane, who was about to help her undress for the night.

The maid regarded the leaflet with surprise. "I don't know, madame."

"How did it get here?"

"I've no idea. Except for ten minutes I've been in the apartment all evening."

Rose picked it up and the first lines inflamed her fury. "It's filthy and libelous. A poem about the Queen of the kind I'm told is handed out in the streets of Paris and elsewhere." She hurled it into the fire.

Interrogation among her other servants did not reveal the culprit. To her relief no more leaflets appeared and she could only suppose one of her enemies had sneaked it into her rooms.

But she had not seen the last of this pornographic material. A while afterwards she accompanied the Queen with others to the Comédie-Française. As she entered the grand box in the wake of the Queen, she spotted to her horror a similar leaflet in the same bold print on the brocaded seat of the royal chair. She would have snatched it up, but the Queen, who must have seen what it was, merely crumpled it up without looking at it and cast it to the floor, keeping her heel on it throughout the performance. It confirmed Rose's belief that the Queen knew what was said about her and simply did not care, for she was as merry that evening as she always was when out to enjoy herself.

Rose took her lead from this action and thereafter concentrated only on what was pleasant in her life at Court, becoming wholly absorbed into the gilded isolation of Versailles, the months speeding by until she had been there for two years, almost without her being aware of the passing of time, her days so full and her evenings lighthearted, dazzling occasions. It was now as important to her which lovely gown she should wear to dance in the Hall of Mirrors, or to play cards or billiards, as it was to the Queen. The days when it had made her irritable to put on fancy clothes were a far distant memory. She and Diane always discussed her wardrobe for the day with a dedication that once she would have thought absurd.

There was competition among the ladies' maids as to whose mistress would look the best on any given occasion and Diane's fever to be the winner led to original and tasteful ornamentation and style that did make Rose stand out from the rest. It suited her that gowns were soft and billowing, supported by many petticoats and a minimum of padding, without hoops or other restrictions, only those with figures less sylphlike than hers still needing the constriction of stays. Mademoiselle Bertin was forever making her new additions to her wardrobe and she wore out her dancing shoes so fast that the shoemaker had a regular order to keep her supplied. Frequently she found herself in debt and had to extricate herself with tedious economies, not daring to ask her grandmother for a loan.

Her supple waist was a target for many a strong arm. She had discovered early in her days at Versailles how delicious it was to be kissed and embraced, but there she drew the line, keeping off all exploratory hands. It was amazing how many men sulked when repulsed or grew angry as if just being male gave them some divine right over a woman they fancied. She did not care a snap of her fingers for any of them, except those who had accepted good-humouredly that, since they could not be her lovers, at least they would be her friends. She talked about the courtiers to Jasmin when they had supper one evening in the summer pavilion at Château Satory. They always made a celebratory occasion of her coming home.

"There's no denying that many of the men at Court are truly handsome," she said, enjoying her favourite version of biscuit manqué which the chef had mounted on a silver dish surrounded by rosebuds, "and lots more are extremely attractive." There was a spot of cream on her lip and she licked it off with the tip of her tongue in a manner of which Madame Étiquette would not have approved. "They all have one fault in common, or that is what I've found in the ones I meet, which is they think they're irresistible." The amusement danced in her eyes and came forth in a giggle. "I teach them that they're not!"

"Poor unfortunate men!" Jasmin replied in the same vein. "What of those who have asked the Queen for permission to court you?"

"She knows my attitude towards marriage." Rose looked thoughtful for a moment, her head tilted and the spoon poised halfway to her mouth. "I may marry someone I like when I've retired from Court to live here again and need a companion to sit with me by the fire."

Jasmin kept her expression composed since this statement was intended seriously. So love had not come yet to this granddaughter of hers, who had turned into a beauty in a strangely fascinating way that had nothing to do with a perfection of features. It was the same witchlike allure that shone out of Marguerite's portrait, had bypassed her, glinted waywardly in Violette and returned again with the streak of wildness in Rose. Surely those rebellious curls, bobbing about her teasing face, should warn all would-be seducers that here was a woman no ordinary man could handle.

Château Satory always seemed empty to Jasmin when Rose had left again. It was as if she took the sunshine with her. Jasmin found herself huddling closer to the fire for warmth and began to feel the cold at all times of the year, reminded of Madame de Pompadour and her almost constant need of a shawl.

Sometimes she wondered if unconsciously she was feeling the chill wind blowing across France. She received many visitors in connection with her charity work, almost all of which she had had to delegate in her increasing frailness. Through what she was told, and from written accounts of developments delivered to her, she was certain she was able to understand many things that were happening better than anyone at Versailles. With her alert mind she saw unmistakable danger signals that made her anxious. People were restless. French regiments had gone to help the Americans in their revolt against England, and now they were returning with talk of new freedoms and the abolishment of class that was further undermining the established order of France. For herself she felt no French King should have supported a rebellion against another monarch, but obviously there had been a golden chance to secure a brash new ally against France's old enemy, England, and it was being said by all that the French had helped to give George III a bloody nose. She only hoped there would not be repercussions of an unexpected kind. It was not just the poor who were growing increasingly resentful, but the bourgeoisie too, breaking new ground in outspokenness against the privileged classes of the nobility and the clergy. Even a number of those bearing high rank, such as the Duc d'Orléans, had become malcontents of the first order to wrest power from the Throne.

Rose was untouched by any of this gloom, absorbed completely into the gilded scene around her, as if all the troubles of the world stopped at the palisades of Versailles. Her days were as carefree as any she had known, marked by extravagances that sometimes ran her into debt. Lucky at cards, she usually managed to win what she needed to make her solvent again, making sure never to play with those whom she knew to be cheats. Rank and position were no guarantee of honesty at cards, but it was a subject it would be grossly impolite to mention and a situation accepted by all.

Being younger than the rest of the ladies-in-waiting gave Rose an advantage that she appreciated. The Queen often took her along to the quarters of the royal children, having noticed her open and warm response to them. They would all go out into the park if the weather was fine, otherwise it would be play indoors with little Princesse Marie Thérèse and her younger brother. Marie Antoinette adored her children. She and Rose would sit on the floor with them, building with bricks or spinning a top or dressing dolls. Sometimes the King would appear and join in a game. Whenever the little Dauphin lisped a need to "pee-pee" the King would kneel to unbutton the child's flap and hold the small silver chamber pot until all was done and the button fastened again. Both children loved to ride on their father's shoulders and the Queen would lift them up in turn. They clutched the King's formally dressed curls as if at a bridle and shrieked their delight at being so high in the air. Rose, watching and joining in the laughter, thought how they all made a perfect family picture. This royal couple was united in love for the children, even though anyone could see that the Queen had no more than an amiable fondness for her big, lumbering husband in spite of his obvious devotion for her.

Yet they had more in their relationship than most married couples, Rose observed, many of whom actively disliked each other and spoke like strangers when compelled by some formality to appear together. Daily her resolve against marriage grew and she became cynical about love. Versailles was full of passionate affairs that fizzled out after a few months, and often less, as one partner became bored with the other. How glad she was to be free of entanglements!

Her first visit to the Petit Trianon was made with the Queen and the children. It was as if Marie Antoinette had suddenly woken up to the fact that Rose was no longer a newcomer to her circle of attendant ladies, but had become a well-liked and amusing companion. The Queen always wore simple white muslin gowns when at her favourite retreat, usually with a pastel-coloured silk sash. Rose was similarly clad, both of them in large straw hats, when they set off in a two-seater calèche, the children tucked between them and the Queen with the reins. They sang together as they bowled along, the little Dauphin giving squeals of merriment. It was only ten minutes' drive away. When almost there they passed the rose marble Trianon where once the Sun King had sought the same kind of peace and rest from the rigidity of Court etiquette as Marie Antoinette had found at the Petit Trianon, which they reached after another short verse of their song.

The gilded gates stood open and they spun into a square forecourt. Rose had seen the neoclassic house many times, but this was the closest she had ever been to it. Compared with Versailles it was a minuscule doll's house and it would not have taken much imagination to see the whole cube-shaped building slotted into one of the staterooms at the Château. The Queen sprang out, always excited to be back at the place she loved most, and lifted out the children. Holding her son on her hip and taking her daughter by the hand, she scampered through the open door as if she were a child herself.

Rose followed more slowly. The Queen and the children were already disappearing up the staircase with its handsome banisters to the main floor. Arriving upstairs, Rose went through an anteroom into what she guessed had once been Madame du Barry's dining room to judge by the fruit motifs on the walls. Then she went on into a drawing room and a company salon of delicate elegance, everywhere light and airy and filled with sunshine, still without catching up with the others. The chatter of the children guided her to the Queen's boudoir.

"Come in, Madame Rose," the Queen called, this form of address to a titled woman having nothing to do with her being married or single. She had both children on her lap and was holding a bowl of sweetmeats from which she was allowing them to make a choice. "Come and see which colour you would like!"

It was the start of the happiest of days. They played hide and seek in the grounds which had been simply landscaped in the English style with woods and meadows, a secret grove, two lakes and a bubbling stream. Rose took the Dauphin with her while Marie Antoinette and her daughter hid individually. Then they went over the rustic wooden bridge to the Hamlet, which was a little farm specially created there, the children eager to see the animals.

Once again Rose was struck with the toylike layout of everything. There was no reek from the byre, no dungheaps, and when the children greeted the goats Rose observed that the animals had been washed and their coats brushed.

"Let's see the cows now, Maman!" Marie Thérèse clapped her hands in excitement.

"We'll get the bells first."

They called at one of the twelve thatched cottages in which lived the peasant families specially selected to work this dream farm. A woman was baking bread and she was not in the least flustered by having the Queen in her kitchen, being well used to it, and smiling and bobbing she took a bunch of blue ribbons hung with bells from a peg on the wall. Before the children left she gave them both a new-baked roll.

The cows were grazing in the Hamlet's meadow, glossy as well-groomed horses. The Queen put the ribbons around their necks and the air became filled with the prettiest tinkling from the bells, no discordant clang of an ordinary cowbell here.

"Don't the cows look pretty, Madame Rose?" Marie Thérèse exclaimed. "When I'm bigger I'm going to be allowed to milk them as Maman does sometimes."

Rose had noticed the royal milk buckets when they had passed the dairy. They were of white porcelain, probably Sèvres, with the Queen's initials in blue. "What will your brother do here when he is older?"

"Drive the hay-cart and the wagons. That is a boy's work."

In spite of the pristine condition of everything necessary for the coming and going of a fastidious woman who did not like dirt or unpleasant smells, this was a real farm and produce from it served both the Petit Trianon and, to an extent, Versailles. They dined on some of its meat, vegetables and salads in the Queen's house in the Hamlet, for she had a retreat here as well. Although rustic in its exterior, it had all the amenities from a billiard room to a backgammon room, a Chinese salon and a library. After finishing dinner with a surfeit of strawberries and cream, the children took a nap. Until they woke again Rose sat with the Queen on the open gallery of the house where they chatted and watched the field workers. The day ended with the children having a ride on the Chinese merry-go-round that stood on the lawn at the Petit Trianon.

There followed many such excursions. Anyone who came to the Petit Trianon had to be specially invited, even the King, who had a small attic bedchamber above the main floor. Rose slept in a neighbouring room whenever she stayed overnight, a privilege earned through creating her own niche in the family circle through her attachment to the children and they to her. Marie Antoinette valued her precious liberty there too highly to have anyone stay under her roof not closer than those dearest to her.

The King was never there when Marie Antoinette gave her exclusive parties to which Rose was now invited. It was partly because gaming bored him as did dancing, his frame too clumsy and his feet too heavy for the frivolous steps; also, although it was never voiced, he was dull company at any intimate gathering and had no light conversation.

The parties were certainly lively affairs and went on until dawn. In the mild summer nights dancing was held on the lawn by the light of coloured-glass lanterns, and in that romantic, relaxed atmosphere it was no wonder that amorous encounters took place. If sometimes a couple passed into the shadows, nobody else took any notice, least of all the Queen who wanted only that everyone there should be happy around her.

"At this place I can imagine I'm back in my native Austria," she said meditatively to Rose one day as they went down the steps of the Petit Trianon to stroll to its own theatre nearby. "The Court was so informal compared with Versailles. My childhood was wonderfully carefree and full of family love. That's why I'm trying to give my children the same blissful beginnings. It is something to remember and cherish all one's life, a bastion to help one withstand whatever misfortunes may come along."

They entered the little white and gold theatre, the Queen throwing off her serious mood as she was greeted by her friends there. She loved theatricals, and performances were put on at fairly frequent intervals, the plays widely varied. Rose was always given a role, usually that of a tavern maid or a saucy servant due to her wicked curls and deep cleavage. She always hoped that next time she would be the leading lady, but invariably that role was given to the Queen, who was an excellent actress as well as a fine singer and talented musician.

At Versailles the Queen often played the harp in her State Bedchamber for the King and her ladies. Occasionally she would accept a larger audience in the Mars Salon where, on a draped dais, she would sing and play the clavichord or the harp. She was giving a concert there on an evening when Rose had been assigned to a special errand. When eventually Rose arrived it was late and the performance well advanced, the salon packed full with every seat taken. On the dais the Queen had moved from the clavichord and was playing her harp, seated on a tabouret with her soft lace skirt spread out about her, her beloved diamonds scintillating like captured stars about her neck and wrists as her tapering fingers plucked the strings.

During applause between pieces, Rose made her way through those standing at the back to follow the wall until she was close to the dais and yet inconspicuous as she stood with her back to a corner. The next piece that the Queen played was a merry folk tune and as she came to the end of it, putting her hand against the strings to still them, Rose witnessed a sudden change in the flawless complexion. The rose colour rushed along Marie Antoinette's cheekbones and receded as quickly as it had come, leaving her exceptionally pale, her eyes riveted across the heads of the applauding audience to the distant doorway.

From her unique position Rose was able to see that a tall, lean and fair-skinned man with thick dark brows, a long handsome nose and a well-cut mouth had entered from the Diana Salon. He was giving the Queen such a deep and glowing look under his romantically long-lashed lids that Rose could almost breathe in the loving tension between them. As yet in the applause and approbation nobody else had noticed their magnetised gaze, but within seconds someone's head would be bound to turn to see who had caught the Queen's attention.

Rose darted forward to clap wildly, deliberately blocking the Queen's view of the newcomer. "Such a pretty piece, madame! What a pity that is the end of the concert."

The spell was broken. Marie Antoinette, momentarily flustered, shot Rose a glance of gratitude, thankful to be saved from playing any more, her concentration shattered by the return from the United States of Axel von Fersen. It was a long time since she had seen him. He had served as aide-de-camp in the French contingent and now he was back. She had read the letters he had written her many times over before burning them, for there were spies everywhere and she never kept anything not meant for other eyes. She had wept to see them curling to ashes in the flames, once scorching her hand when she had pulled one out to read it lovingly just once more.

As she acknowledged the continued applause of her audience, she was thinking that the time for written words was over. He would be able to say at last all that had lain between the lines, thoughts and feelings as yet unspoken, for at all their previous meetings they had both fought against the rising tide of love between them. In that single look exchanged across the crowded salon he had told her clearly that after four years away from her nothing had changed for him any more than it had for her.

The King had risen from his seat as she stepped down from the dais. No doubt he thought it odd that she had decided against playing the two final pieces that he had specially requested should close her concert. She hoped he thought she was tired as she went at his side through to the Venus Salon where a buffet supper was being served. She dared not look in Axel's direction, intensely aware of his gaze as if he had reached out to touch her in a caress. It was as if she were half-swooning when she found herself in a chair with a crystal goblet of wine in her hand and a plate with some delicacy on her lap.

She raised her eyes and there he was again. This time he was coming towards her and nothing was going to stop her bursting into tears of joy before all these people at the first sound of his voice. Then once more her youngest lady-in-waiting saved her.

Rose had exchanged a few words with someone to discover the newcomer's identity. Having seen that the Queen was in a state of mounting emotion, she moved forward swiftly into Axel's path.

"You are back from the new nation, I believe, Comte von Fersen."

"That is so." His Swedish accent was attractive. "The United States is settling down to a new order and I believe everything will go well. Have you perhaps someone of your acquaintance still over there?"

"No, it is simply that I share the interests of the Queen. I am her lady-in-waiting, the Marquise de Chuard."

He understood then that there was a definite purpose behind her addressing him. "In that case may I ask you to lead me to her?"

"With pleasure." Rose felt she had given the Queen time to recover herself and this proved to be the case. Her lower lip was no longer quivering dangerously and to all but a close observer she appeared composed as the Comte bowed and spoke to her. Their conversation did not last more than a few minutes, but when the Swedish nobleman drifted off again she looked radiantly happy.

Later, in the Petits Cabinets, the Queen drew Rose away from the other ladies there into the summer blue of the Meridian Cabinet. No reference was made to anything that had happened earlier, but it was with them as if being shouted aloud by their reflections in the mirrored alcove.

"Tomorrow you and I will go alone to the Petit Trianon, Madame Rose. I have some new books for the library there and I thought you might like to choose where they should go on the shelves."

It was an odd request. Rose was puzzled. The Queen knew she was a keen reader, but there were palace librarians who usually dealt with such matters.

The reason became obvious the following day when the Queen, carrying only three volumes with her, led the way into the company salon and put them down on the inlaid table. "Please sit here and enjoy reading them first. I shall be in the next room with a visitor."

She left a wing of the double doors open as she went back to await the arrival of Axel von Fersen. Rose, unofficial chaperone and guardian to prevent the Queen's emotions from running away with her, recognised his voice when he arrived.

"My darling!"

"Beloved!"

The long silence following told its own tale. They were

kissing passionately, unable yet to spare breath for any-thing more. Rose wished she could have shut the door to give them privacy, but that would have been a disservice to the Queen. Against her will she heard their first words to each other, Marie Antoinette speaking first.

"Are you here to stay now, my dearest love?"

"No, my darling. King Gustavus has chosen me to be his escort on a royal tour."

"How long?" There was a hint of panic in her question.

"At least eighteen months, more likely two years."

She gave a cry. "I can't endure it. To have you back and be able to speak my heart to you at last only to lose you again is beyond my strength."

"You'll never lose me." His voice was fervent in his vow. "I love you. I'll love you till my dying day. Don't weep, sweetheart. We'll have a few weeks together. I promise you. Nobody in Sweden knows yet that I've returned to France. I'll do everything in my power to delay my depar-ture for Stockholm as long as possible."

There was a long and passionate silence. Then they must have moved further away to sit by the window, for their voices came low and quiet. Rose began doggedly to read the book she held, having moved as far from the door as possible.

Even as she read her thoughts danced. What kind of faithful love was this, secret and unfulfilled, that could survive a four-year absence? Her grandmother had spoken of Marguerite's enduring love for Augustin Roussier, but that belonged to a faraway time and what she had seen at Versailles made it as difficult to accept as anything but an ancestral fairy tale. She prided herself on not being the least romantic, able to discern the ultimate purpose be-hind a man's flattery as if it were written on his face, and she was fully experienced in the art of flirtation. But all this between Marie Antoinette and Axel was entirely new to her. The truth of their love throbbed in their voices, shad-owed by tragedy since there was no future for either of them beyond snatched meetings, endlessly painful part-ings and concealment from the rest of the world.

"If you both had any sense you would say goodbye now," she muttered under her breath, inexplicably angry that she was helpless to do anything to aid their dilemma. In a way she wished all those who had ever slandered Marie

Antoinette could have been here in this company salon to see for themselves that even for a great love she was not prepared to break her marriage vows.

The clock above the grey marble fireplace ticked away two hours before chair legs scraped and footsteps approached. Rose stood up as the Queen and the Comte came into the room. She was suddenly shy, a rare experience for her, but she felt as if she had been caught eavesdropping instead of having been deliberately placed there. Axel came forward and kissed her hand.

"We are at your mercy, Madame la Marquise."

"Nobody shall ever learn your secret from me, sir."

"It's a heavy burden for you."

"I carry it willingly."

"You have my undying gratitude."

He left then, the Queen going with him as far as the door of the anteroom. When she returned she kissed Rose on both cheeks. "When you acted as you did for me yesterday evening I knew I had found in you a friend who would never betray me."

There began for Rose many such visits to the Petit Trianon. Marie Antoinette, who had been unable to trust herself in the first mad wonder of her reunion with Axel, had rediscovered the strength of will that had sustained her previously and she took Rose with her for private meetings with him only to keep gossip at bay. He, an honourable man, whose love for Marie Antoinette was of the rare, unselfish kind, put her security and well-being before his own savage desire at all times.

"Are you betrothed?" he asked Rose during a ball in which he was partnering her in a minuet, which was always danced with a vigorous grace, making skirts swirl and coattails swing out from well-muscled thighs.

"No, and I'm not likely to be."

He smiled at her vehemence. "Why is that?"

"My grandmother would never force a *mariage de convenance* on me, because she had such a wretched time of it herself, and the Queen is too kind to press on me anyone I don't want. Sometimes I find myself liking one courtier more than another, but it is never serious on my part and I can't foresee it ever could be. There is nothing better than to be free."

He continued to smile, but his eyes became serious. "I

shall remain free, but not through choice. The woman I would have married is out of my reach and I want no one else."

She saw he meant what he said. As before she felt almost stunned by this extraordinary love that this man and the Queen had for each other. Her heart ached for them.

In spite of Axel's resolve to delay his departure for Sweden, the Swedish Ambassador notified Stockholm of his return, not without a dual purpose. The Ambassador had admired the young man's chivalrous behaviour in leaving the Court for America, when everyone could see that the most beautiful Queen in the world was ripe for his plucking. Now Marie Antoinette was giving herself away again. When singing a love song during a concert for the entertainment of a foreign dignitary, she had been indiscreet enough to look directly at Axel von Fersen as if unable to stop her eyes betraying her heart. The sooner he was back in Sweden the better for his sake and hers. The Ambassador did not want to see a promising career shattered by a foolish indiscretion.

Nobody knew how many tears Marie Antoinette shed in her Petits Cabinets after Axel's departure. It seemed to Rose that it was from that moment the Queen began to change and become more restrained and serious, even patient in giving time to discussing state matters with the King in his library. He liked to be guided by her, correctly assessing her intelligence to be far keener than his own. Thus the slightest mistake or error of judgement was laid at her door, even when a minister might have blundered somewhere along the line, the argument being that if she thought less of pleasure and more about serious matters these incidents would not occur.

Rose could tell that the trips to the Petit Trianon with the children gave the Queen far more pleasure these days than the parties she continued to hold with music and society games in the company salon there. When she became pregnant again her spirits soared, and her cup ran over when she gave birth to another boy in the relative privacy of only two royal witnesses. After that first terrible occasion the King had ruled that such an intrusion should never happen again.

The baby was baptised Louis Charles in the Royal Chapel and was soon introduced to the Petit Trianon. The

Dauphin was proving to be a sickly child, causing the Queen constant anxiety, and she liked to get all three of her children into the healthy country air as much as possible.

It was a brilliant August morning when she drove them as usual in the calèche, Rose holding the baby in her arms, the two older children tucked in on either side of her. The baby's wet nurse and one of the children's personal maids were being driven in a similar vehicle behind. The five-month-old Prince was tearful and Rose suggested they should all sing some nursery lullabies to send him to sleep.

"Oh, yes!" Marie Thérèse bounced on the seat. "I'll choose the first one."

"No, me!" exploded the Dauphin, asserting his male right.

By the time the argument was settled they were well along the dusty lane and the Queen's lovely voice gave volume to the melody. Even as the baby fell asleep three horsemen appeared in the distance with baggage horses bringing up the rear. Rose guessed immediately that they were foreigners, probably English. Ever since good relations had been restored between England and France, at least on the surface, Englishmen had come flooding back. Many of them were on the Grand Tour, extensive travel being deemed necessary to give polish and sophistication to European young men of wealth and good birth. No less important to the families who sent them, whatever nationality, was that they could sow their wild oats far from their home environments.

They all took back souvenirs of their travels, the Englishmen in particular buying up works of art and ancient sculptures to embellish their stately homes and to donate special pieces to a new museum in London. Versailles was the social mecca for all nationalities, Axel von Fersen having first come on a Grand Tour. If they were as noble as he they came with letters of introduction, otherwise they made do with sauntering about the Château and the park, keeping an eye open for a chance to intrude on a social function, preferably when the royal family were present. Since the Queen had abolished the public suppers there was less chance of seeing her or the King for those without an official entrée.

As the distance shortened between the royal calèche

and the horsemen, Rose became more certain that these were three Englishmen. There was an older man who would be the tutor; his task being to guard as much as possible the morals of the young man in his charge as well as to implant knowledge and appreciation of the architecture, paintings and sculpture all the way from France through Switzerland and Italy to Greece. The fellow in charge of the baggage horses was the servant and, drawing them all in single file to give the calèche the maximum room, was the chief traveller himself.

Broad-shouldered and obviously tall from his height in the saddle, he had the cocksure air of the rich and well-bred, a brilliant figure in a coat of emerald green and a black tricorn hat trimmed with an erect white ostrich feather, black riding boots reaching to his doeskin-covered thighs. His hair was unpowdered in the more casual mode that fashionable men were adopting and matched his hat and his boots in colour, a ribbon keeping it tied at the back of his neck. A brutally handsome young man, his tanned complexion gave him the look of a brigand; an illusion heightened when he began to grin broadly at both Marie Antoinette and Rose, showing white teeth as straight as if chiselled by a sculptor, who might easily have added the cleft in the arrogant chin. He had put a hand to his ear as if to catch the singing, the Queen having fallen silent by reason of her status, while Rose and the children carried on merrily. Then as he and the calèche were almost abreast, he doffed his hat and held it to his chest.

"My dear ladies! What a sweet welcome to Versailles! Are you Venus and Diana stepped down from your plinths in the park with cherubs plucked from one of the fountains to accompany you?"

Marie Antoinette inclined her head graciously at the flirtatious compliment, well aware he had no idea who she was, and Rose, not pausing in the song, looked full into his eyes as she spun past. The irises were light green and predatory as a tomcat's.

"What an impudent rascal," Marie Antoinette remarked with some amusement as soon as they were out of earshot. She snubbed unremittingly those whom she disliked, but she would never cut anyone who made an innocent mistake.

"Indeed he was," Rose agreed. It had been hard to resist

turning her head. She would have liked to have seen his expression when his older companion told him that the calèche had borne the royal crest. Laughter rose in her as she imagined it. At the same time there had been something about him that had sent a delicious shiver pulsating through her veins.

She stayed overnight, but left the following morning when Madame Élisabeth, the King's sister, a pleasant young woman who was fond of her sister-in-law, arrived with Madame de Lamballe and some of the Queen's other ladies-in-waiting. The Queen had entrusted Rose with a letter to send to Axel and she had it tucked in the drawstring purse that swung from her wrist as she walked the path by the Grand Canal instead of being driven back to the Château. Once she had changed out of the plain muslin gown that she was wearing into one that her grandmother would like better, she would despatch the letter on her way to Château Satory.

It was a glorious morning on which to walk. She had come to the path by way of the gardens that linked the Queen's cherished abode to the Trianon. The sun blazed down, creating sun-diamonds on the water as dazzling as anything worn by the much-maligned First Lady of France. The path turned at right angles as it left the edge of the cruciform arm to follow the length of the Grand Canal eastwards. Rose, although her eyes were shaded by her enormous hat, blinked in order to see Versailles in the far distance, a mere glimmer on the horizon. It was a long walk, but she was shaded by the overhanging leafy branches of the trees and it was pleasantly solitary, for only a few dedicated walkers ever came this way. Once she took a rest on the grass, trying to picture how the Grand Canal must have looked in the Sun King's day when exotic vessels had cruised along it. There were a few little sailboats in a boathouse for those who wanted to use them, but sailing did not appeal to either the King or the Queen. As courtiers needed to be set a fashion in order to follow it, even on this hot August day there was not a sail to be seen.

By now she was within easy view of the Apollo fountain with its dramatic waters shooting high into the air and she was struck by the vast numbers of people milling about. It was as if a giant hand had shaken hundreds of coloured sequins over the park.

There were many foreign tongues in the air as she left the path by the Grand Canal to make her way towards the Tapis Vert. She took no notice of those clustered around the Apollo fountain until someone addressed her.

"Mademoiselle! One moment, please!"

She turned. It was the Englishman. Tall against the cascading water, he seemed almost to loom at her, no less dramatic than Apollo in his chariot straining for the skies. He was more soberly but no less well dressed today. Perhaps yesterday's parrot-hued attire had been his way of arriving at Versailles with aplomb. He was regarding her quizzically.

"Sir?" She was unaccountably wary. Somehow she felt threatened by him and yet the sensation was as exciting as it was alarming.

"I blundered yesterday. I learned that I addressed the Queen along the road. We had just passed the Petit Trianon and I should have guessed, but who would expect to meet the Queen of France singing nursery songs and travelling with her children and nursemaid?"

Rose drew in her breath sharply, about to let him know in no small measure that he had made another error, but then her sense of humour overcame her. "Doesn't your Queen Charlotte do that?" she asked with feigned naïvety.

He laughed heartily and shook his head. "Never. She's too staid anyway. Tell me, was the Queen offended?"

"She was taken aback, but not angry."

"I thank God for that. I have to present myself to her tomorrow."

So he was one of those with a letter of introduction and therefore of some importance if he was to meet the Queen herself and not some minor member of the Court. "That will be in the afternoon in her own State Apartment."

"So I was told." Momentarily he pressed his lips tightly together, causing one corner to twist as he looked questioningly at her. "How did you know I was English? I pride myself on not having an accent and since landing at Calais I've been taken for a Frenchman all the time."

She shrugged. "Admittedly you speak my language like a Parisian-born and could easily pass for a countryman of mine, but you wear clothes that bear the unmistakable stamp of English tailoring and that gives you away to me. I'm particularly familiar with it, because the Queen likes

English-cut riding habits." She was on the point of adding that she had an English riding habit herself but that would have given her deception away. "Were you born in France, perhaps?"

"No. But I've made many French acquaintances in England whom I'm hoping to meet again here now that, after some delay, I've arrived in the land of my ancestors. It's been a tradition in our family that all the children should be bilingual. Somehow French nursemaids, governesses and tutors were always found even when our two nations were at war." His eyes danced wickedly at her. "But I never had a nursemaid as beautiful as you. What is your name?"

She hesitated for a moment. "Rose de Chuard."

"Richard Aldington." He stepped closer to her and cupped her chin in his hand. "I should like to see you again, Rose."

She jerked her chin away. The joke had gone far enough. "You will," she warned fiercely. "I promise you!"

He called after her as she shot away from him. "I look forward to that, Madame la Marquise!"

So he had known her identity all along. Probably someone at the fountain had told him beforehand when she had come by. She did not know whether to be furious or amused. Somehow she managed to be both.

Jasmin found her granddaughter a trifle distrait during her short visit. It was as if the girl's thoughts were drifting somewhere else all the time. "Is there anything bothering you, dear child?"

Rose shook back her curls as if throwing off whatever was on her mind. "Nothing, Grand-mère. Maybe I'm a little tired. I walked all the way from the Petit Trianon back to the Château this morning."

"In this heat! You must be exhausted."

They were sitting in what was known as the Cool Salon. Most houses of any size had such a room for really hot weather and here at the Château Satory the soft greens of the marble floor and the hangings added to the sensation of coolness. Rose moved from her seat restlessly and paced up and down.

"I might as well admit it. I had a disturbing encounter today with one of those Englishmen on the Grand Tour." She told how it had all come about. "He's bold and conceited and dangerous. I would not trust him for an instant as far as my being a woman is concerned. I've met many such men and therefore he's everything I dislike. Yet in a matter of minutes I found him to be the most attractive man I've ever met and he makes me laugh." Her voice became filled with humorous self-mockery. "Do you think I suffered sunstroke on that walk and it has curdled my brain?" She came back to sit on a stool at Jasmin's feet.

"That's a possible explanation," Jasmin remarked drily. "Personally I've never been able to sum up someone's whole character as you have done. I suggest that you let him get over the excitement of being at Versailles and of meeting you, and then see how he appears."

"Dear Grand-mère." Rose rested her cheek on Jasmin's thin old hand. "If he should turn out to be better than I think he is, I could let you take a look at him yourself."

Jasmin rested her free hand on the girl's thick curls. There was little enough on which to pin her hopes, but she could not help wondering if her granddaughter was on the brink of love at last. The fact that the young Englishman could make Rose laugh was in his favour. Sabatin had not caused her to smile once in all their married life.

In the Salon of the Nobles, the Queen's own Throne room, those persons listed for the day were being received. Marie Antoinette, her figure fuller since the birth of her last child, sat on a canopied, raised armchair that was approached by a few steps. She, and all present, were in finest Court dress and jewels. Rose stood with the other ladies-in-waiting, her back to the portrait of Louis XV in his coronation robes. At every announcement she awaited Richard's name, but so far he had not appeared. There had been two ambassadors and several noble ladies in turn, her impatience growing at the length of time the Queen spent in talking to each. But the woman who ran carefree at the Petit Trianon was entirely different from the Queen regally performing her state duties.

"Lord Aldington."

The announcement sent Rose's pulse racing. Then she thought she would hardly have known him. Serious and almost stern in his countenance, hair dressed formally, clad in dove-grey satin encrusted with silver embroidery, sword at his hip, he advanced to the throne, bowed deeply and then looked straight at the Queen with respect and without servility. She gave no sign of remembering him as the rascal who had tossed the bold compliment.

"You are on the Grand Tour, I believe, Lord Aldington."

"Yes, madame."

"According to your godfather, the Duke of Dorset, and your country's ambassador, you have an interest in botany and depart tomorrow to further your knowledge on your travels."

"That is correct, madame. The Ambassador is most anxious I should spend three or four months in Paris upon my return, and that is what I plan to do. My time is cut short now because I have been fortunate enough to be invited to attend a series of botanical lectures at the University of Bologna."

"Do you speak Italian as well as you speak French?"

"I have sufficient mastery of the language."

"How did your interest in plants come about?"

"My family seat is at Easterton in Kent. It covers many acres of farmland and orchards. I spent most of my childhood there, and as a result my interest in botany flourished."

"Since your time is too short now to visit the Orangery and the botanical gardens at Versailles, perhaps you would like to do that when you come back again?"

"I should be most pleased, madame."

"There are some rare flowers in the hothouses at the Trianon."

"I'd be honoured to present a new variety if such good fortune comes to me on my travels."

"We should be delighted to receive it. Whatever happens we wish you success with your studies. Are the arts to be eliminated by this pursuit of yours?"

"No. I intend to see everything from the Sistine Chapel to the Parthenon."

She asked him a few more questions before expressing the hope that he would have a safe journey. The audience was at an end.

Rose thought he had not noticed her, but as he reached the door he turned his head slightly to widen his reckless eyes at her for no more than a second. As if he had shouted it out loud he had told her that in her Court finery she was a sight to behold. She thought the same of him, unable to keep from smiling to herself until she noticed Madame de Lamballe giving her a curious glance. The corners of her lips continued to dance on their own. What a pity he was not staying longer. It could be two or three years before he returned, probably longer. By then she would have forgotten him as she had all those other men who had captured her interest from time to time. It was odd that her main regret should be that her grandmother would not meet him. It would have been fun to see two such contrasting people together and to hear what the wise old lady thought of the handsome rapscallion.

Rose came down the staircase from her apartment that evening after changing her gown for the fifth time to suit the events of the day. Behind her came Diane holding her billowing skirt free of the stairs while she herself concentrated on keeping the front hems high enough not to impede her step. In this part of the Château the flights were as narrow and turning as in any ordinary citizen's house, glass-panelled doors cutting away draughts from one floor to another. The King's locksmith workshop was a small room not far from her apartment and she could hear the thump of the pedal of his lathe that showed he had forgotten the time and was still at work.

"Careful, madame!" her maid requested urgently. "Not so fast, please."

Rose slowed her pace. She was about to descend the last flight when she heard footsteps coming up and waited, there being little room to pass. Suddenly in the light of the hanging glass lantern illuminating a turn in the stairs Richard appeared and halted at the sight of her.

"There you are!" he exclaimed triumphantly. Then he took the stairs two at a time to reach the one just below where she stood and handed her a particularly lovely pink rose which she knew grew in the South Parterre. "I've been searching everywhere for you in this maze of a place. I want to talk to you."

"Do you?" She inhaled the delicate perfume of the rose, but raised an eyebrow distantly as if untouched by his urgent request. "It can't be now. May I pass?"

"Let me assist you down the stairs." He extended a hand eagerly and then tilted his head to look past her at Diane. "I'll take over."

Rose tapped her foot with feigned impatience on the

wooden floorboards, not in the least annoyed but determined not to be overpowered by him. "Do not interfere, sir! If you want to be helpful go down to the foot of the stairs and see if my sedan chair has arrived."

"It has. I passed it. Where are you going, if I may ask?"

"To attend the Queen."

"In what capacity?"

"If you must know, I'm to be present this evening when a violinist performs for Their Majesties in the Queen's Petits Cabinets." She did not add that the violinist was from Austria, which was why he was to play privately in the Gilded Cabinet. People were becoming suspicious of everything the Queen did and it was no longer politic for her to show her preference for anything to do with her native land.

"Do you have to be there?"

She jerked her chin. "What a question! I can tell you're new to Versailles. Now if you will kindly let me continue down these stairs—"

He went backwards down the flight in front of her. "When will the performance end?"

"I've no idea. Probably about eleven."

"Then you'll be free?"

"No. I shall be at the Queen's *coucher* after that."

"Midnight then?"

"Maybe."

"That's the hour to begin merrymaking in the town, I'm told. Let me take you dancing."

"Out of the question!" If she had had only herself to think about she would have gone with him for the devilment of it, but if she should be recognised and any gossip result it would only reflect on the Queen. "I'd never leave the precincts of Versailles at that hour with a stranger."

"But we have met three times now! How can we be strangers?" Deliberately he blocked her descent by halting with outstretched arms, compelling her to look up from the next tread to meet his smiling eyes. He was saying far more in the way he was looking at her than he was putting into words. "Have mercy! Through searching high and low for you I've made myself late already for a reception I'm supposed to be attending with my uncle in the apartment of a duc in the north wing."

She had noticed his hands as he held them out in a

gesture of appeal. So many of the foppish courtiers had limp, dead-fish hands, but his were strong and broad-palmed with long capable fingers. An unbidden image came to her of him stroking the petals of a flower or probing carefully into the heart of a plant and, to her dismay, a crimson blush soared up into her cheeks on the association of her thoughts. It caused her to answer him more tartly in her embarrassment than she would otherwise have done.

"Then you had better take one of the Château's sedan chairs to get you there or you could be hours finding your way."

His expression became more serious at her sharp rebuff, which seemed to puzzle him. He turned about to lead the way down the last few stairs. Diane, witnessing it all, thought wistfully that if the chance had been hers she would have agreed to an assignation with this physically magnetic man. As she followed behind with her arms still full of the soft folds of the gown, she hoped her mistress would relent. After all, it wasn't as if Madame Rose had not played with fire before and emerged unscathed. Surely this Englishman offered a challenge? It would not be like her to turn aside from that.

They had reached the bottom of the staircase. The sedan chair was waiting with Rose's coat of arms on the sides. She seated herself in the blue satin-upholstered interior and the door was shut. Being a warm evening its windows were open and Richard spoke through one in desperation as the bearers lifted up the supporting poles.

"Tonight! At midnight! In the Ballroom Grove!"

She gave him a tantalising smile, flicked open her fan and was borne away. He stood staring after her.

"Will she be there?" he asked Diane without turning.

"It's impossible to say." The answer came truthfully. "Shall I summon a sedan chair for you, sir?"

"What?" He looked as if he was having difficulty in collecting his thoughts. "A chair? Oh, yes, I suppose I'd better take one."

She went to the door and called, "Bearers!"

A sedan arrived immediately.

It was exactly midnight when Rose left the Queen's bed-chamber. Throughout the evening she had been telling herself that she wouldn't go and now the choice was out of her hands. Not through her being a little late, which he would allow for, but because in her light gown she could not go flitting out like a pale moth without someone seeing her. Then she saw Diane was waiting for her with a black domino over her arm.

"That was thoughtful of you," Rose said to Diane as she put it around her shoulders. The reply came without expression. "I thought you might need it, madame."

Rose pulled the hood up and left the Château by way of the West Front. Flambeaux illumined the park, but not to any extent since there had been no festivities there that evening. She sped down the steps and past the Water Parterres to go by way of the Avenue of Bacchus and Saturn to the Ballroom Grove. With her eyes becoming accustomed to the darkness, she saw ahead a tall cloaked figure being guided by another with a shaded lantern. It was doubtless Richard with a servant familiar with the park. She did not call out, not knowing who might be within earshot in the shadows, but followed swiftly, her silken shoes making no sound. Then, instead of turning to the Ballroom Grove, the two dark figures branched off and she, close behind, saw the pale figure of a woman in a large hat standing by the trees.

Instantly she realised she had stumbled upon somebody else's rendezvous, something slightly inconsistent tugging at her mind, and she would have withdrawn immediately if the servant had not moved away to leave the couple together and take up a stand that barred her retreat. She had no choice but to stay, invisible in her black domino against the bushes. The couple were whispering together and she could see that the servant was straining his ears to catch what was being said and, being closer than she, could probably hear the lovers' exchange. Then, against her wish, she herself caught a single phrase from the woman.

"That is forgotten. The past is over."

The words had a dramatic effect on the cloaked man, who knelt to kiss her hands, whispering excitedly. At that point the servant shifted his position to get a better view and Rose seized the chance to slip away. She arrived breathless at the Ballroom Grove and rushed to the terrace that encircled it, expecting Richard to come forward. A single flambeau showed her the cascades of water forming walls down to the circular marble dancing floor below. The whole place was deserted.

She found it hard to accept that he had not waited. Perhaps he had never come. After all, she had given him no answer. During the evening he might easily have met a pretty woman willing to go beyond the realms of mere dalliance.

Her thoughts went to the couple in the other grove. Why had she supposed at first that the tall cloaked man was Richard? The woman's words seemed to echo in her ears. He had mentioned having friends in France. Was it possible that he had met and made up some past difference with a Frenchwoman he had met in England? The secrecy suggested she was a married woman. Whoever she was it was obvious she was not a woman of fashion to wear a hat at midnight. It was that jarring touch which had marked itself at the time. Perhaps the female was a courtesan!

In a sudden burst of temper she flounced away from the Ballroom Grove, but curiosity drew her to the place of the clandestine meeting. The grove was empty now and something showed pale on the grass. She went forward and picked it up. It was a rose, plucked from the same bushes as the one she had received earlier that evening. Flinging it from her, she ran back to the Château, wishing away the coincidence, but full of piercing hurt and doubt.

In another part of the park, in the Colonnade, Richard continued to wait. He had been in this circular place since eleven o'clock, determined not to risk missing Rose, for he was full of hope that she would appear. The suggestion as to where they should meet had been made on the spur of the moment. He had seen little of the extensive park and when mentioning to someone that he had been in a place within a circle of fountains, he had been told it was the Ballroom Grove.

Somewhere in the distance a clock chimed the half hour. He made no move to leave, but by two o'clock he forced himself to accept that what he had hoped for was not to be; plans that they should correspond and that he would see her again upon his return to Versailles had all come to nothing. He went back through the archway in the circular Colonnade, stricken by a sickening sense of disappointment and loss. Rose's witchlike beauty would haunt him for a long time to come. The second rose he had picked to give her, one of deepest crimson, was left wilting on a marble ledge.

Nineteen

Rose had spent a happy afternoon at the Hamlet with the royal children and their governess, the Duchesse de Polignac. The Queen had been with them until, much to her regret, she had had to leave to return to the Petit Trianon, having agreed to an audience specially requested by her jeweller, Monsieur Boehmer.

It was when Rose judged the audience to be almost over that she also went back to the Petit Trianon, wanting to speak to the jeweller herself about the replacement of a lost pearl from a brooch, which would have to be matched exactly. What she had not expected was that Madame Campan, one of the Queen's ladies whom she knew well, should meet her on the steps.

"Go to the Queen quickly!" she urged. "She is in great distress."

Rose ran up the stairs and found the Queen in her boudoir, her eyes red-rimmed with weeping and her face ashen. She addressed Rose immediately.

"Such a terrible thing has happened! I don't know which

way to turn. Monsieur Boehmer came with some absurd story of my owing more than one and a half million livres on that diamond necklace he tried to persuade me to buy on more than one occasion."

Rose remembered what a glorious necklace it was, a *rivière* of matchless diamonds that dazzled the eye. It was no wonder it was worth a fortune. "I was with you the last time when you told Monsieur Boehmer you wanted nothing to do with it."

"So you were. I may have to call on you to state that fact publicly." Marie Antoinette sprang up from where she was sitting and paced the floor, twisting her hands together. She had wanted the necklace at first sight, but then she learned it had been originally ordered for Madame du Barry as a gift from the late King, who had died before it was completed. Anything to do with that odìous woman was anathema to her, and it had set her against the necklace forever. Recently she had been thankful that she had not let herself get into further debt over it, for she and the King were making personal economies on a considerable scale in view of the country's financial difficulties. Rage soared up in her. "To make matters worse, Monsieur Boehmer told me that Cardinal de Rohan purchased it on my behalf and with written authorisation bearing my signature!"

Rose stared at her in disbelief. "But you have not spoken to him for years."

"That's correct, Madame Rose. Even when he dared to come here I had him sent away by others." She threw up her hands. "What trickery and lies have been used I can't begin to imagine. One thing I do know. The Cardinal shall stand trial for stealing a necklace in my name. He shall be proved a liar and a thief!"

It was the start of a scandal that rocked the nation. Cardinal de Rohan had been the dupe of two infamous swindlers, who had taken advantage of his greedy wish to ingratiate himself with the Queen and his aim to become the most powerful man in France. Rose was aghast to learn that she herself had been an unknowing witness to the trick played on him that had convinced him beyond a shadow of doubt that he had gained the Queen's favour at last. A young prostitute, who in a poor light bore sufficient resemblance to the Queen to pass muster, had been taken to meet him in the Grove of Venus in the park at Versailles to tell him he was forgiven for his past misdeeds.

"I saw them," Rose confided to Jasmin, who raised an eyebrow at hearing she had been on her way to keep a late-night tryst. "It struck me that something was strange. It never occurred to me that the young woman was impersonating the Queen, but I did think that no lady of the Court would wear a daytime hat at such an hour. It was one of those large-brimmed affairs with the swathed crown that the Queen has made so fashionable. If the Cardinal had ever grasped the rudiments of fashion he would have realised the creature was an impostor!"

Jasmin made a remark about conceited men thinking that no woman could resist their charm in the end. "That was the Cardinal's downfall." Then she eyed Rose astutely. "What was the outcome of your tryst?"

Rose made a little face. "Nothing."

Jasmin was too tactful to question her further about it, but she gave some thought to the Cardinal, who had been incarcerated in the dreaded Bastille while awaiting his trial that should clear the Queen's name. Nevertheless, she thought it would have been wiser of the King not to have had him arrested in his vestments in the busy Hall of Mirrors on his way to hold Mass in the Royal Chapel. It had offended many of the nobility that it had been done so publicly and at such a moment. Inevitably the Queen was blamed and, for once, not without reason. It was unmistakably an act of vengeance.

The following year, on the last day of May in 1786, the Cardinal was acquitted and the two swindlers given merciless sentences. As for the diamond necklace, that had been broken up and sold without trace before any arrests were made. Marie Antoinette was devastated by the acquittal. Throughout the whole scandal sympathies had been with the Cardinal, who was believed to have been shielding her, and in giving such a verdict the judges had endorsed this belief. Her well-known love of diamonds had stood against her as had her extravagances and debts of the past. That she was no longer the flighty young Queen of days gone by was completely ignored.

"I see you shed tears for me," she said emotionally to Rose, who had just heard the verdict. "I am in need of them, because I've been made a sacrifice for the crimes of others. I had thought to find honest, unbiased judges, but instead they have created an injustice to ruin my character and my reputation in every way."

Rose despaired that the Queen should be so cruelly mistreated. People in all walks of life, from the nobles at Court to the beggars in the gutter, had turned against her with hatred. Leaflets spilled filth about her at every street corner, pornographic caricatures were passed from hand to hand, even at private parties at Versailles, while she herself was beset with worry about her beloved elder son, who was ailing.

In the whole dreadful affair of the diamond necklace there was not a single glimmer of light for anyone. Rose wished heartily it had been Richard with that woman in the park and the rest of it a myth. All she had left for herself was that he had failed to have enough interest to come to the Ballroom Grove in the hope that she would be there. It was maddening that it should still hurt when he had been no more than a passing stranger. She put it down to pride.

There was some joy for the Queen in the birth of a daughter, Sophie, but within a year tragedy struck again when the child died. The Queen wore the white mourning of the Royal House of Bourbon and her face was as pale. To add to her tribulations, her older son's health had deteriorated steadily with a twisting of his spine and a wasting of his limbs. The Dauphin bore his pain bravely, both the Queen and Rose sitting with him to hold his hand and read him stories when he lay strapped to a board as the doctors tried in vain to straighten his back.

"I'm sure to be better soon, Maman," he said often to his mother when she carried him in a state of exhaustion to his bed.

"Indeed you will," she responded cheerfully, hiding her anguish from him. Only out of his sight and in private did she give way to tears when yet another attempted cure had no effect. She was in such a state of despair, seated on the blue couch in the mirrored alcove of the Meridian Cabinet, when Rose, who was with her, answered a tap on the door. Lifting her head wearily from her sodden handkerchief, Marie Antoinette saw in the mirrored side panel that Rose had slipped from the room, leaving the door open behind her. Puzzled, she turned her head to look over her shoulder in its direction. Then the one person able to bring some light into the present darkness of her life entered and held out his arms to her.

"Axel!" She thought for a breathless moment she must be hallucinating.

He reached her before she could move. "I'm back and this time I'm not leaving again, my darling!"

Once more Rose became the royal chaperone. She was used to riding out with the Queen, long since chosen from all the other ladies for her agreeable companionship. Now these excursions became more frequent, the Queen seizing the chance to meet Axel in the forest because, even when he attended parties at the Petit Trianon, she could never be alone with him any more than she dared single him out for a private word at the social functions at Versailles.

Neither Rose nor Marie Antoinette suspected they were being followed on a sunny afternoon when they set out together. The Queen no longer rode the spirited horses she had always chosen in the past, thinking always of her children and their need of her. It was Rose who more often than not took an ill-tempered mount, revelling in the battle for control and still as wild in her ways as the Queen had ever been. It never occurred to her, as it had to her grandmother, that her seeking of excitement and pleasure might well stem from the original source of sexual abstinence that had once afflicted an equally young, healthy and energetic Marie Antoinette.

As always, Axel was waiting. With the usual procedure, Rose turned her horse away to avoid witnessing their passionate greeting of each other. It had become her custom to leave them alone together while she rode off at liberty until an arranged time. Sometimes in the far distance a hunting horn would sound, for the King hunted every day, and she was on the alert to give warning of approach either by the chase or by any horseman who happened to enter the vicinity. Today she made for the long grassy avenue of a natural firebreak between the trees and took her horse into an exhilarating gallop. It was then that she heard a horseman some way behind her. She slowed her pace, giving him a chance to overtake her, but he remained at a distance, matching his speed to hers.

She took a swift glance over her shoulder but the angle of his brimmed hat hid the upper part of his face and prevented any clue to his identity, which she guessed was deliberate and so became increasingly angry. What game was he playing? Was it some flirtatious idiot from Court forgetting the rules of etiquette that should prevent him from following the Queen and her lady on a private ride? She tried to shake him off, riding at breakneck speed in the hope he would tire and fall back, but his snorting horse kept the same allotted distance from hers all the time. In the midst of her rage came fear that this was a spy, someone who had stumbled on the Queen's secret and was determined to find out what part she had in it. Well, he would learn nothing from her. Let him try! Knowing she was safely away from the lovers, she finally slowed her horse and wheeled around to face him.

"You!" she exclaimed furiously.

It was almost three years since she had met the man reining in to approach her. But there was nothing of the pleasant atmosphere of that past summer day in this present encounter. Richard Aldington's countenance showed none of the impudence of expression she remembered. This was a grimmer, more serious man whose light green eyes held the chill of hostility in their depths, no less dangerous for that change in attitude towards her.

"Good day to you, Madame la Marquise."

"How dare you follow me! You must have realised I wanted to ride alone."

His reply came without the trace of a smile. "I could never resist a little sport."

"Your manners have not improved with the passage of time."

"Neither has your sharp tongue, I regret to say. As for courtesy, is it customary for you to leave the Queen on her own in the woods?"

Suddenly her earlier fear swept back. Perhaps he was an English spy and had been from the start. She answered him cuttingly. "If you were familiar with Court etiquette you would know better than to intrude in this manner. The Queen finds no solitude anywhere else. She is entitled to wander in the forest on her own. There is much on the poor lady's mind."

"As it happens, I came to warn her through you. Probably even as we speak the King is receiving certain incriminating papers."

"What do you mean? The King is hunting."

"A rider has gone after him as is done with urgent despatches. These will tell the King of the Queen's meetings with Comte von Fersen now and previously."

She was alarmed. "How do you know this?"

"Much has happened since I last saw you. The death of my father recalled me from the Grand Tour and once all affairs were settled I returned to Paris where I am now attached to my country's Embassy. My uncle, the Ambassador, has certain sympathies for the Queen, because she never made any secret of her abhorrence that France should support a revolution in the American colonies against an old-established monarchy. In his official capacity he can't warn her personally, which is why this has been my first assignment."

"How did the Ambassador hear about these meetings in the forest?" Immediately she bit her lip at her own question, recalling that only minutes ago she was suspecting Richard of being a spy. She also remembered a casual remark made by the Queen some time ago when they were inspecting her rare plants at the Petit Trianon. "Do you recall that young English viscount—Lord Aldington I think was the name—who promised to bring me any interesting botanical specimens he might find while on the Grand Tour? Well, recently I asked the British Ambassador why he had never come back to Paris and he told me that sadly the young man had had to return to England owing to his father's death. As the elder son he has inherited the estates and the title and is now the Earl of Easterton."

Recovering herself she turned to him. "There's no need to answer that question, Lord Easterton. I'm thankful to hear that the Queen has some friends other than those of us who are closest to her."

It appeared she had got his title right, because he did not dispute it. "I'll not accompany you back to the Queen. It would be an intrusion on my part at this time."

"Then on Her Majesty's behalf I thank you and the English Ambassador." She inclined her head in farewell and rode back at a gallop along the way she had come.

He watched her go. Now he knew why he had come back to France, although he had told himself and everybody else that he needed a few months in Paris to round off his broken journeyings. In spite of rancour at her flouting of their midnight meeting and the spice and variety offered by many beautiful women encountered on the Grand Tour, she must have remained more in his thoughts than he had ever realised.

All at home had expected that having inherited his father's title and become the new lord of Easterton Court, he would be more than ready to settle down. He was a changed man in his outlook, but not through these new responsibilities of land ownership and political position. The untimely death of his father had been a devastating shock. Never before had grief touched his carefree existence. With only twenty years between him and his late parent they had enjoyed a cheerful, boisterous relationship that never suffered from their fierce quarrels, usually when they were in their cups, over the way the estate should be run. He had found it hard to accept that a man so full of energy and bonhomie, who rode with his farmer tenants and held that all men were equal in the hunting field, even as all pretty women existed to be chased, could be snuffed out like a candle through a single sharp pain in the chest. It had made him see that he had rollicked away twenty-five years of his own life with little to show for it except the paintings and statuary he had shipped home from Italy and Greece respectively, and the trays of plants gathered from foreign soil to give forth an alien beauty in his hothouses.

He had waited a year before broaching a possible return to Paris to his mother. She had turned to him more than to the others in her deep sorrow, perhaps sensing that his grief was more on a level with hers. Immediately she braced up as if she had been given back a purpose in life. "Go to Paris, my son. Stay six months or longer if you wish. With the bailiff's help I shall manage everything as if you were here. It will also give me time to have the Dower House renovated and I shall move in there when you decide to come home again." Then all that was French and romantic in her came to the fore. "Perhaps you will bring back a bride."

He dug in his heels to ride by another route out of the forest. Rumour had it that Rose de Chuard had never been ensnared. The challenge lay open to him. He intended to take it up.

As soon as Marie Antoinette arrived back at Versailles she was told the King had left the hunt and returned. It was unprecedented and she was filled with dread. She went straight to his private apartment where she knew she would find him. To her distress she found him sitting bowed over in a chair, sobbing like a broken man. She flung herself to her knees beside him and put her arms around him.

"Louis! My dear husband! Don't weep. I beg you."

"Is it true about you and Comte von Fersen?" He raised his tear-stained face pathetically, his mouth tremulous. "I have received a terrible report."

"The truth is that I'm fond of Axel von Fersen. More than I should be, I know. But I'm your wife, my dear. You are the father of my children and the man to whom I'll be companion and partner to the end of my days. We have grown closer with the years than I ever thought possible when I first came to France. You know that. I have told you in our most secret marital moments." She took a handkerchief from her pocket and unfolded it to wipe his eyes as if he were her son instead of her husband. "I won't see the Comte again. He shall resign the commission in the French Army that has been granted him and return to Sweden."

"No, that's not the answer."

"Yes, it is. I insist. I will not have you upset unnecessarily. It can only be dealt with by my refusing to see the Comte again under any circumstances."

"If he goes away it will be said that I had not taken your word on the matter."

Briefly she arched her back to look into his eyes. "Have you, Louis?" she asked in anxious suspense.

"Yes." He answered her simply. "You would have told me the truth either way."

She was deeply moved by his reply. "Where is that infamous report?"

He indicated the fireplace. "I burned it. Nothing more shall ever be said about it."

She looped her arms about him again and he embraced her with a kiss. For a while they stayed together, he sitting and she kneeling with their arms about each other. When eventually she left the room she was completely enervated by having run the full gamut of emotions from love, fear and compassionate sorrow to intense relief in a short space of time. Her insistence that Axel be sent away had been a gambler's throw and she had won the stake.

In his chair Louis wept again. His wife loved Axel von Fersen with all her heart. He had no doubt about it, but he himself loved her too much to deprive her in the midst of all her tribulations of what little happiness she had in seeing the Comte from time to time. If their feelings for each other had overcome them, so be it.

When Rose saw Richard again he was with the British Ambassador, whom she had met on many occasions. A few conventional phrases were exchanged before she took her seat with other company at the concert they were attending. Although they sat quite far apart she was as tuned to his presence as if nobody else were there, which made her applaud the musicians a trifle more heartily than was necessary and then look everywhere except at him during the buffet supper in the Venus Salon. Pique that he did not approach blended with satisfaction that she must have made him feel ignored and forgotten. Then she happened to meet his gaze head-on in a mirror and felt herself blush with shock and excitement right down to her toes. When she looked again he was in conversation with a pretty woman, both of them laughing and getting on well together. The next time she glanced in that direction they had left.

She began to look out for him wherever she went and then, just when she thought he was keeping to entertainment solely in Paris, he reappeared on an evening when gambling tables had been set up in the Hall of Mirrors and, as always, the room was crowded. With the Queen at the Petit Trianon and the King shut away with his books in the library, the atmosphere was very free. In days past the Queen's presence had added to the high-pitched merriment of any such occasion, but since the affair of the diamond necklace many nobles whose names were as old and revered as the Cardinal's chose to stay away when they knew she was to be there, even though she had become in her demeanour and outlook the Queen they had always wanted her to be, devoted to serious study over politics with the King, striving to be economical in all things and dedicated to seeing France through its present financial crisis, which was getting worse all the time. Others marked with savage resentment her increasing withdrawal from the social life of Versailles for the preferred company of old and trusted friends.

Rose had already seated herself at a table when she saw Richard surveying the Hall of Mirrors from under the archway of the War Salon. With his impressive height, his broad shoulders setting off the perfect cut of his crimson silk coat, he looked extremely handsome standing there. She wondered if he was looking for the woman he had been with on the evening of the concert and wished the creature well of him. Perhaps he would turn up for any appointments he made with her.

Richard's gaze took in every detail of that brilliant gallery. It was as if a flock of gorgeously feathered birds had been drawn by a lustrous net into that mirrored cage with the buzz of voices and laughter, the slap of cards and the rattle of dice from tables almost swamping the strains of the orchestra playing in the Peace Salon at the opposite end. "Blue boys" were in attendance with packs of cards and spare dice as well as a supply of blue velvet bags in which heavy winners could take away their gold and written promissory notes.

He was convinced he was looking at a passing scene. France was in a ferment and yet these inhabitants of Versailles played on as if nothing could reach through those ever-open gates into the Cour Royale and pluck at their sleeves. He had talked to many Frenchmen since his return, listened to the tirades against the aristocracy at street corners, and been to the meetings of intellectuals and to those of agitators, always dressing according to the occasion, his nationality going undetected. He was not a spy in the sense that he was after government secrets, but he had become his uncle's agent in building up a true picture of what they both viewed as a powder keg.

Why could not these noble peacocks and no less richly attired peahens see that their country could not stay locked forever in a feudal system in which they were the sole beneficiaries, exempt from paying many taxes while the burden was carried mainly by the ordinary people. The bourgeoisie and the peasants envied the far more just and liberal ways of England and the comparatively classless society of the United States which held up a mirror as clear as any in this gallery to their own miserable and restricted plight.

"May I show you to a table, sir?" A "blue boy" had come forward. "What is your preference?"

"Faro. There is a vacant seat by the second window. I'll take that."

Rose saw him being led towards the faro table where she sat. In this game where bets were placed on the order of appearance of certain cards, large sums of money could be swiftly won and lost, but she was usually lucky and awaited the start of play with confidence.

"Good evening, Madame la Marquise." Richard bowed to her before taking the seat. She acknowledged his greeting and introduced the two noblemen on either side of his chair to whom she had been talking.

"How are you enjoying your time in Paris?"

"Mightily. Paris has such a wide variety of *divertissements* and I have been invited to many hospitable homes."

"I hear you gave the King and Queen a rare plant that you had collected on your travels."

"That's right. It's an orchid."

"What are its chances of survival?"

"It has done well in my hothouses at home and I brought it from there. Have you seen it?"

"Not yet." She shrugged her indifference. "I wouldn't know where to look for it."

"I'll show you."

She was unable to stop herself from giving him a glare. "I think not," she said icily, his laxness on that previous occasion rankling more than ever. "I'm too busy and have no time to waste."

His cool expression did not change, although his eyes became steely. "That I can believe. I certainly would not want to make another arrangement that you had no wish to keep."

She fumed inwardly, able to tell from the burning in her cheeks that two angry spots of colour had appeared. To think how she had gone to the Ballroom Grove to see him, only narrowly escaping from becoming involved in that sordid play-acting she had witnessed. If she had been sighted Heaven alone knew what lies would have been told about her when it all came to light.

The game was beginning. She placed a bet and then tried to become absorbed in the play, but his presence at the table and her own pent-up annoyance distracted her. Without even looking at him her eyes registered the iridescence of the diamond ring on his finger, the fall of lace at his wrists and the powerful line of his jaw. He was even in her nostrils as if it were possible to discern among the mingling perfumes the clean male strength of him from the opposite side of the table.

She had lost again! It was no consolation to her that he was losing too, but after a while they recovered their losses almost simultaneously. By the time supper was served she had won a little and he had accumulated a small pile of gold. She left the table to join friends for supper, but she met him again in the Cornucopia Salon when he took the crystal goblet of fruit juice that had been poured for her and handed it to her himself.

"Join me in another game when we return to the Hall of Mirrors," he invited. "We can partner each other this time in whatever you fancy. I think we bring each other luck."

She tossed her head. "On the contrary, I connect you with misfortune. I barely won at faro and before that you were a messenger of ill-tidings to a lady whom we both know."

"Maybe if we took a stroll outside away from this atmosphere we might go back to our first meeting and start getting to know each other all over again."

"I'm not interested in doing that."

His exasperation with her flared up. "If you had given me the same straight answer before I should not have stayed listening to a clock chime hour after hour in the Ballroom Grove!"

"You weren't there!" she flashed back. Then realising by his look of astonishment that she had given herself away, she bunched her ribbon-threaded gauze skirt in her hands and fled from the Cornucopia Salon, dodging in and out of the clusters of people through the staterooms until she reached the Hall of Mirrors again. There she almost threw herself into the last vacant seat at a table for four, seeing too late that one of the players was a man whom she usually avoided, but it would have been ill-mannered towards the other two players to leave again immediately.

"This is a rare pleasure," he said to her, his painted

eyebrows raised in his rouged and powdered face, he being one of many men at Court who liked to make flamboyant use of cosmetics. Thirty years old, tall and well built, the Comte de Cordierer was a notorious womaniser, lived beyond his means, and had once had his face scratched by a discarded mistress in the Mars Salon. Fortunately for him neither the King nor the Queen had been there at the time. "We are about to play reversi. Does that suit you?"

She had played it often. It was said to have been the Sun King's favourite game and each player played independently. "Exceedingly well, Comte," she replied, thinking it did not matter what the game was as long as she kept her wits about her. This fellow was a formidable player of the worst kind.

"Pray be the first to cut for the deal, madame," he invited, placing the pack in front of her. But before she could do that a "blue boy" came to speak in the ear of an elderly duc at the table. Immediately the old man rose to his feet and apologised at having to leave on the King's business. Even as he moved away Richard appeared by the empty chair.

"May I join you, madame and messieurs?"

Much against her will she could only match her nod with the Comte's and the other player's, the solemn-looking Baron de Berry, who had no humour in him at all. As at the previous table, she made the introductions and the game began. This time, greatly annoyed by her own foolishness in betraying herself, she played keenly and astutely, wanting above all else to defeat Richard at every hand. She could tell that he was equally determined to beat her and it became like a tennis match played on the Sun King's court, they the opposing players and the other two mere spectators. In reality it was not like that, but it gave her satisfaction every time she won a point over Richard, whatever the result.

She won several times as he did, the Baron lagging behind and the Comte not scoring at all. Then, in spite of all her skill, the Comte began to win and there was no stopping him. All the gold that Richard had acquired left his place as did hers and the Baron was forced to dig deep into his pocket for the next stake. The Comte had an irritating habit of making apologetic gestures with a smug smile every time he swept the board. When yet another set came to an end with him triumphant, Rose decided to pull out of the game.

"I'm afraid I've gone as far as I can, gentlemen," she said, signalling to a "blue boy" who came forward with a promissory note and pen and ink. She filled it in and was about to add her name when Richard spoke sternly.

"Don't sign it!"

She looked up in alarm, guessing what he was about to do and determined to stop him. "It's the custom!" she exclaimed excitedly as if he would not have known that in any part of the world, but there was one main difference between gaming at Versailles and in England that apparently he did not know. He had turned towards the Comte.

"You, sir," he said in a low, deadly voice, "are a cheat!"

She and the Baron and the Comte, even the "blue boy," drew in their breath. A little silence was created at the table like the eye of a hurricane, for all around the cheerful noise from other players continued unabated. Richard's hand shot out and wrenched aside the Comte's pearl-pink satin coat to reveal a lining full of pockets, several with cards.

The Comte hurled himself to his feet with such swiftness that his chair went crashing back, drawing the attention of those at nearby tables. He was mad with rage, his eyes almost starting from his head, veins leaping in his temple.

"You English dog!" he roared. "You're not fit to be in civilised society!"

Richard, who had also risen to his feet, struck aside the furious fist being shaken in his face. "I demand an apology from you for your insult and for your dishonest play."

"Damnation to you!" The Comte almost danced with temper. By now the attention of the whole gathering had been captured, people at the back jumping up onto chairs to see what was going on. "My seconds shall call on you in the morning!"

Turning on his heel, satin coattails swinging, the Comte stalked out of the Hall of Mirrors. The Baron addressed Richard. "One of the best swordsmen in France has just challenged you, sir. I hope you are his match."

Richard smiled grimly. "I hope to prove I'm more than that."

"I wish you well. Are you in need of a second? I offer my services gladly."

"I thank you."

They spoke for a few minutes about arrangements, everybody else watching and whispering. The orchestra was heard clearly for the first time that evening. Richard bowed in turn to Rose, to the Baron and the company. Then he also left by way of the War Salon.

Rose watched him go from where she still sat. People had begun gathering around and pressing in on her. "What happened? Has the Comte de Cordierer been denounced? Whom has he challenged? Is it really a duel?"

She could not bear their questions and threw herself up from her chair. People fell back to let her through. She sped after Richard through one stateroom after another as she had fled from him a while before. When she came in sight of the King's Staircase she found him leaning against the balustrade with arms folded, waiting for her. As she approached he straightened up and held out a hand. "I hoped you'd come. Let us take that stroll I suggested earlier. There is something between us that has to be cleared up."

She kept her hands clenched firmly at her sides. "What foolishness you have committed! I tried to stop you. Why didn't you take notice? The Comte de Cordierer enjoys cheating. Some courtiers cheat because they are desperate for money, but others like the Comte feel it adds spice to the game. Why didn't you pay up and let him be?"

He stared at her incredulously. "You're telling me that you *knew*?"

"Of course I did. So did the Baron."

He drew up his hands in mock despair. "You accuse me of folly and yet you met the stakes as if you were playing for pebbles instead of gold."

"I like deep play. There's no thrill in it otherwise."

"That's your privilege when you were playing faro, but in riversi you were deliberately throwing your money into the Comte's pocket."

"Not at all. I had hoped to manoeuvre him through my own ability. That was the Baron's aim too. It's against all the rules of etiquette to disclose another man's weakness. It's the same with stealing. It goes on all the time."

His expression was stern, an inexorable note in his voice. "No gentleman cheats at cards. It abuses every age-old tradition of goodwill, friendship and even hospitality at the gaming table. In England a cheat, once denounced, whatever his rank, would never be invited by his contemporaries to play again, let alone allowed to flaunt his dishonesty in a royal house."

She sighed impatiently. "I agree with you in principle, but that's beside the point. This is Versailles and not an English drawing room. You have brought trouble down onto yourself."

"I would have spoken earlier but the rogue is a veritable magician. I had to detect his sleight of hand before I could guess exactly where he was putting the switched cards."

"What does a stupid game or how it is played matter when your life is at stake? He may kill you! At best he'll inflict a terrible wound!"

"How can you be so sure that I won't kill him?"

"That's as bad. If you had been French you could have returned to Court, but as an Englishman you would be requested to leave the country."

"Would that be of any concern to you?"

"I'm thinking of your future at your Embassy."

"I don't plan to be there long in any case." He stepped close to her, took hold of her upper arm and gently bent her elbow, which she was still holding stiffly, to capture her hand in his. "I waited three hours for you in the Ballroom Grove with poor Proserpine being raped. How did I miss you?"

She drew back her head, eyeing him half suspiciously. "That sculpture isn't in the Ballroom Grove. It's in the middle of the Colonnade."

In the same instant realisation came to them both as to what had happened. There was a long pause as they searched each other's eyes, she reeling inwardly from what it meant. Neither made any light remark about the error, the same thought in both their minds. He put it into words.

"We've lost three years," he said quietly, raising her hand to cup it in both of his, pressing a kiss to her fingers and not taking his eyes from hers. "What damage have I done?"

"Nothing that can't be mended," she breathed, her face tender and deeply troubled. It could be that all they had left of time together was a mere thirty-six hours. "Shall we go to the Ballroom Grove now?"

"I'd prefer to show you the orchid."

"But that's at the Trianon. Have you a carriage?"

"I have, but I understand it's possible to walk there by the Grand Canal."

"It's a long way."

"Is that important? Will you get tired?"

"I rarely tire from walking."

"Then we have all night to get there and back."

Her slow smile illumined her whole face. "Yes, we have, haven't we?"

Then with fingers linked, they hastened downstairs together and out into the moonlit night. They talked their way past the Water Parterres and the Latona fountain with its spreading skirts of spray. Each described how the waiting had been the night they had failed to meet, she adding her account of her extraordinary experience, which they discussed at length. He was particularly interested, partly because of his involvement in sending that warning to the Queen and also because, having listened to the British Ambassador, he believed with him that she was innocent of any dealings with the diamond necklace.

They were three-quarters of the way down the Tapis Vert when he paused, indicating a side turning. "It was down there I waited for you."

"You were leagues away from me," she declared merrily, pulling her hand from his and speeding off down the tree-arched pathway. He followed at a run, but she reached the circular peristyle a few seconds ahead of him. In that huge ring of marble arches and pillars, the slate blue and purple tones washed pale by the moonlight, she waited with her back to the central sculpture of the rape of Proserpine, her voice almost lost in the play of the fountains shooting up from the twenty-eight basins of the Colonnade. "I'm here now!"

She had flung her arms wide as if to embrace the night itself, but as he approached her she danced away and began a game of threading her way in and out of the sixty-four columns as if she was one of the gambolling children in the frieze of the Colonnade. He watched her with a grin of pleasure, standing with feet apart and hands on his hips. In a gauzy gown and with her cascade of curls softly rising and falling she looked like some mythical nymph instead of the voluptuously bosomed young woman that she was

When she came skipping back to him spray from the fountains had sprinkled her hair and skin like diamonds.

"What did you do that for?" he asked, loving the sight of her.

"I magicked away all the unhappiness and disappointment you felt the night you waited alone here. Did you never do that as a child?"

"Never."

"An only child invents all sorts of little rituals and imaginary companions. My guess is that you come from a large family."

"Four brothers and no sisters."

"Tell me about them and your home and how living in England differs in your opinion from living in France."

He told her that he and his brothers, who included twins, had been born within a span of six years and so their lives had been closely interwoven in childhood, with the same tutors and exploits and adventures. She was able to build up a picture of a large rambling old house in Kent in the midst of gentle, fertile countryside with a family life of hospitality and hunting and harvesting. Then, when he had come of age, he had inherited by his maternal grandfather's will the London house built in the last century by a Huguenot forebear who had settled in England and founded a banking business there.

"I'm the first direct descendant not to become a banker, but my brothers are making up for that. Two of them are presently on the Grand Tour and will enter banking upon their return while Douglas, who is next to me in age, has already entered the office in Lombard Street and has no other interest beyond bonds and shares and figures in a ledger. For myself, I shall be fully occupied with the running of the estate and taking my seat in the House of Lords. Although my botanical interest includes rare flowers and plants, it sprang originally from the more serious aspect of such things as the causes of wheat spoilage and how to combat it. The estate and the husbandry of the land are important to me."

"I never supposed you had a serious thought in your head when we first met."

"Apart from that, there wasn't. In any case all the time my father was alive the responsibility was not mine and when I was in London enjoyment was my only priority. It was in the same frame of mind that I set out on the Grand Tour." He gave her a smiling sideways glance. "You gave me a setback that I least expected and it stayed with me throughout my travels."

He told her of his father's death and of the effect it had had on him, something he had not revealed to anyone, and she sensed it was a confidence, which was gratifying to her. She wanted to get to know him above all else and he was leading the way just as she would have wished.

They had passed the Apollo fountain and there ahead was the Grand Canal stretching away into the distance like a pointing silver finger. "Why don't we sail to the Trianon?" he suggested eagerly. "The north cruciform arm goes all the way there, doesn't it?"

"Not quite, but it's near." She was full of enthusiasm for the idea and knew from what he had just told her that he was used to boats from sailing on the lake at Easterton as well as on a river that ran through the estate. There were two gilded rowing boats moored by the bank, but he disregarded them and took a flaring flambeau from its holder to investigate the boathouse. Vessels loomed up at him, the whole place smelling dank and disused. Then by the side of a ramp in a long narrow pool he came across a little ornamented barge, cobwebs thick upon it. For all he knew it might date from the Sun King's time, but after inspecting it from bow to stern he deemed it to be sufficiently well caulked and tight for a sail of the length he had planned. He thrust open the boathouse doors, doused the flambeau for safety and stepped back aboard to punt the barge out into the Canal.

Rose, watching from the bank, saw him emerge into the moonlight in the smoothly gliding barge, its bow encrusted with fake gems that held the gleam of real jewels in the moonlight. Although its paintwork was flaked in places, it still retained an aura of its bygone splendour. Eagerly she waited for him to bring it alongside for her to board.

"Wait a moment." He pulled a lace-edged handkerchief from his pocket with which he proceeded to wipe away the remaining cobwebs. Then he held out a hand to her. "Come aboard. You're probably the first passenger for a hundred years or more."

"Do you mean that?" Holding up her skirts, she leapt lightly onto the deck.

He chuckled. "No, it's been used since then but not recently. Let's see how the sails run up."

She gasped with delight as the sails unfurled and billowed out. They were pure silk, Louis XIV's device of Apollo's head shining gold on the sapphire-blue spread. "Oh, look! How exciting! Once all the sails on the Canal would have been as grand as this!"

She went exploring herself and found some rolled-up brocade draperies in a locker, which she hung over the sides in the old style, the golden fringes trailing in the water. Unearthing a cushion bright with scarlet tassels, she seated herself on the deck by Richard, who sat higher, holding the tiller as they were borne slowly along by a warm and gentle breeze. Once the deck would have been carpeted but it retained a faint golden sheen in the moonlight. The little barge moved serenely along as if it had been only yesterday that it had carried a merry company on such a cruise. The thick woods of cedars, oaks, maples and pines went slipping past on either side of the wide, shining water.

The night was creating such empathy between them that she was able to talk freely, telling him about Château Satory and her grandmother and what she knew of her parentage, holding nothing back. She recounted her first resentment at receiving a title and coming to Versailles, of the change that had taken place in her and how she had taken her cue from the Queen in letting nothing sway her in taking an independent path to pleasure and excitement.

"There's no more beautiful place to be in than Versailles," she declared, glancing contentedly about her. "Everything happens here."

"What about the outside world? Do you ever give a thought to that?"

She drew in her chin and mocked him with an impression of his tone. "How solemn you sound now! Are we to turn to politics?"

He smiled, shaking his head. "Not this evening."

"Good." She shifted her position, smoothing her billowing skirts into place. "If you want serious talk I'll present you to my grandmother. She never spares me from everyday events whenever I visit her, so I'm not as detached from life outside the palisades of Versailles as you seem to suppose." With a shrug and a sigh she looked up at the stars. "I'm not ready yet to follow any path but the one set for me. There's so much to enjoy! I like to feel carefree. Maybe one day I'll tire of dancing my years away, but not yet." She shook her head vehemently. "Not for a long, long time."

He could see that certain stages of her life had matched his own, even though their backgrounds were entirely different. It had taken tragedy to sober him to the realities of life and he hoped that no similar event would ever happen to her. There was something fresh and new and untamed about her that he wanted to channel only towards himself. As yet she was still managing to keep at bay the full force of the attraction between them.

"Many men must have fallen in love with you since you first came to Versailles" he said. "Have you loved any of them?"

"I've been close." Her eyes were teasing him.

"How close?" he persisted seriously.

She pretended to consider, shaking back her curls in a tantalising manner. "That's difficult to say."

He fixed the tiller and leaned down to grip her by the arms. "As close as now?"

Her gaze was locked by his and she did not seem able to break it. Somewhere in her throat her voice fluttered and came out in a strained, husky whisper. "No. Never as now."

He drew her upright on her knees, drove both hands into her curls and pulled her head forward to bury her mouth in his. She felt herself dissolve totally into love. It was as if she had been on the edge of a tumultuous whirlwind ever since their first meeting and now it had caught her up and was hurtling her away with him. Of all the kisses she had known none had ever been like this as she knelt, hands at her sides, exulting in the almost frantic exploration of his loving tongue while the barge went sailing on in the moonlight and nightingales sang in the passing woods.

When he drew his face away from hers he kept his hold, smoothing her cheekbones with his thumbs and looking deep into her eyes as if searching out her soul. "I came back to France to find you. Whatever reasons I may have presented to others and to myself, I knew all along it was in the hope of meeting you again."

"I tried to forget you. I was hurt and furious, but beyond that I felt I had missed getting to know someone who could have had a deep effect on my life."

"It was the same for me. Darling Rose." He spoke softly, his hands sliding gently down her neck and shoulders and back until he held her in firm embrace. "I love you."

They kissed again. Nothing had prepared her for such joy. Ever since coming to Court she had heard open talk of sexual pleasure, of passion and romance, and she herself had experienced certain sensual delights, but nobody had ever spoken of the jubilant expansion of the heart that came with the full onslaught of deep love. The resistance against letting her emotions run away with her, which had been built up over a long period, had enabled her to stay curiously innocent, her sophistication no more than an outer carapace, and now she was in a state of wonderment.

"I love you, too," she breathed, scarcely able to believe she was uttering these words at last.

They shared more kisses, adoring and gentle and lingering, his hands passing over her face and neck and breasts before he lowered her back to her cushion and resumed charge of the tiller. Apart from an occasional automatic glance ahead of him, for he expected no hazard on the Canal beyond a floating branch, he kept his gaze on her, looking down into her face as she looked up into his, their softly spoken love-talk for no other ears but their own.

Gradually they approached the section of the Canal where it branched in either direction and, handling the old barge expertly, he headed it in a long and easy curve into the north arm. The distant lights of the Trianon came twinkling into view, but the Petit Trianon was too far beyond it to be visible from the Canal.

"We can't see the steps up from the Canal path yet," she said, peering ahead, "but I think that tall flambeau must be lighting the flight." It was then that a chill wetness came seeping through her satin shoes. She jerked her feet towards her and felt the slap of a wet petticoat frill. Then with widening eyes she saw water had swilled up through the deckboards. She sprang up from her cushion. "The barge is leaking!"

He exclaimed under his breath. "I thought I felt a slight

lunge when we took that turn. Perhaps some caulking came away. I'll make for the bank."

He had been steering a middle course and a considerable expanse of water lay between the barge and the grassy bank. Before they were halfway across the deck was awash and he knew they were not going to make it.

"Can you swim?" he asked her, throwing off his coat.

She looked more surprised than startled, not having realised that a perilous situation had developed. "No. I can't."

"It doesn't matter because I shall swim with you. Just keep calm, do as I say and there'll be nothing to fear."

"I'm not in the least afraid."

He saw she meant what she said, looking to him with absolute confidence as if love had somehow made them immune to danger. "Kick off your shoes," he instructed, getting rid of his own. She obeyed and he gripped her around the waist to lead her swiftly to the side of the barge. "Take a deep breath and hold it as long as you can."

She leapt with him into the water as if taking flight and together they plunged down into the dark blue depths. The water was colder than he had expected. Still holding her tight he kicked his way upwards and the moonlight burst onto them as they broke the surface. She spluttered and gulped in air, her curls sticking to her head like a golden cap, but she remained compliant and did not struggle as he struck out with her for the bank.

When they reached it he pushed her up first and shot a look over his shoulder before clambering up after her. The barge had disappeared. One of the brocade draperies lay floating on the surface like a giant lily pad. He collapsed face downwards onto the grass, getting his breath back.

"Are you all right?" she asked anxiously.

He rolled over onto his back. She was sitting up and leaning over him, drops from her hair falling onto his chest like rain. He gave her a broad smile of reassurance. "There's nothing wrong with me. You're shivering. Shall we be able to borrow some dry clothes at the Trianon?"

She grimaced. "I know the courtiers who'll be there. They'd make a laughingstock of us, the pompous loons! We'll go to the theatre at the Petit Trianon. I have some stage gowns in the wardrobe room and there are plenty of men's clothes that would fit you."

"Whatever you wish." He sat up and propped himself on his hand, bringing his smiling face on a level with hers. "I'm sorry that our voyage ended as it did."

She threw back her head on a peal of laughter. "Wasn't it funny! Oh, dear! We've sunk the Sun King's boat. He would have been furious if he'd still been here, wouldn't he!"

"What would he have done?" He shared her mirth.

"Thrown us into the Bastille, I suppose!"

Her bedraggled gown had dragged down from her shoulders, showing him more of her breasts than she knew. He leaned forward and kissed her neck. The laughter stilled softly in her as it had in him. His lips trailed down to the curving mounds of her breasts as if sipping the rivulets running down into her cleavage. Her shivering became more like a violent ague, set off by desire as much as from being chilled. She wished she could throw off her wet garments and lie naked with him in the night-warm grass. All her natural longings, which she had fought steadfastly on many occasions, threatened to overwhelm her in this new vulnerability created by love. When he drew aside a sodden frill of lace to expose and kiss her right nipple, she almost swooned. She did not know whether she had the mental equilibrium to cope with such a crescendo of feeling rising in her. To save her sanity she whispered a faint protest.

He forced himself to draw away from her. "I'm being selfish," he said hoarsely, covering her again and bringing her to her feet with him. "You'll get a raging lung-fever if you keep those cold garments on you much longer."

They ran together to the steps that led up from the path and went by way of the Trianon gardens to reach the vicinity of the Petit Trianon. It was quite far, and by the time they reached the theatre they were both warmed by the exercise and happily out of breath. She led the way up the steps into the porch. The doors were not locked and he followed her into the blackness of an octagonal vestibule. She knew where there were candles and lit one, the glow bringing her face and shoulders into his vision again. He held the door for her into the auditorium, which was equally dark, the high windows shuttered. He glanced about him as the candle-flame glimmered faintly on the blue velvet chairs and the gilded mouldings of the horseshoe-shaped auditorium.

"It doesn't seat many," he commented.

"It's not intended to. The Queen's troupe consists of her friends and those close to her, while the audience is made up of the King, the royal family and sometimes just a few people whom she likes." She gestured to a high gallery. "The staff from the Petit Trianon sit up there."

"So the retainers are permitted to come whereas those holding the highest offices at the Court do not necessarily receive a ticket?" He was intrigued by this situation. It was the first touch of democracy he had met in this autocratically governed land.

"Why not? The Queen lives like an ordinary citizen at the Petit Trianon. Rank at Court means nothing here." She had set off in the direction of the dressing rooms behind the stage and he hurried after her.

"Have you been in many performances?"

"About a dozen, I suppose. They are not put on so often now. The forthcoming performance will be the first for quite a while."

"I should like to see you act."

She threw a twinkling glance back over her shoulder at him. "If you care to light the footlights after you've changed, I'll perform one of my scenes for you."

In the men's wardrobe room some elaborate costumes were draped on wicker frames, many more being in the drawers of the clothespresses. She rummaged through several drawers until she found what she wanted.

"Here you are! This should fit you." She pulled out a yellow silk coat. "It was worn by the Comte de Vaudreuil in Beaumarchais's play *The Barber of Seville*. He's as tall as you and about the same build."

She had lit some more candles for him and left him to change. With the coat there was a shirt still neatly folded from the hands of the laundresses, breeches, stockings and a handkerchief, everything immaculate. When dressed, he looked around for shoes and found rack after rack of them. A pair with silver buckles fitted him well and at the makeup table he found a comb to run through his hair, which he had dried with one of the towels she had taken from a cupboard for him. When he had retied it at the back with a new ribbon, he emerged from the wardrobe room and called to her.

"I'm nearly ready," she replied from behind a closed door.

"Then I'll put a taper to the footlights."

One by one he lit the candle-lamps along the front of the stage. Then he went to investigate the ropes and raised the curtain on a rustic scene. Rose came up the steps onto the boards, her newly dried curls abounce once more, her gown of orange silk. Merrily she handed him the red leather-backed book that she carried.

"Here's the play that's to be the next production. I don't see why I should do all the work, so you shall read a part. It's called *The Secret Promise* and it's the story of a village maid who is really a princess in hiding. I've marked the scene. I'm the farmer's daughter and you're the princess's beau."

"I'd prefer to be yours," he gave back with a grin.

She made an amused little face at him. "In the play I want you to be. In fact I'm out to tempt you, but you forget me as soon as you see the royal village maid."

"Impossible!"

"Be serious!" She indicated a rustic seat set at an angle. "You're sitting there when I come on. You've just arrived at the village."

He glanced over the lines as he settled himself. Apart from charades at winter parties and family gatherings, most English people had little to do with acting. They flocked to the theatre in the cities and in the countryside to see any travelling company, but the passion for amateur theatricals among the noble and wealthy in France did not have a parallel in England. It was because of his mother's French ancestry that his family had made a tradition of putting on a play once a year for the local community. One of the barns had been transformed into a permanent theatre and strolling players were always permitted to perform there. As a result, he felt quite relaxed in the glow of the footlights and threw himself into his rôle as Rose came running onto the stage and then halted, supposedly seeing him before he saw her.

"Who is this?" she said in an aside to the blackness of the auditorium. "He's a grand gentleman fresh from Paris, I'll be bound. I'll make myself known to him."

The flare of interest he showed as she approached him, the eagerness lying behind the assumed bored air, came over well as they entered fully into their parts. It was a hilarious romp, culminating in a chase, which was to end when the royal village maid suddenly entered carrying a basket of flowers. She came right on cue. Neither Rose nor Richard had heard the faint rustling at the back of the theatre as several people had crept in to take seats in the darkness. The Queen had gone out again to enter by a rear door that had enabled her to pick up the flowers en route for the stage.

"What's ado here?" she exclaimed, setting her basket down on the seat.

Rose carried on in her rôle, taking up one of the silk flowers to twirl it before thrusting it into her hair, but Richard, hiding the surprise he felt, snatched the flower from her. With his gaze riveted on the royal village maid he tucked it into his coat above his heart instead of pressing his hand to his chest to express the piercing of Cupid's dart. At that point the curtain descended, lowered by another in the troupe who had gone unseen to the side of the stage. From the auditorium came a burst of applause.

Within the gloom of the curtained stage, Richard bowed low to Marie Antoinette and Rose curtsied as she made a swift apology. "I did not know you would be here this evening, madame."

The Queen smiled reassuringly. "It's of no consequence. At the Petit Trianon the conversation had turned to the new play and I brought everyone here to see that the old scenery we used before will do perfectly well."

Previously the Queen had had new scenery for every production, but in her sweeping economies not even a fresh backcloth was allowed. She turned graciously to Richard. "I liked the touch with the flower, Lord Easterton. That was inspirational and I'm sure the producer, Madame Campan, will want to retain it. You have a flair for acting. I cannot offer you the same rôle in the forthcoming production, but there are two smaller rôles as yet uncast if you would care to take one of them."

"I should be honoured, madame." He could scarcely believe his luck. It would give him the chance to see Rose far more than would otherwise have been the case. Rose was equally pleased and showed it. The Queen spoke to her again.

"What made you come to the theatre at this late hour?"

Briefly Rose explained and the Queen was immediately concerned, well aware of what would have happened if Richard had not been a strong swimmer.

"You shall stay the night at the Petit Trianon, Madame Rose. I think you should retire now and get some rest. Lord Easterton, you will find accommodation at the Trianon. You will be notified of the time of the first rehearsal."

Rose and Richard left the theatre together, pausing to speak to several of those in the auditorium, Axel von Fersen among them. Once outside they threw their arms around each other in jubilation that he had become a member of the royal troupe. He swung her up and round before pulling her close to him and kissing her. Then suddenly the shadow of the duel with the Comte de Cordierer seemed to shatter the enchantment of the evening, falling across them both at the same moment. Deliberately they had kept it at bay throughout all the past hours.

Her eyes were desperate with appeal. "We're already in the early hours of a new day. Let me keep your dawn appointment with you tomorrow morning."

He stroked her face. "Oh, no, my dearest. Without intending it, you would disturb my concentration. If you want to be sure of my coming back to you unscathed you must stay away."

"I need to be within range."

He shook his head. "No. You must do as I ask in this matter. Wait for me here at the Petit Trianon."

"In the park then. I'll show you where." She took him by the hand and led him past the little palace until they could see the delicate white rotunda of twelve Corinthian columns supporting a sculptured, copper-topped dome. As was often the case when the Queen gave an evening party it was illumined by burning faggots in a concealed ditch which gave it the look of floating in the air as did other of the charming edifices similarly lit throughout the park. "There! In the Temple of Love."

"What better choice?" He embraced her again and she leaned against him, her face in his shoulder.

"I'm afraid," she whispered.

He spoke softly and encouragingly. "What talk is this? You weren't in the least scared when the prospect of drowning confronted us."

She raised her anguished face. "We would have gone

together then. This is different. I can't bear the thought of your suffering a scratch, much less a wound."

Had he spoken out at that point he would have said that he foresaw danger everywhere in France to an extent that made his forthcoming clash with a fellow swordsman a mere bagatelle, even if it should prove fatal to either of them. Instead he gave her an answer that was seriously meant, although given lightly. "I can't let anything happen to me, because I promised to show you the orchid I gave the Queen and I never go back on my word."

Her anxious eyes searched his. "You won't disappoint me?"

His arms tightened about her. "Never. Neither shall you ever suffer a moment's unhappiness if it lies in my power to prevent it, no matter what may come."

She flung herself upwards to his mouth, clasping him about the neck and kissing him ardently. They swayed together in the darkness, caressing and seeking, straining towards each other. Then voices coming from the direction of the theatre told them that the Queen's guests were departing and reluctantly she drew away from him.

"Until tomorrow," he said quickly.

"I'll be waiting. God keep you." She pressed a kiss to her fingertips and transferred it swiftly to his lips before she sped away to disappear into the Petit Trianon.

He decided against the accommodation the Queen had advised. Instead he got a carriage at the Trianon that returned him to his own at Versailles and from there he went back to Paris. When the Comte de Cordierer's seconds called on him shortly before noon he received them with the usual courtesies. The venue was arranged. It was a green sward at the far south end of the Swiss Lake at Versailles, surrounded on three sides by trees, the fourth being taken up by an equestrian statue by Bernini of the Sun King, who had never liked it—the reason why he had had it placed at such a lengthy distance out of sight of the windows of the Château. It was a favourite place for duels.

Just before dawn Rose, wearing one of the white muslin gowns she kept at the Petit Trianon, crossed the little bridge over the water that surrounded the Temple of Love. She wanted to keep vigil at this time of Richard's peril.

There were little seats within the rotunda and she sat on

one, leaning her back against a pillar. The stars had faded and the soft hues of dawn had begun to seep across the sky. The pinkish light bathed her and the tall statue of Cupid on its round plinth that stood in the middle of the circular marble floor. The sun began to rise over the gardens of Versailles although she did not see it until it topped the tall trees and its first warm rays touched her. Since coming there she had not moved, feeling numb with anxious suspense and seeming as motionless as the statue, her hands clasped in her lap, her feet together. She had not brought a fob-watch. Time had no connection with this period of waiting. Her eyes were fixed on the path down which her whole future would come. If it was a doctor who appeared through the distant archway in the wall there would be hope. If a priest should come she would no longer have a reason for living.

From the forecourt there came the clatter of hooves and rattle of wheels over the cobblestones. She rose slowly to her feet. Her mind seemed detached and floating. It was as if she were in a void, hovering between life and death. Then she heard a long-drawn-out cry of exultation and realised it had come from the depth of her own rejoicing heart. Richard had appeared from beyond the trees, to all intents unharmed and hurrying to her.

"My love!" He called to her as he came. "There'll be no banishment from France for me! The Comte is not dead. I simply brought him to his knees."

He came pounding across the bridge and she saw there was a streak of blood down the side of his face as if a rapier point had grazed it in passing. She met him on the steps of the rotunda and fell into his arms.

His passionate mouth found hers. As she clung to him their embrace became a fusing of their lives together. Neither would ever again wish to be apart from the other.

Twenty

Although Rose and Richard attended several rehearsals of *The Secret Promise* it was never performed. The Queen had intended it as a diversion from troubled times for herself and everyone else involved, but matters of state overwhelmed her, for she could no longer leave any important decisions to her ineffectual husband. As various political and economic measures failed dismally, it seemed to Rose that the very air of Versailles had become tainted with venom against the woman struggling to stabilise the country's finances and maintain the strength of the monarchy. There was unemployment everywhere; even those in work were on low wages, some earning no more than a pittance on which to keep their families while the the high cost of living rose daily. As if France did not have enough trouble, the disastrous failure of the harvest had caused grain prices to soar.

"Where is it all going to end?" Rose asked Richard with a sigh. He was driving her in a calèche to Château Satory and they had been discussing the recent bread riots in

Paris during which troops had been called out and a number of people killed.

"I wish I knew." It was several weeks since his first visit to her home and he had been often since then, but today was destined to be the most important. He was going to ask the Duchesse de Valverde for her granddaughter's hand in marriage. "The Court and the rest of the nobility, together with the clergy, are making a terrible mistake in clinging to their status as the one privileged class. If only they had agreed to surrender their feudal dues and other tax-free rights it would have eased the financial chaos as well as lifting a great burden from the people. At the moment I see no hope."

"It's the nobles' greed that makes them stubborn," she commented angrily.

He gave her a sideways glance. "For power as much as for gold. They want to govern France with the King as a figurehead. With their self-centred interests they would not be trusted by the peasants, the bourgeoisie or by one another. They would destroy this country completely."

She knew he was right. Had it not been for her grandmother, whose contact with the destitute had never been broken, she would never have known what hatred existed generally against the aristocracy among whom she moved like a goldfish in a crystal bowl. There was also the loathing and deep-rooted resentment among the bourgeoisie, whose sons were denied high rank in the army and innumerable civil positions exclusive to those of noble blood, and who, in many cases, had become the new poor in these hard days. Old grievances died hard and fresh injustices made matters worse.

Yet it was Richard, far more than Jasmin, who had brought her face to face with the urgent need for reform in France. She supposed that over the years she had become too accustomed to her grandmother's complaints about the oppression of the peasantry to consider how matters might be changed. Many times on Richard's visits to her home he and her grandmother had entered into deep political discussions, the old lady's mind being as alert as it had ever been. At first she had not joined in, feeling at a distance from these grim problems about which she could do nothing, but Richard had the ability to involve her with a word or a glance as if determined to prise her out of her detachment, more than backed up by Jasmin as if she had turned her face away too long. Sometimes they had had the look of amiable conspirators plotting to make her one of their band. Her capitulation had been inevitable, simply because her love for him had made her aware of all things as never before. She came to realise that she had shared the haughty egotism of those at Court for far too long and that she and they could not dance forever along a gilded path while all around them France crumbled into ruin and despair. At the moment of revelation she had been full of shame that she had never come to terms with the situation before. At least it had not been too late to adjust to this new clear-thinking and she was able to present outside viewpoints to the Queen whenever the opportunity presented itself.

"One thing is certain," Richard continued, turning into the gates of Château Satory. "The halcyon days of Versailles are almost over. There will have to be a more realistic Court in the future."

She nodded in agreement, turning her head to gaze out at the passing trees and parterres of home. In spite of the King's weakness, the confusion of government, the vice, the avarice, the petty jealousies and feuds and all the futile quirks of etiquette, there was something essentially magical about Versailles. It was as if its spirit rose above all the meanness and merely gloried in its magnificent works of art and matchless craftsmanship that adorned it inside and out. Suddenly, not knowing why, she shivered. Turning to him, she thrust her arm through his and cuddled close.

"Let's marry on New Year's Day," she urged a little frantically, looking into his face. "It's a new beginning and —pray God—it will bring in a better era for France and all of us, no matter how things appear now."

He chuckled and kissed her. "On the first day of January, 1789, it shall be. That's a relief. I thought you wanted a spring wedding."

"Only because a betrothal is expected to be a certain period. I feel sure that when I talk to the Queen she will agree. After all, she knows what it is to be in love."

"That's my next hurdle after today. To gain royal permission to wed you."

"The Queen won't refuse. As soon as I requested a special audience for you she guessed. I could see that." Rose laughed silently out of pure happiness. "Why is being in love so difficult to hide? Everyone seems to know from the moment it happens."

They kissed again. Sometimes such passion seized them that all her resolve to wait until their wedding night seemed doomed. He was unable to keep his hand from her breasts or from caressing the shape of her through whatever soft garment kept him at bay. But for her a period of adjustment to love was essential. It had affected her from the start like some joyous illness as if she had become possessed of a passion too vast for any human heart to hold. She was dazed, certain she had become a little mad, and was both exhilarated and terrified by turns at what had happened to her.

Jasmin awaited them in the Ivory Salon. She had never seen a couple more in love and, as she had always half expected, Rose was ever as near tears as laughter in the enormous happiness that possessed her. To see them squabble was like watching a pair of playful kittens patting each other with sheathed claws. Yet they had had sharpish words on the terrace outside the Ivory Salon one day, forgetting she was within and could overhear. He was unable to see why Rose could not leave the Queen's service when she became his wife.

"Naturally the Queen will not release me in these exceptionally troubled times," Rose had declared on the determined note that Jasmin had recognised well. "I'm the one person whom she can trust completely. I'm privy to her secrets and they will die with me."

Jasmin could guess at something that her granddaughter probably knew. It was whether or not Marie Antoinette and Axel von Fersen were lovers, a topic of speculation at Court and elsewhere. Personally she hoped and believed they were.

"What will happen when I want to take you back to England with me?" Richard questioned urgently.

"That doesn't come into it yet. You told me the Duke of Dorset wants you to stay on at the Embassy for an indefinite period."

"At least let us live in Paris."

"I've told you before. I must remain at Versailles. I'm sure the Queen will see that we have a larger apartment. There is not the demand for accommodation that there

used to be. Even some of the Queen's closest friends have
deserted her because their noses were put out of joint by
her dissolving their lucrative posts at Court in her economies."

It was then that Jasmin added a cough to her thumping
on her cane, already banged twice, to remind them that
they were within earshot of someone who was old but not
deaf. But the message had been misinterpreted. Rose had
come hurrying in to ask her if she was in a draught from
the open doors or did she want a sip of water for her cough.

The Englishman had not requested her permission to
marry Rose that day or on subsequent visits. Her guess was
that they believed they must be conventionally cautious in
approaching her. After all, he was a foreigner and a Protestant, not at all what she had wished for Rose, and, under-
standably, they must be harbouring some doubt about
whether she would give her consent. As it happened, they
had acted wisely in not rushing her, for she had come to
know and like Richard Easterton, whom she judged to
have the depth of character and the qualities necessary
to make Rose a good husband. As for herself, the thought of
Rose going so far afield was agonising to bear, but she
despised selfishness, having suffered enough of it from
Sabatin ever to inflict it on anyone else. She would give no
sign of her own loss when it came to granting Rose's hand
to Richard.

There were the carriage wheels! They had arrived. Jasmin put one thin hand on the arm of her chair and gripped
her gold-topped cane to heave herself up to meet them on
her feet. Unlike many of her friends she refused to seek
sympathy and tolerance through the infirmities of old age.
Michel, who had become a frequent visitor in his loneliness
since the death of his wife, was ever an example to her. He
never spoke of the pain that was always with him, behav-
ing towards her as if they were still young. The truth was
that within themselves they were the same as they had
been in their youth, only now trapped by ageing bodies.
She saw death as a throwing off of that wrinkled, distorted
cage and a release of eternal youth into a spiritual sphere.

"Here we are!" Rose came running into the room, radiant and beautiful. The warm young arms embraced her
with care for her fragile bones and she was kissed on both

cheeks. "You have a lovely new gown, Grand-mère! How it suits you!"

Jasmin kept up with fashion in a modest way that was suited to her years. In style her lilac gown with its fichu was similar to her granddaughter's coral silk with Chantilly lace foaming over the high young bosom and the softly gathered skirt. The Englishman was bowing.

"Madame la Duchesse." He kissed her hand. "It is most kind of you to invite me to dine today."

"You are most welcome, Lord Easterton. We are soon to be joined by an old friend of mine, Monsieur Balaine. I think you will enjoy meeting him."

"I shall be honoured." He knew from what Rose had told him that the artist was her grandfather. The occasion was being made into a family gathering since the Duchesse was prepared for what he was to ask her.

Rose was looking delighted. "I haven't seen Monsieur Balaine for ages. He is such a dear man."

An echo came back to Jasmin. Hadn't Violette used that same description of Michel long ago in this same room? It was an apt appraisal. "Now sit down and tell me what you have been doing," she said, moving back to her chair and hating her own slowness. "But first of all, how is the young Dauphin? Is there any improvement?"

Rose shook her head sadly as she and Richard sat down side by side on a sofa. It was their favourite seat, for it enabled them to hold hands. "None, I fear. He's such a courageous, uncomplaining little boy. It's heartrending to see how he suffers."

"The poor Queen." Jasmin's voice was full of compassion. "What torment she must be going through."

"Yet they continue to slander her. The latest is that when she was told that the starving peasants couldn't afford to buy bread she said they should eat cake instead."

"Pouf!" Jasmin flicked a hand contemptuously. "Has that old chestnut been pulled out of the fire again? Two of our Queens before her have been credited with a similar remark. I don't believe it of any of them. Let us turn to a happier topic. How did you enjoy the ball at the Embassy?"

Rose went into raptures. Anything she did and anywhere she went in Richard's company was magical. Her sparkling gaiety imbued her description of the ball, of incidents at a later reception at Versailles and how she and other ladies followed in carrioles, as was the custom, when Richard had ridden with the King's hunt. It was at this point that Michel arrived. Rose was distressed to see how much slower he had become, relying heavily on the support of his two canes. Yet he had the same dignified air about him that he had always had, much like her grandmother's, and both of them through their individual personalities were able to make one forget their age and disabilities.

"How well you look, my dear," he said to Rose when greetings were over and Richard had been duly presented. "You make me wish I could take up my paints again. What a portrait I could have done of you in that charming gown!"

She put a hand on his arm, Richard having surrendered his seat on the sofa. "I prefer the painting of the pony you gave me to any portrait of myself. I have it in my boudoir at Versailles."

Jasmin entered their conversation at this point, reminiscing about Rose's excitement the day it had been given to her. Richard, momentarily out of the circle, was taking a chair to swing it nearer Rose when his gaze fell fully on a portrait hanging in an alcove. He had been vaguely aware before that a picture was there, but previously he had never given it more than a cursory glance. Now he set down the chair again to go across to the portrait and study it closely. He could have sworn the likeness was of one of his forebears, although at a much younger age than in the portrait that hung in the Roussier banking house. The features were certainly the same. There were the dark green eyes of which his were a lighter version and an arrogant nose similar to his own. He spun round as a pause came in the conversation by the fire.

"It's quite extraordinary! I believe this painting to be of my Huguenot great-great-grandfather on my mother's side of the family. He served with Louis XIV's musketeers."

There was a silence in the room, broken only by the crackle of burning logs in the grate. Rose's eyebrows were raised in astonishment. Monsieur Balaine looked interested and the Duchesse seemed to be holding her breath, having placed a fluttering hand to her throat.

"What was his name?"

"Augustin Roussier."

"That is he."

He looked dumbfounded. "How extraordinary! His son, Edmund, who carried on the Banking House of Roussier, was my mother's grandfather. Many tales of the family's escape to England have been passed down to me but I still do not understand why Augustin's portrait should be here."

Rose slid swiftly to her feet and went to him. "This château was once his. It was built for him by my great-grandfather. He left here after the Revocation of the Edict of Nantes when he was forced to flee from France."

He cupped his hands round her upper arms, frowning seriously. "Are you sure about that? The Roussier family seat, the Manoir, was at Le Havre. I've always heard that he went from there after his father's murder by the dreaded dragoons and his sword fight with them. I went to visit it when I was first in France and found it had become a neglected ruin. There has never been any mention of Château Satory in all my mother's and my maternal grandparents' talk of the past."

Jasmin spoke up. She had risen from her chair. "I think I have the explanation for that. Augustin Roussier gave this château as a gift to Rose's great-grandmother, Marguerite Dremont. She was also my mother." She gestured towards the portrait above the fireplace. "As you are a man of the world, Lord Easterton, you will understand me when I say she was outside Augustin Roussier's marriage and his children. He must have borne in mind the possibility that his descendants might claim the property back from her or from the offspring of any future marriage and decided that Château Satory should never be spoken of again. And as matters were arranged, no claim has ever been forthcoming."

"Nor shall it ever be!" Richard stated forcefully.

A sweet smile curved Jasmin's crinkled lips. "I never doubted that you would say that. Would I be speaking prematurely if I said it seems as if love is about to complete a full circle?"

"If all goes favourably for me in your eyes."

"Then let us send Rose to fetch that book from the library that I promised to loan you the next time you were here. If you are agreeable, I should like Monsieur Balaine to stay."

When Rose returned from the library, having allowed a full half hour for everything to be settled about her dowry, the marriage date and so forth, one wing of the Ivory Salon double doors stood open, a sign that she should enter. She put the book on a side table and went in. Richard was waiting for her and took her hand to lead her forward, his overjoyed expression telling her at once that all was well.

Dinner was one of the happiest repasts Jasmin could remember being served at Château Satory. Her chefs had excelled themselves and Michel proposed a toast to the betrothed couple that was charmingly expressed. She was, however, puzzled to see that once or twice Rose looked unusually subdued and the reason was revealed to her in the short time they had alone together before the visit was over. She had taken her granddaughter upstairs to give her a betrothal gift. Until the Queen had given her consent Rose could not wear the sapphire betrothal ring that Richard had had made for her, but as Jasmin considered the matter settled she wanted her granddaughter to have the ruby and diamond brooch that had been a gift from Louis XV when they had both been young and he already in love with her.

"It's exquisite, Grand-mère." Rose had seated herself on the stool before the mirror in Jasmin's bedchamber and was gazing at the brooch's reflection where she had fastened it to the neckline of her gown. It was odd that the royal donor had been her father whom she remembered clearly from her childhood visit to Versailles. Then suddenly she was touched again by the more distant past as she had been downstairs earlier. In spite of herself a sob choked in her throat and she covered her eyes with one hand.

"Dear child! What's the matter?" Jasmin, standing beside her, became agitated with alarm.

The reply came bursting forth. "I wish Richard didn't have Roussier blood in his veins."

"Why ever not? I can't tell you what it means to me. When you two are married it will bring Augustin and Marguerite together at last."

"No!" Rose threw up her head. "Don't say that! They may have loved each other but they were ill-fated from the start. Suppose their misfortune should descend on Richard and me to prevent our marriage from taking place? I'm terrified, Grand-mère! When he stood there by that shadowed portrait and I heard how he was a descendant of Augustin Roussier, it was as if the ground fell away from under me. Nothing is safe and secure. I could see our love in jeopardy."

Jasmin almost recoiled before such convictions. What horrifying vision of the future had passed briefly before the girl's eyes? Then she collected herself and answered as calmly and as wisely as she could.

"I remember your tirade against the misfortunes that afflicted the women of this family when you first heard that you were to go to Versailles. Think for a moment. Out of what you saw as a disaster has come a love that would never have been born otherwise."

"Yes, that's true, but—"

"You spoke of the Queen's secrets a while ago. Now I shall tell you one." Jasmin lowered herself onto the stool as Rose moved up to give her space. "Michel has come back to me. You see a tired old woman but he sees me as if I were still young. The strange thing is that after years of shutting away my innermost feelings for him, the fact that there is no longer anyone standing between us has made a great difference to me. Once I shut him out of my life because of impossible circumstances and then again when I discovered there was another woman in his life. Now there is no need to harden my heart any more. Despite his affection and deep gratitude to Béatrice, he has never stopped loving me and we have truly found each other again." She gestured gracefully. "Of course it is different from the past. Companionship has taken the place of passion and perhaps my love was never as strong as his, but if I had to go through my years of misery all over again to receive all I have now, I would do it willingly." She put her palm lovingly against her granddaughter's cheek. "I have told you this to dispel your fears. Love has always been subject to tribulation, but what happened to Marguerite and Augustin has not proved true for me and neither should it for you."

She saw she had eased her granddaughter's wave of foreboding even if she had not entirely banished it. Rose was intrigued by this renewal of love in old age.

"Shall you marry him?" she asked.

"Oh, no." Jasmin spoke decisively. "He is head of his house and I of mine. We are content to see each other as often as possible."

When they were downstairs again Rose, still wearing the brooch, drew her relationship with Michel into the open for the first time. "Farewell, Grand-père," she said as she was leaving, kissing him affectionately on both cheeks.

He was gratified by this new development. "Bring your betrothed to dine with me soon, Petite-fille."

"I will."

Later that evening he gave Jasmin a thoughtful glance across the backgammon board in the midst of their play. "What did you say to Rose when you were both upstairs?"

"I told her the truth."

He gave her a steady look. "Good."

She smiled to herself, shaking the dice onto the board. There were many ways of expressing love. The young thought there was only one.

Rose and Richard were married in the Royal Chapel on New Year's Day as they had planned. The King and Queen attended as well as several other members of the royal family and more than two hundred courtiers and their ladies. Richard's mother had come from England escorted by her second son, while her twin sons had arrived in Versailles at the final stage of their Grand Tour and a number of English friends had also made the journey.

Rose wore a gown of silver-striped white silk sewn with diamonds and pearls. Her curls, dressed out into the abundant width that was so fashionable, held silk rosebuds in their depths and her necklace of sparkling diamonds was Richard's wedding gift to her. He was superbly tailored in the English fashion, his coat of silver brocade cut in the new style, double-breasted with high upstanding collar and slim tails. They had eyes only for each other.

Two women present were remembering their own marriages before the high altar gleaming gold against the embellished white marble. Marie Antoinette recalled the hope and happiness that had buoyed her up that day, compensating for her gown not fitting well, beautiful though it was. By then she had already won the adoration of the Court and the people with her youth and charm and eagerness to embrace all things French. It had all vanished like a dream.

Jasmin, at Michel's side, had different thoughts. She had been in such a state of shock and horror that she could recall nothing of the ceremony itself. All that was vivid in her mind was the glowering hatred in Sabatin's face and then, as they went down the aisle, the anguished expression of the young King in the gallery, he who had so swiftly forgotten her. It had always been her intention to give Marguerite's sapphire pendant to Rose on her wedding eve, but since the girl had expressed a superstitious fear that history might repeat itself, she had decided instead to bequeath it to her with all the rest of the jewellery that she would eventually inherit. By that time Rose should have discovered that her fears were groundless.

The wedding feast was laid out in the Hercules Salon. Musicians played, *vin de Champagne* flowed and toasts were drunk and finally there was a ball in the Hall of Mirrors. Soon after the dancing began, Jasmin and Michel decided to withdraw from the festivities. She was feeling extraordinarily tired and on the morrow she was entertaining Richard's mother and brothers who were being accommodated at the British Embassy in Paris.

"It's been a wonderful day," Jasmin said to the bride and groom.

"We'll come and see you soon," Rose promised.

"Your grandmother will not be lonely," Michel assured her. "I shall see to that now just as I will when eventually you go to live in England."

"That won't be for ages yet." Rose spoke firmly. "In any case, when I am there I'll be able to come back to Château Satory whenever I wish. When a letter can reach Paris from London in less than twenty-four hours it should not take much longer for me to get home."

"Would you ride a post-carrier's fast horse, then?" Jasmin teased with a flick of her fan.

Rose answered her seriously. "If I had to, Grand-mère. If you needed me."

"I'd come with Rose," Richard declared.

"I'm sure you would," Jasmin replied lightly, kissing them in turn. "Now Michel and I must go. We have had enough excitement for one day."

It was a long way through the State Apartment to the

staircase. Jasmin wished it could have been possible for
Michel and her to have sedan chairs to carry them, but the
old rule was still maintained that only royalty might use
that form of transport in this part of the Château. Normally
it would have been more difficult for Michel than for her to
traverse the polished floors, but this evening she was the
one who dragged, scarcely able to put one foot in front of
the other. It was an enormous relief when they sat back in
the carriage that was to take them to their respective
homes.

Richard and his bride returned to the dancing. The tall
mirrors reflected them in turn as they skimmed past under
the glittering chandeliers in gavottes and minuets and
lively country dances, partnering each other whenever it
was possible, exchanging silent messages of love in their
glances whenever they were apart.

At midnight Rose was hurried away by her ladies to the
new and larger apartment that had been allotted to her.
She barely glimpsed her maid as she was hustled into the
bedchamber. There was no unhooking or untying of her
garments by the faithful Diane on this night. Jewelled
fingers were plucking her clothes from her, young, laughing female faces surrounded her and waves of varied
scents wafted into her nostrils. It was almost overpowering.

On the outskirts of the ring of ladies around her mistress,
Diane received the discarded wedding gown and took it
into a closet where she draped it carefully over a wicker
frame. Then she returned to gather up the scattered petticoats strewn about the floor together with the wisp of a
chemise, the diamond-buckled satin shoes and the white
silk stockings.

Marie Antoinette came to the bedchamber to be the one
to see the bride into bed since the girl had no mother to be
there and the grandmother was too old to supervise at
such a late hour. She knew also that her presence would
stem any excessive horseplay and this was apparent when
Richard arrived with an escort of his brothers, the wilder
element having stayed outside the door. His silk robe was
taken from him and he climbed into the huge canopied
bed beside Rose. As they sat side by side receiving everyone's good wishes, he found her hand under the bedclothes and squeezed it. The Queen kissed the bride and

the gold and orange bed-curtains were drawn, leaving them in amber-tinted shadow.

They did not move until they heard the door close and the room fell into silence. Then exuberantly they flung their arms about each other and collapsed back into the pillows, rejoicing as they rolled together in a tight embrace.

"It's over! They've gone!" he exclaimed elatedly, looking down into her happy face. Then he saw her expression follow his into one of tenderness and love as he spoke softly to her. "Now it's only you and I. Forever."

"I love you," she whispered in English, something she had planned to please him from the lessons she was taking in his language.

"As I love you, my darling wife," he murmured back to her, the last word lost as he took her parted lips in an ardent kiss. When it ended he sat up again to haul his nightshirt over his head and toss it away through the curtains which swung under the impact and parted to let the candlelight in the room run flickeringly over them. It gave a momentary aura to his muscled body as if for a few seconds he had become Apollo around whom the whole of Versailles revolved. Pagan, beautiful and full of fiery desire.

Yet at first he was almost unbearably gentle, every delicate touch sending her into paroxysms of delicious tremblings. He threw back the bedclothes to take her nightgown by its hem and draw it slowly up, unveiling her body to him, his kisses keeping pace with its progress until at last he took it over her head and her upstretched arms to throw it from the bed. He caught her wrists in one hand before she could lower her arms and pressed her back into the pillows, a willing captive, while he caressed and kissed her breasts, cupping and stroking with such play of lips and tongue that she felt she was drowning in sensual delight. Her spine arched and with a gasp she broke her wrists from his light hold to run her hand lovingly over his shoulder, neck and up into his hair.

The curtain had not quite fallen back after being disarrayed a second time by the flight of her nightgown. He, seeing that all the modesty she had clung to in the past months had flown at last, kicked the drapery back still farther with one foot and their pale entwined bodies became pale gold in the candlelight and the glow from the fireplace.

"I wanted it to be like this from the minute I saw you," he breathed, moving his mouth to hers again. "If I had been able I would have pulled you from the calèche there and then into my arms."

"I saw that in your eyes," she whispered back before his kisses swallowed her up once more.

Then his lips left hers to travel down her body again, his hands splayed over her hips while his lovemaking took on a new dimension, rousing such passion in her that she threshed like some lovely fish. He could no longer hold back from taking her and propelled himself forward to slide powerfully into the dark, moist virginal depths of her. He felt her start on a moment's pain, her eyes flying open, and then all was rhythmic harmony. He carried her with him up and up to sun-god heights and they climaxed together, their gasps mingling and their hearts beating in the tumult of love.

The night hours passed in a pattern of passion and dozing and making love again. They breakfasted in bed, feeding each other in the way of lovers, dazed by this new existence into which nobody could intrude and where nobody could separate them. They left Versailles shortly before noon to drive to a château once owned by Madame de Pompadour, which the Queen had offered them for a sojourn together. Almost nothing had been changed since the royal favourite's day, everything in exquisite and timeless taste. Fires blazed in every fireplace for the weather was bitter, one of the cruellest winters for many years. On the way they had thrown money to starving people in rags who had come running to beg at the sight of their gleaming carriage as it went spanking by on the frosty road.

They made love in front of the fires, locking the doors of whichever elegant room they happened to be in amid walls of pink or blue or green and under ceilings of white and gold. On sharp, clear mornings they rode in the forest and when it snowed an old sleigh was brought out of storage for them to go for drives with little bells tinkling. At night their ornately draped bed became a haven again for expressions of love. The outside world with all its problems had ceased to exist and for once in their lives they gave no thought to it.

"To think I was once afraid that something would prevent our marrying," she said blissfully one morning. They had returned from a sleigh ride and were going up the steps into the château, his arm about her waist, their breath hanging in the icy air.

"What put that idea into your head?"

She stopped and turned to him. "When I learned you were of Roussier descent I suddenly saw us being Augustin and Marguerite all over again."

"That was impossible. Their circumstances were entirely different."

"I know." She gave her head a little shake at her own foolishness, thrusting away the memory of the shaft of foreboding that had pierced her at the time. "Tell me, do you at least think our meeting was predestined because of them?"

Such fanciful notions were alien to his practical mind, but he could see by the way she was looking at him that his answer was important to her. "Only through my being brought up to appreciate my Huguenot heritage, making me determined to see France and visit Versailles." He tweaked her chin gently between his finger and thumb, giving her a smile. "My mother actually wished a French bride on me, not knowing that you were still haunting me. If all these things add up, then I should say that destiny was at work."

"Yes, I see that."

"Only for our good, I hasten to add."

"I agree with you," she said contentedly. "It has brought us so much." He hugged her about the waist as they continued up into the house.

Unbeknown to them, cut off as they were for a little while from any outside contacts, spates of violence had broken out everywhere. Desperate people were breaking into granaries and plundering bakeries and corn convoys. Anyone suspected of hoarding grain to fetch still higher prices went in danger of his life, even a bishop being stoned for refusing to release corn to the needy. Country nobles were being defied, the peasants refusing to pay tithes and dues and defending themselves with cudgels and pikes when attempts were made to turn them off their land. The stench of anarchy was rising and many nervous bourgeois began to form citizens' militias to protect themselves.

All this news and much more burst upon the newly married couple when they returned to Versailles, but the most alarming information of all to Rose was that her grandmother had been indisposed and thus unable to entertain Richard's mother and family who had now gone back to England. While he drove to Paris to see what work awaited him at the Embassy, Rose went straight to Château Satory. She found Jasmin up and neatly gowned, her white hair widely dressed under a lace cap, writing letters in the library.

"What happened? Were you taken ill?" Rose exclaimed anxiously when greetings were over.

Jasmin put down her pen and removed her spectacles. "No, the doctor could find nothing wrong with me. The morning after the wedding I just found it impossible to rise from my bed. It was as if all my energy had deserted me."

"You did too much beforehand, helping me with the lists and gathering all those beautiful gifts you gave me."

"Perhaps, but I was so pleased to do whatever I could. My chief regret was that the dinner for your English relations had to be cancelled. Fortunately Richard's mother came to see me before they travelled home again. She is a charming woman and we had a long talk. Naturally she was eager to hear all I could tell her about Augustin Roussier. I let her roam the château at will to see what had once been his residence."

"How did she accept Marguerite having been his mistress while he was married to her great-grandmother?"

"In the same broad-minded and kindly way she received what you and Richard told her about your parentage." Jasmin gave a worldly-wise smile. "With all that French blood in her veins she is philosophical about such matters. She also told me some of their family history during the intervening years. I gathered that Augustin's greatest joy in his old age was Edmund's little daughter for whom he had his own pet name—Lily."

Rose mused over it. "Lily of France, or lily of the field?"

"Maybe the latter. Is not a simple marguerite a lily of the meadow?"

"He really did love Marguerite, didn't he?"

"Never doubt it. I should say he saw Lily as the child he

and Marguerite might have had. She lived to a good old age, a strict but devoted mother and grandmother. I was told Richard was the best-loved of her grandchildren. In both character and looks she saw in him a marked resemblance to her adored grandfather."

The scare that Rose had suffered over her grandmother's indisposition proved to be the forerunner of still more disastrous happenings in the political sphere. In April some factory workers rioted when there was talk of lowering their wages, which were barely above subsistence level, and troops were brought in to quell them. Richard, dressed as a bourgeois in his role of unobtrusive observer, narrowly missed being bayoneted in error and had his hat knocked sideways by a rioter hurling slates from a roof. He thought it as well that Rose imagined he sat all day at a desk at the Embassy when not attending some sedate diplomatic gathering.

He had twice made swift visits to England to present a report on French affairs to the Prime Minister at Downing Street and spend an afternoon in the House of Lords, calling in to see his mother on the way back to Dover. It was agreed in London that Louis and his ministers were reaping the folly of having supported the American Revolution. Not only had the involvement added to France's enormous debts, but it was becoming increasingly noticeable that those troops who had served in America were often halfhearted in putting down dangerous riots, their sympathies unmistakably with the mobs taking the law into their own hands.

Richard, who never forgot that he had some French blood in his veins, longed to see the people of France enjoying the liberty and justice that was long overdue, but unleashed violence was not the way. In America the battles had been between the revolutionary forces and the King's troops; here in France, if matters should come to a similar pass, it would be a different kind of struggle, for people in every walk of life would find themselves set against one another and all would be swallowed up in bloody turmoil.

If the Queen gave her permission and his commitments at the Embassy allowed, he hoped to take Rose on a vacation to England for two or three weeks in order that she should see her future home and country.

"We'll stay at the town house," he said to her in eager anticipation, "and I'll show you all the sights of London and where to shop for anything your heart desires."

"Shall I buy a new hat?" she teased. It was a joke between them that she had shelves full of plumed and silk-swathed headgear.

"You'll find that in Saint James's Street they'll all be straight from Paris!"

She chuckled. "Then I'll have some English jewellery instead."

"I know just the shop in Bond Street."

Her eyes danced. She was excited by the prospect of visiting England in preparation for time to come. "What else shall we do?"

"I'll take you down to Kent and you shall see the sister orchid to the one at the Trianon."

"How do you know it's feminine?"

"How could anything so exotic and beautiful be anything else? It's just like you. I'd call you Orchid if I didn't like your own name better."

She felt the past brush against her again at his words. "What then?"

"There'll be a ball for all my relatives and my friends in the country and far afield to meet the new lady of Easterton Hall. Then next morning I'll whisk you back to the coast and the packet boat for Calais before all the return invitations come swamping in to take up the time I want to spend alone with you."

"What a trip it will be!" She clapped her hands together in happy anticipation.

These days, in spite of her ebullient gaiety, her seemingly unchanged lightheartedness and her total dedication to love, she was aware as never before of what was happening beyond the palisades of Versailles. Within the Château everything went on much as before. The royal economies had little or no effect on the average courtier, who maintained the same extravagant mode of living that he had always enjoyed, believing that the current troubles would blow over. Other nobles were less optimistic but saw the difficulties as a harassment to themselves, an annoyance that should be set right to suit them as soon as possible.

Even if Rose's concern had not been aroused to the problems besetting her country, it would have been impossible for her not to be closely informed, married as she was to Richard. He had every fresh development at his fingertips and looked graver at every turn. Only in their bed were they away from all the troubles, their murmured talk confined to their love for each other and of every new pleasure discovered within their curtained haven.

One evening when Richard was being driven home from the Embassy, he instructed his coachman to make a detour in order that he could visit Jasmin at Château Satory. Rose was very busy at the present time with her royal duties and he had begun to call quite regularly in order to be able to report to her on her grandmother's health as well as saving the Duchesse from feeling in any way neglected. On this occasion he found a ladies' card party in full swing and would have left again if Jasmin had not given her place to someone sitting out. Together they went into the Music Salon.

"How is my granddaughter?" she asked, her serene expression showing she had no doubt of the answer.

"Extremely well and still busy. That's why I'm here on my own again."

"No matter. It's good to see you. What has been happening since I saw you last?"

When she had heard him out she asked another question. "Have you any idea yet when you'll be able to take Rose to England?"

"Not yet."

"When you do get her there," she said firmly and purposefully, "don't bring her back. I should be happier to know she was safely away from France at the present time. Michel had a brick thrown at his carriage the other day. Fortunately it missed the windows and he suffered no harm."

He expressed his regret that such an incident had occurred and then he regarded her quizzically. "Do you really suppose Rose would agree to such an arrangement?"

She lifted her hands and let them fall again in a gesture of conceding his point. "I don't know why I even suggested it. She would follow you into the mouth of hell if she had to and my fear is that France may come to that."

"It won't if common sense prevails. Have you no faith in the forthcoming convocation of the States General?" He was referring to a body of the three estates, composed separately and individually of the nobles, the clergy and the people, which the King had promised should be allowed to meet in May in order to settle outstanding grievances. Although he had agreed under pressure, it was generally accepted that in spite of everything he still wished to do his best and allow some reforms. As usual, the Queen was blamed for several high-handed and foolish autocratic actions he had taken over the past months, upsetting everyone concerned.

Jasmin's eyes glinted cynically as she held Richard's gaze. "No, I don't hold out much hope for the country when that quarrelsome body gets together. Even the preparation for it has been full of discord. If reforms are passed to bring order out of this present impasse it will be a miracle—for which I pray, needless to say."

"Amen to that," Richard endorsed.

When he arrived back at Versailles he found Rose waiting for him, her face distraught, and he embraced her at once. "What has happened?"

She was barely able to answer him in her distress. "The Dauphin had a bad turn today. He's getting weaker all the time. Now he can no longer stand."

As she began to weep he held her still closer to him, knowing how she loved the child.

On the morning of May 4th, Marie Antoinette sat on the edge of her son's bed. She spent every free moment away from her duties with him and, still in her nightclothes, she had come to feed him with a little breakfast as she did every day. With the half-emptied bowl set aside, she was propping him with her arm to give him a drink when Rose entered the room and spoke to her.

"Madame. Forgive me, but it is time for you to dress for the procession of the States General and the service at the Church of Saint Louis."

The child reached out his arms to his mother when he had drunk all he could manage. "Don't leave me, Maman. Please."

Usually he accepted that duties took her away and it was a measure of how ill he was feeling that he should have appealed to her now. Marie Antoinette thought her heart must break, but there was no extenuating circumstance, not even her child's fatal condition, that would excuse her from attending the assembly. "I'm going to church to pray for you, my little one." There was a throb in her voice. Reluctantly she rose to her feet. "I'll not be long."

"Maman! Stay with me. I'm afraid when you're not here."

Marie Antoinette almost collapsed. Rose made an unprecedented move by clasping the Queen's elbow while speaking to the boy. "I'll wrap you up warmly and carry you to a vantage point where you can see your maman leave with your papa. She can blow you a kiss and you can wave to her."

Recovering herself, Marie Antoinette kissed her son, stroking his hair back from his forehead, and then went from the room. During the past months she had withdrawn into herself, her children presenting the only meaning to her life; even her love for Axel had reached a steady level without emotional ups and downs. It was as if she had been split in two, her heart with those most precious to her and her mind detached to deal with the burden of government for which she had never been trained.

Her thoughts being with her son, she submitted to bathing, having her hair dressed in its simple style and being helped into her gold and silver gown with no more attention than as if those around her were invisible. Out of the Crown jewels she chose the Regent diamond for her hair.

The town had never seen such a procession as on that day. Over a thousand members of the States General, all carrying lighted tapers and preceded by colourful banners and pages with falcons on their wrists, proceeded on foot to the church. Every house along the route, which was lined with Swiss Guards and French troops, was hung with bright silks and tapestries and people had come from far afield to form vast crowds. The jewels and sumptuous garments of the royal family and the nobles were matched by the brilliance of the clergy's rich robes, while the more sombre clothes of the Third Estate seemed only to accentuate the majestic magnificence that was Versailles.

During High Mass Marie Antoinette uttered special private prayers for her child, for these days she never knew if he would still be alive when she returned to him.

At the opening of the great assembly the following day in a large hall, Richard, seated in the space reserved for foreign diplomats and visitors, thought the Queen looked like a pale wraith of her former self as she entered. Although there had been cheers for the King, there were none for her. The icy silence was acute.

"There is the scapegoat," whispered an American voice behind Richard that was imbued with sympathy. "They're showing her she has no part in this national reconciliation."

Richard wished he could have raised a cheer for her himself, but as a foreigner he had to remain silent. He watched her as she sat throughout the long speeches. Sometimes a tear trickled down her cheek, but she did not seem aware of it, the agitation of her fan revealing her nervous tension. Surely there had never been a more beautiful or unfortunate Queen. He was relieved when at the end someone did raise a shout as she was about to leave. "Long live the Queen!"

She looked touchingly pleased and curtsied acknowledgement, which set off applause throughout the hall. Whether or not the approbation was merely to please the King did not matter in Richard's opinion. It had given her one moment of comfort.

The procedure of the assembly lumbered on. Rose heard that pamphlets were being distributed that said the Queen was plotting to sabotage the attempts of the Third Estate to get reforms settled.

"How little the pamphleteers know of her!" Rose exclaimed in outrage to Richard. "She thinks only of her dying child and never leaves his bedside."

In the early hours of June 4th, Marie Antoinette cradled her son as he died in her arms, the King weeping with her. That same day, although she was only thirty-three, her hair began to turn snow-white. Within a few weeks not a trace was left of the pretty ash-blonde hue that had set off her rose and porcelain complexion to perfection. There were no roses in her cheeks now.

On the morning of the funeral, which by royal tradition she was unable to attend, she came through the salon in which hung the portrait of herself wearing a red velvet gown with her three children. It had been painted after the death of her baby daughter, Sophie, symbolised by a draped cradle, and before her elder son had shown the first real signs of the illness that had taken him from her. Rose, who was in attendance, saw how she stopped abruptly to gaze long and fully at the smiling, happy face of the late

Dauphin before she crossed herself, showing she had been in prayer during those moments of contemplation. Then she moved on and to Rose's knowledge she never again looked at the painting, averting her eyes every time as if it gave her pain she did not have the strength to bear.

It was almost impossible for Rose to rejoice in her own happy marriage in the face of such grief, much of which she shared with the Queen. There was also the disappointment of knowing that in the present drawn-out conferences of the States-General there was no chance of Richard being free to take her to England. He could no longer stay with her at Versailles, the Ambassador having recalled him to Paris for assignments about which she knew nothing except that they were important.

They exchanged letters and he came to see her whenever he could, but frequently he had to cancel his visits at the last minute. It was no better when he stopped telling her when to expect him, for then he would arrive to find she was involved in official duties with the Queen, out of which he could not extricate her, or gone to Château Satory, which meant that though he followed her there they had no time alone. Once he did stay the night at the château after arriving late and having no need to leave again until dawn. They slept in the rose and silver bed-chamber that had been Rose's since babyhood.

"This was Marguerite and Augustin's love-bed," she told him as they lay in it, kissing and whispering in the afterglow of passion. She no longer feared the past as she had done, although it was often with her. On the contrary, since nothing had stopped her marriage to Richard, she had become more logical when thinking about Marguerite and felt she had grown close to her.

He nuzzled her neck contentedly. "Could it have been the same for them as it is for us?"

"I hope it was," she breathed, responding to his intimate caresses and the renewed urgency of his body. They were insatiable for each other and his enforced absences were equally hard on them both.

It was a few days later that uproar broke out at the assembly of the States General when the Third Estate, claiming with some right to represent ninety-six per cent of the people, declared that it alone was the only true National Assembly. Richard, who was present, having got wind that something was to happen that day, felt the hair rise on the back of his neck, aware that he was witnessing the first step towards revolution. Centuries of feudalism were hanging in the balance. He saw fear and alarm on the faces of the nobles and the clergy present, followed by outrage on the part of many of the latter when some of their number gave support to this new development.

"It was all most unexpected," he reported to Jasmin when he and Rose visited her later. He then went on to describe an ingenious move to nip the new development in the bud by shutting the Third Estate out of the hall for three days, something he had watched from a closed carriage.

"What happened then?" Jasmin was almost on the edge of her seat to hear the rest of this extraordinary account.

"It looked as if there would be a riot. There were demands that they should demonstrate in the Place d'Armes, but a grim-looking doctor named Joseph Guillotin proposed they should assemble in the Sun King's tennis court near the Château. There they all took an oath. What it means is that they are resolved that in future all government shall be by the consent of the governed and the principles of democracy maintained."

He then proceeded to give Jasmin all the details, for she wanted nothing left out. She seemed relieved to hear they appeared willing to retain the monarchy with probable curtailment of its powers. It never failed to amaze Richard that such a frail old woman, little more than a handful of bones, should still have such an alert mind. It was as if all her energy were concentrated in her brain, for there was almost none left in her movements.

Daily unrest grew, fuelled by agitators on street corners and by the propagandists who were pounding home their message of insurrection with the printed word. The troops became undermined by their influence. There was quite a carnival atmosphere at times when soldiers, drunk on the wine that had been plied to them, together raised a shout that amounted to a war cry against authority. "We'll never fire on any uprising by fellow Frenchmen! Never!"

Richard no longer had time to visit Rose at Versailles, taken up by urgent sorties. He was having a cognac one Sunday outside the Café de Foy, knowing it to be a meeting place for certain agitators, when a young lawyer named Desmoulins sprang up onto a table and loudly began to denounce to a quickly gathering crowd the royal dismissal of the minister Necker. Richard knew that although Necker had been popular with the people, the Queen had disliked him intensely and it was mainly through her influence that the King had dismissed him when he had failed to do what had been expected of him in restoring the country's finances. Rose was a willing source in giving him small items of information that frequently filled in gaps and provided him with an overall picture.

"To arms, my friends!" the lawyer yelled, having a gift for inflammatory oratory that reached out to everyone there. "If Necker has been driven out, what fate awaits the rest of us? Is it a massacre of all patriots that is being planned in high places? Let us all wear cockades as a symbol of hope for our future!" His powerful voice rang out through the clear summer air as he raved on. By now the crowd had swelled to enormous proportions, blocking the street in both directions, incited to terror for themselves and violence against those in power with every fiery word that poured from his articulate mouth. At the start Richard had rescued and drained his glass of cognac, which had been in danger of being smashed by the stamping heels of Desmoulins, who concluded his harangue with a last vibrant summons. "Again I call you to arms! In the struggle none shall take me alive! I do not fear death! The only misfortune for me would be to see France in chains for evermore!"

He sprang down from the table as a huge roar of support went up from many hundreds of throats. The mob turned about like an enormous flock of sheep to follow him as he made his way through to lead the advance on a rampage for arms. Disorder reigned from then on throughout the city. Prisoners were released to join the throng. During the rest of the day and into the next, looting took place. Damage was done as customhouses by the city gates were set aflame in an attempt to wipe out the hated tax on all goods that came into Paris. Every available place was plundered for weapons, armourers standing by helplessly as their stock was snatched from their shelves. In cellars and hovels, as well as in small workshops, pikes were hastily made by those who knew there would not be enough arms to go round when the King's troops came from Versailles to quell the insurrection. Fear was rife, for it was no longer safe to be on the streets and the din of the mob was never far away. The symbolic cockades, advocated by Desmoulins, had begun to sprout like bright flowers all over Paris in the city's colours of scarlet and blue.

Early on the morning of July 14th, a vast mob stormed the Invalides, built to house old soldiers, and cannon and thousands of muskets were seized. No resistance was offered by the inmates who cheered them on, thin blood stirred by the reek of battle that hung about the yelling intruders. The whole scene was watched without any attempt at law-keeping intervention by a troop of foreign mercenaries encamped nearby. Richard, who was present, guessed that the commander believed their sympathies to be with the mob and to order them in would simply have expanded the situation.

Richard was being buffeted about in the crush of the throng, which he had followed almost without respite since the call to arms at the Café de Foy. His dishevelled appearance and workman's garments, a cockade in his hat, bore no resemblance to the well-dressed figure present at the royal opening of the States General. His subsequent attendance at meetings of importance had always been inconspicuous; proof of his full acceptance by the rioters was in the musket being thrust into his hand.

At the same time as he was brandishing it as if triumphant, Rose was awakening at Versailles. It was nearly three weeks since she had seen him and she had received no correspondence since a hastily written message that he was extremely busy and could not say how soon he would be able to see her again. She decided this morning, lying in her bed, that she would pay him a surprise visit instead of going to Château Satory as she usually did when she had a day or more to herself. Richard had rooms at the Embassy and even if he should be out when she arrived, he would find her there when he returned in the evening. She smiled to herself in anticipation, picturing his pleased surprise. Their hours together had been all too few in recent weeks.

"I'm going to Paris today," she announced happily to Diane, who had arrived with her breakfast.

"Should you, madame?" Diane queried uncertainly. "The city is said to be very unsettled."

"That won't affect me. I'm going to visit my husband. If you are nervous, I'll excuse you from coming with me and take someone else."

"No, madame." Diane was jealous of her position and resented any of the other maids intruding on her domain. "When do you wish to set out?"

They left at mid-morning and stopped, on the way, at Michel's house. Rose could never have gone past without calling in to see him, but he had just departed shortly before for Château Satory. They must have passed each other in the crush of traffic her coachman had encountered, the road always busy with many fast drivers between Paris and Versailles. Nevertheless she rested there and took some refreshment, the housekeeper seeing to everything for her comfort. Had it not been for her eagerness to see Richard, she would have waited there for her grandfather's return. She set off again to arrive in Paris shortly after two o'clock. The blackened shell of the customhouse as her carriage bowled through the gates was the first sight she and Diane had of the rioters' handiwork. Soon after there were glimpses of shop fronts shuttered for protection, although trade still went on through the doors.

At first these were the only signs, apart from a smashed window here and there, that everything was not as usual in the city. Then the coachman had to make detours as well-intentioned bystanders called out that he should not take this street or that, the way being blocked by demonstrations. Due to conflicting advice, he drove in a direction that brought him and his passengers into the Rue Saint-Antoine at the end of which the Bastille stood. He had heard the din of a great mob but misjudged its direction and to his horror saw it lay directly ahead in what appeared to be an onslaught on the fortress itself. Even as he would have turned his horses it was too late. Behind him had appeared an enormous sea of yelling people, some armed with muskets and others with pikes, cudgels and pitchforks, cockades worn jauntily. The two grooms riding at the back of the carriage exchanged one frightened glance before ripping off the jackets of their almond-green livery and leaping down in their shirt-sleeves to join the oncoming crowd.

The coachman was made of sterner stuff. Knowing there was a side-turning a way ahead, he lashed his horses who plunged forward, tossing the occupants of the carriage almost from their seats. Fortunately Rose had been clasping the carriage strap by her window as she peered out to see what was causing the commotion and thus saved herself from landing on the floor as Diane had done.

"Are you all right?" she gasped, holding out her hand to her maid.

"Yes, I am." Diane scrambled to her feet again and flung herself back into her place, full of alarm. "What's happening, madame?"

Rose looked calmer than she felt. "We appear to have been caught between two mobs of uncertain mood. I think the coachman fears requisition of the horses, which is why he is making a bolt for it."

The side-turning showed more people streaming up it and the coachman had no choice but to come to a halt. Almost immediately the carriage was surrounded by those on the outskirts of the Bastille mob and many who had come running from behind. The horses represented food to those with empty bellies and when the coachman tried to lash out at the hands unharnessing them, the whip was snatched from him. Then he was yanked unceremoniously from his box to be tumbled roughly from hand to hand until, bruised and battered, blood running down his face, he collapsed against the wall of a shop. He saw the horses taken away to be lost from his sight while the gleaming black roof of the carriage was still just visible over the heads of those streaming on past him. He could not begin to estimate the numbers and feared for the safety of the two young women he was powerless to help. He groaned as he saw the carriage moved, able to tell it was being manned at the shafts to draw it deeper into the mêlée at the Bastille.

Anger had stiffened Rose's spine. She was furious at this interruption of her purpose in coming to Paris and at the lawlessness she was witnessing. No attempt had been made to open the carriage doors but faces, male and female, peered in, some grinning triumphantly, others savagely hostile. She glared haughtily at them all, showing no fear and not blinking when spittle from the most vicious trailed down across the shining glass. Now and again a tattoo of fists on the carriage sides must have given the impression of advancing drums to those ahead and when the hammering came on the roof as well she realised that some of the rioters were perched overhead like monkeys.

"Where are they taking us, madame?" Diane asked in a small voice. She felt stunned with terror whereas her mistress sat as composedly as if on a drive through the park at Versailles in her enormously wide-brimmed hat of champagne silk trimmed with plumes, not a shimmer to her sprigged muslin skirts to suggest she might be trembling with apprehension.

"I can only suppose they want to use this carriage as protection in the case of firing from those defending the prison. If they should not let us out, you are to lie flat on the floor as much under the seat as is possible." Rose gave what she hoped was a cheerful smile. "Don't worry. I shall be down there with you. The carpeting is well brushed and we'll not harm our gowns."

"I'm very frightened, madame."

"So am I, Diane. All that matters is that nobody else should think we are." Rose was clinging to the hope that to show authority was to compel obedience. She had no other weapon with which to defend Diane and herself from whatever the more violent in the mob might decide to do to them.

By now she had a good view of the Bastille. It was a fearsome place of incarceration. Although she had heard that considerable reforms had been made in the treatment of prisoners, the terrible aura of the ancient place remained as if the screams of those tortured throughout past centuries had seeped into its walls and stayed there. Even to Rose in her cosseted existence it represented all that was frightening and evil in the reigns that had gone by. It was understandable that the rioters might see the Bastille as the symbol of feudalism against which they had turned with such an upsurge of hatred. The mob had taken up a chant.

"Down with the drawbridges of the Bastille! Down! Down! Down!"

She could not see the drawbridges from where she sat because the outer buildings of the garrison blocked the sight of them, but rioters were running along the roofs to leap down into the inner courtyard where doubtless they intended some action to get them lowered.

Then above the noise of the mob came the staccato

sound of gunfire, blueish smoke rising into the air. Immediately the doors of the carriage were yanked open. Rose was hauled out on one side and her maid on the other, not with any thought for their safety but to rush them, gripped by the arms, forward with the maddened crowd that had gone charging through into the courtyard at a signal that the bridges were down.

Rose's hat was lost in the first few seconds. The speed with which she was being propelled along did not deter thieves from snatching the pearl eardrops from her lobes, others grabbing off her necklace and her brooch. She lost one of her satin shoes in the running and thereafter the rough ground cut through her stocking to make her sole raw. Ahead was a lowered drawbridge, the smashed chains dangling. All she could think was that her captors, both burly fellows and apparently ringleaders of some kind, had the idea of using her as bargaining power if the governor of the Bastille refused to do as they wished, for they would know from her coat of arms on the carriage that she was an aristocrat of some rank of importance.

"Have mercy! Let me draw breath!" she implored, gasping.

It was doubtful whether they heard her. Her eyes widened with horror as she saw casualties from the gunfire lying ahead and realised she was to be plunged right across them, nothing halting the mad charge. She screamed as her foot came in contact with torn flesh and broken bones, the warm blood splashing up over her skirts. Unable to help herself, she sagged in her captors' grasp and still she was borne onwards as if she weighed no more than a feather.

The drawbridge thundered under the hundreds of feet running across it in an endless stream. There was continuous firing ahead from guards attempting to stem the invasion, but the enraged rioters leapt over the fallen in such numbers that the soldiers were overpowered and disarmed. The Bastille was taken and the elated cheers were as deafening as the roar of rage had been.

Rose's captors, having no need of her after all for the purpose at which she had guessed, hurled her from them. She stumbled helplessly off-balance and fell, hitting her head violently on an ancient cannon used for decorative purposes. There she lay slumped between the barrel and the wheel-spokes, looking like a battle casualty in her bloodstained garments, one arm dangling.

When Richard sighted her he thought for a few throat-constricting moments of shock that she was dead. Then as he gathered her up in his arms he found that she was still breathing.

Twenty-one

Rose recovered consciousness in bed at the Embassy with an English doctor in attendance, her head neatly bandaged, and Richard standing by.

"You'll soon recover, Lady Easterton," the doctor said, surprising her with the still unfamiliar use of her new title. "There's a cut on your head and you have plenty of bruises, but a few days' rest will take care of all that."

As soon as he had left, Richard kissed her and sat down facing her on the edge of the bed. Her first question was about Diane, but he was unable to give her any information.

"I hope she's safe," she said anxiously. "How did you find me?"

He explained that he had been following the mob when he recognised her coach-servants' livery and realised that it could only be she who was trapped in the carriage. "I began struggling through, using my fists and brute force to make a way for myself in the crush. Then when I reached the carriage it was empty and I guessed that you had been taken along as a hostage into the Bastille. If you had fallen to the ground instead of reeling onto the cannon where I found you, there is no doubt that you would have been trampled to death in the fighting and scuffling. We have much to be thankful for, my love."

She agreed. "Let's hope that nothing like that ever happens again."

He nodded, less optimistic about the events that had been set in motion.

Soon afterwards Diane arrived at the Embassy, having come belatedly to seek Richard's help in finding her mistress. She was dishevelled and upset but otherwise unharmed, having been released as soon as it was realised by her simple clothes and lack of jewels that she was not another noblewoman. Yet the crush of the crowd had been such that she was forced forward a considerable distance in the rush to the Bastille before she managed to extricate herself and run from the tumultuous scene. Her shame at having taken flight in panic instead of going after her mistress overwhelmed her as soon as she entered the bedchamber. She dissolved into floods of tears, fearing dismissal.

"I'm so sorry, madame. I behaved in a most cowardly manner. Can you forgive me?"

"Don't blame yourself." Rose was in too emotional a state not to weep with her. "I didn't heed your advice about not going to Paris in the first place. Let us never mention it again."

Only five petty criminals and two madmen had been incarcerated in the Bastille, an anticlimax for the liberators after all the drama, but that was wiped out by fresh bloodshed when the governor's head was severed from his body and paraded triumphantly through the streets on a pike, preceded by the keys to the Bastille.

"How horrible!" Rose exclaimed with a shudder when Richard told her about it. Paris, which she had always loved, was changed more for her by that incident than anything she had witnessed at the Bastille. Her one thought was to go home to Château Satory and she refused even to consider his pressing suggestion that the time had come when she should go to England. "Never without you! In any case, did you not say that the troops sent from

Versailles are being withdrawn to remove the people's fear of retribution? This revolt will soon settle down."

"It's far more than a revolt," he said gravely. "It is revolution."

Her pupils dilated and she turned pale to the lips. "I wanted changes for the better in France, but never that they should come about like this."

"Neither did the majority of people, you can be sure of that. But there'll be no going back now."

On the third day the mayhem and murder subsided as if Paris were drawing breath after its first victory over feudalism in the fall of the Bastille. Richard decided it would be safe to take Rose home, there being little likelihood of harassment in the streets due to a wave of exultation that the King had agreed to come to the city. When they set off from the Embassy they had not gone far when they had to draw up in their carriage as the King went by with a small escort of Swiss Guards.

It was typical of Louis's stolid fearlessness that he should have come willingly into the very eye of the Revolution. It was the same courage that had made him refuse to flee from Versailles with his two brothers and the Princes of the Blood, who had all left for safe havens abroad when news of the uprising had reached them. Several of those ladies closest to the Queen had also taken flight, knowing their friendship with her was enough to condemn them.

"A King cannot desert his people," Louis had said to Marie Antoinette when she had stood ready to leave with him and the children, "however misguided they may have become for the time being."

Misguided! Marie Antoinette had closed her eyes in despair, hearing in his words a foreshadowing of doom.

Now as the ferociously armed crowds cheered him, Louis showed neither surprise nor relief. The Kings of France, in spite of their autocracy, had always been close to the people. He and his forebears had risen, eaten and gone to bed in the sight of their subjects, even as they were born and as those before him had died. He could see that it was as he had hoped; there was little hostility towards him personally, however much fury existed against all he represented. He acknowledged the approbation of the crowds with his customary nod, benign smile and the occasional little wave of his white-gloved hand. Eventually these wayward children of his would return to the fold. He had only to be firm. Nothing should make him surrender the principles of his heritage.

As Richard and Rose continued their journey out through the gates of Paris, a presentation took place in the Hôtel de Ville. The Mayor of Paris, believing as others did that a constitutional monarchy was all but settled, presented the King with the keys to the city as an expression of loyalty and reconciliation. Louis, equally magnanimous, accepted them. He went home with one of the new red, white and blue cockades in his hat. Marie Antoinette recoiled at the sight of his wearing this symbol of the Revolution. Then they embraced each other in tears. She had feared he would not come back alive that day and he knew it had been at the back of his mind that he might be facing a precipice.

All over the country violent acts were being committed and vengeance taken against those that had wrested high prices for grain in the past, all the millers in one district being rounded up and slaughtered. Tax collectors and other such officials went in fear of their lives and many a private grievance was settled with a knife or the sharp end of a pike. Food was scarcer than ever due to the disruption of everyday life and prices rose accordingly. Bands of hungry people went marauding, the women desperate to feed their children. At the kitchen door of Château Satory they came in as orderly a way as they had ever done. Jasmin, unable to hobble more than occasionally to that part of the house, knew she could trust Diane's widowed mother to see that more bread was baked and extra cauldrons of wholesome soup and ragout made ready. For many years there had been servants specially employed for this task.

As soon as Rose was able she left Château Satory and returned to Versailles. Richard and Jasmin did not attempt to dissuade her, knowing her mind was made up. The Queen was touchingly pleased to see her.

"Dear Madame Rose! The present circumstances release you from all your duties to me. Madame de Lamballe has left as well as the Duchesse de Polignac and many others. Some went to Switzerland or Holland, others still further afield. Should you not be in England?"

"No, madame. The time is not yet. I'll be honoured to serve you."

Marie Antoinette gave her a lovely smile. "This is a happy day indeed. Let us go and see the children. The Dauphin has a new governess now in the Marquise de Tourzel since the departure of her predecessor."

They went down the private staircase that led from the Queen's Apartment to the children's rooms, a rope hand-rail set at a distance below that for adults in order to aid the children's comings and goings. Princesse Marie Thérèse clapped her hands with delight at seeing Rose again. She was a pretty child, growing much like her mother.

"You haven't left us! How glad I am, madame!"

The four-year-old Dauphin, impish and pink-cheeked, ran forward to be picked up and embraced.

"We're going to the Hamlet with Maman tomorrow. Shall you come with us, Madame Rose?"

"Nothing would please me better," she replied cheerily.

In many ways life at Versailles returned to normal. People missed friends who had fled the country and took over the duties of those no longer there while the social round went on much as before. In any case, everyone felt safer at Versailles than they would have done elsewhere in France, for, almost daily, word came of damage and bloodshed at outlying properties and distant châteaux where rampaging peasants had taken possession. There was nothing to be done about these outrages, for all feudal rights and privileges had been abolished shortly after the fall of the Bastille.

In Paris many agitators were taking advantage of the new free press to publish any kind of lie and distorted story likely to keep tempers enflamed and the Revolution thoroughly on the boil. It seemed to Rose that those hot weeks of August during which the sun blazed from a cloudless sky were in league with the Revolutionaries in letting nothing cool down. Only at Château Satory and at the Petit Trianon was any tranquillity to be found.

When the Queen, who had held a Court ball to keep up the spirits of the courtiers, invited Richard to a private evening picnic for her few remaining friends at Versailles, the same purpose in her mind, he accepted gladly. It was to be held in the Temple of Love, which aroused both poignant and tender memories for him and Rose. The last time they had been there together was after he had defeated the Comte de Cordierer in a duel.

Persian rugs had been spread on the steps and on the grass for those who preferred to sit there instead of on chairs within the rotunda where a candlelit buffet had been laid out, no servants present. It was a warm, moon-bathed night full of stars, an extra glow given by the hidden faggots that encircled the area where the picnic was taking place. The conversation was quiet, the laughter soft and the outside world far away in this short respite for those who were gathered there.

Axel von Fersen never left the Queen's side. It had been a long time since Rose had last chaperoned them and she knew he often spent the night alone with Marie Antoinette at the Petit Trianon. They had been lovers as long ago as when she had left them on their own in the woods. The Queen had not slept with the King since the conception of the little baby Sophie, whom she had lost, and it was obvious to Rose that he knew of and condoned this passionate liaison. She was thankful that the Court had too much on its mind these days to speculate about the love of these two people.

After supper someone began to play the viol for dancing and several couples made up a set, led by the Queen and Axel. Richard, who had not seen Rose for three weeks, drew her away to stroll on their own through the park and eventually they came to the secluded grotto. Amid mossy banks, pale with little flowers, the water lay still, reflecting the moonlight.

"I wish France could be as peaceful everywhere as it is in this enchanted place," she said, sitting down on the little rustic bench that was a favourite seat of the Queen's whenever she wished to be alone with her thoughts.

He remained standing where he was, folding his arms as he gazed meditatively and unseeingly at the silver water. The bubbling of the stream that fed it mingled with the song of the nightingales in the trees all around.

"It could be," he said with a sigh close to exasperation, "if only the King would meet the National Assembly half-way instead of continually prevaricating. Admittedly he has restored Necker to please the people, but he has virtually dismissed the Declaration of the Rights of Man and Citizen, which Mr. Thomas Jefferson, the American Ambassador, helped to draw up. The whole of France is declaring its liberty from feudalism and the King has blocked his ears."

"It is to be expected that he and the Queen should be hostile to a constitutional monarchy. It undermines all they have ever stood for and they see no good in it. The King would become a puppet of the people." She was full of admiration for Marie Antoinette, who had become a tower of strength in the midst of adversity. All the vagueness and detachment that had been with her through the latter months of her late son's illness and her subsequent bereavement had quite gone, however much she still grieved inwardly. Since she guided the King in many of his decisions, it went against Rose's loyalty to question whether they were always the right ones. She would hear no word against the brave woman. "I know France has never had such a Queen as Marie Antoinette. She has come to the fore like a beacon as far as I'm concerned and put all her predecessors in the shade."

Richard drew her to her feet and took her face between his hands. "Darling Rose. How true you are to those you love and respect. I'd never wish to break that down."

He kissed her and they slipped into a close embrace. Almost instantly their kissing became ardent. They had not made love since before the fall of the Bastille and since it was now early September many weeks had gone by. "Where shall we go?" he murmured huskily between kisses.

"This way." She took him by the hand and led him to the nearby Belvedere, a charming little octagonal pavilion on a grassy mound overlooking the lake. It was here that the Queen often took light meals or rested out of the sun. The glow from the reed-hidden faggots, lit here as elsewhere for the occasion of the picnic, showed up the bas-reliefs on the windows that symbolised the seasons. Once inside they stood amid the pale green walls painted delicately with arabesques, the outside glow enabling them to see each other's faces and throwing their shadows up to the ceiling of cupids on a blue sky.

They undressed each other lovingly. He made a bed for them with cushions on the marble mosaic floor and drew her down to it. There he made love to her with such special tenderness and passion that she knew she would remember all her life every moment of this hour of love spent in the Belvedere.

Jasmin was unwell. Rose, arriving to see her, found the doctor was expected. "What's wrong, Grand-mère?" she asked anxiously after kissing her and then perching on the edge of the bed to hold her hand.

"Nothing for you to worry your head about," Jasmin replied reassuringly. She had kept hidden from her granddaughter and everyone else except her housekeeper and the rest of the domestic staff, who had been sworn to secrecy, that she had twice suffered short losses of consciousness that had been more than a faint. She believed she might have had a prior warning of what was to come on Rose's wedding day, which would explain her dragging limbs and extreme exhaustion on that occasion, but she did not intend to tell anyone about that.

"I want to know what ails you," Rose insisted.

Jasmin sighed as if it was of no importance and explained the symptoms. "I have had to rest after two little spasms. The doctor says it's due to my heart fluttering a little, something quite common in people of my great age. There was really no need for Madame Arnaud to send for him today."

"She did right." Rose was thankful that Diane's mother was such a conscientious woman, not only as housekeeper but in concerning herself with her mistress's well-being. "I'll send Diane back to Versailles to pack some things for me and I'll stay with you until you're better again."

"Heaven forbid!" All along Jasmin had wanted to avoid casting any blight on her granddaughter's first blissful months of marriage, the reason why she had never mentioned her first relapse to anyone. "I'm better being here on my own with Michel's visits and yours to look forward to whenever you can come."

She was adamant. Rose returned to Versailles at the end of the day, far from convinced she should not have stayed in spite of the doctor saying that Jasmin could go on for many years yet, provided she lived quietly.

Rose noticed afresh, as she always did these days when returning from Château Satory, how empty the great salons of Versailles had become. Many more courtiers had left for places of refuge, some being lynched on the way.

Those that remained passed the time as best they could, for what social events there were had become halfhearted affairs. Everyone had been made painfully aware of what was going on in the bloodstained crisis that gripped the country. Gruesome crimes had become commonplace in the name of Revolution. A former minister was hanged by the mob from a street lantern before his head was severed with a butcher's knife and the mouth stuffed with straw in the belief that he had once advocated it for the starving in the place of bread. His son was slaughtered afterwards as a further act of revenge, a pattern being followed in various parts of the country where law and order had ceased to exist.

Everybody became more cheerful at Versailles with the arrival towards the end of September of the loyal Flanders Regiment, numbering over a thousand, who had marched at the King's orders from the north to give their protection to Versailles. On the first day of October, in the afternoon, Rose accompanied the King and Queen with the Dauphin to the Château's Opéra. All the officers were being given a banquet on the stage, other ranks taking up tables in the pit. It was a thrilling occasion with the vivid uniforms, the trumpeters' fanfares, orchestral music and cheers for the royal family on a scale that had not been heard for a long time. Rose was the first to take a white ribbon from her hat to fashion it into a cockade of the House of Bourbon. When she had tossed it to one of the officers he promptly fastened it to his jacket and there were shouts for more. All the rest of the Queen's ladies then followed suit and the white cockades began to sprinkle the gathering, such acclaim being given to the King and Queen that they were quite overwhelmed.

Rose, flushed with excitement at the part she had played in the event, was full of it when she found Richard waiting for her in their apartment.

"You should have heard how those soldiers cheered!" she exclaimed, twirling around the room and tossing her ruined hat into a corner. He reached out and caught her to him, grinning at her sparkling gaiety and then kissing her before sitting down and drawing her onto his knees.

"I know you and everyone else feel safer with the Flanders Regiment here," he began on a serious note that did not suit her mood, "but—"

"Why shouldn't we?" she interrupted, trying to smooth away with her fingers the frown that had clamped down his brows. She felt like making love with laughter and all their intimate little jokes as they did sometimes, although any lovemaking these days was still sparse with his living at the Embassy while she was here.

"It's nothing to do with their loyalty, which is not in dispute, but the current political situation. A new crisis is on the way. The agitators are planning to prevent bread supplies from reaching Paris in order to inflame tempers afresh, especially when word reaches the city of the banquet without stint held for the Regiment here today."

She did not want to talk politics. There was a time and a place for everything and it was not now. She put a hand over her mouth in a mock yawn, teasing him with her eyes. To her surprise, he seized her wrists and pulled her hand down from her face, his expression one of serious urgency.

"You must leave France, Rose. In spite of what you think, it's dangerous for you to remain any longer at Versailles. There's no telling what may be happening three or four weeks from now."

Her patience began to ebb. "There's nothing to be afraid of at Versailles, especially now."

"That's where you're mistaken. The King with his vacillating policies and the Queen, who is hated more than ever, are the natural targets for any future outbreak of violence. I explained to you after your ordeal at the Bastille what I have been doing and now that the Revolution is out in the open I have been asked to shoulder new responsibilities which I cannot discuss at present. The Ambassador is willing that I should have a few days in which to take you and the Duchesse de Valverde to England. I have the necessary papers for you both as well as for Monsieur Balaine, should he wish to accompany us, and for your maid."

She shook her head firmly. Nothing was left of her previously happy mood. "Grand-mère isn't strong enough to make any journey. It would kill her. She has to live quietly with the minimum of exertion."

"Then she will wish you to go without her. She talked about it to me once. For quite a time she has wanted you safely out of harm's way."

She stared at him incredulously, removing his hands from her waist and backing away a pace from him. "Do you suppose that after all she has done for me I would leave her when she is unwell and almost helpless? Neither would my grandfather go off to England without her, let alone that he has his own family to concern himself with here." Suddenly she was livid with him for even suggesting she should take flight at such a time, from those closest to her as well as from her country in its troubles and, not least of all, the Queen. "You go! You're English! There's nothing to keep you here whatever your new responsibilities may be! Why doesn't the Ambassador go too? We French will see to our own affairs and settle our nation peacefully without foreign interference!"

Immediately the words were out she regretted them. The colour had drained from his face and he was staring at her as if she had become a stranger before his eyes. It was as if she had torn open a great gulf between them, revealing all the differences of language, culture and background that divided them. What was worse, the centuries-old enmity that had existed between their two countries, veneered over by periods of peace, had reared up in her as if the past had suddenly made her its spokesman for old scores unsettled and defeats unavenged. Yet she was powerless to cry out to him to forget what she had said. There was too much anger in her and pride had her by the throat.

He addressed her coldly. "You speak as if at heart I care nothing for France. Well, you must think whatever you like. I'm going now to see your grandmother and ask her if she still feels the same way about my taking you to England. Will you abide by her decision?"

Her fury returned. "You know what her answer will be! But however much she will try to hide it from you, she will be upset at the prospect of parting with me. When you first discussed it with her she was well. Now she is not and the doctor impressed upon me that she should not be distressed in any way."

"Are you telling me not to go to her?" he asked, his voice dangerously soft.

There was a determined and aggressive set to her head. "I'm saying that Grand-mère shall not die through some whim of yours to take me away when I'm needed most." Her voice dropped a note to a threatening level. "If you trouble her over this matter I shall not only stay with her whatever she says, but I'll never go to England with you!"

With rigid self-control he kept his temper in check, levering himself up swiftly from the chair to dominate her with his height. "Today is the first day of October. I'll be back in a week. In that time you can prepare the Duchesse de Valverde for your departure and spend final days with her. For all her frailty she has a far stouter spirit than you give her credit for."

She answered him implacably, her colour high and burning. "I've already told you to go to England whenever you like. But without me. I'm staying here!"

He swung about abruptly and went from the apartment without a backwards glance. She was left standing uncertainly in the middle of the room, having expected more from him. Now, in spite of being close to shedding tears of sheer temper, she wondered how much he had taken her threat to heart. It had been a searing quarrel, all the more painful for being the first since their marriage. But she would never retract. He must find a way to reach her again.

The next day and the day after she looked for a messenger with a letter. None came. It was the same the following day. By the fourth evening she felt certain that now nothing would come. She began to feel apprehensive about whether he would turn up on the seventh. If they did not reach out to each other then it would bode ill for their marriage. Pride stopped her from writing to him as it had held back conciliatory words before their quarrel had reached full height. To lower her spirits still further, she read in one of the scurrilous newspapers printed by the propagandists that at the Regiment's banquet the red, white and blue cockade of the Revolution had been spat upon while the Bourbon cockade had been flaunted at the instigation of the Queen.

"Lies!" she fumed to Jasmin when she had come to Château Satory for the day. "In any case there wasn't a Revolutionary cockade in the place."

"At the present time there are those doing nothing else but turning truth into lies and creating foul rumours out of nothing," Jasmin replied sagely. She thought her granddaughter was in a particularly edgy mood and wondered if anything else was troubling her apart from this fresh slander against the Queen. But when Rose left again without bringing up any other matter, she supposed herself to have been mistaken.

On the fifth day Rose began to anticipate with mingled hope and trepidation her meeting with Richard again. Surely he would come even though he could be sure to find her decision unchanged? To distract her thoughts, she spent the morning with the royal children and Madame de Tourzel in the section of the park reserved for their play. Later, after midday, she set out for the Petit Trianon on foot, taking a short cut through the woods and following a path that the Queen had taken earlier that day. It had been arranged that they should walk back together. The trees were looking glorious in their autumnal colours, scraps of blue sky showing overhead through the saffron, russet and crimson leaves, a carpet of the same rich pattern rustling underfoot.

The Queen was hardly ever at Versailles now. It was as if she was drawn by some magnetic force to the peace and tranquillity of the Petit Trianon and its environs as never before. Since Axel von Fersen was ever her constant companion there, it had become a place of love. Rose wondered if she would find him with Marie Antoinette today. When together, away from the Court and all other eyes but hers, they did not attempt to hide the adoring glances they gave each other and were full of secret smiles.

"Where is the Queen?" she asked the footman in the scarlet and silver livery of the Petit Trianon who was on duty at the door. "And is anyone with her?"

"I believe Her Majesty is on her own at the grotto, madame. I have just directed a messenger from the Château there."

Rose went through the archway in the courtyard wall that led to a path she had to follow, which would wind its way to where Marie Antoinette would be sitting on her favourite rustic seat. In that green and mossy place the sunshine would be filtering through the overhanging foliage, while berries dangled like rubies and clusters of late-blooming flowers strained to meet their reflection in the glinting water.

Suddenly Rose heard hurrying steps coming towards her along the path, gravel scattering underfoot. Then Marie Antoinette, her face pale with anxiety, burst into view, the red velvet jacket she was wearing over her white gauzy gown making a brave spot of colour against the dark bushes. Indicative of her hasty departure from the grotto was that she carried her hat in her hand. At the sight of Rose she waved a note that had been delivered to her by one of the "blue boys" from the Château, who came hurrying in her wake.

"I'm on my way back to the Château in a carriage that has been sent for me. Come with me, Madame Rose! It's not safe to be on foot. I have been sent word that the Paris mobs are marching on Versailles!"

Rose felt a lurch of icy fear and ran after her to the waiting carriage.

Back at the Château, Marie Antoinette went straight to her children. The King was out hunting and word had been sent to him. In the Cour Royale the Swiss Guards were struggling to close the main gates, which had stood open since the Sun King's time and had rusted on their hinges. From a window Rose watched their efforts as they shoved and pushed and pulled. They had succeeded in closing one of the two gates when the King returned at a gallop, riding through into the Cour Royale with his huntsmen, their horses sweating and mud-splashed. Lined up in battle order in front of the Château was the Flanders Regiment reinforced by some local National Guardsmen, ready to repel all comers, and they gave him a cheer. Shortly afterwards Rose saw Axel von Fersen arrive at top speed from Paris. He flung himself from his steaming horse and rushed into the Château by way of the arched grille to reach the Queen's Staircase and her apartment. Rose guessed he had but one thought and that was to save the Queen all harm, giving his own life if necessary.

As she stood looking out, others came to peer through the glass. With nothing unusual to be seen they would go again to mingle with the hundreds milling about restlessly in the State Apartment, many talking in anxious groups. In the Hall of Mirrors some courtiers continually ran from one end to the other, not wanting to miss anything when somebody arrived either in the War Salon or the Peace Salon with what was purported to be fresh news. Panic was not far removed and everybody was in a state of confusion. Rose, feeling sick with apprehension, the fall of the Bastille all too vivid in her mind, felt some relief when the second gate, screeching on its protesting hinges, was finally closed. Then it began to rain, the pattering of the drops across the window heralding the distant noise of the mob advancing up the Avenue de Paris.

Straining her eyes through the heavy downpour, she was astonished to see that the mob consisted of women, most of them armed with pitchforks, broomsticks or homemade pikes. As they came into the Place d'Armes the vast swarm spread out like a plague of ants, breaking into a run, shrieking and shouting, to reach the closed gates and the palisades. It was impossible to estimate the number, but she thought there must be six or seven thousand of them. Some screamed for bread as they shook their fists through the railings, yelling obscenities, and others had brought bowls for the macabre purpose of collecting the entrails of the Queen. Most of them were drunk, bottles having been handed out by the organisers in Paris, and wineshops had been looted on the way. Empty flasks were hurled over the gilded spikes of the palisades at the troops to fall harmlessly on the cobbles and smash into glittering smithereens. In the midst of them were two horse-drawn cannon, which were trundled forward to point menacingly at the East Front of the Château. A whole cluster of strong-looking women then unharnessed the horses, which were led away. The barrels of the cannon and the quickly stacked iron balls gleamed darkly in the rain.

Rose tore herself away from the frightening, strangely hypnotic sight and went to the Gilded Cabinet in the Queen's private apartment. Marie Antoinette was still in conversation with Axel in the Meridian Cabinet. When she left, Rose and Madame de Tourzel were summoned there. Marie Antoinette sat on the recessed blue silk daybed, reflected many times over in the mirrors. Although she was in more danger from the mob than anyone else in the Château, she was fully composed and as immaculate in her appearance as if awaiting a Court social event.

"I have special instructions for you both," she said, "because you two out of those ladies still with me are closest to my children. If any attack is launched against the Château I want you to see first to them. They are to be taken to the King and not brought to my apartment, because it would be too dangerous for them to be here with me. Is that understood?"

They both answered her together, Madame de Tourzel unable to hold back a sob as she wiped her eyes. The Queen rose, patted her on the shoulder and told them both to wait in the Gilded Cabinet with the other ladies until she had seen the King to discover the latest developments.

The time of waiting seemed interminable until she reappeared, even though refreshments had been served in the meantime. All stood as she reentered the room and they regarded her anxiously.

"There is a chance that we shall be leaving here for Rambouillet," she told them. "It is only a short distance away, but we should be safer there. However, the King is not yet convinced that the move is necessary and so we must be patient." In her own mind she was screaming for him to be persuaded, thinking of her children's safety, but he was more inclined to listen to the minister advising him to stay than the others counselling flight. In decisions such as his keeping faith with his people, she had no voice.

"Why don't the troops disperse the mob?" one lady burst out.

Marie Antoinette looked faintly surprised that she should ask. "The King would never order them to fire on women."

Another spoke up. "A page informed us that there are men disguised in female dress out there. They are in charge of the cannon and there are many more similarly clad, who are armed to the teeth."

"That is true. The King knows it, but he will not risk any women being harmed." Marie Antoinette's blue eyes went steadily to each of her ladies in turn as if to instill some of her own courage into them and keep them immune from panic. "If you should wish to get a few necessities packed to take with you in case we are evacuated to Rambouillet, now is the time."

As Rose hurried to her apartment she wondered where Richard was in this present turmoil, because he would have heard what was happening before the mob set out from Paris. Somehow he would try to reach her, their quarrel shelved if not forgotten, and the fact that he had not ridden openly like Axel von Fersen suggested that he was with the mob again, even though he had told her he thought the time needed to disguise himself was over. So long as he could conceal his true identity from those harri-

dans he was safe but if he was discovered and believed to
be a spy he would be torn to pieces.

"Oh, no!" She caught her breath with horror, pausing for
a moment on the flight of stairs to grip the rail for support.
Then she hastened on again, her fear all for him and none
for herself.

When a piece of hand-baggage had been packed, she
told Diane to get some of her own things together, for she
did not intend to leave Versailles without her. The maid
hesitated, her small, heart-shaped face revealing her worried state.

"Will the Swiss Guards ride with us?"

Rose regarded her sympathetically, knowing she had a
beau among their number, a fresh-faced, freckled young
man of her own age. The romance had bloomed to a point
where Rose expected any day to have a request from Diane to be allowed to marry. "The Flanders Regiment will
escort us, I'm sure, and the Swiss Guards will be left to
protect the Château in their usual rôle, although they will
be safe enough once the Court has left."

Diane smiled again, relieved to know her beau would
not be in danger, and went to pack her own belongings,
while Rose went to the children's apartment and arrived at
the same time as Madame de Tourzel. The Dauphin was
already in bed and asleep, but Princesse Marie Thérèse,
being almost seven years older, was allowed to be up later.
Rose and the Marquise played a lighthearted game of cards
with her, the child's hilarity in marked contrast to their
inner feelings, which they hid from her. Then Rose supervised the princess's supper and afterwards took over from
the nursemaids to see her into bed. When Rose rejoined
Madame de Tourzel in the adjoining apartment, the connecting doors left open in case of emergency, she was met
by an immense show of pent-up anxiety.

"Please go and try to find out what is happening," the
Marquise begged her. "It's hours since we heard anything
and one of us must be here with the children."

When Rose found that the Queen had not returned to
her private apartment, she went at once to the Bull's Eye
Salon where she could see all who came and went into the
presence of the King who was in his apartment.

"What is the latest news?" she asked Madame de La

Tour du Pin, another of the Queen's ladies waiting there with the same aim.

"The King received a delegation of six women from the mob. They were shown up here with as much pomp as if they were royalty and were much overawed by everything, I can tell you. With them were some members of the National Assembly, who have been meeting all day at the hall in the town."

"Did you know those men?"

"I recognised Dr. Guillotin, who is professor of anatomy at Paris University, but the others were unknown to me."

"How did the audience go?"

"I heard that the spokeswoman fainted with emotion. It certainly wasn't from starvation because she looked to me as if she was of that certain profession that is ever well paid. Anyway, a doctor revived her and the King promised to do everything possible to end the famine. The delegation left in smiles, but judging by the ugly sounds that the mob made afterwards the promises they conveyed from the King were not well received."

Rose left to report to Madame de Tourzel. On the way she looked out of a window again. In the light of the lanterns that surrounded the Château she could see it was still pouring and the Place d'Armes was all but deserted. The mob of women and the men with them had sought whatever shelter they could find. Only a few drenched figures remained on duty by the cannon. Within the Château's palisades there was still a scene of activity and standby. The troops, surely cold, wet and miserable, stood in the same places, officers striding about on the alert. Carriages had been drawn up in a long line in readiness should the King decide on a move to Rambouillet. Judging by the way in which the coachmen and grooms were running about, it looked as though someone had discovered the horses' traces had been cut and carriage wheels loosened. It was a night when any kind of sabotage could be expected.

Later, after being implored again by the Marquise to gather in the latest developments, she passed the same window again and saw an entirely different scene. The National Guard of Paris had arrived in the Place d'Armes, bringing another mob in its wake. The women had run from the shelter to fraternise with the soldiers, tossing their mud-splashed petticoats in invitation and to welcome uproariously those men who had come to swell their number. Was Richard in that throng? She hoped he might see her at the window and know she was thinking of him, but someone in the mob mistook her for the Queen. Immediately there was a rush to the railings to scream abuse at her, using all the names given to Marie Antoinette when the populace had first held her responsible for the nation's debts.

"Bitch! Spendthrift! Whore! Come down here, Madame Déficit, and let us cut out your heart! We'll stew your liver and set your head on a pike!"

Rose retreated from the window in horror and had not recovered when she reached the Bull's Eye Salon. A courtier vacated for her the tabouret next to Madame de La Tour du Pin, who looked at her with concern.

"Are you all right?"

Rose nodded, keeping her terror to herself. The women had reacted like tigresses. It had been a terrible sight. "What has been happening here?"

"Lafayette, Commander of the National Guard, has arrived and is with the King now. He dripped rain all across the floor." Madame de La Tour du Pin pointed with her closed fan at a trail that glistened in the light of the chandeliers. "The Queen is there, too."

The time of waiting dragged on. Messengers came and went; a National Guard officer refreshed the line of raindrops. Midnight had long gone by and it was the sixth of October. Rose thought how Richard had planned to come on the morrow, not suspecting that the violence he had foretold would erupt much sooner than he had anticipated.

It was after one o'clock when the Queen, looking tired and sad, emerged from the King's Apartment. Everyone in the Bull's Eye Salon bowed and curtsied as she went through. Noticing Rose and her companion, she beckoned to them and together they went back to the Gilded Cabinet where the other ladies still waited.

"We are not going to Rambouillet after all," she told them. "Commander Lafayette has given us his assurance that there is no immediate danger. The crowds in the Place d'Armes have agreed there shall be no more trouble tonight. We must hope that the National Assembly will be able to resolve everything peacefully tomorrow, bearing in mind the King's promises. So all go to bed and sleep soundly."

She herself ached in every limb with weariness and was thankful to retire, Rose and two of her other ladies-in-waiting, Mesdames Thibaut and Auguier, attending her. By two o'clock her candles were extinguished with the exception of one always left alight and she was asleep even as her three ladies left the bedchamber. Rose closed the door and immediately all three looked at one another with a single thought.

"I'm not going to bed," Madame Auguier declared.

"I'll keep watch with you," Rose said, having been far from convinced that the mob had been persuaded into settling down.

"So will I," endorsed Madame Thibaut.

Rose had only to let Madame de Tourzel know all was said to be well. That lady promptly went to bed with relief and was also asleep within minutes. It was with caution that Rose approached the window again. Once again the Place d'Armes was clear except for those by the cannon. In the Cour Royale all the troops had been relieved by a token guard. Everything was still. Not a figure moved in the fitful illumination given by the lanterns. Even the rain had stopped, the clouds breaking here and there to reveal the stars. Yet Rose remained only half reassured and went back to keep vigil with her fellow ladies-in-waiting. She could get to the children swiftly enough by the Queen's private staircase if the need should arise.

Diane, who slept in a little room adjoining her mistress's apartment, always rose early in the morning. Since it was not easy to meet her darling Jean-Paul due to their conflicting times of duty, she never missed a chance to slip out to see him when he was on night duty in the grounds. This meant that before the guard was changed at dawn they were able to talk a little with nobody else about, to kiss and cuddle before she left him again. Sometimes she took him a hot newly baked roll from the kitchen on the way, which he would tuck into his jacket to eat when she was gone, and it was their little joke that he should always remember to brush the crumbs away afterwards.

This morning she did not fetch a roll, not sure how many extra guards would be on duty near the kitchens, or if she would be stopped anywhere. With a dark cloak over her blue woollen gown, she made her way down the staircases and out into the morning air, dawn just rising in the sky. She knew exactly where Jean-Paul would be. He was on guard not far from the Orangery, within the locked gates of a narrow courtyard. With a smile of anticipation she came at a run through a passageway to where she would catch her first sight of him. Then she stopped with a shriek in her throat. It went unheard, for a vast mob of men and women, led by a giant of a man carrying a huge axe, was coming like a tidal wave from the direction of the Orangery where the gates must have been treacherously unlocked. In the same second she saw Jean-Paul seized before he could fire his musket and wrenched before the axe-carrier who swung the blade up in the air and sliced her sweetheart's head from his neck. She collapsed in a faint. Had she not been close to the wall, she would have been kicked to death as the mob, giving forth a blood-roar, surged through the passageway to reach the Cour Royale and the Queen's Staircase.

In the room where Rose and her two companions were keeping watch, a gilded bronze clock with a Sèvres face chimed six o'clock just as a sinister rumble resounded from the staircase only two rooms away from where the Queen slept. Rose leapt for the door and flung it open; Madame Thibaut rushed through and Rose followed her across the Salon of the Guards to the anteroom. There the guard, clubbed and wounded, his face a mass of blood, was struggling to make a barrier of his musket against the leaders of the mob fighting to get in.

"Save the Queen!" he shouted in the last moment before he buckled up as a pike rammed its steel point into his stomach. Madame Thibaut and Rose were already rushing back into the Salon of the Guards where they slammed and locked the doors. In the royal bedchamber they did the same. Madame Auguier, having heard everything, was already rousing the Queen, tearing the bedclothes from her.

"Quick, Madame!" she shrieked. "Your life is in danger! Assassins have come! Fly to the King!"

Marie Antoinette half fell out of the bed, her fine silk nightgown clinging to her shape. "Save my children," she gasped to Rose, who had snatched off a petticoat and fastened it about the Queen for modesty's sake.

"I'm on my way to them now!"

As Rose bolted away, Marie Antoinette rushed for a concealed door in the wall that led into her Petits Cabinets and by which she could reach the Bull's Eye Salon and the King's Apartment. But when she came to the door that should have opened into the Bull's Eye Salon it would not give.

"Merciful God! It's locked!" she cried out.

"But it's never locked!" Madame Thibaut cried. "Let me try!"

But the key had been turned. Some overzealous guard or servant had locked it during the turmoil of the previous evening and it refused to give. Marie Antoinette began to hammer on the door and her two petrified ladies-in-waiting joined in. Crashes and thumps from the direction of the bedchamber told them that the insurgents had entered. The three of them redoubled their efforts in sheer panic, knowing the concealed door could be discovered at any second and then all would be lost. Marie Antoinette was beside herself with terror of the obscene indignities to which she would be subjected at the hands of such maddened ruffians if she should be caught and dragged back into their midst. Death itself was nothing by comparison.

In the Bull's Eye Salon, a "blue boy" nervous at the uproar that he could hear, had entered only to hear a further hammering on the door from the Petits Cabinets and what sounded like her voice crying for it to be opened. He turned the key and stepped back in astonishment as she flew past him in a state of undress into the King's Apartment, followed by two of her ladies, dishevelled and seemingly half mad with fright. He had the wit to lock the door again and heard the Queen's shriek of disappointment at finding the King was not in his apartment.

But Louis, who had been awakened by the noise, was hurrying back along the secret passage under the Bull's Eye Salon, having raced to his wife's bedchamber only to find she had already fled from it. He had not traversed that way since they had ceased to share a bed and the hem of his brocade robe caught up little swathes of dust. As he thrust open the concealed door into his State Apartment, Marie Antoinette rushed into his arms with a glad cry.

"My dear!" he exclaimed. "I thank God that you're safe. The intruders broke in just as I left your bedchamber. I fear they are doing much damage there."

She nodded, too emotionally tense for speech, and they kissed each other. At that moment Rose, holding Princesse Marie Thérèse by the hand, arrived with Madame de Tourzel in a peignoir, who was carrying the Dauphin. As soon as the little boy was on his feet he ran with his sister to their mother, who crouched down to catch them in her arms and hold them tight. It was then that the dreadful sound came of an onslaught on the door into the Bull's Eye Salon, the wood splitting and cracking. The Queen's escape route had been discovered.

Louis moved protectively towards Marie Antoinette, who straightened up and would have pushed the children to him, knowing that it was her blood that the rabble wished to shed, but he indicated that she should take them by the hand. They stood as a family, brave and united. Rose and the three other ladies-in-waiting grouped themselves on either side, their spines straight, outwardly as calm as their Queen. All watched the door through which the rabble would come once entry had been made in the salon beyond.

Then miraculously the attack on the door ceased. The same "blue boy" came rushing into the State Bedchamber, not forgetting to bow to the King in his excitement. "The Guards are driving out the mob, Your Majesty! The Château is safe again."

For a few moments nobody moved. Then relaxation swept over them and they turned to one another in thankfulness, although knowing that everything was still in the balance and danger always present. Outside, below the apartment windows and filling the Cour Royale, the rabble like a surging sea was yelling and screeching, thwarted in its purpose. Now and again the shout of "Long live Orléans!" could be heard. This was the renegade nobleman, long an enemy of the King, who was known to be behind the Revolution. Rose did not doubt that he had been the chief organiser of this terrible event. After all, someone who knew the Château well had told the mob exactly which direction to take in order to find the Queen's bedchamber which was never open to the public gaze, it being the King alone who was expected to share his whole existence with the people.

Courtiers and ladies had begun hurrying from all parts of the Château into the King's bedchamber, some in dressing-robes and most of the ladies with their hair tumbling about their shoulders as was the Queen's and Madame de Tourzel's. Madame Auguier had fetched a cream velvet robe for Marie Antoinette to put over her nightgown and petticoat, not mentioning the way the bedchamber had been despoiled or that she had found the bodies of two slaughtered guards lying there, their heads missing.

Axel was among the first of the arrivals, hurrying in to go straight to the Queen and kiss her hand, his eyes telling her all that he could not express in the company of others. After him, at a run, came the King's sister, Madame Élisabeth. She embraced her sister-in-law in relief that she was safe, for they had always been good friends.

There was a stir among everybody present when Lafayette arrived. Although he must have been feeling sheepish at the way the mob had deceived him, he bluffed it out with his customary arrogance. "Show yourself to the people, sire," he urged the King. "They are demanding to see you and it will help quell their mood."

The doors to the balcony were opened. The early morning sun touched the double reversed *L* of Louis XIV's monogram in the metalwork, which had been there since the first embellishment of the Château, and it flashed reflected light across those within the room. Louis went out onto the balcony where once that same Sun King, awesome and flamboyant, had stood proudly with the future Louis XV as a child. Their descendant, lacking their ability to charm, ever at heart a private man and still happier with books than with people, faced the yelling rabble with courage and resignation. The shouts that greeted him were taunts in themselves.

"Long live the Revolution! Long live the Nation! Long live Orléans!"

Then, when he continued to regard them placidly, they remembered they had him in the palm of their hands and became more amenable. "Long live the King!"

He made acknowledgement and as he went back inside there came a fresh demand on a fierce, growling note. "The Queen! Let us see the Queen!"

Rose caught her breath with alarm. There were many muskets in that crowd and the Queen would be an easy target for any one of them. But Marie Antoinette did not flinch and went forward to the open doors. The children refused to leave her, taking her hands, but they burst into tears of fright when the sinister roar broke over them in thousands of angry tongues.

"Send in the children!" came the demand rising above the rest.

She bent her head to speak to them and they ran back in to their father. Then she stood alone, never more noble and majestic in her appearance in spite of her undressed hair lifted lightly by a breeze and her simple attire. She could hear the shouts urging those with weapons to shoot her, scuffles occurring here and there as others tried to seize the muskets to fulfil that aim. In the knowledge that she faced death at any second all fear for her own life left her. It made her realise that even if she should be spared by some miracle it would never return. All that mattered, or had ever mattered to her, was the safety of her children and those dearest to her.

As if in a final gesture she made a graceful curtsey that none had ever been able to match. Such dignified courage struck a chord with the mob and even those tussling for a musket gave in, letting the weapons be lowered. The tone changed and the cry was taken up: "Long live the Queen!"

Although it was not unanimous, it saved her life and gave some hope for the future. She went back into the bedchamber and all present either bowed or curtsied, awed by her cool serenity. While she comforted her children and dried their eyes, for they had wept all the time she was on the balcony, the unsatisfied mob shouted a new demand, voicing what had brought them there in the first place.

"To Paris with the King!"

So the ordeal was not over. Lafayette made speeches to the crowd from the balcony and brought the King out again. Louis, knowing he had no choice, agreed to move to Paris, telling the triumphant mob that he entrusted his family to their safekeeping.

The bodies of the guards had been removed from the Queen's bedchamber, but Marie Antoinette blanched at the bloodstains when she returned there to bathe and dress and make decisions about what should be packed. Servants had acted quickly to right overturned furniture and cover the bed, but the slashed hangings bore witness to the rage that had been released there. Always thoughtful of her ladies, she told Rose and the two who had kept watch with her to go and rest for a while, since others were able to attend her.

"I believe we shall be setting off with the Court to Paris at one o'clock," she said. Then she turned directly to Rose. "Come to me at noon in the Meridian Cabinet. There is something I want to say to you before departure, Madame Rose."

Mystified as to what it could be, Rose went to her own apartment and was surprised to find her bed was still turned down from the night before and there was no sign of Diane. She rang her bell and, when nothing happened, went to her maid's room, wondering if the young woman was ill or, remembering how she had run from the Bastille, if she was cowering there and afraid to come out. But the room was empty.

Rose gave up all thought of rest and began to do her own packing, having sent up from storage the boxes that had brought her belongings to Versailles. She had to wait because all over the Château similar demands were being made and the servants found themselves struggling with one another in the places of storage to grab the right containers. Everything was ready in piles on her bed and on the floor by it and in her boudoir by the time the boxes eventually arrived. She asked the servants who brought them if they had seen Diane and received a negative answer.

At noon, wearing a travelling gown, she went to the Meridian Cabinet. The Queen, similarly dressed, entered just after her and drew her to the daybed where they sat down together.

"This is farewell, Madame Rose," Marie Antoinette said gently. "No matter what you say I release you now from your loyal and devoted service to me."

"Madame!" Rose's protest came with a shake of her head. "Don't send me from you at this time. Later, perhaps, when things are better again."

"I don't want to let you go, but unlike the rest of my ladies-in-waiting who have husbands at Court or no responsibilities outside it, you are a different case. Not only are you married to an Englishman, but there is the Duchesse de Valverde to whom you are devoted, I know. Is Lord Easterton with her at Château Satory?"

"I don't know where he is. Either in Paris or somewhere in that teeming crowd in the Cour Royale." She gave a word of explanation as to why he might be with the mob, not speaking of her fear for his safety which was constant. The Queen had enough troubles of her own.

"All the more reason for you to go home to Château Satory," Marie Antoinette said with emphasis. "Not only will he be able to reach you there, but your grandmother will not be alone. I hope and pray that our going to Paris will mean an end to this dreadful situation. Above all else the King wants to avoid civil war or further bloodshed of any kind." She paused for a moment. "I don't wish to cause you unnecessary worry, but if things don't get better who can say whether the residences of the nobility outside the Court will not be attacked as châteaux have been in distant provinces and as Versailles was today. Lord Easterton, being a foreigner, will be able to give you and the Duchesse de Valverde the protection of his country." She took Rose by the hand and they stood up together. "Don't make this time harder for either of us. Your friendship has been of inestimable value to me many times."

Rose could not hold back her tears. "My prayers will be for you and the King and the children."

"We shall be in need of them. I thank you, my dear Madame Rose." She kissed Rose on both cheeks.

Rose sank into a last curtsey to her. It was a poignant moment never to be forgotten and her tears spotted her skirt.

No sooner had she gone than Marie Antoinette was overcome by the events of the day, this farewell with someone she had long trusted being a final straw. She sank down again on the daybed, covering her face with her hands and sobbing her heart out in the certainty that she would never again see the Petit Trianon that she loved or play with her children in the meadows of the Hamlet amid the cows and the chickens in the sweet game of pretence that she was just an ordinary woman with no queenly duties to dog her steps and twist her life. As for Versailles where she had first come as a fourteen-year-old bride nearly twenty years ago, silence would reign with no echo of her laughter or tap of her heels to show she was ever there.

Paint and powder could not hide her swollen eyelids and the still tremulous line of her mouth when the time came to leave. She wore ruby-red velvet and one of her most elegant hats trimmed with white plumes, but there was still a tragic look to her as she went from her apartment to join the King, whose own expression was sad. She put her hand in a courtly manner on his proffered wrist and with the children following them they went with regal dignity down the marble staircase to their waiting carriage.

It was almost half-past one before some order was made to the departing cavalcade and it was able to proceed. Nearly three hundred carriages bore the royal family and the Court away from Versailles. After them came two horse-drawn cannon and hundreds of baggage wagons piled up with boxes and furniture. Frantic servants, who had no wish to join the mob and did not want to be left behind, filled every vehicle available to them and when there was no more room they climbed up to ride on top or in any spare space amid the goods and chattels. In their blue and silver livery they were mocked as being like monkeys by the rabble, who made up the escort fore and aft and alongside.

All the Revolutionaries were better armed than when they came, for they had taken the weapons of the Flanders Regiment as well as those of the household troops, none of whom had been ordered to fire a shot, and they marched gloomily along. They and everyone else had been given a red, white and blue cockade to wear. A few of the more nervous among the nobility put them on. The rest let them lie on the carriage floors. The din was tremendous, looted regimental drums being banged, and many of the riotous horde set up chants or songs of their own, excitement and a sense of triumph at fever pitch. Gruesomely, the heads of the slaughtered guards were danced along on pikes, several deliberately close to the royal carriage, even though the Dauphin and his sister were riding with their parents.

Rose watched the terrible and lamentable procession from an upper window above the King's deserted bedchamber. She was able to see it go straight down the Avenue de Paris, a seemingly endless river of people, horses and vehicles, and she did not move from her silent farewell until it was finally lost from sight.

She was not to know that Richard had already begun his search of the carriages for her, riding up and down on one of the horses stolen from the royal stables and looking as much of a ruffian as any in the crowd. He had seen little chance of getting her away by using his entrée at Court, able to foresee that if things went wrong he would be trapped with the rest of the Court and as much a prisoner as she. For that reason he had been with the cannon, a woman's cloak over the rough garments he had worn before when mixing with the mob. He had seen Rose come to one of the windows when he had been huddled against the cannon in the rain and had despised the ignorance of those who thought she was the Queen. At least she had conveyed a message that she thought him to be nearby and he regretted not being able to give her a signal in reply.

He was not relieved from his duty at the cannon, which he intended to see was not fired at any cost, until just before an outbreak of shouting told him the Château was being invaded by the mob, something that had been plotted elsewhere that night without his knowledge. He had rushed to join the invaders, but had got no farther than the vestibule of the Queen's Staircase, for by then the guards were forcing the rabble out.

Now as he rode peering into carriage windows for Rose, frequently alarming the noble passengers with his fiercely armed appearance, he recognised many familiar faces. Axel von Fersen glanced at him with disdain and without a trace of recognition, confirming the excellence of his disguise, as did a pretty noblewoman, whom he had enjoyed on the occasion of his return to Versailles before he had won Rose back again. She and most of the women wore the fashionable large-brimmed hats which consistently hid their faces from him. He had to ride both sides of a number of carriages several times before he could be sure that one of the occupants was not his wife.

It took six and a half hours for the cavalcade to reach Paris. Then there was a tedious welcome from the Mayor through which the Dauphin slept, his thumb in his mouth. Afterwards all were allowed to go to the Tuileries, the old palace where the Sun King had spent his childhood. Richard, who watched everyone stepping wearily from the carriages, was making certain he had not missed Rose and he pitied those entering the half-furnished Tuileries, which had not been a royal residence for over a hundred and thirty years. They would suffer much discomfort before everything was put in order for them.

Convinced at last that Rose was elsewhere, he took a fresh horse and set out to search of her once again.

Rose had never been nervous at Versailles before, but she was now. Those servants who had not gone with the Court had made a choice to be with the people and no longer in service to the nobility. When she left the upper room from which she had watched the royal family's departure, she asked one of her own pages to arrange a carriage for her and a vehicle for her boxes. He regarded her mockingly.

"Why not walk and carry your own goods? Nobody here is at your beck and call any more." He went striding off. Two more servants ignored her, passing by as if she had not spoken, and when a fourth leered at her she ran to her apartment, determined to take her jewels and her grandfather's painting and then leave at once. To her huge relief she found that Diane had returned. Then the young woman turned a white, stunned face to her and she saw how muddied and dirtied she was, blood on her apron.

"Diane! What happened to you?" she cried anxiously in the dreadful belief that the young woman had been raped.

"They murdered my Jean-Paul." The maid was in such a state that she seemed to have no control over her features, her mouth and chin jerking awkwardly. "I went out early to meet him and I saw them cut off his head."

"Oh, no!" Rose's mind reeled at what the girl had witnessed and she guided her to a chair. "Sit here. I'll get you a cognac."

It was one that Richard particularly liked and in thinking of him her hand shook, making the crystal goblet rattle against the mouth of the decanter. Diane took a gulp automatically as if she had no will to decide anything for herself.

"I must have fainted. When I came round it took me a while to find him. He had been left in the path of those hundreds of people and I finally found him crushed and broken lying beside some steps." She raised her poor wretched face to Rose. "But his head wasn't there. I searched everywhere. I think I went a little mad and kept crying out because one of the National Guard came from his post to tell me to shut up. I asked him to help me find Jean-Paul's head and he said those Revolutionaries had it on a pike."

Rose shuddered, picturing the heads she had seen accompanying the departure, and she stooped to put her arms comfortingly around the young woman. "How terrible for you. If only I had known what you were going through I would have tried to help. Why didn't you come to me?"

"I couldn't get back into the Château with the National Guard keeping all those people out. I managed to get a gardener to help me with the body. He wrapped Jean-Paul in some canvas and then he and somebody else carried him to the old police quarters. That's where the bodies are. I stayed with Jean-Paul until I heard everybody leaving."

Rose, almost certain of what was coming, hugged the girl tightly. "Hush! Try not to remember!"

"I saw his head. Do you know what those terrible people had done? They had made a barber wash away the blood and dress the hair of all the heads. Jean-Paul's hair was waving clean and golden in the sun. But there was fright stamped on his face!" Her voice rose to a faint scream and she would have started up from the chair, but Rose forced her down again and held her. The sobs came tearing up from Diane's throat in the most awful weeping Rose had ever heard.

It was dark when they slipped out of the Château. Rose had become increasingly afraid of hostile servants accosting them and thought it best to remain quietly in her apartment until she could lead Diane away through the labyrinth of passageways they had both come to know so well. The slamming of doors and shutters told her that the National Guard were supervising the closing up of Versailles against outsiders, and she wondered what its fate would be if the King and Queen and the Court stayed permanently in Paris.

Both she and Diane were darkly clad to be as inconspicuous as possible. She had borrowed one of her maid's working-dresses and capes. The little painting that she treasured was wrapped into a bundle of Diane's clothes while she herself had left everything except her jewels, which she had concealed upon her person.

She had thought it best to leave by a side gate and, as she had hoped, the National Guardsmen on duty there supposed them to be two servant girls and quipped good-humouredly as they went past. Then they walked all the way to Château Satory. Diane, normally strong and energetic, stumbled along as if in a trance.

As they drew near and turned into the drive, Rose was seized by such overwhelming thankfulness to be home that she broke into a run, leaving Diane to jog after her. Flying up the steps, she hammered on the door as she reached it and jerked on the bell.

"I'm here, Grand-mère!" she called joyously, as if she could be heard within.

The door swung open and she froze with shock. One of the hated Revolutionaries loomed terrifyingly up at her against the candlelight within. Then he spoke in Richard's voice.

"Rose! Thank God you're here! I was just on my way to Versailles to find you. Your Grandmother has had an attack. I fear she's very ill."

She fell into his arms for a swift kiss of reconciliation and then rushed from him and up the stairs, crying out in her heart for Jasmin not to die. Such a loss after everything else would be impossible to bear.

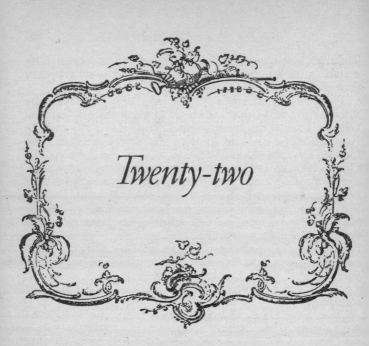

Twenty-two

Versailles had stood empty for more than two and a half years in August 1792 when Rose went to claim her possessions left there. In nursing Jasmin through a long illness followed by as many months of convalescence, there had been no time to think of anything else and neither did she want to go within the gates of the Château again until the horror and sadness of that sixth day of October had lost its freshness in her mind. Not that she would ever forget, and Diane was a changed person since her dreadful ordeal. It was noticeable to Rose how Diane always turned her gaze away from the Château, as she did herself, whenever they drove across the Place d'Armes or shopped in the vicinity.

It had been a terrible time for France with plots and counterplots among those with conflicting politics, the moderates and the extremists struggling for control. Prominent men had fallen from power while newcomers, such as Robespierre and Danton, had taken their places. There had been riots and more than one massacre, pillage and brigandage and hunger unchanged for the poor. At the

Tuileries some months before, the King had been rein-
stated in his functions, although deprived of all arbitrary
powers.

Today as her carriage bore her into the Cour Royale she
missed the Swiss Guards in their bright uniforms. National
Guards stood at the gates, wearing tricolour sashes and the
Revolutionary cockade in their black cocked hats. Yet,
looking towards the gilded East Front where the King and
Queen had shown themselves on the balcony to the shouting mob, she found that other memories of happier days
were coming back to her. It was as if Versailles were exerting its old magic to win her over again just as it had enraptured her when she had first come there, suspicious and
resentful of the change being wrought in her life.

Richard had offered to accompany her on this expedition, but she had felt the need to face the past alone. "If
you're sure," he had said uncertainly.

"I am," she had replied. "Go to the Embassy as you had
intended."

"Very well. I can call in at the Tuileries if you've finished
your letter to the Queen."

"Oh, I have." She entrusted it to him knowing that
Marie Antoinette would be pleased to hear from her, for
the royal family was virtually barred from having any visitors now. Yet there had been quite happy occasions at the
Tuileries when the King and Queen had sustained hope
that all would still go well. The old palace had been furnished and embellished to be a fit setting for a Court even
if it could never be compared with Versailles. During this
period, Princesse de Lamballe, who had fled to England
after the fall of the Bastille, returned to be lady-in-waiting
again to the Queen, who was as grateful for her loyal
friendship as she was to Rose for hers.

Twice Rose and Richard had visited Saint-Cloud when
the royal family had been allowed to holiday there. It had
been such a pleasure to play with the Dauphin and Princesse Marie Thérèse again and to chat with the Queen in
peaceful countrified surroundings without meeting a
Guardsman's eye in every direction. But there had been
no more such respites for the royal family after Axel or-
ganised an escape from France for them and it failed disastrously.

Rose alighted by the grille that stood open to the Château, feeling cast down again with concern for the royal family. Things were going from bad to worse for them. Their lives were in constant danger and hatred was mounting to a fresh peak. She entered the Queen's vestibule. It was deserted except for two National Guardsmen standing on duty and a third sitting at a table. This had always been such a busy place with handsomely dressed people going up and down the green marble staircase while the little stalls, such as the one from which Marguerite had once sold fans, had done a roaring trade.

"Your name?" barked the seated corporal.

"Lady Easterton." She then told him of her claim and he looked it up on a list.

"Identification?" He took her papers from her, nodded and handed them back. "All boxes are in the first antechamber beyond the guardroom. I suppose you know the way."

She ignored the sarcasm in his voice. "Yes, I do."

Followed by the two grooms from her carriage, who were to carry the boxes, she went up by the Queen's Staircase, taking her time. In its marble alcove at the top the gilded group symbolising the marriage of the Sun King and Queen Marie Thérèse gleamed at her as it had done so often before, the murals on either side giving a sense of distance and space.

She went through the guardroom into the first anteroom. Where once the Sun King had taken his supper in the public gaze there were innumerable boxes and containers of every size, some she guessed would never be claimed, the owners dead or gone abroad. A guard there helped her to locate her boxes, all of which were labelled, and as the grooms began to shift them she could not resist going on through the open doorway into the lovely white and gold Bull's Eye Salon. She saw with relief that the door through which the Queen had fled had been repaired, no sign now of the damage inflicted. In fact, care was being taken by the Assembly of the vast building that her fellow countrymen and -women, whether noble, bourgeois or peasant, had always seen as part of their own lives with their innate right of entry. Ironically there were more restrictions now than there had ever been before. Now in its semiclosed condition almost all of the windows were shuttered and whatever furniture had not been removed was hidden under dustsheets.

"Citizeness, your boxes have gone downstairs."

She turned with a nod to the guard who had come to the doorway, and she went past him out of the rooms and back to the vestibule where she signed for her possessions and left.

At home Diane unpacked for her, bringing out gowns she had almost forgotten. Fashion had changed little for women during the period, the Queen no longer in a position to set a pace, or even wishing to with other far more serious matters on her mind. Men had taken to high-standing collars, plain cravats neatly tied, slim-cut coats and frequently tight pantaloons and high boots, a style that suited Richard admirably with his broad shoulders and strong thighs. He had gone off that morning in a new green coat that he had had made in England during one of his visits home. He never suggested that she should go with him, for Jasmin was in such a weakened condition that anything could happen at any time, and Rose was thankful for every day she had with her. He no longer kept permanent rooms at the Embassy, for his diplomatic duties took him far afield, which meant he resided at the Château Satory when not abroad.

Jasmin liked him being there. When he was away she missed him carrying her up and down the stairs, for whenever she was well enough she liked to receive visitors in the Ivory Salon, propped up by pastel-coloured cushions that enhanced her snow-white hair and wearing a different gown every day. Michel Balaine was still her most regular visitor, lonely in his large house with all his family residing elsewhere. The two of them talked more about the past than the present as old people do, although both retained the same interest in what was happening in France and expressed their anxiety.

Rose thought it fortunate that Jasmin believed it was Richard's diplomatic service that kept them in France, not her state of health, whereas he could probably have conducted it equally well from London. Although he never spoke of his duties, Rose knew he had been to the Court of Vienna and had visited abroad many French émigrés who had set up miniature courts based on the etiquette of Versailles wherever they had settled. Her conclusion was that he had two purposes, one to convey to foreign governments his own country's attitude towards events in France and the other to try to win freedom for Marie Antoinette and her children through ransom or, in the case of Austria, in exchange for French prisoners taken in the current war that had broken out between the two countries. He spoke once of meeting Axel in Vienna. She was sure the Comte was still working towards getting the Queen out of France in spite of the previous catastrophe. Yet she was also sure that Marie Antoinette would always choose to stay with the King, whom the French would never release. There was loyalty and courage in the Queen beyond the limits of anyone's understanding of her.

Rose was not unduly worried when Richard was late coming home from Paris. His hours were often irregular, depending on what he had to do. Jasmin always went to bed early, having supper on a tray, and Rose ate hers, as she always did when Richard was absent, with her grandmother. Afterwards she read a chapter from a novel to Jasmin and by that time the old lady was ready to sleep.

The rest of the evening passed slowly. Rose sat with a book until, becoming bored, she flung it aside and went out into the hot, flower-scented August night to stroll all the way down the drive to the gates in the hope of seeing Richard's carriage lanterns approaching in the distance. An uneasiness was growing in her, so that even when she returned to the house she could not think of undressing for bed. It was after midnight when she heard a horse's hooves. Rushing into the hall, she reached the door before the servant on duty arrived and opened it to a messenger from the Embassy. Tearing open the note she read a single cryptic message scrawled in haste.

Do not expect me home for three days. R.

"What is happening in Paris?" she asked the messenger who was waiting for any reply.

"There has been an attack on the Tuileries with terrible bloodshed, madame. Lord Easterton witnessed it but was unharmed."

"What of the royal family?"

"The same, but shut up in a room with iron bars at the Riding School for their own safety. All the male royal servants were slaughtered, from the chefs to the pages, and many courtiers, soldiers and civilians killed. There was more carnage there in Paris today than on a battlefield."

The waiting seemed interminable. When Richard returned late on the evening of the third day he was disheveled and unshaven as if he had had no time to think about himself. His new green coat was ripped at the sleeve and bore some dried bloodstains. He put an arm about her waist and led her into the Crimson Salon. Then he threw himself down in exhaustion onto a chair, his elbow on his knee, his head in his hand.

"I fear the King and Queen are doomed," he said hoarsely. "They've been taken with the children and Madame Élisabeth to the fortress section of the Temple."

She stared at him, appalled by what he had said and scarcely able to find her voice as she thought of the royal family in that grim place. She put a hand on his shoulder. "Is there no hope?"

"I see none. There has been a new Revolution, and a Commune of cutthroats has set itself up in power in the Hôtel de Ville. Hundreds of the nobility have been arrested and thrown into prison, including Madame de Lamballe and the other ladies-in-waiting. The monarchy has been abolished. France is now a republic."

Her knees seemed to buckle and she dropped down on them to bow against him as he put his arms about her. The sights he had seen of ruthless slaughter weighed down on his eyes as if they would never go away. Only in the loving comfort that his wife gave him in their bed was he able to shut them out. It was during these nights abandoned wholly to love that Rose conceived, something they had not planned until she should be safe in England. It increased his anxiety about her whereas she could not help but be overjoyed. It was like a bright light in the midst of all the darkness and sorrow.

Within days of establishing itself, the Commune, flushed with success, ordered a butchering of priests, aristocrats, political opponents and imprisoned unfortunates, including some children. The timely action of a compassionate guard at the Temple in pulling a curtain across a window saved Marie Antoinette from one harrowing sight. She did not see the head and mutilated naked body of her dear friend Madame de Lamballe jogged up and down on pikes in front of her prison window.

Dr. Guillotin's invention, designed originally for the humane despatching of criminals, began to be used more and more for so-called enemies of the Republic. The hiss and crash of the blade on the block could be heard in Lyons and many other cities, as well as Paris, throughout the land. Richard wanted to get Rose away from France more than ever before. The fact that she was the wife of an Englishman gave her some protection, for foreigners were allowed to go about their daily business without harassment. Yet her name was probably listed in a file somewhere as the former Marquise de Chuard, lady-in-waiting to the Queen.

So far there had been no trouble at Château Satory. Jasmin's good name as a friend of the needy had kept her and her property safe from marauders. She was not the only aristocrat to be thus spared; there were others like her in various parts of the country whose charitable works had gained them a reward for which they had never looked.

In January Richard attended the King's trial and was sickened by the whole procedure. The chief accuser was Robespierre, whose articulate venom destroyed any chance of justice. All that stood out in the travesty was Louis's unshakable courage and his devotion to his people. He was sentenced to death with the execution to be carried out the next day.

That morning Jasmin insisted on rising early to dress in black and keep a vigil downstairs with Rose in silent prayer for his soul. Shortly before mid-morning a cannon was fired at Versailles, echoing another in Paris announcing that Louis XVI was dead.

"The King is dead! Long live the King!" Jasmin exclaimed emotionally. Rose put an arm about her grandmother in shared sorrow, her thoughts with the widow and her children.

The distress and exertion took its toll on Jasmin. She collapsed later the same day just as Richard arrived home and he carried her upstairs to bed while Rose sent for the doctor. When he came he said much as he had said before, which was that there was nothing to be done for the Duchesse except complete rest and Rose's good nursing.

"What a nuisance I am to you, Rose." Jasmin's exhausted whisper from the pillows was almost inaudible. "Especially now when you are fully five months into your pregnancy."

"You are never any trouble, Grand-mère," Rose replied softly at the bedside. "I'm always here to look after you."

Jasmin smiled and slept, holding on to her granddaughter's hand. She had forgotten completely all thoughts of Rose going to England at any time. When Richard came to tell her he would be going home for a while it never occurred to her in the insular state of an invalid what it must mean to him to leave his wife behind in such dangerous times. The Commune, enraged that England refused to recognise the Republic, had declared war, even though France stood without a friend in Europe, and across the Atlantic much sympathy had waned through the excessive bloodshed. In Paris the English Ambassador was preparing to withdraw immediately, taking all members of the Embassy with him, including Richard, whom he would not allow to stay under any circumstances.

"I'll be back, darling," Richard assured Rose as they clung together in a last embrace before his departure. "You'll not be alone for long, I promise you, my love."

To the Ambassador's annoyance an escort of the National Guard rode with his party to the coast and waited on the quay until the ship had sailed, no courtesy intended but an insulting show of getting the enemy well off French soil. Richard paid the escort no attention, filling in details as to how he should return. He thought he could be back in France within a matter of three or four days. If Rose followed his advice to stay at home and not go to Paris under any circumstances, all should be well. There was always the secret vault she had revealed to him where even Jasmin could be taken into hiding in an emergency. He had stocked it with weapons and plenty of ammunition, counting on the loyal male staff to help him put up a barrage if the need should arise, and he had taught Rose how to load and fire both a musket and a pistol. While they were in the secret vault she had paused in stacking the shelves with food to open a box for him to peruse the old deeds and architectural plans, drawn by Laurent Picard, and the transfer of ownership to Marguerite Dremont. It had been extremely interesting to study them and to see his great-great-grandfather's strongly penned signature.

Within the first hour in London, Richard officially resigned from the diplomatic service that he had entered only to be of aid during those extenuating circumstances in

France, never having considered it as a career. He went home to Kent, intending to stay no more than a couple of days, but found the family gathering together at Easterton Court. His mother was dying. She had kept from them all the disease that had been gnawing away at her and had been finally overcome. The message sent to him through diplomatic channels asking that he should return must have reached the Embassy in Paris after its closure.

His mother lingered for two weeks, her suffering intense, and he was overwhelmed by sorrow that such a lively, vivacious woman should be so struck down. When the funeral was over he worked in grief to settle her affairs and to deal with many outstanding matters on the estate. He then began to look towards France again, concern for Rose never being out of his mind.

It did not prove difficult to get a Dover fisherman to sail him across the Channel and land him on a deserted stretch of the French coast. He then walked to the nearest town where he made enquiries about a coach to Paris. It meant staying overnight at a hostelry where he presented himself as a bourgeois going on business to the capital, but he thought he would be more inconspicuous with other travellers than riding horseback on his own on a main road from the coast. Under no circumstances could he risk the slightest suspicion as to his true identity, for he had to get back to Rose. A month had passed already since he had left her.

It was not a comfortable journey. Every seat in the coach was taken inside and out, and the early March rain had made a quagmire of the roads in many places. Twice he and the other male passengers had to alight and help push the wheels out of ruts, a wet and muddy process. From conversation within the coach, to which he listened, making appropriate remarks, he learned much of what had been happening in his absence. Political factions were still at one another's throats; there were rumbles of an uprising against the Republic by Royalists and the Queen and Madame Élisabeth in their prison now deferred to the former Dauphin as the new King, Louis XVII.

"The Widow Capet," one passenger said on a roar of laughter, using the new nickname given to Marie Antoinette, "chooses to forget that the monarchy doesn't exist any more!"

The rest joined in his mirth, adding comments of their own. Richard, who was feigning a doze at that point, was spared any risk of showing how the gibe had made his gall rise.

At Paris the coach drew into the courtyard of a large inn. It was late evening, the place well lit and extremely busy. He entered into a wave of heat blended with the aromas of wine, tobacco and cooked food, backed by a din of conversation and the drunken singing of "La Marseillaise" from some soldiers seated at one of the many crowded tables that he could see through a wide archway. Amid the smoke haze the scarlet cap of Liberty, which had become as much a symbol of the Revolution as the cockade adorning it, was in evidence on both men and women. Carrying the one piece of hand-luggage he had brought with him, he had to wait his turn behind a cluster of people wanting attention at a desk. His impatience was at a peak. He had been directed there from the inn stables where he had hoped to hire a horse with the minimum of delay, knowing he could get to Château Satory within an hour. The narrow brim of his steeple hat gave his face little shadow under the iron chandelier that illuminated that section of the entrance hall and, already marked out by his height, he was willing enough to fall into talk of the inconvenience of travel these days with a portly bourgeois waiting with him. It gave him the chance to turn his back on the crowded room, not noticing that a youth in a scarlet cap, who had been staring at him from one of the tables, now rose leisurely to come and lounge against the wall within earshot, smoking the long-stemmed pipe in his hand.

Side by side Richard and the bourgeois moved nearer the desk as those in front of them were attended to and moved away.

"Are you in Paris on business, citizen?" the bourgeois enquired, having proudly given the information that he was presenting a petition at the Hôtel de Ville on the morrow on behalf of his town concerning some land rights that had reverted from a local aristocrat after four hundred years.

"Yes, I am," Richard replied easily. "I'm a dealer in silks from Lyons. Needless to say, sales have fallen off due to a loss of previous clients and I'm here to approach a new market."

The bourgeois gave him a knowing nudge with an elbow. "You should do well. From what I hear the members of the Commune aren't short of female companions eager to deck themselves out when they attend the trials at the courts. They'll all be wanting something new when the Widow Capet comes up before the judges."

"Is that a possibility?" Richard's question was voiced on a casual note.

"I'd say it was a certainty. There are many crimes laid at her door and sooner or later she will have to answer to them." The bourgeois saw that the desk was cleared of those ahead and waved Richard forwards. "After you, citizen."

Richard stated his need of a good horse to the clerk in attendance. Then he paid for the hire and took the necessary slip to exchange for his mount with the groom in charge. The listening youth tapped out his pipe and pocketed it as he went to the table where the soldiers sat and spoke quietly to them. They all turned their heads to watch Richard leave. As soon as he went through the door they sprang to their feet, knocking back their chairs and grabbing their hats, attracting everyone's attention. Then they rushed out one after another in his wake, the informer following last of all.

In the stables Richard strapped his hand-baggage to the back of the saddle and, putting his foot into the stirrup, he swung himself up onto his horse. As he rode forwards to leave the courtyard he found himself faced by a row of a dozen soldiers, all with muskets levelled at him.

"Halt and dismount in the name of the Republic!"

He regarded them coldly, registering there was no other way out, the buildings of the hostelry enclosing the yard on all three sides. "For what purpose?"

"To present your papers and state your identity."

"Since when has a law-abiding citizen had to present himself under threat of fire? I am Augustin Roussier," he said, using his ancestor's name as he had planned, "a silk merchant of Lyons." He took his papers, forged by an expert in London, from his pocket and held them out. "As you will see everything is in order."

His air of authority had its effect. A soldier came forward, examined the papers and nodded to his comrades. "According to these, he is who he says."

The youth in the red cap sprang forward. "Fools! I tell you he's the Comte d'Avignon! I'd know him anywhere! He's a wanted man. His head is for the guillotine!"

Richard swore under his breath. He had met the Comte d'Avignon and although they were not much alike in visage they were of the same height, physique and colouring. He could understand how the error had been made. Without showing his anger at this unexpected turn of ill-fortune, he addressed the youth firmly.

"Take a good look at me. Correct the mistake you have made. You and I have never met."

The youth came forward sullenly, given a thrust by the soldiers. By now a crowd had gathered, people coming out of the hostelry to stare with their wine in one hand and some with a chunk of food in the other. He studied Richard's impassive face, an element of doubt growing. Then he thought of what a fool he would appear if he should admit he was wrong, which served to strengthen his belief that he was right. He flung out a pointing finger of accusation at the hated aristocrat he saw through his own self-conviction.

"You're the Comte d'Avignon! I saw you when you chased a stag through our village! You rode down my sister and two other children, leaving them dead!" All the old fury and outrage boiled up in him and his voice almost reached a scream. "Murderer! The guillotine is too swift for you! I say to the nearest street lantern with a rope!"

Richard jerked at the reins making the startled horse rear, hooves plunging. Then he brought the whip down with such force across the animal's hindquarters that it leapt forward, scattering the soldiers and all those in his path. Muskets fired, men shouted and women screamed. He would have escaped if a chance shot, fired seconds after the rest, had not caught the side of his head. He flung up his arms and fell as though pole-axed to the cobbles of the yard while his horse went thundering on. The crowd rushed for him and he would have been torn to pieces if a sergeant, who had been upstairs with a woman, had not emerged at that moment from a side door to find a bleeding man at his feet. He drew his cutlass and held it protectively over the prostrate figure, making those at the forefront of the rush slither to a standstill.

"Who is this?" he demanded through his long black

moustache. He was a fearsome fellow, hard on his men, and he resented this commotion that had brought him in haste from a pleasant sojourn.

"The Comte d'Avignon. He was recognised and tried to escape." Modest pride crept into the voice of the corporal giving the account. "I brought him down."

The sergeant grabbed the unconscious man by his blood-soaked hair and turned the ashen face towards him. "Bah! This isn't the Comte d'Avignon! He's already been arrested and is in one of the main prisons with a horde of fellow aristocrats."

"This man acted suspiciously in the hostelry, turning his face away from the light."

The sergeant sighed. "In that case he'll have to be investigated." He took another look at the victim. "If he lives, that is. Bind his head or he'll bleed to death."

Richard lay unconscious on dirty straw in a small prison in a narrow mediaeval back street where drunks and petty thieves were usually housed before trial. The sergeant came three times to see if he was fit to be questioned, but he had developed a fever and lay raving about orchids. His name was entered on the gaoler's books as Augustin Roussier and a space left as to his crime. Then the sergeant forgot about him, having more important matters to deal with, and Richard would have died there if the gaoler's wife had not nursed him. Madame Robiquet was a plain, simple woman, terrified of her bully of a husband, clumsy in many ways, but she had healing hands. When Richard eventually began to recover he was thin and wasted from the fever and could remember nothing. He accepted that his name was Augustin Roussier since he could recall no other and the days passed in torment for him as he tried to wrench some memory back from the past to tell him why he was imprisoned and how he came to be there.

On the last day of May at Château Satory, Rose gave birth to a strong, healthy son. Her immense joy was mingled with intense thankfulness that all the anxiety she had endured during her pregnancy had not affected him. There had been so many days of fruitless waiting for Richard to return and countless nights when fear for him had kept sleep at bay. The baby was baptised Charles after Richard's father, which had been his choice when they had

discussed names, and she yearned anew for his presence
and that he could see the boy she had borne.

At first she nursed the baby herself. It was no longer easy
to find people willing to enter the homes of aristocrats,
even though there was a surfeit of valets, grooms, ladies'
maids and chefs adding to the new poor of the land. Their
former masters and mistresses had fled the country or
were imprisoned or, as in Rose's case, lived as much out of
the public eye as was possible with the threat of investigation by Commune agents hanging over them, a danger
most servants wanted to avoid, At Château Satory a loyal
core of the staff remained, but all the young men had gone
to swell the ranks of the National Guard. Diane's mother,
Madame Arnaud, who as housekeeper had been such a
mainstay of the château, had also left, although it had been
a sad departure for her. Her son-in-law, who owned a small
wineshop in Paris, had been a bystander killed in one of
the riots and she had gone to help her widowed daughter
run the business and also look after the three young children of the family.

Few people came to be fed at Château Satory these days,
for the cornucopia that had been Jasmin's kitchens had all
but dried up. Newcomers, who had drifted into the district
through the upheavals of the Revolution, had several times
broken into the outlying storehouses of the château until
eventually new supplies of meat and flour were impossible
to obtain. The floors and shelves of the buildings remained
bare, the windows smashed and doors hanging on their
hinges. What would have fed many had been gorged by a
few.

This new element in the community surged dangerously
about, wearing their red caps and ever alert to seek out
trouble. A party of prisoners brought to the town of Versailles were set upon and murdered before they could be
put in their cells. On one occasion an unruly-looking band
entered the gates of the Château Satory and were only
persuaded to withdraw by the efforts of two local men
among them, who had had cause in the past to be grateful
to the Duchesse de Valverde.

It was after this incident, when Charles was just six
weeks old, that Rose worked alone at night to carry the
family portraits and other treasures into storage in the
secret vault. As yet only Richard knew of its existence

besides herself, for Jasmin had forgotten all about it, just as much else had faded from her mind. A rearrangement of less valuable paintings hid the gaps, but it was odd not to see Marguerite with her Versailles fan and gold gauze gown shimmering above the fireplace in the Ivory Salon.

At least Jasmin was not worried by these changes. She had been completely bedridden since her collapse on the day of the King's execution. Michel still came to see her, although she did not always know him, her periods of lucidity becoming fewer and fewer. It was not easy for him to get up the stairs, but he persisted doggedly, his shoulders and arms remaining strong and muscled due to his refusal to give in to the pain that often made the sweat run from his brow.

"Where is Richard?" Jasmin asked him one day when he had lowered himself into the chair at her bedside. She was quite clear in her thoughts that day. "He has been away a long time."

Michel exchanged a glance with Rose, who was standing on the opposite side of the bed. He had been trying to help her trace her husband, sharing her belief that Richard was imprisoned somewhere. A faithful old retainer, who had been with the Balaine household for many years and was now retired and living in Paris, was spending his time making careful enquiries at various prisons, it being dangerous to appear too inquisitive. The retainer's son had been despatched on the same business to Calais, the port that Richard had always used, and to try to pick up traces of him anywhere along the road to Paris. Through a secret communication with one of Richard's brothers, the date of his departure from England was known, but that had been all there was to guide the enquiries. Richard had not discussed his plans with anyone.

"Rose's husband will be back at Château Satory when his duties permit, my dear," Michel answered Jasmin. "You know what a busy young man he is."

Jasmin was not to be appeased. "His first duty should be to his wife at this time. He hasn't seen his son yet, you know, and our great-grandson is such a lovely baby." For a moment Jasmin's old eyes shone with happiness. "That's not through his choice, you may be sure."

"Rose is pining for him." Jasmin had forgotten her

granddaughter was in the room. "They were always so happy together."

"As they will be again."

Rose went out of the bedchamber and closed the door behind her. She had not realised that her grandmother had noted more from the confines of her silk-draped bed than had been apparent. Slowly she went across to a window and pressed her fists against the glass as she looked in the direction of Paris, far out of sight beyond the trees. Where was the man she loved? The temptation was growing in her to go to Paris herself and try to seek him out. She had a wet nurse available now and could safely leave Charles for a few hours. Although the last instruction Richard had given her was not to go to Paris for any reason whatever, she felt the time was coming to overrule that advice. All along she had refused to consider the possibility that he might be dead already, but she had begun to feel that if she did not intervene soon it would be too late. Waiting in vain for her grandfather's retainer to turn up any information had nearly driven her insane.

She would start tomorrow on a daily basis! In that way she could spend the daytime hours in searching while still being home at night to ensure that all was well with her grandmother and child. Dressed inconspicuously and with plenty of gold to bribe a way out for Richard when the time came, she would have an advantage as an attractive woman over an elderly man and his son making their fruitless enquiries.

Feeling stimulated by the prospect of positive action after months of enforced waiting, she went to her room and rang for Diane to help her sort out the simplest garments in her clothespress and closet.

"Shall I come with you, madame?" Diane asked, pulling open a drawer.

"No. I must leave you in charge of my grandmother and Charles in my absence." Then Rose saw what lay in the opened drawer and stayed Diane when she would have closed it again. It contained the muslin gowns and pastel-coloured satin sashes she had worn at the Petit Trianon. She touched one sadly. Had that happy time ever existed or was it just a blissful dream that had been swept away by what was spoken of as the Terror that now possessed

France? Did Marie Antoinette in her cruel imprisonment comfort herself with memories of those days?

"My mother heard in the wineshop that the Queen's son has been taken from her," Diane said almost in a whisper. She had returned the previous day from a visit to Paris and had not known how to break the news to her mistress. "They let her hear him crying for her in a cell below hers, for days and nights on end."

Rose had let the muslin gown fall back and she clutched the side of the drawer, her knuckles showing white. "How could they be so merciless?" she queried in a strangled voice.

"Now they make him wear a red cap and shout for the Republic. He has been beaten and coerced to do and say whatever they want of him."

"Oh, the poor child!"

"The Queen is being subjected to every humiliation. The guards rarely leave her cell. She has to dress and tend herself in their presence."

Rose fell away from the clothespress and threw herself across a chair in distress. That Marie Antoinette, the most modest of women, should be subjected to such outrage overwhelmed her with grief and compassion. She wept helplessly for the torment of a beloved lady and friend who was beyond her power to aid in any way.

It was an early hour when Rose dressed the following morning, wanting to make the most of her time. She slipped into her grandmother's bedchamber to make sure that all was well and then cuddled and kissed her baby several times before letting the wet nurse take him away for his feed. Then she spoke gravely to Diane.

"I'll be home by this evening. That is how it will be from now on. I shall go again and again until something comes to light." She paused. "If anything should happen to me at any time, take care of my baby until his father comes or the family in England can give him a home." She handed Diane a purse. "There is gold in that for you to use in an emergency."

"Yes, madame, I will."

Rose drove herself in an old cart that had once been used by the gardeners, a nag in the shafts. There were no riding or carriage horses left in the stables, not that she could have used any of them even if they had not been taken for

food in the raids, and she regretted the loss of the beautiful
thoroughbreds. She wore a plain cotton gown and a wide-
brimmed hat tied under her chin with a bow. Her Court
glide, which had long since been second nature to her, had
to be changed to the ordinary walk of a young bourgeois
woman and she had spent enough time with grooms and
stable lads in her childhood to be able to roughen her
speech to the right degree. In her pose as a carpenter's
wife selling a few wares to supplement the family income,
she took vegetables and fruit from the château's kitchen
garden and a basket of eggs from the henhouse, which had
escaped the raiders' attentions, being lodged near the
nag's quarters that stood in a secluded grove.

As she had expected, it was easy to sell outside the prisons. The guards purchased her fruit and eggs, also her
vegetables if they had wives and families in the vicinity.
She had selected the larger places of detention, many of
them convents that had been requisitioned, because it was
here the political *détenus* were housed away from ordinary criminals, and where she could most expect Richard
to be incarcerated. In general conversation with the
guards she would reach a point when she could ask if there
were any foreign prisoners inside. She learned of Italians
and Swiss and a Dane who had brushed with the Commune.

"Any Englishmen?"

"No. They and any Austrians we caught would be shot as
spies."

It was hard not to turn pale before these statements. She
clung to the hope that Richard had retained his French
guise and had not been detected. Her aim was to be allowed to go from cell to cell in the prisons in search of him,
for prisoners were allowed to buy and sent out money to
her. Sometimes the gates of the prison she had chosen that
day would open and horse-drawn tumbrels come rumbling
out over the cobbles with victims for the guillotine. She
always scanned the faces, terrified she would see Richard
there, and had to dip the wide brim of her hat to avoid
being recognised when she saw someone she knew from
the past golden days of Versailles. Once she sighted the
Comte de Cordierer with whom Richard had duelled. He
was staring contemptuously ahead as he stood with others
in the tumbrel, showing that he had stared death too often

in the face on battlefields and in duels to be quelled by the guillotine. She offered up a silent prayer for him as she always did for every one of these unfortunate people, many from humbler walks of life, on their way to their execution.

It never failed to amaze her how the life of Paris went on much as before. People strolled down the Champs-Élysées, went window-shopping and marketing, hurried about their business and patronised cafés and places of entertainment. The tumbrels had become such a familiar sight that in the Rue Saint-Antoine and the Rue Saint-Honoré not everyone glanced in their direction as they rolled on to the waiting guillotine where crowds had always gathered, places that Rose took care to avoid. Yet it was not uncommon when she was driving from one prison to another to find she was following either a cartload of headless corpses on their way to a common grave or a trail left by the dripping blood along the cobbles. She had to fight both nausea and tears, needing to be able to smile when she reached her next destination.

When September came she took loads of kindling from the grounds of her home, often having to gather and tie the bundles herself with only one old gardener left to help her. At least the scratches and stains from the wood took away the whiteness of her hands, which previously she had kept covered with some cheap lace mittens. In the château only Diane, two maids and an orphaned cleaning boy remained where once there had been servants everywhere. She had shut up many of the rooms and spent what little time she had at home with her grandmother and her son. His wet nurse refused to stay under the roof of an aristocrat for her own safety, but came at regular hours from her cottage to perform her task.

The kindling sold well to both guards and prisoners. She could scarcely contain her excitement on the day when she was finally allowed to enter the back porch of Saint-Lazare with a heavy basket of kindling to sell to those within. She had heard that the *détenus* were allowed their own furniture, that their letters were uncensored and that a way of life had been established that adhered in many ways to Versailles, but she had not expected to find such a relaxed atmosphere among those awaiting a terrible death. Having been a convent, the rooms here were high and light and airy and well-dressed people sat chatting, playing cards, painting and sketching. In one room there was a pianoforte where a marquise she knew well was giving singing lessons to several little girls. Other children were playing games together. Meals were being prepared on portable stoves or, if sent in from outside, heated up to give the most appetising aromas.

"Kindling! Just what we need!"

Several ladies and nobles came at once to purchase from her, interested only in what she had to sell and not in her face, which at least half a dozen of them would have recognised had she not kept her head well down as if in shyness, the close-fitting cap beneath her hat concealing her curls.

She made trips in and out with her kindling until she ran out of supplies. Richard had not been in any of the rooms she had visited and she had been in all where the *détenus* were housed, taking advantage of the freedom allowed them in being able to visit one another in all parts of the prison, paying calls and issuing invitations as if still in their apartments at Versailles.

Having crossed Saint-Lazare off her list, she went the next day to another prison where the guards, having heard she had had access to sell elsewhere, also let her in. Here she found many faithful servants had been imprisoned with their masters and mistresses and, although awaiting the same fate, bowed and curtsied with as much deference as they had shown previously in many a rich château. Richard was not to be found there either and another prison left her list. There were many more to visit and although she found herself denied admittance to a number of them she still continued undeterred.

Sadness for the plight of the *détenus* was always with her and there was an extra burden of sorrow to bear when in October the Queen was brought to trial. Newspapers gave full accounts and the verdict was settled from the start. Rose did not go to Paris on the day that Marie Antoinette was taken to the guillotine, not in a carriage like Louis or in a tumbrel, but in a rough cart, seated on a plank with her hair shorn and her hands tied tightly behind her back. Her dignity and composure impressed many in the vast crowd of spectators. As on the day the King was executed, Rose kept vigil in silence, prayers and memories mingling.

In November it turned cold. Rose's kindling was in great

demand and she was in the process of selling one day in a convent-prison, which she had not been allowed to enter before, when the door of the large room was flung open. A National Guardsman with an escort came in with a list of those to go down to the waiting tumbrels.

"The Marquis de Loiseau. The Duc and Duchesse de Villemont! The Comtesse de Berthier and her two children! The Vicomte de Fabiole." On and on he bawled his way down the list of sixty distinguished names.

There was no panic. The paper had been pasted up earlier and people were prepared. Some closed the Bibles and missals they had been reading while others kissed one another goodbye. Voices were quiet, attitudes dignified. Those whose children were going to the guillotine with them lifted the young ones up into their arms and took the older ones by the hand. Rose stood motionless in shock and despair, watching the procession of doomed people go from the room while those who were left stood in respect until the door was closed. When she went out of the prison again the tumbrels had gone. Sick at heart, she almost gave herself away at the gates out of the city by answering the guard in the diction that would have stamped her as an aristocrat. The Terror had fastened such a grip on the country that on the merest suspicion she could have been hauled away to await a tribunal and its inevitable verdict. She was trembling as she passed on through the gates, wondering how long her luck would last.

She made only two more trips to Paris before Jasmin became desperately ill. Rose, able to see that this time her beloved grandmother was coming to the end of life, sent for Michel in order that he could say farewell to the woman he still loved. He came at once.

"Jasmin, my dearest," he said softly to her. "Look at me once more."

Slowly she opened her eyes and met his loving gaze. She knew him and gave back the same look in the last moments before she slipped into a deep coma. He broke down into sobs, his wide shoulders shaking. Gently he kissed her hand and her brow before he went unsteadily from the room, his head bowed, his tears still falling. Rose accompanied him downstairs and saw him into his carriage.

"I shall not come to Château Satory again," he said sadly

to her. "Forgive me, but I could not endure that house without Jasmin's presence. I should expect to see her everywhere."

"I understand, Grand-père." She kissed him and turned back into the château as he was driven away.

Wiping away the tears that continued to roll, Michel wished he could have given Rose the information he had received, but it was too early yet for any certainty and he did not want to raise her hopes only to dash them again in the midst of the present sorrow that they shared. His retainer had learned that in an out-of-the-way prison, a small place of six cells where no political prisoners were held and the most unlikely place for Richard to be incarcerated, there was one young man who recited and sang in what he said was English. Not that the gaoler understood any of it, but the prisoner, who had lost his wits and been unable to remember anything for a considerable time, admitted he must have learned the language. He had once made an attempt at escape, which resulted in double locks being put on the door, preventing any more such ventures. The name given was Augustin Roussier, which seemed to Michel to be too much of a coincidence not to lead strongly to the prisoner being Richard. All that remained was the difficulty of confirmation and in getting him out. The retainer had said the gaoler was dedicated to duty and immune to bribery.

Rose did not leave her grandmother's bedside again and sat holding her hand. Shortly before midnight Jasmin died. It was entirely peaceful.

The following morning the funeral was arranged for two days hence. There were the usual practical matters to be dealt with. Their lawyer came and the will was opened and read, there being no time in these troublesome days for the leisurely procedures of the past. Jasmin had bequeathed Marguerite's sapphire pendant and all her jewellery to her granddaughter together with Château Satory, its lands and everything appertaining to her wealth and possessions. After the lawyer had gone, Rose began the task of going through innumerable letters and papers, discarding what had long ceased to be of any importance and putting anything to be kept in an iron box in the secret vault where the jewellery was also in safekeeping.

On the day of the funeral Rose put on Marguerite's pen-

dant and wore it under her black gown. She felt it linked
her closely with the two women who had made their mark
on Château Satory, one through love and the other
through charitable works. A funeral carriage, the horses
black-plumed, took her behind the cortège to the little
Church of Saint Antoine on the outskirts of the town of
Versailles. She rode alone, Diane staying at home with the
baby. It was Rose's decision that the remaining servants,
who would have attended, should keep away for their own
safety. Spies were everywhere. At the church Michel was
waiting and she entered with him. She was touched to see
how many people had come to the service, almost every
seat taken.

At Château Satory Diane sat in the kitchen with the two
housemaids, having a piece of bread and cheese. They had
all been up extra early that day due to the funeral, some
refreshments having been made ready in the Crimson Salon in case anyone should return with their mistress afterwards. Their amiable conversation was interrupted when
the cleaning boy, his expression full of fear, burst in on
them from the rear courtyard.

"There are soldiers marching up the drive! I was down
in the orchard and heard their orders. They've come to
take the Duchesse de Valverde and the Marquise de
Chuard into custody!"

One of the housemaids sniffed contemptuously, a beaker
of milk halfway to her mouth. "They're too late for the
Duchesse and our madame is Lady Easterton now."

"But they're not too late for us, you silly cow! We can be
condemned just for working here and they'll get Madame
when she comes back from the funeral!"

Both the maids screamed and leapt up from the benches
to rush for the door, Diane with them, the Bastille panic on
her again. But as the cold morning air hit her full in the
face she remembered the baby upstairs. She couldn't leave
him. He would be slaughtered!

She turned back indoors and ran to the hall. The marching feet were getting nearer. As she flew up the sweeping
staircase she heard the first hammering on the château's
door.

"Open in the name of the Republic!"

Charles was asleep in his crib. She snatched him up and
he gave a whimper, but as she wrapped the blankets about

him he closed his eyes again. This time she avoided the main staircase and took the servants' flight for her descent. It brought her out into a corridor near the kitchens and she uttered a distracted moan, seeing through a window that National Guardsmen had come swarming into the court-yard there, cutting off any escape. Wild-eyed with fright, she raced into one salon and then another until she reached the Music Salon. There she unlocked the glass doors that led to the lawn where the summer pavilion stood, flanked by a copse. Pushing the doors closed behind her, she darted under overhanging branches deep among the trees, scattering fallen leaves. Finally she threw herself down, cradling the baby, hoping desperately they would not be discovered.

She saw soldiers go into the summer pavilion and make a search of it before running on. One entered the copse, almost making her heart stop as she viewed him through the undergrowth, but he made only a cursory search and ran off again. Charles awoke and lay gurgling and kicking as if it were some new game to be lying under trees. When she heard a rustle right behind her she sat bolt upright in terror, expecting to find a guard looming above her ready to strike, but it was the elderly gardener.

"You'd better get away from here now as quick as you can," he urged, crouching down stiffly. "The soldiers may carry out a final search of the grounds before they padlock all the gates. My guess is they think the aristocrats in the house got warning and fled. They're closing up the house shutters and bolting doors."

"Where are the maids? Is the boy safe?"

"They hid behind the hen-house. No outsider ever finds the outhouses there. Now they've gone," he said.

"You must warn our madame not to come back here. She might run right into the soldiers. Can you get the nag hitched to the cart for me? I could leave by the far gates and take the baby to Monsieur Balaine. Lady Easterton can find us there."

"Why not meet her on the road?"

"No! I can't risk hanging about. I must take the lanes and cart-tracks. My papers are indoors where I can't get them and you know what it means to be questioned without having identification. You do as I say!"

Together they crept through the trees and took paths

behind box hedges to reach the nag's secluded little stable. The gardener did not like to see the animal go, for he had cared for it a long time, but he hitched the cart to it and saw Diane and the baby on their way. Then with his lolloping gait he left the grounds himself, taking his few possessions in a bundle, because he knew there was no going back. He stationed himself beyond the château where he could halt his mistress's carriage.

At the funeral service Michel sat with his granddaughter and then stood with her outside to see Jasmin interred in the family tomb that Laurent Picard had designed and erected before his own demise. Crowned by a balustrade it had a look of Versailles about it.

Michel parted from Rose in the churchyard. She was anxious about him in the bitter wind and bade him not to linger. There were many people waiting to express condolences and she could see she would be quite a time yet. He agreed only because he was in so much pain from the cold that he feared his legs might give way.

"I shall keep in touch with you about the matter of your husband," he said, regretting that nothing more had come to light to let him tell her what he already knew. "It is still well in hand. Come to see me as soon and as often as you can."

"I will, Grand-père."

His coachman, able to see by the lowering clouds that it was going to rain at any moment, drove him home at a spanking pace. The downpour started as they reached the Balaine mansion and footmen came running out to shelter him with an umbrella and to lend a strong arm for assistance. He thanked them courteously. All his staff liked him and congratulated themselves on secure work for a well-established bourgeois in these troubled times. No taint of blue blood to threaten them in this house.

Michel had not been long settled in his favourite chair by the fire, a glass of wine in his hand, when a visitor was announced. To his astonishment Rose's maid, soaked to the skin, with his bawling great-grandson in her arms, came rushing in, her face full of fear.

"The National Guard are waiting at Château Satory to arrest my mistress! I had nowhere to go with the baby!"

He struggled to his feet in alarm and leaned on his canes. "Lady Easterton must be warned!"

"That is being done, sir. She will come here." Almost beside herself with fright, having expected to meet soldiers all the way, she stood helplessly rocking the baby, rain running from her sodden cap and hair, drips from her skirt-hems soaking into the carpet.

"You're safe here and you have done well. I'll see that you are rewarded. Now you and the baby must have dry garments or you'll both catch a chill." Michel took his canes into one hand to reach for the bellpull with the other. "My housekeeper shall take care of you. I know there are clothes upstairs belonging to the women of my family. When you are fresh-clad come down here again and tell me exactly how it all happened. Bring Charles with you. His mother will want to see him as soon as she arrives."

When Diane reappeared in Michel's salon she had had a hot drink, her hair was dried and dressed and she wore a green silk gown. Charles, who had been spoon-fed in the kitchen by the housekeeper, was already asleep again, dressed in some garments slightly yellowed by storage, which Michel guessed had once been worn by his daughter's child.

"Sit down," he invited. "Opposite me by the fire. That's right. Now begin your account."

Diane rearranged the baby's shawl, cradling him to her as she settled herself, and began to relate all that had taken place. She had hardly finished when they heard someone being admitted into the hall.

"That will be Lady Easterton now," Michel said to her. But it was not Rose's voice that reached them and judging by the heavy tramp of feet the new arrival was not alone.

"In the name of the Republic I demand to see Citizen Balaine."

Diane gave a sharp cry and sprang up with the baby in her arms. "They have come for me! Oh, save me, sir!"

"Nobody shall take you from here," Michel stated determinedly, once again rising to his feet. "You are a member of my household now. Stand by me."

She obeyed as the footman showed in an officer of the National Guard, a burly uncouth-looking man given extra height by the high plumes in his cocked hat. Two of his soldiers followed him and stood with their backs to the door. "You are Citizen Balaine?"

"I am," Michel replied. "What is your business here?"

"You are under arrest!"

"Under what charge?" Michel was wholly confident that this officer did not have the authority to take him into custody for harbouring a maidservant and his own great-grandchild, who was simply a baby as far as anyone was concerned.

"You were the Court painter, were you not?"

Michel stiffened his spine. This was a different case altogether. He could guess what was coming. "I was—a long time ago."

"Then you have Royalist sympathies and are a threat to the Republic." The officer's eyes darted to Diane. "Who are you?"

Michel answered for the terrified young woman. "One of my servants. She has no involvement in the charge you have levelled against me."

The officer ignored Michel. "What is your name, citizeness?"

The reply came in a whisper. "Diane Arnaud."

"Whose is the child?"

"Mine!" Diane clutched Charles closer to her. If nobody suspected his true identity, he still had a chance of survival.

"Indeed." The officer's gaze slid to Michel as if judging the possibility of parentage before regarding Diane thoughtfully again. To her dismay, instead of dismissing her as she had hoped, he repeated her name to himself as if it had struck a chord with him somehow. Then he took a list from his pocket and perused it before his hard eyes considered her questioningly again under his thick brows. "Do you deny that you are really maid to the Marquise de Chuard and have been for several years? It will be the worse for you if I don't have the truth!"

"I was in her employ. That was a while ago."

He glared at her accusingly and tapped the paper he held with a forefinger. "Not by what I have written here! I put it to you that you have only recently changed your place of work! Where are the aristocrats of Château Satory?"

"The Duchesse de Valverde is dead and I have no idea where my former mistress is to be found." She knew that

Michel Balaine must be as much on tenterhooks as she, fearing that Rose might arrive at any moment.

The officer glanced over his shoulder at his corporal. "Search the house. The aristocrat may be disguised as a servant. Round up all the domestic staff."

Michel thumped his canes furiously. "The lady is not here. Neither have you any jurisdiction over her. She is Lady Easterton, wife of an Englishman, and therefore a national of England and no longer of France!"

There was a contemptuous snort. "Why isn't she across the Channel, then? Since she has chosen to remain in France she is still the Marquise de Chuard as far as the Republic is concerned."

"I tell you again you have no right!" Michel was enraged by such flagrant injustice. What happened to himself was unimportant. He was old and had lived long, but his granddaughter's life was all before her. "I demand that lawyers be consulted and your order to seize her rescinded!"

The officer scowled fiercely. "Shut up, old man! You and your kind forfeited your own rights long ago by choosing to serve the monarchy before the people." Then he beckoned fiercely, having made up his own mind why the young woman in the green silk gown had changed her place of employment. "Now out to the wagons with you, Citizen Balaine, and your paramour and her brat, too!"

He allowed them to don cloaks against the rain and to take milk and some pap fit for a six-month-old baby before they were escorted to the waiting covered carts. Michel had to be lifted in and it was a painful procedure for him, his canes shoved along the floor of the vehicle to him afterwards. All his servants, except three who had revealed to the officer that they were wearing Revolutionary cockades over their hearts beneath their jackets, were shoved into the carts after some scuffling which was swiftly quelled by the butts of the soldiers' muskets. The officer had failed to find any trace of the Marquise he sought, but that was no surprise since he thought she was probably fleeing to one of the borders, where sharp-eyed guards let few escape. As for the servants of the house, he was committing them to the same tribunal as their master on the assumption that after much long service they had been tainted by Royalist sympathies. That was treason enough to send them to the guillotine.

Rose came hurrying on foot along the road. After the gardener had halted her returning carriage and whispered his warning to her, she had instructed the coachman to turn about and drive her back to the church. There she had dismissed him and hurried the short distance into town to hire a hackney carriage to take her most of the way to her grandfather's mansion. She had alighted at the hostelry nearest to his home, not wanting to leave a trail that could be traced, and as she followed a bend in the road she was in time to see wagons and an escort of marching soldiers leaving the Balaine residence.

Breaking into a run she reached some cottagers who were about to go back indoors after watching events. "Wait a moment, please! What's been happening at that house?"

They were eager enough to share the excitement with her, for in her plain black garments, the brim of her hat dipped and stretched by the rain, its ribbons sodden, there was nothing about her to suggest that she belonged in any way to the house about which she was enquiring.

"The retired painter who lives there has been arrested and his servants with him. One of the footmen had his head cracked by a musket and was knocked out."

"Was there anyone else with the painter?" It was all Rose could do not to screech her question, for they had begun discussing everything over again with one another.

"There was a young woman with a baby." The speaker, a big red-faced woman, saw how Rose slumped ashen-faced against the wall as if all strength had ebbed and mistook the cause. "Expecting a babe yourself, are you, citizeness? Don't upset yourself. They dash out the brains of the little ones against the posts of the guillotine, but that won't happen to yours."

Rose slithered down the wall in a faint. She was hauled into one of the cottages, her face slapped to bring her round, and then given a draught of rough red wine to drink. While she had been unconscious her purse had been opened to reveal only a few coins of little value and papers stating she was a carpenter's wife. Had she had more she would have been robbed, but she appeared to be poorer than they were in spite of the good cloth of her clothes, and they let her be. When she reeled weakly to her feet she was made to sit down again and asked how far she had to go to get home.

"I'm on my way to Paris." She put forward a request carefully. "Do you know of any transport going there? I could pay a little."

All present scratched their heads and gave the matter some discussion. Then one of the women mentioned a neighbour who owned a donkey cart. He was called and came with his cart. Rose took a seat beside him after the price was settled and he took her to the gates of Paris. Always when she dressed in the morning she encased her waist in a belt full of gold, just as she had always kept her forged papers in her purse for emergencies, and she knew she had enough with which to bribe the most conscientious guard once she had located her baby, her grandfather and her maid. If she should find Richard at the same time her cup would run over.

Only a few miles away Richard sat with his head between his hands. During the past weeks his mind had gradually cleared and memory returned, but now, conscious of the time that had passed, he was almost distraught with anxiety that he would be unable to regain his freedom and rejoin Rose.

It was almost dark when his cell door opened unexpectedly and the gaoler's wife entered. He gazed at her in amazement for she was obviously in a state of extreme agitation, her hair dishevelled, her eyes wide with panic while the lantern in one hand shook and the bowl of soup in the other slopped over with her trembling. "Quick, monsieur," she gasped. "I know you are well now and you can go, but tie me up first." Putting the bowl and lantern down on the ground she produced a length of cord from her pocket together with a bunch of keys. "Quickly now— my hands and feet—I've hidden the gold your friend gave me, but my husband will kill me unless I can make him think you attacked me when I brought your supper and seized the keys. Quick, monsieur—*quick*—while he is still at the hostelry."

Minutes later Richard was outside in the narrow street momentarily disorientated. A figure stepped forwards in the dusk. "Thank God you are out, sir. Monsieur Balaine sent me. Come now." A firm hand took his arm and led him away.

* * *

Rose had gone straight to Madame Arnaud and had to break the news to her and her widowed daughter, Nicolette, that Diane had been arrested and why. In the depth of their distress they made her welcome and she stayed with them, sharing a bedchamber with two of the children, for accommodation was cramped. Madame Arnaud warned her that it was unlikely she would discover the date of the tribunal that would decide the fate of those she was seeking since no advance notice was given.

"The tribunals are nothing but a farce. Prisoners are dragged before the court, tried by villains selected by the Commune and sentence is passed in a matter of minutes while the spectators yell like a Roman audience putting thumbs down to fallen gladiators. Sometimes the executions are carried out the next day. There are so many taking place now."

"Then I must try to get Grand-père and Diane and my baby out before they are brought to trial."

"If somehow you could get them here," Madame Arnaud suggested eagerly, "we have deep cellars where they could be hidden safely out of sight."

That was the plan. Rose purchased a covered cart and a nag more lively than the one she had had before, which should be able to go at speed if the need arose. She gathered all the old baby clothes that Nicolette had saved and set both her and her mother to making more, roughly thrown together or swiftly knitted while she set off to sell what she had.

In the comparatively short time she had been absent from Paris, changes had been made. She met new guards at some of the prisons and they barred her from entry, although sending word to the prisoners that she had baby garments for sale. She was able to judge by the size requested whether or not they might be intended for Charles. At first all were for newborn infants and she pitied the mothers that had had to give birth in prison knowing that neither they nor their babies had long to live. Where she did gain access through previous acquaintanceship with those at the gates, she found no trace of her own child or the two adults she also sought.

She was on her rounds one morning, drawing up outside the Temple, when Nicolette came rushing up to her, breathless and gaunt-faced with despair.

"Your grandfather and Diane! They were incarcerated in this place after trial and left in a tumbrel ten minutes ago! I just heard. My mother has gone to the Place de la Révolution to see if she can get through the enormous crowd there for a last word with my sister."

"What of my baby?" Rose cried, white-lipped. "Is he with them?"

"I don't know!" Nicolette saw that Rose had made room for her on the seat and shook her head. "I can't come with you! I have to get back to my children."

Rose slashed down the whip across the horse's back and it shot forwards to carry her away at a tearing pace. Those dodging out of her path shouted abuse at her, but she did not hear, gripped by such terror and grief that she drove as if frozen, staring ahead and cracking the whip again and again. The wheels rattled over the uneven cobbles and slithered as she took sharp corners, narrowly escaping collision with other vehicles. Knowing she would not be able to drive into the Place de la Révolution, she drew up near an alleyway, left her horse with foam dripping from its mouth and ran like the wind through a maze of murky passageways. She came out by a harness-maker's, not far from the huge square where two or three thousand people had gathered.

The guillotine stood high and dark on a platform in the middle of the square, enabling even those at the back of the dense mob where she had arrived to see well. It was a clear bright day with the sharp iris-blue sky clear of the clouds that frequently accompany wintry sunshine. Executions were already in progress, soldiers with kettle drums beating a rhythm every time the blade was raised for the next victim. Then came the crash on the block and a moment's suspenseful silence followed by a roar from exultant throats as the severed head was displayed. It was tossed into a basket with the body and the procedure repeated, with almost no delay.

The tumbrels were coming in from a street not far from where Rose stood and she began to push her way through, getting nearer the route lined by soldiers leading to the guillotine. When she was only yards away she saw her grandfather. He was standing with others in the rolling tumbrel, holding on to a wooden slat and giving no sign in his proud expression of the physical agony it must have

been to him in balancing against the thumping over the
cobbles. She cried out to him, reaching a hand, but her
voice was lost in the din and although his gaze was scan-
ning the faces in the crowd he neither saw nor heard her.
Then a woman in a shawl beside him turned and she saw it
was Diane with Charles in her arms.

She screamed and began to fight like a madwoman to
get through. Those about her shook off her clawing hands,
thinking she was seized by blood-hysteria, which frequently affected unstable women at the guillotine, and one
man gave her a clout across the head that sent her down on
her knees. When she had struggled up again the tumbrel
was well past and there was no hope of reaching it.

With tears streaming down her face, her arms half cradled for the child about to be killed before her eyes with
the two other persons dear to her, she watched the tumbrel come to a halt. Those in it began to alight and stood to
await their turn for the steps up to the platform while the
guillotine finished its work on the condemned in the tumbrel before them.

In excruciating anguish Rose saw Michel struggle on his
canes up the steps. Diane began to follow him, holding
Charles with his little cheek against hers as she made the
most of their last minutes together. Then Michel made an
extraordinary move. He paused as if for breath and half
turned to speak to Diane a few steps below him, dropping
his canes. She thrust Charles to him and with all his
strength he hurled the baby into the crowd where a pair of
hands received him. Then Michel tottered and fell from
sight, cheating the guillotine of his life as his head struck
the cobbles. Diane, struggling to go to him, was wrenched
up onto the platform and thrust down on the board that set
her head on the block. The drums beat a tattoo, the blade
hissed and in the crowd Madame Arnaud covered her eyes
and wept.

Rose, half out of her mind, grieving for both her grandfather and her maid, was pushing herself towards the place
where she had seen Charles disappear. She was convinced
her grandfather had seen Madame Arnaud in the crowd
and thrown the baby to her. Then, while still a distance
away, she could see in a whirlpool of excitement that it was
a man in a black cocked hat with longer and far more
powerful arms than a woman's who had caught her child

and was balancing him high on one hand, twirling him about.

"It's dog food out of this one!" he roared in a thundering voice, hoarse and triumphant, the crowd letting him through with laughter and slaps on the back. "There's nothing like blue blood to strengthen a fighting hound!"

Her baby was crying. She could hear him above the tumult. His shawl was flying out exposing his little limbs to the cold weather as he was borne like a human banner away from the guillotine. She followed frantically. It was only a little easier to leave than it had been to get near the tumbrels and her efforts were desperate, for the black-hatted man was fast gaining ground ahead of her as the crowd willingly parted to let him through as though he were some kind of hero in his murderous intent. If she lost sight of him in the crush there were a dozen directions he could take and then she would lose track of him altogether with no chance to save her son from his clutches with gold from her belt.

Suddenly she could no longer see her baby. He had been lowered and the bobbing black hat could only be glimpsed now and again, threatening to vanish at any second. With a scream she drew on all the strength that was left in her to get through, beating with her fists at those who came in front of her and receiving angry pushes that inadvertently helped her on her way. It was one such push that sent her careening beyond the outskirts of the crowd to find that the man with her son had gone. Crying and moaning as if demented, she ran this way and that, every street riddled with side alleys, and she thought her heart must explode in her agony.

"Rose!"

She halted as if jerked by the throat and turned her head to see Richard in the black hat, barely recognisable with unkempt hair hanging about his unshaven face, holding their shawl-wrapped son to his shoulder and beckoning to her from an arched passageway. His arm received her as she flew to him and they kissed frantically. Only caution made him check their emotional reunion, all three of them being in the utmost danger.

"We need some transport," he said first, explanations to come later, "to get out of Paris and away to the coast."

"I have a horse and cart," she exclaimed, taking Charles into her arms and cuddling him close. "It's not far away."

They hurried to where she had left it. The horse had moved a little way on its own volition to drink at a fountain's trough. When they were seated Richard took the reins and they drove in the direction of the north gates, to all intents an ordinary couple who had spent a few hours disposing marketable wares in the city, some bundles of still unsold baby clothes in the cart to prove it.

He had forged papers for the three of them, supplied by Michel's retainer, who had continued faithfully with his task even after his master's imprisonment, having already received the necessary gold to unlock Richard's prison door. In spite of her fear of her husband, the gaoler's wife, who had never been allowed a sou of her own, had finally succumbed to temptation at the sight of the gold.

"Michel's retainer was able to tell me all that had happened, except that he knew nothing about your whereabouts," Richard explained. "He found out details of the arrest at the Balaine mansion from a drunken servant making free with the wine there. One of the soldiers had said to this fellow that the prisoners were being taken to the Temple. The retainer used bribery to find out the date of execution. All I could do was hope that you would be in the Place de la Révolution when this terrible day came. I went early to the guillotine to be sure that I stood a chance to catch our son if Diane should see me holding out my hands for him. Instead your grandfather restored our son to us. It was bravely done."

She nodded, too choked for speech. They passed through the gates of Paris and out into the countryside without any holdups. The road to the coast was long, but they covered it in easy stages, sleeping in the covered cart at night under home-woven blankets bought at a village market, which Richard thought would be safer than staying at hostelries. At the coast he had no difficulty in finding a fisherman willing to ferry them across the Channel at a price. On a still, dark night they set sail. When the white cliffs of Dover rose out of the sea at dawn, all danger was behind them.

The dower house in the park of Easterton Hall, last lived in by Richard's mother, became a halfway haven for

French émigrés fleeing to England from the Terror. Then when Robespierre fell from power to meet the guillotine himself the terrible days of massacre came to an end. From that time on the dower house was used to accommodate overflows of guests when a social occasion of importance took place at the Hall. The most recent event had been a family christening on the summer's day when Richard rode there accompanied by his young son on his first pony. He and Rose now had a baby daughter, whom they had named Lily, a natural choice for them both.

"Shall you be long here, Papa?" Charles asked him when they had dismounted.

"No. I have only to discuss some redecoration. Be a good boy and play until I call you."

Charles was familiar with the dower house, having been there many times. While his father talked with a steward about the dining room walls he went running off on his own, seeking a diversion to while away the time. His attention was caught by a collection of quill pens on a rosewood desk, which he knew had belonged to an old lady in the family who had died a long time ago. Pulling a chair into place, he clambered onto it and began a game of make-believe that the pens were horses, racing them across the polished surface. Happily absorbed, he was still there when Richard entered the room in search of him.

"Come now, Charles. It's time to go."

In the way of children, Charles had to have one more race with the pens and in his haste almost shot them to the floor. In reaching to save them, he inadvertently pressed his small elbow on a secret spring in the desk. A hidden drawer shot open, hitting his hand.

"Oh!" He was more surprised than hurt.

"What have you found?" Richard exclaimed. The existence of the drawer had been unknown to him. Together he and his son peered into the drawer and saw that it contained a slim, wrapped item, bearing a label. The ink was faded, but as Richard held it to the light of the window he recognised his grandmother's handwriting. *For Richard's bride.* When he had removed the wrapping he smiled at what he found within.

After leaving his son with a nursemaid at the Hall, Richard went in search of Rose and sighted her from afar. She was on the brow of a grassy knoll from which it was possi-

ble to see the sea. Her gaze, shadowed by the straw brim of
her hat, was directed towards France.

As he supposed, her memories that day were poignant.
She was thinking of Marie Antoinette's little son, Louis
XVII, whose short and unofficial reign within the walls of
the Temple had ended when he died there in suspicious
and unexplained circumstances. Mercifully his sister had
been handed over to the Austrians and was with family at
the Court of Vienna from which their mother had left at a
similar age for a fateful marriage many years before. Poor
Madame Élisabeth, friend to the Queen to the end, had
been guillotined with so many others known and remembered with love and affection. As for Versailles, it had been
stripped of its treasures, even to the chandeliers of the Hall
of Mirrors, which belonged nowhere else. The *Mona Lisa*
and other masterpieces had been removed to the Louvre
palace for safekeeping, together with other works of art.
Much of the finer furniture had gone to enhance the more
important government buildings of the Republic and everything else sold abroad to all corners of the world.

"Rose darling. I have a special gift for you."

She turned to see Richard coming up the slope towards
her, one hand concealing the surprise behind his back.
With a smile she raised her eyebrows in anticipation. "Yes?
Whatever can it be?"

He kissed her before he brought forward the love-token
and presented it to her. It was a fan, its silk tinged by age.
Gracefully she flicked it open and saw that it was one she
recognised from a portrait secreted in the vault of Château
Satory that she hoped to recover in time. Across the leaf of
the fan, shimmering its delicate colours in the sunshine,
was an exquisite painting of Versailles before its first embellishment and before it was enlarged.

"Marguerite's fan," she whispered in wonder.

"Yours now, my love."

She nodded and held it close to her heart as she looked
again in the direction of France. Maybe one day Versailles
would rise again. It was something for which she would
never cease to hope.

ABOUT THE AUTHOR

ROSALIND LAKER, who has had a lifelong fascination with Versailles, is the author of *Banners of Silk, The Silver Touch, This Shining Land*, and other novels. She lives with her husband in Sussex, England.

DON'T MISS
THESE CURRENT
Bantam Bestsellers

THE LATEST IN BOOKS
AND AUDIO CASSETTES

Paperbacks

☐	27032	**FIRST BORN** Doris Mortman	$4.95
☐	27283	**BRAZEN VIRTUE** Nora Roberts	$3.95
☐	25891	**THE TWO MRS. GRENVILLES** Dominick Dunne	$4.95
☐	27891	**PEOPLE LIKE US** Dominick Dunne	$4.95
☐	27260	**WILD SWAN** Celeste De Blasis	$4.95
☐	25692	**SWAN'S CHANCE** Celeste De Blasis	$4.50
☐	26543	**ACT OF WILL** Barbara Taylor Bradford	$5.95
☐	27790	**A WOMAN OF SUBSTANCE** Barbara Taylor Bradford	$5.95

Audio

☐ **THE SHELL SEEKERS** by Rosamunde Pilcher
Performance by Lynn Redgrave
180 Mins. Double Cassette   48183-9 $14.95

☐ **THE NAKED HEART** by Jacqueline Briskin
Performance by Stockard Channing
180 Mins. Double Cassette   45169-3 $14.95

☐ **COLD SASSY TREE** by Olive Ann Burns
Performance by Richard Thomas
180 Mins. Double Cassette   45166-9 $14.95

☐ **PEOPLE LIKE US** by Dominick Dunne
Performance by Len Cariou
180 Mins. Double Cassette   45164-2 $14.95

Bantam Books, Dept. FBS, 414 East Golf Road, Des Plaines, IL 60016

Please send me the items I have checked above. I am enclosing $_____
(please add $2.00 to cover postage and handling). Send check or money
order, no cash or C.O.D.s please.

Mr/Ms _____

Address _____

City/State_____ Zip_____

FBS—11/89

Please allow four to six weeks for delivery.
Prices and availability subject to change without notice.